Trust No Bitch

Lock Down Publications
Presents
Trust No Bitch
A Novel by *Ca$h & NeNe Capri*

Lock Down Publications
P.O. Box 1482
Pine Lake, Ga 30072-1482

Lock Down Publications
Ca$h
Email: ldp.cash@gmail.com
Facebook: Cassius Alexander
Like our page on Facebook: Lock Down Publications @
www.facebook.com/lockdownpublications.ldp
Amazon: http://www.amazon.com/Ca$h
NeNeCapri
Facebook: NeNeCapri
Twitter: @NeNeCapri
Instagram: @NeneCapri
Cover design and layout by: **Marion Designs**
Book interior design by: **Shawn Walker**
Edited by: **Shawn Walker**

Acknowledgements

We would first like to acknowledge our fans nationwide. Thank you for supporting our individual careers and this collaboration Trust No Bitch. To our loyal supporters on the social websites, in the book groups, and the distributors, you fuel our drive. To the readers, you make us what we are authors. Thank you Shawn Walker for your boss editing. Keith, we thank you for the cover and look forward to more of your work. Friends, family, associates, and fellow authors we thank you all.

Dedications

CA$H: To the one who prefers to remain anonymous, they can't destroy what they can't see.

Nene Capri: To My beloved daughter Princess Khairah everything I do is for you. Mommy loves you.

Chapter 1
Mentor and Protégé

Kiam was putting the last of his things in the two boxes he had placed in the middle of his bunk. As he lined his things neatly from one side to the other his mind shifted to the work that lay ahead. His blood rushed through his veins as he felt the reality of impending freedom. The thoughts were sweet in his mind but bitter in his belly. He had spent the last eight years living how many would consider beastly.

At age twenty-six the trail of blood he had left behind was long and thick. And honestly it was only going to get thicker. As he turned to check to see if he had everything, one of his boys entered his cell appearing to be all about business.

"Ay, Kiam, one of your homeboys just came on the compound. Some cat who calls himself Supreme. He says he's from the eastside of Cleveland. Isn't that your hood?" asked Philly Cat, a straight up G from South Philadelphia who was serving thirty years behind a snitch nigga's testimony.

Philly Cat was one of the dudes responsible for checking new arrivals' credentials when they first came on compound to make sure that they were solid. The rule stood firm, snitches weren't allowed to live amongst real niggas at Lewisburg.

"Yeah, that's my hood," Kiam attested. "But the name Supreme don't ring no bells. Did you check out his papers?"

"Nah, he says he sent them home." Philly stood, rubbing his hands together.

"Well, you know the rules, if the homie can't prove who he is, he has to get off the compound. It don't matter where he's from. He's not my muthafuckin' homie." Kiam wasn't claiming nobody that couldn't prove their officialness.

He stood contemplating for a minute then rendered his verdict. "Take me to that nigga."

Philly Cat led Kiam outside on the yard where other solid men were questioning Supreme. Kiam walked up and studied the newcomer. He didn't recognize the nigga's face so he kept quiet and listened to his responses.

It was obvious that if Supreme wasn't from that city once dubbed The Mistake by the Lake, he had at least lived there for a while. He knew the names of all the shot-callers, and he knew all the hoods. He claimed to have once had the notorious Garden Valley projects on Kinsman Avenue on smash before they were torn down and rebuilt, but something didn't seem right about ol' boy.

"Fam, what's your government?" Kiam cut in.

"Michael Gresham," Supreme replied, mean-mugging, with his thick arms folded across his chest.

Kiam ignored the weak intimidation tactic. Instead he entertained him with a small chuckle which was his signature stamp of death. Instantly Supreme knew he had stepped through the gates of hell and Kiam appeared to be the devil himself.

Supreme was a big muthafucka, but size doesn't determine a man's gangsta. His biggest mistake was he hadn't looked Kiam in the eye. That in itself hinted at a flaw in his get-down. Boss niggas could match a man's gaze with one better.

"Homie, I'm gonna make a few calls and check out your street cred. If you're not who you claim to be, you better check off compound now," he warned Supreme.

Kiam didn't stay a second past his words; he turned his back on Supreme and walked away. *That nigga frontin'. I can see fear in his eyes. If it turns out he's a rat, hiding under a different name, I'm gonna send him up out of here in a body bag.* It didn't matter that his release date was upon him, his gangsta was never on hold.

Kiam used his celly Pop's contraband cell phone to reach out to the streets. It only took a few calls to find out that Michael

Gresham was indeed a thorough dude. But the nigga that also called himself Supreme was not that Michael Gresham.

By evening Kiam had learned that the Michael Gresham that had Kinsman on smash got thirty-five years and was at ADX Florence, the super max federal prison in Colorado. The description nor the reputation fitted this clown down here. What the fuck is this nigga hiding? wondered Kiam.

The question rang strong in his mind, but he damn sure didn't have time to figure it out. Kiam hated fake niggas with a passion. He believed that they all should be killed. Weak, fake niggas had cost a lot of good men their lives, taking the stand to testify and selling their souls. In that moment the decision was made. Supreme's fate was death. In fact, Kiam felt that he deserved the most gruesome death just for calling himself some real shit like Supreme when he was not anything close to it.

Late that night he pulled a homemade ski mask over his face to hide his identity in case the wrong nigga saw him moving. He eased out of the broom closet, where he had strapped up, and crept up behind Supreme in the television area. "Welcome to the grave muthafucka," he gritted, shoving a knife between the imposter's shoulder blades.

Warm blood poured down Kiam's arm as he stabbed Supreme repeatedly. The surge of testosterone that filled his body as he took another man's life was priceless. And even with the victory of maxing out on his bid holding in the balance, nothing felt better than the kill. Kiam had well-established that he would stand on principle regardless of the consequences.

The next morning...

Kiam stood in front of his celly and mentor with a heavy heart that contradicted the beast that lied within. In the three years that they had bunked together, Alonzo, whom he affectionately called Pop, had become his surrogate father and his only trusted friend. As anxious as Kiam was to return to the streets and apply all the things that Alonzo had instilled in him, he still felt some kinda way about leaving Big Zo behind.

"Pop, you know I would give anything for you to be able to walk out that door with me." Sincerity covered his face as he looked his guru in the eye.

Big Zo showed no expression. He appreciated the love but the reality was that he wasn't walking out of that door with his protégé. As things stood he wasn't ever walking out of those prison doors, he had life in the feds and that was that.

"Don't worry about Pop, I'm built to last. My life is in here now. That's the bed I made, and that's the bed I'm going to sleep in."

Kiam nodded his understanding. He admired the strength that Pop had in spite of his predicament. Big Zo hadn't let the sentence break him. At fifty years old, he worked out every day to stay in top shape, and he was impeccably groomed. His mind was a vault of knowledge and wisdom that extended far beyond street life. But Pop was about that life too.

He put a fatherly hand on Kiam's shoulder and spat a jewel in his ear. "I see how you're looking at me. You're feeling bad because you're leaving me behind. But there's no time for that. You have to forget about what's on this side of the fence, including that business of last night, I'll handle that. I need for you to focus on what's on that other side. Do you understand me, son?"

Kiam just nodded because he did not trust himself to speak. It wrung his heart to be leaving him behind.

"Go out there and put your hustle and murder games down like I've prepared you to do," Pop continued. "I have schooled you to become the strongest street general to ever fuck with the game, and I expect nothing less of you."

"Failure is not an option," Kiam intoned.

10

"It is not." Big Zo put the other hand on Kiam's shoulder. Standing at about 6' 2 they were the same height. He looked at his understudy and implored, "Remember, you are to leave no enemy alive or they'll rebuild then come back to overthrow you. Never forget that the only people that can hurt you are those closest to you. No matter who it is—family, friend or foe— if they show one glint of treason you must execute them with extreme prejudice. You bury the muthafucka, let Allah worry about forgiveness."

"I understand, Pop. And you already know how I live."

Indeed Big Zo did. He quickly reflected on the countless sacrifices Kiam made on his behalf. In the past three years there had been several incidents that tested Kiam's loyalty and his gangsta; he had aced each test.

Big Zo's mind returned to the present. He tightened his grip on Kiam's shoulder and continued to drop jewels on him. "Son, you're a throwback. There's not many dudes your age that honor the code. Self-preservation is the only code that still stands today. Fuck anything else you heard."

Pop's brow furrowed, he wished that he had known that when the feds began snatching up his comrades and pressuring them to flip on him.

"Real men like you and me always suffer the greatest penalties because we won't compromise our principles to save ourselves." Kiam's voice almost broke. He knew Big Zo's story well; he had read the trial transcripts more than twenty times.

"I let certain men live because I thought that they were built like me. Death before dishonor is what we were all taught. But at the end of the day, muthafuckas saved themselves and left me for dead. Don't let them do that to you. Do you understand?" Pop questioned needlessly.

"Yes, sir."

"Now you must remember, you can trust yourself and you can trust my daughter. Lissha has been taught by the best. She is just as comfortable carrying a Glock as she is carrying a Gucci bag. She is to be your conduit to the top, but she is not to be your woman. You can have everything that I left out there but my daughter. She is beautiful and any man will be tempted to want more from her than a business relationship, but you are not to fuck her. Is that clear?" He studied Kiam with intensity that was as hot as burning coals. Kiam did not blink. His loyalty was concrete.

"Temptation befalls many. If you succumb to it, I will not be forgiving. I will use everything that I have to reach out and touch you – by any means possible," Pop warned.

"On everything that I love, I won't betray you. And if any amount of money can bring you home, I'll be back to get you," Kiam promised.

"Death before dishonor soldier."

"To the grave," Kiam vowed. He saluted his mentor then walked toward freedom, prepared to conquer the game.

What he was not prepared for was Lissha's beauty.

Chapter 2
Home Coming

Lissha was posted up against her apple red 2012 Dodge Magnum in the parking lot of the prison at nine o'clock sharp. She reflected on her specific orders from Daddy as she awaited the man of the hour. Forty minutes later, Kiam emerged from the front doors of the penitentiary. Lissha noticed that the pictures she had seen of him did not accurately reflect what he looked like in the flesh.

"Got damn," she fidgeted as he drew near. His chocolate, well-chiseled, frame moved swiftly toward her. Instantly she felt the kitty tingle as his eyes met hers. She crossed her legs at the ankle to slow the pulse that was beating fast below.

Kiam put some stride in his step as he looked up and saw Lissha waving him over. Her pretty pecan tan glowed in the sunlight. Her sandy brown shoulder length hair draped the sides of her face accentuating her high cheek bones. His eyes moved all over her 5'8" 135 pound figure, enjoying the journey.

Her breast sat up like two ripe melons and the curve of her hips in those skinny jeans had his dick asking him questions that he damn sure wanted to answer. Then Big Zo's words echoed loudly, *Temptation befalls many. If you succumb to it...*

Damn, Pop, he shook his head. Sensing that Lissha was probably picking up on his vibe, he quickly threw a little smile on his face.

"Look at you, all cheesed up." She smiled and extended her arms to receive him.

"What's up, ma?" He reached in and hugged her tightly.

Kiam felt the magnetism between them as the heat from her body embraced him. Her scent caressed his nostrils as her silky skin melted in his hands. It had been years since he held a woman in his arms and her perfect frame was the welcome he needed. He inhaled deeply, wanting to grip tighter, but Pops warning rang in his ears as if they were being shouted out on a mega phone. *"Don't fuck my daughter."*

Kiam abruptly pulled back.

"Why you acting all scary? Did Daddy threaten you?" She flashed him that pretty smile of hers, then giggled.

"Nah. None needed. His instructions were clear and I'm going to carry them out or die trying." He got real serious erasing the smile completely from his face.

"Well, let's go," Lissha popped the locks with the remote, and headed to her side.

Kiam hopped in and sank into his seat. He knew that everything from this point on would be a test and he intended on passing with flying colors.

Lissha and Kiam drove for hours before they reached Cleveland, Ohio. Kiam was looking out the window taking in the many changes that had been made to the city since he last set foot on its soil. Traveling down Superior Avenue he saw that some of the hoods had received a facelift, but he knew without a doubt that those grimy streets were the same cesspool that they had always been.

The laughter and conversation that filled the vehicle was cut short when Lissha pulled into the 7all apartments, looked up and saw her right hand, Treebie, coming toward them at a rapid pace.

Lissha threw the car in park and jumped out.

Kiam watched as the intense conversation between the two went back and forth. He reached over to the driver's side and let the window down to get a better idea of what was going on.

Kiam eyed the female Lissha was talking to. There was a slight resemblance between them, but not a strong enough one for him to mistake them for family. Like Lissha, she had soft brown skin and high cheekbones. Her hair was a little shorter than Lissha's and a small dimple in her left cheek stood out. Even though she was rocking baggy clothes Kiam could see she was well put together.

"What the fuck you mean the spot got hit?" Lissha questioned vehemently.

"I know that nigga Finch was behind that shit. Bayonna called me about an hour ago and said that nigga is holed up at his girl's house on 144th and St. Clair. I'm ready to do this." Treebie pounded her fist in her hand.

Lissha angrily about faced back toward her vehicle. She gripped the steering wheel tightly as she calculated her next move.

Treebie retrieved a black bag from her truck and passed it to Lissha. "The *whistles* are inside," she instructed before she peeled off.

Lissha quickly unzipped the bag and handed Kiam a 9mm German Luger, a Glock .40 and two silencers. Kiam didn't hesitate accepting them. He hadn't even set his feet on the ground yet, but that didn't faze him anymore than the shit he did to Supreme last night. He instinctively began to assemble his new toys.

Lissha pulled her custom-made pearl handled .380 from the bag, checked the clip, and then slid it between her legs. Satisfied that her "baby" was ready, she threw the car in gear and mashed out.

The ride was silent as Lissha zipped through the streets. Kiam asked no questions. No words were necessary; he wasn't new to the game. He was set to killah mode. A nigga had fucked up and a strong example was about to be set.

Twenty minutes later, Lissha pulled up a block away from Finch's girl's house. She surveyed the area, spotting Finch's red BMW 6 Series in the driveway. She grabbed her sneakers out of the back seat, tossing her heels aside. Kiam stood watch as she laced up, rising to her feet with her heat in hand.

"What this nigga look like?" he grimaced.

"Medium built, short afro, and he has a tattoo of a diamond under his left eye."

"Let's go."

Lissha turned toward the house and Kiam was right on her heels. He moved with the stealth of a panther. As they approached the driveway Treebie, who had already been waiting, emerged from the side of the house. She moved low-key with her fo-fifth at her side.

"You know what to do," Lissha whispered between pursed lips.

"If that nigga buck out the back I'ma put his insides on the outside," Treebie spat with flared nostrils and squinted eyes before disappearing.

Lissha and Kiam moved to the door and she gave the secret knock. Seconds later a knock came back. She hit the door twice more then it opened.

Her gut filled with disgust when she looked at the lineup that painted the living room. It was Finch, his number one, and one of her young boys that ran weight from one side of town to the other. Apparently there was some fishy shit brewing because all of them had guilty looks on their faces as if they had gotten caught with their dicks in some underage pussy.

"What's up, LiLi?" Finch's speech slurred with nervousness pitted from his belly.

"You tell me?" Lissha positioned herself near the door leading to the kitchen. "Do you know what happened at my spot today?" Her voice was real calm as she studied Finch's body language.

"I don't know what the fuck you talking about." Finch reached forward, grabbed a cigarette and lit it. He then sat back in his chair, crossed his legs and blew smoke in Lissha's direction.

"Who the fuck is this?" Finch's boy questioned, pointing at Kiam. "We ain't talking business in front of a fucking stranger," he spat.

"Don't worry about who the fuck I am," Kiam gritted, pulling both bangers from his waist and resting them at his sides.

"What the fuck is going on, Lissha?" Finch roared. "You got this nigga being all disrespectful in my house."

Kiam's head tilted to the side. The nigga fit the description of the one Lissha had said violated, plus he was talking reckless. That was two strikes against him and Kiam didn't even allow one. Without hesitation, he shot Finch in the stomach.

"What the fuck is wrong with this muthafucka?" Finch clutched his gaping wound, buckling over in pain.

Beebop put his hands in the air and began to plead his case. "LiLi. Hold up, let's talk this shit out."

She shook her head no, rejecting his plea. "The only thing I want to talk about is the whereabouts of my shit?" She waved her piece in the air.

"I know where it's at." Her little runner panicked. Sweat beaded across his face as tears threatened to fall from his eyes.

"Shut the fuck up." Finch squawked. He was folded over at the waist, holding his stomach. Blood gushed between his fingers and anguish filled his face.

Just as the young boy started to reveal their hands, the three men began arguing back and forth.

Kiam and Lissha looked back and forth before Kiam got fed up and shot Beebop in the face. He flew back in his seat and his brains hit the wall behind him hard and slippery.

The young boy hit the floor covering his head and begging for his life. "Where is my shit?" Lissha repeated with finality in her tone. She pointed her .380 and aimed it between youngin's eyes.

"It's in the closet," he speedily rushed his words as he pointed across the room.

"Get up and get it. Punk muthafucka." Kiam growled, gripping both gats so firmly his hands ached from the clench.

The boy returned apprehensively, dropped the bags at Kiam's feet while raising his hands all in one swift movement. "I don't want no trouble y'all." The words trembled off of his quaking lips. But trouble is what he declared when he got involved. Lissha shot

17

him in the back of the head causing him to fly onto the coffee table, shattering glass in every direction.

She picked up the bags as Kiam headed over to a dying Finch who was breathing short and heavy. Leaning in, Kiam placed the gun in Finch's mouth and forced eye contact. He wanted to make sure he stole his last minutes by filling them with fear and torment.

"Oh god, please. Have mercy. I wasn't trying to cross her," he stuttered.

"Prayer ain't acceptable at times like this. God don't love niggas like us. Make it up in the next life because you leaving this muthafucka. And the next time around, be loyal nigga."

Kiam shoved the gun to the roof of Finch's mouth and let off several shots, spraying the top of Finch's head, decorating the ceiling.

He stepped back, looked at his work, and smeared the blood from his face onto the back of his hand. His breathing was steady but his adrenalin moved rapidly through his body. It was official he was home, back on the killing field. This first taste of blood was merely a catalyst to the terror his return would cause in the hearts of many, and the conflict it would cause in the heart of one.

Chapter 3
Welcome Home

Over the next few hours Lissha drove through the streets, taking Kiam to several of the trap spots to see how shit was moving. Things were gravy at her spots up and down 30th, 55th, and out in EC on Hayden. On Euclid Ave, where it first turned into East Cleveland, on up past Shaw High School she had things on smash. There were other spots in the city under Lissha's control, but she would show him those another day. She figured that he was tired from his long, eventful, first day home and was ready to kick back and cool his heels.

After placing a few calls, she headed to the Ritz Carlton downtown. She had reserved the Presidential Suite for Kiam and a little treat to go along with it.

Lissha pulled up to the valet. She got out, tipped the young boy a c-note, popped her trunk and grabbed a medium sized Louis Vuitton bag. She closed the trunk, then headed toward the entrance. Kiam slid out of the passenger side with his own bag slung over his broad shoulder. He took in the opulent exterior of the hotel, it was a welcome sight after spending almost a decade in a prison cell.

Looking up the block, he saw the new casino that was due to open its doors next month. Downtown was blossoming. There were lines of newly built skyscrapers that sprouted up from the ground toward the sky, helping Cleveland to live up to its new moniker Tower City. Kiam was going to capitalize on the city's growth from the underworld's view.

With an easy stride he caught up to Lissha at the front desk. After getting the keys they walked to the elevators in total silence.

Kiam was worn out, the long drive from Pennsylvania had taken a toll on him. Then, as soon as Cleveland greeted him like a snaggle toothed relative, he had made his first kill of freedom. With the smell of death still in his nostrils, he had toured the city collecting Intel. Now all he wanted to do was take a hot shower, get some rest, and plot his takeover.

When the elevator stopped on the 14th floor, Lissha stepped out, looked down at the key card then walked to the left where the room was located. The moment the doors to the suite opened, Kiam immediately became relaxed. Deep shades of olive green, tan and blue surrounded the expansive living room. The carpet was plush and on key he took off his boots just as he had been raised to do.

He walked over to the floor to ceiling windows and looked out over Lake Erie. The view was breathtaking if one were a romantic, which Kiam wasn't necessarily. He chuckled because he had dumped his first body in that same muthafuckin' lake that now represented something tranquil.

Lissha walked to the wall and flipped the light switch. It beamed a little too bright so she dimmed it.

"This is you for the next couple weeks, player," she stretched out her arms in a behold manner."

The luxurious 1,065 square foot suite offered a view of the city, partial view of the river and lake, one king bedroom with sitting area, one and one-half bathrooms, Jacuzzi tub, expansive living area, a formal dining area with seating for eight, and a kitchen with full-size refrigerator.

It was a far cry from a prison cell.

Lissha walked to the back of the couch and pulled out several bags. Kiam walked over to her and took a quick look inside, there was an assortment of high end labels.

"Thanks, ma," he responded.

Lissha just smiled, then handed him the Louis Vuitton bag.

Kiam unzipped it and to his surprise it was filled with neatly stacked hundred dollar bills.

20

"Daddy said this is just the beginning." She looked up at Kiam's expressionless face and slowly ran her hand up his arm.

Kiam took a deep breath as he battled to control himself, there was a full war going on with his conscious and his duty.

"I have something for you," Lissha mentioned above a whisper.

"What's that?" he asked, unsure if he really wanted the answer.

"Come with me." She took his hand and led him to the bedroom.

Kiam was conflicted. His mind was saying, Nigga you better not! But his dick was tapping against his zipper and screaming *eight years, nigga.*

"Lissha." He called out her name in an attempt to gain control of the situation but his feet didn't get the message because them muthafuckas kept on moving. "Ma, hold up," he protested.

Lissha didn't respond, she used her free hand to open the door and again Kiam was taken by surprise. In the middle of the floor was a huge Jacuzzi with a sexy brown skin honey wearing nothing but a smile and bubbles.

"Didn't I already tell you about acting all scary?" Lissha asked while looking over her shoulder, giving him her sexy low-eyed glare.

Kiam just shook his head.

"Her name is Donella, she is to do whatever you want. For as long as you want it." She let go of his hand. "I gotta go. A bitch needs a shower and a long ass nap. Stupid niggas are tiring as hell," she said, referring to the Finch situation, then she hugged Kiam tight.

"Tell Pop, I send my greetings." He broke their embrace.

"I got you. Now worry about getting that nut off your back. I know if Daddy was in some pussy he would not be thinking about you." She laughed then headed toward the door.

Kiam took inventory of the bad ass female before him.

"You gonna stand over there all night?" Donella slowly lifted her leg from the water and draped it over the edge of the tub.

He didn't utter a sound. He used only his eyes to communicate. Pulling his shirt over his head, Kiam moved closer to where she was.

Once he was completely nude, he stepped into the tub leaning his back against her chest. Her soft breast and the hot water relaxed every muscle in his body except one; that soldier was at attention and doing a full salute.

She pulled his head back onto her shoulder as she ran the sponge over his neck and chest. When she got to that rock a smile came over her face. She took all of him firmly into her hand and began to ease his pain. Slowly she stroked and squeezed. "You are such a beautiful man," she cooed in his ear. "I know your sacrifice." She squeezed harder as her wrist rotated to his pleasure. "It's your time. Make this city bow to you," she encouraged as she ran her tongue inside his ear.

Kiam closed his eyes and enjoyed her handiwork. Just when he was on the edge Donella released him. "Stand up, I want to taste you." She commanded.

Kiam rose to his feet, towering over her. Water and suds ran over his chest and abs as she took him in her mouth. The tightening of her jaws sent chills up his spine. Slippery wet moans filled the room as she slurped and stroked. Kiam placed his hand on her head for balance and watched the show. In and out her mouth his dick disappeared and flutters formed in his gut as he threatened to release what felt like tons.

Grabbing his ass she took him to the back of her throat causing a low hiss to leave Kiam's lips. He grabbed a fistful of her hair and prepared to let go. Pulling back a little, Donella sped up her movements until he released long and hard to the back of her throat. She cupped her tongue allowing him to see the thick white evidence of her effect on his soldier. Then she smiled up at him erotically and swallowed every drop.

Licking her lips Donella moaned, "Mmmm. The taste of power."

Kiam slid down in the tub, put his head back and recuperated. Donella straddled his lap ready to feel all that thickness.

"Nah, we good." Kiam shut her down.

Donella leaned back and made eye contact. "You don't want none of this?" she asked while seductively grinding on him.

"Nah, you put in work. I'm good. Lift up." He pushed her back so he could get up. Wrapping a towel around his waist he walked into the living room and snatched a few bills from the Louie bag that laid on the couch.

"Did I do something wrong?" Embarrassment dripped from her question just as the water slid down her body and dripped from her flesh before she quickly dressed in the complimentary robe.

"You straight. I need to get some rest." He handed her the stack.

"No," she waved it off, "Baby, I'm good." Things were much bigger than that. Donella grabbed her things and got dressed. "If you need anything just let me know."

She wrote her number on the note pad, walked over to him, stood on her tippy toes and kissed his cheek. "You official." She looked down then back up. "The woman that gets all that is going to be a lucky bitch."

Kiam didn't reply, he was the type that kept his words at a minimum. Muthafuckas didn't know what you were thinking until you opened your mouth. He knew nothing about Donella to trust her with his thoughts no matter how trivial they were.

She smiled at him understandingly. "Rest well."

Kiam walked her to the door, locked it, and then headed for the shower.

A different type of man with less control would have been balls deep in baby girl, but Kiam was of a select breed. He needed to get his shit right first, plus he didn't know her. *Fuck around and my dick fall off.* He had got his nut; he was satisfied. Now he needed to get focused.

As the water ran over his head and down his face, Kiam began to plot. First, he wanted to make sure he took care of all the business he had pending. Second, hit the long list of shit Pop needed him to do. He knew he was indebted to Pop, but he also had some unfinished business of his own to settle. He needed to make sure he wasn't under no one's thumb and mercy.

Kiam walked out the bathroom with a foolproof plan in the front of his mind. He lotioned his skin before throwing on the hotel robe and lay across the king sized bed. It had been a very long time since he laid in such comfort. It felt like the bed had grown arms and was hugging him.

He tucked the fat goose down pillow under his head and began to doze off. *This city is like a fat pussy and I'ma fuck her hard until she cum. When she pass out, I'ma grab her purse and be out. They will never know what hit 'em.*

Lissha pulled up in front of the hotel and picked up Donella twenty minutes after receiving her text. Quickly, Donella jumped in the car and fastened her seat belt.

"What happened?" Lissha asked as they drove off.

"Only what he wanted to happen. Pussy will not be a problem," Donella reported.

Lissha didn't respond. She knew that if Dee said it then that's what it was, because Donella had the type of sexiness that could tempt God. She thought back to when Big Zo first recruited Donella to the team. He had met her in a strip club up in B-more where she was wasting her beauty and talents popping her ass for a little bit of a nigga's trap.

24

"What do you want with that trick bitch, Daddy?" Lissha questioned him.

Big Zo laughed. "I don't want the pussy, I want the power she possesses with it. When you look at her, you see a stripper. What I see is a bitch that can lure a muthafucka into the gates of hell. Trust me, she'll be a valuable asset to us."

As usual Big Zo had been right. Before the feds came snatching him and his people up, Donella had seduced and led three of Big Zo's enemies into his hands for execution. Not once had she failed. If Kiam could resist that sweet chocolate candy between Donella's legs, pussy most definitely wouldn't be his downfall.

Lissha phoned Big Zo.

"Hello." His deep voice rang in her ear.

"It's confirmed," she said with satisfaction in her voice.

"Um. Go to phase two."

"Got it. Love you, Daddy."

"Love you, too."

Chapter 4
In Search Of Answers

Kiam was awakened by a soft but persistent knock at the door. He sat up, rubbed his eyes, and swung his legs over the side of the bed savoring the plush carpet underfoot. Looking up, he squinted his eyes against a beam of morning sunlight that peeked through a part in the cream-colored blinds over the main window.

He slid the German Luger from under the pillow and walked bare-footed to the door with the strap down at his side.

"Who's there?" His deep baritone was a little coarse from sleep.

"Room Service," came the feminine reply from the other side of the door. Which was a shock to him since he hadn't ordered anything.

The mention of food caused his stomach to growl. He suddenly recalled that he hadn't eaten since he and Lissha had grabbed a couple of Philly steak sandwiches before leaving PA yesterday.

"Leave it outside the door," he directed.

He allowed a few seconds to pass, then pressed his ear against the door just in time to hear soft footsteps patter away. Cautious by nature he waited a half minute longer before opening the door. He stuck his head out and peered up and down the hallway. Satisfied that everything was good, Kiam pulled the cart inside and relocked the door.

When he uncovered the trays on the cart, the aroma of a decent breakfast wafted up his nose. Kiam licked his lips and inspected the meal more closely. There were egg omelets, hash browns, turkey sausages, toast, cereal, milk, coffee and orange juice. As he began to move the dishes around the tray he saw a folded small card. He flipped it open and quickly read the accompanying message.

Welcome home, Kiam, Please enjoy your breakfast. I'll see you in a couple days.

Lissha xoxo.

Placing the note back on the tray, Kiam cracked a little smile. He pushed the cart over to the dining area, sat at the table as he wasted no time digging in.

An hour later he had fed his belly, showered, and threw on one of the outfits that Lissha had purchased for him. The cream and brown True Religion gear graced his frame like she had gotten it tailored for him. He checked his reflection in the mirror on the wall in the bedroom, pleased with what he saw. His features had matured while he was on lock but his cold black eyes hadn't changed one bit. They made his youthful face appear unreadable.

"Kiam, what's going on in your mind that causes you to look so serious all the time?" The lady that raised him had often asked when he was growing up.

Kiam could never quite answer the question. At least not honestly, because the truth might have sent Miss Charlene to an early grave.

He rested his thoughts on her. She had been murdered in her home a year after he began serving his bid. Somebody had to pay for that, and he already knew where to begin looking for answers.

That nigga DeMarcus better have some names on the tip of his tongue when I find him or it's gonna be a bad day for Cuz.

He sat on the side of the bed and reached for the phone on the nightstand to hit up his dude Czar. He finally picked up after his phone had rung a half dozen times. Surprise rang from his voice when he realized it was Kiam.

A short while later, with the April sun kissing the back of his neck, Kiam slid into the passenger seat of Czar's black 2010 Mercedes Benz GLK 350.

"What's good, Bleed?" Czar greeted him with a genuine smile. He skipped the routine gangsta hug because he remembered that Kiam wasn't a touchy-feely type of dude. "I see you did the time instead of letting the time do you," observed Czar. "Anything else would have been asinine, right?" replied Kiam. "True. Damn, nigga, welcome home. You lamping at The Ritz so you must be good." "I'm alright." "Man, I know I didn't send you nothin' on your books but—" "You don't owe me any explanations," Kiam cut him off. Czar didn't owe him anything which meant Kiam didn't owe him a damn thing either. "Where that nigga DeMarcus at? He still around?" he inquired. "Is he? Hell yeah, he's still around. And he has Miles Road turned up from 93rd all the way up to Lee Road. Man, that lame ass nigga has gotten rich since you've been gone. I know he was looking out for you, wasn't he?" "Something like that." Kiam's response was evasive.

Czar, who was five years older than Kiam, had known him since he was a little badass, so he recognized the bitter tone in which Kiam had replied. He didn't know what DeMarcus had done, but he knew that boy wasn't built to beef with a goon like the one in his passenger seat.

Czar wasn't a groupie type dude, but he had no qualms with giving props to those that deserved them. Although he had never witnessed Kiam take a man's life, he knew what he knew—Kiam's murder game was prolific. Czar knew that just as he knew a pig's pussy was pork. Every dude that had beefed with Kiam had ended up with his shit pushed back— that wasn't a coincidence.

Before he went away on gun charges, at eighteen years old, the streets trembled when Kiam came on the block. Established hustlers had him pegged as a growing force to be reckoned with if his quick trigger finger didn't take him down first. More than a few ballers from over his way secretly rejoiced when Kiam caught time in the feds. They had peeped that he was a hungry lion that would not have been content until he was King.

Czar had peeped the same thing. He wondered if the bid had changed Kiam any.

"So what's up, nigga? You gon' turn it up or are you all rehabilitated and shit?" He asked with a chuckle in his tone.

"I'ma do me." Kiam kept it brief.

"Meaning what?" Czar pried.

"Meaning nothing and everything."

Czar couldn't figure that shit out and it made his head hurt to even try. "I hear you, nephew," he steered the conversation back to DeMarcus. "I'm not tryna plant no seeds because I know you and DeMarcus grew up drinking out the same cup, but it seem like he didn't bubble until Miss Charlene died."

"And you said that to say what?" Kiam put him on the defensive.

Czar turned right on 116th and Union heading toward Miles Road.

"I hate to spread rumors dawg, 'cause that's not my get down but I fuck with you hard so I gotta keep it one hunnid," Czar went on. "Word on the street is that DeMarcus killed Miss Charlene and used the life insurance money to sponsor his come up in the game"

Kiam said nothing. He knew from Miss Charlene's own mouth that any money left over from the policy after her burial went to the church. DeMarcus would have known the same thing.

"I raised y'all to be men, y'all can take care of yourselves when I'm gone," she had explained before that day ever arrived.

So what Czar was saying meant nothing to Kiam. He didn't discount the possibility that DeMarcus had killed Miss Charlene for money, but it damn sure wasn't insurance money.

Kiam was silent, contemplating, preparing. He looked out the window at the changes that had taken place since he went away. Some apartment buildings had been demolished, and empty lots stood where corner stores once thrived. Houses were boarded up and the streets were littered with potholes. Destruction and despair was as visible as a dark, gray cloud filled with rain. But the city hadn't witnessed nothing yet, what he was going to do would surpass the darkest imagination.

Chapter 5
The Foundation

Lissha was comfortably seated in her black, white and silver living room flipping through an Essence magazine. There were several Hawaiian glaze candles burning, and the sound of Trey Songz Passion, Pain, and Pleasure CD was playing in the background. She reached forward, grabbed her huge mug of green tea, and brought it to her lips. As she placed it back on the coffee table her doorbell rang.

She removed her legs from their folded position and rose to her feet. She walked to the door, rested her eye against the peep hole then clicked the locks.

"Damn, bitch. What you got some ass up in here?" Treebie barged past Lissha headed to the living room looking around with a suspicious eye.

"Good Morning, Lish," Bayonna said as she followed Treebie.

"Hey ma, and why is this bitch always so loud and ignorant? This bitch would fuck up a good nut right on the brink."

"Whatever." She palmed her hand in the air. "What you got in this cup?" Treebie inhaled deeply.

"Put my shit down. Who the fuck walks into someone's house and sticks their nose in cups and shit?" Lissha twisted her mouth, walked over to Treebie and took her cup out of her clutch.

Bayonna took a seat in the high back chair, crossed her legs and shook her head.

"Is this bitch drunk?" Lissha turned her question to Bayonna.

"No, I am not but I'm about to be," Treebie announced as she walked to the kitchen, snatched a bottle and three glasses from the cabinet, then sashayed back into the living room.

"Alright, let's get down to business." Lissha watched Treebie pour their glasses of wine as they took a seat across from hers.

"Okay, so Kiam is on deck," Lissha began. She paused to look at both ladies. "We need to introduce him to Gator so he can take over that operation and reinforce our power on the streets. Then we need to set up a meeting for him with the drug connect so he can take that shit over and we can turn down and handle all this other shit we got on the table."

"So, Gator is not calling shots anymore?" Treebie curiously raised her eyebrows.

Lissha cut in. "No. Daddy wants Kiam to take charge and we're gonna back him one hundred percent."

"I'm not comfortable with that. We don't know this nigga." Treebie was getting agitated.

"Hold the fuck up. Don't forget your place in this shit." Lissha turned to Treebie with a wrinkled brow. "This nigga is official. Daddy sent him to us and if you got a fucking problem with that, address it to Daddy and see how that turns out." Lissha stared directly in Treebie's eyes and did not blink.

Treebie glided her tongue across her teeth then sucked them. "I ain't got no problem with Big Zo's decisions. I'm just saying we been working with Gator for years. I know his get down. I ain't got time to be holding no new nigga's hand and then have to worry about him turning on us when shit get tight."

"Have I ever crossed you? Have. I. Ever. Crossed. You?" Lissha emphasized each word waiting for her to say the wrong shit.

"No, and hopefully you never will," Treebie got up. "I gotta pee." She headed to the bathroom.

Lissha's heart began to pick up speed, she was heated. For the first time her right hand and most trusted confidant was challenging her authority. If Treebie's rebellion was a sign that she no longer wanted to take orders she would be wise to order herself a casket because that's how it was going to play out.

"Lish. You know it's not you she don't trust. None of us knows anything about Kiam, so of course Treebie is a little uncomfortable," intoned Bayonna, breaking Lissha's train of thought.

Lissha studied her like maybe she was Judas in disguise. Bayonna felt the burn from her intense gaze and correctly interpreted it. But she knew that there was no flaw in her loyalty so she was unfazed by any uncertainty that might have crept into Lissha's mind.

"Let's just follow the script and put Kiam to the test so Treebie can see what he is made of." She tried her hand at reasoning with Lissha who had a look on her face like she was getting ready to do something to somebody.

Treebie emerged from the bathroom drying her hands with a paper towel. "Look, Lissha. I apologize if I was out of line. I'm not trying to oppose you or Big Zo. It's just that I have sacrificed a lot. We have been through the trenches." She pounded her fist in her hand.

They had indeed been through it together, going back to when it was just the two of them holding down the fort for Big Zo, trafficking blocks up and down the highway to keep lawyer money coming in as he fought a futile effort to win an acquittal.

The day that Big Zo was convicted and sent away, Lissha and Treebie had gone out and gotten drunk, then went back to Treebie's place and cried on each other's shoulder vowing death to everyone that turned informant on him. Together they had murked three of those faggot ass, snitch muthafuckas and to this day they were hunting for the others.

Lissha couldn't overlook Treebie's sacrifices; she had walked away from her husband, Wa'leek, in New Jersey to get down with Big Zo. But had time begun to eat away at her loyalty?

Lissha studied Treebie's face as her mouth continued to move. "Li Li, I love you to the death of me," she proclaimed with sincerity in her eyes. "I will give my life for you, but I will tell you this—if Kiam is foul, Big Zo ain't going to have to touch him. I'm going to put heat all over that ass. That's my word."

Treebie looked in Lissha's eyes searching for approval. Lissha thought long and hard about Treebie's words. If nothing else she was genuine. She had to admit that they had run hard together. Many had folded when things got hot, but Treebie had always stood firm. However, Lissha needed to reaffirm that regardless of all that, they were not equal in authority.

"Apology accepted. But I need you to understand something that should already be overstood. This shit right here belongs to me and Daddy. He makes the decisions and I carry them out." She paused.

Treebie waited for her to continue.

Lissha wet her lips with her tongue then went on. "As far as Kiam goes, you won't have to worry about him crossing you. Because if he does I will kill him myself. But if I find out you stood in the way of him carrying out Daddy's orders, we gonna have a serious problem." The warning was subtle but unmistakable.

Lissha got up, walked to the door and opened it. "Y'all can bounce. I got some shit to do. I'll get up with y'all at the spot in two days," she said.

Treebie headed to the door and Bayonna followed. As they passed by Lissha, Treebie stopped and said, "Either you about to come on your period or you need some dick. But I still love you." She kissed Lissha on the cheek.

Lissha just curled her lips and watched her go by. She wiped her face with the back of her hand as she watched the two ladies walk down the driveway. *That shit felt like the kiss of death.*

She stood staring at them until they drove off.

Chapter 6
Suspicions

The car turned left off 116th Street onto Miles Road. They were headed toward 131st then on up to Lee Road. Trees were barren of leaves because winter hadn't decided to bow completely to spring yet, but the early morning 70 degree temperature lent hope for a beautiful day.

A small group of people were huddled at the bus stop on the corner, in light jackets, waiting on the slow running #50 bus to come. A pair of teenaged girls eyed the whip like they wanted to fuck the grill. Czar honked the horn at them and they waved.

"Lil' hot asses," Kiam remarked with a grin.

Czar pushed on up the street, pointing out all the spots that DeMarcus had on lock.

"I'm telling you, Dee done got his weight up out here. I don't know who put him on but that nigga is doing it. He got runners handling weight and selling steezies for him all up and down this bitch," lamented Czar.

Kiam just listened. There was no reason to comment because he knew that before long the streets would be his. DeMarcus damn sure wasn't built to stop him.

"Who else is gettin' serious money on this side of town?" He questioned his man.

"You got those Gore brothers off Princeton Avenue eating good. They've been locking down a lot of spots, chasing other nigga's off corners up and down East 116th, from Buckeye Road all the way to Harvard Road."

"Greg and Fat?" asked Kiam. He had heard their names mentioned a few times when he had reached out to the streets.

"Yeah. They rock these platinum chains with MBK across the pieces in diamonds. It's supposed to stand for *My Brother's Keeper*. Wherever you see one of them, you see the other. That's how they roll. I figure they're touching about ten whole ones a week."

They'll either get down or get laid down, Kiam decided.

"How many bricks you touching?" he asked Czar.

"Oh, I do a'ight," he replied.

Kiam didn't press him, in time Czar would reveal his hand or get it chopped the hell off. *Take no prisoners,* Pop had lectured Kiam every day. *You'll be able to exert your will over most dudes. Kill everybody else that stands in your way.*

As they drove on up Miles Road, he directed Czar to make a left on 123rd. Czar followed his directions and without being told stopped in front of the house where Kiam had grew up.

Memories came rushing back through Kiam's mind.

"Baby, Miss Charlene is going to watch you while I run downtown to see these white folks about my damn food stamps," his mother told him, handing him a quarter so that he wouldn't act up when she drove off.

Five year old Kiam took the quarter and kissed his mother on the cheek. "I ain't gon' cry, Mama. I'ma go play with DeMarcus until you get back."

"That's my little man. Mama loves you," she said, hugging him tightly.

When she let him go, tears ran down her face, ruining her makeup. "Why you crying, Mama?" He looked at her curiously.

"Mama just got a whole lot of problems." She wiped her eyes and sniffled.

Miss Charlene came outside and told Kiam's mother to be back for him by 7 o'clock. "I gotta go to Bingo tonight. I feel lucky," she said.

"I'll be back way before then," his mother promised. But something in her eyes made Kiam cry as he watched her leave.

When they got in the house Miss Charlene gave him some cookies and told him to go and play with DeMarcus.

He was still crying when he reached the basement where DeMarcus was located, kneeling beside his toys.

"You a sissie," DeMarcus teased.

Whap! Kiam punched him dead in the nose. "Fuck you talking to, bitch?" he snorted.

Now DeMarcus was crying harder than him. "I'ma tell my grandmother," he whined.

"And I'ma fuck you up."

DeMarcus told anyway, and Miss Charlene scolded Kiam something fierce, threatening to beat the skin off his behind. But she was all bark. She loved children too much to do more than pop them once or twice.

"Boy, why you so bad?" she asked, giving him another handful of cookies.

Kiam hunched his shoulders and sat at the window looking for his mother to return. Hours passed and she hadn't shown up. Then hours turned into days and days turned into years.

"You alright, nephew?" asked Czar looking at him quizzically.

"I'm good. Who lives here now?" The house looked ready to fall down.

Czar didn't know so Kiam got out the car and walked up to the door. He had to get inside the house and check something out. That would determine his next move, and whether or not DeMarcus would be the next nigga he killed.

The six raggedy wooden steps strained and squeaked under his weight as Kiam walked up on the porch. At the top of the steps he paused and took in the exterior of his childhood home. The paint had long ago peeled from the banisters, and they sagged like the shoulders of an old, tired man.

In one corner of the porch sat a worn couch with different sized bricks for legs; a rat strolled fearlessly across the back of the soiled piece of furniture fearing no consequences. The rodent suddenly stopped and looked at Kiam, then quickly scurried away.

Instinctively it had recognized the presence of a killah. Kiam liked that. Now niggas needed to do the same.

He proceeded up to the front door and stuck his hand out in search of the doorbell. In its place was nothing but a small gutted out hole. The door frame was freshly painted, like makeup applied on the weathered face of a hundred year old woman, in a futile attempt to disguise the wear and tear that life had taken on her soul. Miss Charlene had to be rolling over in her grave at what had become of the house that she had kept up with a loving hand.

Kiam brushed those melancholy thoughts aside, he had no time for sentimental trips down memory lane until he had the answer to the question that was most prevalent in his mind.

He knocked on the door and waited for someone to answer.

The rap of his knuckles against the cheap wooden door brought no response. He knocked a second time, much louder than the first, but still no one came to the door.

The years of incarceration had trained his ears to pick up the slightest sound or movement. Without pressing his ear to the door he could hear voices coming from inside and they weren't the recorded sounds of a television set. These were live voices. Hood villains talking.

So bring y'alls asses to the door. He pounded on the door like he had some business up in those people's spot and it could not wait.

The door was snatched open and Kiam stood eye to eye with a tall, reedy dude whose melon head was way too big for his rail thin body and pencil neck. Slim's lips looked to be permanently puckered and his jaw twitched. "Fool, why is you banging on my door like you's the goddamn police?" he gritted.

Kiam looked him in the eye, he had already sized ol' boy up just that fast. "Calm the fuck down, nigga, before you get smashed on your own front porch."

"Say what?" Slim asked, adding bass to his voice

"I said what you thought I said," Kiam restated. "But I didn't come here for that. I need to come up in here for five minutes and I'll be out." He reached in his pocket and pulled out a band.

The fiend's eyes bulged at the sight of that fat $1,000 rubber banded knot in Kiam's hand.

"It's either this," said Kiam, indicating the stack. "Or this, nigga." He lifted the bottom of his shirt to reveal the butt of his uncompromising negotiator.

"Man, who are you? You not the police, are you?" asked dude. One eye was on the money and the other was on Kiam's strap.

"Never mind who I am, but I'm not the rollers. I don't care what you have going on up in here. Five minutes is all I need and I'm out," Kiam reiterated.

"A'ight." Pencil Neck licked his dry lips as he accepted the mula from Kiam and stepped to the side.

As soon as he entered the house, the strong pungent smell of burning crack cocaine assaulted Kiam's airway. He walked through the living room toward the back of the house. In the kitchen he encountered another man, and a frail, pock marked face woman, sitting at a cheap card table passing a crack pipe back and forth between them. The card table and the chairs that they occupied were the only pieces of furniture in sight.

The two smokers were in their own world, they didn't even look up and acknowledge his presence. Slim was on his heels.

"Fall the fuck back," commanded Kiam, stopping at the top of the stairs that led to the basement.

"Five minutes," Slim reminded him, then scurried off like the rat.

The old rickety stairs squeaked as Kiam descended them. In the basement memories rushed up on him like a gust of hot air. This was where he and DeMarcus, as little boys, spent most of their time playing. This was also where Miss Charlene had been beaten to death, he had been told.

41

Kiam ducked under several exposed pipes that hung from the ceiling as he passed by the hot water tank. He recalled the day that he and DeMarcus had tussled and he had rammed DeMarcus's head into that same appliance. They were kids back then, now they were men. If DeMarcus had violated like Kiam suspected, he wasn't gonna ram his head into anything, he was going to cut it off.

He stood back up to his full height once he cleared the last overhead pipe and reached the storage room. It was dark and dank. Kiam left the door open to allow in a little light. He stepped over small puddles of water on the floor as he proceeded to the rear of the storage room where the answer to his question lied.

Kiam ran his hands along the cold concrete wall, feeling for an indentation that was imperceptible to the eye and the touch unless you knew it was there. He had built this stash spot himself yet it took several attempts before he was successful in locating the groove that he was searching for in the wall.

He pressed his weight on the spot and a door that had been camouflaged as a section of the wall opened with a squeak, revealing the hidden wall safe. Its own door was shut and locked.

Kiam didn't have to search his mind for the combination to open it; those numbers were indelibly etched in his memory like his birth date. Besides himself, Miss Charlene had been the only one that knew of this clever stash spot. But DeMarcus would have figured that Kiam had left a bank with her. And he was the type of thirsty dude that would brutally murder his own grandmother for a come-up. Well, Kiam was the type that brutally murdered, period.

Squinting his eyes in the dimness of the light that shined through from the outer room, Kiam unlocked the safe then hesitated before opening the door and peering inside. He knew that the contents would be gone, but he needed confirmation. Proof that his surrogate mother had been murdered over what had been inside.

He opened the door to the safe and reached inside. His hand came into contact with what he was feeling for. He grabbed ahold of it and pulled it out, surprised that it was still in there.

The backpack was musty from years of sitting, but its weight told Kiam that it had not been bothered even before he opened it and looked inside. Stacks of money threatened to spill out onto the floor. Kiam stood there in a daze. If DeMarcus or someone else hadn't beaten Miss Charlene to death while robbing her for the money, what the fuck had happened?

The answer came to him almost instantaneously. Miss Charlene had died because she wouldn't give up his stash spot. In that moment his love for her doubled and his anger quadrupled.

"What you got there, man?" The question came from behind him.

Kiam whirled around and in one smooth motion the banger was off his waist and in his hand. He stepped toward Slim and stuck the Nine in his gut. "You wanna know what I got, nosey muthafucka?" he snarled.

"Nah, not really," dude reconsidered, but Kiam told him anyway.

"I got your muthafuckin' epitaph right here if you don't fall the fuck back." He raised his arm and slapped the curious ass fool across the head with the burner, drawing blood.

"Nigga, you don't have to follow me around. I told you five minutes. Five goddamn minutes! But you on some nosey shit." He pistol whipped the white meat out of the smoker's head.

Standing over the fallen man, he reached inside the backpack and grabbed a stack. He tossed the money on the floor beside the bloodied dude and gritted. "Nosey people get it too. Dark Man X. Check him out sometime."

Inside the car, Kiam was quiet as Czar drove off. He stared out the window at nothing in particular while his emotions tested the strength of his mind.

"Did you find what you were looking for, nephew?" asked Czar, glancing down at the backpack that sat between Kiam's legs.

"Nah, man, I didn't find nothin'." His answer was the truth; the backpack raised more questions than it provided answers.

"You still wanna hit Lee Road and try to catch up with DeMarcus? He has a car lot out in Cleveland Heights."

Kiam thought about that for a minute. If he ran into DeMarcus now he would act on emotion and push the nigga's hairline back. Wrong or right, he didn't give a fuck. But Pop had schooled him to be a thinker and he refused to let those lessons be in vain.

"I wanna put that on hold for a minute. DeMarcus isn't going anywhere." He left it hanging in air, because Pop had also stressed that you never let your right hand know what the left one is thinking.

Changing tactics, Kiam said, "Take me on Benwood. I want to check on somebody and see what she's been up to."

Czar didn't have to ask who lived there, he already knew. She had been Kiam's little wifey before he went away.

The Past...

Faydrah Combs had been a tomboy all of her early life, playing ball and stealing out of stores right alongside of Kiam, DeMarcus, and the other little bad ass boys. When those same knuckleheads put their basketballs down and started slinging rocks, she was down with that, too. Running up to cars and slushing through the snow for that next sale.

Back then she was just one of the homies. Then around thirteen years old, her titties started sprouting out and she grew a little bump for an ass. Those jeans that used to sag started fitting tight. That's when things changed, because that's when those same boys that she used to shoot ball with, and now hustled with, started trying to cut something with her. Every one of them except Kiam. The funny thing was, that's what made her want his mean, black, skinny tail. One day she had built up her courage and walked right up to him and kissed him in the mouth. "Nigga, you're taking my cherry," she regulated.

Kiam shoved her up off of him. "Fuck you doing, girl?"

"You're going to be my man," she declared, stepping right back in his space and wrapping her arms around his neck.

He shoved her back away from him, harder this time. "Eyez, you trippin'. You're my homie, I'm not tryna get with you like that," he spat.

She loved when he called her Eyez, but she hated that he still saw her as one of the boys. He had crushed her little feelings. But she hadn't let him know it.

"Boy, I was just playing with you anyway. Don't nobody want your little boney ass," she shot back, throwing the bit of booty she had as she walked away.

She left the block, went home and cried in her pillow. She cursed God for not blessing her with the type of ass and femininity that Kiam would not have been able to resist.

From that point on she hid her feelings from him, but whenever they were out hustling and his body came close to hers, her virgin flower begged to be watered.

Two years later, she was still hustling with him. Not because she was as hooked on that street shit as Kiam and them were, but at least hustling alongside of him kept her in his presence. But it was pure torture for her to have to watch him push up on other chicks.

One night seeing Kiam caked up with a female at a party they had attended, Faydrah abruptly left and trekked three miles home, tears running down her chin.

When she got home, she walked in the house and slammed the door behind her, awakening her mom who was asleep on the couch.

"Do you have to make so much noise?" Rebecca complained.

"Sorry." Faydrah ignored the crack pipe on the end table. They had already had it out about that more times than either of them could count.

She sat down on the couch, laid her head on her mother's shoulder and screamed, "Ugh! I swear I hate him."

Rebecca put an arm around her only child. "Okay, tell me what Kiam has done now." She was well aware that he was the source of all of her daughter's frustration.

"He won't notice me unless I'm flipping a brick with him or busting a gun beside him. I could walk butt naked in front of that boy and he wouldn't even look twice." Faydrah poked her lips out.

"Honey, how do you expect him to notice you when you dress and act just like he does?"

"I don't care," she mumbled.

"Tomorrow I'm going to dress you up and do your hair, and if Kiam doesn't notice you I'll quit getting high."

Faydrah laughed. "You should quit anyway."

The next day when Faydrah went out on the block, all the homies mouths were on the ground. Her jeans hugged her booty like leotards, and her breasts commanded notice. Her hair, which she had religiously worn in a ponytail, flowed loosely down her back. Her lips were glossed and her nails were painted in a girlie design.

The block huggers were transfixed.

"Uh, put y'alls tongues back in y'alls mouths because there's only one nigga out here that I want," she announced with confidence.

"Who, me?" said DeMarcus.

"Nigga, you wish." She shut him down. *Then walked up to the one she so desired.*

Kiam was posted up on the hood of his Yukon. He had been watching her since she walked up. She was looking all the way sexy.

"Hey, baby," she said in a sultry tone that she had rehearsed all morning long.

"What's good, Eyez?" He spoke back.

"You," she said. *"When are you going to quit playing and be my man?"* She threw her hand on her hip, feigning confidence. But inside she was so nervous she was about to pee on herself.

"Just like that, huh?" He flashed a cocky smile.

"Yep, just like that."

"Girl, go on home." He quickly extinguished her hope.

Faydrah bit down on her lip to keep from crying. Then she turned on her heels and held her head high. She would break down when she got home, but not out there in front of all of them.

"I'll be over to pick my woman up when I come out the trap."

Faydrah stopped in her tracks! She couldn't trust her ears. She slowly turned around and stared at Kiam, afraid to ask him if she had heard him correctly.

"I said what you think I said," he clarified. *Then he walked up to her and kissed some of that lip gloss off of her lips.*

Faydrah almost fainted.

Kiam felt her legs weaken. He held her close and kissed her again. "Go on home, baby. I'll be through around nine."

When he took his arms from around her, she didn't walk home, she floated.

Later that night, she drifted to the sky as Kiam tenderly deflowered her. That was the beginning of a young love that lasted until Kiam went away.

Kiam recalled it all. He had thought about her many times during his bid, but he still felt he had done the right thing by telling her to go on with her life. He had heard that she was in corporate America now. That proved that letting go had been best for her.

Kiam was out of the car as soon as it came to a stop in front of Faydrah mother's house.

"I'll be right back," he told Czar.

Ten minutes later he returned with a glint of light in his coal black eyes. He had Czar to drop him back off at the hotel so that he could stash the backpack and change clothes, then he hailed a taxi over to the address that Rebecca had given him.

Chapter 7
Long Time No See

"**E**xcuse me, Miss, can you tell me where the rest room is?" Kiam's voice boomed at Faydrah's back.

For a brief moment she was frozen in her spot. Even though time and circumstances had separated them physically, the connection that they once shared made his voice feel like water to a thirsty soul.

Turning slowly and barely able to breath due to the excitement that rose up in her chest, Faydrah pulled her glasses from her face to make sure that her eyes weren't fooling her just in case her ears were.

"Kiam?"

"Who else you letting get up behind you?" Kiam jokingly stated.

Faydrah turned completely and gasped at the beautiful sight before her. She put her arms around his neck, closed her eyes and hugged him tightly. "Oh my god, when did you get home?" She asked breathlessly.

"A few days ago," Kiam nuzzled his face against the crease in her neck. "You act like you missed somebody."

"I did miss you," she whined. She secured her hold around him.

After a few more seconds of body to body embrace, she backed up and looked him up and down as she ran her hands over his chest. "Look at you, all buff. I guess I can't call you skin and bones no more," she teased.

"Nah, I got my weight up. Been eating my Wheaties." Kiam blushed a little as the warm memories of their knee-high days flooded his mind.

"So, what's up? How did you know to find me here?" She asked as her eyes kept wondering all over his body.

Kiam stood there letting her soak him up.

"Never mind, you don't have to answer that. I already know who told you where I work. Mama still loves you," she added, unconsciously running her tongue over her lips.

"Damn, Eyez. Why you keep looking at me like that?" He affectionately called her by the childhood nickname he had given her due to her pretty diamond shaped light brown eyes.

Faydrah blushed.

"I can't believe you're standing here that's all."

"When is your lunch break? I need to sit and talk to you."

Faydrah looked at her watch. "I had my break already, but I get off at 1:00. I came in early. Let me go up and get my things, then we can go."

"Hurry up, a man is hungry," he said, rubbing his stomach.

"That is the story of your life. Just sit down, I'll be right back." She pushed him toward the seats in the lobby.

"You still think you can beat me," Kiam joked as he sat down.

"Whatever. Just don't leave."

"I'ma wait right here,"

Faydrah giggled as she headed to the elevator.

Kiam's eyes wondered over her curves as she moved away. Everything was swollen in all the right places. *Damn she ain't a teenager no more.*

Faydrah's stomach filled with butterflies as she rode to the seventh floor. When the elevator came to a stop she damn near ran off.

"Damn, girl. What the hell happened in the lobby that got you showing all thirty-two?" Gina asked from behind the receptionist's desk.

"I ran into an old friend. Cover for me, I need to clock out," she replied, whizzing by. Quickly, she moved around her office grabbing her briefcase, cell phone and keys. Cutting off the light she took one last look then shut the door. "Alright girl I'll call you tonight if I can," she said to Gina as she headed to the staircase.

"That must be a hell of an old friend. He got you taking the steps," Gina yelled out.

"Shut up," Faydrah laughed as she entered the stairwell and moved swiftly down to the lobby.

Reaching the last flight, she took a few deep breaths to calm herself. Then she reached in her pocket and popped the other half of her mint in her mouth and exited the hallway. When she got to the seats Kiam wasn't there. She immediately went into panic mode. Her eyes moved all over the lobby in search of him. Damn, she hadn't even gotten his number.

Just as disappointment set in, Kiam came up from behind and put his arms around her. Faydrah jumped, he had a chick's nerves scrambled with excitement.

"Stop, you play too much." She hit his arm.

"You still scared of me? Damn, you a grown woman. What you afraid of?"

"I'm not scared of you," she said in a low voice.

"You ought to be," he teased.

Faydrah sucked her teeth "Whatever. Come on, I thought you were so hungry." She wrapped her hand in his and pulled him toward the exit.

Kiam didn't respond, he was hungry alright but not for food. He was ready to feast on what she had under that skirt.

They walked a few blocks, laughing and talking, and bumping shoulders with the many pedestrians that crowded downtown as she led him to the warehouse district where the good restaurants were. It felt like they were sixteen all over again and had skipped school to hangout. When they arrived at the Blue Point Grille, the city's best seafood restaurant, he opened the door for her and they walked inside.

"You ate here before?" He looked around.

"Yes. I eat here all the time. Come on." She walked over to the hostess and requested a table for two.

Once seated, Faydrah flipped through her menu. Kiam picked his up and scanned the different selections. It had been years since he had sat and ordered from a menu and it felt like he was reading a foreign language.

Picking up on his slight insecurity, Faydrah took control. "I got you, baby."

Kiam just smiled. Faydrah was always very attentive to him and he appreciated that about her.

When the waitress walked over to the table Faydrah ordered for Kiam and herself, keeping in mind that he loved seafood. "The gentleman will have the Shrimp and Scallop Sauté, and I'll have the Lobster Chicken Pasta."

"And what will you be drinking today?" asked the young blonde-haired waitress with a toothy smile.

Faydrah glanced back at the menu, then she looked up and replied, "I'll have a Strawberry Daiquiri." She looked over at Kiam. "Do you still abstain from alcohol, sir?" She teased.

"I don't know what I do anymore." he answered with a slight chuckle. "But I damn sure ain't gonna sit here and sip on no damn daiquiri."

Faydrah and the waitress laughed, "Can you bring him a Coke please."

"Put some Rum in it," he requested before the waitress left the table.

"So, when did you get home?" Faydrah folded her hands and stared in his eyes.

"I been home a few days."

"Okay, taking it into consideration that we haven't been in contact with each other, I'm not upset with you for not finding out where I was your first day home."

"I didn't have to find you, you've always been right here in my heart." He tapped his chest.

"Good answer. Now, what are you doing with yourself? What are your plans?"

"I'm not sure yet. I'm just trying to get adjusted."

"Well, if you need anything just let me know."

Just as Faydrah was getting ready to ask her next question the waitress came to the table placing their drinks down.

Faydrah grabbed the stem and slid it close to her. Taking the straw, she swirled the whip cream around then brought it to her mouth, closed her eyes and slowly ran her tongue down the length of the straw.

Kiam looked entranced as a bit of enticement rose in his gut.

"Damn, maybe I should have gotten one of those."

Faydrah opened her eyes "This is the bomb. You want to taste it?" She swirled the straw again and slid it toward him to try.

"Nah, I want to sample it from your lips," he countered in a smooth as butter kind of way.

Faydrah brought it to her mouth and ran it over her tongue. She leaned across table, meeting him halfway, and they their mouths became one.

Faydrah released a faint moan as Kiam greedily kissed her, this time melting under the command of his passion.

A rush of emotions moved through her body like a current.

Pulling back, Faydrah covered her face, allowing her hair to fall forward and shield her eyes. Those almond-shaped windows to her soul threatened to rain tears down her cheeks.

"Many days the memories of your smile and your kindness got me through," Kiam said as he reached out and gently ran his hand along her cheek. Her skin was as soft as crushed velvet.

"I never stopped thinking about you, Kiam." Her eyes reverted back to the table, blinking back a cadre of emotions. "I'm sorry I didn't write or visit. Even though you told me to go on with my life, I should have did something to—"

"Shhh." Kiam interrupted. "It's all good. I'm happy that you were able to go forward and become someone."

"I needed to hear that," she responded looking up into his eyes. "I never stopped loving you."

"I know." he said with understanding that eased the moment.

Just as he pulled his hand away the waitress approached. "Here you go." She sat the plates down in front of them and the aroma instantly filled their lungs, causing Kiam's stomach to growl.

"Damn, this look good," he unwrapped his silverware from the linen.

"It is good," attested Faydrah, placing her napkin on her lap.

"Do you need anything else?" The waitress smiled politely.

"No, we good. Thank you," Faydrah answered as she watched Kiam put his fork to work. She savored watching him take his first bite.

Kiam was unable to say a single word. As soon as he sunk his teeth into the shrimp his taste buds exploded. He forked a second one and chewed with delight.

Setting his fork down for a moment, he looked up at Faydrah who was delighted in his enjoyment. "So what you doing for the rest of the day?" He asked.

"You." Faydrah was now wide open from that kiss.

"So, I don't have to worry about nobody blowing up your phone, or having to look over my shoulder?"

"No, I have had it on lock for months. I'm willing to give you the key." She paused. "Or is there somebody I have to worry about?"

"Yeah, there is somebody you have to worry about," he replied with a smirk on his face. "But, I'll make him be gentle."

Faydrah smiled. "You so nasty."

54

They talked comfortably back and forth over their meal. The food was delicious and the conversation was even better. They declined dessert, but enjoyed a few rounds of drinks before he paid the tab, called a cab and headed to Kiam's hotel.

Anticipation...

Kiam opened the door and hit the lights. Faydrah sat her brief case down next to the couch and looked around.

"This is nice," she complimented, continuing to peruse his temporary pad.

"It'll work for now." He located the remote and turned on the radio. Maxwell came through the speakers, crooning lyrics that were perfect for their situation.

I should be crying but I just can't let it show/ I should be hoping but I can't stop thinking/ All the things we should have said but we never said/ All the things we should have done but we never did...

Kiam walked over to Faydrah and pulled her close to him. "You're so beautiful," he said, moving her hair back so he could look right into her eyes.

"Kiam. I don't want to be your drunken desire," Faydrah lightly protested as his hands began to roam all over her body.

"I'm not drunk. I'm in total control. And only what you want to happen is going to happen," he said, leaning in and kissing her collar bone.

She purred like a kitten. Kiam reached up and ran his hand through her hair. Pulling her head back, he traced the outline of her neck with his tongue. Gently he pulled her blazer off of her shoulders, allowing it to drop to the floor.

Faydrah simply closed her eyes and allowed him to have every part of her. When he unzipped her skirt it fell to the floor effortlessly. She placed her hands on his shoulders and stepped out of it giving him full access. Kiam slowly unbuttoned her shirt and dropped it on top of her skirt and jacket.

Faydrah felt as shy and nervous as the little blooming flower that had given him her bud years ago. The difference this time was that she was no young girl. She was all woman. No more baggy jeans and hoodies. Her grown woman was on full display in bra and panties—titties perky and pussy fat.

Kiam's dick rocked up at the mere sight of her silky skin. It was as if he was seeing her for the first time, and he was pleased with what he saw from head to toe.

"Eyez, you good?"

She nodded her head, unable to speak.

Kiam released one of her breast from the bra. Placing his mouth over her nipple he sucked lightly, sending heat waves through her body.

Clutching him tightly, she leaned in and bit into his neck.

Kiam reached down and lifted her up slightly, fitting her against his waist. Faydrah wrapped her legs around him and held him between her thighs. Her soft breast pressed against his chest as he walked into the bedroom. He laid her down and stripped out of his clothes.

Faydrah looked on as he released his steel from its enclosure. Her eyes widened slightly; he definitely was not the sixteen year old boy she first gave it to. He was a man in every sense of the word.

"I want to feel you," she whispered while pulling off her panties, allowing him a view of her pretty rose.

"You sure?" He asked, stroking his growing erection to full potential.

"Yes," she responded, reaching out and pulling him to her.

Kiam slid between her legs and rested his dick at the base of her throbbing opening. Her wetness seeped from her lips, kissing the head of his thick rod. Kiam slid back and forth stimulating her clit, causing her to squirm under him.

"Baby, I've missed you so very much," she whined.

"I missed you too," he whispered, tracing circles around her pleasure button.

"Let me have it."

"You want it?" He teased, licking and sucking her breast.

"Yesss," she moaned.

"Get it," he responded as he flicked his tongue across her nipple.

Faydrah took him into her hand and brought him to her moist opening. Slowly he entered her inch by inch, breaking down the tension between them. Faydrah inhaled as he went deeper. Her moans began to fill the room as he stroked faster.

Kiam closed his eyes and tried to focus as her grip became hypnotizing. He stroked from side to side, going deeper with every thrust, causing her to tense up and try to escape.

"Kiam," she moaned as he picked up speed.

"Mmm, yes?"

"Baby, slow down," she panted.

Kiam held back and began giving it to her slowly. "This how you want it, ma?" His strokes became gentle and her muscles tighten around him.

"Ooh, you feel so good," she moaned.

"Go ahead baby, cum on this dick." He steadied his pace as Faydrah pushed the pussy at him so he could hit the spot just right. Her breath quickened as she dug her nails into his back.

"Oh, my god," she cried out in ecstasy lashing her head from side to side. "Put this fire out."

"I'ma put it out, baby girl. Damn, your pussy feels so good. This is how you fucked my head up way back then." He spoke softly in her ear causing her fire to burn more intense. "I used to dream about being inside you again, but even in my dreams it didn't feel this good."

Kiam threw her leg over his shoulder and went to work. She was getting ready to feel the hardness and the raw passion of the years that he longed for her.

"Ohhhh...baby, baby, baby," she cried biting down on her lip.

"You wanted it, now let me get it," grunted Kiam. He grabbed her other leg and placed it on his other shoulder.

"Yes, get it Kiam. Get it all," she cried out as he went deeper than she knew existed.

The room was filled with loud moans and the slippery sound of every stroke. Kiam held on as long as he could. When he couldn't hold on any longer he stroked faster and deeper until he released months of pressure and years of pain. She felt his thick muscle swell up inside of her and spread her wide open just as his hot seeds began to spill out within her buttery cup. Her own love rushed up upon her and caused her back to arch off the bed. "Kiam! Oooohhhh baby, I'm coming!" she screamed.

Kiam kept stroking and his semen flooded her as her body went into pleasurable convulsions. Faydrah's honey spilled down warm and plentiful on his engorged shaft, and she panted as his strokes induced multiple orgasms from her, one right behind the other. "Oh my god. Oh my god." She tried to catch her breath.

Releasing her legs he looked down into her face, then placed soft kisses on her lips. "I never stopped loving you," he whispered.

"I know," she responded on short wind."

Laying there between her legs was his refuge, loving her was easy because she made him feel like a man. With her there was no pretense. She didn't care about the money or the murder, she only saw him.

Faydrah held him tight as he rested against her. Tears ran down the side of her face as she released all the agony of the years she had spent missing him. Through her tears there was happiness; she relished in the pleasure of having him between her thighs.

Kiam was insatiable. Her breathing had barely returned to normal when he flipped her over and began sucking on the back of her neck. In an instant she caught fire again and her legs automatically opened themselves for his desire. She was slippery inside from both of their cum, so he slid right in. "Let me give it to you slow," he crooned huskily as he nibbled her ear lobe and gave it to her gently.

"Anyway you want, baby, I'm yours." She submitted her body to his needs.

Kiam took her to the Mountain Top, and then higher. As orgasm after orgasm rocked her inner soul Faydrah felt like she had soared to Heaven. "Come inside me again, fill me with your essence," she breathlessly moaned.

Once they had exhausted the pleasure of every position possible, they showered and just laid next to each other. Within minutes Faydrah was fast asleep. Kiam watched her as she rested. Tracing his finger along her back and legs, he embraced the silence and cherished the moment he had prayed for nights on end. He lay his head upon his pillow, took a deep breath and began to doze off.

Today was a blessing but tomorrow he was back into killah mode. His only hope was that he never caused Faydrah another day of sorrow or pain.

Chapter 8
The Introduction

Lissha got on the elevator and hit the up button. As she rode in silence her mind turned while processing the meeting that was about to transpire between Kiam and Gator. She had been given the instructions from Big Zo weeks ago to inform Gator of the impending change in command.

Gator definitely wasn't going to like being stripped of his power, no matter how good the change would be for the family. He was going to take things real personal, then do something about it. Lissha hoped that whatever that something was it wouldn't be betrayal, because that would get him much more than a demotion. If he bucked on Kiam, that would be just another test of his mettle, and she already knew how that would play out. Gator had proven that he would bust his guns, but was he built to defy Big Zo and go up against his handpicked protégé? That was the million dollar question.

Lissha hadn't acted on Big Zo's instructions because she had decided to wait until Kiam was on the scene, to feel him out for herself. The fate of that decision would soon be revealed.

Exiting the elevator she quickly put on her game face. After about five knocks Kiam still hadn't come to the door. She pulled out her cell phone and dialed the number to his room. After three rings the door came open. The mood was calm and Kiam had a semi-smile on his face.

Lissha looked at him with her nose scrunched up. "What you doing? Why it took you so long to let me in?" She looked around the room with a caution.

Kiam didn't have to reply because Faydrah emerged from the bedroom answering the question with her presence; she was wearing a three piece business suit and a wide smile.

"So, will I see you later?" she shyly asked as she leaned in and kissed him sweetly.

"You can see whatever you want, whenever you want."

"Time will tell." She leaned over and grabbed her brief case. "Enjoy your day." She flashed him a look that confirmed that he had handled his business. She looked at Lissha and held her gaze briefly before walking past her as if she wasn't there.

Kiam walked behind Faydrah. At the door he tapped her butt lightly. "Be good," he warned.

She looked back over her shoulder at him, then preceded out the door. No response was necessary, her body language told the whole story.

Kiam looked on until she disappeared. Lissha stood back watching the interaction between the two and a bit of jealousy brewed within.

"You ready to take care of this business?" Kiam's demeanor altered.

Seized by unexpected feelings of envy, Lissha delayed feedback, but her hustle mentality quickly resumed. "I was born ready. Get ya shit and let's roll."

Kiam picked up on her slight attitude, chuckled as he positioned his gun and collected his thoughts. "Why you acting all salty?" He toyed with her.

"What?" Lissha folded her arms and shifted her weight. "We got shit to do and you all late, up here fucking around with these ho's." She avoided eye contact as she headed for the door.

Kiam's suspicions were confirmed. "You want me to smack your ass too? Maybe that will help you get your shit right." He followed Lissha to the elevators.

"I don't think so," she replied with heavy sarcasm and sucked her teeth.

Emerging from the lobby of the hotel, Lissha handed the valet her ticket and he hurried off to get the car.

"I'm driving," Kiam yelled out as he came up behind her, ducking his head against a suddenly cool spring wind that came off of Lake Erie.

"What makes you think you're driving my shit?" Lissha tossed her long brown hair over her shoulder and gave him the side-eye as she stepped to her silver 2012 Lexus LFA.

Kiam didn't even answer. He opened the passenger side door for her, then headed to the driver's side. The young valet rushed up and gave Kiam the car keys. Lissha accepted that the issue was not up for negotiation. Kiam was driving and that was it.

Huffing, she settled in her seat.

"What happened to the whip you was pushing the other day?" he asked.

"It's at the house. Why?" she questioned him back.

"I hope you're not out here flossing and shit. Fuck the shine, it's about the paper and the power."

Lissha felt like she was being scolded. Within the few days she had been away from Kiam his whole attitude had changed. It was evident that he was settling into his new role and was not tolerating games. This only made her more nervous about the interaction he was about to have with Gator.

Kiam cruised through the streets with her directing the way. He took a careful eye to every block. Different faces, same game. The streets he had left had not changed at all. His intentions were not to come in shaking things up all at once. He was going to make a few good examples and the mouth pieces he would leave behind would spread his reign of terror.

Pulling into the condos out in Beachwood where Gator rested his head, Kiam parked and slid down in his seat. "Sup? Is this nigga going to be a problem?" He asked.

"Not really, but he may resist a little. Daddy told me to tell him a few weeks back about the change in power. But I figured I would let you do that so I could see where this nigga's heart is at. A man can't hide under the element of surprise."

"I hear you. But do me a favor and don't try to figure shit out. Me and Big Zo already did all the figuring. Just do what we tell you." He looked over at her.

Lissha was literally biting down on her lip to keep from responding with something slick. She knew how to play her position but she was not a punk. Gauging her body language, Kiam added, "No disrespect, its business, not personal." He popped the locks and got out.

Lissha checked her guns and got out, lightly slamming her door. For the first time she was caught off guard. She knew she had slightly fucked up and would probably have to deal with Big Zo later, but for right now she had to get into character. In the time it took for them to walk up on the porch the transformation was complete.

Gator opened the door bare chested with the butt of his fo-fifth peaking up from the waistline of his jeans. His shoulder length dreads were tied back in a ponytail.

"Hey, LiLi."

He looked over her shoulder at Kiam as he reached in and gave her a half hug.

"What's up Gator?" She reciprocated. Breaking the embrace, she introduced, "This is Kiam, the brother Daddy told you about."

"Welcome home, little bruh." Gator extended his hand.

"What's up?" Kiam shook his hand but maintained an icy face.

Gator picked up on Kiam's coldness and adjusted his attitude as well. His brows became one and his mouth morphed into a tight line.

"Damn nigga, move back and let us in. It's windy as hell out here. And you need to put a shirt on before you be laid up in somebody's hospital with pneumonia," Lissha chastised.

Gator gradually backed up allowing them to pass him, keeping a careful eye on Kiam as he closed the door. "So what brings you to my neck of the woods?" he asked Lissha.

"You know me, always about this paper." She took a seat on Gators all white couch.

Every time Lissha came over it always boggled her mind how this blue black gorilla had all white furniture throughout his whole house.

Gator flexed his chest muscles before snatching his t-shirt off the back of the sofa. He sat across from Lissha while Kiam chose to stand behind her.

"So what's good?" Gator took a few swigs of his drink.

"Daddy told me to come out here and make the introduction so you can get Kiam familiar with how shit is ran. I'm stepping back," she announced, leaning forward in her seat and looking Gator right in his eyes.

Gator looked at her, then up at Kiam, then back at her. He moved his glass in a slow circle causing the ice to clink from side to side as his face hardened. "Let me get this straight. So Big Zo told you to bring him to me and for me to show him how shit go?"

"Yeah," she replied.

"Then, what?"

"Don't answer that shit, Lissha," Kiam broke in, taking over the meeting, and changing the whole tone of the conversation. "He heard what the fuck you said, and he can figure out what it means. As a matter of fact, wait for me in the car. Let me holla at this man."

One of Gator's eyebrows went straight up. "She ain't gotta go no fucking where. This is my shit. I say who goes and who fucking stays." He tried to flex his dwindling authority.

Lissha stood up. "I'm good. I'ma let men do what they do. I'll hit you later." She exited.

"Yeah, you do that," Gator spat, now heated from his first interaction with the man that Big Zo had spoken so highly of. He hadn't known Kiam a full five minutes and he was ready to kill him.

Once Kiam heard the door shut he went into beast mode.

"Let me explain something to you. I ain't no bitch made nigga. I don't make friends and I don't have time to fucking babysit. Big Zo gave me a mission and I'ma handle it. Period." He sliced his hand through the air in one swift motion to finalize his declaration.

Kiam paused briefly to let his words sink in and to scale Gator's reaction. He looked him in the eye and spoke clearly. "Now this is how this shit is going to go. I'll call you later tonight with a time and a meeting place. We're about to set the tone amongst our own. Don't get held up in traffic, I hate a late muthafucka. Secondly, everything from here forward goes to me and comes through me. Last, but definitely not least, it's business as usual. Handle your end and don't come up short."

Kiam stood staring into Gator's eyes as if he was reading his soul. He had heard that the nigga had a few notches on his belt, but he wasn't impressed because if Gator was truly about that life, Big Zo wouldn't have needed him to step in and run things.

Just as he suspected, Gator had the scent of pussy on him. He knew that there was no way a real thug would let another man stand in his house and talk noise without making the ten o'clock news real interesting.

Inside Gator bristled, he thought about wetting Kiam's shirt, but he figured he needed to go along and see where things would end up. At the end of the day he held a trump card. He intended on holding, then slamming it on the table when it was time to collect. But still, he wasn't about to get chumped off.

"Bruh, you come up in my shit talking real breezy, like you think I wear a thong. If Big Zo didn't tell you, you better find out some other way—I'm not that nigga to handle like a pussy. Now we can make this transition smooth or we can make it bloody. Really, I don't give a fuck, I do or die for mine," Gator let it be known. His hand was inches from his tool.

"You talking but I ain't felt no heat, so what you saying?" Kiam disarmed him with words that did as much damage to a man as hollow points.

As Gator looked at Kiam he fought back his rage and pasted an accommodating look on his face.

"You done?"

"For now." Kiam left.

When Kiam got to the car, Lissha was sitting with her legs crossed, smoking a Black. "Put that shit out," he ordered.

"Hold the fuck up. This is my shit," Lissha quickly responded.

Kiam cut his coal black's over at her. "Don't make me ask twice," he said real calmly as he pulled out the parking spot.

Lissha looked back at him and wrinkled up her nose. The tables had turned and the change of power was now in Kiam's hand. His air of confidence and leadership was sending a surge throughout her body. Daddy had warned her about Kiam but he did not prepare her for the feelings that would develop once she saw him in action.

Lissha took one last pull, blew the smoke in the air, then plucked the Black out the window.

Coming to a stop at a red light, Kiam calmed the situation a bit. "Thank you. You're too pretty to be smoking anyway."

Lissha pouted her lips and looked out the window.

Kiam put his hand on her leg. "We got a lot of work ahead of us, you need to be focused and on point. There is no place for weakness on this level. I interpreted a look in your boy's eyes back there that don't sit well with me. If he shows the slightest sign of shade I'ma get him a headstone, so I hope you haven't been fucking with the help on the side." The strength of his voice commanded that she look at him. When she did, he looked directly into her eyes.

Lissha saw in his face that he was sincere. Just as she was about to respond he flashed her that sexy smile, causing her mouth to turn up at the corners. "I'm just saying," he stated, leaving it hanging out there.

When the light turned green, he removed his hand and placed it back on the steering wheel. The sexy smile evaporated in a flash, as if it had never existed. Lissha frowned again.

"Don't take shit so personal," said Kiam, observing her expression. "It's not even like that with me. I'm on some business shit, point blank. I don't have time to fuck around or to cater to anybody's feelings.

"Shit is about to get serious real fast, so either you're built for this shit or fall to the side. I'm not placating you because you're Pop's daughter, you're in your feelings or on your cycle. So get that in your head right now." He glanced over at her again.

Lissha remained monotone.

"Do I make myself clear?" he asked, returning his eyes to the road.

"Humph."

Kiam didn't acknowledge her grumble; he allowed silence to make his point.

"I understand," she replied through tight lips.

"Good, because I'm going to need that for something. I don't know what y'all have been doing out here but apparently it's not good enough or Big Zo wouldn't have asked me to step in and take over. As I understand it, business has leveled off. A few of our spots have started coming up with short money, and other squads are out here feeling themselves. All of that is about to change."

She wondered if he was insinuating that because she was a female she couldn't handle the business. If that's what he thought, he had the game twisted. She had just shown him the other day that her gun popped off just as lethal as his.

He was pissing her the hell off. But at the same time he turned her on. She had always been attracted to a nigga that knew how to take command of things.

"Who is our fiercest competition?" he asked.

"Wolfman," she answered without hesitation. "He has the biggest name in the city right now?"

"He had the biggest name," Kiam corrected.

Lissha nodded her understanding. She had wanted to get at Wolfman for the past two years but Gator forbade it.

"Tell me everything you know about him, and watch me make the nigga disappear."

Kiam's confidence was music to Lissha's ears. She eagerly dispensed with the information that she had compiled on Wolfman, the city's largest drug dealer. When she had reported all that she knew about him she outlined the rest of the hierarchy.

Some names were already familiar to Kiam through Big Zo. These were people that had come into hood prominence after Big Zo's demise. Dontae, Money Bags Carter, Frank Nitti. He knew their names but the only one of them whom he knew personally was Frank Nitti and he had never liked that bitch.

Kiam listened in silence until they pulled up to Lissha's condo out in South Euclid. He had already made up his mind that he was going to rearrange everybody's position. Muthafuckas could accept it or get wiped out completely.

"What time you need your car, I got some shit to do?"

Lissha cocked her eyes at him as if he was crazy. "Hold up. So you just gonna talk shit to me all day," she counted out on her fingers, "boss me around then take my car? Where the fuck they do that at?"

Kiam didn't budge. "You didn't answer the question."

"You know what; I'm not doing this with you right now. Just bring me my shit in the morning." She hit the locks and got out.

She closed the car door and leaned in the window. "That ho must have fucked you good last night. Because you up this morning with an S on your chest. Today was free; the next one will cost you." She stood up to walk away.

"LiLi," Kiam yelled out. "Be good."

Lissha turned to watch him drive away.

Kiam went right back into game mode; he could feel his adrenaline pumping. Wolfman and all the others that sat below him were about to have their worlds shook up.

Kiam's first stop was at the Verizon store. He bought himself a prepaid cell phone then hit the important people with the number. Afterwards, he cruised his old stomping grounds up and down Miles Road. He wanted to see things through his own eyes, without Czar's commentary.

He stopped at the tire and rim shop on the lower end of Miles Road to holla at some other homies that were hanging out there. Most of them were the same faces from years ago. They were still stomping the hood and hustling the blocks.

Everyone told him that DeMarcus was doing it big. Kiam took that information in and pondered its implications. DeMarcus hadn't shown him any love while he was away, that didn't bode well for him at all.

Back at the hotel, Kiam mapped out his strategy. He was sure that word would get back to DeMarcus that he had touched down, but he was not stepping to the nigga until he had decided his fate. He was going to let him shake in his boots while trying to figure out what state of mind he was in now that he was back.

Kiam undressed and got a few hours of rest because starting tonight he was putting niggas to sleep.

Gator pulled up at the meeting spot with a few minutes to spare. That was a good look because Kiam was in beast mode and wouldn't have excused tardiness. As soon as Kiam saw him pull up in the black Nav' that he had described, Kiam walked up to the passenger door and slid in.

"Where we headed?" Gator asked over the thump of the music coming out of his speakers.

"Wherever the first problem is that needs to be fixed." Kiam turned the music completely off.

"What kind of problem are you talking about, cuz?"

"I'm talking about in-house problems. The situations with the short money. We have to take care of home before we can regulate anything outside of it. Big Zo told me that we have a spot on 102nd and Sophia that constantly comes up short. Either those niggas can't count or they're on some grimy shit. What's your take on it?"

"I don't think the dudes that run that spot are stealing from us, if that's what you're asking." Gator pulled out of the lot and the dark truck blended into the murky night.

"Big Zo does."

"No disrespect to Big Zo, my nigga, but he can't see what's going on from where he's at. Losses are part of the game. I've known the niggas that run that house for ten years, they don't get down like that."

"Well, explain to me how the trap is coming up short five and ten racks a week?" Kiam countered testily.

"Mistakes happen," Gator defended.

"Oh yeah?" Kiam wasn't buying it. A nigga that couldn't count cheated himself; if he cheated you, he could count damn good. "Take me over there so I can have a talk with these fools."

"Alright, but I'm telling you before we get there that Vic and Cantrell has been loyal to the team from day one. You can ask Lissha."

"Lissha's not calling the shots anymore, and neither are you. So just drive and shut the fuck up before I start thinking that you got something to hide."

"Hold up, Bleed! Fuck you talking to? This Big Zo's shit so I play my position, but ain't nothing soft about me. Check my street resume."

"I already did."

The statement left Gator wondering if it was a compliment or a slap in the face. He knew that he had put in work but for some reason Kiam didn't seem to respect his gangsta. It was all good; the cemeteries were full of niggas that had slept on the next man's G.

They rode on in silence until they reached the crack house. Gator called inside and they were let in as soon as they reached the side door. They followed Vic into the kitchen where Cantrell was whipping crack in the microwave. Two of their young workers were seated at a round glass table bagging up rocks.

Gator made the introductions all around. "Kiam has something he wants to talk to y'all about. Whatever he has to say is not to be contested."

Cantrell looked at his cousin Vic. They both had the same question in their eyes. *Who the fuck is this nigga? And why is Gator acting like this muthafucka run something?* Kiam was about to answer that question real soon.

"Rest your feet," he charged.

Vic sat at the table with the two younger boys, but Cantrell chose to remain standing. He leaned against the refrigerator and folded his arms across his chest.

"Fam, you hard of hearing or something?" Kiam grilled him. Cantrell looked at Gator, but Gator looked away. "I don't like to have to repeat myself." Kiam said.

Reluctantly, Cantrell took the last empty chair at the table.

Gator leaned back against the sink and watched Kiam in action.

"I'm already in a foul mood so don't nobody test my patience or this meeting is gonna end with some bodies sprawled out on the floor," he began. His hand went to his waist as he looked from man to man. Nobody said anything but their expressions spoke loud and clear.

"I don't know how things have been done up until now," Kiam continued. "But from this day forward a short trap is unacceptable. Anything missing comes out of your pay to make it right. I don't tolerate stealing or disloyalty. Is that clear?"

Vic waited to see how his cousin was gonna play it. Cantrell spoke his mind.

"Bruh, I have a problem with you walking up in here talking to us like we're your do-boys. Up until five minutes ago you didn't even know me, and you damn sure don't know what's been going on over here. I mean, who the fuck is you? How in the fuck you gon' just pop up out of nowhere giving orders and shit?"

Kiam chuckled. That hinted something real ugly was about to go down, but those boys didn't know his ways so they were at a disadvantage that they couldn't even fathom.

Kiam's chuckle was followed by a half smile, he liked Cantrell's heart. Maybe in the next life the little nigga would be a shot caller, but not in this one.

Kiam's Nine came off his waist spitting something real hot. Cantrell's head exploded in a spray of skull and blood. His body toppled over in the chair and crashed to the floor.

Vic shot up out of his chair, dashing to the counter where he had placed his trey-eight on top of the microwave. Before he could reach his strap, Kiam aimed his nine milli and opened up his back.

Vic's face slapped the floor and he groaned in pain. He tried to crawl but his legs no longer worked.

Kiam walked around the table and stepped over Vic on his way to the counter. He searched the drawers until he found what he was looking for.

Walking back over to Vic, Kiam tucked his banger back down in his waist and knelt down beside the paralyzed and dying man. He rolled Vic over on his back and plunged the butcher knife in his heart. Blood squirted out three feet in the air.

Kiam stood back up and looked at the two young workers who were still seated at the table frozen with fear. "I don't do insubordination, either," he stated. "Remember that, and what happened to them won't happen to you. Do I make myself clear?"

Their heads bobbled vigorously up and down.

"Alright. From now on y'all are in charge of this trap. Get the dope out and torch the house. We can open another spot down the street somewhere. And remember what I said about my coins," Kiam reemphasized. Then he turned and looked at Gator.

"Pick ya mouth up off the floor, homie. It's just another day in the life of a G," he said, strolling toward the door with his nuts hanging low.

Across town, his female counterpart was on her G shit too.

Chapter 9
Blood Money

Lissha moved around her three bedroom apartment preparing for the arrival of her Blood Money Crew. When the bell rung, she had just taken the last piece of chicken out the pan and placed it on a platter. Wiping her hands on the dish towel, she moved to the door and she opened it wide.

"What's up, ladies," she asked as Bayonna, Treebie and Donella piled into her living room.

"What's up, momma?" Bayonna returned the greeting, giving Lissha a half hug.

"It smells good up in here." Donella placed her purse on the coffee table and headed to the sink to wash her hands.

Treebie did her usual. "Damn bitch, I see food but nothing to drink," she remarked.

She pulled two bottles of 1800 from her oversized Gucci bag and started laughing.

"This bitch," Lissha sighed, closing the door and shaking her head.

"Put some music on so we can make this meeting both business and pleasure," suggested Treebie as she strolled to the kitchen to grab four shot glasses.

Lissha attached her iPod to the Bose Sound Dock, it was on and popping. Beyonce's *Love on Top* came blasting through the speakers.

Honey, Honey/ I can see the stars all the way from here/ Can't you see the glow on the window pane/ I can feel the sun whenever you're near/ Every time you touch me I just melt away...

Everybody's head started bopping and their hands and feet were moving to the beat.

Bayonna put chicken wings and potato salad on everyone's plates and brought them to the living room. Donella grabbed the ice bucket and filled it up. Minutes later the Blood Money Crew was seated Indian style around the coffee table in the living room.

Treebie poured the first round of drinks and held her glass in the air, offering a toast. "To the takeover."

Lissha and the others clinked glasses and took the shot to the head. Slamming the glasses on the table in unison, they all did a little shake with their bodies, then poured and downed another.

Once they felt that first buzz they began attacking their food.

"This shit is good as hell," Treebie said, showing her chicken no mercy.

"You know how I ride for my bitches, I got you." Lissha snapped her fingers and did a dance in her seat.

The crew joked back and forth as they devoured the food. After they finished eating and cleared the table, Bayonna pulled a Ziploc of weed from her purse and started rolling.

Treebie hummed along with the music and went back to pouring. Within minutes they were good and fucked up.

"So what's on the menu?" Treebie asked, sitting back and lighting up her third blunt.

Lissha grabbed the remote and turned the music down a little. "Well, I introduced Kiam to Gator. That shit was craze."

"What you mean?" Treebie blew out smoke and passed the Kush. Then she listened attentively.

Lissha took a couple hits and then continued. "That nigga, Kiam, ain't shit to be played with. He put Gator on point, which was the first time I ever saw that nigga reaching for a clue."

"Damn," Bayonna gushed as she took the blunt and started pulling hard on it. "So, is it going to be a problem between them or what?"

"I don't think so. But we gotta make sure that Gator falls in. We gotta have Kiam's back no matter what. Daddy says he needs this transition to be smooth." She reached for her drink, and took a few sips.

"And on our end, if Kiam can take over and put the streets under his foot, that will free us up to do this other shit we got cooking outside of him and Daddy," Lissha explained.

"Have we made any progress?" asked Donella, leaning in for Bayonna to blow her a gun. When that hot smoke hit the back of her throat she started coughing and choking.

"See that's why I don't fuck with you. You can't hang. Bitch, you act like you just started getting high yesterday, silly ass rabbit." Treebie said, shaking her head.

"Fuck you, she tried to blow my head off. Fucking around with y'all I'll leave up out of here with my lungs in my purse."

They all burst out in laughter.

When the clowning ceased, Lissha turned serious and answered the question that Donella presented to her. "Yeah. We real good. I got with Spank and he told me about a few card games coming up with some intense money. If shit is like he says, we can hit them muthafuckas and be in and out." This was their thing outside of the business with Big Zo.

"What's Spank's cut?" Treebie shot back.

"He don't want shit from one of the spots. That one is personal. Spank got wind that them niggas be running some card tricks, they beat his ass outta fifty bands. He want them niggas put on they ass. But if we hit the other two, our split is sixty/forty."

"Fuck outta here! We going in, we taking all the risk, then that nigga want forty percent to sit at home and scratch his nuts? Nah, fuck that." Treebie wasn't feeling it at all. She poured herself another drink.

"I agree. Maybe thirty but not forty," said Donella, who usually just went with the flow.

"I don't have a problem with it, he's doing the ground work," Bayonna reasoned.

Treebie cut her eyes over at her. Bay was the least tenured of the crew, and she was the only one of them that Big Zo hadn't recruited himself. LiLi had brought Bay in three years ago after recognizing that she had what it took to be down with them.

As far as Treebie was concerned, Bay was still on probation so she often discounted the young girl's opinion.

"Yeah, but Spank ain't gonna be the one standing there with his dick in his hand if them niggas get active," Treebie hotly contested.

"Look, I already approved the amount." Lissha cut back in. "We gotta show them it's real, then we up the price on em'. Let's do these couple jobs and then we can have something to bargain with. Right now we just riding on our word."

"You're riding on your word. I'm riding on my rep. We do one job— the free one. We kill everything moving except one witness to tell the tale after it's over. Then we make that nigga bow to our demands or he can get it too." Treebie looked at Lissha seriously. When it came to the money she didn't play.

Lissha took a few sips of her drink. She kept her eyes fixed on Treebie. "Why you always want to kill somebody?" Lissha asked. "I think you need counseling and some fucking Prozac."

They burst out laughing again.

"Nah, on the real I feel you. And you're right. One on the house and the rest will cost him," Lissha agreed. "The first lick is going down Friday night so everybody be ready to roll. Salute." They brought their glasses together.

Just as the glass left Lissha's mouth her phone started vibrating on the table. When she looked down at the caller ID, it read Daddy. She grabbed the remote, paused the music and put her finger to her lips, gesturing for them to be quiet.

"Hello," she answered in an eager tone.

"Hey, baby girl," Big Zo's voice flowed into her ear.

"Hey, Daddy." She tried to perk up from her drunken state.

"What you up to?" he asked trying to feel her out.

"Nothing much. Just sitting here chillin' with the girls."

"Hey, Daddy," Treebie yelled out teasing Lissha.

Lissha kicked her under the table and waved her hand.

"Is that Treebie?" asked Big Zo.

"Yes, and as you see, she's loud as usual."

"Tell the girls I said hello, then excuse yourself and go somewhere private so we can talk."

"Okay." She dropped the phone to her waistline. "Daddy said hello ladies." She relayed the message as she got up and went toward the bedroom.

"Hey," Bayonna and Donella chorused as she walked away.

Closing the door, she dove on her bed. "Okay, go ahead. I'm alone."

"So what's up with Kiam? Is he getting around the city good?" Big Zo went right into code talk.

"Yeah, I took him on a few job interviews. You know all this application shit is new to him, but he met all the right people," Lissha related.

"Okay, good. Make sure he gets the wardrobe he needs. Tell him I said 'shop around' and don't just go with the first thing he sees."

"Okay."

"We just need a couple more months and everything should line up."

"I know, Daddy. I'm doing everything in my power to make sure I keep shit in line for you."

"First of all, watch your mouth. Second, I heard different. You know ol' boy called and said he was caught off guard by your surprise party." Big Zo was speaking of her not telling Gator about Kiam.

"I know, but I wanted to make sure everybody was legit," she explained.

"I understand. But don't grow a fucking brain in the middle of progress. Do what I tell you. I got this. I need you to hear and obey. Save judgment calls for real important shit like when you can't reach me. Other than that, do what I tell you."

Lissha was quiet. She already knew she had rocked the boat but she was not in the mood to hear his mouth.

"LiLi," he called out.

"Yes," she answered feeling like she was five years old and had wet the bed.

"I know I put a lot on your shoulders, but I need you to be my eyes, ears and hands. We have to be on the same page or none of this shit is going to work. You got me?"

"Yes. I got you."

"I love you, baby girl. Be careful. And make sure that you come to visit me soon. I need to put something in your ear."

"I love you too, Daddy. I'll be down next Saturday," she promised.

"Alright. Good night." He disconnected the call.

Lissha put her phone down on the bed and rubbed her hands over her face. She had to quickly regroup so she could go back out there to the girls without looking like she had just gotten chastised. When she emerged from the room she had a big smile on her face. She got the remote, pumped the music back up and grabbed the bottle and took it to the head.

"Well, damn," Treebie remarked with her head cocked to the side.

"Let's get fucked up. I don't want to know my name in the morning," Lissha said, taking the bottle up once more.

Treebie knew that the sudden change in Lissha's attitude meant that Big Zo had got in that ass. She suspected that he had something cooking. It was only a matter of time before he had Lissha doing sneaky shit that might put them all in a jacked up position. But one thing was for sure and two things for certain, Treebie was not that bitch. She was already making moves to separate herself from Lissha and Big Zo's operation. She just needed to sit back and let her tactics materialize.

Chapter 10
The Heist

Friday night came fast. The Blood Money Crew was in Treebie's basement getting suited up. Lissha stepped into her third pair of sweat pants while Treebie pulled on her second hoodie. Bay and Nella was already geared, lacing their boots. Thick, loose-fitting clothing helped disguise the girl's weight and gender.

Lissha, Donella, and Treebie pulled their hair back into tight ponytails and tucked it under fitted skull caps. Bay wore her hair in an extremely low cut that only a cold broad like herself could rock without looking butch. She covered her hair with a skully too, and they all pulled their head gear low over their brows. The bottom half of their faces was covered with black half-face masks. Nothing showed but the slits of their eyes.

Lissha strapped on a bullet proof vest and waited for the others to do the same. There was no way to predict how marks would act once you run up in their spot so the girls covered all angles.

Treebie walked to the lock boxes and spun the combination. Every time she opened the door to her arsenal chamber, a smile came across her face and her nipples stiffened. If she had a dick, that too would've been rocked up.

"These some sexy bitches," she stated as she reached for her Carbon.

She picked it up and caressed it before swiping her bullets and loading up. A twinkle of anticipating danced in her eyes as she looked to her left at Bayonna and passed her a Calico.

Two months shy of turning twenty-three years old, Bay was the baby of the crew. She was a diminutive chick but her heart was colossal. Her method of operation was no words, only action. The others called her the silent killah because when it was time to rock, she grew a pair of big balls; she didn't let air slide when they threw down on a spot. And if a nigga uttered one wrong word, Bay's Calico made it his last without reasoning.

Donella was next to Bay, tightening up her vest. Amongst the crew she was known as The Negotiator. Whatever information she couldn't get with words and her sex appeal, she negotiated with her banger. Her Glock .50 made a muthafucka spill his guts in one form or another.

Treebie was the live-wire of the crew. She would much rather bust her gun than talk shit out. It was like she was more turned on by the killing than the hustle. When Treebie ran up in somebody's spot their futures weren't longer than the time it usually took her to click clack one in the chamber.

Lissha, on the other hand, was the most level-headed. With a team of women that weren't afraid to bust a gun then come home and drop a grand on the Mac counter, she knew she had the deadliest crew on the streets. By day, they were the baddest by the coldest definition. But by night, they were the wrong bitches to fuck with. And tonight would be no different.

"Check your weapons, ladies," Lissha said. "Make sure they're cocked and locked."

Once everyone affirmed that their guns were ready, she passed them each a voice distorter. One by one, they fitted the contraptions around their throats. After a quick check to make sure everything was in place they moved to the counter and opened the four small containers.

Each woman carefully placed a pair of blood red contacts in their eyes. They allowed a moment for them to adjust, and then they looked each other over.

"We go in this muthafucka as four and we come out as four," said Lissha. She had given this short pep talk dozens of times before. It was part of their ritual but it was not to be taken for granted.

She looked around and read her crew's body language. Satisfied with what she saw, Lissha said, "Let's get it."

"Blood Money!" They chanted in unison.

When they got to the spot they were targeting on Wadepark, they rode by to make sure everything appeared to be as Spank said it would be. From what they could tell, it was legit. They parked a half a block down, eased out of the car, and then moved in the shadows of the night.

Moving up to the door they all went into beast mode. Treebie did the secret knock. A minute or so passed before they heard the door locks click open.

It was on!

They forced their way inside. Treebie pulled her gun and blasted the first two fools to stand up. She watched their bodies drop, then planted herself firm in the middle of the room.

Donella went to the left and Bayonna went to the right. Lissha took up the rear, closing the door.

The startled doorman opened his mouth to say something and got his face blown off. Lissha popped two more in his chest and watched him slide down the wall. She stepped over the man's body and planted her back firmly against the door.

The card players were in clear murdering range. They sat stock still, staring at the red-eyed intruders.

"I need all that shit on the table in a big bag, or I'ma put me a muthafucka in a black one." Lissha's distorted voice commanded respect.

"Hurry the fuck up. Donella yelled out. She waved her gun around the table, daring someone to test it.

"Hold up, nigga, do you know whose game house this is?" A fat yellow skinned brother at the head of the table yelled out.

Without pause Bay let off in his chest sending him hard to the floor. "The next sound I hear better not be anything but paper or plastic. Get that shit packed the fuck up!" she barked, tossing two large shoe bags on the table.

"These niggas think we playing," Treebie spat. Her eyes peered and her breathing thickened. The evil in her soul beamed through those red contacts making her appear bizarrely unnatural.

"Hold up, nigga. We got you." The dude at the other end of the table shouted. He and the two cats next to him began clearing the money off the table and shoveling it in the duffel bags.

When they had given up all of the dough in sight they sat there thinking that they had played the robbers. "Now let's take a walk over to the wall safe, and if you don't have the combination you can start praying," said Treebie.

A look of surprise flashed in the eyes of one of the dudes left breathing; he wondered how in the hell did they know about the safe? Common sense told him that they were going to kill him whether he opened the safe or not, so he might as well have taken the combination to the grave with him. But even a man that's facing imminent execution holds on to hope until the very end. "I can open the safe, just don't kill me," he blurted out like his dick had turned into a clitoris.

Treebie put her gun to the back of his head and marched him to the real prize. He shook like a stripper on a Friday night as he opened the safe and filled the duffel bags.

"Now walk that shit to the door. And if you make a wrong move it will be your last," Lissha said as they kept the guns focused on their targets.

Once the money was safe by Lissha's side the delivery boy turned to walk away with his hands in the air. When he passed Treebie he mumbled something under his breath. Lissha caught a syllable or two, and sent heat to the back of his head. His body flew into the card table, tumbling it over.

"What the fuck?" cried an older gambler. "We gave y'all what you came for. What else y'all want?"

"I need one more thing," Lissha said in a calm deep voice.

The man looked at her and hesitantly asked, "What's that?"

"Your soul," she responded.

Treebie stepped up and served his ass up something hot and heavy. Another gambler reached for his waist and Donella made that his final act in life. Her sistahs chopped down anything else that moved.

When they were done there were only two men left standing. One was a bald older man with a thick gray beard. The other one looked to be in his early thirties. They both had their hands suspended in air with fear enveloping within their hearts as they sat awaiting their execution.

"This nigga shaking like a stripper?" Treebie chuckled, placing the gun on the bridge of the younger man's nose.

Narrowing down at him with unforgiving eyes, she saw the color literally drain out of his face. "Nigga, loosen your ass cheeks. This is your lucky day. We need a mouth piece and you've just been nominated."

Sweat beads ran from his race as the cotton in his mouth made it impossible for him to swallow.

In one move Treebie shot the older man in the face. She looked back down at the young dude who was trembling in his seat. A smell assaulted her nose. She couldn't tell if it was pussy or shit, but she knew it was fear.

Bayonna and Donella moved closer to the door, keeping their weapons focused on him. Treebie shook dude down for weapons, ran his pockets, then handcuffed him to his chair.

Her crew members looked on as she reached in her pocket pulled out a dollar bill. She rubbed it the dead man's blood next to him.

"Make sure you tell them niggas this is Blood Money," she said, stuffing the bloody dollar in his mouth.

The young dude gagged. Easing backwards she lifted her gun to his face so that his eyes were level with the barrel.

"Be easy, nigga," she spat.

She raised up and they formed two lines, back to back, to make their exit.

Within seconds they were gone. The die was cast and the word would go out. *Don't fuck with Blood Money.*

Chapter 11
Business is Business

Lissha opened her eyes slowly and looked around the room. Stretching her arms and legs she prepared to get out of bed but was stopped by the strong arm and leg of the man lying next to her.

"Don't get up yet. I need you to ride this morning wood," he said, placing that hard muscle against her butt.

"Nah, I got some shit to handle," she said, removing his arm from her waist.

"Damn, why you always ready to jump out a nigga's bed and get into the streets?" Gator spat.

"It's not like that. We laying in the middle of a war zone and you wanna cuddle. I fucked you real good last night, you should be straight," she said, rising to her feet and wrapping a towel around her naked flesh.

"Last night is over. I'm trying to get you to make this tent go down." He was laying on his back with his dick holding the sheet in the air.

"You so crazy," Lissha chuckled as she crossed her arms over her chest. He had been her way of winding down after the job she and the girls had pulled off last night.

She stared down at Gator. He had his hands behind his head on the pillow and he was looking up at her invitingly, with his dreads splayed out all over his head. He slowly ran his tongue over his lips, reminding her how he could make it pleasure her.

Lissha weighed her options. She had to meet her bitches in an hour. They were going to celebrate last night's successful caper by hitting the malls. Later they were driving to Akron, Ohio for dinner at The Diamond Grill, then they would come back home and cap the night off downtown at The Horseshoe Casino, gambling and getting buzzed. But right now she had some fire head and good, hard dick just a few feet away. Another orgasm sounded good to her ears.

Walking back to the bed she grabbed a condom off the nightstand. "Strap up, nigga, and consider this the fucking Lottery— prime pussy back to back."

"I ain't mad at you," he laughed, humored by her audacity. He ripped open the pack and strapped up.

She dropped the towel to the floor and straddled Gator's lap backwards. Easing down on all that hardness, she let out a soft moan and went to work. Her ass began to bounce and jiggle, and her moisture slid up and down his rigid length. Gator grabbed her hips and closed his eyes.

When she heard those familiar groans leave his lips she rode harder and faster. She closed her eyes and imagined that the thick, hard, muscle inside of her belonged to someone else—someone she should not have been fantasizing about. Thinking of him immediately took her over the top. She bit down on her bottom lip to keep from crying out his name as her body trembled and she began to release.

Gator felt her walls contract around his dick and he gave up the fight to hold back his seed. He grunted and filled up the Magnum. Lissha rose up off of him, allowing his dick to ease out of her.

"Goddamn, you know how to make a nigga relax in the morning," he whined in a deep, raspy, and satisfied voice.

"I always handle my business, player. No matter what it is."

"Yeah, you do. And I handle the hell out of mines. I love to hear you moan when I'm running pipe all up in your stomach. I'm telling you, ain't no better feeling than fucking the boss's daughter and making her come." He reached out and patted her ass.

Lissha slapped his hand away. "Hold up. Let me clarify something because you're really feeling yourself this morning. You don't fuck me. I'm fucking *you*. It's a difference."

"So you say," Gator lightly disputed.

"Fuck up and you'll see. Don't confuse what we do with what has to be done. Because if you slip up with what Daddy is doing, it won't matter if you make me quote scriptures when I cum, your ass will fall just like the rest."

"What, you gon' replace me with Kiam? Is that why you're so slick out the mouth lately? If so, fuck that nigga. I don't know why Big Zo trust him over me anyway. The way he's coming in wanting to crush everything, we'll all end up in the feds," he fumed.

With a scowl on his face he sat up and fired up a Newport. He blew smoke rings toward the ceiling and recounted to her what Kiam had done to Cantrell and Vic.

"So what? You wanna dig them up and apologize to 'em?"

Gator's expression hardened. "While you joking about that shit, those niggas had been down with the team from the onset. Kiam just killed them for no reason. That shit ain't cool at all. I think Big Zo made the wrong call on this one," Gator objected.

"Well, if you want to question Daddy's decisions, you can do that the next time he calls you. Let me know how that works out for you," she hurled over her shoulder as she headed to the bathroom to jump in the shower.

Gator sat pulling hard on his cigarette. His forehead was creased as he thought about everything that had happened lately. Anger resonated in his gut. He was still caught in his feelings about the way Kiam was moving. He was on some real gorilla hustling. This whole transition didn't sit well with Gator. But he was going to sit back and watch, and when Kiam failed Big Zo, he was going to be the first one to put that shit all in his face.

Chapter 12
A Boss Move

Lissha was lying comfortably in her bed; it was 3:00pm the next day. The rain beat a soothing melody on her windows, welcoming her slumber. She had been up all morning hugging the toilet and calling Earl from the night out at the casino with her girls. Now her stomach and head were paying for her over-indulgence in the free drinks that had been provided to her and the crew. The only relief was in the fact that she had won seven bands at the black jack tables. How she had made it home without wrapping her car around a pole was a mystery to Lissha.

She had just dozed back off when her phone began to ring. She didn't look at it, she merely pushed it to the side, turned over and put the covers over her head.

The phone rang back to back four times before she decided to answer. Pressing the send button on her phone to accept the call, she had already made up her mind to cuss out whoever was on the other end.

"Yo, why the fuck you keep ringing this number?" Lissha growled at the caller.

"Why the fuck are you hollering into the phone?" he replied, remaining smooth and unfazed by her grouchy attitude.

"Kiam?" Lissha asked, pulling the phone back and checking the number.

"Yeah, who did you think it was blowing you up?"

"I didn't recognize the number," she said as she pulled the cover back over her head. "What's up? Where in the hell is my car? You were supposed to return it three days ago."

"Don't sweat that, I got you. Anyway, I'm on my way to pick you up. I need you to take a run with me real quick."

"Nah. I can't leave the house right now. Maybe later."

"Ain't no later, I'll be at your house in twenty minutes. Get your shit together." He hung up.

"That muthafucka gonna be mad as hell when he get here." She huffed, tossing the phone on the nightstand and closing her eyes.

Thirty minutes later Lissha's doorbell chimed loud enough to wake the dead. She felt like her head was about to explode.

"Is this nigga serious?" she mumbled.

Turning over on her back, she stared at the ceiling while contemplating if she should move or just lay there. Just when she was about to get up, her phone rang again. She snatched it up, checked the ID, and then threw it back on the night stand.

"This nigga is crazier than I thought!" She slipped on a t-shirt and walked to the door.

Her pressure went straight to the roof when he began pressing the bell like the jump out boys was after that ass.

Lissha snatched the door open and gave Kiam the dirtiest look she could muster.

Her appearance shocked him. Her hair was wild, her nostrils were flared, and the bags under her eyes looked like you could throw some clothes in them and take a trip.

"Damn. You look fucked up," Kiam remarked as he walked into her house like he was invited.

Lissha stood holding the door knob tight in her hand in an effort to not go ham on him. "What do you want, Kiam?"

"Fuck you mean what do I want? You act like I didn't call and tell you I was on my way," he casually stated as he took a seat on her couch. "It's nice up in here," he said, looking around.

"Thanks," she muttered insincerely.

Kiam snorted. "Too bad, you fuckin' up the good vibes with all that nasty attitude."

"I told you on the phone, I am not going anywhere. I don't feel well. So if you could kindly raise your ass up off my couch, you can catch the door on the other side just as I'm slamming it," she spat.

"I'm not paying you no attention. Get your shit together and pack a small bag, we're taking a trip."

Lissha stared out the door at the rain showering down her walkway. She wanted to go off. Instead, she took a deep breath and closed the door. "Where we going Kiam?" She asked dryly.

"I need to meet that connect," he announced, trying not to watch Lissha's sexy legs as she passed him on her way to the loveseat.

"We are not scheduled to see him until next week."

"There has been a change of plans. I need to see him tomorrow."

"Tomorrow? He's in New York. That means we have to drive all night."

"Exactly, so get your shit together like I said ten minutes ago and come on."

Lissha just looked at him. She took his smug ass in real good. He had on crisp jeans, a black Ralph Lauren pullover shirt and fresh kicks that she had not purchased as part of his welcome home package. He was rocking a fresh haircut with a razor sharp line. Even when he was trying to piss her off, he was still sexy as hell.

"Why you still sitting there?" Kiam lifted his eyebrow. He pointed toward the bedrooms for her to get it moving. Every time he spoke it gave her body a jolt of energy.

The movement of his hands crossed Lissha's line of vision and broke her train of thought.

"Whatever." She tsked, then slowly got off the couch and headed to her room.

"Hurry up," he yelled out behind her.

Lissha's response was to slam the bedroom door behind her.

Unfazed, he called Faydrah.

"Hey, baby," she answered with excitement in her voice.

"What's good, ma? You miss me or what?"

"Boy, get out of my thoughts," she giggled. "I was just going to tell you how much I miss you."

Kiam settled further back on the couch and rocked his foot. "What you miss, me or what I did to you the other day?"

"Both. Humph, I'm not going to lie. Matter of fact, I'ma need you do it again real soon."

"I got you, baby," he promised, looking forward to that replay just as much as she was. "I gotta go on a short trip out of town but I'll be back in a few days, and when I get back I'ma blaze it for you real good."

"You promise?" She sat behind her desk clamping her thighs together.

"Yeah, and my shit already boned the fuck up. I can't wait."

"Ooh, me either baby. I wish I could feel you inside me right now." She closed her eyes and imagined him moving in and out of her with long powerful strokes. "Damn. Why you gotta get me all wet and I have a meeting in five minutes?"

"I thought you stay wet?" he said.

"I do for you," she replied in a sultry tone.

"Don't make me come down there and bend you over your desk."

"Don't be teasing me, Kiam." He had her kitty purring. Unfortunately she had to get off the phone. "Baby, can I call you later?" she asked with regret.

"That's cool," he said. "I'll talk to you later, bae."

"Love you." She blew him a kiss.

Kiam ended the call and sat back silently hurrying Lissha.

Lissha showered and got dressed. Sitting on her bed, she tried to get her mind right for the long drive and the unexpected drop in on their connect. Riz could be real extra sometimes, and Kiam was certifiable. She needed to be mentally prepared for the reality that she was about to put two beast in a cage and the outcome just might be death.

Tucking a few pairs of jeans and tops in a tote bag, she released a long sigh. She then grabbed her toiletries, underwear and bras, and placed them inside the bag as well. She took a jacket out of the closet to carry along in case the weather up in New York was ugly. Finally she placed her Prada sneakers in a shoe bag and set it down on the bed beside the tote bag.

She hit the closet safe and grabbed a couple bands and two credit cards, and put them inside her purse. She retrieved her .380 from the nightstand, checked its clip to make sure it was fully loaded, tucked it inside her purse and headed for the living room.

When she emerged from the bedroom, Lissha was looking refreshed in a pair of light blue jeans, Fendi sneakers and belt to match. A brown tight fitting shirt that hung long in the back and was high in the front showed off a section of her flat, toned stomach. A double piercing accentuated her navel.

Kiam's eyes wondered over her frame. Her facial features where more pronounced with her hair pulled back in that neat ponytail and the loose fitting material of her shirt clung to her chest allowing him to see her pronounced nipples right through the bra.

"Damn, nigga, take a picture it'll last longer," Lissha spat as she noticed him looking a little too long and hard.

"Well, shit, when you left outta here you looked like a deranged killah, now you look more like America's next top model."

"Shut up," Lissha chuckled. She walked toward him and tossed the tote bag in his lap.

Kiam stood up and moved to the door.

Lissha followed behind him, set the alarm and headed to the car.

The rain had stopped and the sun was attempting to peek through the clouds.

Lissha sank into the seat, slipped on her shades, and reclined back.

"We need to take 70 all the way over then get on 78. It's pretty much a straight route," she said, preparing to take a nap.

"Yo ass ain't going to be sleep." Kiam looked over at her.

"Why not?"

"You're a co-pilot. You better recognize," he made known as he pulled off en route to the highway.

Lissha just stared at him for a few minutes then looked away. She could see this trip was going to be pure torture. Before it was over she might have to choke the shit out of him.

Temptation...

When they got to the Holland tunnel Lissha almost did a happy dance in her seat. She was ready for some good food, a hot shower and a long slumber.

Kiam pulled into the Trump Soho hotel, Lissha got out to get the room keys while Kiam secured the car with the valet and gathered the bags.

When he got to the front desk he walked up on Lissha arguing back and forth with the receptionist. He sat their bags down on the floor and asked what the problem was.

"They messed up the reservation, that's what's wrong," Lissha huffed, talking with her hands flying all over the place. She accidently slung the debit card that she was holding.

"Shit," she fumed. She was tired and in no mood for bullshit.

"Ma'am I'm sorry for the mix up, but like I told you we can upgrade you to a suite with two king size beds."

"We requested two rooms, you need to make that happen."

"Look, we good. Let us have the room," Kiam cut in. He picked the debit card up and calmly placed it on the counter.

"I need my own room, I'm not trying to shack up with you," Lissha said, looking to the side at Kiam like he had the coodies.

"Why? Are you scared?" he asked flashing that sexy smile.

"No. I just need my own space." She turned back to face the receptionist who was smirking at their banter.

"Don't worry it's only for two days. Trust, you're not that goddamn irresistible," Kiam affirmed.

Lissha turned up her lips.

The receptionist ran the debit card then returned it to Lissha who was in a tiff.

"Here's your card, ma'am. We will be sending up a complimentary bottle of champagne, and your dinner is on us for the trouble. Is there anything else I can help you with?" asked the young woman as she passed them the room key.

"That will be it for now," Kiam said. He reached down and grabbed the bags. "If you have anything for a bad attitude please send that up immediately," he joked.

"Yes, sir. Enjoy your stay," the woman answered with a chuckle.

"Ya' ass ain't funny," Lissha snorted, heading to the elevators.

When they got to the room the décor took their breaths away. The white and tan room was spacious and airy. There was a living room, dining area and kitchen. Lissha walked through the huge glass doors out onto the balcony. By itself, the view was worth the thousand dollars a night they were paying.

Kiam placed their bags next to the dresser and joined Lissha on the terrace. Together they stared out over the New York skyline.

"This might be the last bit of peace we get. Hold on to it, we're going to need it," Kiam said as he left Lissha to enjoy the view.

After laying out his sweat pants and t-shirt, he grabbed the menu from the side of the bed.

"What you want to eat?" he called out.

Lissha returned inside. "What they got?" She took the menu from his hand and plopped down on the bed.

Scanning the pages she made a few mental choices then picked up the phone.

"Hello. Yes, I would like to place an order. Can I have an order of Shrimp Alfredo with extra shrimp, a side of asparagus and a salad with blue cheese dressing?" She paused to listen to the woman read back her order. "That's correct. What you want, Kiam?" she asked.

"I want a T-bone steak, medium well. A baked potato with sour cream and cheddar cheese, string beans, and ice tea." His mouth watered with anticipation.

Lissha placed his order and hung up.

"Place the call to the connect. Tell him we want to have a sit down tomorrow around five."

"Don't you think we should ask if he'll be available? People don't like it when you're abrasive, Kiam."

"Fuck I care what the next nigga like? And just so you know, I never ask—denying me ain't an option. Now make that call."

"Alright," Lissha said.

Walking over to her bag she grabbed the prepaid and placed the call. Surprisingly it went well and the date was set. "Everything is a go," she informed Kiam when she hung up from Riz.

"Aiight, we 'bout to make it happen."

"I'm about to make a bath happen," Lissha quipped. "I'm going to hop in the tub before the food comes."

"Do what you do," said Kiam.

She walked over to the table and took the complimentary bottle of champagne by the neck, then headed to the bathroom grabbing her bag along the way.

Lissha looked around the bathroom, the huge glass shower was inviting but that big white shiny tub was whispering her name. Turning on the water and adjusting it to her comfort, she began filling the tub then added her David Yurman shower gel.

Quickly she undressed and sank her weary body into the hot bubbles. Lissha poured herself a glass of champagne drank it down, closed her eyes and relaxed.

Lissha was soaking for only ten minutes when she heard Kiam entering the bathroom. When she opened her eyes he was passing the tub on the way to the shower butt naked.

"Ummm, excuse me," Lissha said, face wrinkled up.

"What's up?" Kiam asked as he turned on the shower.

"You don't see me over here?"

"Yeah, I see you," he responded.

"What are you doing?"

"What do it look like?" he asked, stepping into the shower.

"It looks like your standing in here butt ass naked."

"You seen a dick before right?" he asked sarcastically, closing the door and positioning himself under the water.

"Not like that," she mumbled.

Kiam acted as if she wasn't there. He lathered his body and let the water rinse the suds away.

Lissha watched every second of it.

When he was done, he dried off and headed out the bathroom the same way he walked in, dick swinging. As he passed by the tub Lissha crossed her legs.

"You need more bubbles," he said, looking down at her then pushing on without further comment.

"Close the door," Lissha yelled out.

She dipped her washcloth in the tub and put it on her face. She needed to cool off. Kiam had just given her fever. She spent another twenty minutes becoming one with the porcelin and putting to bed the thoughts that seeing Kiam's naked body had awakened.

As Lissha lotioned her skin she heard a knock on the door. She threw on her robe and joined Kiam in the dining area.

"Damn this looks good," she said as he uncovered each dish.

"I'm about to be on some real fat boy shit," announced Kiam as he took a seat.

Lissha sat across from him and they dug in.

Once their meal was done they retired to the living room. Lissha put her iPod on the docking station and sat by Kiam.

"So you ready for tomorrow?"

"I'm always ready. Business is business."

"Riz can be a real asshole."

"Don't worry I got it. Real recognize real," Kiam assured her.

Lissha sat looking at Kiam's oiled chest. She allowed her eyes to wander down to that print that sat up in his sweat pants.

Kiam picked up on her gaze and decided to defuse the situation, "So, when is the next time you going to visit Pop?"

"When we get back, I know he is going to want to know what is going on and how you are adjusting."

"Probably so. But Pop knows I'm about this life. That's why he entrusted me to come out here and oversee everything."

"Is that right?" A provocative look flashed in her eyes.

"Stop being fast," Kiam admonished like Lissha was a little hot tail girl.

"Shut up," she teased, giving him a little shove.

"On the real, your father is proud of you. You're out here standing stronger than most niggas. I respect that. Now I see firsthand why Big Zo speaks so highly of you," he said looking in her direction.

Lissha lowered her gaze. "I'm all he has."

"What about your mother? Pop never talked about her. Were they still together when he got locked up?"

"No. She's dead. She died when I was sixteen?"

"How? Was she sick or something?" he asked, hoping to get inside of her.

"No. She was gunned down."

Kiam noticed that her responses had become clipped. He saw no emotion on her face so he didn't feel that he was opening a wound that hadn't healed. "Was your mother as pretty as you? You must look like her because you don't look like Big Zo," he said.

"If you don't mind, I would rather not talk about my mother. She wasn't down for Daddy and she and I didn't get along. She's dead, that's all you need to know, and I'm all that he has."

"Well don't ever think he doesn't recognize your loyalty. Trust me, he knows," he confirmed.

Lissha smiled because Kiam was looking at her like he wanted to hug her. She stared at his lips and she became compelled to taste them.

Drifting into each other's gaze and feeling the heat that resonated between them, they both knew what was inevitable. Lissha was so ready to act on her feelings, but Kiam couldn't just throw his promise to Big Zo to the curb. At the last second he pulled back, leaving Lissha's eyes closed and her lips pursed to be kissed.

"Nah, ma."

She looked at him like, *you gotta be kidding!*

Kiam was as serious as the method of takeover he was primed to implement. He slid down to the other end of the couch, putting much needed space between them. "It's not safe over there," he quipped.

"Whatever, Kiam," she replied.

Before he could respond his cellphone rang. He answered it with relief in his voice.

"Hello."

"Hey baby," Faydrah's voice serenaded his senses.

"What's up with you?" he asked, getting up from the couch, heading to his bed.

He lay sideways across the bed, engrossed in what Faydrah was saying. When he burst out laughing, Lissha cut her eyes at him.

"Send me a picture, baby," Kiam said into the phone.

Overhearing him, Lissha's stomach turned. She stood up and tightened her robe, walked over to the mini bar and mixed herself a drink.

The more Kiam talked and laughed the more Lissha drank. By the time he hung up she was good and fucked up.

Walking to her bed adjacent to his, she looked on in disgust as Kiam smiled while flipping through the pictures Faydrah had just sent.

Lissha dropped her robe and let him get an eye full of what she knew he wanted. "I don't even see you standing there," he said, fighting the war between duty and desire.

"If you didn't notice your mouth wouldn't be moving." Lissha climbed in bed, pulled the cover over her head and went to sleep.

Kiam knew she was pissed but he needed her to be. They had almost crossed the line, and he would not be able to forgive himself if he did. He turned off the light, turned over and fell into his slumber.

Chapter 13
Back To Business

The next day Kiam and Lissha had a late lunch. Neither of them spoke a single word as they ate. Lissha felt a little awkward after last night, but Kiam wasn't even thinking about that, he was in full business mode. After lunch, they got dressed and prepared to go see Riz.

Kiam barricaded Lissha at the door. "Leave the money here," he said, noticing a satchel in her hand and correctly guessing what it contained.

She looked at him curiously.

"This is just a meeting, were not copping anything. Matter of fact, after this get-together he'll meet us halfway with the delivery."

Lissha was skeptical. Riz didn't travel.

"Don't doubt me," Kiam said, reading her mind. "I'm very persuasive."

Lissha didn't debate, she hurried back and stashed the satchel, then caught up with Kiam at the elevators.

When they reached the lobby, she stopped at the front desk and left explicit orders for their room not to be disturbed. She looked up and saw that Kiam was scanning the premises, eyeing everyone and everything. Kiam was in that zone.

They exited the hotel side by side. Lissha was wrapped in a leather jacket, stepping briskly to keep up with Kiam's pace. The wind whistled between the buildings as they headed to the car. Kiam had one thing on his mind and Riz was gonna respect it or get *disrespected*.

Pulling up to Riz's Brooklyn apartment building, Kiam and Lissha checked their guns and exited the vehicle. As they approached the steps a hot surge filled Kiam's body—he was ready.

When they reached the entrance, loud music blared through the door and the scent of weed funneled out into the hallway.

A barrage of bangs eventually summoned someone from inside. A tall, slender man with a nappy afro swung the door open, giving passage to Lissha and Kiam. "LiLi. How you been, ma?" He greeted her warmly.

"Hey Bean. I'm good," Lissha said, giving him a big hug.

"This your boy you told us about?" he inquired instantly, reaching out to shake Kiam's hand.

"What's good?" Kiam responded.

"I can't call it, come in." Bean moved to the side allowing Lissha and Kiam to pass.

"Riz, it's LiLi," Bean yelled out as he came up behind her and Kiam. "Y'all wanna burn something?" He sat down on the couch and pulled out a Dutch.

"Nah, we not here for that," Kiam answered for the both of them.

Bean looked at Lissha. "You sure?" he asked.

"Yeah, she sure," Kiam restated. He wanted it known that his decisions were not to be challenged.

Bean could already sense he was going to be a problem. He picked up the remote and turned the music off.

Riz walked in from out of the back sporting a black t-shirt, a pair of green army fatigue pants, and black Goretex boots. His short dreads were sticking up all over his head and his clothes were wrinkled like he had just rolled out of bed. Two massive Rottweilers were at his sides.

"Sit," he commanded. Each dog went to an opposite side of the couch and posted up.

"What's up LiLi?" he spoke, leaning in and hugging her neck.

"Tired as hell, you know that drive be kicking a bitch ass."

"Yeah, but the money we make together makes it worth it." Riz reminded.

He turned his attention to Kiam and flashed his iced up grill. "So you're the man that's running the show now?"

"With an iron fist," Kiam spat, looking on with a stony stare.

Riz sat next to Bean and propped his feet up on an ottoman. He looked up at Kiam trying to assess him.

Kiam stood firm with his arms folded across his chest.

Riz grabbed a blunt from the ashtray and lit it up. Kiam watched his pallid mouth as he puffed and blew out smoke.

"So, what can I do for you?" Riz asked.

"I'm here to talk bricks and prices."

"I thought we already had an understanding on that?" He looked from Kiam to Lissha. Her expression told him that she was not calling shots.

Riz nodded his understanding and looked back at Kiam. "I'm not prepared to deliver any less than what Gator gets and I'm not excepting any less than he pays," he stated as he continued to inhale and exhale smoke.

"Fuck what you and Gator agreed to, that was then, this is now?" Kiam laid down his stake.

Riz looked at Bean, as if to ask if he was hearing Kiam right. Bean silently communicated that he was on point if Riz wanted him to lay Kiam's ass down.

Riz shook his head no and returned his full attention back to Kiam. "I see Big Zo has finally found a man in the mode of himself to take charge of his operation. But even Big Zo didn't come up in here and talk to me as hostile as you do."

"I'm not hostile, Bleed. But don't try to hold me to what another man agreed to. Gator has been demoted, therefore, anything he agreed to has to be renegotiated," Kiam made it clear, as he looked Riz dead in the eye without blinking.

Riz nodded his head in acknowledgement of Kiam's stance and decided to hear him out. "Talk numbers. Let me hear your proposal."

Kiam unfolded his arms and cupped his fist in the palm of his hand. "I ain't paying no more than fifteen. But I'm prepared to double the amount we usually get, and before long our order will quadruple," he predicted.

"In the meantime, you want to pay fifteen?" Riz laughed.

"Bleed, you see something comical about what I proposed?"

Lissha heard a slight chuckle behind Kiam's words and immediately tensed up; she hoped he wasn't about to air the room out. But Riz didn't respond to Kiam's unspoken challenge, and she was glad for that.

"Let's roll, Lissha," Kiam said.

Riz shot up off the couch waving his arms. "Hold the fuck up. Lissha we been doing business with you for years. You're one of my most loyal customers. Then you let this nigga come in here standing between good business?" he questioned harshly.

"She ain't got shit to say, you're talking to me. Lissha wait for me in the car," Kiam ordered.

"Lissha, is this how you're doing business now?"

"You heard him, Riz. Whatever he says, I back it." Lissha got up and headed to the door. When she touched the door knob the dogs began to growl.

"Stand down," Riz spoke out, calming the killer canines.

Lissha posted herself outside of the door gun drawn. If she heard ruckus she was going in blazing.

Inside the apartment Kiam remained poised and ready for whatever. He held Riz's stare with one just as confident. Fuck the odds, he had a full clip.

"I see you got big gorilla nuts," said Riz, coughing on the blunt he was blowin'.

"Nah, gorillas got big Kiam nuts," Kiam clarified.

"This man right here is the truth," Riz said to Bean, his long-time bodyguard. "I think I like this muthafucka. If he has the balls to come up in here by himself and challenge me on anything, I can just imagine how he crushes niggas back home."

Bean co-signed with a nod of his head. Real recognized real as Kiam had predicted to Lissha it would.

"Now I see why you're in, and Gator is out. I believe we'll do great business together."

"At fifteen a piece," Kiam maintained.

"No, I can't do fifteen. I can do fifteen-five if you get twenty. That's a ticket that reflects my confidence in your ability to tremendously increase your purchase in the near future."

Kiam pretended to think the offer over, but inside the deal was already sealed. He had been willing to pay up to seventeen a block so fifteen-five was gravy. Now he pushed for Riz to have the work delivered to him at a location that would be halfway between their two states.

Riz wrestled with him over it for a while before partially giving in to Kiam's proposition. "Ok, I'll have the product brought to Williamsport, PA. But you have to purchase thirty—for that amount I'll make it happen."

Kiam conceded the battle because he had won the war. He reached out and shook Riz's hand. "We can continue doing business," he said. "I'll have someone get at you in a few days."

"I look forward to it," replied Riz. "You need to smoke some of this heat wit' me." He held the blunt out to Kiam.

"Nah, I don't indulge," Kiam declined.

Riz could respect that. He nodded his head and sat the blunt back in the ashtray.

Kiam took a seat on the couch across from him. They talked over a few other particulars, then Kiam bid Riz goodbye. As he walked Kiam to the door, Riz threw an arm around his shoulder and whispered something in his ear. Kiam's expression revealed nothing and he said even less.

Lissha eased her hand out of her jacket and relaxed when Kiam came out looking like everything was good with him and Riz.

"You okay?" she asked as they strolled back to the car.

"You didn't hear any gunshots did you?"

"Is that a yes or a no, Kiam?" she sighed. *This muthafucka gets on my nerves. Just like a pair of panties that keeps crawling up my ass.*

"Do I frustrate you?" he asked, waiting for her to pop the locks.

"Yes, you do." Lissha slid behind the wheel. She pulled off and left him standing there looking stupid.

Kiam gritted his teeth and tapped his foot, counting the seconds in his head.

Lissha circled the block then pulled up to where he stood. The passenger window eased down and she leaned over in the seat. "You need a ride?" she asked playfully.

He slid into the passenger seat and turned up the music to tune her out.

"Eww! Why you always so uptight? Don't you know how to relax and have a little fun?" She wrinkled her nose. "What, that bitch you were booed up with at the hotel the other day didn't fuck you good enough? I can always find you one of these BK hos to break you off."

"Why your mind always on my dick?"

She stuck her middle finger up at him and pulled off, determined not to say anything else to him unless it was absolutely necessary.

Through his peripheral, Kiam noticed Lissha's expression but he didn't have time to assuage her aggravation. His thoughts were occupied by what Riz had put in his ear.

Chapter 14
Hidden Alliances

Back in Ohio, Gator literally had his tongue in shorty's ear. She moaned and wrapped her legs tighter around his back as he thrust deeper inside her honey pot.

"Umm, baby, you know that's my weak spot. Please, I'm not ready to come yet."

"Nah, don't hold back. Come all over this black ass dick. It's yours, get it all," urged Gator, carrying her throughout the house, fucking her well.

"Is it mine?" she asked, feeling him all up in her stomach. His length and girth filled a bitch up.

"Hell yeah," he said, pressing her back against the wall. He gripped her ass with both hands and long stroked in and out.

Her nails dug deep into his back and she bit into his shoulder to keep from screaming. "Ooh, shit!" she cried as her love began to come down.

Gator felt her body tense as her walls re-gripped his thick wand. He slammed in and out of her with powerful gyrations, pulling all the way out to the tip, then ramming in balls deep. She yelled out his name. He grunted out hers, and they both exploded simultaneously.

A short while later they were back in bed. Gator was smoking a blunt; she was stroking his dick lovingly. "It gets better every time," she told him. "I want it to be mine for real."

"It can be, if you do what you gotta do," he said. He didn't have to expound, they had talked about it before. Now that Kiam was on the scene and had replaced him as boss, it was time to really press her to slump Lissha.

"I told you, we don't have to do it like that. We can just strike out on our own," she said, releasing his meat and sitting up.

He passed her the blunt. "You know it's blood in and blood out with that bitch. And now that she has that nigga Kiam rolling with her, she would really be on some vengeance shit," Gator predicted.

"We could talk to Big Zo."

"What the fuck for? You think he's gonna go against his own flesh and blood?"

She thought about that for a minute. "You're right," she had to agree. "But getting rid of LiLi now won't set us free. We would have to do Kiam too because from what I'm hearing he ain't nothing nice."

"Don't you hop on that nigga's dick too," he chastised.

"No, baby. You don't have to worry about that. I'm your bitch even though we have to keep it hid. I believe in you." She looked down into his eyes convincingly.

Gator pulled her head down and covered her mouth with his. He kissed her deep then stared up into her eyes. "That's why I'ma wife you, boo. Because you ride hard for a nigga. I know you and Lissha and 'em go back further than you and I do, but it's time for us to make our own moves."

"I agree," she said, contemplating his insistence that she kill one of her Blood Money Crew members for the sake of being with him.

"I'ma have that nigga Kiam smashed," he vowed before blowing her a gun.

Shit was about to get hectic.

Chapter 15
A City Under Siege

Now that Kiam had the connect firmly in his corner it was time to turn up. He had Lissha and Gator to take him around to each one of their dope houses and introduce him personally to the people that ran them. If a spot wasn't pumping hard enough, he replaced the person running it with a younger, hungrier trap boy under their employ. A couple niggas protested their demotion and got something real hot put in their domes.

"Niggas get a little rank and grow content. The problem is that y'all have them on salary. So they get paid the same whether the trap makes five bands or fifty. What incentive do they have to trap harder? Muthafuckas probably been laying up in some pussy when they were supposed to be serving," he said as he sat in Lissha's study looking over the numbers that each spot produced.

The cryptic figures were stored in a program on Lissha's laptop. She stood over Kiam's shoulder decoding the numbers for him.

Gator scowled from across the room where he sat in an over-stuffed lounge chair with his feet resting on a mauve and grey ottoman that matched the chair. *This nigga has something to say about everything, he said to himself.*

Kiam pushed away from the desk. He steepled his hands under his chin, closed his eyes, and thought everything over. The numbers were pitiful for an operation the size of theirs. When he opened his eyes he had a clear plan.

"From now on the workers were going to get paid off of commission. The more A.C. they sold, the more they'd make." A.C. is what they called crack in Cleveland.

"We're gonna give them 60/40 packs."

"What the fuck is that?" questioned Gator.

Kiam explained that 60/40 packs meant that they would give the trap boys bundles of pre-packaged rocks and they would split the proceeds 60/40.

"We'll get the bigger slice of the pie, and it'll still be gravy because we get sixty percent from all of the houses. On the flip side, this allows the workers to make much more than they had been making on salary."

"That sounds good," Lissha co-signed, processing the math in her head.

"I don't like it. They'll be eating as good as we are," voiced Gator.

"I didn't ask you if you liked it or not. Some niggas didn't like being demoted," Kiam reminded him. He didn't have to elaborate, it was still fresh in Gator's mind what happened to those that bucked the changes that Kiam was initiating.

Gator fought hard to keep his feelings from showing on his face. He got up and went to the kitchen to get a Heineken out of the refrigerator.

"I don't see how y'all made it this far following that clown nigga's lead," Kiam said to Lissha.

"He wasn't always like this. When he first came aboard he was on point. But now I think the money and the bitches has made him soft. He's not trying to elevate higher because he saw what happened to Daddy and others when they reached the top in their game."

"Did he work for Pop before he fell?" asked Kiam, wondering how Gator had wagged an indictment.

"No, Gator saved my life, that's how we met him. As appreciation Daddy plugged him in and he rose from there. Like I said, he was hungry back then, now he's not. Daddy must've recognized that," Lissha shared.

Kiam didn't press her for details on how Gator saved her life, he knew the story would come out sooner than later. It didn't matter though, that was then. He had the nigga figured out.

"Niggas like Gator are afraid to reach for the top because they believe that once you get to the pinnacle, there's nowhere to go but down," he said.

"Is he wrong?"

"If we're talking about the average nigga, he's not. For a nigga like myself, it don't apply. Once I reach the top, I'ma just ascend to another stratosphere," Kiam said.

"You're so fucking humble," Lissha remarked sarcastically.

Kiam looked at her and shrugged his shoulders. His arrogance made her secret treasure throb.

Gator returned with a beer and a sandwich in hand. The three of them talked business strategy for the next hour. After hearing Gator's input, Kiam was better able to comprehend how he had at least helped rebuild Big Zo's operation to its present status.

Gator received a text and announced that he had to leave and handle a personal matter. As soon as he left, Kiam stared at Lissha silently.

"What?" she asked, gathering up the empty Heineken bottle and the plate that Gator had left on the floor. Kiam continued to stare. *"What?"* she asked again with more emphasis.

"You're fuckin' that lame," He said, coming from left field. "I can tell because that muthafucka is very comfortable in your house. That nigga 'round here moving like he paying the mortgage on this bitch. All up in your refrigerator and shit."

"I didn't snatch your dick outta Mrs. Corporate America's mouth. So don't be all in my shit," Lissha said, never breaking eye contact until she sashayed past him and into the kitchen.

A minute later Kiam came and sat on the padded stool at the kitchen's island.

Lissha had already made up her mind that she was not having it out with him about something that wasn't his concern. His directions from Big Zo was to take over the organization and elevate it to a new height, not sniff her fucking thongs.

She busied herself at the sink apprehensively waiting for Kiam to try to go there.

"So what's up, LiLi? You in your feelings now?" he asked.

"Not hardly."

"Good. Because we have a whole lot of work to do. You're slipping, shorty."

"And how is that?"

"Storing numbers in your computer is straight reckless. It don't matter that they are coded, the feds got big head geniuses that can decode that shit in the blink of an eye."

"I'll uninstall the whole program and delete that from my hard drive," said Lissha, turning off the faucet and drying her hands on a towel.

"No. Get rid of the whole computer," ordered Kiam.

Lissha didn't argue about it, she agreed to burn the computer ASAP.

"In the meantime, go strap up. I think I know why our trap on Avon is pumping small numbers."

"Strap up? Wait a minute. I'm not defying you, but I put my life on those boys that run that house. They're on the square, Kiam. We don't have to kill them," said Lissha in the defense of three of their most loyal trap boys.

Kiam smiled at her incorrect conclusion. He had already collected his Intel. "Nah, I'm not gonna crush JuJu and 'em, we're gonna crush the niggas that are in their way," he revealed.

"Greg and Fat?" She had done her homework too. Long before Kiam came home.

Kiam nodded.

"You don't even have to get your hands dirty with their blood. I have some killahs on it already," she revealed.

"Oh yeah? Who are you talking about, ya boy?" Cynicism rang loudly.

"I'm not going to dignify that with a response," she tossed back.

"Who are these so-called killahs you're talking about?" he probed with an eyebrow raised.

Lissha came and sat on a stool next to Kiam. She smiled at him reassuringly. "You don't have to worry about these killahs, I put my life on them. They're tested and proven, and it's about time you meet them."

"I bet they're as soft as ya boy," he wise-cracked.

"Softer." She smiled. "But much more deadly."

It was time for her to introduce him to three gangsters in high heels and Maybelline.

Chapter 16
Distracted

Lissha pulled into her driveway blasting her radio, feeling like a beautiful black goddess. She had just gotten her hair, nails, and feet done, everything waxed, and did a little shopping. She popped her trunk, jumped out and grabbed her bags and headed inside.

Placing the bags in her bedroom she ran a tub of water and hit her satellite radio to set the mood. She had been running hard all day but the girls were set to come over later. *Damn.* She still had to cook and get the house ready. But she still needed to grab a few hours for herself.

She put all of her clothes away, then stripped down to her birthday suit and stepped into her bubble filled hot tub. Laying her head back against the cushion, she settled in and dozed off.

She awoke an hour later still feeling tired. She stood up in the tub, turned the shower on and quickly washed and rinsed off. The water put some pep in her step. She oiled and scented her skin and slipped into a pair of tight white boy shorts and a tank top.

Walking into her living room she picked up the remote and turned the radio all the way up. Frank Ocean's *Thinkin' Bout You* blared from the system. Singing along Lissha poured herself a tall glass of white wine, rolled a blunt and plopped down on her soft loveseat and went into chill mode.

After a few sips of wine and a half of a blunt, Lissha was feeling relaxed. In between songs she heard her cell phone ringing in the other room. "Dang, can't a bitch chill," she sighed, jumping up and hurrying to reach her phone.

By the time she reached the bedroom they had hung up. She checked the Caller ID and saw three missed calls from Kiam. They hadn't spoken in a couple days so she called him right back to find out what was up. Strolling back into the living room she held the phone to her ear with her shoulder and waited for him to pick up.

"Hello?" he answered.

"What's up?" she plopped back down on the loveseat.

"Come outside,"

"For what?" she asked, reaching for her glass of wine.

"I need to talk to you for a minute."

"Well, come in," she said, throwing her hand to the side.

"Shorty, just come outside real quick."

Lissha sat the phone down next to her then put her head back. This negro must think I'm his puppet. She sat forward, looked at the window, and blew her breath out real hard. Kiam could really work a nerve when he wanted to and it seemed like he took pleasure in doing so.

Rising to her feet she walked over to the door, slipped into her flip flops and headed outside. As she walked down the walkway Kiam's eye's settled on her 2 carat diamond belly ring that sparkled in the sunlight. She walked up to the car and got in with her attitude on max.

"What's up?" she asked, looking at him with her eyebrows raised.

"Why you outside naked?"

"I'm not naked, Kiam. Anyway what's up, man?"

"Why you giving me all this attitude? You missed me?" he asked, locking eyes with her

"Yeah, I missed you like a thorn in my ass," she turned her head to the side.

He started to say something else slick but decided to get back to business. "I need to have a sit down with your girls tonight."

"Why tonight? What if I have something else planned?"

"Cancel it. I rearranged everybody else, now I need to get with the girls to see where their heads are at before I put them on this mission."

"I told you, I got them." She huffed.

"So you trust them bitches with your life?"

"I certainly do."

"Well, you may know them like that, but I don't. And I'm not taking a fucking gamble on my shit. Oh yeah, and let's not forget that you sent one of them 'trust them with my life' bitches to suck my dick."

"Fuck you," Lissha spat then turned and grabbed the handle to get out the car. Kiam clutched her thigh and gripped it tightly, preventing her from exiting the vehicle. Lissha turned toward him with her whole face bald up, her eyes low, and her breathing quick.

"Get your hand off my leg," she said through clenched teeth, as if each word was a warning all by itself.

Seeing his smug expression made her want to punch him in the face. She balled up her fist, but his words were quicker than her hands.

"No disrespect, ma. I know those are your girls. My bad," he apologized.

Lissha just looked at him. The apology was half ass but it was a start. More than he had given before.

"Look, on the real, I need to feel them out," he explained. "Don't take it personal, Lissha, I'm just the type of man that don't like to leave anything to chance. I gotta make sure that every aspect, and everybody, is on point."

"I'm not new to this Kiam. If you're such a boss nigga, recognize that I'm that chick who'll be the eyes in the back of your head," she spat as she opened the door.

"You mad at me?" Kiam teased, giving her that disarming smile that he could turn on and off in the blink of an eye.

"Your ass is bipolar." Lissha looked down. "You gonna move your hand or what?"

"Stop frontin', you know you want my hands all over you."

Lissha shook her head. She had never met anyone like him; he was the kind of nigga a bitch loved to hate. She grappled his wrist and moved his hand. "You wouldn't know what to do with me," she replied tersely.

Kiam's eyes settled on her ass as she rose from the seat. "I bet you're itching to find out," he said as she walked away.

Lissha hurried up the walkway; she needed to get as far away from him as possible. The way he made her feel she wanted to invite him in so they could just fuck out all that aggression and get it over with.

"LiLi?" Kiam called out.

She kept her stride, ignoring his arrogant butt. When she reached the door she turned around with an exaggerated flourish, "What?"

"Be good."

Lissha flipped him the bird. Kiam just laughed and pulled off.

When Lissha got inside she sparked up her blunt. She took a few deep pulls and sat it down. Kiam always caused her emotions to do summersaults. She was trying to follow Daddy's orders but every time she got around Kiam it got harder and harder.

She sat for a few more minutes then headed into the kitchen to start cooking. As she went through the refrigerator gathering everything she needed for the meal, Kiam's question played in her head: *You trust them bitches?*

Hell yeah, without reservation she trusted her girls. When they ran up in someone's house to take that blood money or had to push somebody's scalp back, they had never let her down. She placed the food on the counter and thought back to the countless missions they had been on and how each one of them held their own. *Damn what Kiam thinks about them.*

Lissha went out in the backyard and put the beef ribs on the grill, marinating them in her homemade sauce. Her taste buds salivated in anticipation as she headed back inside to prepare the potato salad, baked beans and corn on the cob. In a short time she had everything prepped. She placed the beans in the oven and the potato salad in the refrigerator then made a toss salad to go with the meal.

While the meat simmered she hopped in the shower, threw on some jeggings and a t-shirt and got ready for the girls. Quickly she rolled a few blunts and made sure that the wine and the 1800 was on deck. It was about to go down.

A few hours later…

Lissha walked over to her iPod station and programed some music, turning the volume up loud. Just as she headed to the kitchen the doorbell rang. On the way to the door she grabbed a blunt off the glass cocktail table and put some fire to it.

She checked the peephole, and then opened the door singing, "Alriiight…." Lissha was happy to see her ladies. She smiled and blew cloud smoke in Treebie's face.

"That's what the fuck I'm talking about," Treebie said, taking the blunt from Lissha's hand.

Lissha moved back allowing the girls to pass. Bayonna was wearing a pair of red, tight-fitting skinny Jeans. She snapped her fingers and did a two-step to the music that boomed throughout the house. Donella followed suit doing her signature move, dropping to the floor and bringing it back up.

"Let's get this shit going," she said, throwing her purse on the floor next to the couch and going for the wine bottle and a glass.

Lissha went into the kitchen and grabbed the 1800 out the freezer along with the shot glasses. Bayonna lit another blunt and started it into rotation. "Damn, LiLi, it smells good as hell up in here," she complimented.

"Yeah, you know I put my ass in it this time," Lissha joked.

"I hope the fuck not," coughed Treebie, choking on that good ass loud.

"You know you love my sexy Apple Bottom," Lissha said, making her cheeks jump.

"Bitch you nasty," Treebie laughed.

They all sat down and immediately began taking shots to the head and passing blunts. Lissha puff puff passed, then began her tutelage.

"Alright, we got another hit to do this Friday. Everything is lined up and we stand to make a grip. After we do this one, we get two of our own." Hearing that, the girl's ears perked up.

Lissha took another shot of 1800 before continuing. It went down smoothly. "Also, we got this new deal with our connect," she sat her glass down and folded her hands. "From now on, y'all will have to pick up in Pennsylvania."

"Riz agreed to that?" interrupted Treebie.

"Yeah, him and Kiam worked it out. Actually, Kiam just demanded that shit and stood his ground," Lissha replayed.

Bayonna and Donella nodded their heads respectfully because they both knew that it took a man with a strong will to get Riz to bend. Treebie didn't say or do anything; she wasn't ready to jump on Kiam's jock.

"Now, just because the pickup spot and the route have changed, we still need to make sure that shit arrives safely and in a timely fashion," Lissha strongly emphasized.

"You know how we do," Treebie said, pulling her gun from her waist sitting it on the table.

"You know I hold's my own," Donella chimed in.

"Enough said." Bay sealed the deal.

Lissha nodded her head. "That's what I like to hear. And don't forget about Fat and Greg, they're in the way of business."

"We're on it like yesterday." Donella assured her.

"That's what's up." She poured each of them a shot.

They grabbed their glasses and brought them together. "Let's get this money." Lissha toasted. The women clinked glasses then threw back their shots.

Setting her glass on the table Lissha announced. "Ladies, Kiam will be here in a little while. He wants to bring us up to speed on this next move. Now, I'm warning everyone beforehand that he can be a little forceful, but Daddy put him in charge so it is what it is."

Donella didn't see a problem with it, she just hoped for some of that prime beef Kiam selfishly walked around with. Bayonna had yet to meet him, but from all that was being said she knew that he would be impressive.

Treebie grabbed a blunt and sat back. She hadn't seen Kiam since they put Finch and them on their backs.

"Let's eat," suggested Donella. Her munchies had kicked in and the smell of those ribs caused her mouth to water.

"Bay, come help me fix the plates," said Lissha, rising to her feet and looking at Treebie puffing away, lost in thought. Lissha silently prayed that her right-hand didn't bump heads with Kiam.

Lissha and Bayonna went into the kitchen and fixed the plates, then headed back to the living room. "I'm about to hurt this," Bayonna said as she sat down and began to dig in.

Just as Lissha brought her fork to her mouth the bell rang and a sinking feeling rose in her gut. She used the remote to turn the music down on her way to the door. Bayonna and Donella looked over at Treebie whose mood had gotten very serious.

Lissha pulled the door open and her eyes unconsciously roamed up and down Kiam's frame; he stood tall with his white t-shirt clinging to his form and giving a slight hint of his well-developed chest. His black Seven jeans fitted just right resting on top of his boots. He looked as scrumptious as the ribs, like his beef would melt in a bitch's mouth just as fast as the barbeque.

"Can I come in?" he asked, breaking Lissha's stare. When he wasn't fussing and bossing her around he had a nice smooth baritone.

"You gonna let me in or what?" he repeated, flashing his sexy smile.

"Whatever," she replied nervously, like a school girl with a crush.

Kiam stepped pass her and the trace of his Gucci Guilty Black cologne caressed her nostrils. Lissha closed her eyes for a second and inhaled deep. Damn. She was going to have to control of herself.

Back in the living room, she made the introductions. "You met Treebie and Donella," she gestured to the two. "This is Bayonna." She nodded toward Bay.

Bayonna wiped her hands and stood to shake his. "Nice to meet you," she extended, looking no more than sixteen to Kiam.

"No doubt," he replied then spoke to the others. "Ladies."

"Good to see you again," Donella smirked.

"What's up?" said Treebie, nodding her head slightly.

Kiam took Lissha's seat. Leaning slightly forward, he was ready to jump right in to the business.

"Um, excuse you, I'm sitting there," Lissha said, coming over to him.

He looked up at her. "Well, you can't sit on my lap so you might wanna sit somewhere else."

Lissha frowned. And with a theatrical huff she picked up her plate and sat across from him by Treebie. The girls watched their little back and forth exchange.

"Ladies, I know this is your girls night, so I'll make this quick," began Kiam condescendingly, but his tone still carried command. Everyone stopped eating and sat up.

"I've been moving shit around a lot, and quite a few things have changed in a very short time. If you're wondering where you fit in, and what your new roles are gonna be in this organization, I'm about to break it all down."

Kiam rested his arms on the back of the sofa and looked from one face to the other. It was clear to him that he held their attention. "I want y'all to slide further into the background, no more hand-to-hand sales or dealing with the workers.

"What I do want is for y'all to make the pickups. This first pickup is scheduled for next week. We gonna meet them in Williamsport, Pennsylvania. I need everyone to be on their A game. No slip ups."

Kiam detected a slight wrinkle in Treebie's forehead that hadn't been there a second ago. He would deal with that. In the meantime he went on. "I don't know these niggas we're dealing with, just like I don't know y'all. But Big Zo said y'all official and Lissha confirmed that, so my trust is in their assessment only. Y'all might not want to make them look bad."

"Let me get this shit straight." Treebie cut in. "You want us to ride out to PA and meet these niggas. Make the transfer and bring you the shit, then what?"

"What you mean then what?"

"Just what I said," Treebie shot back.

Kiam smiled at her audacity, recalling her get-down from the first ecounter. *Just like I figured, a pit bull in a skirt,* he assessed, and then got serious. "There ain't no then what. I got it from there," he declared.

"Nah. That sounds like you'll eventually cut us out. We in this shit all the way with you or you can take the fucking ride," Treebie countered. She sat back, crossed her legs and lit up.

Kiam looked at her sideways and his coal black eyes turned even darker. Lissha noticed the change and pounced in. "Look, we're not doing this," she said, directing her words more to Treebie than to Kiam. "This is the way Daddy wants this shit handled. We need all hands on deck." She looked over at Treebie who had her eyes fixed on Kiam.

Treebie took another deep pull on her blunt and blew the smoke out in Kiam's direction. "You right Li, it's business. You got my full cooperation." She looked Kiam up and down and smiled, then picked her gun up off the table and headed to the bathroom. Her intended disrespect rung loud and clear.

Kiam chuckled.

Lissha, who had already figured out what that meant, stood up. "Kiam, can I please talk to you in the other room?" she asked.

"Hold up!" He brushed past her and headed to the bathroom.

When Treebie opened the door she was startled by Kiam standing in the doorway. He pushed her back in the bathroom and closed the door. "Let me explain some shit to you. I don't have time for petty bullshit. I know you official but don't test that shit on me. I don't fold like them other pussy ass niggas. You here because Big Zo and Lissha say you cool. But if you make me feel differently, I know how to make my problems disappear." His eyes bored into hers.

"You ain't talking 'bout nothin', I feel the same way," she said.

"You can feel however you want to, just respect my position so I don't have to reinforce it on you,"

Treebie stared him in the eye and her lashes didn't blink. "I know what your position is, Kiam. The problem is I don't know what you did to earn it,"

Kiam moved dangerously close grabbing her by the jaw applying a little pressure. "Some shit ain't for you to know, just play ya fucking position. Or did you fuck your way into it?" Kiam slapped her with words.

Pulling her face back she gritted. "You don't know shit about me." Her breathing rapidly increased.

"I know more than you think I do. But I'll let you worry about that." His wry smile unnerved her but Treebie remained cool.

"There's nothing for me to worry about," she calmly asserted.

Kiam chuckled as he stepped back out of her space. "Enjoy the rest of your evening," he stated politely. Like he really did know something.

When he swung the door open. Lissha was standing in the hall with a look of nervousness all over her face. She looked past him at Treebie. "What happened?"

"Nothing I can't handle," Kiam said moving past her.

She turned her attention to Treebie who looked like she was ready to kill somebody. "Tree, what the fuck is going on?"

"Just leave me alone for a minute." She pushed Lissha back slamming the bathroom door in her face.

Resting her hands on the counter she stared in the mirror replaying Kiam's words in her mind and wondering what all Big Zo had told him.

When Lissha walked back in the living room her wheels were turning. She looked over at Kiam engrossed in a conversation with Donella and Bay and cut in. "I need to speak to you Kiam," she said in a demanding tone.

Just as Kiam was about to answer her request his cell rang. He looked at the screen and smiled. "Another time," he said to Lissha as he stood up and headed for the door.

"Hello," Kiam said into the phone.

"Hey baby." It was Faydrah. The happiness of her tone let him know that she was smiling. Kiam loved that.

"Hey you," he spoke back, using an affectionate greeting from their past.

"*Hey you,*" she echoed with sweet familiarity. "What you doin'?"

"Thinking about my girl," he answered reaching for the door knob.

"I have something special for you. Can I see you tonight?"

"Of course."

"Hit me when you get close,"

"I can't wait to hit you." He turned to look at Lissha coming his way.

Faydrah giggled as the thoughts of their last time together filled her mind and moistened her panties. "You so bad," she cooed.

"I work hard at it," he boasted jokingly, and then added, "I'll see you in a minute." He disconnected the call and returned his attention to Lissha. She was eyeing him with a face of stone.

"Anything else?" he asked

"No, I'm good," she said with a little attitude in her voice.

Kiam smiled "I'll catch up with you in a couple days. Make sure the girls are on point." He opened the door and started down the short walkway.

"They're on it, just chill and go lay up with Mrs. Fax and Copy," Lissha hurled, resting one hand on her hip and the other on the door preparing to slam it.

Kiam didn't dignify her smart comment with a response, he got in his truck and drove off.

As soon as she reached the living room the girls went in. "That nigga there. Whew!" Donella shouted out. "Fo' real, did you tell Big Zo how he is?"

"Trust me, daddy knows how Kiam is, he schooled him for three or four years. True, he can come off a little too hard but he's the butt-naked truth."

"That nigga ain't shit just like the rest," Treebie gritted looking at Lissha with homicide in her eyes.

"What the fuck did he say to you?" Lissha asked with a deep crease in her forehead.

"I just don't like that muthafucka. Call it my in-tui-fuckin'-tion."

"Sheeeiittt, what's not to like about him?" Donella disagreed. She tossed a shot back and shook her head in regret of a lost opportunity. "I still can't believe I let that sexy muthafucka leave the room without coming up off some dick?"

"What can you say, he knows what he wants," Bayonna surmised.

"Girrrlll, that nigga ain't nothing nice. Maybe we can pass that nigga around like this blunt," laughed Donella as she lit up.

Treebie turned her lip up. "Fuck that nigga. His ass on borrowed time, and I hope I'm the one that gets to punch his clock," she intoned bitterly, reaching for the blunt.

"You need to calm the fuck down," Lissha said grabbing a couple plates from the table and walking to the kitchen.

Bay took the blunt from Treebie, inhaled deep then served them up with some jewels. "Kiam is just carrying out Big Zo's instructions," she reminded her. "Ain't no telling how many nights they stayed up planning all of this. We do have to be on point.

"None of us has ever been on this level. Gator always handled the pickup and we just played our roles once it made it to Cleveland. We in the big league now, ladies. Let's woman up and do what he needs us to do," she encouraged the crew. She looked at Treebie to see if she comprehended, then she sat up and poured her and Donella a glass of wine.

Lissha stood in the kitchen door looking at the girls. Kiam had just shaken everything up, his presence changed the whole dynamic of everything they were doing. She knew that it was only a matter of time before this whole situation would come to a head. She was just praying shit didn't get bloody.

Ca$h & NeNe Capri

Chapter 17
Something Special

Kiam pulled into Faydrah's driveway and deaded his engine. He picked up his cell and called inside.

"Come open the door," he said, and then hung up.

He hopped out the car and strode to the door; with each step a little bit of excitement crept into his usually cool demeanor. Faydrah was the peace in the middle of his storm.

He approached the door and knocked a few times. Within seconds the door came open and his eyes were treated to her standing in the doorway with a light blue, silk lace bra and a matching G-string peeking out from under an open sheer robe.

"Hey babe," she said, moving into his arms.

Kiam received her tenderly. He squeezed her tightly as he walked her backwards and closed the door. Her baby soft skin was a comfort to his hands as he ran them down her back and over her butt.

"This is what a man needs after a long day," he whispered in her ear.

Faydrah melted in his strong arms, inhaled the masculine fragrance of his cologne, and began placing tender kisses on his neck and face. "I missed you," she confessed as her lips found his.

Kiam gave in to her kisses. He happily closed his eyes and enjoyed her soft lips and tongue as her hands gripped his back. He pulled back and sank his teeth into one of her breast then ran his tongue up her neck and kissed her again. Faydrah's entire body caught on fire.

"Baby wait," she whispered. His touch was taking over the moment and she did not want that.

"I thought you had something for me," he cooed in her ear as he fumbled with the back of her bra.

Faydrah reached up and grabbed his hands. "I do, but you need to let me be in control for a little while," she panted, pulling back to look into his eyes.

She could see the unbridled passion, and the fire from his soul pierced hers.

"You gonna come to the door wearing an outfit that says 'fuck me', then say hold up. Where they do that at?" Kiam said, stepping out of his boots.

"Don't worry, I got you. Just relax and let me do me," she said, taking his hand and leading him to the backyard.

Kiam's eyes settled on the string that lay perfectly between her ass cheeks.

As Faydrah slid open the patio door Kiam rested the rock up against her softness. "My boy wanna holla at you.,"

"Tell him I'ma have a long deep conversation with him if he'll just be patient." She moved forward and walked onto the deck.

Kiam was pleasantly surprised. Her yard was like a resort. She had a huge deck with a Jacuzzi on it surrounded by sheer white curtains. There was an in-ground pool and a huge gazebo surrounded by netting with a white cushioned lounge chair swing in the middle. There were flowers in an array of bright colors strategically placed throughout the yard and tall, potted palm trees. Flickering lanterns lit the area, setting the mood just right. Kiam gazed up into the pitch black sky; there were a few stars which flickered dimly in the far distance.

"You hungry," Faydrah asked as she opened the lids on the platters.

"You know I like to eat," he responded with a sexy smirk on his face.

"Come sit down." Faydrah smiled. She had prepared his favorite foods and couldn't wait to see his reaction.

Kiam took a seat at the table. His eyes lit up when he looked down at his plate and saw deep fried catfish nuggets, baked macaroni and cheese with five cheeses, collard greens and a bowl of banana pudding. She had remembered that these were the dishes that Miss Charlene used to make for him every Sunday.

"Thank you, baby," he said, standing up and kissing her lightly.

"I told you I got you," she replied affectionately.

They shared a few sweet kisses before they began to eat.

The food was delicious, and the ambience was perfect. They talked and laughed about the old days and how bad Kiam was. It felt good to him to have someone that he could just be himself around, someone who shared his past and was a perfect addition to his present.

When their plates were empty, Faydrah began clearing the table.

Kiam stood up. "Where's the bathroom, baby?"

"It's down the hall on the left." She pointed through the curtain in the doorway.

After Kiam disappeared into the house, Faydrah prepared the next stage of her plan.

She turned on her Pandora, hit the remote to dim the yard lights, lit a few candles then started up the Jacuzzi.

After washing his hands and rinsing his mouth with the Listerine he found in the medicine cabinet, Kiam grabbed a wash cloth and towel and hopped in the shower. It had been a hot, muggy, day and he wanted to get refreshed.

While Kiam showered, Faydrah poured them both a drink and placed them in the cup holder on the side of the Jucuzzi. Looking up at a full moon, she slipped out of her robe and bra then stepped into the warm water.

The music was playing and the candles were flickering. Against this romantic backdrop Kiam emerged from inside wrapped in a black fluffy towel.

Faydrah enjoyed looking at him, he was sexy without effort, and he was all hers again.

Kiam stood in front of the tub gazing down at her with hunger in his eyes. He licked his lips slowly and let the towel that was wrapped around his thirty-four inch waist fall to the ground. His iron rod stood straight up, ready to do damage.

When he stepped in the Jacuzzi, Faydrah leaned up and kissed the head of his dick, sending chills up his spin.

Pulling back, Kiam said, "Tonight let me please *you*." He went to his knees and lifted her out the water. Placing her on the edge of the tub, he slipped off her G-string.

Faydrah's center throbbed as he gripped her firm in his arms, threw her legs over his shoulders, and placed tender kisses on the insides of her thighs. His tongue slid to the crease of her leg causing her breath to quicken as he came closer to the furnace that burned at her center.

Kiam continued his tease until he felt she couldn't take anymore. He delicately ran his tongue up and down her pulsating kitty, then he zoned in on her bud of pleasure and alternated between sucking it gently, and firm.

Faydrah moaned and gripped the back of his head, prodding him to suck harder and take her to the point of no return.

Kiam knew what she wanted, but he wasn't ready for her volcano to erupt. He continued to tease and please at the same time.

Faydrah threw her head back as Avant and KeKe Wyatt crooned through her speakers My First Love.

Long as I live/ You will be my/My first love/My first love/ and my only love...

Faydrah gyrated and quivered as Kiam ran his tongue up and down her wet lips.

Showing no mercy, he held her firm in place, sucking and circling her clit with the tip of his tongue until she rained h.er sticky sweetness inside his mouth.

Releasing her legs he came up and looked in her eyes. "Thank you, baby" he whispered softly.

"For—what?" she asked breathlessly.

"For just being you."

"Kiam, I love you," she rasped, wrapping her arms around his neck and tracing his lips with her sweet tongue.

"I love you too, baby. Now come ride this dick," he commanded.

He definitely didn't have to ask twice. Faydrah stood up and looked down at his mammoth erection with desire. Kiam leaned back, positioning himself for her to straddle him. He put his arms out along the edge of the Jacuzzi and prepared to get the royal treatment like the king he was.

Straddling his lap Faydrah wrapped as much of her hand as she could around his throbbing thicknesses and guided him inside of her. She took her time sliding down on his pole, inch by wonderful inch, until she had all of him inside her.

"Ooh, yessssss," she moaned, rocking her hips and sliding up and down his length.

Kiam stared into her eyes taking each breath as she released it. She was riding his dick like she owned it. Kiam placed one hand on the small of her back pulling her into him. She leaned back angling his dick just right to hit that special spot deep inside of her.

Faydrah closed her eyes and gripped his shoulders as her pussy began to contract. "I'm about to cum," she moaned.

"Get that shit baby,.."

"Kiam," she cried as she rode faster, teasing her spot until she came long and hard. She bit into his neck while continuing to ride.

Rain drops began to drizzle down on them as he held her in place.

"Kiam, baby, it's starting to rain," she whispered feeling another orgasm coming on.

"Mmmmm, fuck the rain, ride this dick."

Her soft breast rested against his chest and he held her in his arms, never wanting to let her go.

Faydrah felt so connected to him she could read his thoughts. "Kiam, you're all I need," she moaned. It came out as a cry of pleasure, from a place no other man had ever touched.

Her eyes became misty as she felt his thrusts pleasuring those tight walls that caressed his steel.

"All this dick is yours, ma," he said, pulling her all the way down on him.

The rain came down harder, but Kiam paid it no mind, he was caught up in the enjoyment of her muscle play. Faydrah was the only woman that could get him wrapped up in every emotion of sex and make him let go when he wanted to hold back.

He pressed his lips lightly against hers and probed into her mouth with his tongue. Faydrah shuddered to his every touch, he was the air she needed to breath and she inhaled him deeply.

She felt as if she had stepped outside of her body. Becoming overwhelmed by the love they shared, she broke down. Tears slid down her face as they both exploded.

"Kiam, I never want to lose you," Faydrah cried.

"You won't." He held her tighter.

Wrapped in each other's arms they both breathed heavily while the rain poured over them.

"What else you got for daddy?" he whispered into her ear.

Faydrah looked into his eyes. "I think I need you to make me touch my toes," she purred.

Kiam was about that. "Stand up and grab the edge of the tub," he directed.

Faydrah wasted no time getting into position. She braced herself while looking over her shoulder. He looked sexy coming up behind her stroking his dick as rain water rushed over his smooth chocolate skin.

He grabbed her ass and spread her round cheeks. Looking down at her flower opening up for him turned Kiam on. He wrapped his hand around his stiff muscle and guided it inside her wet, hot walls.

Faydrah held in her breath and bit down on her lip. With each deep stroke she tossed that ass back at him.

"All of this belongs to me," he proclaimed, gripping her hips and forcing deep grunts to escape her lips.

"Yes Kiam," she mumbled.

"Make this pussy suck my dick," he growled.

Faydrah pushed back and rotated her hips and squeezed her muscles. "Like this?" She slow grind as he filled her up with every inch.

"Sssss. Just like that," he said, enjoying her every move. "Put your foot up on the edge of the Jacuzzi. Open that pussy up for me." He took control.

Faydrah gave him whatever he wanted.

Positioned perfectly, he made a few more power strokes and hit the spot that gave them both intense pleasure.

Faydrah's moans became louder and her breathing increased as a soul rocking orgasm came over her. "Oh my god," she cried out, gripping the edge of the tub.

"Oh shit," he quaked. "Hold it right there, ma."

Faydrah wanted to beg him to flood her until it ran down her thighs in rivulets, but she was out of breath and couldn't speak.

Kiam sounded like he was howling at the moon when he released his hot cum inside of welcoming tightness. Faydrah cried out in ecstasy then babbled his name.

After they recuperated, Kiam pulled her up into his arms and kissed her deeply. "Your neighbors gonna be looking at you funny tomorrow," he joked.

"So," she said not caring. "If they ain't having good sex and cumming then they should kill themselves."

"Let's go inside and dry off," he chuckled.

"Only if you let me wet you up afterwards."

"You know what I like."

They stepped out of the Jacuzzi, still touching and kissing. Faydrah gathered up the towel and her underwear and they headed inside.

When Faydrah woke up the next morning with Kiam lying next to her, her heart fluttered. Kiam was her everything. Just having him near was all she needed to cope. But a cloud of uncertainty always followed the warm feeling he gave her; he was in that life and the reality that at any minute she could get a call telling her that he was gone was more real than the warm body lying next to her.

Faydrah sighed deeply and snuggled closer to him. She needed to become full with his presence to last her when he wasn't there.

Chapter 18
Unfinished Business

The good loving Faydrah gave him did not keep Kiam from getting up and handling his business the next day. A man with huge ambitions couldn't afford to lay up in pussy 24/7 regardless to how good it was or how he felt about the woman. The streets were his wife, everything else was a mistress.

After leaving Faydrah mumbling in her sleep and dreaming of a house full of little Kiams, he hit flip mode and took to the streets checking traps and making sure that his workers were on their grind.

Just when the sun was about to go down and most cats were thinking about what club or which female they were gonna hit that Saturday night, Kiam decided it was time for him to deal with a situation that had been heavily on his mind. He rode through and picked Czar up.

"Where we headed, fam?" Czar asked as they drove off from his house.

"To get some answers," Kiam said.

Czar rubbed his hands up and down his legs as he settled in his seat. Kiam's tone made him nervous.

They rode in silence from out Indian Hills with the sounds of the streets growing louder as they drove down Euclid Avenue, through EC, toward Lee Road.

"Where's DeMarcus's car lot?" asked Kiam, coming to a stop at the traffic light.

"Bust a left, it's not too far down," said Czar, feeling a bit more relaxed. It was gonna be fun watching Kiam confront DeMarcus. *Man, I wish I had some popcorn.* Czar smiled in anticipation of the drama.

An icy cold glance from Kiam wiped the grin off his face.

Kiam made the left and drove down Lee Road until Czar pointed out DeMarcus's car lot. Kiam pulled into the lot and parked at the front door.

He saw that DeMarcus sold some real nice new and previously owned cars and trucks. It was near closing time so only a few customers were around. *Perfect*, Kiam thought as they got out the car and went inside.

An attractive mocha complexioned woman greeted them at the entrance. She was wearing a dark blue business suit with a skirt that stopped just above her thighs and showed off smooth, well-toned legs. She had a long, beautiful and expensive Asian-hair weave that flowed down to her generous ass. She wore small black, square-framed glasses that showcased an undercover freak type of look.

"May I help you gentlemen?" she asked, averting her eyes away from Czar's.

"Is DeMarcus around?" he replied, looking at her with a hard gaze of unfriendly familiarity.

"No, but he's on his way over from the other lot. Maybe one of our sales representatives can help you. Are you looking to buy an automobile?" This question was directed to Kiam, she knew that Czar already had a small fleet.

Kiam didn't respond at first, he was busy looking around the office. There were two high-end seating areas with 60 inch flat screen televisions. There was also a coffee/cappuccino station with all the fixings and two small refrigerators with several name brand drinks and snacks, all free to accommodate the customers. On the walls were plaques and awards of excellence that the sales people had earned. This wasn't any half-operation, from the looks of things the lot was doing well.

"How long before DeMarcus gets here?" he asked, ignoring the question that passed through her sexy red lips.

"DeMarcus should be here any moment. You can wait for him here in the lobby," she said, grabbing the remote and turning on the television. "We'll be closing in fifteen minutes but he should be back by then. Please enjoy some refreshments while you wait." She extended her hand toward the snack area.

Kiam disregarded her hospitality. "Where's DeMarcus office?" he asked Czar.

Czar pointed to a room on their left and Kiam walked in that direction. The female was dead on his heels.

"Oh no, you can't go in there," she protested and jumped in his way when he reached the office.

"Chill, ma, it's all good. Just send him in to see me when he gets here." Kiam swept her aside.

She looked back at Czar questioningly.

"Daphne, it's cool, he's DeMarcus's people," he explained.

Kiam walked in the office and closed the door. Looking around the plush, brightly colored room he began to take inventory. He stood looking at the photos on the wall; there was dozens of pictures of DeMarcus and different guys who had purchased vehicles.

Kiam slowly walked to the other side of the office with his hands clasped behind his back. His eyes settled on a framed picture of Miss Charlene that sat on a shelf. He picked it up and stared at it; a small pain pinched his heart. He silently vowed to find and destroy the man responsible for her death.

He sat the picture back in its place and took a seat behind the mahogany desk.

Ten minutes later he heard DeMarcus' voice outside the door; he was assuring Daphne that she was not in any trouble. When he came into the office and saw Kiam leaned back in the chair with his feet propped up on the desk, he frowned but quickly changed his expression.

"What's up, nigga? I heard you were home, what took you so long to come holla at me?" He flashed a phony smile and closed the door.

Kiam's expression was blank. "If you wanted me to holla, you would've let me know where to find you and I wouldn't have had to come looking for you. But it's all good," he responded, taking his feet down and folding his hands on the desk.

"I see it *is* all good. You don't look like you're hurting for anything. But you know if you need something, I got you." DeMarcus propped himself up on the edge of the desk.

"You ain't got shit I need, but you do have something I'm demanding—just on general principle." Kiam chuckled.

"Demand?" DeMarcus nervously fidgeted.

Reflexively Kiam's hand went to his waist; it was just a habit. A little chuckle then he would put a nigga on his ass. But this wasn't that, at least not yet. So he brought his hand up and placed it on top of the desk. "You're a funny nigga," he said.

"What you mean?" DeMarcus asked.

"We grew up in the same house so you know better than most that I'm the wrong person to piss off, yet you sit there and insult me."

"How am I insulting you, Bruh?" DeMarcus gestured with his hands.

"Cancel that *bruh* shit," spat Kiam. "A brother don't leave you dead in the water for eight years. So don't even come at me like we're family, nigga. I shouldn't have had to ask you for a damn thing, you should've laid the red carpet out for me as soon as I touched down. But fuck all that, I just wanna know if you've heard anything about who killed Miss Charlene."

"Nah, I haven't heard nothing." He looked over at her picture as sweat began to form on his forehead.

"I went by the old house and my stash was still there, but I'm willing to bet whoever killed her was looking for it. Now, who the

144

fuck else besides yourself would've known that I had money there?"

"Ain't no telling, but if I were you I'd start with that snake muthafucka that's out in the lobby," said DeMarcus.

It was funny because Czar had said the same thing about him.

"If you felt that way, why haven't you handled the situation by now? You mean to tell me that you're letting—"

A knock on the door stopped him in mid-sentence.

"Come in," said DeMarcus.

Daphne stuck her head in. "Everyone else is gone. Do you want me to hang around?" she asked.

"No, you can go on home I'll be there later on," he said. "Lock everything up before you go."

"Okay, see you later on."

Czar came into the office as Daphne was leaving. Lust danced in his eyes as he watched her switch off.

He grabbed a chair and straddled it backwards. Kiam noticed that Czar and DeMarcus looked at each other with unbridled contempt.

Kiam wasn't the type to say anything behind a man's back that he couldn't say to his face thus he continued the conversation. "Like I was saying, if you suspect that this nigga right here had something to do with Miss Charlene getting killed, why is he still breathing?" he questioned DeMarcus, point

Czar's eyes went from Kiam to DeMarcus then back to Kiam. He shot up off of the chair and grabbed DeMarcus by the collar. "What type of bullshit are you trying to put in the game?" he snarled, pushing DeMarcus against the desk knocking shit over in the process.

DeMarcus slapped Czar's hands off of him. "Nigga, you know what I'm talking about," he spat. He regulated his breathing and straightened up his tie.

"Nah, I don't know shit besides you seemed to come up good in the hood after your grandmother got killed. The way I see it, you're pointing the finger at me to keep the light off of your punk ass. What I'ma rob and kill Miss Charlene for? My money been grown up for years."

"So you say," DeMarcus disputed. "But don't nobody know what you got but yourself. I hear all of that boss hustla shit coming out ya mouth but I know for a fact your pockets were leaking back then."

"What?" Czar laughed dismissively, backing up a little. "Boy, you'll catch a rabbit fucking a grizzly bear before you'll catch me broke."

"That's what ya mouth say," DeMarcus shot back.

Kiam sat back, crossed his legs, and watched them hurl accusations back and forth.

"You a bitch nigga trying to disguise your jealousy with anger. But don't worry, I fuck her real good," DeMarcus chided him, causing Czar's his smile to retreat.

Finally part of the truth came out. DeMarcus turned to Kiam. "Bruh, this clown is still mad because I snatched Daphne off his arm. See, he tricked a lot of money on her but the bitch wanted me. That nigga's beef is about a ho."

Czar's face balled up and the thick vein by his temple almost bulged out the side of his head. DeMarcus had struck a nerve.

"Fool, I don't beef with no nigga over pussy. I'm just putting it out there; I think you killed your grandmother because she wouldn't tell you where Kiam's stash was."

"You sound stupid!" He turned to Kiam. "Bruh, I know you don't believe that shit. Me, kill Mama over some money? Hell, over anything! Nigga, I would take dick in my ass before I would do some foul shit like that. For real, Bruh. Fuck what this jealous-hearted nigga trying to put in your head, it's all love, and that's how I felt about Mama."

146

Kiam didn't need to hear anymore to know that the DeMarcus's vow was insincere. Ever since they were small DeMarcus had been a cruddy muthafucka, and Czar wasn't much better. Either one of them could have been lying. One thing for sure, he wasn't about to sit there all night trying to figure it out.

The two men shouted back and forth like cackling hens. When Kiam couldn't take anymore he put an abrupt end to it. "Shut the fuck up!" he barked, sending an eerie vibration throughout the room.

Both men abruptly stopped talking and sat down glaring at each other. Kiam reached in his pocket and pulled out a coin. Looking at DeMarcus, he said, "Heads or tails?"

"Huh?" DeMarcus was slow to catch on.

Kiam cut his eyes at Czar and held his stare.

Czar swallowed hard.

"Heads or tails?" said Kiam.

Czar understood what was at stake; this was a cold-hearted form of Russian Roulette. He threw his hand in the air. "Hold up, my nigga. I don't understand why you're putting me in this." His voice quivered.

Kiam pulled his tool from his waist and sat it down in front of him on the desk. "One of you niggas better choose or I'm deading both of you. Best to decide your own fate."

Czar swallowed again.

DeMarcus finally got a clue, but fear held ahold of his throat and wouldn't allow him to call the coin toss. The only sound that came out of his mouth resembled a whine.

Kiam reached for the forty-cal that he had sat on the desk.

"Heads," called Czar.

Kiam flipped the coin. It turned over in the air several times, almost in slow motion, before gravity brought it back down from the ceiling. Kiam caught it in the palm of his right hand. *Whop!* He slammed it down on the desk with his hand covering it.

Czar and DeMarcus rocked nervously in their seats. Kiam lifted his hand just a bit and peeked up under it to see how the coin had landed. When he saw it he chuckled, and one of their fates was sealed.

The banger came up off the desk in Kiam's hand in one smooth motion. In that fraction of a second before he aimed at the loser and squeezed off a perfect shot, Czar's ass hole tightened and DeMarcus pissed his pants.

Boom!

Czar's head snapped back and his brains sprayed against the wall behind him as he toppled over in the chair, crashing to the floor onto his back with one leg grotesquely twisted under his body.

DeMarcus's mouth was agape.

Kiam's expression had not changed, it was just another kill. He flipped the quarter to DeMarcus. "That's your lucky coin. Put that shit on a chain and wear it around your neck for good luck. Trust, you're gonna need it if I find out it should've landed on tails."

He stood up, walked around the desk, and put another slug in Czar's cranium as casually as if he was looking at his watch.

He looked back up at DeMarcus and now his eyes were squinted. He said in a real low tone, "You been out here eating good the whole time I was on the inside and you didn't do shit for a nigga."

"All you had to do was call or write and let me know what you needed, Bruh," stuttered DeMarcus.

Kiam raised the gun and pointed at his head. "Call me that shit again and I'ma change the color of the walls up in this bitch."

"Okay, man, what do you want? Just tell me how I can square things up."

"I want half of everything you own. Your drug spots, your businesses, your stash. Everything! Even your bitch." He fired a shot mere inches over DeMarcus's head.

DeMarcus damn near jumped out of his skin.

"Test me if you want to," gritted Kiam, and then he strolled out the door as nonchalantly as he had walked in.

Chapter 19
The Chase and the Catch

The week flew by as Donella and Bay looked forward to Saturday night with excitement and morbid anticipation. Bayonna moved around her apartment rushing from one room to another trying to get ready before Donella arrived to pick her up.

It was Ladies Night at the Tequila Ranch and the place would be overflowing with d-boys, athletes and other made men. After dealing with all of Kiam's demands lately the girls were in need of some loud music, drinks and male attention.

Bayonna stood looking in her wall length bathroom mirror. She was definitely feeling the reflection that stared back at her. She looked too cute in her black skinny leg jeans and silver sparkling bra. She was styling her hair when she heard her door bell ring. Placing the flat irons on the sink she hurried to the door to let Donella in.

As soon as she opened the door Donella looked at her over her Chanel shades and shook her head with slight disappointment. "Why your ass ain't never ready?" she asked.

"Just come in." Bayonna grabbed her by the hand and pulled her into the living room.

"Damn, Bay. What the fuck happened in here?" Donella asked, looking at the piles of clothes, shopping bags, shoe boxes and cleaner's plastic all over the floor and couches.

"You know I have a hard time finding shit to put on," replied Bayonna, rushing back into the bathroom to finish her hair.

"This shit is ridiculous. Bitch, you gotta do better than this," said Donella, stepping over the debris. She shook her head again and reached in her bag and pulled out two small bottles of Ciroc.

"Whatever, open that shit so I can get the night started."

"Here, and hurry up its 10:30. I wanted to get there before eleven." She passed her the open bottle.

"Bitch don't start. You can't rush perfection," Bayonna chirped, taking the bottle to the head. "Wow," she crowed as the coconut flavored liquid ran down her throat.

Donella laughed then began downing hers. Just before she finished it she held her bottle up so they could toast. "To the chase."

"And the catch," Bayonna added as they clinked bottles.

They downed the rest of their drinks and threw the bottles in the trash. Bayonna completed her look by putting on a little eye liner and glossing her lips. After she put on her black see-through shirt and silver Red Bottom stilettoes she was ready to go.

The ladies left out the house looking delectable and hot. Donella sashayed down the street in her dark blue Seven jeans, leopard Red Bottom open toe six inch heels and brown halter top that rested at the top of her jeans exposing her toned shoulders and arms. They jumped in Donella's silver metallic 2012 BMW 335i sports car and threw on a club CD to set the mood, with their mission in full focus.

They popped their fingers to the music and zoomed toward their destination. The Beemer rode so smooth Bayonna thought about buying her one just like it even though she already owned a Jag' and a Infiniti truck.

When they reached the club, Donella pulled onto the street and drove at a crawl, scanning the area for a parking space. As luck would have it some chicks were pulling out. She drummed her fingers on her thigh, impatiently waited while they fumbled around their little Honda Accord.

"These silly bitches," Bayonna said as she watched the drunken females laugh and play instead of getting the hell out of the parking space. She reached over and beeped the horn.

Donella looked over at her, surprised. "Bay, chill. Why you all hyped?"

"Fuck them; they need to hurry the fuck up,"

One of the females flipped her wrist and yelled out. "Wait your turn!"

Without hesitation Bayonna grabbed the door handle and was out the car. "Wait my what?" she said, walking over to the car, hips swaying, heels clicking.

"Oh shit, my bad, Bay," the driver said as she realized who her friend had gotten slick out the mouth with.

Bayonna squinted her eyes trying to remember the girl's face. "Gail?" she said. It was one of Gator's groupie ho's.

"Yeah, girl how you been?"

"I'm good now, but for a second it was about to get ugly out here," she said, looking over at the bitch with the mouth.

"Oh, she cool Bay." She looked to her girl. "Kaleese, this is Gator's people." She tried to calm the situation.

"Yeah, well if she cool tell her to watch her fucking mouth," Bayonna said.

She peered at Kaleese, holding eye contact until the woman wilted. Kaleese didn't dare open her mouth again. As soon as Gail mentioned Gator she already knew she had better keep her mouth closed.

"It ain't nothing Bay, I got it. Let me pull out so you can get in. I just left your brother inside; it's turned up in there. Y'all have fun," Gail said, getting in the car. She didn't want any problems, she had heard about Bayonna and her crew and she was not built for a war with them.

When Kaleese got in the car Bayonna headed back to Donella's vehicle and hopped in.

"What was all that about?"

"Nothing, that was that bitch that Gator fucks with."

"Bitch, you off the chain lately." Donella shook her head, Bay was bursting out of her shell.

Once they were parked they walked past the long line of people waiting to get in. Being that they were VIP, they went to a side entrance and knocked three times. The door came open and they were hit with weed smoke and loud music.

"What's up Bay?" The 6'5", 300 pound muscular bouncer took her hand, pulling her toward him.

"Hey Bones," Bay said giggling.

"Hey Nella," he said as she followed Bay into the basement of the club.

"Don't call me that," muttered Donella, crunching up her face.

"Why you so damn mean?" Bones remarked.

"Whatever." She brushed him off, moving past him and Bay.

Bones stood there scratching his head for a second. He looked at Bay, showing all thirty-two teeth. He had the biggest crush on her but she just played with his mind and pockets. Donella couldn't stand his black ass; it was something about him she didn't trust.

"Come on, Bay," she yelled over the music.

Bayonna threw up her hand for her to wait a minute. She was trying to get in this nigga's pocket and Donella's bad attitude was about to fuck that up.

Donella twisted her lips up and turned to scan the room for Gator and the crew. There was money all over the place. The owner of the club had the basement set up for all the ballers and celebrities that wanted to party without having to deal with a gang of groupies.

The VIP room was jumping, strobe lights bounced off of the walls and the music thumped. The stools at both bars were occupied and there weren't many empty tables or booths. Both small dance floors were crowded and the ratio of women to men was at least seven to one, which meant it was cutthroat as usual.

Donella's eyes roamed the room, watching the chickens that had made it to the basement. They were damn near naked, working hard trying to come up on some paid dick.

She shook her head. "Thirsty bitches," she mumbled.

When her eyes settled on Gator sitting at one of the bars, she started in his direction. "Come on," she hurried Bayonna.

Spotting Gator, too, Bayonna walked around Donella mumbling, "You'll fuck up a wet dream."

"If ugly ass Bones is in it, it's a nightmare," Donella shot back following her over to Gator.

Their boy was in his element. He was rocking a button down shirt with gray Armani pants that lay smoothly on top of his suede Ferragamo 'Giostra' loafers. His dreads were twisted down tight in the front and pulled back into a pony-tail, allowing the diamond earrings in his ears to sparkle as brightly as the strobe lights. Two thickly built females clung to his sides, getting high off his swag.

Bay and Donella walked right up to where he was seated; ignoring the hungry ho's he was entertaining.

"What's up, nigga, you buying?" Bay asked as she rested her hand on his back.

"What's up sis?" Gator leaned in and kissed her cheek. The icy piece on his platinum chain brushed against her chest.

"Hey Dee," he said to Donella as she reached in and hugged his neck.

"Hey you," Donella responded.

The two women that he had been entertaining looked at Bay and Donella with hard faces.

"Don't worry honey; we're not the competition," said Donella.

Gator smiled, he loved the attention. He stroked his newly grown goatee, showing of the shine on his wrist. The boy was a stunna at heart. He pulled out a bankroll and peeled three bills off for each of the women. "Order some drinks at the other bar while I holla at my fam," he said.

They took the money and sauntered off to do exactly that. Donella shot him the evil eye. Bay caught it but didn't think anything of it. Gator shrugged his shoulders and smiled arrogantly. *This is the muthafuckin' life.*

"Where's the rest of the crew?" he asked, looking around for Lissha and Treebie.

"Lissha about to go see Big Zo, and Treebie probably somewhere terrorizing, you know how she do," Donella brought his drink to her nose. "What's this?"

"Gimme my shit," he said, snatching it from her hand.

"You ain't gotta snatch it, nigga," Donella said, hitting his arm.

"I hate that shit, Treebie ass love to stick her nose in people's shit. That bitch rubbing of on you. Yo, give them whatever they want," he yelled over to the bartender then got up. "Get y'all drinks and meet me in the back room." He placed a hundred dollar bill on the counter and walked off.

Bayonna and Donella got their drinks then headed to a private room in the back of the basement.

When they stepped inside Gator was seated comfortably in a tall leather chair sipping his drink.

"What's up?" Bayonna asked as she took a seat across from him

Gator laughed, looking at her with a drink in each hand, "Damn, Bay, you trying to get fucked up."

"Hell yeah, I'm out trying to have a good time," she said, taking a sip of her Hennessey and Coke.

"So what's good? Y'all happy with new management?" Gator asked, searching for any discord in the ranks.

Donella looked over at Bay then back at Gator, she knew that she needed to keep her mouth closed and let her handle it.

"You know me, as long as my money right I don't give a fuck who in charge," Bay replied, taking another sip.

"So I guess you done jumped on the nigga's dick too?" He turned his question to Donella.

"I ain't on nobody's dick. Big Zo put this shit in motion. If you got a problem with Kiam then speak to Big Zo. You got his number," Donella stated, holding a firm gaze.

"Don't get smart with me. I'm just taking a pulse beat."

"Well, don't ask dumb ass questions if you don't want smart ass answers," Donella shot back.

"Just as I thought, that nigga got all of y'all on his nut sac," he spat, taking down more of his drink.

"Look, Gator, we came out to have a good time. If you want to shake things up, do it. But what you ain't gonna do is have us in on some conspiracy type shit, I don't get down like that." Bayonna said, rising to her feet.

Donella stood also. "I guess we'll catch you later," she said, heading to the door.

"We bigger than this," Gator called out as he watched her leave.

"I'm out too," said Bay.

"You ain't taking your drinks?" he asked, looking at her two drinks on the table.

"Nah, I'm good. This whole little meeting left a bad taste in my mouth."

"I'ma remember you said that when all this shit turns upside down."

"You do that," she said as she went to catch up with Donella.

"We gotta watch that nigga."

"Already on it," Donella responded as they headed up to the main club.

The catch...

As Bayonna and Donella moved through the crowd their eyes scanned the room for Fat and Greg.

"There they go," Bayonna said, giving Donella a light elbow to the ribs.

"Where?" she asked, looking in the direction of Bayonna's finger.

"Over there in VIP, come on," she said excitedly.

They marched over to the VIP section and tapped on the glass door. The bouncer cracked the door like he was the police. "You got an invite?" he grumbled.

"Tell Fat and Greg, Bay is out here."

The man looked them up and down then shut the door.

"This nigga," Donella spat.

"I know, every week he act like he secret service in this bitch," Bay added, looking through the glass and seeing Money Bags Carter and his King Kennedy Projects' crew balling a couple of booths down from Fat and Greg.

A minute later the door opened, "Come on," said the bouncer with an attitude.

Bayonna just shot him a dirty look.

Donella sucked her teeth as she walked through the small space he provided.

When they were in the room Bay looked over at Greg and Fat, they had strippers popping pussy all over them. They were throwing hands full of money at them ho's as if they were caked up.

Bay's stomach started to turn as she studied them from across the room. *These are the little niggas causing all the problems?* They didn't look over twenty-one. They were skinny, their jeans were skinny and from the looks of it so was their money because it looked like they were throwing ones.

"Come on girl, let's get this shit over with," Donella whispered in Bay's ear.

Bayonna shook her head and went into character. She threw her hips wide as they walked over to Fat and Greg's booth. "Damn, nigga, can I get some?" she yelled out over the boom of Trey Songz hit *Bottoms Up.*

As she continued walking toward them she wiggled her hips and snapped her fingers to the music.

"Oh shit, look at you," Greg hollered as Bayonna teased him with the rotation of her hips and ass.

Donella walked over to Fat and sat right on his lap, fingering the piece that hung down on his platinum chain. The letters MBK shined across the fist-sized piece in diamonds.

"I heard this was a baller's party, can we join?" she asked, grabbing a bottle of Patron off the table and popping it open.

"Hell yeah," Fat cheesed, and his lil' dude became alert as soon as Donella's fat ass began grinding on his dick. He had been trying to get at her for months and hadn't gotten pass hello, but tonight seemed to be his lucky night. He knew all along that he was gonna tap that ass sooner or later.

Bayonna pushed through the thirsty tricks and took a seat on Greg's lap, causing him to rock up immediately.

"Oh, so you trying to give a nigga some play?" he asked, looking at her nipples through her shirt.

"You know we don't fuck with no bum ass niggas, we trying to chill with the best tonight." She gassed him up further by stroking the sides of his face.

Greg looked over at Fat who was all in Donella's ear putting his mack down. He looked back at Bayonna and started to do the same.

Bayonna leaned in and whispered in his ear. "Uh, don't you think you should get rid of these trick bitches? I sure don't want them popping their nasty pussies in my face."

Greg waved the bouncer over.

"What's up G?" he asked, standing there with his chest about to burst out of the tight shirt he had on.

"You can get the rest of these bitches outta here, we good," boomed Greg.

The burly bouncer began grabbing strippers by the arm and escorting them to the door.

For the next two hours the foursome popped several bottles, danced, and laughed. As the empty bottles stacked up, Donella and Bay got them real comfortable.

"So what else y'all got planned?" Greg asked.

"We trying to chill with y'all," responded Bayonna. Looking into his eyes she mouthed, "I'm ready to fuck."

Greg shot up out of his seat with his tongue hanging out of his mouth. "You ready to roll out?"

"I'm ready to do more than that," she answered, straightening her clothes and placing a single kiss on his lips.

He looked over at Fat and Donella, she had his platinum and diamond chain twisted around her finger pulling him close and whispering in his ear.

"Let's roll nigga." Greg interrupted their moment with his urgency.

"Chill, Bleed," Fat responded, looking up barely able to see through the slits in his glassy eyes.

"Let's go," Donella said as she ran her hand between Fat's legs sealing the deal as she rose to her feet.

Greg and Fat followed the ladies out of the club. They happened to be parked only a short distance from Donella's car.

"Ya'll following us?" Donella asked as she popped the locks.

"Nah, let me ride with you. Bay can ride in my car with Greg," Fat responded.

Bayonna walked to the parking lot and jumped in Greg's Audi S5 Cabriolet. She leaned back in the cool leather seat and they followed Donella and Fat.

When they reached their destination in Shaker Heights the streets were quiet. Donella drove slowly toward the house, turning down her radio as they pulled into the driveway of the ranch style dwelling.

Greg pulled behind Donella and turned off his engine.

They all filed out of the vehicles and headed to the door. Bayonna turned her key in the lock, opened the door, and hit the lights.

Greg and Fat were filled with excitement from the mere thought that they had come up on some untouchable pussy. Every hustler who was getting money in the city wanted to bag those boss ho's.

"Have a seat. Let me roll up some loud and get us something to drink," Bayonna said as she walked to the kitchen.

Fat and Greg took a seat on the couch and Donella walked over to the window, closed the blinds, then turned some music on.

"We about to get fucked up," she said, walking over to the fireplace and lighting the candles to enhance the mood.

Greg and Fat looked at each other and smiled. Their crew wasn't gonna believe that they had smashed those two top-notch broads.

When Bayonna emerged from the kitchen she had a drink in one hand and a baby Luger in the other. Treebie was on her heels with a pump.

"What the fuck!" cried Fat.

"Relax," Bayonna said, taking a swig of her drink. "You wanted to get fucked, didn't you? Be patient and you will,"

"Y'all bitches for real? Y'all about to try us like dat?" Greg erupted. "Y'all must be muthafuckin' crazy!"

"No, y'all the muthafuckas that's crazy," Treebie corrected, pulling one in the barrel.

Sweat beads popped up on Fat's forehead. "Look, you can have whatever we got," he hurriedly offered, digging down in his pockets and tossing his bands on the table.

"Bitch nigga, do we look like we take small change?" Treebie groveled then blasted him in the knee.

Fat howled.

"Oh shit," Greg jumped, putting his hands in the air. Now he realized it was not a game. "You ain't gotta do this." He had lost all the bass in his voice.

Fat rocked back and forth in pain, holding his right knee and watching the blood ooze between his fingers. Breathing heavily and beginning to panic he did the only thing that came natural. He begged. "Please, Treebie. Please, I got kids."

"Good, then I'm saving them the embarrassment of being raised by two bitches," she growled then shot him in the other knee.

"Owww! Come on, please don't do this shit," he cried out. Tears ran down his chubby face as her attempted to stand up on legs that could no longer support his right.

Screaming out in pain he collapsed to the floor and began crawling in a desperate and painful attempt to reach the door. Treebie aimed the pump at him stopping him in his tracks.

Behind them, Greg tried to negotiate their freedom. "Look, whoever put y'all on us, we'll pay you double."

"You still think you going home? Awww," Donella knuckled her hand under her eye in a half circular motion. "Poor baby," she taunted.

"Please, we'll give y'all anything. just don't kill us," he begged.

"You ain't got shit we want but real estate, nigga," said Donella. Her face showed no compromise as she pulled on a pair of driving gloves then grabbed a piece of rope from under the back of the couch.

Greg shifted nervously on the couch. "Go ahead and make this bitch roar," warned Treebie, raising the pump to his chest. Greg looked down both barrels and shuddered. Behind him Donella tightened each end of the rope around her hands. In a nanosecond it was around his neck.

Greg fought to keep her from cutting off his breath. As he struggled to get his fingers underneath the rope his eyes bulged with plea. The restricted blood flow in his neck capsulized into his pulsating veins, threatening to explode. "Please, I'm begging you," he cried.

"Nigga, shut the fuck up," Treebie barked.

"Please!"

"Alright," said Donella, releasing her grip and stepping to the side. For just a second Greg thought he had gotten a reprieve. He looked over at his man who was lying on the floor going in and out of consciousness. The pump sounded off with a boom that echoed throughout the room. Greg felt an excruciating pain shoot through his shoulder. "Bitch you shot me." He grabbed his arm and winced.

"No shit," Treebie responded then shot him in the other arm.

"What the fuck is wrong with you?" he grimaced in pain as blood poured from his wounds. "It's enough for all of us to eat."

"Is that what you were thinking when you came at our young boys talking about fuck Kiam and them bitches?" Bayonna asked, sitting her drink down and walking over to her bag.

She grabbed a needle and a small bottle and shook it up. Sticking the needle into the bottle she drew the acid into the syringe until it was full. Donella wrapped the rope back around his neck. His arms were useless now and he couldn't fight, so he pled.

"Fuck them bitches, huh?" Treebie repeated his words to him again.

"It wasn't like that. Look, you can have whatever you want. We will give you any one of our corners. Y'all want Avon? LA— Lenacrave and Angelous? I'll give y'all all that." Greg grunted as his arms began to burn.

"*Give?* Muthafucka you ain't no position to give, this is a straight up jack move." Treebie said then chuckled as she moved a little closer.

Donella kept pulling on the rope causing him to gag and his eyes to water.

Next to him Bayonna bent down and smacked Fat in the face. "Wake up, nigga." Her voice was dispassionate and hard, nothing like the purrs she had whispered just a while ago.

Blinking back the pain, he opened his eyes slowly as tears ran from the corners. He could hear his boy being prepped for death a few feet away.

"See, Greg, you probably made some good choices in life, but you made three very costly ones. Rule number one, never go anywhere without your strap. Rule number two. . . *Trust No Bitch?*" said Treebie.

Greg looked at her like no one had ever taught him that.

Treebie shook her head, those lames weren't about that life. *How the fuck did they blow up?* she wondered.

"Besides going somewhere without your *whistles* and trusting the wrong bitches, y'all made the biggest mistake of all, and that was fucking with Blood Money," Treebie said through gritted teeth.

Greg's eyes got wide when he heard her utter the words that haunted the streets. His mind started running the countless stories he heard about the niggas who were jacking muthafuckas and killing wholesale, leaving behind their signature of blood money. Now, at the door of death, to find out that they were really women fucked his head up.

"Surprised?" she asked, holding her barrel firm in his face. "See, now that you know our little secret, you gotta die. But don't worry, playboy, you're about to become part of our urban legend," she snickered, then nodded at Bay and Donella.

Donella pulled harder on the rope around Greg's neck, tightening both ends. Greg clawed, trying to get his fingers up under the rope to release the pressure but the gunshot wounds to his shoulders made him weak. He kicked and struggled but it was all in vain—his life was almost over.

Bayonna took the needle and stuck it in the side of Fat's neck releasing the toxic fluid. His body began to jerk and convulse.

Donella turned Greg's head toward Fat so he would spend his last minutes watching his boy suffer.

"Fuck those bitches?" she gritted. "That's what y'all said? Maybe in the next life, but never in this one!" She pulled harder.

Greg tightened his eyes when he saw Fat's face swell up from the acid that coursed through his veins.

Fat began to gurgle and spit up blood as gapping wounds formed around his eyes and mouth.

Bayonna grabbed a five dollar bill from her pocket and rubbed it in Fat's mouth then began to force it into Greg's. He squirmed and tried to clamp his mouth tight in a last show of bravery.

Bayonna grabbed her gun and smacked him in the mouth causing it to open wide enough for her to stuff the bloody bill.

Greg choked and gagged as it settled to the back of his throat. Donella pulled harder and harder as the excitement of the kill turned her on.

Greg's legs began to lash out violently as he fought for his life. Bayonna came up behind Donella and pulled tightly on the rope with her. The force of both of their grips pulled at Greg's neck causing it to snap.

Treebie stood over the two men and smiled at their condition. "Punk ass niggas, hope it was good for you," she spat.

Bayonna and Donella released the rope and stepped back to look over their work.

"Damn that felt good," Bay said, breathing quickly.

"Hell, yeah. I think I came," Donella said and they all bursted out in laugher.

"Bitch, you need to see somebody about that shit," said Treebie.

"Let's get these niggas wrapped up. Bay bring their car around back," Donella directed.

"Alright roll some shit up, I need some motivation," Bay said, grabbing the car keys from the coffee table.

Treebie rolled up, while Donella opened the bags and spread them out. When Bay came back inside they smoked two blunts, took a couple shots of Patron, then went to work.

When the bodies were secure in the bags, Treebie reached down and removed Fat and Greg's worshipped chains from around their necks. She dropped the icy pieces in a small black velvet pouch and pulled it closed.

Together the girls drug the bodies outside and hoisted them up in the trunk of Greg's car.

"Dang, I didn't know dead muthafuckas were so goddamn heavy," said Bay, exhausted. It was her first time dragging a body, usually she just turned someone's lights out and breezed in the wind.

"You have to eat your Wheaties," quipped Treebie, wiping sweat from her forehead with the sleeve of her shirt. They all laughed, then went back inside to clean up.

Pulling their hair back they got strapped up in their blood money uniforms. They drove the car down to 123rd and Lenacrave where they knew it would be found and left it parked at the curb.

The next afternoon Treebie put a call into Kiam to meet her at the Red Lobster on Warrensville Road. When she pulled up he was sitting in his car leaned back listening to Meek Mill *Dreams and Nightmares.*

Kiam watched as she walked over to his vehicle; he had to admit Lissha's crew was sexy as hell, each with a different attribute of beauty.

Treebie leaned in his window. She didn't smile or say hello. She simply said, "Don't ever question our get-down."

She tossed proof in his lap that they were official, then walked off.

Kiam picked up the bag and looked inside. He pulled out the shine that Fat and Greg wore religiously and saw sparkles of blood on both chains. A large splotch of dried blood was caked up between the letters on one of the MBK pieces.

A smile hit the corner of his mouth, he had already heard how they were found and now he beamed with pride to know it was someone from his camp that did it.

As Treebie pulled off she looked at him and winked. Kiam nodded his head as her tires screeched on the way out the lot. It was official, Kiam was more than comfortable with sending the girls for the pickup.

"A bitch that loves to kill," he said aloud as he pulled off. "Every nigga needs one."

Chapter 20
Debriefing

Lissha pulled into the parking lot of the prison and tried to steady her mind to sit through eight hours of visitation. She looked over the grounds and saw the same heart-wrenching sight, concrete and barbed wire. Even though the sun was shining bright there was a cloud of hopelessness and despair that seemed to hover over the penitentiary.

Lissha inhaled and began to transfer her driver's license and money from her purse to a small clear clutch. She combed her hair then flipped the visor up and got out the car.

As she walked toward the gates a few regulars waved and struck a conversation. She was almost to the doors when she heard, "Hey, Lissha."

She looked back to see the wife of one of Big Zo's old cell mates. Though the woman was only a few feet behind her she yelled out like she was a block away.

I can't stand her loud ass.

"Hey, sweetie," Lissha half-heatedly spoke.

"I haven't seen you in a while," the woman continued then tried to hug her.

Lissha rolled her eyes as she patted the woman on the back. "I know, I been running girl. You know how it is," Lissha said, pulling back.

"Yeah, girl, we been coming here for a long time," she blabbered as Lissha tried to walk away.

Lissha moved to the doors hoping that she would get the hint, but she didn't. She followed Lissha inside the jail, talking her to death.

When they entered the drab visitation room, Lissha got depressed. Going through this process year after year could break the strongest person. But unlike others she would not give up on her loved one.

Lissha waited until her talkative stalker found a seat, then she bolted to the vending machines and purchased all the items that Big Zo usually wanted. She bought him hot wings, burgers, a salad, chips, soda, and two fish sandwiches. He never ate everything that she bought, but it didn't matter, she just wanted to have it there for him.

After she was settled in her seat, she looked at her watch and counted the minutes. Time ticked at the pace of drying paint. After a forty minute wait, Big Zo emerged from the back fixing his shirt and looking over the room for Lissha. When his eyes settled on her, he smiled. She was seated with her head resting on her hand with her eyes closed.

Big Zo walked toward her nodding and waving at a few guys and their families along the way. He walked up and stood right in front of Lissha then tapped her leg. Lissha slowly opened her eyes and a smile spread over her face.

"Hey, baby girl." Big Zo smiled back at her.

"Hey, Daddy," Lissha responded and got up to give him a hug.

Big Zo held her tighly in his grip, it had been over a month since he saw her and her presence was comforting to his soul. His baby girl was indeed a rider. Time would never make her stop visiting.

When Lissha pulled back, Big Zo rubbed her face and gave her another smile "So how have you been?" he asked, sitting down and folding his hands in his lap.

Lissha sat down, too. "I'm just trying to maintain, Daddy," she casually replied, opening a soda.

"How are the girls?"

Lissha shook her head. "Well, Donella and Bayonna are never a problem. Treebie, that bitch be on some other rebel type shit." Big Zo looked at her with the side-eye, he always had to remind her about her mouth. "My bad for the language," she quickly apologized. "Like I was saying, Treebie is way too extra sometimes. She continues to test me."

Big Zo squinted his eyes. "Does she handle business?"

"Always. But…"

"But what?"

"Nothing." Her words recoiled back into her throat.

"Speak your mind, baby girl."

With little convincing she continued. "Treebie just needs to calm her ass down. We got into it a few times over Kiam. On the real, she doesn't trust him. That's it in a nutshell."

"Look, the bitches are your business. If she's outta line, that shit is your fault." Big Zo got serious. "I don't have time for rebellion in my camp. I sent you someone who will handle business and put me in a better position. Don't let anyone stand in the way of that. Family. Friend. Or foe." He gave Lissha look that made her want to crawl under her chair. She never wanted to disappoint him.

She looked down rubbing the side of the soda bottle and wondering if she was built for this mission after all.

"Look at me," he said calmly.

Lissha lifted her eyes.

"Everything that I have—everything that I'm willing to sacrifice is for us. You gotta stick to the plan, if we got one weak link, then the whole fucking chain will break. You understand?"

"Yes," Lissha said a little above a whisper.

"Okay. Now tell me about Kiam."

Lissha took a deep breath. "He reorganized everyone. He put all the strength in the right places, and he had us fall back with the exception of pickup."

"So, Gator doesn't handle that part anymore either?"

"That's the way Kiam wants it. Should I tell him to put Gator back in charge of the pickups?"

"No, I was just asking," he said.

"Okay. Kiam also negotiated to have our squad meet Riz's team half way instead of us having to go all the way to New York to pick it up."

"I don't want you trafficking the shit period. I don't care if it's just from one end of the street to the other, because if you get cased up everything falls apart."

"I know. Treebie and 'em are picking it up. The first pick up is this week." She paused and separated her thoughts, so she would say the right thing. "I know you put Kiam in charge and he is handling business, but he is very arrogant. I always worry that he will say the wrong thing to the right person then we're back to step one."

Big Zo rubbed the bottom of his chin as he processed his thoughts. He could see that her judgment was coming from more than business, there was also some emotion attached. "You got feelings for Kiam, don't you?"

"No," she quickly denied.

Big Zo steepled his fingers under his chin and chose his words effectively. "Look, I know Kiam is very charismatic and has a powerful aura, but I need you to stay focused. I can't afford for you to mix the relationship."

"I haven't," she protested.

"I hope not. Remember, this is serious. It's the only shot I have to ever get out of here so don't fuck it up by thinking with your butt."

"I won't, Daddy. You taught me better than that," she reassured him.

"Good. Under no circumstances are you to allow that man into your bed." Big Zo formed a small frown on his face. "We clear?"

"Yes Sir," she pouted. They sat in silence thinking about what he forbade her to do.

Lissha brightened up first. "Are you ready to eat?" she asked, smiling to let him know that his baby girl was always on his side.

Big Zo nodded yes and she went to the microwave to heat up his food.

While Lissha was away Big Zo was in deep thought. So many had failed him, would she be next? He couldn't see that ever happening; not his baby girl.

Lissha returned with his food piping hot. She sat it down on the table and handed him some napkins, then unscrewed the top off his fruit drink. "Thanks, baby," he said, picking up the burger and chomping off a big bite.

Lissha sat back down and waited for him to look up. Big Zo's eyes wandered around the visitation room as he ate. Lissha leaned over and wiped the corners of his mouth with a napkin. "Daddy," she said. "I spoke with the lawyer that I told you about months ago. He says he sees some things in your trial transcript that he may be able to use to get your conviction overturned."

"Yeah? What he want, fifteen million?" he asked sarcastically.

"No. He'll do the appeal for one hundred and fifty thousand. That's nothing."

"We might as well flush that hundred fifty down the toilet. I don't believe shit any attorney says."

"He's supposed to be one of the best. He worked on BMF case down in Atlanta years ago."

"Is that supposed to make me feel good? Did he get Big Meech off?" The question was rhetorical because they both knew the answer was no.

Lissha fought to keep the look of fatigue out of her eyes, she wanted very badly for something positive to happen in his appeal process, otherwise he would die in prison. She would do anything to prevent that from happening.

Big Zo knew her better than she knew herself sometimes, so he understood the look in her eyes. He reached across the table and pinched her cheek like she was a little girl. "Lissha, has Daddy ever led you wrong?" he asked directly.

"Never," she confirmed without hesitation.

"And I never will," he promised. "Forget about attorneys, those muthafuckas are nothing but leeches." Lissha nodded, she would not bring the topic up again. "Now what's up with Blood Money?" he quickly changed the subject.

She moved a little closer and began telling him what they had on the table. Big Zo listened attentively, downloading each piece of information and plotting on how he could use it to enhance the plans he already had in motion. His astute mind put each piece into place. The time flew by and the next thing they knew it was time for her to go.

Big Zo took one last sip of his soda then rose to his feet. Lissha stood up and gave him a big hug. "I'll be back in a few weeks," she said with sadness in her voice.

"Don't worry, baby girl, when this is all over we'll be set. Just do like I tell you and it will all work out."

"Yes sir."

"Tell Kiam I said I'm proud of him. Remind him that he is to do everything in his power to keep you safe. Nothing else comes before that."

"I will. Love you, Daddy."

"Love you, too." Big Zo turned her a loose and watched as she joined the long line of visitors waiting their turn to exit the facility. At the door she turned back around and waved.

"Talk to you soon," he mouthed.

"Okay." She motioned with her thumb and index finger.

Big Zo turned to look at Lissha one last time before she left, he noticed that the sadness had washed over her face. He knew it wasn't just because she missed him. He strongly suspected that she was torn between his orders and feelings that she had developed for Kiam. He had to make sure that if he didn't get through to

Lissha, he'd surely get through to Kiam. Under no circumstances could they cross that line, and he would defend that order with his life.

Lissha filed out the prison door and moved swiftly to her car, choking back tears. The thought that Big Zo might never get out of prison, and the weight of his demand, was overwhelming. As soon as she shut the door and started her engine tears began to roll down her face. She had begun to want the very thing that he would not permit her to have.

As she headed to the airport, she knew that she had to make a decision. Everything depended on that.

Chapter 21
Putting It Down

While Lissha was away visiting Big Zo, the shipment arrived without incident or delay. Kiam had Gator disperse it to those he had put in position to handle it from there, then he sat back and counted the evidence of other niggas' broke pockets. They had the whole Eastside turned up with their product which Kiam had renamed *Schizophrenic*. He learned years ago that one must do what others won't, in order to have what others don't.

Most dealers were selling whip to increase their profits, but Kiam's team had that real fish scale still in the casket, meaning the kilos were unopened and uncut. Low prices and fat weight had fiends twerking to the rock houses. Niggas were checking their calendars because it felt like it was '87 all over again when crack first hit the scene.

True to his word, Kiam had strong-armed half of DeMarcus's Miles Road territory. From 93rd all the way up to 131st every nickel sack, gram, ounce or brick sold was that Schizo'. And their other territories were pumping just as hard.

Besides the dope money, Kiam had stiff armed his way into ownership of a few profitable gambling houses on the Eastside. The city was bowing to his power. *All hail to the king.*

Since Kiam didn't trust Gator to walk and chew gum at the same damn time, he only allowed him to make small drops and oversee part of the daily operations. Gator could barely handle that because pussy had his mind on the type of shit that brought entire empires down.

Kiam felt there was something funny about a man who always wanted to be pretty. *That muthafucka might as well put on some lashes and pumps,* he thought. With that in mind he chose the young boy JuJu to handle the brick sales and to oversee a gambling house on 117th and St. Clair that he had took from an old head.

There was something Kiam saw in little man that reminded him of himself. JuJu was about his paper and he took no shorts.

The three of them were riding in Gator's white Expedition. They pulled into DeMarcus's car lot and Kiam got out as soon as the truck came to a stop. "Come on youngin', let's go upgrade your status, you ain't gonna get no good pussy with that bus pass," he said, closing the front passenger door.

"I'm cautious but I damn sure ain't slow, I need some pussy that will make a little nigga feel tall than a muhfucka," he shot back, sliding on his Aviators.

Kiam chuckled as he headed for the front door.

JuJu climbed out the back rocking a pair of crisp black jeans, a grey T, and brand new J's. He stood only 5'6" but size didn't mean shit, he packed two fo-fo's resting against his waist, and they damn sure weren't there to hold his belt up.

Youngin' wasn't afraid to act a fool. When the opposition didn't bend, he folded 'em, and today Kiam was rewarding him for his loyalty and obedience. He had Faydrah looking for a condo for little man, if JuJu stayed down his blessings would be plentiful.

"Y'all good, right?" asked Gator, looking down at his cell phone at a text that had just come through.

"Yeah, we straight, you can bounce. Don't forget to go over on Star and make sure that *that* money is right. When you scoop it up take it to Lissha," said Kiam as he swung the door open and stepped inside.

Gator nodded while struggling not to show that he didn't like taking orders from Kiam. He sat with his poker face until both men were inside. When he drove off the frown that he had held back forced its way on his face.

He quickly glanced at his phone and read the text message. It was *her* asking him to call. They hadn't really talked since they'd seen each other at the club. He knew she would be a little salty but he didn't care, baby girl was Team Gator all day. Pulling up to a stop light he hit her back right away. "Yeah, what's up?"

"What you doing?" she asked accusingly.

"Damn, why you make it sound like you think I'm up in some pussy?" Gator laughed

"Ain't no telling with you, if a bitch blink too long yo' ass be right up the next bitch's ass," she flat out charged.

"Go 'head with all that bullshit, I'm on my way over to the trap then I'm coming your way. What's up?"

"What the fuck do you think is up? A bitch needs something stiff and cooperative."

"Well, you know what I'ma need?"

"What you gonna need?" She folded her arms and waited for his answer.

"I'ma need to hold on to the back of your head while you give me a knee bending experience."

"How come every time I ask you for some dick you wanna put it in a bitch mouth?" she asked with her lips twisted to the side.

"You know this nigga don't act right unless he gets to have a conversation with some tonsils," he stated with a slight smile on his face. His dick jumped as the last word left his lips.

"Well, you keep a bitch eyes rolling so you know I'ma do whatever you want me to," she promised.

Gator's foot got heavy on the gas with that thought. "I know you got me. But on the real, you know what I really want you to do."

"Don't even go there." She stopped him before he could get started. Ever since they had switched up the pickup, he had been pressing her to let him know when and where it went down.

"What, that bitch got you shook?" Gator asked as he eased his window down, honked his horn, and blew a kiss at a lady that was driving beside him.

The lady smiled at him, but then a big headed dude that had been reclined back in the passenger seat sat up and grilled him. Gator reached in his waist and flashed his steel. "This ain't what you want," he yelled out the window and the guy swallowed whatever slick words he had started to say.

"Who are you talking to?" she angrily asked.

"Nobody, just some clown that almost got his face splattered. Anyway, what's up? You gonna do that or what?"

"You gotta give me time, Gator. Damn. We've only done one pickup. Let me peep everything out and get Riz's people more comfortable with bringing the shit halfway so they'll relax a little."

"Fuck dat. They don't have to relax. I got something that will relax 'em for eternity," he said, patting the banger that he had put back on his waist.

She smiled, envisioning him doing something demonstrative with his hands. "I know you will, boo." She chuckled. "But, baby, they had a small army riding with them to protect their product. They had everybody but Jesus and his Disciples."

"Okay, but I'm gonna stay on you. It's time for me to make some moves of my own. The way I'm feeling, fuck Lissha, Big Zo, and Kiam."

She didn't respond. Gator was on a suicide mission, allowing his hatred of Kiam to get the best of him.

"I'ma call you when I'm through handling business and I'm on my way," he said.

"Okay, I'm waiting. Hurry up, you know a bitch will start without you," she purred.

"Get it wet for me baby, I'll be right there." He disconnected the call.

"Pick out any whip you like, I'll be right back," Kiam instructed his young boy.

While JuJu browsed the cars Kiam walked inside. This was not the first time since smashing Czar that he had seen DeMarcus, but it was the first time that he had been back to the lot.

Daphne perked right up when she saw Kiam coming. She had family that lived on Miles Road and they had all told her how he was putting it down.

"Hi, Kiam." she spoke, coming up to him with a wide smile on her face and a look in her eyes that said more than any words could ever convey.

Kiam looked at her with a sneer and nodded almost imperceptibly. *Bitch don't know me.*

Daphne had on a cream-colored Michael Kors pants suit. Huge diamonds sparkled on her fingers and two carats dripped from her ears. A diamond heart-shaped pendant hung around her neck on an invisible chain.

It don't matter how you dress them up, Kiam wanted to tell DeMarcus, *a ho was still a ho.*

Kiam didn't give her a second thought as he proceeded back to DeMarcus's office.

Daphne rushed up behind. "Um, I'm sorry but DeMarcus is in a meeting with his banker," she said hurriedly as he reached for the door knob.

Kiam stopped, pulled his hand back, and turned to look at her. "When he's through let him know that I'm outside," he said in a gruff voice.

"You can wait for him in my office if you'd like," she quickly offered. "It has air conditioning. I know you don't want to wait out in the hot sun."

Kiam caught her flirtatious tone. *I'd rather burn the fuck up than sit in her little air conditioned office.*

"Be happy with what you got before you run into something you can't handle," he warned, then turned and walked outside.

Daphne stared at Kiam's back. *Whew! That muthafucka turned me the fuck on.* She liked her men the same way she liked a dick—hard.

As Kiam walked out the door onto the lot Daphne promised herself that she was going to get that, one way or another.

JuJu was with a salesman looking over a brand new white 2012 Land Rover Evogue. It was sitting on 22 inch rims whispering his name. The sticker price on the front window read $55,000. Kiam had told him to pick out whatever he liked but he didn't want to seem greedy.

"What's up, Ju? You like this or what?" asked Kiam, coming up behind them.

"Yeah, this bitch is real nice but I'm not trying to make you spend a grip. Really, I'm good with my Tahoe until I can cop this myself," said JuJu.

"Never mind all of that, you want this right here, it's yours." He opened the driver's door and checked out the interior of the SUV.

"You want to test drive it?" the sales guy asked Kiam, sensing that he carried the wallet.

Kiam looked at JuJu, who nodded yeah. He could already picture himself profiling through the hoods in that sexy muthafucka. He knew that girls were gonna be trying to fuck the grille, but he wasn't going to allow pussy to cause him to lose focus like Gator had.

While JuJu and the salesman took the Land Rover for a cruise, Kiam walked over to a black murdered out 2012 Cadillac Escalade that he had noticed. The sun bounced off the pearl paint, glistening up into his face. He used a hand to shield his eyes from the glare as he walked around the vehicle, checking it out.

Satisfied that the truck was built to represent a man like himself, Kiam patted the hood. "This me right here," he said, not concerned with the sticker price.

DeMarcus emerge from inside. He was wearing a blue suit and canary yellow tie, walking alongside of an older man. They shook hands and the man walked to his car. When DeMarcus noticed Kiam standing there a look of apprehension shadowed his face.

DeMarcus retreated to his office with Kiam right behind him. The first thing Kiam noticed was that DeMarcus had replaced the blood soaked carpet.

The door banged when Kiam closed it causing DeMarcus to slightly jump.

"What's up, *bruh?*" Kiam said. "I must make you nervous?"

DeMarcus didn't respond.

Kiam walked around the desk and took a seat behind it, leaning back in the chair and propped his feet up on the desk.

"Really, is all of that necessary?" asked DeMarcus.

"Is breathing necessary?"

DeMarcus took in a mouth full of air in an attempt to remain as calm as possible.

"This is how this shit is going down. I'ma talk, you're gonna listen," Kiam made it known. "First, you have a white Land Rover Evoque and a black Escalade out on the lot. I want both of them, draw the paperwork up."

"How you paying for them?" asked DeMarcus suspiciously.

"I'm not. Those two are on the house."

"Man, that's over a hundred grand!" protested DeMarcus as he slouched down on a couch.

Kiam stared at him with a coldness that sent a chill up his body. "Nigga, shut the fuck up and get to working on the titles."

"Man, you're killing me," complained DeMarcus.

"Be careful what you ask for. Fuck around and speak your own death into existence." Kiam smiled sinisterly.

DeMarcus sighed with resignation as he got off the couch and walked behind the desk and stood waiting for Kiam to relinquish his chair.

Kiam saw the defeat in DeMarcus' eyes. He didn't pity him, he felt the muthafucka owed him more than that. He rose from the chair and propped himself up on the edge of the desk while DeMarcus got on the computer.

"What else besides the trucks?" he asked in a clipped tone.

"Nothing else from the lot, but like I told you the other day, I'm your connect now. I expect you to start buying your work from my young boy JuJu. You'll meet him in a minute." Kiam looked down at him. His press game left DeMarcus little room to breathe.

DeMarcus looked up from the computer. "Man, I already gave you half of my corners and I didn't even trip it. You felt I owed you that and I respected how you felt."

Kiam shot up off the desk and leaned down into DeMarcus' face. "Nigga, you didn't respect nothin'. You feared this shit, that's what made you surrender those corners. And you were wise to do so because I'm not fucking around."

Kiam grabbed ahold of DeMarcus's collar and held it with a firm hand. "You're buying ten whole ones a week at nineteen-five apiece. If that steps on your connect's toes, *fuck him*, tell him to come see me. My blood pump boss not bitch." He released DeMarcus' collar then moved back to his seated position.

DeMarcus shook his head but said nothing. This was going to be a huge loss he'd have to eat, but he saw no other way to continue living. The vision of how Kiam had done Czar was still fresh in his mind. He knew Kiam's tool didn't discriminate. The question was, what was his connect going to say when he told him that he had found another supplier?

Chapter 22
Playing Both Sides

Daphne pulled her ear away from the door just in time. She heard the door open, then the sound of footsteps behind her as she made her escape. She hurried back to her office and used her cell phone to place a call

"Yeah? What you want? I'm busy," he said in a deep bear-like voice that always seemed to make her nervous.

"Um, I need to see you," she whispered, fidgeting with the ring on her thumb.

"For what?"

"It's about DeMarcus, and it's very important," she said, peeking out her office door to make sure he wasn't walking up on her.

"Okay, meet me at the house on Lakeview. Be there in a half hour, I don't have time to waste so be on time. I got a lot of shit going on today." He hung up.

Daphne took the phone from her ear and stared at the blank screen. "Damn, can a bitch get a goodbye?" she said under her breath. "Heartless ass black bastard."

She couldn't wait for the day she reshuffled the cards and dealt herself the better hand. Then, that muthafucka was gonna pay for all the shit that he had ever done to her.

She went to DeMarcus' office and told him that she had a doctor's appointment. He was seated behind his desk looking like somebody had just violated his asshole and he was trying to decide whether or not he was still a man. *We might as well switch genitals*, she said to herself, leaning down to kiss him goodbye.

Forty-five minutes later, she was getting carpet burns. Wolfman grabbed the back of her head and made her gag. He looked over at his man, who was sitting in a chair on the other side of the living smoking a blunt and playing a video game.

"Nitti, you see how this bitch swallows the whole dick? Nigga, you ain't never had a ho with head like hers," he bragged.

"The bitch tight with her shit, huh?" replied Frank Nitti, never taking his eyes off the Xbox. He didn't wanna look at no other man's wood.

"Fuck yeah. Nigga, I done had my dick sucked in all fifty states. Nah, make that fifty-two, cause an Eskimo bitch sucked it in Alaska and a Hawaiian ho brained me in Maui. I'm telling you, ain't nan sucked it better than this bitch right here."

Frank Nitti laughed.

"You want her to bless you after she gets done with me?" offered Wolfman, closing his eyes as Daphne began working her throat muscles on his long, thick pole.

"Nah, I'm good," Nitti declined.

Wolfman's ass rose up off the couch, Daphne was doing her thing. "Yeah, make me bust all down your muthafuckin' throat," he growled.

"Come on, then. Gimme that nut," she said, as she sucked and stroked him simultaneously.

Wolfman forced himself deeper down her throat and howled as he erupted inside of her mouth. He pulled out before he emptied his nut and shot the rest on her face. "Bitch, you the best," he said, slapping his dick against her forehead.

"Umm," she smiled, licking her lips.

While Wolfman fixed his clothes she went upstairs to the bathroom and brushed her teeth and gargled. Inside the bathroom Daphne looked in the mirror and fought back the tears. He always made her feel like a two dollar ho and she hated him for that. At one time she had loved him with all her heart, and he had seemed to love her just as much until she made the biggest mistake of her life. After that she was nothing to him.

Daphne didn't want to think about that right now. She blinked back her tears, took a deep breath, and thought with a coldheartedness that matched his. *Get your game plan together first,* she reminded herself. *Let him laugh now and make him cry later.*

When she returned a few minutes later Wolfman was seated on the couch stroking his thick and unkempt full beard. Now he was all business.

"What's up with your boy?" he got straight to the point.

He listened as she recounted everything that she had heard. When she was done, he looked at Frank Nitti and asked, "You ever heard of this nigga Kiam?"

Nitti smiled. "Yeah, I know him well. We almost bumped heads years ago before he went to the feds. He used to be a ski mask kid back then, and he was ferocious with that hammer."

"You sound like you ready to bend over and let him fuck you," snorted Wolfman.

Frank Nitti wasn't soft. Even though Wolfman fed him, he didn't hesitate to shoot him a cold stare. "I'm just saying, nigga," replied Wolfman softening his tone.

Nitti let it ride. He thought for a moment before adding, "I been hearing Kiam's name a lot lately, but I thought it was a different nigga because I had never known him to fuck with the work like that. Plus I thought he was still on lock."

"Well, now you know he's not. And he's out here fucking with my mula." Wolfman cracked his knuckles.

"They say he fucks with that bitch Lissha and 'em. They're dropping work called Schizophrenic all over the city. I think that's why our profits have slowed down."

"What happened to Gator? I thought he ran that crew?" asked Wolfman.

"I don't know. I guess they're under new management. Kiam has that whole clique turned the fuck up. Damn, I should have known it was him. We might have to shut them down before they get too big. You want me to send some goons at him?"

Wolfman didn't answer right away. When he did, he said, "Nah, let's see what's really up with him first."

Frank Nitti set the game control down and looked at his boss man. "I already know what's up with him, that nigga a killah. He probably soaked up game in the pen and now his hustle match his gangsta. Let's hit him before he gets too big."

Wolfman shook his head no, he was thinking of a way to bring Kiam into the fold and make his team stronger. He looked at Daphne. "You met the nigga, can you put the pussy on him and reel him in?"

"I doubt it. The nigga is a boss," she replied. "But I can try."

"I don't need you to *try*, I need you to make it happen." Wolfman pulled out a wrinkled hundred dollar bill and tossed it at Daphne's feet. "Step your game up. I want Kiam."

Letting the money remain where it lay, Daphne stepped toward the door with a purpose, but it wasn't exactly the one Wolfman had set for her.

As soon as she was out the door, Wolfman said to Nitti, "We're gonna have to cancel that bitch after this, I can see the double-cross in her eyes."

Chapter 23
Let Me Go

Lissha was emotionally worn out after her visit with Big Zo. She had gone home and locked herself up in the house for days as a result. As she moved from one room to the next she tried to talk herself into a good mood. She stood in her kitchen door staring at the sink full of dishes and felt defeated.

"This don't make no fucking sense. Bitch, you live alone and got dishes pilling up," she chastised herself as she walked over to the sink, put on her pink rubber gloves, and turned on the hot water.

Once she got started, it was on. She cleaned her kitchen, pulled open her curtains and blinds and went to work sweeping, mopping, dusting and changing her linen. The bathroom was her last task, she cleaned it from front to back and put up a fresh shower curtain then she hopped into the shower.

When she emerged from the bathroom, she oiled up, threw on some sweat pants and a t-shirt and checked her messages. There were several calls from Kiam which she wasn't planning on returning. She knew if anything went wrong he knew what to do and, if not, he would surely bring his inconveniencing ass right to her door. She had come to the conclusion that she was going to back way up off him.

She flipped through her contacts and hit Bay. "Hey momma what's good?" Lissha said into the phone.

"Ain't shit. I'm getting my nails done. What's up with you?"

"Nothing really. I need to get out of this house. Where's Donella and Treebie?"

"Donella is on her way to pick me up. I don't know where Treebie ass at. But we about to go out for lunch."

"A'ight, come scoop me up on the way."

"Okay. See you in a minute. And bitch be ready."

"Whatever. Bye."

Lissha disconnected the call and hit Treebie's phone twice, back to back, but got no answer. "Where this bitch at?" she said aloud, placing her phone on the dresser. Treebie never missed calls so that shit had Lissha wondering.

She pondered for a minute then headed to her closet to change clothes.

Treebie sat on the plane playing back in her head the conversation that she had with Wa'leek.

"You need to come see me." He was straight to the point.

"I got too much going on right now."

"We ain't having a conversation about this shit. Get on the flight, see you when you get here," Wa'leek said into the phone then hung up.

It had been two months since she'd seen him and she knew if she didn't make the trip that nigga would find her and act a fucking fool. When she landed at Newark International airport her stomach began to ache.

She walked briskly through the airport to baggage claim, grabbed her small Gucci duffle then headed for the exit. As soon as she stepped out the door she saw him standing there looking fine as hell, clean from head to toe. He was mobbing in jeans, a pair of icy white sneakers, bright white V-neck t-shirt, and he was clean cut with a mean look on his high yellow face.

"That's all you got?" he asked, reaching in and taking her bag.

"No, I got some more shit, they gonna bring it to the car," said Treebie sarcastically as she headed for the passenger side of the car.

"Watch your mouth, before you get fucked up." Wa'leek smacked her ass on the way past.

"That shit feel good don't it?" She said as she ducked her head and slid inside the car.

Wa'leek shot her a quick smile, popped the trunk and tossed the bag in the back.

When he got in the driver's seat, Treebie's eyes roamed all over his body, he had added several more designs and color to his sleeve tattoo. He rested his hands on the steering wheel and shot her that hard stare.

"Why you eyeing me like that?" he asked, looking at her through his low gray eyes.

"Ain't nobody looking at you," she said, rolling her eyes.

"Stop shooting a nigga all that heat and let me taste them lips."

Treebie took a deep breath then turned and leaned toward him. She pulled him to her by the back of the head and kissed him deep.

His soft, juicy lips pulled her in. She turned her head allowing him to slip his tongue damn near down her throat. Their lips remained locked until a car horn blared behind them.

"Damn," Wa'leek said, ignoring the car behind them, as he stared at her breast sitting up in her shirt. "You done fucked around and made my soldier salute. You know what that mean?"

"No, I do not," she responded, sitting back in her seat.

"Don't worry, you will," he said as he pulled off.

When they got to his West Orange home Treebie was pleasantly surprised. He had redecorated with a very tasteful array of reds, blacks and whites. The brown throw rug that she hated had been replaced with a thick, black wall to wall carpet that felt like fur. She eyed the 84' Plasma mounted to the wall and the high-tech stereo equipment in a glass case in the corner.

"Why you acting like you never been here before," he asked, coming up behind her.

"I'm just admiring your decorating skills. This must be an upgrade for your little ho's you bring home," she stated accusingly.

"Let me explain something to you. You're my wife but you ain't here. I ain't no fucking homo so you know I get pussy. But them bitches know they fuck me, they suck me, but after that, I call they ass a green or yellow. Because they gotta get the fuck up outta here." He rested his hands on her waist and pressed his lips to her ear.

Treebie turned her head.

"Your legs are the only ones I slide in between with my heart involved. And any bitch I fuck with know that." He put his arms around her.

Treebie leaned back into his embrace and wrapped her mind around what he had just said. At the very least she had to respect his honesty and she knew that no secondhand bitch could take her place.

Wa'leek bent his head down and nibbled on her neck."Now go hit that shower and get sexy so we can hit the streets. I'll be right back, I gotta take care of something real quick," he said, removing his arms from around her waist.

She quickly spun in his direction. "I did not come all the way out here to sit around the house while you run the streets." She frowned.

"You better save all that tough shit for them bitch ass niggas in Ohio. Do what I told you." He kissed her lips and walked off.

Treebie was staring at his back when he turned around. "I want you to wear that dress I laid out. And hurry up, I'll be right back." He opened the door and walked out slightly slamming it behind him.

"That nigga get on my nerves," she said with a sigh as she walked to the bedroom.

When she opened the door what she saw confirmed his claims. A large picture of her hung on the wall over the head of his bed. Several small framed pictures of them on vacation in the Caribbeans sat on his dresser and nightstand.

"A bitch know her pussy good when a nigga got a shrine," she joked aloud as she pulled her shirt over her head, walked into the bathroom and hopped in the shower.

Two hours later Wa'leek returned with several bags in his hands. Treebie was sitting on the couch in her bra and panties, flipping through channels.

"Why you ain't dressed?" His eyebrows drew inward.

"Because I knew your ass would take forever, I didn't want to wrinkle my shit up.,"

"Yeah a'ight," he said, walking past the couch and down the hall into the bedroom.

Treebie turned off the television and followed him. When she walked in the room he was dumping clothes out of one bag and money out of the other. She watched him stack and organize the neatly wrapped bills and head to his closet.

Out the corner of her eye,

she saw him put the money in a stash door in the wall.
"You ain't gotta peek, what's mine is yours, all you have to do
is ask. Never give me a reason not to trust you," he said over his
shoulder.

"What?" She felt like she had been caught with her hand in the
collection plate.

He turned back around to face her. "I don't repeat shit when I
know people heard it." He hit the light and shut the closet door.

Treebie sat on the bed with her hands folded and her mouth
turned down. "Get dressed," he ordered, pulling his shirt over his
head moving toward the bathroom. "When I come out the shower I
wanna bounce."

As soon as Treebie heard the shower come on she got up,
scented her skin then slipped into her clothes. Wa'leek had chosen
for her a tight red, off the shoulder, knee length body dress and
Red Bottom stilettos. Wa'leek came out the bathroom butt ass
naked. Treebie's mouth watered when her eyes settled on all that
dick. She watched every muscle in his body flex as he moved
around the room.

"Dick look good don't it?" he asked then took it in his hand
stroking it slow, bringing it to attention. "Why don't you talk to
him real quick?"

Treebie sashayed over to him and took position. "Don't mess
up my dress." She looked up at him as she took him in her hand.

"Make sure you swallow like a good girl and you won't have
no problems," he instructed while watching his dick disappear into
her mouth. Looking down at her, he tried to control his breathing
as she spat all over his rod and slurped it right back up then took
him to the back of her throat and gave him an oral massage.

"Ssss . . ." he hissed. "Work that shit," he moaned. After a few
more jaw breaking movements he released long and hard to the
back of her throat. Treebie pulled back, careful not to spill one
drop.

Rising from her squatting position, she ran her tongue over her lips then kissed his. With a dramatic flair she turned and switched off to the bathroom. She stopped at the door and looked back at him over her shoulder. "A bitch bad ain't she?"

"Fucking trooper," he agreed, walking up to smack her shapely ass before she closed the bathroom door.

They arrived at Bella Italia for dinner. Not long after they were seated the waitress appeared with drink menus. "You know I don't like you drinking. Bring her some water with lemon," he told the waitress before she scribbled down the order.

Treebie looked up at the girl reproachfully. "Sweetie, please bring me a tall glass of Chianti, and you can bring *him* some water. Thank you." She handed the waitress the menu and the girl sauntered off.

Wa'leek shook his head. "You so hardheaded."

"You are not my father," she said, rolling her head to the side

"Why when I hit that spot you call me daddy?"

"Shut up," Treebie said then laughed.

When the drinks arrived the waitress cautiously placed the wine in front of Treebie and the water in front of Wa'leek. Treebie smirked. "Don't be scared. He is way more bark than he is bite."

The waitress smiled. "Are you ready to order?"

"Not yet, give us a minute," Wa'leek answered, giving Treebie an intense stare.

After the waitress left, Treebie began sipping her drink. Wa'leek drank his water then they caught each other up on what was going on. The conversation was going good until Wa'leek started his shit. "So when you coming home?" he questioned, touching on a subject that always ignited a fight.

"I don't know." Treebie braced herself for the battle.

"Fuck you mean you don't know?" Wa'leek sat forward placing his elbows on the table.

She looked into his eyes and saw that his mood had changed just that quickly. She tried to choose her words wisely before answering but no matter what she said, or how she said it, there was going to be a problem. "You know I got things I have to do. When I'm done, I'll be home," she said.

"What the fuck is that supposed to mean? You done left some dick to follow behind some pussy."

"Don't do that, I never come between you and your team."

"I didn't leave my fucking family to go bust a gun for the next bitch," Wa'leek replied bitterly.

"You fucking left me out here by myself. If it wasn't for Big Zo I don't know what I would have done—I owe him," Treebie countered.

"You don't owe that muthafucka shit. I did four years for our loyalty to Big Zo, all debts are paid. So fuck him," he gritted.

Treebie's blood was boiling. The more he talked the angrier she became. "You made your choices. And I made mine. You know where my loyalty lies but right now I gotta hold Lissha down."

"Man, fuck that bitch." The boom of his voice caused the couple at the next table to look in their direction.

"No, fuck you," returned Treebie. "I'm not doing this shit with you, you must be outta your mind."

"Why you so loyal to that bitch?"

"Big Zo is my people. I am loyal to him, plain and simple. Lissha is his daughter and I do what I gotta do with her to keep the peace and make my money."

"I don't give a fuck about none of them muthafuckas, and that new nigga you working for, he ain't shit either. I'll fuck around and come out there and rob and kill all them niggas."

Treebie had heard enough. She got up, knocking into the table so hard that her glass tipped over. Red wine spilled onto the white table cloth. "Take me home!"

Wa'leek grabbed her arm. "Sit the fuck down," he ordered, looking up into her eyes. Treebie stood there ready to defy him. The manager rushed over to their table. "Is everything okay?" he asked.

"We're fine," said Wa'leek holding on to Treebie's arm firmly. With his other hand he reached into his pocket and sat a hundred dollar bill on the table. "Sorry for the inconvenience. He released Treebie's arm and stood up.

Treebie brushed past them and stormed to the car. When Wa'leek got outside she was breathing fire. He let her go off for a minute then explained his position. "My bad," he offered in apology. "But I'm fresh outta loyalty to that nigga. I want to put my family back together and I can't do that with you outta state risking your life for them. You feel me?" He put his hand under her chin and tilted her head up so that she could see the sincerity in his eyes.

Treebie didn't respond. She stood there burning up. As soon as she heard the locks click, she slid into seat and stared out the window with her elbow resting on the door. Wa'leek climbed behind the wheel and turned on the music. Not a word was uttered between them as they drove back to his house.

Chapter 24
Mind Fuck

Treebie jumped out the car and double timed it to the front door. The sound of her heels clacking on the concrete echoed in the silence of the night.

Wa'leek walked up behind her and opened the door. Treebie stormed in the house, moved to the bedroom and began gathering up her things.

Wa'leek turned on the stereo in preparation for the yelling match that was about to ensue. When he looked up Treebie was headed his way with her bag.

"Where the fuck you think you going?" He questioned harshly.

"Take me to the airport," she demanded.

"Fuck you mean? You ain't going nowhere." He reached in and tried to snatch her bag from her hands.

"Stop, Wah. Move! I should have never came here," she yelled back, refusing to let go of her bag.

"You gonna turn on me for them niggas?" he barked.

"It's not about them. Now get off my shit and move."

Wa'leek yanked her bag out of her arms and tossed it across the room. "Yo ass ain't going nowhere," he said forcefully, grabbing her by both arms and pulling her to him. Treebie tried to snatch away but the more she tussled with him the tighter he held her.

"Get the fuck off me," she spat.

"Shut the fuck up."

"No, you shut the fuck up," she disobeyed. "Get your hands off of me, Wa'leek. Right fuckin' now!"

Wa'leek pinned her against the wall forcing her arms above her head. "Wah stop," she cried, struggling against his body.

Wa'leek put both of her hands together and grabbed her by the throat. "Gimme a kiss."

"No, get off me."

He released her throat and reached in his pants, releasing that steel. Treebie squirmed between him and the wall as he reached under her dress and yanked her panties down around her ankles. "Wa'leek no, stop it!" Treebie fought as his fingers slid effortlessly between her thighs.

"You know this what you need," he said, staring at her with those hypnotic eyes.

"Wah, don't!" She continued to resist as she felt his finger push deep inside her.

"Don't what?" he whispered, picking up speed.

"Don't—do—this."

"Why not?" His voice dropped to a deep bass as his fingers delicately stroked her.

Treebie's cries of protest slowly turned into moans of pleasure. Wa'leek continued to reach for that spot as her breathing confirmed that she was ready to submit.

"Get it wet for me, baby," he whispered in her ear placing light kisses on her neck.

"Wah," she panted and her body began to tremble. He released her hands and wrapped her legs around his waist. Slowly, he slid all the way in. Treebie closed her eyes and sucked in her breath. Wa'leek went in deeper and stroked with command.

Treebie climbed the wall in an effort to escape his thickness. "Ain't nowhere to go," he rasped, holding her in place and thrusting harder. Treebie wrapped her arms around his neck and gave in to his command. She rolled her hips in harmony with his.

Wa'leek held her as he walked to the bedroom bouncing her up and down on all that dick. Each time she rose and descended Treebie's moans grew louder.

The next morning, Treebie awoke wrapped in Wa'leek's arms. When she opened her eyes he was staring into them with a tenderness that was foreign to his character. He kissed her good morning and said, "I need you, baby. I don't wanna fight with you."

"I don't want to fight with you either, Wah. I love you," she replied with sincerity.

"Come home, baby," he said stroking her cheek.

She didn't reply because she refused to lie to him. Wa'leek understood what her silence meant but he could not accept it. "You gotta let them go, ma," he said softly.

"I will when the time is right," she promised.

"Fuck that, the time is now."

"I thought you didn't want to fight?" she reminded him as she stared into those gray eyes.

"A'ight ma," he relented, but he knew how to get her to bring her ass home.

Over the next two days, Wa'leek worked on Treebie's mind and body. When the weekend was over and it was time for her to return to Cleveland, he was confident that he had her back under his control.

On Monday afternoon, he drove her to the airport confident with the seed of dissention he had sewn deep in her heart.

"When you bringing that wet back?" Wa'leek calmly asked, looking over to Treebie from the driver's side of his Ranger Rover.

"Soon," she answered, leaning over to taste those sweet lips.

"Hurry up, don't make me come for you."

"I won't. Just have a little more patience, baby," she said.

"I can't promise you that."

Treebie knew that time was running out. When she got out of the car she grabbed her bag and switched to the entrance for flight departures. Wa'leek beeped the horn and she slowly turned around. "You walking like something happened to you." He grinned.

Treebie just smiled big, flagged her hand, and disappeared inside.

Dropping his smile, Wa'leek pulled off and hit his Bluetooth. "What's up, my nigga?"

"Long time no hear," Riz slurred into the phone "What's good?"

"What you know about this new nigga Big Zo got working for him?"

Riz got quiet. "Maybe we need to sit down."

"I'm on my way." Wa'leek hung up and headed for the Holland tunnel.

Chapter 25
Heated Exchanges

Kiam hopped out of the truck with a black and burgundy backpack in his hand and strolled up to Lissha's door and rung the bell. He only had to wait about thirty seconds before she swung the door open.

"Hey." She stood there in a wife beater and a pair of yellow boy shorts.

"What's up?" His eyes ran from the top of her head down to her feet. She noticed him staring but made no comment. Usually she had something slick to say. Today was different.

"You're early. It's six o'clock, you said seven," Lissha complained.

"So what? You want me to come back in an hour? You must got a nigga up in here."

"No, I don't. But if I did, why should that concern you. Daddy told you to oversee the business, not me. This is grown woman shit over this way, and I'm perfectly capable of managing my own personal life."

"Grown, huh? I got something that makes big girls feel like little girls," he teased.

She shot him a look that told him not to go there, and in case he didn't get it, she reprimanded, "You better keep your mind on business before you find yourself wondering what the hell hit you and who was behind the wheel."

"I bet you been rehearsing that little comeback all day. I would clap for you but I got shit in my hands. And don't be fooled, I might tease and joke but when it comes to business, nothing gets in my way. Not even little pretty girls like you," he replied unperturbed.

"Whatever. Come in and handle your business so I can watch your best feature."

"What's that?"

"Your back." She turned and walked to the living room with him watching her booty bounce with each step. Lissha looked back just in time to see the lust in his eyes. He was looking at her like he wanted to bend her over the arm of the couch and show her that he was running more than just the business.

"I just wanna know one thing," he said.

"What?"

"Is it as good as it looks?" his eyes traveled down to that fat V between her thighs.

"Better," she shot back. "Too bad you'll never get to know for yourself."

"Don't bet on that," Kiam said arrogantly.

"Don't you bet against it," she matched his confidence.

"I never let what people say I can't do stand in the way if I wanna do it. Real niggas write their own script. If I wanna hit it, I'ma hit it. Just hope you can handle it when I do."

Lissha ignored his comment; he wasn't hitting nothing over that way. "You can have a seat, I'll be right back," she said, sauntering off into another room.

Kiam sat the backpack down at his feet and took a seat on the couch. Lavender scented candles burned in various areas around the living room. The soft sounds coming from the IPod dock relaxed his body and his mind.

When Lissha returned she had changed into a pair of baggy sweats and a loose-fitting top. Kiam looked up at her and laughed.

"What?" she asked.

"You're still sexy as a muthafucka, ma," he said. "You can't hide that no matter what you put on."

"Ain't nobody trying to hide nothing," she lied. "Anyway, don't worry about how sexy I am, you just keep up with that little goodie-goodie chick you've been seeing?" she said, sitting down across from him with her legs folded underneath her.

"Eyez? Goodie-goodie? Nah, you got her all wrong. You should know better than to judge a book by its cover. Baby girl used to hug the block with the big dogs. She's corporate now, but she's still gangsta with her shit."

"You said all that to say what? All bitches bleed."

"I ain't come over here to tongue wrestle with you." He stopped her. "I guess Gator ain't taming that pussy right so you giving me all that attitude. But it's all good, that's what happens when you give a little boy a job that was meant for a grown ass man," He rested his hands on each leg only inches away from his dick and stared at her trying to figure her out.

Lissha felt his eyes all over her and her body began to heat up. Her nipples tingled and her kitty purred. She hated that she couldn't stop herself from wanting him. Her mind told her to follow the script that Big Zo had written, but the epicenter of her womanhood had a mind of its own. She unconsciously squeezed her thighs together and tore her eyes off of him.

Kiam seemed to sense her dilemma. He smiled knowingly and patted a spot on the sofa right next to him. "C'mere, shorty," he said, his voice thick with primal seduction.

"Nah, I'm good." Lissha shook her head. She knew that if she went over and sat beside him and he didn't push her down and get all up in that pussy she would end up throwing his ass down and taking her some dick.

"You sure?" he asked.

"Yeah. I'm not going to let Daddy down. One of us gotta be trustworthy." She was determined to stand firm.

She turned her head away from Kiam before his mouth watering gaze made her change her mind. The moment of weakness passed. She was good now.

Her words were like a punch in the chest. The warning was clear. She had just set things on the right track with that statement. Kiam knew exactly what he needed to do.

"Okay. Well, I wanted to drop this off to you." He reached down and picked up the backpack and handed it to her. Lissha opened the flap and looked inside at the bands of dead faces. "Take care of the girls and make sure Pop is straight," Kiam instructed.

"You don't have to remind me to take care of Daddy, that's what I do. I been doing it long before you showed up, so what makes you think I would stop now?"

Kiam cocked his head to the side. "Fuck is your problem?"

"Fuck is yours?" she asked right back.

"You know what, I think you want me to do to you what Gator can't."

"And I think you want Daddy to do to you what you know he *will.*"

Kiam was up off the couch as soon as the comment left her lips. He grabbed her by the face and gritted, "You trying to disrespect me?" His voice was low but lethal.

Lissha said nothing.

"See, when you be around pussy ass niggas too long you forget how you should never talk to a man." He tightened his grip on her face and forced her to look in his eyes. "You see any bitch in me?"

"No, I don't. Now get your fucking hands off my face." She dug her nails into his arms.

Kiam accepted her half-hearted submission. He released her and allowed himself a minute to cool off. When his chest stopped heaving up and down, he said, "You almost got fucked up, shorty. Don't ever try to pit me against your father again. I love and respect Big Zo to the utmost but I fear no man." He turned his back to her and walked to the door.

"Kiam," Lissha called out.

"Fuck you want?"

"I apologize," she said. "I would never pit you against Daddy."

He shot her the deuces and kept on pushing. He didn't know what the fuck he was doing playing with her anyway. His loyalty to Big Zo had to trump lust, and his love for Faydrah should have extinguished any flame that sparked between him and any other woman. It was time for him to dead the bullshit and stand firm on principle.

Ca$h & NeNe Capri

Chapter 26
New Beginnings

Faydrah moved around Kiam's new condo opening appliances and carefully putting them in their place. Uncovering the couch and love seat, she smiled at the idea of her finally being able to see Kiam enjoy life.

He watched her joyfully move about the rooms hanging curtains and arranging the furniture that she had helped him pick out. While he walked off to answer a call from Lissha, Faydrah opened several boxes looking for the lamp that she had bought to go with the living room furniture.

Her eyes popped out of her head when she saw that she had opened the wrong boxes. Two of them were full of money and a count machine. The third box that she opened contained guns, a silencer, vests, black clothing and boots. She snapped the boxes shut like she had seen somebody's dark family secrets.

Faydrah wished like hell that she hadn't mistakenly opened the wrong boxes, because now her mind was racing and her joy was gone. When Kiam returned to the living room she was still bending over the box which contained the weapons. His eyes roamed over her body admiring her curves in her tight leggings and tank top.

Coming up behind her he wrapped his arms around her waist and whispered in her ear. "Let's go break that new king-size in." He pressed himself against her butt and began walking her up the stairs.

"I have work to do, Mister," she giggled.

"Me, too, I gotta see how these springs work," he shot back, steering her into the bedroom. Playfully, he tossed her up on the bed then crawled between her legs.

"Stop Kiam," she screamed with laughter as he bit and tickled her stomach. In spite of what she had seen, she could not stop herself from enjoying his rare playfulness.

He pressed his body down onto hers and planted soft kisses on her lips. She parted her lips, demanding his tongue, while her hands went on an expedition. The surge of testosterone that shot through his body had him ready to put that ass to sleep.

"Kiam wait," she pleaded as his hands slid under her shirt and gently caressed her breast. Kiam ignored her plea as he traced her lips with his tongue. "Baby, we need to talk."

"About what?" he asked, grinding his steel against her clit while planting soft kisses on her neck and collar bone.

"No, seriously." She pushed him up slightly to look into his eyes.

"What's on your mind, shorty?" he asked, still in full fuck mode.

"What's going on, Kiam?"

"We about to fuck real hard for a little over an hour then fall asleep and start all over again," he rasped, leaning in and kissing her again.

"Kiam, wait. I need to talk to you for a minute." She gently pushed him up.

"What's up?" He paused to hear her out.

"What are you doing? I saw some things that let me know you're back in the streets."

"What you talking about, Eyez?" he asked.

"I don't have to explain. You know what I saw." Kiam sat all the way up and rubbed his hand over his face.

Faydrah sat up next to him. "I wasn't being nosey, I was looking for that lamp I bought you," she explained, then her expression turned somber. "I guess I knew before I saw those things, because I know you. You're right back in that life," she accused.

Kiam laid on his back resting his hands behind his head. "I gotta do, what I gotta do," he said.

"What you gotta do? What does that mean?"

"You know what this is Eyez."

"No, I don't. I know that you just gave up eight years of your life over some bullshit." She glared down into his face.

Kiam sat up. "I'm not doing this with you right now." He shook his head.

"Why not, Kiam? Because I'm touching on some truth?" she challenged.

Kiam stood up and headed out of the bedroom. Faydrah hopped up and caught up with him at the door. She grabbed his arm and planted herself in front of him. "Where are you going? Really, you're going to just walk away in the middle of a conversation?"

"For real, shorty, I'm not trying to talk about it. Move out the way." His words hurt, because they confirmed her suspicions, but she choked back the pain and continued trying to reach him.

"Baby, I love you," she said. "I always have. Many days I thought about moving on. But I couldn't because I knew I couldn't let go of you. It didn't matter that we didn't keep in touch, you owned my heart. I kept dreaming that you would come home and leave these damn streets alone so we wouldn't ever have to be apart again."

Kiam stood quiet as she took him by the face and continued her plea. "You are a brilliant man, the same effort you put into hustling and killing, you can put into something positive and become just as successful."

Removing her hands from his face Kiam affirmed his position. "I hear you. But I'm not in that place right now. I got things I have to do. I got mad love for you, but it's you who has to decide what you're gonna do. I already know what I gotta do. Now you can either ride with a nigga or hop off," he said as he walked away.

"What kinda statement is that?" she railed. "I guess that's some bullshit those jailhouse niggas put in your head."

Kiam turned on his heels moving back in her direction. "I'm my own fuckin' man. I don't need no nigga to validate who I am." He raised his voice, peering down at her.

Faydrah gritted her teeth and stood up in his face. "Who you trying to convince, me or yourself?" Unlike the niggas on the street she had no fear of his reputation. With her he was just Kiam.

"I don't have to convince you of shit. I'm a loyal nigga, you know that. I made promises to a man that I love and respect like a father, so I'm going to keep my word. That's my get down, you already know that. I would never disrespect you, but if you can't roll with what I gotta do, then you know what you gotta do."

She rested her hand on his chest. "Yeah, you're right," Faydrah agreed. "You are loyal. But the person you need to learn to be loyal to is yourself."

Kiam looked away as her words threatened to shatter his illusions of what being official meant. As mad as it made him for her to challenge the code that he lived by, he knew deep inside her words came from a caring place. But the ego that lay within him would not let him submit.

Faydrah saw that in the stubborn set of his jaw. *Why in the hell am I wasting my breath?* she asked herself. She removed her hand from his chest and set her own jaw. "You're right. I am going to get off," she stated as she walked downstairs to gather her things.

Kiam rubbed his fist in his hand. He wanted to stop her but a false sense of pride took the wheel and was driving a wedge between him and the only woman he ever really loved.

As Faydrah hit the door, struggling with her shoes, her purse fell to the floor. Snatching it up, she flung it over her shoulder then franticly searched for her car keys.

Kiam walked into the living room, plopped down on the couch, and silently watched her. He was too stubborn to utter what his heart demanded that he say.

212

Faydrah said, "I was just going to walk outta here and not say anything else to you, but I'm not built like that. All this shit you got going on up in here." She waved her arms around. "It's all going to crumble around you. And the very muthafuckas you vow loyalty to are gonna be the ones to stab you in the back." Her voice cracked and her eyes filled with tears.

Kiam's heart ached over the pain he was causing her, but his response didn't show what he felt inside. "You done?" he asked bluntly.

Faydrah held back her tears and forced a smile. "I damn sure am," she replied with strength. She grabbed the door knob and snatched the door open, slamming it as she stormed out.

When she got outside the door all of her emotions spilled over. She leaned up against the wall, held her purse tight in her arms and let the tears fall. She slid to the ground as the pain in her spirit no longer allowed her legs to support her weight.

Placing her face in her hands, she wept. She cried for who Kiam could be and who he was determined to remain. She never wanted to upset their bond but she knew that she could not live with herself if she didn't tell him how she felt.

On the other side of the door Kiam was dealing with the same feelings. His heart told him she was right, but the beast in him had made commitments he was not going to ignore. Conflicted and angry, he got up and headed to the door to return to the streets. He looked down and saw her sitting on the floor with her back against the wall, sobbing.

"Baby, what you doin'?" he asked softly.

Faydrah looked up with pain and sadness in her eyes. "I don't want to live without you Kiam," she said from the heart.

"Come here ma." He reached down and gently lifted her to her feet. Faydrah went into his arms and leaned her forehead against his chest.

"Baby, please get outta the streets. Do that for me," she asked in a desperate tone.

"I'm not going to lie to you. I can't get out right now. But I promise, nothing I'm doing will hurt you. I need you to chill and let me do what I do," he maintained.

Faydrah had to allow that, because letting go was no better option than trying to live without air. "Okay, Kiam," she agreed, "but you have to promise me that when shit is piled against you, you'll get out."

"I promise, shorty." He held her closer to his chest. "Now let's go back inside. You out here embarrassing me in front of my neighbors." He pulled her inside and closed the door with his foot.

"Shut up." She hit his arm. "You should be glad somebody cares about your black ass." Faydrah sat her bag down and pouted her lips.

"What?" Kiam smiled. "Does this mean I can't see them legs on my shoulders?" He licked his lips enticingly.

"You think your ass is cute."

"Girl, you see all this." Kiam put his arm up displaying his bicep. "Nigga on point."

"Whatever. You just better be careful. And that chick I saw at your hotel room. You watch her. I don't trust that bitch."

"I got it. Now come make up with me. You got my little nigga all upset." He walked over and picked her up.

Faydrah wrapped her arms and legs around him as he carried her to the bedroom and laid her on the bed. He took his time undressing her, then he slowly undressed himself.

Naked and wrapped in passion Faydrah laid tenderly under his precise push. Each stroke affirmed their love but she could tell that he was no longer the Kiam she fell in love with, he had morphed into something else.

With each pleasure-filled release she wondered what had changed him. Was it the time in prison or the feeling of abandonment each time he lost someone he loved or trusted? Either way she knew it was only a matter of time before she would be lying with a stranger. She wondered how much of herself was she willing to lose while trying to save the broken pieces within him.

Chapter 27
Treacherous

Lissha moved around her house trying to get her mind right to deal with Kiam. She had not seen him since their little altercation the other day. It was pick up time and he insisted that she go with him. She both dreaded and looked forward to seeing him.

A moment after she grabbed her gun, her phone rang. Checking the screen revealed that it was Big Zo. "Hello," she answered.

"Baby girl." His voice boomed into the phone.

"Hey, Daddy." She forced her voice to sound chipper.

"You alright?" he asked

"Yeah, I'm good. How are you?" she replied, trying to shift the weight in the other direction.

"I'm good now. I'm just checking on you. I had a feeling that you might be going through something because you haven't called in a few days." He gently probed.

"Everything is fine. I'm about to go to the store with Kiam."

"Yeah?"

"Mm hmm, they just got some fresh watermelon in and I know it's on sale." She shot him some code real quick.

"Alright handle your business. Hit me when you get back."

"I will," she assured him, reaching for the button to disconnect.

"Lissha?"

"Huh?" She put the phone back to her ear.

"Get your shit together. We got too much on the line," he reiterated, pacing back and forth in his cell.

"What you mean, Daddy?"

"You know what I mean. I know you, I can hear the wavering in your voice. But I taught you better than that. Don't make me regret my decision. Talk to you later." He hung before she could respond.

Lissha wanted to throw her phone against the wall, run to her room and jump back under her covers and pretend that none of this was happening. As soon as she started into her feelings she heard a car horn outside her door.

"Oh, boy, here we go," she sighed, heading for the door. And as if the day couldn't get any worse she looked up and saw the bitch from the hotel propped up in the front passenger seat of Kiam's truck like the fucking Queen of England.

Lissha took a deep breath, closed the door, and strutted down the walkway. She climbed into the backseat and closed the door, staring at the back of Kiam's head with disgust in her eyes.

Sensing she was shooting him prisms he reached up and adjusted the rearview mirror and gave her a smile. "Good afternoon, Miss Lissha," he said all formally, like he was driving Miss Daisy.

"Ain't shit good about it. I thought we had business to handle, I didn't know it was bring your friends to work day."

Faydrah looked over at Kiam and smiled. She was not frazzled by the heat that was coming from the back seat.

Kiam looked over his shoulder at Lissha. "This ain't no friend," he clarified. "This is the result of what happens the next morning after you make that pussy purr." He leaned over and kissed Faydrah's lips.

Lissha wrinkled up her nose.

"I take it your man didn't come home last night," Kiam jeered, then turned the music up, put the car in gear and pulled off.

"Fuck you, Kiam."

Faydrah gave him a look telling him not to even entertain the bullshit. Kiam nodded his understanding. He looked up in the mirror watching Lissha put on her shades and turn toward the window.

As Kiam drove downtown to drop Faydrah off at work he periodically looked at Lissha who was becoming angrier by the minute. Being that Faydrah was a true team player, she fed right into Kiam's little games and giggled and rubbed all over him as he drove.

Lissha sat fantasizing about pulling out her heat and blowing both of their minds all over the front window.

When Kiam pulled up in front of Faydrah's job he turned down the music, reached in his pocket and pulled a nice stack out and handed it to her. "Get that shit that makes a nigga act the fuck up," he said.

"And bring you home to me?" she added.

"No doubt."

"Okay, baby." She leaned over and kissed him passionately while sliding her hand over his print.

"Don't be sleep," he said.

"You know how to wake me, don't you?" she cooed, giving him her sexy gaze. Stepping from the vehicle, she grabbed her purse and looked back at Lissha. "Have a good day."

Lissha threw her an evil smirk. "You have a *safe* one."

"Oh, trust me I intend to, because anything that could prevent that from happening, I know how to remove it." She held a short eye lock with Lissha before flashing Kiam a smile. "Bye, baby," she said as she walked away.

"Eyez, behave," Kiam yelled out.

Faydrah waved her hand over her shoulder and kept it moving.

Lissha was not amused. "Your bitch ain't house trained, you better make sure she know who is running this shit before she gets fucked up," she said to Kiam.

"The only thing you running is ya mouth," he laughed.

Lissha mumbled something slick under her breath that Kiam didn't quite catch, but he recognized her attitude for what it was. "You jelly?" he smiled.

"Of what? A bitch that gets good dick because her man's mind is filled with how good *my* pussy feels? Fuck outta here. I'm a product of Big Zo, that bitch ain't got shit for me. And neither do you." Her mouth tightened as the words left her pretty glossed lips.

Kiam smiled. "You're so cute when you're trying to be mean."

Lissha shot her middle finger straight in the air.

"Get in the front, I ain't no fucking chauffeur." Kiam hurled back at Lissha.

"Kiam, please don't fuck with me right now. Because if I come up there I might do something we both will regret."

"You ain't talking about shit, you wanted distance between us, so you got it. Deal with it." He threw that killer glare her way then pulled off.

Lissha quickly picked up on the fact that his words said one thing but meant another. A smile came across her face as she realized she had succeeded in getting in his head just like he was in hers.

"Take me by Treebie's before we start picking up. I need to get at her real quick," she said as he turned up Prospect Avenue.

Kiam didn't respond, he drove in silence with only the music as a buffer between the discomforts they both were feeling.

When they pulled up to Treebie's townhouse, Lissha jumped out the back seat, walked up on the steps and rang the bell. She waited a half minute then knocked on the door a few times.

Treebie opened the door in her robe looking as if Lissha was a Jehovah Witness. "Why the fuck you on my shit like that?" Treebie asked with a mean mug.

"Why the fuck you ain't answered your phone in three days?"

"I was taking care of some business. What's up?"

"Taking care of business?" Lissha threw her head to the side. "We got shit pending and you just disappear? What the fuck is going on with you?" Lissha asked, as her eyes settled on a few light hickies on Treebie's collar bone.

"I'm a very grown woman. I don't question your actions, so don't question mine."

"Have you bumped your muthafuckin' head?"

Treebie smiled looking over at Kiam whose eyeballs were focused out the front window. His body language read aggravation. "What happened, you and your little boyfriend get into it?"

"First of all, don't do that. Second, you need to get your ass on point. We ride on these niggas in two days. Its's blood money, bitch, you know I don't play with my shit."

"And I don't play at all. I'll be ready, snatch your thong out ya ass and try to have a good day. I'll be over tomorrow."

"You get on my nerves," Lissha clacked as she turned to walk back to the car.

"LiLi, you need to go ahead and give that nigga some pussy so you can get your mind right," Treebie said and began cracking up.

"Fuck you, Tree."

"Not me bitch, fuck the nigga that has your ass on fire. A good nut might calm you the fuck down," she laughed then shut the door.

Treebie's laughter echoed in Lissha's mind as she jumped in the back seat. She was pissed and feeling like she was back at square one in her feelings. Kiam shook his head. *She gon' hop her hard headed ass right back in the back seat, huh?* He turned the music back up and pulled off.

They encountered Gator at their first stop in East Cleveland. He came out of the trap house on Hayden and passed a shoe bag full of mula through the window to Kiam. He cut his eyes at Lissha and held his stare. She knew what he was thinking but she didn't give a damn. Just because she wasn't dealing with him anymore, didn't mean she was fucking Kiam. She mean mugged Gator right back.

"That's what happens when you fuck with the help," shot Kiam as he bent a corner and hopped back on Euclid Avenue.

Lissha ignored the trite remark and Kiam let the subject die. He hit JuJu up real quick to let him know that he was coming by his place to pick up the money he had for him.

"That's cool, I got it on deck," replied JuJu. The weekend dice games at the St. Clair joint was beginning to do big numbers. Kiam was glad that he had decided to get down with that hustle.

Lissha welcomed the brief reprieve because as long as Kiam was on the phone he wasn't talking to her. She stared out the window tuning out his conversation.

After collecting from JuJu they hit a few of their other houses around the city. Within two hours they had successfully made every stop. They had the money tucked tight in the trunk, now they just needed to drop it off at the safe house and then they would be out of each other's hair.

"Why did I have to ride with you to do this?" she questioned him as they drove down East 116th toward Kinsman.

"You need to know where our new spots are in case something happens to me," he explained.

"I'm not that lucky."

Kiam ignored her sarcasm. Reaching 116th and Union, he pulled into the Sunoco station. "I need to get some gas real quick," he said.

"Do you, boo boo," she shot back, keeping her face to the window as if that would make her invisible.

Kiam pulled up to the pump and jumped out. "You want something?"

"Nah, I'm good," she answered making sure not to look in his direction.

When he was inside the store, Lissha jumped out the truck and stood next to it while flipping through her cell phone. She shot Big Zo a quick text letting him know she was safe and would be transferring money into his account in the morning.

She looked up into the store and saw Kiam engaged in a heavy conversation. Lissha sighed loudly, she was ready to get home. Aggravated, she turned to get back in the truck.

"I guess you a big shot now, huh?" The feminine voice came from behind her.

Lissha whipped her head around and every muscle in her body seized up. "Get the fuck outta my face," she hissed. Her eyes nervously searched for Kiam.

"You ain't shit." The woman lashed out at her.

Lissha moved toward her with her lips pulled back. "That's because the pussy I dropped from wasn't shit," she said, bristling inside.

"I don't know how the fuck you can live with yourself."

"And I don't know why you're still living."

Lissha and the woman began slinging heated remarks and curse words back and forth. They both had wicked tongues and plenty of ammunition to hurl at each other.

Kiam looked up from his conversation inside the store and saw Lissha and the woman standing nose to nose, going at it.

"I'll get with you another time. Hit me up." He touched fist with Frank Nitti and hurried out the door.

Moving swiftly in Lissha's direction he heard the woman say, "Fuck Big Zo, I hope his punk ass die a slow, painful death,"

"Be careful that the grave you wish on him doesn't grab your ass first."

"Yo, what the fuck is going on?" Kiam stepped in and pushed them apart. He looked from Lissha to the woman, waiting for either of them to explain. All of a sudden Lissha's mouth was on mute.

"This dirty bitch is the worst thing that ever happened to me," said the woman. She turned back to Lissha and hocked a glob of spit in her direction. Lissha jumped back then lunged forward punching her dead in the face.

"Oh yes, bitch, I been waiting for this day," the woman snarled, bouncing on her toes as she reached up and wiped blood from her busted lip.

Kiam backed up a little as fist flew back and forth with unleashed fury. The sound of the punches bounced off their faces causing bystanders to flinch in pain.

Kiam grabbed Lissha by the waist and lifted her off her feet and moved her to the truck. "Calm yo ass down, you drawing too much attention. We dirty," he whispered tersely.

"Get the fuck off me." She kicked and pulled at Kiam's arms trying to break free.

"Let that bitch go," the woman begged.

Lissha wiggled out of Kiam's arms, snatched his whistle off his waist and pointed it at the woman, "I fucking hate you!" she yelled out.

The woman tore her shirt open and began pounding her fist over her heart. "Do it. Don't be no punk as ho. Do it. Pull the trigger!"

Lissha was shook up, she stood with her arm extended and her trigger finger frozen as tears began to run down her face.

"Do it!" The woman egged her on. But this time the woman's voice cracked. "I ain't got shit to live for. You and that man took everything I had!"

The gun shook in Lissha's hand as she re-tightened her grip to keep from dropping it. The woman stared at the weapon, inviting the end to her pain.

Lissha looked at her with no pity, but she could not bring herself to put her out of her misery. Their eyes held each others as the past ran through both of their minds. Lissha interpreted it one way. The woman interpreted it the opposite, but what had happened between them was irreversible.

Sweat and tears ran down the woman's dark brown face, trickling past her bloody mouth. Lissha's chest heaved up and down as she tried to calm the many emotions that fought for control over her. Squeezing the trigger would put an end to everything that had happened between them.

"Fuck you doing?" Kiam's voice jarred her from her thoughts. She let her arm fall down to her side.

Kiam cautiously took the gun from her hand. She relinquished it without protest, but the anger in her soul remained red hot. She casted an evil eye at the broken woman and snarled, "Stay the fuck away from me because the next time I see you, there will be no mercy."

"Likewise bitch," said the woman, about to get hyped all over again.

"Come get in the car, Lissha," urged Kiam, grabbing her by the arm. "Fuck all of this drama. This that hot shit."

"Get the fuck off me." She snatched away and walked off.

"Where the fuck are you going?" Kiam tried to move behind her.

Lissha didn't say anything she high tailed it to the corner where people were boarding the #15 bus. She pushed pass a few people in line and hopped on.

Kiam turned back to the woman, he needed answers. "Who the fuck are you?" he demanded to know.

"I'm her dirty little secret," she replied, lowering her eyes. "You better be careful. That bitch is treacherous. I wouldn't trust that heifer with her own thoughts." She pulled her shirt closed and walked away.

Kiam wanted to go after her and force her to explain, but the sirens in the background trumped all that. He jumped in his truck and pulled off, puzzled over what he had just witnessed.

After dropping the money off, he made a beeline to Lissha's house. He parked and sat outside, determined to get every question he had answered either by will or by force.

Chapter 28
A Test Of Loyalty

Two hours later Lissha, slid out of a cab and moved quickly toward her door. Kiam jumped out of his truck, walking with long stealth-like strides. They reached her door at the same time. "What the fuck was all that shit about?" he barked.

"None of your fucking business." She put her key in the door and pushed it open.

"Fuck you mean it's none of my business? We was out there with mad money and you creating fucking heat, 'bout to get our asses snatched the fuck up." The vein in his neck was like a whip cord as he followed her into the kitchen.

"Look, you were probably out there waiting to see if I made it home safe. Well, here I am, so you can be on your merry fucking way." She tossed her keys on the counter and turned to go in the living room.

Kiam snatched her little ass back around so that she was facing him again. "You think I sit out in front of bitches houses to make sure they get home safe?" he blared.

"I don't know what you do, and I don't care." She marched away from him.

Kiam was right behind her.

Lissha sat down on the sofa and reached for a half of blunt that was in an ashtray on the end table. Kiam stood over her, seething. "You must be fucking stupid." He placed with his fist in his hand while trying to regain his composure. "Now, this is the last time I'm gonna ask you what the fuck that shit was about."

Lissha sat the blunt back down and looked up at him. "It could be your last time or your third time, and my answer will be the same. None. Of. Your. Business." She dragged each word out, making sure to drive her point all the way home.

Kiam started to explode, but thought better of it. "Yeah, you right, it ain't none of my business. But if you ever put me in that type of situation again, I'll blow your fucking head off," he warned then turned to the door.

"Muthafucka I ain't scared of no nigga. You ain't saying shit." She pounced up off the couch and walked up on him.

Kiam turned around. "Don't ever walk up on me," he said.

"Or what? What?" Her arms flew out to her sides animatedly, challenging him to release his rage.

Kiam fought back the impulse to slap the shit out of her. Had she been any other nigga's daughter he would've rattled her teeth.

"Yeah, that's what the fuck I thought," she continued to mouth off. He knew what the fuck her problem was. It was time he shut her up.

In one move Kiam pulled her into his arms and put his lips to hers. Kissing her deep, he took her breath and finally shut her up. She received him as if she had been waiting all her life for that moment.

Lissha allowed his tongue to command all her attention and his hands to follow. When her pussy started to throb her thoughts boomed Big Zo. She tried to slam the doors to her mind shut and just follow the command of her body, but Zo hadn't schooled her to get down like that.

All of a sudden Lissha pulled back. "Kiam, no. We can't." She pushed him back and tried to catch her breath.

"Why not?" he asked, then pulled her back into him and took more of what he wanted. Lissha gave it willingly. She sucked on his tongue as he gripped her ass and walked her backwards toward her bedroom. Lissha was panting with an anticipation that had her pussy screaming.

As they reached the bed he pulled at her clothes. The heat between them was incinerating. "Kiam," she cried out, trying to stop what was destined to be.

"Let this shit happen," he responded on lust-filled breath.
"I can't betray Daddy. Please Kiam remember your promise."
Kiam's hands stopped where they were. He pulled them back,
breathing hard and standing there with a dick even harder.
She looked up into his eyes as tears left hers. "We can't," she
mumbled regretfully, shaking her head from side to side. They
looked at each other in silence for what felt like forever but was
actually only a few seconds. Kiam spoke first. "You right. I'm sorry, get some rest." He
kissed her forehead then turned to the door.
When Lissha heard the door close, she yelled out in frustration.
"Why?" She sat hard on the floor, put her face in her hands and
cried.

Kiam moved as if his life depended on it. When he got in the
car he slammed his palms down on the steering wheel and let out a
loud and frustrated sigh. He had almost crossed the line.
He was beyond conflicted, he had a woman whom he loved
and another one that was his forbidden desire. And he had accepted
a mission that could bring everything crumbling down.
He drove off thinking he needed to readjust his priorities
because the last thing he wanted to become was a muthafucka a
nigga couldn't trust.

Chapter 29
Retreat

Kiam felt the weight of his actions pounding in his head and heart as he inserted the key in the door and walked into his condo. He walked upstairs with the burden making his legs feel like lead. Inside his bedroom, he hit the light and his attention settled on a picture of him and Faydrah on his nightstand. He was giving her a piggyback ride; her arms and legs were wrapped around him tightly and she wore a smile that reflected the love she had for him.

When he tallied everything up, she was the fuel that replenished his dark soul when the streets threatened to turn it into an abysmal dungeon.

He removed his gun, placed it on the nightstand, and sat down on the bed. The day played back in his mind in slow motion. The situation with Lissha and the strange woman, and the fact that he had almost done something he swore he would not do—sleep with Big Zo's daughter.

He shook his head as Lissha's words cut into his heart confirming that he needed to get on point and keep it like that. *Remember your promise,* she had pleaded. What he needed to do was get money and find a way to free the man that had given him the keys to an empire. Too many niggas forgot about loyalty once their feet touched down on the outside of the prison fences. *Death before dishonor*, he reminded himself.

He thought about the only two women he had ever loved. He had lost one while caged. Now that he was out, he wasn't going to lose the other. Eyez loved and knew the man he was when his gun wasn't blazing. Their bond was impenetrable; it had held her heart captive while he was away, and it had led him to her doorsteps the moment his feet touched back down in the grimy city streets that had first introduced them to each other as kids. It was time for him to show her that he appreciated what they shared.

He reached for his phone and Googled some resorts in the area. A list of them popped up on the screen. He scrolled down until an advertisement for Big Rock Cabins caught his eye. It was a nice little getaway spot in the Appalachian foothills of Southern Ohio, secluded far from the hustle and bustle of the city. It seemed to offer exactly what he was looking for.

Kiam secured a reservation for the weekend. He needed a few days to get his mind right, and with strong lieutenants in place this was the perfect time for him and Faydrah to get away and strengthen their love.

Satisfied with his plans, Kiam hopped in the shower and began to mentally prepare for the little getaway. The water cascaded down his body and helped eased the tension that came from the life he had chosen.

With his priorities back on track sleep came easy for Kiam that night. When morning came he packed a few things then headed to the store to pick up some essentials that would make the weekend just right. Once he had all of his bags of tricks he stopped through the spots and gave out specific orders. His last stop was to see JuJu.

"Look, make sure you keep your eyes on these niggas, and if shit go wrong put a nigga on his ass. I'm only comfortable with casualties being those of the next nigga's team," he imparted.

"I got you," JuJu assured him.

They shook hands and bumped shoulders, then Kiam jumped in his truck and headed downtown to pick up Faydrah.

Faydrah was at her desk pounding away at her keyboard and talking loud into the speaker phone to colleagues in two different states. They were trying to iron out problems with a special project that they were working on.

When she saw her door open and Kiam standing there, her pretty light brown eyes brightened a bit more and the serious expression on her face quickly turned into a wide smile. He held a large bouquet of yellow, orange and blue assorted flowers wrapped in pink shiny paper with a big bow.

Faydrah instantly lost interest in the business call. Her eyes sparkled as she waved him over to her desk. Kiam handed her the flowers, and leaned down giving her the sweetest kiss she had ever tasted.

Excitedly, she put her finger up and mouthed, "*One minute.*"

Kiam took a seat in a chair across from her desk and watched as she buried her nose in the flowers and inhaled their fragrance. She sat the bouquet on her desk and finished typing the report as she glanced up at Kiam and made funny faces.

He shook his head at her silliness, it reminded him of that time when they were twelve and his appendix burst. She came to his hospital room and blew up the rubber gloves and drew faces on them in an attempt to cheer him up.

"Okay, I believe that sums everything up. I will email the proposal to both of you by noon Monday. Enjoy your weekend," she announced to the parties on the conference call, then disconnected.

Now she didn't have to hold back. Rising from behind her desk, she squealed, "Aww, baby." She walked around the desk and climbed on Kiam's lap, hugging him around the neck and placing tender kisses on his lips.

"Thank you, baby, I love them." She reached over and fingered the bouquet.

"I love to make you smile," he said.

She laid her head on his shoulder. "I needed that," she said. The day had been a stressful one up until then.

"You need something else too," he grinned, placing his hands on her butt.

"So, what you want to do tonight?" She wriggled her behind on his dick.

Kiam kissed her on the back of the neck. "I wanna do you on your desk right now."

"Down boy." She slapped his hand and giggled. She got up off his lap, pirouetted, and walked back behind her desk to wrap up her end of the project. "So am I getting some tonight?" she asked.

"I'm leaving town."

Faydrah snapped her neck to the side and looked at Kiam like she was ready to choke him. "Leaving town? Where you going?" She couldn't keep the disappointment out of her voice.

"Not me alone, baby - *us*."

"Going where? I can't just leave town, I don't have anything to wear. Besides, I have work I need to finish up before Monday. Really baby, I can't get away this weekend," she sighed.

"Yes, you can," he said. "I picked out everything I want to see you in for the next couple of days. Get your laptop and let's go."

"Baby!" She stomped her feet like a five-year-old.

"Wrap that shit up, I want to get on the road before rush hour." He looked at his watch.

"You serious?" Kiam didn't respond he just raised one eyebrow. Faydrah thought for a minute then grabbed her thumb drive, downloaded her files and emailed herself a backup. Quickly, she left the room to give instructions to her secretary and to copy a few documents she would need.

Returning to her office where Kiam sat tapping his foot in mock impatience, Faydrah packed up her laptop and three manila envelopes. She grabbed her briefcase, her purse, and the flowers. Kiam shook his head.

"Baby, let me carry that for you," he said, relieving her of the briefcase.

He frowned at her when she tried to hand him her purse. "I'm just kidding," she laughed.

"Don't play, shorty," he feigned a mean mug.

Faydrah locked up her office and they headed out. "This better be good," she warned, looking at him flirtatiously.

"Isn't it always good?" He licked his lips and flashed that sexy smile.

"You saw a bitch throwing shit in a bag like it was a state of emergency issued, didn't you?" Faydrah said, and they both chuckled.

When they got in the truck Faydrah kicked off her shoes and surfed his satellite radio for an old school station. Marvin Gaye was singing *Let's Get It On.* Kiam and Faydrah snapped their fingers to the beat and sung along.

We're all sensitive people/With so much love to give, understand me sugar/Since we got to be/Let's say, I love you/There's nothing wrong with me/Lovin' you/And giving yourself to me can never be wrong/If the love is true /Don't you know how sweet and wonderful, life can be...

As they drove, Faydrah beamed from the inside out. This was the Kiam she fell in love with. She bottled up every moment, carefully tucking them into her memory as if they were her last.

Three and a half hours and many old school songs later they arrived at their destination. When they pulled into the wooded area Faydrah's eyes were all over the place. They settled on the sign that read Big Rock Cabins. Kiam parked the car in front of the registration office and walked inside to retrieve their keys. Faydrah continued to look in every direction enjoying the serene backdrop of trees and flowers.

Kiam jumped back in the truck, passed her the keys, and then drove along the path deeper into the woods. Pulling alongside a wooden staircase outside their cabin, he turned off the engine and hopped out. Faydrah got out as well and moved to the back seat to get her things. Walking to the trunk where Kiam stood gathering bags she enjoyed the grass below her feet.

"What's all that?" she asked, looking at the many bags in the trunk.

"Stop being nosey and take these." He handed her the bag with the sheets, pillows and comforter, then grabbed the ones with the food and drinks and cleaning supplies.

Placing his bags on the porch he went back to the car to grab a few more items.

Faydrah opened the door and fell in love. There was exposed timber framing and natural wood throughout. The only thing modern was the TV, fireplace and the stereo. The open living room had a long couch, two arm chairs and a fire place right in front of it. The medium sized kitchen and island sat off the left. Huge picture windows brought all the scenic surroundings inside.

She placed the bags on the floor next to the table and moved to the small sun porch that had a grill, a small table, two chairs and a hot tub on the elevated deck. A forested ravine view topped off the moment. It was like time stood still, but her heart raced with excitement.

Kiam walked up behind her and wrapped his arms around her waist. "We needed this," he said softly, kissing the back of her neck.

Faydrah took a deep breath and leaned back against his chest. "Thank you, baby," she gushed as they stood looking out and enjoying the sounds of life. It seemed like several birds were having a very interesting conversation.

They took it all in for a few more minutes then headed inside to get situated for the night. Faydrah walked up the quarter-turn staircase that lead to an open loft with a pillow-top queen-sized bed. She turned on the ceiling fan that hung overhead in the vaulted living room.

Stripping the bedding, she folded it up neatly and sat it on the chair across from the bed. Next she began putting on the sheets, pillow cases and comforter Kiam brought. She reached in the bag and removed the scented candles and began lighting and placing them around the cabin.

Kiam put away the food and set up their toiletries in the bathroom. They met back up in the living room where Faydrah helped him light the fireplace.

As the flames licked at the firewood, Kiam placed a black fur throw rug right in front of the fireplace then they hit the shower.

When they emerged from the bathroom Faydrah got comfortable on the couch while Kiam prepared dinner. She sat watching him move around the kitchen with a focused expression on his face.

Faydrah's stomach started growling as the aroma of the steak and onions, candy carrots and yellow rice wafted out to where she was relaxing. Kiam was throwing down in there. When he was done cooking, he prepared their plates then joined her on the couch.

"You hooked a sistah up," she beamed as she tasted the succulent T-bone.

"Damn, I did this?" he said, chewing the tender meat.

"Yes, baby you did, and it's so sweet of you. Is this what I have to look forward to the rest of my life?" she asked, looking up at him lovingly.

Kiam leaned over and kissed her softly. "This and a whole lot more," he promised. He knew she was wife material and he damn sure wasn't going to let the next man have her.

When they were done eating, Faydrah helped him clean the kitchen then he sprawled across the rug in front of the fireplace. Faydrah went upstairs and grabbed the comforter and a book out of her purse. By the time she returned Kiam was relaxing on his back with his hands behind his head, thinking about a hundred different things.

Faydrah turned the radio on, adjusting the volume to low, then she spread the comforter on one side of him and sat down on it

Indian-style. "Grab that remote, let me see what's on TV real quick," said Kiam.

"Nope, I'm about to read to you."

"Read to me?"

"Yes. Is that a problem?" she asked.

"I guess not."

"Come here." She pulled him up. Kiam positioned his head against her chest, resting his back between her legs. Faydrah smiled, looking down at him staring at the book like it was capable of robbing him.

"Relax, it's not going to hurt."

"That's what I said to you nine years ago, but I was wrong," he joked.

"Shut up, nasty." She tapped him on the forehead.

Kiam chuckled as she opened the cover of *Sweet Persuasions* by Maya Banks and began reading. He had to admit to himself that he was enjoying her animated tone as she eagerly turned the pages. Faydrah was all into it. When she got to the first sex scene Kiam began making her pages come to life.

He turned over and positioned his face between her legs. She slowed down as his hands began to glide over her lower lips. Tingling all over, she looked down as he stole her concentration. "Keep reading," he whispered as he ran his tongue slowly up and down her sweetness.

Faydrah continued to read on but with labored breathing as music played softly in the background. Her eyes rotated back and forth between the pages and Kiam as he produced a flood between her thighs.

When he began sucking on her clit the book hit the floor and her moans filled the room. Kiam was handling his business and she was rewarding him with her sweet nectar all over his lips. She rubbed his head as he kneeled before her royal throne and allowed his tongue to worship her.

238

"Yessssss," she cried out as her honey poured. Her thighs gripped the sides of his head and her body arched off the floor in an inverted C.

Kiam kept tasting her until the room began to spin. Faydrah had gone to the edge and back and now it was his turn. He rose to his knees, released the beast, grabbed her ankles pulling her under him then pushed himself deep into her wetness.

Faydrah held onto him tightly while trying to make sure to shift beneath him just right. She knew that he loved it when she moved her hips in a slow circular motion and stared up into his eyes.

"You like this, baby?" she asked softly.

Her pussy felt better than freedom. The light moans that left his mouth confirmed that she was pleasing every inch of him. Kiam rested his gangsta— something he was comfortable doing only with her— and enjoyed her every movement. Between her soft thighs there was nothing for him to prove but his love and desire.

The crackle of the flames that danced in the fireplace accompanied the heat-filled strokes he gave her. Passion surged through their bodies like electricity. No words were needed, every movement spoke volumes as they rolled on the rug from one pleasure-filled position into the next.

As if the universe heard their hearts, Silk began to sing lightly in the distance.

Baby won't you let me look inside your soul/Oh my baby, let me make you lose control/Let me be the one you need, baby just come to me...

Kiam covered her pretty face and lips with soft wet kisses as she tensed up with every powerful push.

"Baby," she moaned. Her legs trembled from the pleasure that he gave.

"You're my everything," he whispered causing tears to release from the corners of her eyes.

She squeezed him tightly while rotating her hips faster, pulling him in deeper.

Bracing himself for the release, Kiam bit softly into her neck and let his essence flow into her core. It felt like he would come forever and her natural sheath welcomed it. They both moaned each other's name as the last of his thick, warm fluid fed her womb.

"I will love you forever," she whispered, holding him gently against her breast.

"I know," he said softly.

There in the middle of the log cabin the past, present, and future came together in harmony. She was his and he was hers, and only death could break their bond. They fell asleep in each other's arms satiated by their intense love-making.

The next morning Faydrah got up and showered, threw on a short sun dress, grabbed her laptop and started working. She looked down at Kiam and shook her head. He was out like a light, snoring softly. Constantly running the streets on little rest over the last few weeks had caught up with him.

Shortly after she was done with her work Kiam got up and staggered to the shower. She giggled to herself because she could see the results of last night's heated passion.

A quick shower brought him back to life. He reappeared talking smack and denying that she had that behind weak in the knees. They traded kisses back and forth then he went off to prepare some things, but he wouldn't say what.

Faydrah prepared some chicken shish kabobs with peppers, onions, pineapple and shrimp; she marinated them in a garlic butter sauce.

Kiam's timing was impeccable, he returned just as she was taking the kabobs off the grill. "You ready," he asked, walking out on the deck.

"Ready for what?" she questioned as she placed the last of the food on a tray and covered it with foil.

"To go on a little picnic."

"Huh?" she exclaimed, wiping her hands on the dish towel and setting it on the table.

Kiam took her by the hand. "Come on." Faydrah grabbed the tray with the food as Kiam dragged her off. When she got to the other side of the cabin she saw that Kiam had set up a blanket on the soft green grass, with a little straw basket filled with fruit and chocolate and a can of whip cream. Bottles of Moet & Chandon sat chilling in an ice bucket with two glasses beside it.

"Let me find out," she said, looking over at him with surprise sparkling in her eyes.

"They only locked up my body, my mind was always free to create and this is something I always imagined us doing," he said.

Faydrah smiled at him as he assisted her to sit. She breathed in the fresh air and lavished in the warm sunlight as it danced in the open field.

Kiam opened the drinks and filled both of their glasses. He held up his. "To the rest of our lives."

"Cheers." She clinked her glass against his, confirming that she shared his vow of forever.

They sipped champagne then Kiam fed her grapes and strawberries and shook up the whip cream. Faydrah tilted her head back and allowed him to spray it in her mouth. Slowly, he leaned in and kissed it off her lips.

Faydrah savored the taste of his berries and cream flavored kisses. "You like putting white stuff in my mouth," she joked.

"Sure do."

They laughed then continued to eat the treats he had set up along with the food she had prepared. When they were done Kiam reached inside the basket for another treat. All of a sudden he snatched his hand back. "Oh shit, what the fuck was that?" he shrilled, leaning back.

"What?" Faydrah became alarmed.

Kiam peeked in the basket then slowly began to reach inside a second time. "No, Kiam, don't!" she shrieked, afraid that a snake may have gotten inside of the basket. Her eyes were filled with a little fear.

"I got it, hold up," he said bravely.

Faydrah closed her eyes and pulled her hands close to her face.

"Oh shit, I got it." He pulled his closed hand back.

Faydrah peeked through her fingers. "What was it?"

"This shit movin'." He shook his hand with a nervous look on his face.

"Kiam, throw it!" she cried.

Instead he held his hand up for her to see. "Look."

"Nooooo!" She shut her eyes again and tried to move back.

Kiam grabbed her leg and held her in place.

"Stop, let me go," she yelled out.

"You don't want to see it?"

"No, stop it."

"Look, it ain't that big."

"Kiam stop."

"Just look."

Faydrah slowly opened her eyes to see him smiling and holding a beautiful diamond ring between his forefinger and thumb. She gasped.

"Scary ass," he joked.

"You play too much," she whined, holding her chest.

"Eyez," he said, suddenly becoming serious. "I can't do this life thing without you." He dropped his smile and took her h placed five carats on her finger.

Faydrah lost her breath. Tears welled up in her eyes as she looked into his. "And you won't have to," she cried, wrapping her arms around his neck.

"You promise?"

"Yes, baby I promise. I've been dreaming of this day forever. I'm going to make you very happy."

"You can make me very happy right now," he replied with a look that could not be mistaken.

"You ain't saying nothin'." She reached for his zipper and pulled out her best friend. Kiam instantly stiffened to her touch.

Climbing onto his lap she eased down on his steel. "You didn't say yes," he moaned.

"I'm about to," she said as she began riding him to the rhythm of her heart.

With all of nature as their witness they consummated their vow to be together forever. The last thing on Kiam's mind was Lissha and the violation that he had almost committed with her.

Chapter 30
A Wrong Move

While Kiam was three hours away from the city with all thoughts of her eradicated from his mind, Lissha wasn't exactly sitting around regretting what hadn't happened. It was in a corner of her mind but other things demanded her attention.

Lissha, Treebie, Donella and Bayonna moved calculatedly around Treebie's basement getting into character for tonight's caper. They had already fulfilled their obligations to Spank so everything they collected from tonight's job would be one hundred percent profit.

Treebie pulled on the blunt, then sat it down. She strapped on her vest and covered it with two thick t-shirts. Then she completed the hookup with a black hoodie. She sat back down on the couch and looked over at Bay and Donella who were already completely dressed and loading their guns.

Lissha was at the counter a few feet away downing shots and getting into beast mode, but it seemed like there was something else fueling her fire. Something more than her love of the carnage.

"LiLi, you good?" asked Treebie.

"Yeah, I'm straight," she said, taking another shot of Rémy to the head.

Treebie rose to her feet, walked over to where Lissha stood, and put a hand on her shoulder. "Regardless of what may go on in our personal lives, we in this shit together."

"I know," Lissha said, making eye contact with the one who was like her left arm. She knew that no matter what, Treebie would never cross her or fold up.

Treebie had a look in her eyes that mirrored the sign on her soul that read *kill or be killed*. "We almost ready?" she asked, looking around the room.

Bay put the clip in her Nine and said, "Hell yeah, I'm ready."

"Me too," announced Donella, picking up her pump shotgun with the rubber pistol grip handle.

Treebie looked at Lissha, who gave her a look that meant she didn't even have to ask. "I was born ready," Lissha replied click-clacking one in the chamber of her ratchet.

They all met at the counter where they performed the final part of their ritual: tight ponytails, fitted nylon hats pulled to their eyebrows, voice distorter, face mask, and lastly, the blood red contacts.

Pulling thick black hoodies over their heads, they raised their shot glasses. "We go in this muthafucka four and we come out four," Lissha gritted.

A clink of their glasses emphasized the vow. They downed their drinks, slammed their glasses on the counter, and headed for the door one behind the other.

The small one bedroom dilapidated house on 117th and St. Clair was rumored to be one of the biggest paying gambling spots in the city. The girls parked a few houses down and quickly got into position. Lissha and Donella crouched down by a set of garbage cans on the right side of the door. Treebie and Bayonna were crouched behind a set of bushes on the left side.

Treebie had done all of the foot work finding out that inside there would be two guards at the front door and one at the back, and as many as ten gamblers. All the men were very familiar with the other end of a trigger. These were street niggas true and through. The girls knew they had to go in quick, loud, and deadly.

Patiently they waited for their mark to arrive. It was funny how no matter how hard a team tried to fill their circle with strong rings you could always find a weak link.

When Treebie saw Lil' Bump coming up the walkway her blood rushed through her veins. She gnashed her teeth, gripped her gun, and slowly stepped from the shadows. "Bleed, if you make one country move I'll turn your mother's sweet dreams into nightmares," she growled.

"Fuck is this?" He instinctively moved his hand to his waist. Treebie raised the gun to his chest and his arms shot above his head. "Don't kill me, Cuz," he pled. *I'ma play along, but the second you slip I'ma push ya whole forehead back.* What he would soon find out was that slipping wasn't part of their get-down. Donella stepped out shoving her gun right in his spine. "You better cooperate then, or I'ma make you a muthafuckin' paraplegic," she muttered.

"I don't ha—"

"Shhh!" Treebie put her finger to her mouth, silencing him. Damn all that talking, time was valuable. They had to get in and out because *johnny* rolled by frequently in this hood.

"I need you to put your ugly ass face to that peek hole. You better not blink, yell or make the wrong move or your little sister Aniya, and your mother, Selena, will die a slow, agonizing death. Cooperate and they get released in an hour," said Treebie. She had the names right so Lil' Bump couldn't chance that it was a bluff, and the voice distorter made the threat come out very ominous.

Taking him by the back of the neck, Treebie pushed him to the door. There was fear in his heart and a big ass gun pressed to the base of his skull. Bayonna and Donella formed a line behind Treebie and Lissha took up the rear.

"Smile, muthafucka," Treebie ordered him.

Lil' Bump knocked on the door.

"Who is it?" a gruff voice asked from the other side.

"It's me, Cuz. Lil' Bump."

Treebie heard those locks click and her nipples hardened. As soon as the door opened a crack she shoved Lil' Bump forward and blasted a hole in his back, sending his insides all over the card tables.

The crew ran up in the house like body snatchers, changing the pulse of the whole operation. The two guards at the door reached for their bangers but their reaction was a second too slow. Bay and Lissha's guns popped off in sync. *Boc! Boc! Boc! Boc! Boc! Boc! Boc!* They put the two men down with a deadly burst of gunfire that let the others in the house know that they were not fucking around.

Donella dashed toward the back of the house, running into the man that had been guarding the back door. As he reached to his waist, she hit him with two shots in the head. He staggered back and his body slid down the wall leaving a streak of blood all the way to the floorboard.

Behind them Treebie slumped two at each table, then the girls positioned themselves around the room. Lissha closed the front door and put her back up against it.

"Put your muthafuckin' hands in the air," Treebie barked to the card players that still had their body parts intact. Slowly hands went up. Each man held a stone face as they searched their minds for a way to turn the tables.

"Y'all know what the fuck this is," Treebie shouted. Donella and Bayonna grabbed black cloth bags from their back pockets and threw them on the table.

"Do y'all know who you're fucking wit'? This ain't no street you walk baby nuts on. This 117th and muthafuckin' St. Clair. You gotta have big ass balls to run up in here," a young thug shouted from his seated position.

"Well, I must be in the right fucking place, because my shit grande," Treebie gritted and grabbed her crotch.

"Nigga, fuck you," yelled out a tall slender nigga. In a flash his hand went under the table. When it came up he had his whistle in his hand and he let off several shots. Two of them caught Bayonna in the chest and slammed her back against the wall. Her ratchet fell from her hands as she hit the floor, unconscious.

"Muthafucka!" screamed Treebie. She aimed her Glock at him and emptied the clip. His body jerked with each round that pierced through it and he slumped down to the floor bloody and crooked. Treebie zoned out, she was still squeezing the trigger after there was no more ammo in her gun and no more life in his body.

"You see that," screamed Lissha, using her gun to point at the dead bodies lying around the room. "Don't be the next muthafucka to get it." She held her whistle on the remaining men as Treebie snapped out of her zone and slammed a fresh, fully loaded clip in her piece.

Donella blasted a nigga on GP before bending down to check on Bayonna who was just regaining consciousness. Her bullet proof vest had saved her life but she was momentarily in shock. Her breathing was labored and her chest burned.

Bayonna gathered her wits, picked up her hammer and climbed to her feet. Methodically, she walked over to the dead man that had tried to murk her. Half of his face was blown off and his chest was opened up like a busted can of tomato paste. Bayonna stood over his corpse and showed it no respect. "Bitch ass nigga," she spat and pumped three in what remained of his head.

While this was going on the others kept their guns trained around the room in case another fool had big nuts. They eyed every one of them and were ready to place them in a church looking up at the roof if they so much as flinched.

"Everybody just chill," said a short dude with dreads. He was sitting in a chair away from the table, unshaken by the gore around him. His voice was level and his eyes were alert. Lissha looked at him and almost blew her disguise. It was gotdamn JuJu.

"Aw, fuck!" she muttered under her breath. Donella and Bayonna was thinking the same thing. Somebody had really dropped the ball. Treebie didn't give a flying fuck. JuJu could get it too.

"D-double, fill them bags up," he ordered his runner from his reclined position.

"Do that shit slow muthafucka," Donella yelled out with her pump tight in her grip and his head sharp in her sight.

D-double, JuJu's lieutenant, jumped up and went over to the stash spot and filled the bags then dragged them over to Donella and Bayonna's feet. On his way back to the table he accidently bumped into Treebie. Donella and Bayonna cut his ass down, swiftly and without mercy.

"Clumsy ass muthafucka," snorted Bayonna. She was blood thirsty now.

With their friends' bodies dropping all around them, two other dudes decided not to sit there awaiting their executions. They silently communicated with each other with their eyes, then tried to get up and reach for their guns. In the process they knocked over the card table to create a distraction, but they were fucking with stone cold killahs that were trained to go.

Lissha's trigger finger went crazy, she hit one of the men in the chest with five successive shots. Donella's pump made carnage of the other brave heart. "Y'all niggas still think it's a game?" she barked.

Silence filled the room as the remaining three men held their lips tight with contempt. Bayonna glanced at Lissha who gave her a slight nod. She grabbed the two bags and pulled them to Lissha's feet. Lissha gave a second nod and Donella hit one dude and Bayonna hit the other leaving JuJu as the one to tell the tale.

Treebie moved over to JuJu and put her gun to his mouth. "If you gonna kill me, Bleed, handle your business, but I damn sure ain't gonna bitch up," he said in a voice that didn't tremble.

"Is it worth trying to be tough over the next nigga shit?" She stood ready to air his ass out.

"It's all good because this shit right here comes with the life I signed up for. But I promise you, my nigga will find you. And when he do, he's gonna give pain a whole new meaning."

"Oh, so you're somebody's right-hand man?"

"Fuck you."

"Nigga, you a bitch. Open your mouth so you can suck my dick like you sucking his," Treebie gritted as distasteful thoughts of Kiam filled her mind.

"Bleed, you got the game fucked up. I'm not opening up shit. You gonna have to knock my fucking teeth out."

"Oh yeah?" Treebie forced her gun into his mouth almost pushing it to the back of his throat.

JuJu winced and gagged but he didn't fold. Lissha was wondering what Treebie was about to do. JuJu was on *their* team. *This bitch done lost it.* Lissha silently looked on.

"Get this muthafucka down," Treebie ordered. Bayonna walked over and grabbed him around the neck restricting his breathing. His eyes glistened as his airway tightened. Blood and fragments of teeth slid on his tongue and settled on both sides of the barrel.

"Get this nigga secure," commanded Treebie, running out of patience. If the gunshots had been heard, johnny could be on the way.

Donella moved fast. She pulled out a roll of duct tape and strapped JuJu tightly to the chair. Treebie continued to run the show. "Grab this nigga's hand," she barked.

Donella grabbed his wrist and forced him to hold his hand out. Lissha looked on as poor JuJu suffered at the hands of her crew. She felt some kind of way because he went hard for the team, but there was no pulling back now.

Treebie looked down at JuJu from up under her disguise. "I bet when you woke up this morning you never envisioned this shit, huh?" she taunted him.

JuJu said nothing, he couldn't see their faces so he studied their mannerisms, anything that would help him hunt them down later. There was something peculiar about the way they walked and moved. He filed that in his memory.

"I almost gave you a pass," Treebie went on. "But since you work for a bitch, the penalty is misery." She pulled the gun from his mouth, grabbed his right wrist and blew a hole straight through the palm of his hand.

One foot reactively slammed against the floor as he yelped out in pain, "Shit." His lips quaked as his adrenaline coursed through his veins, settling his trembling body to a slower vibration.

"Now you can be his *left hand* man," snickered Treebie.

Bayonna grabbed a bill from her pocket and shoved it in JuJu's bloody palm, closing his fist around it. Pain shot up his arm and sweat dripped from his collar. Valiantly, he did not scream out in pain or beg for mercy.

Removing the bloody bill from his hand and stuffing it in his mouth, Bayonna said, "Tell your bitch ass boss man that Blood Money said thank you."

Treebie stepped forward and toppled the chair over. Juju's head cracked against the floor.

Carefully, with their heads on a swivel watching for any sign of the police, they moved out the door and to the car.

When they walked into Treebie's basement. Lissha began snatching her clothes off. "Shit! Why the fuck didn't we know that was Kiam's spot?" she asked, resting her hands on the counter.

"I don't know, we checked everything out just as we always do," Donella responded as she pulled her hood over her head.

Bayonna pulled off her hoodie and vest and examined her chest. It was bruised and sore.

"Man, this shit is fucked up," Lissha said.

"Why? Because you got feelings for the nigga?" Treebie shot some shade in her direction.

"Bitch don't play with me. We done fucked around and robbed ourselves. You don't see a problem with that?"

"You don't see a problem with the fact that Kiam got shit going on behind your back. Big Zo supposed to know everything that nigga doing." Treebie looked at her, waiting for a comeback. When Lissha didn't retort, she smiled. "Yeah, that's what I thought." She proceeded to take her off her gear.

"It don't matter, knowing whose spots we're hitting is your fucking job. Now we gonna have Kiam's crazy ass on our heels."

"If you mention that muthafucka's name one more time," Treebie said, gnashing her teeth.

"You issuing threats, bitch?" Lissha came from behind the counter.

"Don't fucking test me." Treebie stood firm, looking into Lissha's red eyes.

"Test you?" Lissha threw back at her. "Bitch, I'll *bless* your muthafuckin' ass, that's what I'll do." She stepped in Treebie's grill.

"Bitch, don't get your shit pushed back." Treebie stuck her finger in Lissha's mug.

Lissha slapped it down.

Donella ran over and stepped between them. "I'm not letting y'all do this shit. We ride together not *against* one another." She pulled Treebie back a step.

Lissha was still spazzing. "She fucked up, plain and simple. Now I gotta fix this shit." She blew out an exasperated breath.

"Bitch, you ain't in this shit by yourself. You worrying about what that punk ass nigga got to say and Bay almost lost her fucking life," Treebie yelled as she pointed over to Bayonna. "Look at her! She over there fucked up. You holla out that 'go in four' shit, well tonight we almost came out as three. Burn that shit in your mind."

Lissha looked over at Bayonna and the severity of the evening began to feel heavy on her heart. She took a deep breath and sat on the couch to gather her thoughts. "We gotta cover every end of this shit," she calmly stated.

"No shit," Treebie said as she sat across from her.

When they locked gazes no more words were spoken. They knew they had to be smart and make sure that from now on they paid closer attention to detail. The also realized that now their relationship would be different. The trust had just taken a turn and it was only a matter of time before one of them would push the envelope. When that inevitable day came more than friendship would be lost.

While the girls disrobed and began putting their gear in black plastic bags, Lissha stood there thinking. She had to admit Treebie was right. Big Zo knew they were hitting spots. If Kiam had told him that he had his hand in gambling houses Big Zo would have told her to steer clear of those particular houses. So if Kiam hadn't told Big Zo about his gambling houses, what else was he doing on the low?

Lissha now wondered if Kiam was really loyal or if his allegiance had grown cold with the rise of the money and the power. She grabbed her phone and walked in the other room. When Big Zo picked up she unleashed the coded report and his icy silence confirmed that something definitely wasn't right.

Chapter 31
Good Times Never Last

Kiam was chilling in the passenger seat, listening to Eyez hum along with a Keyshia Cole song on the radio. She had volunteered to drive back and he hadn't refused. He looked over at his baby and smiled; she was still radiant from their weekend retreat.

She reached over and held his hand. "I really enjoyed this weekend," she said sincerely.

"Me too, baby. We have to do it again real soon, something about being up in the woods brought the freak out of you," he teased.

"I'm always your little freak." She released his hand and slid hers between his legs and grabbed a handful of dick .

"A'ight, mess around and make me give it to you on the shoulder of the highway," Kiam warned.

"Give me some of that back woods *wood*," she replied stroking him. "You can't hang."

"You feel my little nigga, don't you? He hard body." He looked over at her.

"Yes he is. All swole up and ready to take a chick down through there."

"Pull over." It was dark outside plus the windows were tinted. He was game for a quickie.

"I'm not messing with you, Kiam, you already got me walking sideways." She giggled and removed her hand from off that steel before she became tempted to pull over and ride it.

Kiam was looking over at her to see if she was really game but the kitty was sore from all that good lovin' he had put on her. "Look at who can't hang," he boasted.

"Be quiet, baby." She cheesed and reached over and play-punched him on the shoulder.

"For real though, ma, I really enjoyed this weekend. A nigga could get used to that."

"Yesssss," she sang, savoring the memories. She didn't want the weekend to come to an end. To wake up in his arms and receive all of his attention had her floating.

Faydrah glanced down at the engagement ring on her finger and prayed that the fairytale would last forever. All she had ever wanted was to be his wife. The diamond on her finger was his promise to make her wish come true.

Halfway back to the city Kiam decided to get his cell phone out of the compartment between the seats and check his messages. They had turned their cell phones off and left them in the truck the entire weekend so that they could focus entirely on each other.

As Faydrah steered into the fast lane, passing a slow moving Suburban, Kiam powered up his phone and saw a half dozen text messages from JuJu and several voicemail notifications. A line creased his forehead, something had to be wrong. He didn't bother opening the text messages or listening to the voicemails, instead he called JuJu's cellphone.

"Man, I've been trying to reach you since Friday night," JuJu said as soon as he answered. Kiam could tell from the tone of his voice that something serious had taken place.

"What happened?" he asked.

"Niggas ran up in the gambling spot on 117th and St. Clair."

"Who ran up in there, undies?" asked Kiam, referring to the vice squad.

"Nah, it was those Blood Money niggas. Man, they killed everybody in the house, and they took all the spread. Something like a hundred racks."

Kiam's face hardened. "Fuck the money. They killed D-double?"

"Yeah, man, the homie gone," he sadly confirmed." And Lil' Bump too. Bruh, that bitch ass nigga got them in the door."

Kiam's blood boiled as he listened to JuJu give him a full report of the robbery. When JuJu told him what they did to *him*, his whole face washed over in anger. He didn't know who in the fuck the Blood Money crew was but he was gonna kick down every door in the city until he found them. Then he was gonna execute them without trial or jury.

When Kiam hung up the phone Faydrah looked at him out the corner of her eye. She had clearly heard his end of the conversation and she recognized the expression on his face. This was the reason she wanted him to leave the streets. She didn't give a damn about street principles, revenge, and loyalty to people who weren't loyal to themselves. She just wanted him to be around to love her and not wind up back in prison or lying on a cold slab at the Coroner's. That's all she cared about.

Kiam was quiet, which she knew meant somebody was going to die real soon, he was just calculating his moves. Steaming inside, she got off at the next exit. Kiam looked at the gas needle and saw that the tank was three-quarters full. "What you doing, ma?" he asked suspiciously.

"I'm turning around and going back to the resort. I am not letting you do what's on your mind."

"No the fuck you not," he growled.

"Yes the fuck I am."

Kiam reached for the steering wheel and yanked it. Faydrah slammed on brakes barely avoiding crashing head on into a passing vehicle. Her heart was beating fast and her hands trembled. She threw the truck in park and snapped her head around toward Kiam, glaring at him. "What the fuck is wrong with you?" she screamed. "You almost got us killed. Is the streets that fucking important to you." Tears formulated.

"Don't fuck with me right now, shorty," he warned her. He hopped out the truck and stormed around to the driver's side.

Faydrah got out but she sure wasn't getting back in. She took off up the dark four lane road on foot.

Kiam pulled up alongside of her and rolled down the window. "Girl, get your ass in the truck," he ordered.

"Fuck you. You can have the streets." She quickened her pace to a sprint.

"I don't need this shit right now," Kiam fumed as he sped up and caught up to her again. He put the truck in park and hopped out.

Faydrah felt Kiam's fingers brush against her back in an effort to catch her and she kicked into a full gear run. By the time Kiam ran her down he was out of breath and not in the mood for anymore of her shit. He snatched her up, threw her over his shoulder. Faydrah squirmed around. "Put me down," she cried.

Kiam ignored her theatrics, and carried her back to where he had left the truck. He strapped her in the passenger seat and slammed the door. "Play with this shit if you want to," he warned.

Faydrah sat there with her arms folded across her chest as he climbed back behind the wheel. Kiam took off doing ninety all the way back. Neither of them said a word to each other the rest of the drive home.

As soon as they pulled up at her place, Faydrah was out the truck before it came to a complete stop. She ran inside her apartment and slammed the door, locking Kiam out.

With her back against the door and her heart aching, she waited for him to bang on the door and tell her that he had changed his mind, he was not going to seek revenge on anyone. But the only sounds Faydrah heard were his squealing tires and her own sobs. She snatched the door back open to call out to him, but all she saw was fading taillights. Distraught, she closed the door and walked up to her bedroom, wiping at the tears that ran down her face. She fell across her bed then slid to her knees.

Dear God, I only ask that you protect him and those that he encounter tonight. Watch over him Lord, and please hear my prayer.

Ca$h & NeNe Capri

Chapter 32
Beast Mode

Kiam blocked out Faydrah's emotions, this was not the time for him to be affected by her tears. The only wet faces he wanted to see were those of the family members of the niggas that called themselves Blood Money and flaunted that shit like they couldn't be touched.

His knuckles were white as he gripped the steering wheel and drove through the city with that toe-tag shit on his mental.

One of JuJu's bout it chicks let Kiam in as soon as he knocked. Juju was in his bedroom, sitting on the edge of the bed with an arsenal of weapons at his feet. His mouth was hideously swollen and his right hand was heavily bandaged. Pain medication had him drowsy, but none of that diminished his gangsta, he was ready to ride.

"They handled me like I was a ho. But they fucked up when they didn't kill me. On my hood, I'ma body every one of them when I find 'em," he vowed. The heat in his eyes was intense enough to set the room ablaze.

Kiam laid a hand on JuJu's shoulder and spoke in a low tone so that the girl out in the living room couldn't hear him. "Don't worry, they're gonna die for what they did to you. And it's gonna be painful and slow."

"I'm ready to ride," JuJu said. *Tonight.*

"I know you are, lil' homie, but fall back for a minute and let me collect some Intel on these niggas, then we'll ride. Now tell me everything you can remember about those Blood Money boys, no detail is too small."

Leaving JuJu's place a half hour later Kiam went over to Lissha's. It was past midnight but he didn't care about the time, murder never sleeps. Muthafuckas had tested the crew's get-down on his watch and that shit was unpardonable.

Lissha came to the door wearing a long t-shirt and wiping sleep from her eyes. She looked in his face and saw the blazing heat behind his pupils. He brushed right past her and headed to her living room.

Lissha closed the front door and followed. She already knew why he was there, but she was nervous about how much he had been able to find out. She quickly replayed the events of Friday night in her head. Had they done anything that may have given their identities away? Lissha tried to recall.

Kiam flicked on the light and sat down on the sofa. "Have a seat," he said. Lissha studied his face before complying. Three lines creased his forehead and his jaw twitched.

This muthafucka hotter than fish grease. Damn, Treebie fucked up and now I'm left to face the music if he knows. Lissha instantly regretted answering the door without her strap. Now she had to use guile, act like she normally would with him, and deny all accusations.

"What the fuck is going on, Kiam? Why are you barging in my shit at one o'clock in the morning bossing me around?" she hurled.

He ignored her question and his look hardened even more. "What do you know about Blood Money?"

Lissha swallowed nervously. "Um, I heard of them, they're a stickup crew. Why?" She dummied up.

"Is that all the fuck you can tell me? Do you know who any of them niggas are?"

"No. All I know is that they have a lot of hustlers shook. Why are you asking about Blood Money, did something happen?" She had recovered her poise, it was evident he didn't know shit.

Kiam told her what had happened.

"Wait a minute. When the fuck did *we* get into the gambling business? You doing shit behind me and Daddy's backs now?" she asked, deflecting his attention off Blood Money.

"Fuck you talking to? I'm doing what the fuck I do. And as long as the money is proper you just play your position. I don't answer to no fuckin' body. Big Zo knows my get-down, I'm a loyal nigga, that's why he chose me to run this. Now get your panties out your ass and do something constructive, like tell me anything you can to help me find out who Blood Money is. That's what the fuck you do."

Lissha stood up and smoothed her t-shirt down over her brown thighs. "Since you're so power struck find them yourself. I'm going back to bed. Don't let the door hit you in your ass too hard on your way out."

When she turned to head back to her bedroom, Kiam sprung up off the couch, snatched her by both arms, and spun her around to face him. Instinctively Lissha fixed her mouth to snap, but Kiam went there first.

"Look," he snarled, "this is not the time for your slick ass mouth. Money and lives got took tonight. From this point on, the games stop. Get that through your head or I'ma force it inside that muthafucka. Now take your ass to bed and wake up with a brand new attitude." He shoved her toward the bedroom and walked out the door.

After she heard Kiam drive off, Lissha grabbed her phone off the dresser and hurriedly got Treebie, Donella, and Bayonna together on a conference call. It was imperative that everyone understand that Kiam was on a warpath and there could be no more slip-ups. "That muthafucka is boiling," Lissha kept saying.

"You told us that five times already. Damn bitch, if you scared increase your insurance policy," said Treebie.

"Fuck you," Lissha replied.

The ladies argued back and forth about what, if anything, should be done to thwart all efforts of Kiam's to find out who Blood Money were.

"If he gets too close I'ma put him in the dirt," said Treebie.

Chapter 33
A Gangsta's Reaction

Kiam had been turning the city inside out searching for the identities of Blood Money. He offered fifty bands for each of their names but so far no one had exposed the crew.

JuJu was chomping at the bit to get his revenge; he had bought a Tommy gun and a brand new AK-47 with a Larry Bird *extenzo*—thirty three shots. How he was going to shoot either weapon with one hand, Kiam wasn't sure, but he respected his G.

As he headed downtown to a sport's bar to meet with Frank Nitti, Kiam's cellphone rang. He answered the call without identifying the caller. "Bitch nigga, you don't look for Blood Money, we look for you," The caller said then line went dead.

Kiam stared at the blank screen. As he suspected, the call came from a restricted number but he knew that it was authentic because the caller had sounded like he was talking into a wind tunnel or some type of voice distortion device like the one JuJu had described. Whoever Blood Money was, they had just made their first mistake.

Kiam knew that he had them worried, otherwise they wouldn't have made the call. They would have just struck. They were killahs, no doubt, so what was it they made them fear him? He pondered.

He knew that if he found the answer to that question it would reveal their identities.

A half hour later Kiam sat across from Frank Nitti.

Nitti used his steak knife to cut a piece of the rib eye in front of him. "I'm hearing your name loud in the streets," he said, chewing and flashing a fake smile that couldn't hide the envy that was underneath it.

"You must be listening too hard, fam," shot Kiam who was not one to mince words.

"Bruh, you know the streets talk. I hear that Schizophrenic got the whole Eastside jumping. They tell me you got the work for the low, still in the casket. And you got shit sewed up from Miles to Hough, all the way out to EC. You came home and hit the ground running, didn't you?"

"What's your point, homie? You a groupie or something?"

"Nah, nigga, you know better than that," Nitti sat the knife and fork down, pushed his plate back, and sneered at Kiam.

"Get the fuck off my dick and get to the point, then." Kiam's hand slid under the table just in case Nitti didn't let the disrespect pass.

Nitti peeped the move and let his own hands remain on top off the table, palms down. "Damn, Bleed, we go way back. What did I ever do to you to make you come at me like that?"

"Number one, let's not pretend we're close or nothing. Just like you, I haven't forgot about our run in back in the day."

Nitti recalled their old beef as one he still wanted to settle. *Keep your friends close and your enemies closer.* That was how he played the game. "Fam, I let the past stay in the past. Why you think I hit you up? Fuck the bullshit, nigga, it's all about the paper and I hear you're locking shit down these days."

"That's neither here nor there, Bleed. But why you wasting my time reading me my own resume? I already know what the fuck I've done, 'cause I'm the muthafucka that did it. Just say what's on your mind. Time is money." Kiam had did his homework since running into Nitti at the Sunoco station. He knew who the nigga rolled with.

"A'ight. Long story short, you're stepping on toes. And the toes you stepping on are attached to some big ass feet. You ever heard the name Wolfman?"

"Long story short," Kiam reminded him.

Nitti finally got to the point. Kiam listened as he explained Wolfman's offer. When Nitti was done, Kiam chuckled. "Do I look like a worker to you?"

"Don't be arrogant, man. You don't wanna fuck with a nigga like Wolfman," warned Nitti. "Just think about the offer."

"Yeah, a'ight. I'ma think about it and get back wit' you." Kiam stood up, preparing to leave. He looked down at Nitti whose hands were now folded on the table in front of his plate. Kiam chuckled again. In one swift motion he snatched the steak knife and brought it down with force, plunging it straight through Nitti's hand and pinning it to the table.

"I thought about it, Bleed, and that's my muthafuckin' answer."

Chapter 35
Time Is Up

Treebie moved up her walkway juggling bags and her cellphone, trying to retrieve her keys. She fumbled with the locks while listening to Lissha angrily insist that a meeting was needed as soon as possible.

"What the fuck happened now?" Treebie was rushing, they had to leave in an hour to make the pickup from Riz's people.

"Bitch, I don't want to talk about it on the phone, meet me at the Winking Lizard out in Independence."

"Way out there!" Treebie held the phone with her shoulder as she slid the door key in the lock.

"Yeah, way the fuck out there," Lissha said.

Treebie stepped inside her house and almost fainted. Wa'leek was sitting in her living room with his arms rested on the back of the couch and a look on his face that said he was ready for a war. "Oh shit, let me call you back." Treebie dropped her bags and ended the call over Lissha's heated protest.

Wa'leek was eyeing her like a hawk.

"What you doing here?" she asked, laying her phone on the counter and frowning at him.

"What did we agree on?"

"Wa'leek I told you, I need time."

"Well, times up. When I leave this city, you're coming with me."

"That's not happening."

"It's already in motion." He stood up wearing all black, heading in her direction.

"Baby, please. I have something I have to do first," she maintained.

"Yeah I know, pack. Get ya shit together and be ready to roll and none of this shit is up for discussion. I'm about to shake this whole muthafuckin' city up." He peered through those gray eyes and her heart sank to her toes.

Wa'leek turned to walk to the door and Treebie grabbed his arm. "Wah, please. I got a lot of shit on the line."

He turned back around and locked eyes with her. "Like what, running to get that pussy ass nigga's shit from way out in fuckin' PA?" His revelation made her very quiet and confirmed her worse fear, Wa'leek was back in contact with Riz. But what all had he told him.

"Yeah, shocked the shit outta you with that one. I had a sit down with my boy."

"Why the fuck are you going behind my back and getting in the middle of this? This ain't got shit to do with you." She began heating up.

"What the fuck is you talking about? If it involves you then it involves me."

"I'm fucking grown, I don't need your approval, I'ma do me and I suggest you do you. Please stay the fuck out of my business. And for the record, I ain't going nowhere with you." She stood breathing fire.

Wa'leek moved closer to her. Only an inch remained between them. "When I get finished with these muthafuckas, it ain't going to be shit to stay for. I'm giving you an out. Because I promise you this, I never show mercy to my enemies. I love you, but please don't fuck around and make yourself a problem I have to solve," he calmly warned.

Treebie took a half step back. "Why are you doing this to me?"

"Why the fuck are you doing this to yourself? You act like you owe this bitch. You don't owe her shit," he boomed, causing her to jump.

"It's not about owing her, I gave her my word." Treebie's voice sounded feeble under his attack.

"Did she give you hers?" he challenged.

270

Treebie got quiet.

Wa'leek pounced. "Let me ask you something, and I want you to weigh the question real good. Why is it that Lissha don't go on the pickups? You don't think that shit is a little foul that she gets to sit home blowing Gator while you out there risking your fucking life and freedom?"

Again Treebie didn't respond.

"Yeah, toss that shit around for a little while." He turned and walked toward the door. "I'll be back in a little while so start getting your shit together," he ordered then rolled out.

Treebie walked to the counter and grabbed a glass and a bottle of 1800 and poured herself a drink. As she downed it Wa'leek's words played back in her mind. She hadn't looked at it in that way. But now it was crystal clear. Lissha and Big Zo weren't taking any of the risk but collecting all the dough.

Treebie's phone started ringing, interrupting her thoughts. When she looked down at the screen it was Lissha. "What's up?" she answered, feeling some kind of way.

"What the fuck happened? You just hung up."

"Ain't nothin'."

"Are you on your way?"

"Yeah, I'll be there as soon as I can. I gotta throw my shit in the car."

"A'ight, see you in a few." Lissha hung up as she cruised through the streets worried about why Kiam wasn't answering his phone and what was going to happen if he found out who Blood Money was.

Treebie walked into her bedroom and gathered her road clothes and loaded her guns. Her mind was all over the place. They had to pick up later tonight. Lissha was all heated behind them hitting Kiam's spot. And now she had Wa'leek's crazy ass wandering around the city getting ready to make things worse than they already we're.

"Fuck it," she said out loud as she grabbed her bag, phone, and keys and headed to the door.

On the other side of town...

"Oh, shit! What's up, fam? What brings you to the Midwest?" Gator said with a semi smile as he opened the door for Wa'leek.

"You know how I do, never know where a nigga gonna show up next," replied Wa'leek as he passed Gator and walked right into his living room and took a seat on the coach.

Gator closed the door and followed suit, taking a seat across from him, "So what brings you this way?" Gator said, reaching over and grabbing his cigarette off of the cocktail table and lighting it up.

"Don't do that shit right now," Wa'leek ordered.

"Same old Leek," Gator said as he put it out and placed it in the ashtray.

"What the fuck is going on with this nigga Kiam?" Wa'leek went straight to the point.

"Man." Gator dragged the word out real slow as if he was considering how to respond. "That muthafucka done came out here and took the fuck over," he reported.

"On whose orders?" Wa'leek questioned him.

"Big Zo's."

"And you just let that shit happen?" Wa'leek raised an eyebrow.

"You know how Big Zo do." Gator sat forward and folded his hands, ready to get it all off his chest.

"Yeah I sure do. And I got four years behind the shit that he do."

"Well, he spent three years preparing that nigga to come out here and take the food off the very tables of the people that held shit together the whole time he been gone. That nigga Kiam killing everything that gets in his way.

272

"So what you gonna do, just sit there with your thumb up your ass or you gonna handle your business? What, your gun don't pop off no more?"

"You already know how I get down. I got some shit on the front burner and when that shit finish simmering it's on like a muthafucka."

Wa'leek stood up. "I hope so. I would hate to have to make this trip bloody." He turned to the door.

When his hand touched the knob, Wa'leek stopped and slowly turned back around to face Gator who was right behind him. "Oh, you might want to make sure you put some shit on the fire for Riz while you at it. He told that nigga one of your little secrets."

"What secret?" asked Gator.

Wa'leek smiled. "Happy hunting. I got my own rat to smoke out of a hole. Good luck." He turned the knob and walked out, slightly slamming the door behind him.

Gator returned to the living room, grabbed his cigarette, lit it up and began taking long hard pulls. He sat back down with his mind ran a mile a minute. If Riz had told Kiam what he thought he did, then Kiam had more than a head start. That wasn't good at all, in fact it was deadly.

Gator jumped up and grabbed his gun, tucking it in his back. He threw on his boots and left his apartment to head over to see Wolfman.

Wa'leek sat slouched in his rental car watching as Gator pulled out his driveway. "That was easier than I thought," he said to himself as he pulled off following Gator.

Chapter 34
One Thing after Another

As Kiam drove from one block to another, it was like he was seeing the city for the first time. The air was turning crisp as the leaves threatened to fall from the trees. The pulse of the city was idling at the moment, but at its heart was a thirst that needed to be quenched.

Behind the cloak of darkness that casted a shadow over the hoods, there were strong feelings of poverty, death and despair which seeped from every alley and crevice. The season was changing and Kiam was changing with it. It was the autumn of a new day, the whole way he dealt with muthafuckas from this point forward was going to change.

Kiam was in total beast mode, his temper was high and his patience was short. So much had gone on in the last couple of weeks that it had his mind and spirit in an uproar. The one thing he knew he definitely had to repair was his relationship with Eyez.

They had barely spoken since their argument on the way home from the retreat a week ago. Here it was the Eve of their new day and already he had managed to draw a wedge between them with the very things he promised her he wouldn't let tear them apart.

Hitting the Bluetooth in his truck he spoke out, "Call Eyez."

The voice command dialed her number and he waited to hear her voice flutter through his speakers. "Hello," her soft voice called back to him. Its sound was medicine to his soul.

"Hey you."

"Hey, baby, where are you?"

"I'm on my way to Bw3 on Mayfield. What you doing?"

"Laying here thinking about you," she admitted with a purr in her tone.

"Put on some clothes and come meet me."

Faydrah looked over at the clock on her nightstand. It was 10:15 and she had to be at work at six o'clock in the morning. She started to just tell him to come on over but she knew that they had things to rectify. If he came over she would sacrifice what really needed to be said to satisfy her yearning to have him in her bed.

She decided that it would be best for her to go to him. "Okay, let me get dressed, I'll see you in about thirty."

"A'ight, baby girl, drive safe. See you in a minute," Kiam said as he disconnected the call.

Faydrah rolled over and climbed out of bed, mentally and emotionally preparing herself to have this sit down with Kiam as she wiggled into her jeans.

Once in the car she took a deep breath, turned on the radio and cleared her mind.

Twenty minutes later, she pulled into the parking lot in her red Mustang convertible and parked next to Kiam's truck. Exiting the vehicle she straightened her shirt and hit the locks.

When Faydrah walked through the door Kiam stood up to greet her. Smiling, she walked right up to him and stepped into his arms. Kiam held her for several minutes, trying to comfort her weary mind and ease the tension between them. "Have a seat, ma," he said releasing her from his embrace.

Faydrah slid into the booth and Kiam slid in next to her, affectionately pressing his knees against hers. She smiled at the gesture, but the first few seconds were filled with a pregnant silence as she fidgeted with her keys.

"I'm sorry," they both said at the same time.

"Don't be trying to steal my lines," Kiam smoothly stated, taking her hand into his and bringing it to his lips. "I missed you, Eyez," he confessed.

"Kiam, what are we doing?" she asked as she connected her pretty brown eyes with his.

"I love you, that's what *I'm* doing. I know what it is to have you, and I know what it is to be without you, and that's not even an option. No matter how hard I search, I would never find another woman like you. Hurting or losing you is never my intent."

Faydrah listened and blinked back tears.

Kiam went on, staring deep into the windows of her soul. "I made a promise to a very solid man who has given me all that he has left. That man became like a father to me when I was behind the wall. What happened the other night was a direct threat to some things that I'm doing for him so I gotta handle it. All I'm asking is that you don't ask me to let him down. Just let me see this mission through." He begged of her to understand.

Faydrah *overstood*. She knew that with men like hers it was loyalty or death, but too often it was both. "Baby, you don't have to see this shit through." She bit down on her lip to quell the anger that bubbled in her soul every time she thought about what the game did to those that refused to walk away.

"This ain't you anymore, Kiam. All your life you have been taking on missions to save everyone else. But who is going to save you?" She rested her hand on his chest.

Kiam got quiet.

"I understand your need to rule; you're built like that. But baby, these niggas out here have changed. Eight years have passed since you were out here, and with each passing year the game has become grimier. Ain't no code anymore." She paused to swallow some of the emotions that fought to spill out. Kiam looked in her eyes and saw her deep concern for him.

"These niggas don't respect nothing," she continued in a voice that was on the verge of breaking with each word uttered. "I don't want you to be the next man's badge of honor." Her eyes became teary as the thought of him laying in some gutter on a dark street flooded her mind.

Kiam put a reassuring hand on top of hers. "I know, ma, and that's why I'm not sleeping on these fools. Just hold me down until I do what I gotta do, then I'm out. Please, Eyez, I need you."

That was the one proclamation she could not ignore. Her heart just wouldn't allow her to deny him what he needed. Faydrah put her hands on the back of his head and pulled him to her. She kissed him gently on the lips, then pulled back holding his face between her hands and surrendering to his plea. "I'm not going anywhere. But please don't force me to live without you,"

"You have my word. I'ma do everything within my power not to let that happen."

"You better do what you gotta do, and I mean that," she reinforced, then the corners of her mouth turned up again.

Kiam smiled back at her.

She lifted her hand up and flashed her jewelry. "Now that you done put a ring on it, you owe me some t*ill death do us part*. And I want that to be when we can't tell whose teeth is whose in the little cups on the sink."

Kiam chuckled. "You crazy."

"Yup, and that's why you love me." She stuck her tongue out at him teasingly. It was amazing how quickly he could take her frown and turn it upside down.

"Forever, baby." He leaned in to kiss her again.

"You better know it." She savored the feel of his lips against hers.

Kiam stole another sweet kiss. When their lips parted Faydrah asked, "Where is that waitress? I done got hungry messing with you in the middle of the night."

Kiam looked around then flagged the waitress.

After the last wing vanished, they sat and talked and laughed until Faydrah realized that she had better take her butt home and get some sleep.

"You know I still didn't get my fix," Kiam reminded her as he opened her car door for her.

"You been fucking these streets so hard, you forgot that you had something hot and wet waiting on you," she replied, twisting her lips.

"You talk a lot of shit."

"And I can back it up."

"I got something you can back up *on*," he boasted as the thought of getting up behind that fat ass and making her submit hardened his dick.

"Let's see if your punk ass Cadillac can beat my four horses to the house." She tapped the roof of her car and looked over at his truck.

"You ain't taking about shit." Kiam got a little charged up.

"Well, let's go." Faydrah threw down the challenge.

"A'ight, it's on." Kiam put his fist out and Faydrah hit it. He nodded in agreement then turned to get in his truck.

Out the corner if his eye he noticed a black Cutlass creeping toward them with its headlights turned off. Inside the vehicle were evil eyes and faces half-covered with bandanas. "Eyez get down!" Kiam barked and shoved her to the ground just as loud gunshots erupted from inside the Cutlass.

Faydrah screamed as her elbows scraped the pavement and bullets pelted all around them. Kiam covered her body with his and hurriedly snatched his banger off his waist. When he brought it up, his Nine barked back loud. Boc! Boc! Boc! Boc!

Fearing for Faydrah's safety, he pounced back up on his feet and swiftly moved away from her. The shots from his assailants' guns whizzed by his head as he dashed behind his truck, crouched down and busting back at them over the hood.

Faydrah's screams pierced through the rapid gunshots that clapped in the quietness of the night. Kiam rose up and got hit with two up high. He stumbled back against a car that was parked beside his truck. Heat exploded in his body and hot blood poured from the wounds, but he refused to go down.

Fuck death, I don't fear that shit. If this was how it was written, well, bring that shit on! Either way, he wasn't dying with bullets still in his clip. He was bout to show them why niggas in the streets called guns whistles.

With his left arm rendered immobile and hanging limp at his side, Kiam pulled himself upright and raised the Nine in his right hand. "This what the fuck y'all want!" he yelled out, death-struck. Then he sparked up the night.

Bullets whistled through the air and tattered holes in the side of the Cutlass. The gunmen blasted back, then zoomed away, tires screaming.

Kiam staggered around the front of the Escalade, barely able to hold himself up. He was losing a lot of blood and he felt weak. "Eyez! Baby, where you at?" he called out.

"Kiam!" She was on her feet running toward him. Crying and babbling incoherently. She had feared that he'd been killed.

Kiam winced from the pain in his shoulder when she ran into his arms and sobbed against his chest. Sticky wet blood coated her forehead. "Oh my God!" she cried, realizing that he had been shot.

Kiam blocked out the pain when he heard the sirens heading their way. His head was beginning to feel light but he had to think fast. He was a convicted felon. If the Jakes caught him with a tool he was going back to the feds.

"Faydrah," he groaned loudly, cutting through her emotions. "Take this and get out of here!" He handed her the Nine.

Faydrah understood. She took the gun, hurried back to her car, and got in the wind.

As soon as she pulled off Kiam slumped to the ground and lost consciousness.

Chapter 35
Enough Is Enough

Faydrah sat up in Kiam's bed and stretched her tired limbs. With one hand covering her mouth to stifle back a yarn, she looked over at the empty spot next to her. Last night was the first night in almost two weeks that she had a chance to in a bed and her body was relieved for the much needed rest.

She slung her feet over the side of the bed and walked slowly to the bathroom, moving like an old lady. Her body was still very sore from the close brush with death, and sleeping in a chair next to Kiam's hospital bed night after night only made it worse.

She looked long and hard in the mirror at the evidence of the pain and confusion she had been going through since that night. Bags were beginning to form under her eyes and worry lines seemed to be etched into her forehead. Beyond that, her soul was in total turmoil. Kiam was alive and for that she was grateful, but with all the police attention and having to look over her shoulder, a part of her wished that she had left the past in the past.

Pouring facial scrub in her hands, she brought them to her face and tried to wash away some of the restlessness that wore thick around her eyes. After brushing her teeth, she hopped in the shower in an effort to mentally prepare herself to go back to the hospital.

A fresh shower gave her renewed energy. Humming a happy tune, Faydrah threw on some leggings and a t-shirt and a pair of sneakers. Quickly checking some emails she downloaded some files then packed her briefcase. She was thankful that she had some vacation time so she could look after her man.

As she drove to Hillcrest Hospital to see Kiam, she called in to a restaurant and ordered them some food. When she stopped at a red light she looked down at her engagement ring and suddenly found herself crying. Kiam was her everything and within a split second she had almost lost him.

Faydrah decided that as soon as he got home they were going to have a very serious conversation. Things had to change because the one thing she was not prepared to do was bury the only man that she had ever loved.

When the light turned green, she was still sitting there thinking. A horn honked behind her, drawing her mind back to where she was headed. She drove on, stopped to pick up the food she had ordered, then proceeded on to Hillcrest.

Faydrah walked into the hospital speaking to the receptionist and a few workers that she had grown familiar with over the last week. Exciting the elevator and reaching Kiam's door she became alarmed when she saw that it was closed. Her heart thumped wildly against her chest as fear grabbed ahold of her. Could Kiam's condition have taken a tragic turn since she left the hospital last night? She wondered nervously.

Pushing the door open slightly, she held her breath and peeked through the crack. There was no white sheet covering his head and the bed wasn't empty. Faydrah let out a huge sigh of relief. Of course her baby was okay.

Her eyes widened when she saw the two females from Kiam's crew. *Bang!* She swung the door open causing it to hit the wall and moved swiftly past the women and to Kiam's bedside.

Sitting the food on the tray and her briefcase on the side of the chair, she stood up and looked at Kiam with her head to the side.

Treebie and Lissha were silent waiting on Kiam's lead.

"What are you doing, you're supposed to be resting?" Faydrah asked with her lips drawn tight in a straight line.

"Baby, you know I have to take care of my business," he humbly stated.

"Fuck all that. You need to be concerned with getting better. Those streets and the trash that they produce will still be there when you get out." She looked over at Lissha.

"The streets? Bitch, ain't that where he found *you*?" Lissha piped up.

"Yup, and this street bitch got pussy worth claiming." She held up her hand. "But you wouldn't know anything about that, you got that spend the night pussy."

"Bitch, don't get fucked up," Lissha clacked, balling up her fist.

"Struck a nerve." Faydrah leaned in.

"Fuck you," Lissha spat, feeling herself about to leap on Faydrah's ass.

"No, fuck you."

"Both of y'all, shut the fuck up!" Kiam yelled out, wincing in pain.

"I guess ain't nothing wrong with his balls," Treebie cracked.

Kiam shot her a fierce look.

"My bad," she said, holding her hands up in surrender.

Kiam jerked his head back toward Faydrah. "Eyez, sit down."

She looked down at him and folded her arms.

"Don't make me repeat myself," he growled.

Faydrah looked at him with low eyes and flared nostrils and sat in the chair by his bed.

Kiam trained his eyes on the most hard-headed one in the room. Speaking in a low but stern tone, he said. "Lissha, don't disrespect my woman. You give her the same respect you give me."

"Your *woman*? You better make that bitch respect me." Lissha was hotter than a stolen pistol.

"Bitch, if you want respect you better give it," Faydrah cut back in, springing up out of her chair.

"Sit down!" Kiam ordered.

"No, fuck that. This bitch can get it. I'm tired of all this shit. Your fucked up promise to her father got you in all this bullshit."

"Bitch, you better watch your mouth," Lissha exploded. "Say one more thing about Daddy and I'll take your fucking life." She moved toward Faydrah with hot aggression.

Treebie's arm shot out, restraining her. "No, sis," she said. Leaning closer so that only Lissha could hear her, she whispered, "Always move in silence."

Faydrah was ready to move some furniture. "Bitch, you ain't the only one with bullets," she spat, moving closer to where they stood.

Lissha snapped open her bag and reached inside. "Not now," Treebie said, looking into Lissha's eyes.

"Fuck her. I'll knock her fucking head off." Faydrah continued to rail.

"I swear to God, if I gotta get the fuck up all y'all gonna regret the day y'all met me," Kiam said through gritted teeth.

"I already do," remarked Treebie. "Let's go, Li Li."

"No, y'all can stay. Because I'm done. I'm not doing this shit," Faydrah said, seething inside.

"What?" Kiam boomed.

"You heard me. Let this bitch take care of you." Faydrah turned to grab her bag.

"Eyez." He reached out for her but was restricted by his pain.

Snatching away, she tried to catch the tears that pushed at the corners of her eyes but it was too late. "No, Kiam, I cannot do this."

Kiam was about to apologize but she cut him off. "You want these streets? You can have 'em. But I can't be a part of it," she stated with conviction.

Kiam looked up at her with regret as she slid his ring off her finger and sat it on the bottom of the bed. "You remember this, the very muthafuckas you're loyal to ain't gonna be loyal to you." She walked past Lissha and Treebie. "Go ahead, lead him to his grave—that's what y'all want to do anyway." She purposely bumped up against Lissha on her way out the door.

Lissha stared at Faydrah's back and put her name on her hit list.

Kiam was past heated. He rubbed his hands over his face and thought carefully for a minute before rendering his verdict. Just as he was about to let Lissha have it, his phone went off. He looked down and recognized Riz's number flashing on the screen. "Yeah, what's up?" he answered.

"Nigga, you think I'm the one to test?! I promise you, you won't get away with that shit," Riz blared.

"Hold up! What the fuck are you talking about?" Kiam was lost.

"Nigga, you know what the fuck I'm talking about," Riz accused then went on to explain his anger. Curse word after curse word assaulted Kiam's ear.

Kiam was too shocked by what he was being accused of to go back off on Riz.

Lissha and Treebie watched as the vein in the middle of Kiam's temple got thicker. They could hear Riz yelling through the phone. Then silence. Riz had hung up. Lissha and Treebie looked at each questioningly.

Kiam was breathing heavier and heavier, trying to figure out what the fuck had gone wrong. "Muthafucka!" he yelled out then slung the phone across the room.

Kiam snatched tubes from his body and jumped up out of bed. He walked to the bathroom then grabbed his clothes from the closet and began getting dressed.

The women looked on silently. They could see blood seeping through the bandages on his shoulder. They could also fell the rage inside of him.

"Go get the car," he said as he tried to deal with the pain that was coursing through his body.

Just as Lissha and Treebie hit the door, in walked the nurse. She looked at Kiam and gasped. "Oh no, what are you doing? You can't leave, you're not well," she panicked, pressing her palms in the air as if to stop him.

"Watch me," he said as he put his feet in his boots. Passing the bed he grabbed Faydrah's ring and put it in his pocket. "Have a nice day," he said to the nurse who was standing there with her mouth open as he walked out the door in search of answers that was gonna get somebody killed one way or the other.

Chapter 36
Playin' With the Devil

Kiam sat in silence on the burgundy Italian leather sofa in his living room. His ratchet sat on the marble and glass cocktail table in front of him fully loaded with one already in the chamber. Next to the Nine sat a half empty bottle of Jack Daniels and a bottle of pain pills.

Kiam's dark eyes seemed more frightening with the two week old beard that framed his normally clean shaven face. His left arm hung down by his side in a sling but there would be no doubt after this evening that he was still deadly.

With his free hand he stroked the hair on his face as he looked around the living room at the upper echelon of his team. Lissha sat across from him on the loveseat studying his expression. She knew that something real serious was about to go down, but even her wildest imagination couldn't have prepared her for what she would soon witness.

Lissh could see Treebie in the dining room loading a plate with food that Kiam had laid out. *That bitch would have an appetite at her own execution*, Lissha thought.

Donella and Bayonna sat across from each other in twin recliners with plates of untouched food in their laps. JuJu however chose to stand close to the door. He had already decided that if one of them were flawed, the only way they would be leaving was twisted, wrapped in sheets and black plastic.

Lissha's eyes rotated from Kiam to the Nine on the table, and the half bottle of Jack Daniels. Donella fidgeted with her hands and Bayonna rocked her foot as the silence became thick with anticipation.

Treebie entered the living room and sat down on the other end of the loveseat. She was cool as a breeze with her legs crossed and a heaping plate of food balanced on her lap. She bit into the drumstick then filled her mouth with fork full of spaghetti. "What kind of meat is in this? Ground turkey?" she asked, looking at Kiam.

"Humph," her grunted.

"Whatever that's supposed to mean. Anyway, it tastes like damn jerky."

Kiam didn't comment, he was steady staring her down.

Treebie felt his gaze hot on her face but she kept on eating. She didn't know why Kiam had called them all together; she suspected that it had something to do with the angry phone call that he'd received from Riz the other day, but she wasn't sure. She knew she was strapped and if he was planning on acting a fool she would surely aid in his venture.

Kiam cleared his throat, then spoke with words that were carefully chosen. "I sat and thought long and hard before I called y'all here tonight," he stated a little over a whisper. All eyes were focused on him and there was no other sound in the room aside from his voice.

He looked from one face to the other. "The last thing a general ever wants to do is wonder about the loyalty of his men," he continued as he picked up the medication bottle, popped it open and threw two pills in his mouth.

He poured himself a shot of Jack and locked eyes with Lissha. "I'm going to start with you. My product made it back here, but the money never made it to Riz, his people got jacked leaving the exchange spot. Now unless I'm stupid that tells me that it was set up on this end. You told me that you'd put your life on your crew."

"And unless you have proof that I can't, don't even bring that shit to me," Lissha defended her girls.

Kiam chuckled. "Besides you and me, they were the only ones that knew when and where the pickup goes down."

Treebie stopped chewing and sat to the edge of her seat. "What the fuck is that supposed to mean?"

Lissha held her hand up gesturing for Treebie to be quiet. She sat up and looked him square in the face, the way Big Zo had taught her to face opposition. "Are you accusing me of something?"

"Until I find out exactly what happened, I'm accusing all of you muthafuckas," he said point blank.

"If Riz's people got jacked, why the fuck couldn't the cross come from his end?" Lissha contested.

"That's what I'm saying," Treebie angrily agreed. "And ain't nobody seen Gator's slick ass in two days, how we know he didn't have something to do with it? You need to find out where that nigga at."

"I already know where he's at," Kiam replied matter of factly.

"Well, enlighten the rest of us, please," shot Treebie, impatiently.

Kiam smirked. "You're chewing him."

Treebie gasped and spat out the spaghetti. She cocked her head to the side and looked at him crazily. "What the fuck, man!"

"I skinned that bitch nigga alive, then I ground him up real good," said Kiam.

Treebie slung the plate off her lap and bolted to the bathroom. Lissha, Donella, and Bay stared at Kiam with their mouths open.

JuJu was still covering the door. He was not surprised by Kiam's revelation, he had helped him dice Gator up.

Treebie returned to her seat still gagging and waiting for Kiam to tell her he was only kidding, but the look in his eyes confirmed that he was dead ass. *This nigga craze.* Treebie shook her head in utter disbelief. The others were thinking the same thing.

Kiam looked at them as if to say they hadn't seen shit yet. "Gator was stupid," he said. "He should have known that he would be the first person I suspected. I thought he had something to do with the attempt on my life, but I was wrong. He jacked Riz's people. I couldn't get him to admit it before I ended his suffering, but it don't matter, I know that he was skimming money for years. Riz told me that."

"You put a whole lot of faith in what Riz say. That nigga could be wrong about all this shit," Lissha voiced.

"You got a problem wit' it? Cause if I'm right about Gator having something to do with the jack then one of you had to help set it up." He paused and looked in the faces of the women one by one. He had to admit that they were tight lipped and unified. But in a minute Gator's accomplice would fold.

"I'm gonna give the guilty one a chance to own up to what she done. If you do that I'll show some mercy, but if you sit here and play innocent I'ma do to you the same thing I did to your boy," Kiam promised ominously.

Neither of the girls expressions changed a tad, noted Kiam. "Y'all gon' play this shit all the way out, huh?" Still he got nothing but four blank stares. The silence in the room was profound.

Switching tactics Kiam said. "I give that soft nigga, Gator, credit; he wouldn't tell me nothing. Nah, he took that to the grave with him. But I'ma still find out which one of you crossed me."

On cue Daphne came sweeping into the living room. Four sets of eyes focused on her.

Kiam chuckled and picked his gun up off of the table. He looked at Daphne and said, "Point out the bitch that you saw with Gator when he met with Wolfman."

Daphne locked eyes with the guilty one and did not bat an eyelash as she raised her finger and pointed directly at the traitor. "That's her right there," she said.

To be continued...
Trust No Bitch 2:
Available Now!

BOOKS BY LDP'S CEO, CA$H

TRUST NO MAN

TRUST NO MAN 2

TRUST NO MAN 3

BONDED BY BLOOD

SHORTY GOT A THUG

A DIRTY SOUTH LOVE

THUGS CRY

THUGS CRY 2

TRUST NO BITCH

TRUST NO BITCH 2

TRUST NO BITCH 3

TIL MY CASKET DROPS

Coming Soon

TRUST NO BITCH (KIAM EYEZ' STORY)

THUGS CRY 3

BONDED BY BLOOD 2

RESTRANING ORDER

BOOKS BY NENE CAPRI

PUSSY TRAP I, II, III & IV

DREAM WEAVER

TAINTED

291

Coming Soon From Lock Down Publications

RESTRAINING ORDER

By **CA$H & COFFEE**

GANGSTA CITY **II**

By **Teddy Duke**

A DANGEROUS LOVE **VII**

By **J Peach**

BLOOD OF A BOSS **III**

By **Askari**

THE KING CARTEL **III**

By **Frank Gresham**

NEVER TRUST A RATCHET BITCH

SILVER PLATTER HOE **III**

By **Reds Johnson**

THESE NIGGAS AIN'T LOYAL **III**

By **Nikki Tee**

BROOKLYN ON LOCK **III**

By **Sonovia Alexander**

THE STREETS BLEED MURDER **II**

By **Jerry Jackson**

CONFESSIONS OF A DOPEMAN'S DAUGHTER **II**

By **Rasstrina**

WHAT ABOUT US **II**

NEVER LOVE AGAIN

By **Kim Kaye**

A GANGSTER'S REVENGE

By **Aryanna**

<u>Available Now</u>

LOVE KNOWS NO BOUNDARIES **I II & III**

By **Coffee**

SILVER PLATTER HOE **I & II**

HONEY DIPP **I & II**

CLOSED LEGS DON'T GET FED **I & II**

A BITCH NAMED KARMA

By **Reds Johnson**

A DANGEROUS LOVE **I, II, III, IV, V, VI**

By **J Peach**

CUM FOR ME

An **LDP Erotica Collaboration**

THE KING CARTEL **I & II**

By **Frank Gresham**

BLOOD OF A BOSS **I & II**

By **Askari**

THE DEVIL WEARS TIMBS

BURY ME A G **I II & III**

By **Tranay Adams**

THESE NIGGAS AIN'T LOYAL **I & II**

By **Nikki Tee**

THE STREETS BLEED MURDER

By **Jerry Jackson**

DIRTY LICKS

By **Peter Mack**

THE ULTIMATE BETRAYAL

By **Phoenix**

BROOKLYN ON LOCK

By **Sonovia Alexander**

SLEEPING IN HEAVEN, WAKING IN HELL **I, II & III**

By **Forever Redd**

THE DEVIL WEARS TIMBS **I, II & III**

By **Tranay Adams**

DON'T FU#K WITH MY HEART **I & II**

By **Linnea**

BOSS'N UP **I & II**

By **Royal Nicole**

LOYALTY IS BLIND

By **Kenneth Chisholm**

Trust No Bitch

Lightning Source UK Ltd.
Milton Keynes UK
UKHW020757020323
417909UK00012B/1340

The Winter Sparrows

Mary Rose Liverani

The Winter Sparrows

Growing Up in
Scotland & Australia

NELSON

Thomas Nelson Australia
480 Latrobe Street Melbourne Victoria 3000

First published in 1975
© Mary Rose Liverani, 1975
First paperback edition published 1978
Reprinted 1979, 1981, 1982, 1983, 1984

Printed by The Dominion Press - Hedges & Bell
Maryborough, 3465

To Charles Farquharson

Acknowledgements

Of primary importance in the writing of this book was the persistent and determined encouragement of Mrs Geraldine MacNeill, Senior Lecturer in Linguistics at the University of Newcastle, the unstinted co-operation of my husband, Ermete, and the generous, unconditional financial assistance of the Australian Government, to all of whom I am most grateful.

Contents

Part I   My Ain Countree

1 Our Daily Bread

'Hop o' my Thumb' was a fairy story to which in my early childhood I returned again and again. Its theme fascinated and frightened me. A man and a woman had seven children, of whom Hop o' my Thumb was the youngest. They all lived in extreme poverty existing on crusts of bread that grew staler and scarcer until the day came when the woman persuaded the man to take all the family into the forest and abandon them to the generosity of nameless spirits. The youngest child overheard his mother's plan and managed once or twice to foil it by scattering a trail of stones that led the children home. In the end, however, he failed to accumulate a hoard of stones and the children were successfully surrendered to the benignity of the wilderness. The happy ending never interested me. We too were seven children. My father, a ship's rigger, earned enough to provide only an hour by hour existence and my mother never ceased to worry at the problem of survival. This problem, she would regularly announce at intervals, was insoluble, irresolvable, and when I heard this, lying in our bed, I would mentally project my ears to the bedroom wall and listen for plans to abandon us. Maybe she would try to entice us to the bluebell woods and sneak off, leaving us without the tram fare home. Although I was the eldest and had been to the woods once or twice, I simply could not remember how to find our way back. I couldn't even remember the name of the tram. My mother had a different plan, however.

'It's no go trying to carry on making a bob in this place,' she told my father one night when even the kettle had been scoured to brilliance and thrust upon Archie McIntosh, the pawn man. 'It's well enough when there's work at the yards, though ye

1

do have to knock your pork out to get a few quid, but the whole business is so uncertain. Two allnighters this week, and sweet eff all the next. Jesus, Mary and Joseph, it's enough to drive ye to madness, trying to manage wi' a pay that's never the same twice running. I'm sick, sick, sick of the whole shemozzle and', here her voice grew tense with threats, 'if ye don't try to find a way out for us I'm going to get to hell out of it and leave ye with the lot.'

This was an alternative I had never considered before. My mother would run off into the woods herself and leave us in the house. This was far, far worse than the fairy tale solution. Out there was something which might happen upon us and after a bit of tribulation, save us as in 'Hop o' my Thumb'. But who would come to the house? We would never find gold here. Stiff with horror, I lifted my head from the bolster and screwed up my eyes to hear how my father would reply. There was only silence and weeping. And then my mother began to scream.

'Well, go on, go on,' she called out. 'Don't just sit there staring at that bloody paper.'

I heard the rustling and crackling that told me she'd snatched the paper from my father and thrown it down somewhere.

'All right,' I heard my father say tiredly. 'You're the one with the big ideas in this family. Let's hear what you have to suggest.'

My mother sniffed, loud with contempt. 'Typical, isn't it, passing the buck to me. That's something you're always good at.' Then her tone brightened as anger was supplanted by excitement. 'Wi' all that reading you do,' she said accusingly, 'you miss the important things. Have you no' seen that ad in the paper about getting a job in Australia, working for a firm called B.H.P.?'

My father sighed in exasperation. He sounded as if he were counting ten under his breath and his voice was the one he used when we kept on being stupid.

'That ad's for miners, for God's sake. I'm no' a miner. I'm a rigger.'

'Don't flatter yourself,' my mother responded tartly. 'You're an engineer's labourer. That's what's written on our marriage certificate. So stop bummin' your load. A miner's only a labourer anyway. It says here you don't need to be trained. They'll take anybody.'

2

I'd heard people talking about Australia from time to time. Mr Smellie who lived up the next close to us, Archie's close, and was dying with T.B., not only him but his whole family Mrs Gibson had said, had a sister in Sidney. Blackfellows and bananas. Everybody said Australia was full of black people, and bananas grew on the streets for anyone to pick. It would be smashing to live there. I wondered, however, how the people got their jobs. If there were ships in the yards then your father could work allnighters, but if the yards were empty he would come home with his piece uneaten. No one had said anything about ships or yards in Australia. How did the people get their jobs? That's what I would like to know. Joe Gibson had told us when we were talking about Mr Smellie's sister that Australia was bigger than Scotland by a hundred times. Imagine it. Even a giant with his seven league boots would never get to the other side till he was old and grey, and his soles would wear out. So if the people there didn't have jobs they could take their children far away right into the centre and they would never find their way back. Snakes too. They were everywhere, everybody said. They hid in the trees, disguised as branches, and at night they dropped down on you and strangled you to death. And then you became a big lump inside the snake's skin and slid down it till you disappeared. It was a terrible place. There were insects called mosquitoes, after the aeroplanes, and they sucked up all your blood like vampires till you quietly dropped dead. And spiders. Poisonous ones that made you screw yourself into knots and die choking and screaming. It was boiling hot all the time. People usually just threw their eggs on the pavements to fry them. It was so hot that if you stayed there a long time you turned black.

So I never mentioned to my friends that my mother was wanting to go to Australia. I didn't want their sympathy. In any case she forgot about it. One day Labour won the election. Everything was like Hogmonay. My mother and father had been crouching over the radio since early in the afternoon while a voice kept talking about the Conservative party and the Labour party and seats. They were having a big party and trying to get into each other's seats. It was a bit like musical chairs for grown-ups. My father wanted Labour to get the most seats. All the neighbours were in our place because we had the best radio. 'It's an export model,' my mother used to tell everybody, and all the best things were kept for exports. The news of the seats

3

and the parties was coming from Lahore on the radio. People were sitting on the table and were sprawling on my mother and father's bed in the lounge room. Mr Gordon was cuddling his bottle of Haig's Dimple and there were bottles of lager in rows on the floor. My mother had on her new dark wine dirndl skirt with the high waist and her long-sleeved pink striped blouse. She'd done her hair with the tongs and she looked a right smasher. Was she in a good mood! She was laughing and patting people on the shoulders on her way in and out of the kitchen where she was fixing up the table. I was waiting for the right time to go to the bakehouse in Blackburn Street to get the hot rolls for the bacon and sausages.

Every little while, when the man on the radio said that Labour had got another seat, my father would thump his right fist into his left hand and his face would go purple with excitement.

'C'mon Atlee,' he was shouting, 'ye wee smasher, gie it tae the old swine.'

Everybody in the room agreed with him. They all nodded their heads together like golliwogs and sang:

'Aye, gie it tae him, gie it tae the Tory sods.'

They seemed to be shapelessly drunk, but in fact, the bottles hadn't been opened yet. My father was turning into a madman, laughing hysterically, punching Mr Gordon on the shoulder, ruffling my mother's hair. I squeezed under the table and groped my way to a spot directly under the radio trying to hear what was making my father so queer. Suddenly everybody started whistling like ships' sirens; they were shouting and singing so loudly I could hardly make out the words on the radio.

'The first Labour government in British history . . . a victory for socialist forces . . . Mr Churchill is likely to meet the queen . . .'

So that was it. I knew who Mr Churchill was. He was the enemy of the workers and in 1926 had shot all the miners dead when they wouldn't work. Well, he couldn't be dead if he were going to meet the queen. What were they all so happy about? Maybe she was going to put him in the Tower of London. At this point my mother dragged me out from under the table and thrust five shillings into my hand.

'Here, hen,' she said, 'get on your horse and gallop down to the bakehouse. It'll be open by the time you get there.' There

4

were 350 cracks in the pavement to leap over before I got to the bakehouse. If I touched each space between the cracks only once I would arrive at the bakery almost before I'd left the house. That's how fast I was. Even so, by the time I got back the whisky bottles were nearly all empty. My father was tipping one upside down to catch the last dribble on the tip of his tongue.

'Oh Jesus, isn't it smashing?' he was yelling to everybody. Suddenly he became elaborately quiet and serious and put his arm round Mr Gordon's shoulder.

'This calls for a song, Joe,' he said, 'and there's only one song called for.'

So the two of them began to sing. My mother came rushing in from the kitchen with one of her black looks and her eyes staring out of her head with rage.

'Here you lot, that's enough o' that. I'm no wanting any Communist shit in my place. Stop it, Joe Gordon. Anybody who sings the International here can get tae hell out o' it. And that goes for you especially, Robert Lavery. If ye want tae sing something why don't ye try 'Now thank we all our God'. Aye that would be the proper thing tae sing instead o' that atheistic rubbish. It's a victory for the Labour Party, no' the Communists.'

'Aye, but it's a victory for us too,' said my father earnestly, paying no heed to my mother's vexation. 'The people are gradually being enlightened. First they'll be Labour and then they'll be Communist. And it'll be a great day for us a'. Even for you too, ye silly wumman, though ye're too dense tae appreciate it. Communists gie a fair deal tae women as well. Equal pay for equal work and nurseries for the weans.' His face lightened again at the future he envisaged and linking his arm in Mr Gordon's he began to sing in a virile baritone:

Oh, it ain't gonna rain no more, no more,
It ain't gonna rain no mo-o-o-re.
For ah'm on the broo and the parish too,
And it ain't gonna rain no more.

Everybody took hands and joined in and the walls of the house shook with excitement. In a little while I edged my way over to my father and touched his arm lightly. He grinned when he saw me and reached out to the table for a roll with fried bacon inside.

'Here, hen,' he said softly, patting me on the head, 'There's a roll for ye and ye can gie this one tae Margaret. Are the others sleeping?'

5

I nodded, having already stopped my mouth with a huge bite of the crisp bacon and hot bread.

'Right then,' went on my father. 'Nick off tae bed because Mrs Gordon's watching ye and it embarrasses her tae be seen drinking by kids.' He glanced across the room at our upstairs neighbour who was wiping her mouth anxiously and clutching her glass for dear life. 'She's got a funny notion, that woman, that being proper means no' being human. That's the trouble wi' all these religious maniacs. They were made human for a good reason but they choose to forget it and try tae become a new breed o' animal. Here, just a minute,' he said, as I started to sidle off. 'Have ye got it straight what's been going on today? Do you know why we're celebrating?'

'Sort of, Da.'

'Ah, but my lass, sort of isn't ever good enough. You should never be content with "sort of" knowing something. This,' he said, pausing for effect and oblivious of the din around us, 'is one of the most important days in the history of the world. The men who're going to govern us are guid blokes, Labour men. Labour means for working people, like us and a' the people who live in Plantation. They're going tae tax the rich and use the money to help the poor. Isn't that a grand thing, hen? We've got a champion at last. Mr Atlee's no' really one of us, he's quite a wealthy chap, but he cares aboot the poor. He wants tae give them a chance, where Churchill wanted to keep them in their place—an' that place is the gutter.' He stared absently at the pink walls that had been stippled with blue and green dyes by my mother for last Hogmonay, and then went on. 'These hooses here'll all be pulled doon and everybody'll have a place of his own wi' a garden maybe, and a toilet inside, an' nae bugs behind the wallpaper.' His dark blue eyes, piggy eyes my mother called them when she was fighting with him, narrowed thoughtfully. 'In a few years, a' the folk here will have moved out into the country wi' fresh air and grass. We'll see the back o' this dump.'

My father was speaking as a provider, because the Scottish husband is primarily a provider. When my mother used to run off to her mother with a tale of woe, she would be given little sympathy. Doubtless the prospect of being landed with a somewhat irascible and unpredictable daughter trailed by her seven brats horrified my grandmother. So she would listen to my mother's plaints which always began: 'I can't stand that bastard any longer . . .' and would respond always in the same way.

'Well, ye know how it is, Rose. He's no' my cup of tea, but he's a guid man. He doesnae drink tae excess nor run around wi' filthy wimmen . . . and he's a good provider.'

This was habitually seen as my father's greatest virtue, not only by his wife and his mother-in-law but also by himself. What he wanted from his political system was economic redress: seven beds for seven heads and he wanted the heads lying in a row, not alternating with feet. He wanted parklands for us to play in instead of dark closes foul with men's urine. He didn't want allnighters, but neither did he want short time. Steady work, better-paid work and freedom from the fear of 'getting his cards'. The Labour Party was going to realise his pastoral dream. We would be turned out to graze on the new housing estates and the tenement dockside dunnies would rot away from disuse.

Behind us we would leave the Clyde that was curtained off from sight by high wooden fences crusted with barbed wire. These were the protectors of property, of the great warehouses full and running over with crates of oranges from Jaffa, peanuts from the Gold Coast, dates from the Lebanon, exotic names that first seeped into our vocabularies as brands indelibly inked in blue on the fruit that we stole and ate in triumph. We would put behind us, too, the great ships with funnels that always reached comfortingly higher than the barbed wire, musical chimney boxes whose sirens swept through the dirty tenements along the river banks like searchlights of sound probing the dark, musty corners of recessed beds in dingy single-ends and piercing the sleepers with knowledge of a life beyond the periphery of black granite.

My own dream was a little more particular than my father's. I longed for a country where there were no pawnshops and where tobacco companies were doomed to grind out forever and a day nothing but Will's Woodbines. Turkish Pasha were the only cigarettes freely available in the post-war cigarette market in Scotland. My mother loathed them and refused to smoke them.

'Woodbines, I must have Woodbines,' she would tell me, counting out the coppers into my reluctant grip. 'Go and get Woodbines and don't come back without them.'

'But where shall I find them?' I would wail despairingly.

'Everybody wants them and there aren't any around. And they don't give them to wee people anyway.'

'Get out, get out,' my mother would yell at me, throwing the door open and leaping at me with her right arm raised in a violent gesture, 'get out that bloody door and look for these cigarettes. If ye come back without them I'll lay ye in your own blood.'

Will's Woodbines were advertised on every imaginable available space in Glasgow, but the little green and gold boxes themselves were never on display. Why the firm sought to stimulate demand for its product when the supply never approached being adequate was one of the seven wonders of my world. Another was why my mother didn't adapt herself to Pashas that she could have smoked night and day in perpetual motion instead of suffering long smokeless hours for a few minutes spiced with the unique savour of Will's fretted amber. They must be wicked, that firm, I thought, to make people long for their cigarettes and then make only a few.

And so, oscillating between resignation and impotent fury, I would set off on my near-daily odyssey through Glasgow to hunt out the minuscule hoards of Woodbines from newsagents, and cafés and small corner shops through Plantation and Govan and Elder Park and sometimes over the river to Anderson. My first stop was always at the papershop of the two spinsters, the Misses Alexander, Sara and Susan. 'The cinnamon sticks,' I called them, because their tall, skeletal structures were generally covered by drab brown frocks, unrelieved by buttons or belts. Never once did these women sell me the Woodbines and they never would, I knew, for they believed that I smoked them myself. Still, it was part of my ritual to ask them. Then I could add them to my list of places attempted, of dangers faced in the quest for Woodbines. As usual they smiled thinly and said in a prissy duet:

'No Woodbines today, only Pasha and Turf.'

I hesitated. Turf was sometimes acceptable to my mother depending on how desperate or amenable she was. There was no doubt today, however, that she was in a pretty bad mood. My father had lost time again this week and there would be no over-time at the weekend to make up for it. So I nodded curtly to the two miserly women and went out. What a waste. They had all these Woodbines stashed away under the counter, I was sure of it, and no kids who wouldn't have to go and look for them. They didn't smoke anyway. Probably had lungs like punctured bladders and couldn't draw enough breath.

In the cafés and corner shops I wasted no time.

'Got any Woodbines?'

'No Woodbines.'

'Got any Woodbines?'

'None.'

'Got any Woodbines by any chance?'

'By no chance.'

Outside the newspaper shops, however, I always hung around till two or three people had gone inside and then while they were waiting or absorbing the newsagent's attention, I would quickly scan the latest editions of the comics.

'Here you, are ye wanting tae buy these comics?'

'No, I was wondering if you had any Woodbines.'

'Fine well, ye know I havenae any, you cheeky thing. You asked me yesterday. Next time I catch ye going through these comics I'll make ye pay for them.'

Today I'll have to go through the tunnel over to Anderson. It's a smelly hole right enough, all that thick green scum trickling down the walls. There must be cracks in the walls or how could the water get in, and if there are cracks they must get bigger every day. What if the walls and the roof all suddenly cave in and press me flat into the river mud, like those giant sting-rays I read about? My father says that's a lot of nonsense. Scottish engineering is the finest in the world, but what does that mean after all? Only that other people are worse. Well, I'm out now, thank goodness. Nearly. I can see the light at the top of the stairs.

No luck so far, but I haven't found a newsagent's yet and those wee shops are never much good. I'll go in the swing park for a bit. Woodbine, be mine, Woodbine be mine, be mine Woodbine. That fits in very well with the rhythm of the swing. If I swung high enough I could see all of Glasgow and if I had the hundred eyes of Argus I could see all the little boxes of Woodbines hiding in the drawers and I could see under the cinnamon sticks' counter and could say to them 'Liar'. They wouldn't like that. They go to church every Sunday. If I were a giant sting-ray, an immense one with wings, I could hover over the city and say:

'Right. Get out all your little boxes of Woodbines from your secret drawers and throw them here at my feet or I'll come down and suffocate you all and press you into the Clyde.' Then I would ram the fags into my ears and up my nose, and fill my knickers and make a bag out of my jumper and stuff it with them and take off my shoes and socks and fill them too. Then I would go home in my bare feet and say to my mother:

'Here ye are, Mammy, I got you some Woodbines.'

And she would say:

'Ah, but I've changed to Pasha.'

I know this newsagent's got Woodbines. I can tell by the look on his face.

'But you're not a regular customer of mine, are ye lassie?'

'No, Mister, but I would be if I lived in Anderson.'

'What are ye doing here then, if you live in Plantation.'

'I'm looking for Woodbines for my mammy.'

'Well, I see from your fingers that ye havenae any nicotine stains, though your nails need cutting. Here's five for ye.'

To market, to market, for a packet of cigs.

Home again, home again, jiggity jig.

A small packet of Woodbines was always worth a pat on the head and other fleeting expressions of gratitude from my mother. I never took any lasting delight in these, however, for circumstances forced upon her two roles: she was the grateful princess who acclaimed the hero returning with tokens of mighty deeds but she was also the villainous king, the princess's father, who insisted on still more and more quests and combats. The endless peregrinations around the city, prompted by the need for either cigarettes or money, fell to me as the eldest because my mother was continually immobilised by pregnancies that she rushed into to avoid cancer of the breast in old age. A Catholic doctor, observing that my mother had successfully practised birth control for three years after her first two pregnancies, warned her that she might thereby bring damage upon her breasts, such as they were, and so for the next six years her womb laboured almost without rest. This relentless procreating ceased only after a Presbyterian doctor hinted at disastrous consequences for the womb, should the routine continue undisturbed. From then on, contraception became the order of the night.

In the day, my mother's ferocious energies were expended in cyclonic gusts that whirled her from bedroom to bathroom, to kitchen to lounge room and back again, pounding and pumelling lumpy kapok mattresses, battering the shabby carpet piece, flailing the curtains, boiling the nappies, kneading the dough, zooming over the starched shirts with hot flat irons, and then, suddenly finished, she stood in all the doorways glaring at the rooms to smell the dirt.

'I don't need to look to see if a room's clean,' she always told me before inspecting my efforts. 'I can smell it.'

So she straddled the lobby, staring suspiciously into every sullen corner and snuffing the air like the giant in Jack and the Beanstalk:

Fee fie foe fum,
All the dirt has been and gone,
But if a single mote I smell,
I'll take my broom and gie it hell.

So you see, my mother's search after God, through attention to personal and household hygiene, left her very little time for hunting up Woodbines or for getting money. Money, money, money, money. For us there were three ways of acquiring it: working, stealing and borrowing. The last may be categorised as borrowing from moneylenders (unsecured loans), borrowing from pawnbrokers (secured loans) and borrowing from relatives (disguised begging). Work and theft were undertaken by my father but the third activity was laid to my charge.

I hate borrowing but if I have to I would rather go to Mrs Dorin. It means I can go and visit Granny Lavery afterwards and say I had to wait a long time for the tram.

'Tell her your Granny's Mrs McGiffin and she'll give it to you. Ask her how much interest you have to pay on ten shillings.'

'Why should I tell her my Granny's Mrs McGiffin when her name's Lavery?'

'Lavery's your father's father's name, stupid. He was her second husband. She takes the name of her last husband, Pop McGiffin. Imagine it, she's outlived three men. Your father's family are all the same. Too bloody lazy to get out of their own way. She never wanted to work and so she got herself married to all these old dock-wallopers.'

She always talks like that about Granny, but I don't care. I love going to her place, especially on Saturdays when she's got me all the comics and sends me down to Cecchi's to get a jug of ice cream. It's lovely and quiet at her place. Nothing to do but read all the time and have cups of tea. Maybe I could bargain with Mammy and say: 'I'll go to Mrs Dorin's if you let me stay

11

overnight at Granny's.' But that would be no good. She can't wait till tomorrow for the money.

She's a weird old wumman that one, living up that smelly close when she's got all that money. Fancy hiring out tablecloths and sheets for wakes. You can't eat from this tablecloth unless you've got a dead relative. Imagine it. They're a special kind of living that eat from this tablecloth. The living that've survived the dead. Who'd want to join that club?

Well, she's unlocking the door. What a wait! Three locks and three keys and then that big wooden latch. I'm sure she turns the key a certain amount of times to the right and then to the left but I can never catch the number. Must be scared stiff. What would she say if I shouted through her letter box: 'Hurry up Mrs Dorin and let me in. I'm Raskolnikov come with my claymore to axe your head in.'

Maybe she sees that kind of thought on everybody's face who comes here, she stares at you so suspiciously. Never takes her eyes off you even when she's feeling in the bag. Might have worked as a tram conductress when she was young. All right, I can stare too, without blinking. You look like Irene Dunne being Queen Victoria, especially with that 'I'll fix you m'lady' look on your face and the mouth like a rat trap. Thank you very much, Mrs Dorin, two and six interest for every week. Yes I'll tell my mother that. Yes she'll be sure to pay it back inside a month. My granny's the guarantor? Oh yes, I think so. Poor Granny, I hope Mammy pays it back this time.

I wish we had enough money never to borrow and never to go to the pawn. It doesnae bother Mammy at all. She's not a bit ashamed.

'Why should I be? You never see the Chancellor of the Exchequer going around with a red neck, do you? And think of what Britain owes America. He's as proud as Punch when he comes back from America having negotiated a big loan. All smiles and written up in the paper and he puts us in American power. You ask your father about that. We're no' in Archie's power, are we. Anyway, as my Chancellor of the Exchequer, ye're doin' a swell job, but I wish ye'd negotiate for a lower rate of interest.'

Isn't Mammy funny? She never cares about anything so long as we've got something for the tea tonight.

The loans from Mrs Dorin were generally negotiated about the middle of the week, that is when the money from the pawn had been used up. Mondayitis was an illness that afflicted me very early in life, because Monday was pawn day. My father's only suit, a tatty, navy blue pinstriped affair, carefully sponged and pressed to remove the shiny spots, was sent to the pawn almost every single Monday within my memory. For this, my mother was lent thirty shillings. One quarter of the basic wage. It was redeemed (a word whose religious usage was always very confusing to me) every Friday night, when my father got paid. Sometimes, unfortunately, there wasn't money enough even to redeem the suit till Monday morning, so my mother instructed me to take the interest to the pawnbroker and ask for a 'loan' of the suit till Monday so that she and my father could go out on Saturday night. Not that they did. On Monday morning, however, she sent me to another pawn where twelve and six was lent on it and then when work at the yards picked up, the suit was redeemed from both pawns. Our regular pawnbroker must have guessed at my mother's shady financial transactions, but he never said anything except:

'You told me you would bring the suit back on Monday. It's a week (or a fortnight, or three weeks) late.'

'I know, Archie, my mother forgot and left the suit in the wardrobe.'

Searching for Woodbines was a trial to me partly because it consumed so much of my leisure time and partly because there was the fear of not finding the cigarettes and having to endure my mother's anger and disappointment. Pawning was a different kind of activity altogether. The pawnshop was in the next close to us, practically up above. So little time was lost in going there. There was rarely any doubt as to the outcome of the transaction between Archie the pawnbroker and me with my father's suit. Each week Archie netted five shillings on the loan so that over a fifty-two week period he had little to complain about and we were only one of his many customers. Pawning, however, even in a dockside area was a source of shame to some, and certainly to me. The Dombeys of the world, with their attendant respectability, have always set themselves up and been accepted as the arbiters of manners and mores and the Dombeys have handed it down that poverty is a sin, a little below

13

prostitution and murder. The poor too accept this dictum with the others and pawning, to the poor with two children, was a sin committed by the poor with seven children.

My mother scoffed at such snobbishness when I protested at ducking under the brass balls with my little bundle wrapped in newspaper.

'To hell wi' them,' she snarled. 'When they start paying your rent they can start telling you how to live.'

But then she never went to the pawn. In fact, for some years the neighbours' children weren't exactly sure if any of us went there. I was the only one in the family who took the suit and no one had caught me. But they would give us children meaningful looks and smirks:

'You go to the pawn, don't you?'

'Does your mother go to the pawn?'

'We know who goes to Archie.'

To this baiting, I generally responded with a cold stare and: 'Some people are right nosey parkers in this place.' Because some of the neighbours actually lived up Archie's close I never went up the stairs of the tenement with my parcel before taking elaborate precautions to make sure no one was about. First, I walked up and down in the street outside the close entrance, idly looking in shop windows to ensure that none of the local children was near enough to see me entering it. Then when I got inside the close I listened at the bottom of the stairs for any sounds of feet or talk that would indicate people were upstairs. When everything was absolutely still I raced up the stairs and darted into the endmost cubicle where I huddled against the walls with a gasp of triumph and relief. The relief, however, was only of ten minutes duration, as long as it took for Archie to give me the money and write out the ticket. You couldn't very well hang around inside once he'd given them to you. He always suspected you were trying to pinch some of the pledges. You couldn't wait, either, until the stairs were empty because customers from other parts of Plantation were climbing the stairs with their bundles all the time. I always chose a cubicle right away from the entrance to the pawn so that when I came out no one could see me unless he popped his head into the vestibule. In that case you could pretend to be looking in the display window with a view to buying something since Archie always sold off his unredeemed pledges. The other children mightn't believe you but if they didn't actually catch you coming out of the cubicle they couldn't prove anything, could they? It was a silent compact between us that I must be caught in the act.

Today I wish I were dead. I feel all strangled in my stomach. My head and neck are boiling hot and I'm never going out into the street again. I'm going to tell my mother the school said I've got T.B. and I'll have to stay in bed for at least a year and by that time we might have gone to Australia. How could he have known I was there, that's what I would like to know. I always speak very softly so that no one can hear me from outside and you can't tell exactly who's in a cubicle because I've tried before to look through the smoked glass to see who's inside. You can only see the blob of a head, not the features. He must have known it was me, he was so quiet. I listened like I usually do and I didn't hear a sound in the hall. If people are looking in the display window they always move a little bit. You can even hear them breathing. But he was absolutely quiet, so he must have been waiting. What a shock I got when I came out. I didn't even see him. He saw me. I was walking out of the hall on to the landing when he ran up behind me and put his hand on my shoulder like a policeman and said:

'Hullo.'

That was all. And he smiled at me. I could see his chest getting bigger with all the air he had sucked in with satisfaction. It was a huge sigh. Then he smiled again and said:

'Just been to Archie, hmm?'

I couldn't say anything. I stared at him and tried to pretend that I wasn't there and he wasn't there and that I was in bed dreaming. Then he said:

'Cheerio, I'd better go. I'm late for my dinner. Mammy'll wonder where I've been all this time', and he ran up the stairs whistling 'The Cock o' the North'.

I just feel so sick. My mother says I've got a rash all over my shoulders and I can go to bed and read a book. But I'm going to sit here all afternoon and hate you, Joe Gibson.

When there was nothing left to pawn, not the suit, not my Sundays only coat, nor Margaret's smaller Sunday coat, not the kettle that my mother scoured to a high polish with steel wool and brazenly sent to Archie with a request for three and six, when nothing more was left to pawn and there wasn't tuppence for the tram to Mrs Dorin's, then it was time to tap our relatives.

The most tapworthy of these was my maternal grandmother, Bygroves. She was a queer hybrid person like one of the lesser monsters of myth. Her hair was regularly permed with 'Toni' home permanent lotion and tinted light blue but her huge feet trod heavily along in men's black lace-ups and men's grey socks so that one end of her appeared to mock the other. Once I tentatively hinted that ladies' shoes of even the very sober sort might regularise her appearance, but she scoffed at the suggestion:

'Here, away wi' ye. Ah'm no' one o' your young things ye know. Ah'm sixty-three and ah'm no oot tae catch a man. Ah'm passed a' that, thank God. Mah shoes are right comfortable. Dae ye think ah would still be workin' strong as ah ah'm if ah'd crushed mah feet intae uncomfortable wimmen's shoes? Ah'm a workin' woman ye know, no' one o' your Chinese aristocracy.'

It was always a mystery to me how the Chinese aristocracy could rightly be considered mine, but I never liked to harry the point.

Granny Bygroves lived round the corner from us in one of the most dejected, filthy looking tenements in the whole of Glasgow. Unlike ours, which were built of red sandstone, the McLean Street tenements were hewn from granite, black and haggard in the bleak winter light and sourly grey in mid-summer. They were a triumphant expression of laissez-faire and Scottish thrift. There was nothing jerry built about them. They weathered the wind and rain, soot and grime as hardily as the raw material they had been wrought from and even after the war, though some of them had been blasted to mortar by German bombs, the bulk of them prevailed, overshadowing the docks as gloomy testaments to the Christian truism: 'the poor ye have always with ye'. Clearly the nineteenth-century ironmasters and ship builders who had these tenements erected that the labour force might conveniently live on the premises, did not regard workers' dwellings as a variable cost. They were a fixed cost, meant to be everlastingly fixed, built once and for all, not for a single generation but for succeeding generations. And indeed, more than one entire line of undersized, undernourished, bugbitten, bandy-legged Glaswegians coughed and sputtered its way into and out of life within the granite cells. The generations did not always succeed to one another, however. In the hardest times three or four of them crowded into the one or two room dwellings where no words were required to express kitchen, lounge, bedroom and bathroom since the concepts did not exist. Such tiny flats, for few were larger than two rooms, reflected the optimistic belief of the architect that the poor would succeed in family planning where the wealthy had failed. Like all species that have a high mortality rate, however, the poor multiplied with the horrifying celerity forecast by Malthus, and the tall tenements became powder magazines jammed with human explosive. Violence shouted and screamed and cursed from despair and thwarted growth. Violence smashed chairs, gouged out bolts of plaster, shattered windows and cracked skulls. In the fearful silence afterwards, Lethe was drained from bottles of lager and whisky and human waste seeped out under the doors, collecting in stagnant puddles that filled dark corners on the stairs.

My grandmother lived in an attic room four storeys above the street. To climb directly the one hundred and twenty or so steps between her and ground level would have been a physically daunting, psychologically debilitating task, but the upward climb from storey to storey was an ascent of the magic faraway tree, a grotesque and distorted tree admittedly, whose separate levels, in contrast with the Enid Blyton fantasy, were crowded with hobgoblins and foul fiends, spitting cats, jellied legs that stuck out whitely from smelly corners, the whole blurred in a musky gloom. One never simply climbed stairs.

There was most light in the close mouth, so the first flight of stairs was for legitimate play. Nearly all the tenement children would run up a certain number of steps and leap from the top one to the ground, each time adding to the distance. The boldest boys could hurl themselves from ten stairs but I finished the game when I had jumped from six.

On the first landing, at the top of the stairs, shadows began to gather and the sources of interest became more furtive and sinister. Here was a lavatory shared by four families all of whom had formerly owned a key, now either lost or stolen, so that the toilet often stood open. One peered at the grimy walls, tracing out the graffiti with an eager forefinger, or sniffed disgustedly but with satisfaction nonetheless at the accidents on the seat or the floor. At rare times the lavatory startled one with a sudden effort to revert to a long forgotten pristine stainlessness. Its walls were whitewashed, the door scrubbed, the bowl saturated with lysol, and one's eyes rolled astonished over this new whiteness, marvelling at the miracle. Someone somewhere in the tenement was taking a new grip on life.

From this landing to the next, everything was murky. You took a deep breath and aimed to dash to the top step of the next flight before drawing a second. Pitch black at the first storey where the gas light was broken; sniff the damp and acrid air for a presence, a drunken body lolling semiconscious in a corner, and then grope your way up the stairs, patting the stone walls like a blind man. Another toilet, with an enormous keyhole that can be peeped through, is on the second landing. To catch someone on the seat is a tantalising objective, though the keyhole is too far to one side and all that can be seen is part of a left arm. Apart from that you can't loiter too long for the occupant, who is listening attentively to your hesitant footsteps, will realise that you have stopped outside. And wonder.

On the second storey the gas light works. A pity. The angry yellow light exposes you in any corner. Here live my enemies, the Muirs, who are always exciting, often dangerous.

Jimmy Muir, the father of the family, was a terrifyingly huge coal carrier of Irish stock, a Celtic supporter and notorious foe of Orangemen and masons. He frequently boasted of the time he had spent in 'college', his ironic name for Barlinnie Prison, and there was little doubt in the minds of those who were unfortunately acquainted with him that Barlinnie would one day welcome him as a permanent boarder. He saw it as his religious duty to unleash his two sons on 'Proddy dogs', particularly those who were female and small; on one occasion the little Muirs bashed up my sister Margaret and tried to tie her to the tram lines. Consequently, you watched the handle of the Muirs' door very intently when climbing the stairs and if it turned, then you leapt down the stairs five at a time and hid until whoever it was had gone.

You might, of course, try running up the stairs instead of down. That would save time and energy. Once I did. Before I had quite turned the corner, however, and started up the next flight of stairs, Tommy Muir looked up and saw me and came bounding up after me.

'You're for it now, ye proddy dog,' he yelled, while I ran for my life, thinking:

'Dear God, don't let him catch me and don't let me trip and let Granny be home.'

My grandmother kept very irregular hours and more often than not she wasn't at home when you called. I suspected that she deliberately tried to avoid callers, particularly me, since we never dropped in for a chat but always to 'tap' her. Visits to her therefore often took the form of a siege, for sometimes she was in fact at home, but wouldn't answer the door. There was no alternative but to wait, even for one or two hours, a very boring time since her landing was always midnight dark, and there was no light to read by.

By God's direct intervention, however, or so I was convinced, she was in the act of leaving her attic when I panted on to her lobby with Tommy Muir just about to grab my jumper.

'Granny, Granny!' I called. 'He's going to bash me, he's going to smash me, he said!'

My grandmother looked up from the lock she was in the process of shaking to ensure that her little attic could not be burgled.

'What's that ye say,' she cried out indignantly, coming forth out of the gloom.

'Here you,' she shouted, grabbing the boy by the scruff of the neck and shaking him. 'Don't let me catch you pestering my grand-daughter when she comes to visit me, or I'll boot ye in the backside from here tae Kingdom Come. Noo, get tae hell oot o' here and ah'll be doon tae see that faither o' yours tae tell him about this.'

'But Granny,' I said, snuffling loudly now that the danger was over, 'it's his own father that siks him on us, because we're Protestants.'

'Och, for God's sake, ye're no still on that tack, are ye, young Muir?' my Granny asked, frowning vexedly and staring right into his eyes. Her own eyes always looked slightly mad for she had huge whites that dazzled you most disconcertingly when they shone on you.

'And why shouldn't ah be?' the boy answered sullenly. 'The Protestants are always bashing us up and they keep a' the guid jobs for themselves. And what aboot a' those songs they sing aboot us and the things they say aboot the pope?'

Both my grandmother and I stood embarrassed. Tommy Muir

19

was quite right in his criticisms. Only recently, when the Orange walk had been performed, threats had been issued to Catholics to keep indoors or take the consequences, and crowds of children had followed the bands singing:

It's the sash my father wo-o-ore,
It's the sash my fa-a-ther wore,
It was orange and white with a yellow stripe,
It's the sash my fa-a-ther wore.
Kick the Pope!

The Catholics peered from behind their curtains, livid with resentment and plotting revenge. They were too outnumbered, however, to risk a street battle, and so when the police drew up near my house, people were astounded.

'What were they here for, no one had been fighting?' Suddenly someone called from the crowd:

'Hey, look up there!' and the crowds swung over to one side of the street so as to see better the roof of the tenements opposite. I couldn't see anything.

'He's up there by the chimney,' a man yelled, pointing almost directly upward. 'He's trying tae push it down on us.'

There was uproar among the Protestants. Some Fenian was trying to bomb us with a chimney pot! Wait till they caught him, he would get what for!

It turned out to be the local bookie, Billy Mathieson. Funny, I never realised he was a Catholic. Fancy trying to tip a huge chimney pot on to the crowd from the top of a tenement. He could have killed a lot of people.

'Jesus, look who it is,' I heard men say when the police appeared hanging on to Billy's arms. His face was all red and his tie had twisted round his neck.

'Ye'll get nae mair o' mah man's lines,' a woman screamed at him, 'ye dirty Catholic sod, trying tae kill decent folk.'

They were trying to push the police out of the way to catch hold of Billy but by this time other bobbies had arrived from the station and they formed a circle round the bookie.

'Back, back,' they yelled at the crowd. 'Anyone who tries to interfere with the law will be charged. Go back to your houses. There's nothing to worry about. Go back home, please, every-one.'

'Ye ought tae string the bastard up,' another woman screeched from the crowd.

'Aye, why didn't ye throw him oot o' the four storey windae.

He'd make a fine chimney pot, the Fenian swine. Trying tae kill us.'

'Why don't ye take him to Ireland,' called another, 'and put him back wi' the pigs.'

Billy was shaking, but his eyes glared with hatred and defiance as he was half thrown into the police car. Men and women crowded round the windows shaking their fists and threatening him with fearful bashings when next they saw him in the street. My mother had been looking through the window and had picked up what was going on from the comments of the crowd. When she saw me watching from the kerb, she called out to me:

'Here you, Mary Rose, get intae the house this minute.'

'They're a bunch o' no hopers that lot outside,' she commented when I rushed in to give her more details. 'Ah'm no a Catholic, but ah don't blame them for getting mad when the Orangemen start singing these stupid songs. They'd provoke a saint.'

Tommy Muir had pulled himself free from my grandmother's loose grasp, and begun to make his escape down the stairs.

'Noo, nae mair o' this silly business,' my granny called down to him. 'Ye've no call tae hit my grand-daughter when she's done nothing to you. And ah'm a Catholic myself ye know.'

'You're an old shitpot,' the boy shouted back irreverently, 'and next time ah'll do her in.'

We heard his door slam as he went inside, and I went on down the stairs with my granny.

'You're no really a Catholic, are ye, Granny?' I asked her.

'Indeed I am,' she answered proudly. 'I'm a convert. Did your mither no' tell ye that?'

'Goodness, no, she never did,' I said, 'but why did ye change your religion, anyway?'

'Because,' she replied, 'ah'm convinced it's the only true religion. The others are breakaways and Roman Catholicism was the original Christian religion.' Then to my astonishment she added, 'Your late grandfather was a Catholic, ye know.'

'But he couldnae have been,' I said, 'Mammy told me he was a mason.'

'Aye, that's right, but that was after he became an Orangeman. He was born a Catholic and your Uncle Brian is a Catholic. Only your mother and your Uncle Jim are Protestants. Your Granny Lavery's a Catholic but your father and his lot are Protestants because Mr Lavery was Orange.'

There was a puzzle extraordinary indeed. Catholics married

Protestants and had babies, some of them Protestant and some Catholic. And when the babies grew up they hated each other. How could you hate your own brothers and sisters? Yet the teacher at the Bethel had told us of Cain and Abel and of Jacob who cheated his father and stole his brother's birthright. His mother had helped him. She had helped one brother to cheat another brother and her own husband. This was very strange indeed. Families should stick together. My father always said this when we were fighting.

There was little sense in looking for clemency, therefore, from the Muir kids, when we met them. They enjoyed hating us, as many Protestant children delighted in hating them. So I always passed their door very carefully indeed. On rare occasions during the week, for the weekend was usually Mr Muir's drinking time, I heard terrible shouting and screaming coming from inside their flat. His wife was a thin little woman who loved the great drunken sot, as my mother called him, and she had an arrangement with her neighbours whereby they left their door unlocked on Saturday nights. When her husband went for her with a chair or a broken bottle, she ran next door and slept there in an armchair until the morning, while the husband lay in his piggish stupor. He was usually repentant by then and went to confession, lashed along by his little wife's sharp tongue, for she had no fear of him when he was sober.

'He's a good man, really, Mrs Bygroves,' she had said to my granny once. 'It's the drink that goes for his brain. It turns him intae a madman. But ye know, he gives me all his pay and I never have tae ask him twice for something. He gets his drinking money from the dogs and horses. He takes the lads tae the fitba' and he's really a guid father. It's the drink.'

But he never sounded to me like a good man when I listened outside his door to his shouting and swearing and heard his wife crying:

'Don't Jimmy, don't hit me.'

'I'll murder ye, ye bitch,' he swore at her, 'ye're a bloody whore. Ah know what ye get up tae when ah'm at work an' as Christ's my judge, ah'll swing for ye one o' these days.'

Sometimes the boys called out in protest.

'Here Da, leave Mammy alone, don't hit her, Daddy.'

I put my hands over my ears and fled up the stairs to the next storey.

'God,' I thought, 'why don't you strike him dead! He's a wicked animal. Why don't you visit him with a plague or something like ye did tae Job and never let him get better!'

On the third storey I passed the door of poor Mr Pearson—God rest his soul, my granny always said when you mentioned him.

'That dirty old swine,' my mother said of him, 'he's better dead or he'd be in gaol.'

Mr Pearson was about the same age as my grandmother. But he didn't work. He lived with his daughter and son-in-law and their three children in the flat below Granny Bygroves. Most days he used to stand at the corner with the other 'corner boys' who were really men, just talking or looking up the football results. I knew him only by sight. I had never spoken to him as my mother warned me every morning before I set foot outside:

'Now mind—don't talk to any men and if any o' them offer ye sweeties, come straight home and tell me.'

One day when I had been to my granny's and she, as usual, was out, I decided to wait downstairs at the closemouth, rather than outside her door in the dark and Mr Pearson was standing there too. He began to chat to me, saying all the usual things that adults say to children: how old was I, what class was I in at school, was I a good scholar, what did I want to be when I grew up, and, finally, was I waiting for Mrs Bygroves. I answered him perfunctorily, not because I disliked him, but simply because my mother had told me not to carry on any conversation with men who were not of the family. Just when I decided to move away, he himself turned into the close and said:

'Well, I'll away up then, lassie. Cheerio!'

I nodded, and turned to face the street looking up and down to see if there was any sign of Granny. She was a long way from coming. The old man was standing at the top of the stairs. It barely registered in my consciousness that the footsteps had stopped on the landing. Then I heard him calling to me:

'Hey, hen, come here a minute.'

I turned round and saw him. He had undone his trousers and in the gloomy light of the stairhead I saw he was holding some darkish object in his hand and making stroking movements.

'Come on up a minute, hen,' he said, beckoning and pointing to the open toilet door. 'I've got something to show ye.'

I was astonished. Though I couldn't see clearly what he was

23

stroking like a cat, I knew from its position what it was. He had taken oot his wullie which meant he was one of those men my mother had warned me against.

'You're wicked,' I shouted at him angrily, 'and ah'm goin' home tae tell mah mither on ye.'

Then I ran home. When I got there I told my mother I'd waited ages for Granny and she hadn't come, whereupon my mother remembered that my grandmother was working a late shift and wouldn't be home till about 11 p.m. I didn't quite know how to broach the subject of old Mr Pearson's strange behaviour and tried out a few beginnings in my mind.

'It isn't right if a man shows ye his wullie, is it, Mammy?' That didn't sound much good. 'Do you know anything queer about Mr Pearson, Mammy?' That might be a more delicate introduction. Or—'You shouldn't have sent me round to Granny's today, ye know, Mammy.' Instead, my mother brought the subject up herself.

'You look very guilty about something,' she said to me. 'What have ye been doing?'

'Nothing.'

'Don't give me that shit. You've been up tae some monkey business or other.'

'It's no' me that's been doin' something. It was that old Mr Pearson, and it was your fault for sending me round when you know Granny wouldn't be home.'

When I explained what had happened my mother sat gnawing her knuckles for a bit.

'Well,' she said afterwards, 'that's it. The first time. There'll be many others. This place is full o' people like that old swine. That's why I want your father to get that job in Australia. Anyway, ye did the right thing. Tonight when your granny comes home we'll go and see her because I've a mind tae charge him, the dirty old sod. Jesus, what a place to bring up kids. It'd gie ye the shits.'

My grandmother came to see us that night, however. She often did when she was working a late shift at the hotel. She would drop in with pieces of chicken and left-overs of various sorts from the pantry and say:

'Here, Rose, ye're still up? Here's a few bits and pieces I've brought from the hotel. Put the kettle on an' we'll have a tightener.'

24

That night, while my mother was attending to the preparations for supper, she told Granny what had happened.

'Aye well, he's an old man,' she said unperturbedly. 'Ye've got tae make allowances. Ah mean he didnae do any real harm tae her, did he?'

'Only because she ran away,' my mother exclaimed indignantly. 'But what aboot the harm tae her mind? These things can affect a kid's mind long after.'

Granny looked at me skeptically over the chicken bone that she was sucking with zest.

'Aye? They do say. But ah'm thinking it hasnae done anything tae her mind. She's gey crafty that big yin, old Lavery over the back.'

Both my mother and I ignored these aspersions on my innocence and my mother went on to point out that if old Mr Pearson were left to continue his indecent exposures without reproof, he might advance to greater things.

'Well, ye're no' goin' tae the polis aboot him,' Granny announced determinedly. 'He's lived in that close as long as ah have, over thirty-five years, and his daughter was born there. It would be a terrible scandal, insupportable, no' to be thought on. Ye'll have tae speak tae his daughter and tell her she has tae keep a better eye on him.'

It was decided we would go immediately after supper to the third floor flat of Annie McGarrigle, the daughter of old Mr Pearson, and get her.

'Ah told her ah'd call in on her the night when ah was on my way tae the attic,' said my grandmother. 'Ah try tae put a few bits an' pieces aside for her.'

The three adults sat on Granny's bed, which was the only seating accommodation available.

'Ah've no need for anything else,' she would explain craftily, when visitors complained of there being no chairs. 'Nae-body comes tae see me unless they're wantin' something for nothing and ah certainly don't want tae encourage them to hang around. An' if ah want tae entertain mah chinas, ah take them tae the fish and chip shop.'

Mrs McGarrigle clutched her greasy chicken pieces and smiled uneasily at me. My mother sat with her 'wrath of God' look on her face so it was clear that any smiles would be as effective on her as on the Gorgon. When she was acquainted with the nature

25

of her father's peculiarity, Annie McGarrigle began to cry. Rather, she whimpered quietly for she was too insubstantial a stick to cry with gusto. The skin on her limbs curved inwards towards the bones until it reached her joints, which in other people are nearly invisible, but in a runty wee woman (as my mother described her later) swelled like blown glass on the end of a tube. I had never seen anyone so thin, nor heard a voice so whiney.

'Ah cannae tell mah man, ye know. He'd kill him. He doesnae like him anyway and has never wanted him in the hoose wi' us. But where can he go? He cannae work because o' his heart. He'd have tae go into the old men's model and ah couldnae hae it on man conscience.'

My granny folded her lips inward till she'd nearly swallowed them.

'Well, lassie, ye'll have tae talk tae him aboot it. Point out that he's tae keep away from wee girls or he'll end up in the chokey. There's nothing else can be done. Ye cannae follow him every time he goes oot because he stays oot nearly all day, doesn't he?'

So we all went home to bed and Annie McGarrigle reflected as she left the attic that it was a blessing she had all boys and thank you very much for the chicken and such-like because her husband had lost a lot of time at work; his T.B. didn't seem to be getting much better.

'That Mrs McGarrigle looks like Pop-Eye's girl friend,' I remarked to my mother as we were leaving the attic.

'Aye,' she agreed. 'Did you see her face? Her skin's pulled over her bones like a piece of plastic. Ye can practically see through it.'

'Aye, Mammy, and did ye see that big varicose vein going down the front of her left leg like a big worm? It was nearly as fat as her leg. Why is she so thin, that's what I'd like tae know?'

A week later, at another supper, eating another piece of chicken from the same pantry of the same hotel and sucking the bone with the same zest, my granny asked casually:

'Well, what did ye think aboot old Pearson?'

'What aboot him?' my mother answered. 'Ye know fine well what ah think about him.'

'Aboot his death, I mean,' said Granny. 'He had a stroke and they buried him yesterday.'

Visions of judgement and hellfire blazed up before my eyes.

'Goodness, it looks as if God punished him, doesn't it?'

'Is that the kind o' crap they teach ye at the Sunday School now?' Granny returned disgustedly, tossing her bones into the middle of the table and reaching for the teapot. 'If God punished all the people that do stupid or bad things we wouldnae hae to wait for Paradise. It'd be right here now. Death's no' a judgement, it comes to every man.'

'Yes, but the time and the place, Granny,' I pressed her, 'isn't there something special about when and where and how we die?' The subject was to be closed, however.

'Here, what dae ye take me for?' she asked me indignantly. 'Ah'm no' one o' your professors o' theology, ye know. Away up tae the Varsity and ask them aboot these things. Anyway, ah say, God rest his soul just the same.'

And thereafter, when I passed the McGarrigles' door, I envisaged old Mr Pearson standing on the stairhead with his trousers undone and my granny saying, 'God rest his soul, just the same.'

Getting money out of Granny was never a straightforward business. Strategy had to be used when you approached the fourth floor where she had her little attic room. You had to tiptoe very quietly down her lobby, careful not to tread on the creaking floorboards. Then you listened with your ear to the door, to hear if she were home. Whenever she was at home, she was usually asleep, but if you listened long enough you could hear her bed groan as she changed position. Sixteen stone on the move was a massive undertaking. Once satisfied she was inside, you simply settled down to wait. If she were moving around, making a cup of tea on her little gas ring, you were really in luck. Even then, however, strategy was not at an end. You had to disguise your knock, because if she suspected a child, namely my sister or me, she would often climb into bed again and go to sleep. So I rummaged in my mind each time I visited her to find an interesting knock. Once I tried the police knock. Very loud and peremptory. No nonsense kind of knock. This is the police. Open up at once.

She opened up at once and glared at me with shock and annoyance.

'Here, what's a' this sounding like the polis! Knocking like a big dick. Ye scared seven years' growth oot o' me. Away hame tae your mammy, ah havenae got any money.'

Whatever knock I used I always got the same welcome.

27

Granny had the same attitude to borrowers as the Greeks had to the bearers of bad news.

'It's you is it, again? What dae ye want? Ah havenae got any money so it's nae use hanging around.'

I said nothing at this stage because I knew what was going to follow.

'Look, ah've got two bob between me and the bailiff.'

'Well, Granny,' I would say gratefully, 'two shillings would be a start. We could get some potatoes to make chips. Mammy hasnae got a bite tae eat in the hoose.'

'Aye, ah like your cheek. Ye mean you'd take my last two bob, the only thing between me and my Maker!' Then looking anxiously down the lobby, she would say with exasperation: 'Here, c'mon in and don't be standing there a' day letting every Johnny know my business.'

Once inside the attic I scrutinised the significant features of the room, while Granny looked into all her little hidey holes and didn't look under the statue that stood on a shilling. There was the window like the one Bess the landlord's daughter hung out of, opening outwards on to the deeply sloping roof of grey slate. To its right was the dark red chimney pot, nearly as tall as I was, and too wide to put your arms round. You couldn't see down to the ground for the roof was too wide and long; you could only see the attics opposite. I often wanted to throw something out of the window to see if I could hear it clink on the ground, but I never had the courage of my sister Margaret, who once tossed an empty condensed milk tin, like a discus, right out into the middle of the street. Granny told us that even a penny dropped from that height and landing on someone's head could kill him. Margaret could have been a murderer but she didn't care.

'Och, they're sure to see it coming,' she said nonchalantly, 'and duck oot o' its way.'

Inside, at right angles to the window and along one wall, was the sink, very dirty.

'It's only for getting water from,' my granny said, when I pointed to its grime. On the sink usually stood a bottle of Barr's Iron Bru. When Granny went to a neighbour's for a few minutes I often used to have a drink and fill the gap with water. She never seemed to notice the difference. An orange box covered with material was opposite the sink and next to the gas ring and served as a locker. That was where she had her cake tin. On really exciting occasions it contained large fondants, pink and white, that melted in your mouth twice as sweetly for being pinched when she wasn't looking. Such a coup brought oohs and ahs of frustration and envy from Margaret when reported to her.

'Ah'm goin' tae ask her for the money next time. You shouldn't get tae go all the time.'

Not much else in the attic was of interest to me. On Granny's dressing table there were funny little plastic dolls wearing crinolines. I hated plastic dolls, but I marvelled that such a great bear of a woman like Granny Bygroves could sit there with her men's shoes and socks crossed and patiently sew with her huge hands, dainty dresses for these little dolls. She was like Gulliver's nurse in Brobdingnag. The little statue above her head always stood on a shilling. I never liked to ask why, for she would have known I had been looking at it and touching it. In the night it glowed phosphorescently.

'Well, ye've seen a' there is tae see, ah take it,' she always said, leading me to the door. 'Don't think ah don't know who's been at mah cakes and fondants. And the next time ye try on mah Californian Poppy you should make sure it doesn't stink out the whole landing. Ah'll make certain mah door's locked next time I go doon the street for a few minutes.'

'Thanks for the money, Granny,' I answered, pointedly ignoring her accusations. 'Mammy'll gie it back tae ye on Friday night.'

'Aye, if ah'm in the front line o' her creditors,' she scoffed disbelievingly. 'Ye can put your mother's promises where the monkey put its nuts—and tell her ah said it.'

That was it. The door slammed on the full stop. Suddenly deflated, I went slower and slower down Granny's lobby, bumping my left shoulder unhappily against the wall. There was no more energy left for the descent, no desire to seek the hidden delights of the toilets, to expose myself to the exhausting histrionics of the Muirs or to savour the regurgitation of old Pearson's last stand at the lavatory with his trousers undone. No energy to jump the stairs four at a time. My substance was turning into aspic and then into fluid, and I began to trickle down the stairs drop by drop. Hours and hours passed before I reached the ground and saw the close mouth at the end of the dark tunnel. I moved outside, squinting into the light and stared up at the sky, looking for the little attic. It couldn't be seen. Down here you were cut off from it, as up there you had no touch with the ground. But it was up there, I knew, up among the clouds, being lightly rubbed out by the swirling, viscous light.

2 Honorary Citizens

Light and darkness in the city held me continually in thrall, impinging on my consciousness almost every waking minute as supernatural forces that were at work enchanting the buildings and the people, springing changes from minute to minute so that nothing ever remained as it seemed: Jekyll was always in the process of turning into Hyde.

To the tenements, the cruellest light of all was the long transparent light of midsummer. Its bright whiteness yanked the hard, ugly slabs of granite right into the open and held up to censorious scrutiny their pitted surfaces choked with two centuries of dirt, and their grimy windows as useless as cataracted eyes. The gaunt, bleak buildings hung helplessly in the glare, exposed to all as black, scabrous monsters reeking like compost in the summer heat. Out of their innards came the children in their new cottons, thin white legs and arms eager for their yearly ration of sunlight, the cod liver oil bottles pushed well back in the cupboards. White faces and white bodies taken out of dark closets for an airing. But all tough and alive-o. The others had been silently excreted by the tenements under cover of winter gloom.

Summer made of the slum children honorary citizens of the city of Glasgow. They were free to roam at will and they did; they went walkabout, runabout and for tuppence, tramabout, to Queens Park, the Bluebell Woods, Rouken Glen, Milngavie, and Linn Park, where they dragged ponds for minnows and tadpoles, threw bread to ducks, stood amazed at the beauty of swans, climbed trees, played Swiss Family Robinson, fell into burns and crammed their stomachs with unripe crab-apples, gooseberries, raspberries and plums, finally staggering home at night clutching their distended abdomens. Straps in hands, their mothers waited at the doors with one eye on the clock and another on the street.

'Where have ye been a' this time! Ye've been away since nine o'clock this morning and look at the time now. It's nearly eleven o'clock.'

'But it's no' dark yet. Ye cannae go tae bed when it's daylight. That's no' for sleeping in.'

We devoured the daylight hours, raced through our sleep and ate absent-mindedly in minutes that inadvertently escaped our notice.

'Aye well, get something intae ye and get straight tae bed after ye've had a wash. Tomorrow ye're goin' tae take Jack and Sadie with ye' because ah want tae gie the place a real good clean-oot.'

They had already gone to bed in preparation for an early rise in the morning. Oh God, what utter agony to have young brothers and sisters when you wanted to play.

'Humph, we're lucky,' my sister Margaret said in bed. 'It's a wonder she didn't tell us tae strap Anne tae oor backs and go roon like one o' those Red Indian wimmen.'

In the morning, after 'going the messages', we strode through the streets with Jackie and Sadie half running, half falling along beside us, each clutching tightly a grudgingly extended finger.

'Don't go sae fast, don't go sae fast,' they whimpered, 'ah cannae keep up wi' ye.'

'Well, ye should've thought o' that before, shouldn't ye, stupid appearance. We're no' going tae crawl along like a baby in nappies. Oh for goodness sake, he's fallen over. Look at him, filthy! Here, get up on mah back an' ah'll gie ye a coal carry.'

We got on the tram and Margaret raced upstairs to 'book' the closed-in compartment. It had seats only for five but I could sit Jackie on my knee. The tram driver was down below. I peered over the railing and could see the top of his cap. Then we turned down the window at the front and leaned out to see the destination written in its long glass box. There was a little handle the conductress turned when they were going to change the destination but we never had the nerve to do it ourselves. The driver could see what you were doing by looking up into a mirror above his head.

'Here, you kids up there, stop jumping around and shut that window or ah'll send the conductress up tae ye.'

She was coming along the aisle anyway and we all sat quietly in guilty silence and fear that she might send us downstairs.

'All right,' she said slamming the door open and parking her spine on the edge of it. 'What's your ages?'

'These two are under five, he's six, she's seven, she's ten and ah'm twelve. We're going tae Gorbals Cross.'

'That's a rum place tae be going for a day out, isn't it?'

The Gorbals was a rum place to be in at any time, for a day or a minute, I thought. Once we'd lived on the outskirts of it and I'd gone to the pictures that were right in the Gorbals. It was a dreadful place; Plantation was a paradise compared with it.

'Oh, we're not going to the Gorbals,' I said, in my correctest English, anxious to dispel any impression we might live there, 'we're going to Milngavie, but we have to catch the tram there.'

'Aye, ye're right there,' the conductress returned, nodding her head approvingly, 'Milngavie's a different kettle of fish, isn't it son?' she asked, ruffling Jackie's red hair. 'Noo, watch your wee brother doesnae fa' doon the stairs.'

'Ah'm holdin' him tightly,' I said.

Both tram rides were a delight in themselves, for the suburbs we passed through were fairly strange to us. So nobody spoke a word all the way to Milngavie. There was too much to look at and think about.

Milngavie was a little village on the outskirts of Glasgow, right at the tram terminus. A burn flowed by it and it was this we made directly for. The water in one part was only a few inches deep and so clear that if you found a little pool you could see to comb your hair or wipe your mouth. Flat, smooth stones covered the bed, almost like a Roman road, and we sat on these in our knickers, our dresses tucked up round our waists. The youngest ones took their pants off, but the heat was never strong enough to risk letting them lie naked. My mother was always warning us to keep our chests covered. We drank the water, washed in it, stared into it for hours, dug up the stones to see what was underneath, splashed ourselves, jumped into the burn, played leapfrog and fell into it. Usually we ended up soaked with our chests all wet and had to run around to get dry. Some of us walked the parapet of the old stone bridge that crossed the burn

33

while one stayed with the young ones; it was too dangerous for them. Sometimes we 'dreeped' from it, that is, hung by our hands from the parapet and dropped into the water, a dangerous game, but its risks never occurred to us. When the bridge and the burn had been exhausted, it was time to take our sandwiches and sit beside the pond on the other side of the disused mill. Although no one had warned us not to go into the mill pond, we never considered doing it and we kept a tight hold on the young ones to make sure they didn't fall in. The water was completely still, unearthly so, and dark green. You couldn't see into it, but we suspected that some monster might be lying in wait in its depths—'the Milngavie Monster', we called it.

'Wouldn't it be funny if a frog jumped out of that pond and turned out to be a handsome prince,' my sister asked, when we were lying on our bellies and peering over the edge. 'You know, like in the fairy story.'

'What story?' asked Jackie immediately. 'Ah want tae hear it.'

'Well, ye're no' goin' tae,' I said, 'for ah'm no' in the mood for telling stories, so shut up.'

'Aw look what ye've done noo, he's startin' tae greet.' Margaret glared at me. 'Here, come over here tae me,' she beckoned to Jackie, 'and ah'll tell ye. She's a mean pig.' She sat him on her knee and biting her finger to help her remember, began:

'Well, ye see, it was aboot this beautiful princess. She had a ball o' pure gold and she used tae play wi' it near a pond like this yin. Then it fell in . . .'

When that one finished, Susan said: 'Och, ah like the one aboot the horse-shoe nail better,' and so we spent unmeasured time telling between us all the stories we could remember and, when they were used up, the monsters we had seen in pictures, making them up as we went along.

The time had gone again and we would be for it.

'Gosh, ah think it's late, ye know,' Margaret said, beginning to gather up our things. 'We better get their faces and hands washed. Mammy'll kill us if we take them home all dirty. His dungarees are still wet.'

'Here, run up and down, Jackie,' I told him, 'and they'll dry a bit. We'll have tae ask somebody the time. Look at that. No' a soul on the street. That's the trouble wi' these posh places, there's never anybody on the streets walking. They all go by car.'

'Hey look over there,' Margaret pointed, 'there's a man

34

sittin' in that panel van. He might be waiting for somebody. Go and ask him, and we'll walk along tae the tram stop.'

'Excuse me, Mister, have you got the time on ye?' I said, poking my head in the cabin window.

'Aye,' he answered, 'time for this.'

I ran all the way up the street after the others and said to them: 'C'mon, gie's your hand Jackie, we'll run tae the next tram stop and get away from him.'

'What did he say tae ye?' Margaret panted while we were running.

'Time for this—and then he did the same as old Pearson.' Her eyes popped open with astonishment and then she bit her lip wonderingly:

'Well, fancy posh people doin' that too. They're just the same as us, the dirty things.'

As we got near the tram stop, Jackie slowed down and hugged his knees together.

'Ah have tae go the lavatory,' he cried.

We all stared at him in horror.

'There's nae lavvy here ye wee pest. Why did ye no' tell us before when we were at the burn?'

'But ah didnae want tae go then,' he wailed. 'Ah want tae go noo, and ah have tae. It's comin' oot.'

'Oh try and haud it in,' we pleaded with him. 'It won't take long tae get home.'

'Ah did it,' he said unrepentantly. 'Ah told ye it was coming oot.'

Oh God, what a misery, what a misery.

'Here, wait a minute,' Margaret suggested helpfully, 'it might be one o' those hard yins ye can throw away.'

'Well, you can look,' I said, shuddering at the thought, 'ah'm no' goin' tae. It makes me sick.'

Margaret got hold of Jackie's dungarees and pulled the seat of them, looking down and holding her nose. She sighed hopelessly:

'It's a big messy one. And look, here comes the tram. What'll we do? He'll smell terrible and everybody'll know he's dirtied his pants. Oh, ah could kill you,' she shouted at Jackie, giving him a little shake.

Robert and Susan moved off a little way. 'You can go upstairs wi' him and we'll sit doonstairs. Ah don't want tae be associated wi' him,' Susan called, screwing up her face in disgust.

'Oh no you're not,' Margaret shouted at her, balling her hand threateningly. 'We'll all go upstairs and we can sit all round him and that might keep the smell inside.'

So that was what we did. We made Jackie stand up all the way so that anything that slipped out would fall on the floor and not on the seat. When we were leaving, we decided to put him in the middle of us, three of us at the front, and two behind him, so that nobody would see him walking with his legs wide apart. But the smell was dreadful and when we started to go down the aisle, grown-ups pushed between us and split us up. Those beside him started wrinkling their noses and looking round them. I heard one of them say:

'Hey, one o' those kids must have shit himself, can ye no' smell it?'

'Heavens,' I thought, 'what if they think it was me', because I was right behind Jackie and he was so small people couldn't see him very well.

As we started to go down the stairs, a youth of about twenty turned his head round towards us and called out for everybody to hear:

'Hey lassie, ye left your calling card on the floor', and when I looked back along the aisle, I saw little mounds all in a line —some of them flattened, where people had stood on them.

When we got home that night, we complained loudly to my mother.

'That Jackie's never coming wi' us again, the dirty little pig. If he comes, we're staying home.'

Jackie, however, remained defiant.

'Ah told ye,' he said, 'ah told ye it was comin' oot.'

Sometimes, after repeatedly disobeying injunctions to return at a 'reasonable' hour, we were confined to the local streets and forbidden to stride out to the waters and the woods on pain of lying, all of us, in a welter of our own blood. Where the tenements were cramped, the streets, fortunately, were wide and relatively free of traffic. The commonest obstruction, welcomed with grins and sly looks, was the coal carts drawn by the monster Clydesdales. Who minded jumping aside for the beautiful beasts! They were the day's treat to look at, but though we beamed into their serious white faces, some of them rolled their eyes when they saw a press of tenement boys crowding the lamp post.

36

'All right, who's goin' tae ruffle their feathers?' said one. 'Ah managed it last time.'

I detested this kind of diversion. It meant sneaking alongside the cart and suddenly thrusting your hand into the long hair that grew from the horse's hock to its heel, and giving it a tug, usually on the near back leg. The horse would kick backwards—part of the skill was to leap out of its way before you got kicked—and rear up screaming with rage, whereupon the carter would lash out with his long whip on both sides of the cart, cursing the boys foully and threatening to flog them if he laid hands on them. Sometimes the girls would prepare for flight before the horses drew level and then run off shouting:

'They're after the horses' feathers.' This generally provoked a long and frightening chase through the street of the girl who had spoiled the fun, with curses and stones being hurled after her until a new diversion presented itself.

At other times, we all waited till the cart had passed and then caught hold of the tail end, holding ourselves on with one armpit until we fell off, or someone shouted:

'Hey mister, look behind ye!' and the driver would turn round yelling at us and cracking the long whip over our heads.

The street games were intensely active and required extraordinary stamina to keep at them all day, which was half the night too in summer. The morning, however, was generally set aside for the tenement olympics, activities that tested courage as well as agility.

All the tenement blocks were shaped like rectangular black picture frames. The outside edges faced the streets and the empty space inside was cut up by rows of spear-shaped railings or by high brick walls (dykes) into back courts, commonly called 'backs', each of which was the territory of a group of flats. It usually contained two brick structures: one, a wash-house with two tubs and a boiler, none of which would have functioned within memory, and the other, a three-sided midden that lodged the bins where people unloaded their rubbish and ashes from the coal fires. The bins were often invisible beneath a mound of ash that reached almost to the roof. These middens were favourite hideouts of little children who loved scavenging in them when they weren't gouging out the hard-packed dirt that formed the ground surface of the back courts, to make 'glabber pies' from a dirt and water mixture, generally considered very tasty by the children.

For the older children, like us, the high dykes dividing the backs separated the lions from the mice. The walls were only about four inches wide on top and it was no achievement at all to walk along them. You had to run, hop on your left leg (if you were right-handed) without lowering your other leg, skip along them with a rope and then do all that backwards.

My sister Margaret did most of these absent-mindedly, simply to vary the monotony of traversing one wall after another that would take you from the bottom of the block to the top, a distance of half a mile or so. My efforts, however, provoked mirth, exasperation, annoyance, and finally dismissal from the gang. It took me about twenty minutes to cross one wall, only about twenty feet long, and I did it in a sickeningly craven manner by sitting astride it and with my hands in front of me, jerking or dragging myself along, rasping my thighs on the rough bricks. All the time, I was terrified I would fall.

'Here she comes,' the others would shout from yards away, looking back to see if I was still aloft. 'Here, stand clear you blokes, or she'll knock ye doon in the rush.'

'God, your sister's glaikit, Margaret,' others complained to her. 'What's the matter wi' her, she's a right feartie.'

'Well, don't complain to me,' answered Margaret belligerently, 'ah didnae make her. Anyway, she's a good scholar.'

However, I was more successful in the 'dreeping' from high walls, since being tall for my age, I had less distance to drop. This gave me a formidable advantage over many of the others who were typically undersized, Glaswegian 'wee nyaff's', short on inches and long on cheek.

'Here, ah bet ye can't dreep from the bakehouse dyke!' This was higher than the wall, more than fifteen feet from the ground.

'Ah could if ah were Daddy long-legs like you, ye great misery.'

'Aye, but ye're scared, aren't ye and ye don't like tae be laughed at when ye're scared.'

'Aye, but you're scared o' stupid things that anyone can do, gettin' along the wall like a bug.'

'But fear's fear, isn't it? Yours an' mine is the same. It means as much tae me as it does tae you, doesn't it? Ye shouldnae laugh at me when ah'm scared on the wall. Ah'm nae different from you when ye try tae dreep from the bakie dyke.'

They always looked slightly embarrassed at this and squinted slyly at each other, brushing their temples with their fingertips, meaningfully.

'Ye're a right good talker for your height. Here, let's get a ba' an' have a game.'

Out on the streets, once the interminable games of rounders, cricket, soccer, headies, and juggling had been wrung dry of every last drop of sweat, a slight breather was taken and then the ropes were set up. French skipping, for the older, more skilful of us. The two best turners, called 'cawers' in Glaswegian, very often two boys, held a long rope in each hand and turned the two in opposite directions. Then the champions, of whom my sister was one, got inside them and gave fascinating displays of balance and timing that made the others hold their breath, until the jumper, suddenly aware of the tension and the intense eyes upon her, giggled nervously and faltered. The ropes snaked around her, pinioning her arms and knotting her ankles.

'Here, that was great, can ah have a go?'

'Away wi' ye, it's mah turn. You had a turn that last time we played, d' ye mind o' it when Joe Gibson and Freddie Goode were cawing.'

'So who cares! That was aboot a month ago. Get oot o' the way or ah'll knock yer teeth doon yer throat.'

'Aye, you and whose army? C'mon up the brae an' we'll hae a go then, misery face.'

At such embarrassing moments which exploded in an atom of time some tenement diplomat would call out:

'Hey, let's hae a game o' kick the can afore it gets dark,' and the two sullen antagonists, not infrequently a boy and a girl, their faces dark and lowering, shadowed over by their black brows and furious eyes, would leave the ropes and run with the others to find an empty tin.

By the end of summer many parents were sighing for the shorter evenings of autumn and winter, when children were home punctually for their tea and anxious to go to bed before eleven o'clock, for although no child wanted to stay indoors, his shouting and fighting annoyed fathers wanting a quiet night reading the papers or listening to a radio play. And doors were constantly being thrown open or banged shut, as first one, then another came hurtling inside to whine:

'Mammy, Tom Smellie's hitting our Robert.'

'Mammy, can ah have a piece an' jam?'

'Mammy, Susan won't let me have a go wi' the peever. She says ah'm too wee, but ah know how tae play.'

'Mammy, Rita Gordon says can we go up the Maxwell wi' her next week and her brother's goin' tae England tae be a jockey.'

Mammy, Mammy, Mammy, till finally, my mother, maddened by the unending attacks on her peace, grabbed a broom and flayed about her like Goliath run amok:

'Jesus, Mary and Joseph, can ah no' get a minute's peace in this bedlam. Here, Robert, get aff yer backside and dae something aboot this lot. They're driving me up the bloody wall. Look at that wee bugger. He's gone under the bed. Here, Mary Rose, get under that bed an' drag him oot.'

She got down on her knees, spitting with frustration and fury, and tried to ram the broom under the bed where Jackie was pressed tightly against the back wall.

'Get oot from under there, this minute, or ah swear tae God ah'll swing for ye when ah lay hands on ye. Jesus, he's grabbed the brush.' She pulled at her thick hair in raging impotence and shook her clenched hands despairingly. Then, throwing herself at the door and wrenching it open in one movement, she streamed out of the close, wailing like a banshee.

'Ah've got tae have peace,' she told the world, 'ah need peace.'

On these occasions she headed for Granny's attic like a wild beast returning to its den and there she renewed her plaint, cursing fate, my father, us, the mother who bore her and life itself.

'Ah'll throw mahself intae the Clyde,' she would vow extravagantly, 'that's what ah'll dae. Ah just cannae take any more.'

'Aye, aye,' Granny would croon, rocking her head backwards and forwards to emphasise her agreement with anything and everything my mother had to say. After a while, when the savage noises dulled to quiet snortings and snuffles in the corner and then to odd sniffs broken by long silences that indicated my mother was making comforting plans for renewing life, Granny put the kettle on and set out two cups of tea with condensed milk. When my mother agreed to a second cup, it was time for the placebo:

40

'It's a big job ye've taken on yerself, lassie, tryin' tae cope wi' seven kids. It's a terrible burden, right enough. But they'll be a godsend tae ye when they're grown up. And think what ye've got tae be thankful for—they're a' healthy and active and bright enough, tae. They might bring fame and fortune tae ye when they're up. Ah mean tae say, ah know that man o' yours isnae what ye'd call the exciting type, he's no mah cup o' tea, but he's a guid man . . .' and the rest followed like the refrain of a hymn: 'he doesnae drink tae excess or run aroon wi' filthy wimmen an' he's a guid provider.'

My mother always considered these propositions like new thoughts, incredible as it seemed to me. She and my grandmother were like weird sisters taking part in a religious ceremony where demons were exorcised through the repetition of formulae. Once the magic words were pronounced and the cup taken, there was a rebirth of life. My mother returned to the house, went to bed, and got up in the morning with plans for revolutionising our existence. By lunch-time, these were put aside for reconsideration after the next crisis and she got on with the washing.

Sometimes, if Margaret and I were at home when my mother was coming apart, one of us would scoop up the other children and stuff them under the blankets, threatening them with Chinese torture if they didn't get to sleep straight away, and the other would ease up to Mammy and say very quietly:

'Will ah make ye a cup o' tea, Mammy?' She would whirl on us like a wild beast and glare, her eyes smoking with strain, and then in a moment, while we waited without breathing, the look would be drawn backward into the dark whirlpool of her mind leaving her dazed and childlike.

'Aye,' she would say dreamily, 'aye hen, that would be fine. Ye're a guid lassie.' She would pat me absent-mindedly and flow bodilessly into the old, brown armchair, like a grey spirit.

She's drinking the tea noo. I wonder if she notices me watching her over the rim o' the cup. Her face is smoothed out now. Jings, she looks like a crazed mask when she's like that.

'Would ye like me tae make ye toast, Mammy?'

She doesnae want any. What else can I say?

'Did ye clean the windaes today, Mammy? They look great. Oor windaes are the shiniest in the street.'

My mother stared at me unblinkingly, suddenly shrewd again. Then she burst out laughing.

41

'You're a fly yin. Don't think ah don't know what ye're up tae. Ah'm no' deid yet.'

In bed later, after we'd settled in with the other two, plonking their feet into the middle of the bolster, Margaret looked up at the ceiling and said laconically:

'Well, we did it. She didnae go tae Granny this time.'

I never really knew what made my mother run amuck like this and she did it regularly over all the years that I can count. It was easy to see specific causes of irritation: the children's noise, the money worries, my father's apparent withdrawal from the minutiae of our daily lives. He was committed to bringing justice to his working fraternity, a mighty theoretical problem, but in fact, he often worked more than a hundred hours a week and was cosily insulated from the dreary comforts that were my mother's lot: juggling economy with nutrition in selecting food for nine, keeping the precious coal bunker filled, cutting out boys' trousers from the shabby men's ones that had been passed along to her. Out there in the yards my father and his friends revelled in a drama that made Titans of them. Even the rich had no greater excitement or colour in their lives. And when the conflict was done, there was the right and proper Scottish harmony at home. The meal and its accompanying odour would be there, the fire blowing vigorously, the children washed and quiet and my mother all made up, her hair curled and crisp, her face freshly powdered. In the morning my father was up very early, but never as early as my mother. The kitchen would be warm and rosy, the porridge boiling gently, spurting and popping on the fire. At night when my father returned, the day's strains and failures would be carefully tucked away, for a working man needed tranquillity.

My mother and father lived entirely different lives and he seemed strangely insensitive to the wildness in her.

'It's your mother, it's her nature,' he would say as we shuddered and quivered, waiting for the crisis to pass.

To me, however, there was more in it than that, some strange longing in my mother, something she could not articulate and that I could only feel. Queer times, she would stop washing at the sink, all of a sudden, and raise her head, staring silently through the bars of the kitchen window, as if something out there were calling her. There was no way she could explain it to me and I watched her with a queasy feeling in my stomach. Later, on

42

encountering *The Forsaken Merman* and *Wuthering Heights,* I thought that the anguish of Margaret and Cathy had the grey, alien quality of my mother's.

3 Any Old Iron?

When school reopened in mid-September the summer of our minds at last took leave of our senses. Till then no child would pull on his long woollen socks with the matted darns or squeeze into his shrunken jumper. If it was summer holidays, then summer it was and the wind could blow till you were blue in the face. With the start of the school year, however, there was a great turning inwards. Inwards on our selves, and inward to the waiting tenements that were wearing the thicker, darker light like new season's makeup: to gloss over their surface defects, their greasy pores, their rough scale, their unsightly furrows. Our attitude to them changed subtly. Freed as they were from comparison with the fresh, clean, summer light, they no longer seemed glaringly ugly. And they were the only alternative to the wet cold street. Summer had piped us over the hills and far away from the tenements, but autumn and winter were shovelling us into the stone bunkers, like the dross we scrabbled for when there was no money for coal.

On Thursday nights when we sang and screeched in the Bethel:

'Our shelter from the stormy blast
and our eternal home'

it was the tenements we were apostrophising, not some ill-defined, capricious, supernatural landlord.

And well they knew it. They doubled in size, for as the light became more and more opaque and river fogs circumscribed the dockside like greasy hawsers, space contracted rapidly. Sight braked with a jolt at the granite walls whose limits were now infinite, lost beyond definition in the clouds. In the fogs, they were our only contact with each other: we groped along their length, fumbled round their corners and crossed the streets with hands outstretched to touch the security of their stone. They lowered over us, the flinty spawn of the factory system, who had outlived it but were sustaining the legend and the fear.

'Go to the ant thou sluggard,' had thundered God and the Victorian Calvinists. 'Go to the ant, and set about it smartly, man. This is Scotland ye've living in, no' the South o' France, ye know. Get tae the yards or the repair. Make money. Lay up my treasures on earth and I'll buy mothballs. Consider the parable o' the talents. Who doesnae double my capital, gets his cards. Go, put money in my purse.'

And in the mornings early, when my mother had got up and lit the fire in the kitchen to cook the porridge and had gone next door to the bakehouse to buy hot rolls that she spread with margarine (our two ounces of butter per person were saved up for my Granny Lavery) then she went to where my father was sleeping in the room where we had visitors and our hogmonay party, and shook him awake:

'Hey Robert, it's six o'clock. Time to get up.'

At the repair, the time keeper was watching the gates with impatience.

'How long wilt thou sleep o sluggard? When wilt thou arise out of thy sleep?'

And all the fathers straggled over the brae, their greasy bunnets pulled tightly down over one side of their faces to stop the north wind roaring down the tunnel of their ears. Their jackets, too, were quite oily, supple and shiny like seal coats, made water repellent with grease from the engine rooms. The pockets hung down below the hemline from years of being weighted with the man's piece—and other things. Inside the gates of the repair yards they disappeared, into the maw of the huge ships lying in dry dock, and were seen no more for twelve hours, twenty-four hours, three days. They were putting money in the purses of John Brown and Company, Alexander Stephen and Sons, Harland and Wolfe and Company, Barclay Curle and Company, the Anchor Line and Company and company and company, for miles along the Clyde, in Glasgow, Renfrew, Clydebank, Dalmuir, Ardrossan, Burnt Island and Dumbarton, putting money in purses at a rate that would never be known again.

Sometimes we didn't see our father for over a week. He came home at 1 a.m. and went out again at five or six of the same morning. When he did come home, he sat in the chair by the fire and snored with his mouth open, his paper slipping down his knees. My mother glared at him with disgust and shook him a bit.

'Here, how long are ye goin' tae sit like that? It's nearly five o'clock and ah want tae go to the pictures. Ah havenae been oot for nearly a month. Ye should take your bed to Stephen's.'

My father pulled himself up straighter in the chair and blinked at us through his red eyes. They really did look piggy, all screwed up and bloodshot.

'Listen,' he said angrily, 'if ah don't bring home the bacon ye throw the pay packet doon and ask me: "how ahm ah expected to manage on that!" When ah bring home a fat pay packet then ye're whinging that ye never go oot. Ye're helluva hard tae please.'

'There's such a thing as a happy medium,' my mother returned, sniffing disdainfully. 'But you Communists are a' extremists.'

My father went red with indignation.

'Ye don't know the first thing aboot it, ye silly wumman. Ah told ye the government had agreed tae pay for a' the repairs needed to ships commandeered during the war. And the companies are doin' their damnedest tae make sure that they pay through the nose. There are ships in those yards that have never been touched in the war. Their damage is pre-war stuff. But the companies are gettin' the government tae fork oot for their repairs tae. That's what's meant by the Welfare State; the biggest charities are given tae the richest beggars. Jesus, the workin' man never wins. An' so there they are settin' us on wi' their penalty rates tae work every bloody minute. Ah had tae knock back a trip tae the tail o' the bank today because ah'm buggered oot. An' there you are whinging because ye canne go tae the pictures. Well, ah'm goin' tae bed. Ye can wake me up at eight an' we'll go tae the second half.'

Whereupon he pulled himself out of the armchair. The springs had gone and it was like fighting your way out of a huge wash-basin. I could see by the changed expression on my mother's face that she was remorseful, and she called out after my father as he slammed into the lounge-room:

'Och, it doesnae really matter, Robert. Sleep for as long as ye want, and we can go tae the Cessnock before it shuts.'

This meant that my father could sleep for four hours, but he never minded going to the pub for a drink, so that would probably be as long as he wanted.

My father was quite right in his criticisms of my mother. She was always wanting the money and demanding querulously: 'What's this taken oot for, and this?' when she noticed the discrepancy between his gross and his net wages. It was as if she thought the deductions from his pay had been made by the government with his connivance, each of them getting a secret cut. But if my father was out all the time at the yard, or if he came home late because he had to work overtime unexpectedly, then she harangued him with accusations that he was irresponsible and undomesticated and that he thought bringing home the bacon was all there was to married life.

Sometimes my father was late for other reasons and then there was real trouble.

'You drunken sot, your tea's been waiting on the stove for nearly two hours.'

I always kept my head down at these meal times, eyeing my stew and potatoes with a stomach that was churning round like a cement mixer. If only she would shut up, there would never be any fighting, for my father never quarrelled. It was always her. What if he did drink a bit before he came home? The world wouldn't come to an end. Why didn't she make the tea later? It was her who was always doing the shouting. My father at first tried to humour her.

'Look Rose, ah had tae drop off at the pub tae discuss a scrap deal an ah' had only two whiskies. Ah mean, you get your cut from it. If ah didnae go tae the pub ye wouldnae have got that hand-out on Saturday night, fifteen quid ah gave ye—nearly four weeks' wages, for Christ's sake.'

'Just leave Christ out of it,' my mother shouted at him. 'He's no' for the likes o' your mob. Marx is the one ye should be calling on. See if he can save your soul.'

My father got up from the table and threw himself out of the kitchen. He seized the paper as he was going and tramped noisily into the lounge-room where he stretched himself out on the bed, sighing and snorting like a fussy walrus. Escape from

47

my mother was not so easy, however. She picked up his plate, laden with stew and dumplings and ran in behind him.

'There,' she said, with a beatific smile of complete satisfaction, 'there ye are, see how ye like that wi' your paper,' and she slapped his dinner right on to his face.

Margaret and I had run in behind my mother and were looking round the door anxious to see what she was going to do with the plate. Poor Da. His face had disappeared and he was in danger of smothering from the potatoes that were choking his nose and stopping his mouth. The stew, fortunately cooled down, was spreading over his chin and neck like river mud, and the walls and pillows were splattered with brown stains and lumps of sticky dumplings.

Thereafter, when my father came home late, he opened the door and put his cap round it, proffering it like a collection plate. In it there would be a couple of pound notes and some silver, and he waited with the saccharin outstretched till my mother came and took it. Then he called through the letter box:

'Can ah come in?'

My mother found it difficult to ignore the money and the humour of the situation appealed to her, so she usually let the lateness pass without a brawl, though she could never resist a few sarcastic remarks. I was always relieved when things went on smoothly but there seemed to me something not quite right about my father's solution.

The money that was proffered in the cap came from scrap. I never knew what scrap was, only that it was something secret, that it involved stealing and that you made money from it. When my father came home straight from work with his pockets sagging to his knees, then he was in scrap. For years, I longed to see it, but he was too smart for me. As soon as I appeared in the lobby he said to me:

'Here, buzz off, quick smart. Intae the kitchen, go on!'

I had been thinking that I would suddenly thrust my hand into his pocket to feel what was inside, no matter if I did get a slap. But he never let me get within touching distance. He went straight into the lounge-room and shut the door. Sometimes I pressed my ear almost into the wood trying to interpret the strange noises I could hear on the other side, but almost immediately my father would shout out:

'Hey Rose, make sure Big Ears isnae at the keyhole', and my mother would come and lug me off. The next day I would rattle the handle of the big press in the lounge. That's where he would put the stuff from his pockets, but he always kept the key on him. I looked in every drawer in the house, on top of the wardrobe, and tried every key I could find, even those that were palpably unsuited to the lock. One or two days later the door would be open, but I knew then that it was no use looking. Whatever had been there was gone. I felt in every corner of the press, but it was always empty, except for two of my mother's irons, heavy ones, that she only used for sponging and pressing. When my father came home he always knew I had been looking and would ask me:

'Well, how has old Nosey Parker been today? Turned up anything yet?' Then he roared with laughter, and his little eyes shut with glee. I would punch him and feel in his pockets:

'Tell me, tell me Da, honest ah'll never tell anyone, ever. What dae ye do in the press? Ah want tae know.'

'Aye, ah know ye want tae know,' he would say, grinning delightedly, 'but that's something ye'll never know,' and he'd point his two fingers at my face, 'because ah'm too smart for ye, see.' He was, too! But I found out just the same.

One night my father hadn't come home and it was very late. I thought my mother would be angry, but instead she was worried.

'Ah've a feeling something's up wi' your Da,' she kept saying.

There was a knock at the door, and when I opened it a workman stood there.

'Is your mammy there, hen?' he asked me. 'Ah'm Chris Cullen from Stephen's, Mrs Lavery,' he said to my mother when she came to the door. 'Big Bob's been held up but he asked me to bring ye his pay packet.' He held out the envelope and started to leave the close in a hurry:

'Ah've got tae get home myself, Missus,' he said as my mother started to question him. 'He'll be home later. He said no' tae worry.'

My father didn't come home later. Instead, a policeman came to the door. Detective Lynch from Orkney Street police station and he would like to inform you, Mrs Lavery, that your husband Robert has been detained at Orkney Street Station pending trial for the theft of scrap iron from the shipyard of Alexander Stephen and Sons. Bail can be arranged for ten pounds and you can visit your husband tomorrow morning at ten o'clock.

Oh dear, oh dear. My father was going to prison like Mr Muir. Barlinnie was the biggest prison in Glasgow. They would put my father in an iron cage and he would be there for years and years till he was old and white-haired and everybody had forgotten about him. Poor Da. He would never be Big Bob again, the giant of the yard who swung hammers weighing twenty-eight pounds to slacken the nuts on the propellers, or who swung on spanners of three hundred pounds to loosen nuts that weighed a hundred-weight. What would happen to us all! What would happen to him?

My mother put her coat on, saying, 'Put the tea out. Make sure the kids get washed after they've eaten. You bath Jackie and Anne, and Margaret'll do the washing up. Ah'm goin' tae the station tonight. Ah'm no' waiting till any ten o'clock in the morning, an' ah'm getting on tae a lawyer.'

She went out, after fluffing her hair up and straightening the seams of her silk stockings and we all sat down to tea by ourselves. I sat Anne on my knee, feeding her spoonfuls of soup ladled from the big iron pot my mother had filled with ham bones and vegetables earlier in the day. Jackie was soaking pieces of bread in his broth pushing in more and more till the liquid had become almost solid.

'Here you, stop making a mess,' I told him. 'You've got enough bread in that soup.'

'Look what ah've done, Mary Rose,' he beamed at me, quite unperturbed. 'Ah've made a swamp for Hereward the Wake to hide out in from the Normans. If we had matches, we could make stilts.'

So that was the result of telling him stories at night! I put Anne down in the armchair with a pillow behind her to hold her upright and went round the table to where he was sitting.

'Right, get your swamp all eaten up or ah'll belt you.' Then he started to cry. How could anybody eat a swamp that was all dirty water and full of beasties? It would make him sick. After trying unsuccessfully to convince him that it was soup in his bowl, and that the solid lumps were bread, not bog, I threw the stuff out and filled another bowl which I made him drink in a hurry.

Susan was sitting beside her empty plate, staring into space, her long narrow eyes slit-like with concentration. She was a taciturn girl who preferred watching and listening to speaking. Suddenly she said:

'When do ye think Mammy'll be back, Mary Rose?'

'Oh, ah don't know,' I answered, 'ages, ah think. She said she was looking for a lawyer. Why?'

She looked at me sideways and then at Margaret.

'Come intae the bedroom and ah'll tell ye.' When we left the kitchen, she whispered to us in the lobby:

'Why don't we make some tablet—Mammy's got condensed milk in the cupboard.'

'You must be daft,' I said to her in horror. 'Mammy could come back any time and catch us. And in any case there's only a pound o' sugar left and no more in the ration books. Mammy gave Granny Lavery half our sugar ration this week. You had better get washed and get to bed, and don't be thinking of such silly things.'

Susan stamped her foot in temper and her pale cheeks reddened in anger.

'Don't try tae fool me,' she cried, tears in her eyes. 'Ah know you and Margaret make tablet and puff candy when Mammy and Daddy are oot and ye never let me have a bit. Ah found a pot under Mammy's bed one morning and it had all the toffee stuck in it. Ah could've told somebody, but ah didnae.'

Margaret giggled and I felt embarrassed. My authority as eldest in the family would be under attack now. How could I force the others to do the right thing, and set myself up as an example of sisterly rectitude, when here I had been unmasked as a sly hypocrite, slapping the others for digging into the condensed milk with their fingers, and commandeering whole tins for my own feasts, sharing out a tray of tablet between Margaret and me when the others were all asleep.

Susan was waiting, regarding me with her lips pressed stubbornly together and her jaw rigid with determination.

'Look, we've only done it twice,' I told her. 'Next time Mammy and Daddy go to the pictures, we'll let you help, but we cannae do it tonight because we don't know when Mammy'll be coming back. She might catch us.'

I cocked my head to see how the argument was appealing to her but her eyes were still like black slate. A more powerful bribe would have to be forthcoming. There was only one thing for it.

'All right then,' I said, resignedly, 'we'll let ye help us make the monopoly money on Friday night. You can make some pound notes.'

She swelled up like a fat duck, her face regaining its normal round contours and nodded her head vigorously as a sign that the contract had been made.

'Jings thanks, Mary Rose. Ah'll be really careful wi' the drawing.'

Margaret scowled at me behind Susan's back. We had been making a monopoly game for weeks, whenever we could borrow a real game from Rita Gordon who had nobody to play with because her big brother had gone to England. She had the game and no players and we had the players but no game. So, for every time we played with her, being careful to let her win or she would go off in a huff, she let us have the game for a night, to copy out the board on to a big sheet of cardboard taken from a box. We scoured the gutters looking for cigarette packets and used the flat parts for the cards, carefully printing the names in coloured inks. Susan was always nagging us to let her help but she was only nine and her letters were too big. Still, pound notes weren't all that often used and we could make sure her efforts stayed on the bottom of the pile. I decided, however, that it would be better to wait till my mother was in a good mood and confess to her about the tablet, otherwise Susan would play the piper evermore.

While Margaret did the washing up, I took from a rack at the bottom of the oven the four bricks we used to heat the beds. I wrapped them in flannel and carried them gingerly into the huge room where we all slept, putting two into each bed. By the time everybody was bathed, the beds would be warmed up. Our house was actually a converted shop. That's why we had bars on the kitchen window. The kitchen used to be the back shop. Our bedroom had a stone floor which, while it had you hopping up and down with cold when you jumped onto it in the morning, was excellent for playing hopscotch on rainy days or just for chalking pictures. So long as we wiped them off with a wet cloth when we had finished, my mother let us write what we liked on the floor. The room was so big that the two double beds where we slept took up only half the floor. Since there was no other furniture in the bedroom, there was plenty of space to skip with ropes, to whip a top, or play leapfrog. Sometimes, if Margaret and I were feeling particularly amiable, we would haul a blanket from our bed and toss the younger ones till they were hysterical with excitement and terror. In winter, especially on drizzly Sundays, our bare bedroom was the envy of the neighbourhood. Three of us were supposed to sleep in each bed, Margaret and I at the top of one and Susan at the bottom. Robert and Jackie slept at the top of the other and Sadie at the bottom. Anne still fitted into her pram. Most times, however, everybody, at least the younger ones, wanted to squeeze into our bed because Margaret and I took it in turn to tell stories, ones we had read, or ones we made up. The scarier they were the better. Daytime quarrels tended to cause a constant realignment of the sleepers. Tonight Robert wouldn't sleep with Jackie; Margaret wouldn't sleep with me. Bedtime always began with sorting out the partners, hushing the recriminations flung between the beds and arranging the legs.

We had a bathroom and that made us unique in the tenement. Other families bathed in their kitchens in front of the fire, but we had a proper bathroom, with a bath and a wash-hand basin and a toilet. Just the same, we used it only on Sundays, because we preferred to wash at the kitchen sink where it was warm and there was plenty of company. Bathing by yourself in the long stony room was very lonely and eerie.

Finally Margaret and I got everyone down and I told them the story of 'The Fatal Skin' which I had only just read. When I had finished, Robert said:

'Go and get Mammy's chamois leather, and we can try wishing on it to see what happens.'

Balzac's fatal skin was shagreen, not chamois, but I got the leather from under the sink and wet it, so that it became soft and malleable. Then I took it into the bedroom and spread it out on a sheet of newspaper.

'All right,' I said, drawing round the chamois with a coloured chalk, 'that's the outline. If it works, then the one who takes a wish on the leather will get his wish, but the chamois will shrink—and so will his life!'

I looked around them. They were hanging over the edge of the beds looking at the leather spread on the floor.

'Well, who's going to wish?'

Nobody wanted to. Finally, Jackie, who was silly anyway, said he would try, since he hadn't used up much of his life. It was to be a secret wish. I took the chamois away and said we would measure it tomorrow. Then, I hoped, they wouldn't notice that the chamois would be dry and consequently considerably smaller. That should produce some tremendous reactions.

So, with the house quiet, we sat in the kitchen reading and waiting for my mother's return from the prison.

She was very late coming home that night. When she threw open the kitchen door and hurried to the fireplace the surface ashes were cool.

'Och did ye fall asleep?' she asked, shaking me awake. 'Look at the fire, it's nearly oot. Here, put the kettle on, hen, an ah'll gie the fire a poke. Ah think there's a couple o' wee coals still hot. Aye it's comin' up again. This lum's got a rare draught. Look at mah hair, for Christ's sake.'

She straightened up and went over to the little mirror screwed high on the wall to one side of the sink, and eyed with disfavour her shoulder length, thick, wet hair, reflected blurrily in the clouded glass.

'A' that time ah spent doin' it wi' the tongs this afternoon and the curls were just the right size. They would've stayed in for days if it hadnae rained tonight. It's this bloody climate that gies people the shits. If it's no' rainin' on your hairset, then some joker's pissin' on your doorstep. Ah cannae wait tae get tae Australia. If,' she added darkly, 'we ever get there.'

I was reaching up for the tea caddy that lodged on the edge of the mantelpiece, but my mother's suddenly altered tone of voice shocked me into immobility.

'Is mah Da goin' tae prison, then?' I asked fearfully. Already I could hear my father tapping out a dying message to some new, young cellmate who would escape from Barlinnie and uncover a huge cache of scrap from Stephen's yard.

'If it's left tae him aye he will,' my mother answered fiercely. 'He's a bloody numbskull, an idiot. No wonder he only went tae the advanced division o' Copland Road. Reckons he never went tae high school because his faither died, but that's a load o' rubbish. The Laverys are a' dopes. "Ah'm goin' tae plead guilty," he tells me. "The detective says ah'll get off light." Did ye ever hear such shit? We just filled up that form for Australia. "Have you any criminal record?" they ask you. "No, not at the

moment kind sir, but just hang on a minute and ah'll get me one.''
As if a detective would ever tell ye tae plead anything else. They
havenae got any proof. It's only one bloke's word against his,
and ah'm damned if he's goin' tae plead guilty.'

She sat frowning moodily into the fire.

'Ah went tae Orkney Street Station tonight. He's goin' tae
pass the bar on Monday morning and then they'll take him tae
Barlinnie tae wait for the trial. Probably Wednesday, they told
me.'

She tugged open her old black handbag and emptied some
pound notes and silver from it, onto her lap.

'Ah've been roon' everybody wi' the hat. Your Aunty Margaret and Aunty Mary put in three pounds each and your Uncle
Angus gave me the rest. Ten pounds bail it'll likely be if he gets
remanded after the trial and five quid for the lawyer. Ah'm goin'
to get one tomorrow.'

I gaped with noncomprehension when my mother uttered all
the legal terms so authoritatively. They obviously meant something to her. 'Passing the bar'. What on earth was that? The only
image I could call up for it was a herd of seals rising up over a
sand bank. Clearly, however, this did not fit my father's situation. There was Palfrey's bar, the pub on the corner, but I
didn't really think the police would let my father have a drink on
Monday morning. 'Remanded' sounded vaguely familiar. Every
Friday, the *Weekly News* reported all the people who had committed crimes in the city.

'At Glasgow Sheriff Court today, appeared John Alexander
Leckie before Sheriff William Mackay, on a charge of having
assaulted his wife Barbara Leckie, thereby causing her grievous
bodily harm. Leckie denied the charge, saying he was away from
home on the night of the alleged assault. He was remanded until
the second of February. The court granted bail on lodgment of
ten pounds.'

So 'remanded' must mean you got off for a while, maybe to
get a lawyer, or maybe so that the police could get more evidence
against you. They had no proof, my mother had said. But if my
father had taken the scrap, then he should plead guilty. He
shouldn't have taken it in the first place. Stealing. And I always
thought he was a good man. He never shouted at us, or swore if
he thought we were listening, and he always gave my mother the
pay packet unopened. He got his pocket money from betting on

the dogs or the horses—or from stealing, I realised now—and from his pocket money he'd bought me all these new books I was reading.

'Great writings,' he'd told me, thumbing through the indices. 'It's time ye were reading some o' these stories,' he'd said. 'Ah know the Hotspur and the Rover an' a' these stories are great stuff; ah read them mahself when ah was a kid. But ye cannae go on stuffing yourself wi' fairy stories and suchlike for ever. These blokes'll tell ye what life's really all about. Look at this—*Nicholas Nickleby*. Ye'll see that Lorne Street Primary's no' such a bad school after a' when ye read this. An' *Oliver Twist* an' *David Copperfield*—they'll show ye what life was like before the workin' man started to fight for the right tae live.'

He went on reading out the authors' names, obviously looking for one in particular:

'Flaubert, Daudet, Balzac, Hugo, Dostoevsky, Gogol, Turgenev. Hm, no Sholokov. They're a' too early. Anyway, ah'll have tae get ye later *Quiet Flows the Don* and his other books. They'll help tae explain why the Russian Revolution took place. Here, look, there's another great story: *Les Miserables*. Och, there's a whole lot o' smashing stories here. You get stuck intae them.'

Though my father talked very little to me, the books became a kind of shorthand communication between us. When I had finished one and mentioned it to him, then he would say:

'Och, aye, and there's another one by him, or another one like that written by someone else. See if ye can find it in the library.'

My mother was too impatient to read and she would never shiver in terror or pull her hair madly, in sympathy with Raskolnikov, but I knew my father must have done so once upon a time.

His greater sensitivity and noble sentiments, however, didn't alter the fact that he was a thief and 'thou shalt not steal' had been brought down very clearly, without any qualification. My father was no innocent man to be unjustly sent to prison for another's misdemeanour. Like Raskolnikov he had done the deed and he ought to be punished for his crime.

'Why don't you let mah Da plead guilty, if he took the scrap?' I suggested to my mother. 'If you're a thief you should own up and take your punishment.'

My mother stared at me incredulously, her mouth slightly open and her face pale with disbelief:

'Are you some kind of an imbecile or something?' she demanded furiously. 'Is that what a' these fancy books fill your heid wi'. Your Da will be tickled pink tae know that's what ye got from a' the money he spent on ye. Oh yes, Daddy, you must take your punishment. Get up off your knees, for God's sake. If your father pleads guilty, he'll go tae gaol. G-a-o-l. Dae ye understand what ah'm saying? Gaol. Barlinnie Prison. An' who's goin' tae feed us? An' how are we goin' tae get tae Australia! Dae ye think they're goin' tae welcome a fee-lon intae their midst?'

'But ye shouldnae steal anyway,' I shouted at her, sudden tears making my eyes hot. 'What did he have tae go an' steal for? You said Mr Pearson should've gone tae prison because he did something wrong, but when your husband does it, that's a different story isn't it?'

'Here, don't you talk aboot your faither like that,' my mother returned indignantly. 'He's no sex pervert. Look,' she said, thinking a bit, 'taking scrap's nothing. Everybody does it. How dae ye think it gets there in the first place? Because the shipowners are dishonest themselves. They've put in a' these ships for repair that werenae damaged in the war, because the government's goin' tae pay for it. An' who's the government? Us. So they're robbing us. We're only stoppin' them from gettin' a double fortune. They'll sell that scrap tae Japan an' places like that an' make a profit from that as well as gettin' their ships fitted oot or converted tae oil burners for nothin'. Are they no' more dishonest than us? They're better educated and they've got enough tae eat. They thieve tae double their fortunes. We wouldnae steal if we didnae need tae. Ye've got tae live. If ye're no' livin' ye're dyin' an' by God ah'm no' dyin' afore mah time for any cock-eyed morality oot o' books.'

I stared down at my shoes and said nothing. My mother too sat in silence, thinking. Of concrete things, however. She jumped up suddenly, knocking her chair backwards with a clatter onto the patched linoleum.

'Here, ah just thought o' somethin'. Pour me oot another cup o' tea, ah'm goin' tae get the irons. They might come an' hae a snoop aroon here,' and she went off in a hurry into the lounge-room, yanking open the door of the big press. I could hear her scrabbling around inside it and in a minute or so she was back, carrying the two big flat irons that I'd seen inside the press each time I'd been rummaging around, seeking evidence of my father's secret activities. She laid the irons down on the floor beside the smaller ones that she normally used for pressing.

'They might just catch on your Da was using them tae weigh the scrap,' she said. 'Oh aye,' she went on, noticing the look of surprise on my face, 'ye never worked that oot, did ye? Your faither had a wee see-saw affair that he used as a scale: the irons on one end and the scrap on the other. That gave him a rough idea of the weight, because the weight o' the irons is stamped on them. Of course,' she added, 'that was only when there was nae big deal on at the yard. Ah mean, ye don't make much from these wee crumbs o' copper an' lead your Da was carrying hame in his pockets. Ye need a truckload tae make any money.'

'A truckload,' I said, rolling my eyes in astonishment.

'Aye, an' don't make your eyes roll like that. They'll stay fixed one day an' then ye'll be a right sight. Aye, he paid the gate-keeper to let the truck intae the docks, and the crane driver to unload the scrap from the ship, an' of course the truck driver got a fair whack because he took the most risks. But the bloke who usually drove the truck got sick, an' that's why that new man took his place. A right squealer, he was. The old yin would never hae put anybody in. It was that foreman who tipped off the police. Your Da told me he deals in scrap himself an' he wanted it a' for him. An' the driver named everybody in the business. But, ah mean tae say,' she let out a huge sigh and shook her head uncomprehendingly, 'your faither's a nitwit. It's only his word against your Da's. That's no evidence in a British Court. Och, he makes me so mad,' she said, getting up from the table and clenching her hands with frustration.

'Your Da's that bloody woodenheaded. Wantin' tae plead guilty. Anyway ah'm goin' tae the lawyer tomorrow an' we'll see aboot that.'

'My father is guilty, just the same,' I thought later, when stretched out on the bed beside Margaret. Mammy was still up. I could hear her turning taps on and splashing water, washing out some things at the kitchen sink. There was something not quite right in her argument, and yet I knew well enough what our situation would be if my father went to gaol for a month or even if he got a heavy fine. What was right? If someone took something from you and you took it back, was that stealing? But it wasn't as simple as that. Thoughts kept spinning me like a top, whirling my mind giddily round and round in the narrow wynds of my brain, growing and growing in momentum until I thought my head was going to burst.

On the Monday morning my father 'passed the bar' with his five friends, that is, he was formally charged with theft, and was taken away to Barlinnie to await the trial which was set for the Wednesday. My mother found a lawyer whom she sent out to the prison to persuade my father to change his plea from 'guilty' to 'not guilty.' The little solicitor came out from the cell, very gloomy and looking smaller, if possible, than his five feet nothing.

'Your husband's a very stubborn man, Mrs Lavery,' he observed mournfully. 'I can't seem to get through to him. He won't change his plea. Says he'll get a stiffer sentence if he pleads "not guilty".'

'But you're the one to determine that,' my mother returned impatiently. 'Go back and point that out to him. You know more about those things than a detective wi' his eye on promotion.'

'You'd better tell him that,' the lawyer said. 'He told me never to come back.' My father had actually said to his legal representative 'Piss off, mac. Ah don't want any o' your kind near me. Ah've got enough troubles o' mah own without coping wi' sharks like you.'

My mother sat thinking for a bit. 'If he gets a conviction lodged against his name, even if he's only a week in gaol, that's our plans to go to Australia kaput. They won't take you if you have any criminal record. I tell you what,' she said to the lawyer. 'You go to the court, just the same. My husband's a very slow-moving sort of a bloke. When the sheriff asks for his plea, you jump up and plead for him, before he gets a chance to open his mouth.'

'He won't like it,' the lawyer commented, frowning anxiously. It was easy to see what was going through his mind. He was small and slight. My father was six feet tall and around thirteen stone.

'Don't you worry about anything,' my mother reassured him. 'I'll pay the money and I'll talk to my husband afterwards.'

At the court on Wednesday, my father's friends all pleaded guilty. They were sentenced on the spot to thirty days hard labour. Then the sheriff called to my father:

'Robert Lavery, 74 Craigiehall Street, Plantation, charged with theft of scrap iron from the premises of Alexander Stephen and Sons on the fourteenth of January, 1951, How do you plead?'

'Your Honour, I plead . . .' when the little lawyer bounded from his seat and waving his arms vigorously in frantic semaphore, called out:

'I am here to represent Mr Robert Lavery, your Honour and I plead "not guilty" on behalf of my client.'

My father, who hadn't noticed his legal spokesman in the court, spun around at the interruption and glared threateningly across the room, first at the lawyer, and then at the sheriff, undecided for a minute as to what he should do. Then my mother started yelling at him: 'Robert, Robert,' in a loud whisper and when he finally looked over at her, she waved at him with a down-pointing hand and hissed:

'Sit doon, ye great fool.'

Some woman in the courtroom tittered and my father sat down hurriedly, the back of his neck scarlet, his big hands bunched on his knees in nervous annoyance and embarrassment.

He was remanded for six months and released on ten pounds bail. The second time he appeared at the Glasgow Sheriff Court, the Scottish verdict of 'not proven' was handed down and he left the courtroom with his record still officially clean. Our plans for going to Australia could still be implemented, much to my mother's relief. My father, however, was not a bit grateful, then or later:

'That stupid wee sod,' he kept saying, 'comin' at me wi' a' his yap yap yap. He would do this, an' he would do the other. Ye were damned lucky it wasnae old ferret-faced Cockburn on the bench or it would've been a different story and you would've been for it. So would he, the wee upstart.'

My mother was too pleased with herself to begin a disputation with my father. She regarded her five pounds as well spent and forever after denounced my father's behaviour in the situation as pigheaded and typical of a Communist ignoramus whose class hatred blinded him to his own advantage.

4   God Almighty!

My school was Lorne Street Primary. It was beautiful on the outside. The walls were of dark red sandstone, a deep stain like oxblood shoe polish and not flat walls, rounded bulging walls like blown out cheeks, full of dimples and hollows, smooth and gritless to the drawing finger. The long arms of two playgrounds, segregated by the stubby building, stretched outright to fend off the unwelcome advances of a galvanised iron making factory on the one side, and a little sweet shop on the other. Girls played on the school's left flank and boys on the right. In school hours they met only inside the walls of the classroom where the teacher watched them with a rolling eye. But that wasn't the worst of it, the teacher's watching us.

'Now boys and girls, I want to introduce you to a new word today. It's a long word, four syllables long, so watch the board carefully and note the spelling. There we are! Om-nis-ci-ent. Say it all together, after me. Om-nis-ci-ent. Omniscient. That's the way. That word means knowing everything. Know-ing everything. Now I know you children think we teachers are omniscient but of course, that's not true. Only God is omniscient. God is omniscient. Remember that. This means that he knows everything you do and everything you think. Can He see everything? Of course. God sees everywhere, because GOD IS everywhere. Every single where.'

Gawd! God is every bloomin' where.

'How long is God? That's a silly question. God has no dimension.'

Then if God has no dimension He's like a point, and a point occupies only one position in space. So that's a silly answer. Maybe God is like a line, infinite in length. If you remove a

61

point from a line you get two half lines. God might equal two half lines plus a point. But that's only a thread in space. Maybe God is infinite like a plane. If you remove a line from a plane you get two half planes. God could equal two half planes plus a line. That's only like a sheet in space. If you remove a plane from space you get two half spaces. Two half spaces plus a plane. That's all space. That's God. An infinity of pointed eyes seeing everything and knowing everything.

It's prepositions again in grammar today and God is still omniscient. He is near me, far from me, beside me, below me, above me, under me, over me, for me, against me, in me? Hm. Above all God is omniscient. I can really spell that word now.

The awareness of God's omniscience spoiled half my enjoyment in the classroom. It was difficult to sort out my home-made stamps and envelopes and plan how to deliver notes consigned to me by my customers for delivery in lesson time, without someone roosting in my brain and muttering all the time:

'Now that's not really the right thing to be doing, is it? Look at you, not a bit repentant. Remorseful at the time, yes, but not repentant.' Or when I was really engrossed in *The Children of the New Forest*, clicking His tongue reprovingly like my Granny Bygroves and scolding:

'You really should put that away. It's very dishonest to be reading under the desk when the teacher thinks you're looking at your grammar book.' Sometimes the voice became menacing and hissed:

'If you don't put that away this minute I'll go into Miss Brown's head and tell her what you're doing. She'll put your book in the bin like she did before and where will you get the money to pay the library? You know what your mother said last time.' In a sudden fright, I would shove the book into my bag and cram the capitals of Canadian provinces into my head till I got mental indigestion.

My God was a kind of genie of the lamp, half servant and half mentor. He was all space, thanks to the hymn we sang every morning for a fortnight:

'Immortal, invisible, God only wise,
 In light inaccessible, hid from our eyes,
 We blossom and flourish, like leaves on the tree,
 And wither and perish, but nought changeth thee.'
The daily hymn came immediately after 'Our Father' which we

recited as soon as we'd said, 'Good Morning, Miss Brown'. Whenever it came to 'forgive us our debts as we forgive our debtors' I ground my sounds very carefully in case God didn't hear properly because I felt my mother was going to be shovelled into hell by all the creditors who bayed at our door on Friday nights and went away unfilled. I never said the last line of 'Our Father' because that's when I listened for Catholics being 'fancy'. We Protestants, in our properly severe and precise manner, ended our petition with 'forever, amen'. The Catholics, however, endorsed God's right to the kingdom, the power and the glory, with a roccoco flourish characteristic of their sensual approach to religion. 'Forever AND EVER' they hammered out. This inclusion or excision of 'and ever' was the essential distinction between us, outranking even papal infallibility which enraged all the grown-up Presbyterians. Papal infallibility meant nothing to us children, but the uttering aloud of 'and ever' in our hearing was a public witness of the Catholic child's uniqueness. Sometimes, in reckless and fearful defiance of the universe, I gabbled the bipartite addendum under my breath and cocked my head to see what would happen. Nothing ever did. Nonetheless, there was always a lapse of weeks between the 'and evers' in case my bravado might call forth clouds of smoking wrath from the Catholic or Protestant spirits, or, without my noticing it, I might gradually turn into an ar see. Every Protestant child fancied that the Catholics were powerful enchanters and if you didn't watch yourself every minute, they would cast a spell on you that could make you love the pope. So when I passed St Gerard's, the Catholic secondary school formerly attended by my mother's Catholic brother, I walked on the other side of the street, pressing myself tightly against the wall but squinting furtively over at the playground as I sneaked past. Strange and evil things went on behind the big double doors, I knew. The sprinkling of holy water, frantic crossings, and weird witch-like chantings that made your flesh creep right up over your ears.

Sometimes my Catholic uncle came to visit us and I sat staring at him, changing my corner spy posts as he walked from kitchen to lounge and back again while he was talking. He was already queer in that he spoke with an English accent and called my mother 'Rouse' instead of Rose. It made us giggle when he said:

'Ell just be with you in a minute Rouse.'

My mother didn't giggle, however. She pressed her lips

together in annoyance and nodded her head as if to say 'aye, ah know what ye'll be doin' in the minute'. 'He's a bloody little snob,' she said every time he left, 'and as mean as cat's shit.'

It certainly impressed us as odd that he had lived for twenty-three years in Scotland and only a few months in England yet now he spoke like the B.B.C. His 'minute' activities, however, were even odder. Our kitchen had a walk-in closet used for covering up brooms and dustpans, hanging up coats—mainly visitors', of course—and for hiding in. That was what Uncle Brian used it for. Every time he said 'I'll just be with you in a minute, Rose,' he hurried into the closet and partly closed the door. He had to leave it ajar to avoid suffocating. We could hear him poking around inside and then the rasping sound of a match being struck on the heel of his shoe.

'Mean little sod,' my mother muttered angrily, jerking her head sourly in the direction of the closet. 'He thinks ah'm punch drunk or somethin'. As if ah'd want his bloody weeds anyway. He can stick 'em where the monkey puts its nuts.'

If he heard my mother's imprecations, Uncle Brian gave no sign. He had developed another English mannerism, a perpetual smile, a sunny streak that shone ruthlessly no matter how bleak or thunderous the surrounding skies. If you were rude to him he smiled. If you were pleasant to him he smiled. If you just stared at him mutely, he went on smiling. It was no expression of mirth, just an outing for his teeth. He ignored my mother's loud, wet sniffs and jabbing comments and tossed them aside with smiling remarks of his own. Just the same, he had a problem. He smoked even more heavily than my mother, lighting one cigarette always from another so that he rarely asked for a match. Once he'd got the cigarette clamped between his thin lips, his back molars ground together, his cheeks were sucked backwards and the tobacco rushed down the rice paper like milk through a straw. Two sucks and a long finger of ash was flicked into the saucer. Then out frothed the smoke from the black chimneys that were his nostrils. He sighed and opened his mouth gently and another puff billowed out and wound in and out, drifting ever so slowly downwards.

'Jings, Uncle Brian,' Susan said once, watching him intently through her long eyes, 'you're like a dragon.'

Uncle Brian nodded pleasantly and smiled. Then he began to feel around inside his jacket. Momentarily his smile shut and an intensely worried, frowning, dark look immediately replaced it, deepening into an expression of sick anxiety as his hand emerged with the cigarette packet hoarded and curtained off behind the fingers. This was his 'em just on my last cigarette' look. It was an alternative to sneaking into the closet every time he wanted to smoke.

'Eh feel rayally shitty, Rouse,' he would murmur unsmilingly, playing hangdog, 'but em just on my last cigarette. We could halve it if you lahk.'

Once, out of patience with him, she slung five Woodbines across the table.

'Here,' she said contemptuously, 'take these an ye'll have five more tae go before ye need the chorus.'

I sat glowering in my corner. Five Woodbines less meant you-know-who would be on the prowl again. Uncle Brian, however, utterly indifferent to my exasperation, covered the Woodbines with his knobbly fingers, long and clutching, and sliding them towards him negated the gesture with:

'Ow, thet's ofly kahnd of you, Rouse, bet eh downt think eh oat. Eh know Woodbines are ofly scarce' by which point he had stuffed the cigarettes deep into his side pocket and was smiling once more, overcome by his noble words.

When he departed, having dunked his bread in our soup, I raced over to my mother and squeezed her neck between my hands in mock throttle.

'I could kill you, Mammy Lavery. What did ye have tae dae that for, gi'ein' him oor cigarettes? The mean pig. He should smoke Pasha.'

She loosed my hands and nodded her head sagely.

'Ah know what ah'm doin'. He'll no' be game tae talk aboot last cigarettes in future. Jesus, ah don't know where he gets his meanness from. There's naebody like that in mah family.'

'Well, he couldnae get it from mah Da's family, could he?' I said. 'And he *is* your family. He's your brother, isn't he?'

'Aye, well, as to that ah'm no sure,' my mother answered, astonishing us all. 'Your granny ye know, was converted tae Catholicism no' long after Brian was born an' she told me later she'd done it tae redeem herself from a great sin, an' your grandfather was always away at sea. Ah think she might have played up wi' some joker.'

Playing up, I suspected, meant melting, burning and trembling and all the rest of it.

Uncle Brian's oddities, however, even to the most rabid

Protestant (and I was only a scared one) could hardly be considered religious in origin, and despite my constant scrutiny when he visited us I was never able to determine how his attendance at St Gerard's had influenced his being. Catholics, I secretly felt, were holier than we Protestants because of their mysteries. They seemed to know things we didn't. Yet the Muir boys were foul-mouthed and violent. And look at Billy Mathieson, wanting to clobber the Protestants with his chimney pot. In what real way was a Catholic different from us? What was the use of his religion, and ours?

In class, Miss Brown never mentioned either faction. She kept her prayer to herself when she said it, so we didn't know what she was and no one had the nerve to ask her. She talked more of God than she ever did of Christ and in retrospect, it seems quite likely that she could have been a Jew.

When the prayer was done, it was time to begin our secular chantings:

'To say I seen or I done, is worse than murder.

'To say I seen or I done, is worse than murder.'

The words were thumped out on the desk in a voice that sounded like the horrific tones of John revealing the Last Judgement. No one ever questioned the dictum and we shivered dreadfully when we heard bold heathen shouting out for all to hear:

'Come oot, come oot wherever ye are. The game's a bogey. Ah seen ye.' Our smallest actions in the classroom were always judged as the spawn of sin or virtue. We never simply made mistakes, or were lazy or dumb. If you hadn't learned your tables you were strapped and blasted back to your seat by the raging wind of Miss Brown's wrath.

'The slothful man saith: "There is a lion without and I shall be slain in the street".

'Do you hear that? Slain in the streets. That's what happens to lazy people. Because lazy people are ignorant. They have no store of knowledge and you know what it says in the bible about knowledge. "Hear instructions and be wise, and refuse it not. Receive my instructions and not silver; and knowledge rather than choice gold."'

For those whose margins were crooked, whose lengthy additions not quite accurate, whose light strokes were too dark, and whose dark strokes too light, Miss Brown delivered a peroration on the virtues of excellence and perfection.

66

'Whatsoever thy hand findeth to do, do it with thy might; for there is no work, nor device, nor knowledge, nor wisdom in the grave where thou goest.'

Some of us found this a little discouraging and wanted to drop our pens straight away, but Miss Brown would never let you.

'Being excellent means doing twice as much as you're asked to do. So If I tell you to do ten sums in half an hour, you're to try and do twenty. And if I ask you to look up a reference in Proverbs, then read something else on both sides of it. If your neighbour asks you to help him parse a noun, then help him to parse the whole sentence.'

The fear of having to write out 'go to the ant, thou sluggard' fifty times, the standard punishment for defectors, made me try to pick my way down Miss Brown's narrow road to excellence. That was how I discovered the Song of Solomon.

5   Love for All Seasons

In our house, the only four letter word never voiced aloud was love. Nobody ever said, I love you, do you love me, if you loved me, and no definition was ever offered of sudden, inexplicable cuddles or squeezes, or spiny defences of our bodies or honour. Love came to us from the outside: from the church, from books and pop songs. 'For God so loved the world that he gave his only begotten son . . .' and you felt that God cried dismally ever after. Jesus loved and died a horrible death. God must be sad, and love was something very discomfiting that it would be better not to think about.

Then there was the true love mournfully recounted in the big print of *True Romances*, *True Confessions* and *True Love Stories*. These were American imports sold with Zane Greys, Ellery Queens, James Hadley Chase's best selling 'blue' books, and hundreds of comics: love comics, war comics, Dick Tracy, Li'l Abner, Archie and Veronica, Superman, Captain Marvel, their war wounds roughly bandaged up with Scotch tape or paste, by the owner of Yankee Mags, the shop in Blackburn Street that sold second-hand American magazines and comics. He was a tightwad, the owner, and would never admit to having a corpse in his shop. The tatty magazines sold at the same fixed price though only the covers remained. This was simply exploitation of the market. Demand for the American dream far exceeded the supply. Anybody who was literate among the tenement dwellers and was interested in life on the range, cattle rustling and shooting, or in a newspaper office where the star reporter came from the planet Krypton, would squeeze his way into the little room, feverishly hunting out copies he hadn't yet read. And the girls, they were after love, love, love. They held

68

their True Romances close to their noses, reading with slack jaws and glazed eyes, irritable when the romance had finished and smiling again only when they had exchanged the old story for a new one. When they weren't reading the magazines, they hurried off with a bundle of Archie comics, all about high school love.

Love in Yankee Mag literature meant outdressing other pretty girls so as to steal their boyfriends and go off into the margin with a simpering smile once you'd got the innocent, almost dopey male. If you were ugly you could forget about love. It wasn't for you. Only the pretty girls got the boy, though you had a chance if you were really only an ugly duckling who, when you took off your glasses and unloosed your bun, became, to everyone's surprise, the most beautiful girl in the office. Then the boss's son, too blind and stupid to have noticed your good bones, wide eyes and double row of eyelashes immediately fell in love with you and that was the last frame in the comic.

The object of your love was always handsome and rich, or if poor, only pretending, so that he could find a beautiful girl who would love him for his looks and not his money. Sometimes, not often though, he was a homebody who, while not exactly rich, had his own humble service station where, with gritted teeth and noble heart, he mended the flat tyre of his rich, flashily handsome rival who was off to date poor homebody's sweetheart. When it turned out that the rich rival was more interested in receiving than in giving, the girl saw in a twinkling that the love worth having was he who stood with the wrench in his hand and the doggy devotion on his face. A new story began at this point. That is, the story was retold with the heroine a brunette instead of a blonde and equivalent changes made in the physiognomy of the heroes. So, love in the love comics was left to the imagination. All that the writers donated were tips on how to get it, and these all distilled to 'be beautiful': that is, have long hair curling slightly at the ends, and big breasts that stick out and stick together to make two little lines like a snake's fang above your undone shirt button. No mention was made of those who weren't elements of the set, like my mother, for instance, who had shortish hair and was always bewailing her flat chest.

Even in the True Love Magazines, always read in hidden corners away from grown-ups, love was never defined. What was discussed until the concluding paragraph of three or four large pages was false love. This, it was hinted, made you melt and dissolve with disastrous consequences. The false love was a response to intense, smoke-coloured eyes, usually heavy lidded, a sensual, loose-lipped mouth, heavy breathing and hands that started to wander. That was when you said no, no, and lost consciousness. There was always a huge photograph of a blonde woman, with her head hanging down her back. After her mistake was born, this woman met another man who kissed her tenderly on the cheek and smoothed away a wisp of hair from her wide brow and they got married. Such a conclusion directly contradicted the tenement teachings on virginity. If you had a baby before you were married or if you 'did it', no man would look at you afterwards. That was what the older girls told me anyway. My mother, thankfully, hadn't yet commenced her series of comprehensive lectures on sex with illustrations taken from a tampon box, so I wasn't quite sure what 'doing it' meant. However, by all accounts it was something devilish but alluring.

The only distinction between false love and true love, so far as I could see from Yankee Mags, was that true lovers were a bit like fathers, stroking your head and drying your tears, while false lovers were like ship's stokers, turning their bellows on hidden cinders that were best left to go out.

This was clearly impressed on me by a James Hadley Chase book whose name I have forgotten; the implications of the story haunted me for years. It was set in gangsterdom, an ambiente remoter to me than Hans Anderson's kingdom of the Snow Queen. Unbeknownst to his wife a man became involved with gangsters trafficking in liquor and when he couldn't settle a debt he had incurred with them, they killed him. That was the first time I encountered the term 'a wooden overcoat'. The wife came from a small town to look for her husband and after questioning various men, each more ugly and offensive than the one before, she was finally directed to the gangster chief, the one who had ordered her husband's death. It was emphasised that the woman was quiet, modest and uneasy in her surroundings. The gangster, after telling her that her husband had been a 'hood' and thereby causing her to faint, attacked her. This was the first time I came across the 'he ripped her blouse open and exposed a naked breast' formula. When the woman righteously cursed the villain and threatened him with retribution, he sneered and told her that in a short time she would be on her knees 'asking for it'. Most astonishing of all, at the end of the story, so she was. Nothing had ever shocked me like the unexpected transformation of this woman who had even been described as a scripture teacher.

Why, exactly, had the woman changed? The innuendos of the plot meant nothing to me. Was the woman some kind of Trilby and the gangster a Svengali? But what hold did he have over her? Maybe the woman had really been like that all the time, a hypocrite like the Dickensian characters who were smarmy with their superiors and nasty to poor people. Yet the writer hadn't shown the woman to be different with different people and her transformation seemed to have shamed her, at least at first. Maybe she was a Mrs Jekyll. But she didn't leap backwards and forward from role to role. She must have changed, even against her will, and why was that? Maybe my teacher Miss Brown could go like that, a fearfully thrilling possibility that I considered many times afterwards when I was supposed to be listening to formulas for calculating simple and compound interest. Finally, the most horrifying implication insinuated itself into my mind. If Miss Brown, who was so good, why not you? Yes, you. That was me I was considering. And if you, then why not everybody? People aren't what they seem. You can't trust them and you can't trust what you see: not people and not things. The tenements, after all, changed their makeup with the season. The big question, therefore, is: what can you touch and hold that won't change? What is real? And who's going to tell you where to find it?

As for love, who wants it? Nothing but misery. Listen to Eddie Fisher or any pop singer on Radio Luxemburg broadcasting on 208 metres.

Love's always a wail. God lost his son by loving. His son got crucified from loving. In Yankee Mags, in *Crime and Punishment*, in *Madame Bovary*, always tears and trouble. Nothing to delight in. In the closes people are always in a hurry and scared that someone's coming. And what joy do you hear through the letterbox? Muttering in the dark.

It was about this time that Miss Brown gave us another terrifying lecture on the nature of excellence, and when I had finished looking up the reference to the vanity of riches in Ecclesiastes, I scurried through the pages to the end, and then came to the Song of Solomon.

Startling poetry. Nothing like 'Lucy' or 'How we Brought the

Good News from Ghent to Aix' or the 'Pied Piper of Hamelin'. What kind of beauty was this? 'My beloved is white and ruddy, the chiefest among ten thousand. His head is as the most fine gold, his locks are bushy, and black as a raven. His eyes are as the eyes of doves by the rivers of waters, washed with milk and fitly set. His cheeks are as a bed of spices, as sweet flowers; his lips like lilies, dropping sweet smelling myrrh... his belly is as bright ivory overlaid with sapphires.'

Where was there such a man? What did he look like with lips like lilies. Weren't lilies white? Lily white skin. And marble legs set on sockets of gold. This man wasn't to be found walking up and down or giving lifts to prettily stranded girls. Not in the love comics or the magazines. And where was the peaches and cream complexion of the woman? 'I am black but comely, o ye daughters of Jerusalem, as the tents of Kedar, as the curtains of Solomon.' Comely like a tent, or curtains?

I read the song over and over, my senses flustered and disturbed by the exotic imagery and the strange, honeyed sounds. Finally, the similitudes that initially struck me as the conjunctions of a deranged but exciting mind took shape, not as photographs of objects familiar to me and the others but as pictorial representations of feelings. The beauty of the loved one was being expressed subjectively. You couldn't imitate it by doing your hair a certain way or by wearing mascara. It wouldn't matter whether you wore glasses or had buck teeth or a flat chest. If someone loved you, you would be beautiful to him and the beauty would last as long as the love. And the poem made it clear that love could be a delight. I didn't understand exactly why, but enough to know that more was to be sought than you found in James Hadley Chase, or True Romances, or in the pop song ululation, and the language of these irritated me thereafter.

Of my discovery I said nothing to Miss Brown at this stage, partly because I was afraid she suspected I'd noseyed in her desk one evening after school and partly from an inarticulated feeling that she might not approve of my reading the Song, though it did lie to one side of Ecclesiastes and though I had been executing the teacher's directives to aim for excellence.

I discussed it with my mother, however, sideways. It was on a Saturday afternoon and my father had just gone off to the match. My mother had sponged and pressed his suit and polished his shoes.

'Here, Rose,' he said, preening himself, 'gi'e me the once over and see if everything's a' right.'

My mother straightened his tie, brushed his shoulders with her fingers:

'Ye'll have tae watch that dandruff ye're gettin'. It'll leave ye bald,' she said anxiously. 'Aye, well, that's it. Ye look a million dollars. Ye better get a move on an' remember, half-past five on the knocker tonight, so we can make the first show at the pictures. An' make sure ye can walk straight when ye get back.'

My father gave his deep, piteous sigh, the one that meant o ye Gods witness the unbearable torments of this your faithful servant, and have mercy on his sufferings.

'Look,' he explained in the let's be reasonable voice that always went with the sigh. 'The soccer match finishes at five. Right?'

'Here, don't stand there catechising me as if ah were some kind o' an idiot. Ah know when the match finishes, an' it doesnae always finish when the whistle blows. Sometimes the result's known well in advance. You just make sure you're here at the right time.'

My father ignored the interruption: 'The soccer match finishes at five an' it takes nearly half an hour tae get from Hampden tae Plantation. Now how ah'm ah goin' tae get drunk? Honest tae Christ, ah'd have tae be Mandrake tae dae the things you think ah'm capable o'.'

'Aye well,' my mother answered softly, nodding her head up and down meaningfully, 'there are those that think ye've got your capabilities, aren't there? But we'll no go intae that for the time being.'

'Aw lay off, will ye,' my father pleaded. 'C'mon, dae ah look all right? Ah'll have tae go or ah'll be late. Here gi'e us a kiss.'

He leaned over my mother, patting her hair, and kissed her, quite a long sort of kiss. As he was going out the door, he turned and gave her a wink:

'Tonight's the night, turtle dove.'

Margaret and I giggled round the table at this, but my mother sat smiling happily, her face that had begun to lower, light once again. She was wearing what I thought of as her 'fond' look. So I leaned across the table and asked her:

'Was that Mrs Perkin ye were referrin' tae Mammy, when ye were talkin' aboot Daddy's capabilities?'

'Aye,' my mother answered, looking angry again. 'The old bitch. She's damned lucky she didnae land herself wi' a slander suit. For two pins ah'd've laid charges against her. Anyway,' she added, getting up from the table, 'it's a' water under the bridge noo. Ah've got the laundry and she's as sweet as pie tae me noo.'

Mrs Perkin lived two storeys up from us. She was quite old and fat with black hair parted in the middle and tied back in a bun, and she never bothered to take off her apron when she went outside shopping. She had two nearly grown up daughters who were both working. We didn't have much to do with her at first, except to say hullo if we passed her in the close, but then the washhouse business came up and Mrs Perkin turned into an old witch, screaming and hissing like steam off the hob and Margaret and I took to putting a hex on her, sticking pins into a little doll we kept for hexing our enemies, including from time to time, my mother. We never actually had proof that sticking the pins into the doll produced agony in our enemies, but it was enough to relish the thought. So we pierced Mrs Perkin's beady eyes, her little putty nose, jabbed her bottom with joy, and yanked her hair out in handfuls, all by proxy, when she went for our mother.

In our back there was a little brick building which was a communal laundry. No one ever used it. Most people went to the steamie in Mair Street, about a mile away. Like my mother, they loaded their washing into the big tin bath every family had, tied it to a board that moved on old roller skate wheels, and lugged the bath behind them by means of a rope that hung over their shoulders. If they got to the steamie early, for sixpence they could have a machine, but if the machines were all taken they had to be satisfied with two stalls, that is, tubs, which were fitted with hot water. Then the rows of women would stand over the tubs, plastering their men's dungarees with part of their month's soap ration, and squeezing the dirt to death on the hard, corrugated wash boards.

We had been in our house a year before it occurred to my mother that the washhouse had a different function from the midden, though that's what it seemed to be when you peered in through the wire mesh protecting the window. In the tub under the window lumps of coal lounged on bits and pieces of junk. An old wardrobe leaned over the copper, broken chairs sprawled on the floor and piles of sodden and chewed news-paper took rest on every other unoccupied surface. The wash-house was locked and the key wasn't even a memory to the women my mother questioned. Finally, one who had been there longer than any other, suggested that Mrs Perkin might have a key and that it was she who used the building as a storehouse.

My mother went upstairs to find out if this were so.

Mrs Perkin was immediately alert to danger. Her territorial privileges were about to be rescinded and she scowled blackly when my mother asked her if it were true that she had a key to the washhouse.

'Aye, ah have the key,' she admitted, raising her fat arms and placing her pudgy hands on her hips, an attitude of aggression that didn't go unnoticed by my mother. 'What's it to you?'

'The washhouse is a communal building. It's full of junk and I want to clean it out so that I can use it.'

Mrs Perkin's face swelled up with choler. Her cheeks were threaded with tiny veins that bespoke a history of heavy drinking, and now the narrow ducts were being flooded with angry blood that spread out under her skin in mottled pools.

'Nobody's ever used the washhouse before, and ah've been here over ten years. Is the steamie no' good enough for you? It's good enough for everybody else. In any case, everything's broken doon inside the washhouse. Ye couldnae use it even if ye wanted tae.'

'Well that remains tae be seen,' my mother answered. 'In the meantime, if ye don't mind, ah'd like the key, and civilly too,' she added, as Mrs Perkin opened her mouth to bellow. 'Ah don't see any reason why ah should fork oot good money for a machine and a stall at the steamie when there's a perfectly good copper and tub in mah own back. Dae you?' she asked challengingly.

Mrs Perkin started to take a deep breath, hauling her huge breasts slowly up from her big stomach, till they stopped just under her chin.

'Piss off, ye lantern-jawed bitch,' she hissed, and shut the door in my mother's face.

My mother's lantern jaw dropped in astonishment. 'That cheeky swine,' she howled, 'ah'll lay her in her own blood. Ah'll lay ye in your own blood,' she shouted through the door, 'ye ignoramus that ye are. An' ah'll be up at the Corporation in the morning tae see aboot this washhoose. You'll get your come-uppance, ye shitpot that ye are.'

And she stalked off down the landing, shaking with fury and indignation. At the Corporation she was given a key to the laundry. Every tenant was entitled to a key. They were very sorry, this had been an oversight on their part and of course not, of course you couldn't use the washhouse as a private storeroom. Indeed not, it was for the use of every tenant.

So my mother unlocked the little brick building, watched in silent curiosity by dozens of hidden eyes looking sideways from their kitchen windows. The filth inside was sickening. Beetles, cockroaches and spiders scuttled round in panic-stricken circles, darting in behind lumps of coal, under the newspapers, into the copper.

'Jesus, Mary and Joseph,' my mother groaned, sagging at the prospect, 'did ye ever see such a sight? It's a bloody disgrace this should have been allowed. These others are a lot o' crapbags tae let that old biddy get away wi' this. Here, give me a hand wi' this wardrobe.'

Together we pulled the heavy wardrobe, furred with mildew and pockmarked with the tiny holes of woodworm, out of the laundry and into the back court. We parked it by a wall. Then began a tiring transport of hot water in buckets from the kitchen to the washhouse, all morning long. My mother scrubbed and scoured and scraped, and gouged and poked, till the washhouse reeled from the blows. Then the dirt began its retreat: the copper boiler sloughed off its scummy green skin and began to shine reddishly in its scrubbed, rough brick fireplace.

'Hey that's a great copper,' my mother said, admiringly. 'They don't make them like that nowadays. It'll boil up like winkie. Ye'll no' need much wood tae get it hot.' She shook her head incredulously. 'An' tae think that it's a' been goin' tae waste because naebody noticed it. No' even me, for a year.'

By mid afternoon, the washhouse was spotless, my mother bearing on her own shoulders and head its dirt and stains. The tenement children had come home from their travels and stood around sucking iceblocks and watching with interest. When it was finished they all pushed and squeezed their way inside the laundry, lifting the lid off the copper, opening the little door of the fireplace to peer inside, turning the taps of the tubs off and on until my mother said:

'Right, that's enough. Tell your mothers the washhouse is

operational now and they can go to the Corporation for a key, or they can borrow mine.' She lifted her head upwards to the two-storey window of Mrs Perkin's flat: 'It'll be nobody's monopoly in future.'

After we had gone inside and my mother was slumped in the armchair, happily exhausted, we saw Mrs Perkin and her husband, who was a quiet chap like my father, carrying all their things away. They went up and down the stairs about three times, helped at the last by their daughters who had arrived home from work. Our kitchen window was open, and we could hear what they were saying quite clearly. My mother was sitting, with a cup of tea in her hand, listening intently to the older woman's grumbles and plaints.

'Who the hell does she think she is, anyway, the Orange upstart!' Mrs Perkin was a Catholic. 'Comin' here an' thinkin' she runs the place. Naebody ever wanted tae use the washhoose before. Everybody goes tae the steamie. They're oot o' fashion, these back washhooses noo, anyway. Even in the other backs, they're a' locked up an' broken.'

My mother hauled herself up out of the chair and marched to the open window.

'Aye,' she shouted out, 'they're probably locked up because o' a lot o' selfish old buggers like you that want tae hog communal property for themselves. That's a bloody good laundry, noo that ah've cleaned it oot, an' ah'll bet it'll be comin' back intae fashion gey quickly.'

Old Mrs Perkin was bending over a box, when she heard my mother yelling at her. She straightened herself up, slowly, glaring balefully towards us, her two daughters ranged on both sides of her for moral support. The husband had moved a little to one side, a bit embarrassed by the hostilities.

'You,' the old woman spat vindictively, 'you're nothing but a whoremaster's wife, ye bitch.'

My mother goggled. She was expecting some jibe about the washhouse and the sudden change in subject stunned her for a minute. Margaret and I, who were pressed behind my mother, shuddered nervously. I didn't know what a whoremaster's wife was, but I knew a whoremaster was something very bad. Granny Bygroves hated Robert Burns and every time his name was mentioned she wrinkled her nose as if she were sniffing a bad smell and growled:

'It's nae matter tae me whether he's a poet or what have ye.

In mah book he was a dirty old whoremaster, an' may he rot in hell, treatin' a' those wimmen the way he did.'

Now if my mother was a whoremaster's wife, that meant my father was a whoremaster, like Robert Burns. I wished I knew what the word meant. 'I'm definitely going to find out about that,' I vowed to myself. How absolutely frustrating not to know. I should've tried before, but I kept forgetting and my mother wouldn't tell me when I asked her. Nor would my Granny Lavery.

'Och, don't you worry about it, lassie,' she answered, when I had asked her. 'Your Granny Bygroves is a good woman, but I think she had a bad experience in marriage and it makes her a wee bit intolerant of some men. Robert Burns was a good man. He liked women a lot, that's all, but he was never mean or nasty to anyone.'

My mother was clutching the bars of the kitchen window and shaking them, like King Kong in his cage.

'What—did—you—call—me?' she gritted savagely, 'what was that you called me Mistress Perkin!'

Mrs Perkin was delighted with the sensation she had caused. Her husband had somehow slipped away, but the daughters were still standing there, smiling quietly.

'You heard,' she said in a very loud voice, looking all round at the sky. 'Ye know fine well what ah said,' and she repeated it again. 'You're a whoremaster's wife.' She started waddling fatly towards the back entrance which was just beside our door. 'You're the wife o' a whoremaster, ye swine, an' ah don't care who hears me.' Then she disappeared from sight and we could hear her climbing the stairs, gaily, like a two-year-old.

'Go an' bash her up, Mammy,' Margaret cried, shaking with fear. My mother had gone as white as death and was staring into space with fixed eyes, as if she were mad. 'Bash her up, Mammy, bash her up,' Margaret kept on saying. She shook my mother by the shoulders. 'Mammy, don't look like that,' and she began to sob. I was trying to imagine what a whoremaster was. It must be something really terrible, like a murderer. God. Maybe my father had murdered somebody. But that was stupid. Robert Burns had never killed anybody, I was sure. Whoever heard of poets being murderers? In any case, the teacher would have told us. But then she hadn't told us he was a whoremaster, either. Margaret had run to the door and wrenched it open.

'You're an old pig,' she shouted up the stairs, 'and my mother's comin' tae bash ye up. Pig, pig, pig,' she bellowed through her tears, her face all red and sopping. But Mrs Perkin had had her day, and the door slammed shut without her speaking another word.

My mother was still standing with that strange look on her face.

'Mammy,' I said, patting her on the back, 'don't worry aboot it. She's an old liar. She just said that because you took the washhouse away from her. Ah'm sure Daddy has never done anything wicked like being a whoremaster.'

'You shut your mouth,' my mother snapped, turning on me. 'You don't know the first thing aboot it. Noo shut up. Ah'm goin' up tae see her this very minute,' she went on. 'There's no smoke without fire an' ah'll get the truth oot o' that old get if ah have tae choke it oot o' her.'

She hurried to the door and went out, nearly slamming the door off its hinges. We listened to her climbing the stairs. We thought she would run up them, but she was moving very slowly, not with her usual confidence. I opened the door quietly and went silently up behind my mother, stopping on the landing below her. I heard her rapping on Mrs Perkin's door, and listened intently as the door opened.

'Well, what do you want?' Mrs Perkin demanded nastily, 'and mind what ye say, because mah two daughters here will stand as witnesses if ye start any funny business.'

My mother sounded surprisingly calm for her. I'd expected her to punch Mrs Perkin or at least shout at her. She'd cracked a woman over the head with a chamber pot once. However, there she was speaking quietly like my father, almost friendlily in fact, to the old bag.

'Ah want tae know exactly what ye meant by calling me a whoremaster's wife,' she began. 'Ah take it ye've got facts at your fingertips because if ye havenae ah'll be right out tae get a lawyer.'

'You bet your sweet life ah've got facts,' I heard Mrs Perkin voicing triumphantly. 'Ah've eve·‌ got a photograph. Come away in a minute, an' ah'll show ye.'

My mother followed her inside. There was nothing more to be heard there so I went back to our place. Well, that was weird. A whoremaster must have a special appearance or something

79

if you could tell by looking at a photograph. I was bursting with impatience to know what my mother would say when she returned. That was in about five minutes. Margaret and I looked at each other anxiously as my mother came into the kitchen. She had a little snap in her hand.

'Here you two,' she said, holding out the photograph. 'Take a good look at this and tell me who ye think it is—and think before ye say anything, because it's very important.'

It was a photograph of a little boy, about three years of age. He was dressed in dungarees and a sloppy joe. Margaret and I examined the photo closely and she spoke first. I didn't want to say what I saw.

'He looks awfully like oor Jackie except he's older.'

'What dae you think?' my mother asked me. Now I understood roughly what a whoremaster was. He was someone who went around with women and gave them babies. And this little boy was obviously intended to be my father's child. God. What a mess. This boy was only about three, which meant my father must have been playing up, that's what they called it, not very long ago. How could he be so mean! And this kid must be my brother.

'Come on, don't stand there like a leek,' my mother said impatiently. 'What dae ye think? Dae ye think he looks like Jackie?'

She was looking directly at me and I felt my stomach cramping in spasms. Oh boy. What would I say?

'Och, ah don't think he looks like anybody,' I finally answered, screwing my eyes up at the photo as if to see it better. 'He just looks like a wee boy.'

'That's no surprising,' my mother rejoined sarcastically. 'He *is* a wee boy, ye great dolt. Does he look like Jackie, that's what ah want tae know. What if he had red hair?' she pressed me. Then added, to herself almost, 'he's got red hair.'

'Well,' I said slowly, 'he's no' that much like Jackie, He's wearing the same kind o' clothes, that's what. An' his face is too long. Jackie's got a kind o' round face. No,' I repeated, decisively this time 'ah don't think he's like Jackie at all.'

'Jings, you need glasses,' Margaret gabbled, completely ignorant of the significance of the photo, 'he's Jackie's spittin' image. Here, look, can ye no' see properly?' she demanded, thrusting the picture under my nose.

'Hey, quit it,' I protested, grabbing the photo and throwing it on the table, 'you're dumb. You're only looking at his dungarees and his haircut.'

My mother sat in a state of confusion holding the photo away from her and staring at it hard. Then she got up and went outside to where Jackie was playing in the dirt with a spoon and a tin can. She wiped his face with a wet cloth and sat him up on the table, peering first at him and then at the photo.

'Ah want tae go oot,' Jackie started to whimper, 'it's no' bed-time yet. What are ye doin' wi' the photie?' He caught hold of it and glanced at it incuriously.

'Dae ye think that looks like you, son?' my mother asked him. I nearly spilled into giggles. How would he know? In fact, he didn't.

'Ah don't know,' he said, without interest, 'ah don't know what ah look like, do ah? Can ah go oot tae play noo?'

He was quite right. We only had one tiny mirror, the one above the sink, and Jackie had never seen himself. My mother sighed, then, and put the photo away in her apron pocket. Wait till my father came home. Goodness what a fight there was going to be. I'd better get out of the way. So I went into our bedroom with a book and tried to concentrate on a story. It must be a strange coincidence, I decided. My father would never do a thing like that. He didn't even like women anyway. Only my mother. She used to laugh at him, in fact, because if Mrs Gordon or somebody came into the house to talk to my mother, he always rushed into the lounge-room and hid behind the newspaper till they went away. And if they spoke to him, to say, like:

'Hullo Mr Lavery, how are you?' he always mumbled a reply that nobody understood and offended the women.

'Your husband's no' really a sociable type, is he?' Mrs Gordon commented sourly one evening when my father had mumbled at her.

'Och, he's a bit shy,' my mother answered. She sounded apologetic, you know, what can ye do with a man like that, but I knew she was secretly pleased the other women were peeved that my father didn't pay any attention to them.

And what now? Was my father another Jekyll and Hyde? Was he like the scripture teacher in James Hadley Chase? I could hardly imagine it. What would my mother do! Things would have to change in some horrible way. Once Sally, my father's cousin by marriage, was talking with my mother about husbands and saying what she would do if she caught her husband with other women. In her ugly step-sister voice she said:

'I'd cut if off, Rose. Make no mistake aboot that. I'd cut it off and ram it doon his gullet, the swine!'

Aunt Sally (I called her aunt) disgusted me a bit. She had a fleshy face and a piggy nose with nostrils that stared straight at you like a pair of empty eye sockets. My mother used to tell Aunt Sally she was doing the wrong thing.

'Ah think you're making a big mistake, Sally,' she'd say, 'chasin' after Angus like that. Ah mean, tae think o' a grown woman howkin' herself over fences tae catch her man, it's humiliatin' for him and for you. And goin' intae the pubs an' that, shoutin' for him tae come hame this minute, ye'll no keep a man like that. He'll want tae run away for good one day.'

'Listen,' my Aunt Sally rejoined in her loud, brassy voice. 'That man o' yours is a bit o' an old saps sucker and a homebody. You don't have tae keep your eye on him. But ye know what a lady-killer Angus has always been. If ah took my eyes off him for a minute, he'd be Joe the Toff before ye could say we're a' Jock Tamson's bairns. But when he knows ah'm watchin' him a' the time, he's got tae be careful. Ah've warned him what ah'd dae tae him if ah ever catch him at anything.'

Yes, she would cut off his head, she'd said. But I wonder what she thought Uncle Angus would be doing while she was rasping away at his neck with a saw. It wouldn't be as easy as she thought, I bet. I wondered if my mother was thinking of doing the same thing to my father. She was awfully quiet there in the kitchen. Probably looking at the photo again. After a time I became engrossed in the book I was reading and I didn't even hear my father come in. The first I knew he was home was when my mother's voice, harsh like a crow's, came shrieking round my head.

'What's up, ye're asking me?' she was blaring. 'Nothing's up wi' me . . . *my* reputation's intact.'

I got up and went into the lobby and stood listening behind the kitchen door.

'Your reputation's intact, is it?' my father repeated kind of dopily. 'Well, ah'm glad tae hear it. It's a great relief tae me.

And what exactly are ye gettin' at wi' a remark o' that sort?'

'Aw, come off it,' my mother sneered, 'don't play Holy Wullie wi' me. That old bag upstairs has got your measure taken, and if she knows it, ye can bet your bottom dollar it'll be in the *News o' the World* this Sunday.'

'Whit the hell are ye goin' off aboot?' my father spluttered. 'A man comes hame dog tired from working a doubler an' he's met at the door by a ravin' loonie. Whit old bag are ye meaning? If ye don't stop talking in riddles ah'm goin' oot an' hae mah dinner at mah mother's.'

'Aye, an' ye'll take your brood wi' ye,' my mother returned indignantly. 'All o' them—or at least those that've got your name.'

I slipped into the kitchen quietly and sat in a corner. They were so busy shouting they didn't notice me. My father threw himself into an armchair and kept pushing his fingers through his hair, in a frenzied gesture of non-comprehension.

'Oh, Jesus, Jesus,' he began to groan, 'ah'll go stark raving mad in this place.' Suddenly, he jerked his head up and glared at my mother. 'Right,' he snapped, 'tell me what fancy story ye've got hold o' noo.'

So my mother told him. 'That kid is the double o' oor Jackie, and he lives roon the corner in Blackburn Street.' She started to cry hysterically and loudly, moaning the while:

'Ah've had chances, ye know. Don't think ah havenae. But ah'm a very moral person. Marriage is sacred tae me, however, I feel, especially after seeing what came oot o' mah own parents' separation. But your family are a' the same. Multiple marriages they go in for. Your cousin and your mother had three husbands. Ye're a lot o' loose livin' sods an' there's proof o' it. Look at that,' she screamed, throwing the photo on his lap, 'ye cannae deny that's a Lavery.'

My father picked up the snap and regarded it thoughtfully. I expected him to say 'don't be so bloody silly' or something like that, but he didn't. He laid it on the table and nodded in agreement with my mother.

'Ye're right,' he said. 'He's a Lavery, true enough. But he's no' mine. He's Angus's.' And with that, he picked up his paper and started to read.

My mother goggled. So did I. Uncle Angus's. Wow! What

would Aunty Sally do to him now? Somebody had better warn him. My mother suddenly jumped up from the table and grabbed the paper from my father's hand.

'Here, don't just start reading the paper like that, as if nothing's the matter. It's Angus's, he says, as if he were talkin' aboot a workin' cap or something; some old thing he just left behind him. Tell me more. How do you know?'

'Ah heard he'd had a kid roon here somewhere,' my father sighed, 'but ah don't know anything aboot it because it's no' mah business. And it's no' yours either,' he added vehemently. 'If ah ever hear o' ye sayin' anything tae Sally, ye'll be sorry, ah'm warnin' ye.' He suddenly noticed me sitting beside the table. 'Christ, it's no show withoot Nosey. What are ye doin', sitting there wi' your lugs flapping?' He turned angrily to my mother. 'There's nae blasted privacy in this place. That big yin listens tae everything. It's got its lugs glued tae the door from the time it gets up tae the minute it goes tae bed, an' it wouldnae surprise me if it works a night shift as well.'

'Well, ah don't have tae listen,' I retorted indignantly, 'the way everybody in this hoose shouts a' the time. Ye'd have to go roon wi' ear plugs no' tae hear. Even when ah'm in the bedroom ah can hear ye talkin'.'

'Ah don't doubt that for a minute,' my father rejoined sarcastically, 'ye've got these bloody ears o' yours on the end o' elastic.'

'Anyway,' I went on, ignoring his jibes, 'ah wouldnae tell anybody anything aboot Uncle Angus; Aunty Sally once told Mammy she'd cut his head off and ram it doon his gullet if she found him goin' aroon wi' other wimmen, an' ah like Uncle Angus.'

'She wasnae really talkin' aboot his head,' my mother remarked to my father, giving him a funny look, 'but in any case, Mary Rose never carries anything oot o' these walls. Dae ye, hen?'

My mother was so relieved, so was I, that she was beaming all over her face, asking my father would he like a cup of tea while she got the dinner on, because she'd been too upset to be bothered before. The point was, what would she tell old Mrs Perkin? She couldn't very well say Uncle Angus was the whore-master instead of my father, because Aunty Sally might get to know.

84

'Tell her it's nothing like oor Jackie,' my father said, 'and if there's any more talk aboot it ye'll slap her wi' a slander charge. If ye deny it often enough she'll get tae believe ye. Anyway, how did ye go wi' the washhouse?'

The washhouse was a great success, as it happened. In the end, even Mrs Perkin lugged her washing downstairs and boiled it up in the copper and after a while she didn't seem to mind any more that she'd lost her storehouse, and came to have a cup of tea with my mother while she was waiting for the water to boil.

My mother didn't question my father's interpretation of the photo, partly because to believe otherwise would have been disastrous but also because my Uncle Angus was a very gay, jolly chap who never had a penny in his pocket but always gave you a shilling if you met him in the street. He would ruffle your hair and give you a hug, then turn to one of his friends and say:

'Here, one o' ye gie me a loan o' a bob. Ah want tae get this wee smasher an ice cream. She's mah second cousin and a right bonnie singer, aren't ye, hen?'

I would hang my head with embarrassment. 'It's no' true, Uncle Angus, ye know that,' I would confess shamefacedly. 'Ah cannae sing a note. Margaret's the one wi' the good voice. She's in the choir.'

'Och, stop your havers,' he would admonish me, chucking me under my chin: 'If ah say ye're a guid singer, then ye're a bloomin' nightingale. Isn't that right you blokes?'

I always ran off with a red face but feeling tickled pink inside. I liked Uncle Angus because he was never serious. Everybody liked him and he loved them all. He always had his arms round somebody, his children, us, old women and young ladies and when he sneaked out at nights away from my Aunty Sally, he had friends posted on every corner to warn him when his wife was out on the prowl, and he would climb over dykes and railings to give her the slip. But she always caught him for she knew every pub and hidey hole in Plantation and Govan. Then she would strut along the street in front of him proud as the trumpet major, with her head high and her chest out, ignoring my uncle's friends who took off their caps in mock mourning when the two marched past. Behind her scampered Uncle Angus, his wife's fool, winking betimes at his friends and at others, pleading:

'Aw Sal, have a heart.'

So my mother accepted my father's explanation but she

pretended that she was never quite sure; hence her references to the neighbours' faith in my father's magical properties.

Anyway, when my father left for the match, I asked my mother if she thought he was handsome.

'My word,' she asserted firmly, astonished that I had even asked the question. 'He's a fine looking man, your father. I wish ah had a penny for every woman that's wanted tae put their shoes under his bed.'

This seemed an extraordinary thing for a woman to want to do, but my mother was talking on enthusiastically:

'Mind you, he's improved a lot since ah first knew him. He used tae have a right plooky skin, from stuffin' himself wi' chocolates an' rubbish like that, but his skin's no' bad noo. An' of course he's tall, ye have tae remember. That counts for a lot. Tall men get the plums.'

'Ye mean,' I said incredulously, 'that you're a plum, Mammy?'

'Sour apple's more like it,' Margaret put in.

'Ah was considered a bit o' a catch in mah day,' my mother said, ignoring our jibes, and smirking at the memory of it. 'Cathy Thompson and I went intae a beauty competition once and they couldnae get anybody tae fit every requirement so they gave Cathy the prize for the best figure and ah got it for the best legs.' She stretched her legs out and regarded them with satisfaction. 'Ye see that,' she pointed, 'ye couldnae get a sheet o' paper between them at the calves, the knees, or the thighs. That's what a good pair o' legs should be like.'

I looked at my own legs. There was a space of about four inches between my calves. You could fit an encyclopaedia there. Margaret's legs touched at her calves but she had no ankles.

'What was wrong wi' your figure, Mammy?' Margaret asked winking at me.

'Nae bust,' my mother said disgustedly. 'Ah've never had much o' a bust and Cathy Thompson had a beauty. However,' she added, 'ah did every bit as well as she did wi' the blokes. She hadnae much personality an' ah used tae make them laugh. Your faither was damn lucky tae get me. Before he met me, a' he used tae dae was study the form an' gorge himself on bananas and chocolates. Anyway,' she said, suddenly suspicious, 'what were ye asking me for, aboot yer faither?'

'Nothing,' I answered. 'Ah just wanted tae know, if you

stopped loving Daddy would ye still think him handsome?'

My mother pondered this a bit. 'Well, ah don't know aboot that. They say love's blind, so maybe when ye love someone ye don't see their defects and every eye forms its own beauty, after all.'

'What, what do they say, Mammy?' I cried excitedly, 'Aboot beauty?'

'Every eye forms its own.'

I was dumbfounded. That was Solomon's Song in a nutshell. And everybody knew it except me. A thought occurred to me.

'But if every eye forms its own beauty, how is it most people like Jane Russell and that sort o' thing? All the eyes must be seeing the same way.'

'Well, ah suppose,' my mother reflected, 'people who grow up in the same kind of place have the same tastes. They get to like the same things, like you kids, for instance, all like dolly mixtures.'

'Aye, and grown-ups all like whisky,' Margaret threw in.

Well, that was another headache. If people did see things differently sometimes, seeing marble legs and things like that in their minds, then you'd wonder what was real again. Yet it was true that there were some things everybody thought were beautiful. I would really have to ask the teacher, because I just couldn't understand the situation.

'Miss,' I began, one afternoon when we were filing out of the classroom, 'Miss, I read a poem where a person saw his love as beautiful but in a strange way. You know what I mean? Not like a real human, but beautiful. And I thought the person was really saying how he felt about his love, not how he actually saw it. Do you know what I mean?'

The teacher looked at me curiously and I began to blush. But all she said was:

'Yes, I think I know what you mean. Go on.'

'Well, I think that's the same as every eye forms its own beauty, but there are some things everybody sees as beautiful, like, you know, film stars and the Trossachs. What I want to know, Miss, is do people see the same thing as beautiful all the time, or just some of the time, and how is it you see something as beautiful the way other people do, and sometimes in your own way?'

The teacher burst out laughing:

'Well, that's a tricky problem and you've put it a bit confusingly, haven't you? I'm not sure if I understand what you're getting at, but perhaps I can say this. Most people don't look closely at what they see or think about what they see, and they tend to accept what papers and the radio, or writers, consider as beauty. The ones who see beauty in their own individual way are generally artists, poets and painters and suchlike and they're the ones who cause us to open our eyes with our minds, not just hold our eyelids open in the general direction of. Do you know what I mean?'

'Hmm,' I said, a bit doubtfully. 'If my mother thinks my father is handsome when everybody else thinks he is ugly, is she an artist?'

The teacher scratched her head. 'Well, halfway there, you might say. If she could convince others your father was handsome when they originally thought he was ugly, you might consider her an artist then.'

'Thank you Miss Brown,' I said gratefully. 'It was making my head ache.'

As I was leaving the class, she called me back:

'What was the poem you were reading?'

I stared at my feet. 'I can't remember, Miss. Just something I saw in a book.'

She held her head on one side and regarded me quizzically.

'We usually remember very well the things that make our heads ache.'

'Not me Miss,' I lied. 'Can I go now, please Miss? My mother'll be waiting for me.'

Life was like a high tension wire slung out in a void and I crawled my way over it with the same fear and hesitation that marked my crossing of the backyard dyke. Every progression left me tense and exhausted. School, even more than home, was a source of continual tension, a perpetual challenge not only to your intellect, but to your survival as a free being, besetting you on all sides with bogey men that sprang up like dragon's teeth: you seized one by the throat in desperation and another grinned in its place. There was little rest. Play was never simply play, nor learning simply learning. You were always being tested. Tested in the morning for tables and whack with the pointer if you were too slow. Tested for the names of capital cities and dead kings, tested for writing, up light and down heavy so that your fingers clawed in cramp from the strain of controlling your pen, tested for spelling, and spelling, and spelling, tested for the dozen rule, tested for the score rule, tested every Friday so that your fingers trembled independently in anticipation when you sat down at your desk. But inside the class there were other, non-academic causes of tension.

It was one of Miss Brown's moral adjurations that the strong should support the weak. In particular terms, good spellers and arithmeticians were to help less able or willing scholars. Thus, for most of the year I was in Miss Brown's class, Jimmy Donleavy was my responsibility. When Miss Brown first directed him to carry his books and pencils to the desk beside mine, I was sick with dread. He was the filthiest boy in the class. His family, all eleven of them, lived in a single end in the most squalid part of McLean Street, near the dry dock, in a close that Margaret and I hurried past with our eyes down if we ever had to be up that end. To catch anybody's eye there was to invite a punch or worse from any of the youths lounging against the walls. Jimmy Donleavy fell somewhere in the middle of the nine children and as three of his elder brothers were working he should have been better turned out than he was. But he always came to school in trousers that had no zip and were held together with a big kilt pin. His woollen jumper, felted from poor washing and shrunken so that at the back it curved up above his waist, never had elbows in it. On wet days his feet were saturated because the soles of his boots were either hanging loose from the uppers, or if top and bottom joined, then only the circumference of the soles remained and wads of newspaper were stuffed into the shoes to replace the vanished leather. Miss Brown always made him wash his face and hands when he came to school because no one at home bothered, and she kept a little bundle of toilet papers for his nose which ran almost continually so that your eyes were blighted by looking at him, or your ears itched when you had to listen to him sniffing up. His loud, sucking sniffs were the only voluntary response he made to Miss Brown's absent-minded injunction:

'James—your nose!'

He stank, of course, even to those who sat in the next aisle, a sour smell much more nauseating than the stench from the middens. The boys kept their distance from him most of the time, though many of them were little better than he, but that little bit they cherished. As for the girls, they regarded him with awe and giggled nervously when his name was brought up in one of the many hushed anecdotes that were always being whispered in quiet corners of the playground.

'See that Jimmy Donleavy, he makes me sick. Ah could kill him. He's so embarrassing. Dae ye know what he did the other day when ah was goin' hame from school?'

'Ah can imagine. He's always doin' it. Did he go like that?'

Here the speaker formed a circle with her forefinger and thumb and poked her other forefinger up through the ring.

'Aye, that's right. Ah mean, ye don't know where to look.'

'Ah know,' added one, her eyes brilliant with the scandal of it. 'Ah told mah mammy. She said tae ignore him and he'll get fed up.'

'Aye, but it doesnae do any good. If ye ignore him he runs after ye, and shouts "up your hole" an' he's doin' that all the time. Ah hate clyping but one day ah'm goin' tae tell the teacher.'

'Och that wouldnae do any good. He gets the strap a' the time as it is. Sometimes six, and he doesnae care a bit.'

'Aye, an' he's a real swearie beast. Such filthy language ye never heard.'

'Isn't it funny how he never says anything tae us when he's in school? He doesnae even talk tae ye in lines or anything, or pull your hair, the way the other boys do. But when he gets oot the school, boy does he go tae toon.'

In my direction at least, Jimmy Donleavy's obscene gestures stopped after he was forced to sit beside me and that was some relief. One aspect of his neglected hygiene, however, demanded my constant attention and kept me in a state of continual suspense. His head was almost always infested with lice. There was never a month that he didn't get a green card from the visiting nurse. The days when he sat beside me with his head all greasy and reeking of D.D.T. emulsion were the only ones when I could relax and sit straight up, instead of leaning sideways with my neck stretched out over the aisle.

My mother raged when she went through my hair with her fine-toothed comb. This had short, tight-fitting teeth and was generally black or white, both of which colours threw into relief any lice that were reluctantly drawn out of our heads. When it was my turn, I sat tautly waiting at each pause when my mother was examining the tiny rake. If she said nothing, then nothing was there and I sagged with relief. If she said: 'Hmm' and cracked something on her thumbnail, then I'd been leaning too close to Jimmy Donleavy.

'Ah'm buggered if ah know why ye won't tell that Miss Brown aboot sitting next tae him,' she complained, washing out the comb in an enamel bowl of Dettol. 'Ah hope ye think it's a barrel o' fun for me daein' this sort o' thing every night.'

'But ah cannae be getting them from him all the time,' I returned, 'there are other dirty kids in mah class. He's no' the only one, ye know.'

'Well, it's helluva funny how ye never had them as often as this before,' my mother said, 'an' the whole point is, when you get them, it goes through the others like fire. It's costing me a fortune for D.D.T.'

I hated the D.D.T. It stung your scalp and made your hair black and greasy and you smelt like fly spray. But when I whinged, my mother dropped the cotton wool and said:

'Right, have it your way. Get eaten up, if that's what ye want.'

This nearly threw me into convulsions. Lice were parasites, my mother had told me. They fed off your blood. It was just sickening to think of it. I used to wonder how many meals a day they had—three, like us, plus supper, or perhaps they were like cows, grazing and munching away all day long. Munching me. I knew practically every hair on Jimmy Donleavy's head, I watched it so closely, but never once did I see anything. If I had, I would probably have leapt from my seat and run screaming from the classroom. My own hair, which was long, was plaited so tightly to my scalp that my Aunt Margaret often threatened to report my mother to the R.S.P.C.A.

'That's terrible, Rose,' she would say, 'the way ye've got that kid's hair plaited: her scalp's lifted up in the air, the way the Indians do when they're preparing to slice it off.'

'Och, stop romancing,' my mother replied, 'we'll see what you would do if ye had tae contend wi' those filthy heids she sits beside in class. At least,' she added grimly, 'if there are nae hairs flying aroon, there's less chance o' catchin' anything.'

Miss Brown said we had to whisper when we were working together but it was very difficult when you were leaning to one side, holding your head as far out as possible.

I was the one who did the talking for Jimmy Donleavy was mostly silent in class. If he got the strap, it was for pea-shooting, not at anyone in particular, just across the room, or for not doing his work or for tipping his chair on to the floor. But he rarely talked. Whenever I looked into his face if I were trying to explain something to him, he was always smiling in his eyes. He had very blue eyes, deep blue like Susan's, with the same secretive and mocking expression. But his lids were red rimmed and sore looking round the edges. A patina of scurf overlaid the top lid like caked soap. Many children of Irish origin had eyes like that and my mother said they got gritty lids inside from the dust and scales that fell from their dirty scalps into their eyes. Once I leaned my cheek on the desk while I was waiting for Jimmy Donleavy to add up his quarters, tons and hundredweights. Suddenly, to my surprise, he let his pencil slide out of his fingers and laid his own cheek on the desk. Oops, beasties swinging out on a trapeze. I slid my head along a bit, out of reach.

After a minute he said: 'Think ah've got scabies?'

I was taken aback and started to blush.

'No, but ye've got lice, ah think, and mah mother goes off pop if she gets any in mah head.'

'Aye,' he said flatly. 'Ah've always got them.'

'Have ye?'

'Ah get a green card a' the time, don't ah?'

He seemed quite unperturbed, as if he were talking about someone else's head. His eyes still had that smiling expression in them.

'Miss Brown's looking over here,' I whispered warningly. 'Have ye done the sum?'

'Nope.'

'Dae ye no' want tae do it?'

'Och, ah keep forgetting how many quarters in a hundredweight.'

'Four,' I reminded him. 'It's printed on the back o' your exercise book, anyway. There are always four quarters in anything, ye know.'

'Aye, ah daresay. You're awfy clever, aren't ye?'

There was nothing in his voice that expressed admiration,

envy or even interest. It was the same voice that said, 'Ah get a green card a' the time, don't ah'.

'Ah don't think I am. If ah were awfy clever ah wouldnae be frightened a' the time, would ah?'

'Aye,' he was smiling openly now, showing teeth that were uneven and corrugated with shallow grooves. 'You're a real feartie, aren't ye?'

Then he sat up and went on with his sum.

That afternoon when we were going home from school I turned the corner of Craigiehall Street and found myself some yards behind a few girls from my class. They were chirrupping and twittering together, their arms tightly linked in the indissoluble blood brotherhood that was resworn each week with new partners. I started dawdling, so as not to catch up with them, for groups such as this were aggressively exclusive and spitefully hostile to any who tried to join the union. Their intensest pleasure derived not from the many joys of brotherhood but from relishing the longing expressions of those who dreamed of joining them. If they were alone, they sulked and bickered and scuffed their shoes against a wall, but if an outsider appeared, they leapt into each other's arms laughing deliriously and loving with extravagant embraces. They whirled their ropes in frantic delight or spun their tops, oohing and aahing and pressing their hands together in prayerful ecstasy over the colours that had never before been so brilliant or gay, or so exclusively theirs, for the eyes of the gang only. Feet away, mutely grateful for being allowed to watch the spectacle from the periphery, stood the outsider in one of her various forms: clumsy, fat and inarticulate with her bag of liquorice allsorts loosely held in her puffy fingers, a schoolgirl's mite brought to win favour from the high priestesses. Or she might be a thin, light-boned creature, shy and voiceless, a nonentity with enormous round white forehead and vacant eyes, who stood hypnotised, her fragile jaw hanging slack and stupid. The gang played on, completely ignorant, so they seemed, of the wistful worshippers, but watching acutely from the sides of their heads like sharp birds. If the audience drifted off in despair, the play instantly stopped by common, unvoiced consent and the group moved away, arms linked, to find another solitary, whose sense of isolation they could intensify with yet another parade of the clan spirit.

Sometimes, in a grand gesture, they admitted an outsider as

an honorary member on payment of a bag of sweets, or box of chalks, or a ride on a new bicycle. But this membership was very temporary, even momentary, and was often terminated violently, abruptly, with slaps or kicks and no apologies, hissed insults being pitched after the luckless victim, who ran off weeping and fretting over the injustices of life.

Margaret and I scorned these groups. From time to time a boys' gang would invite Margaret to join in some of their activities that involved roaming the back streets or throwing stones at another gang. No one ever asked me to be in, but I was happy to play at home with my family or with the ones who lived in the neighbouring closes. I watched the classroom cliques with interest, noting how their unity was fluid rather than solid and was constantly assuming new shapes with the same old elements. The outsiders remained a constant. Those who were unwilling solitaries had no appeal, even for each other, and they relied completely and unashamedly on buying fellowship. Those who held themselves outside the groups, like Jimmy Donleavy and me were intrigued and entertained by the group rituals: their passwords, secret codes, ostentatious embracings and loudly uttered vows. But we regarded them and their paraphernalia with semi-contemptuous disbelief.

Well, there was one of the gangs ahead of me now, putting on their little turn, for both sides of the street were marked at intervals by stragglers, scuffing their feet home. I barely heard the footsteps clattering behind me, and by the time I turned my head, Jimmy Donleavy had already passed and was hurtling for the girls in front. He gave Ina Brogan's pigtails a jerk and slapped Jean McKay's bag out of her hand.

The girls stopped their chatter abruptly and glared at Jimmy Donleavy.

'Och, it's that scunner,' said blonde Dora Woods, talking through her long, fine nose. 'Ignore him, girls. Don't pay him any attention,' then turning to look directly at him, she announced in her clear, hard voice: 'we don't associate with scruff. Come on girls!'

They, however, giggled and clutched their bags tightly against their chests.

'Don't you go saying any dirty things tae us, Jimmy Donleavy,' Jean warned him enticingly, 'cause mah mammy's goin' tae see your Da if ye dae.'

94

The boy grinned happily, baring his ragged teeth. He straddled the pavement in front of them, containing them behind the wall of his outstretched arms.

'Aye, she can dae that,' he said in affable agreement, 'but she might be awfy sorry efter. Mah Da, he knows a few dirty things tae.'

He made a sudden leap to the right where Dora Woods was trying to sidle off, and began mocking her with feint attacks, stabbing her with splayed fingers and making queer faces. Dora drew back in alarm.

'Watch it, you,' she threatened him, her voice trembling a little. 'You put another finger on me and it'll be mah Da who'll come tae see ye, no' mah mother.'

'Here, ye've got me scared half tae death,' Jimmy Donleavy said, shivering in mock terror. He made a run at Ina Brogan who was sneaking along the wall and shouted at her:

'Back, back, ye wee rascal, back tae the fold,' and he began to run round them, huddling them together, pretending to hex them, throwing his fingers at them like spears, and gnashing his teeth.

'Woo, woo, woo,' he wailed, rolling his eyes.

Then, of a sudden he stopped:

'Watch,' he said. 'The magic circle!'

Slowly, while the girls watched with suspicious eyes, he curved his forefinger and brought it round to touch his thumb.

'Ye see,' he said, 'we now have a circle. And now we take the index finger of our right hand and go like—this!' And he rammed his finger up through the ring, pulling it down again and pushing it up. 'Look, look,' he cried, waving the image under Dora's disdainful nose.

The girls burst apart, screaming abuse at him.

'You're a filthy pig!'

'Dirty beast.'

'Wait till ah tell mah Da, tell the teacher, tell the government, tell the preacher. Ah've never seen such a filthy creature. Makes ye right sick.'

They fled, still loosely in their group, their fused bloods boiling in common turbulence, running all the way down to the cross street where the traffic was passing still, chattering with their teeth and claws. Oh, my dear!

Jimmy Donleavy stood for a minute looking at them waiting

to cross the street. He lifted his hands to his mouth to form a trumpet and blew three blasts:

'Up—your—hole!'

They had been waiting for it, hunched together in nervous anticipation and they birled round on one foot, all horror and mime. One hand covered a mouth. One arm rose in the air as if waiting for a sword. One body disappeared into hiding behind the two in front. Two stood with their elbows jutting out, pointed as sharp as dirks, the knuckles hard on the hips. Their mouths were wide open, but the wind blew the words back down their throats. Then the crossway was empty and they all moved off as one, holding their dresses down against the wind.

Jimmy Donleavy turned his back on them. He threw his arms out from his sides, stiffly straight and wooden. Round and round he veered in circles, arcing first towards the ground and then to the sky, warming up his engines. Barrroom, Barrroom! His wings lifted, his engines roared, and he zoomed off, up the top end of McLean Street.

We sat beside each other for only a few more months before we were all reorganised as Miss Croal's qualifying class.

6 Miss Croal's Qualifying Class

Miss Croal. She was as ugly as her name. Her face was covered with pinkish brown face powder. Goodness knows it made little difference. She had bushy eyebrows that grew into each other making a heavy black line right across her forehead, underlining the crooked wrinkles that she got from scowling all the time. She had thin lips that usually disappeared inside her mouth. The purplish, greasy lipstick she wore was only a guideline to where the lips would have been if she had had any. All over her head were the tight little curls that you got when you curled your hair with pipe cleaners. They were harsh curls, not the big soft ones my mother made with the tongs.

'She's a right ugly mug, her, isn't she?' Ann Bell whispered. We were all standing out the front of the classroom with our bags, waiting to be told where to sit because Miss Croal didn't allow you to pick your own seat. Miss Brown did most of the time. It was only when she wanted you to help somebody that you had to sit where she put you.

Miss Croal was looking at a sheet of paper that was lying on her desk lid. When Ann Bell whispered, the teacher's head lifted sharply, with a suddenness and conviction that startled us.

'That girl who's talking. Come here at once!' Her voice was even uglier than her looks. You felt she might have been cursed by some old witch she'd refused to help in the forest and toads would come tumbling out instead of words. Nobody spoke. We all waited, including Miss Croal.

'Well,' she grated. 'I'm waiting. Come out the girl who was whispering.'

Ann Bell tried to melt into the back line. All our eyes were on the ground because we knew by experience it was dangerous to catch a teacher's eye. Miss Croal pushed a few girls and boys to one side and surveyed the others, scrutinising their faces with her Gorgon's eye.

'You, boy! What are you hanging your head like that for? Like some dumbcluck. This is the qualifying class you're in and anybody who tries to pass for an idiot will be out. Out, before he can draw breath. So look intelligent, look intelligent. The look's enough these days,' she added.

While she was speaking, her eyes never stopped searching. Then she said:

'You, you were the girl who was talking.' She grabbed Ann Bell's arm above the elbow and dug her thumb into it. 'Speak up girl, when I ask you a question.'

Ann's eyes, or at least her good one, began to water. She had a glass eye that filled the hole made by a boy's home-made arrow.

'I didn't think you asked me a question, Miss,' she answered timidly.

'Don't be impertinent, girl. You're the one, aren't you? Speak up.'

'Yes Miss.'

'Hah. I knew it.' A satisfied smirk crawled over her face. Then she turned to address us.

'There is nobody who can do anything in this class that I don't know about. I see everything, and I hear everything. Nothing is hidden from me. Nothing!' she added emphatically.

Freddie Goode, who was smart at his work but a bit daft, spoke up.

'Miss Brown cannae know about you, then, Miss,' he asserted boldly. 'She said no teachers were omniscient.'

Miss Croal stared at him as if he were some kind of white bed bug that had just crept out from behind the wallpaper. In fact he did look a bit insect-like, with his bulging blind eyes that peered at you from behind his nickel-framed glasses. These were always slipping down his nose and a hundred times, when he was speaking to you, he would push the bridge up with his forefinger. Apart from the glasses, which were an eyesore, he had thick red hair that sprouted up from his head like a hedgehog's quills and he was fat. The girls treated him as a joke. If we ever played C.C.K., chase, catch, kiss, we always ran like mad to make sure he didn't catch us. To be latched onto by him and to have to pay the forfeit made many a girl run home crying. No one thought of not kissing him. That would have been cheating. But if some sly boy, noticing it was getting dark and the girls were puffed out with running, suggested a game of C.C.K.—no girl would have dreamed of nominating it—then someone was sure to say:

'If Freddie Goode's playing, ah'm no' in it.'

Freddie would get very indignant.

'What's up wi' me anyway?' he would complain. 'You're no' such an oil painting, yourself. Ye neednae worry, ah'm no' goin' tae chase *you*.'

'Och, ye say that every time,' the girl would reply, unimpressed, 'but ye chase anything ye think ye can catch.'

'Aw, come on girls, don't be mean,' some boy, usually the best looking, would intervene. 'Freddie's no' sae bad. He cannae help it if he's got tae wear specs.'

'Aye, an' he cannae help it if he's got red hair an' he's fat, tae,' was the acid rejoinder, 'but we're no' a first aid society ye know.'

Sometimes Freddie went home in a huff. Other times he waited till a decision was given in his favour, then chased vigorously any poor girl who was short of breath. The girls kept their eyes out for him and would call to his selected prey:

'Watch it, Freddie Goode's efter ye.'

This produced phenomenal bursts of speed, for a short time at any rate, but Freddie got his prize eventually though some of the more attractive boys missed out, their stamina sapped by sudden attacks of shyness.

Miss Croal was still staring at him. Freddie, however, his mouth slightly sagging and his eyes wide with innocent curiosity was quite unput out by the fierceness of her scrutiny. She was the Living Duchess, Miss Croal. If the Corporation had allowed her, she would have bellowed forty times a day 'Off with his head', until all the children in Glasgow had been used up and she could have sat in her empty classroom teaching paper dolls.

Finally, seeing that Freddie wasn't going to drop his eyes, she whispered in a tiny little voice:

'You, boy, what's your name?'

Miss Croal's tiny little voice worked the same way as a tidal wave. All her breath got sucked in, drawing her voice backwards right down to the toes. Silence for a second. Then the breath would come rushing back up at a terrific speed, crackling and roaring through her massive chest, squeezing into her windpipe, and storming along with the resonance of thunder. It would burst out of her mouth like an explosion, breaking in terrible waves that came and went about our heads, battering our ears and blasting our brains into dizzy insensibility. Her tiny voice was horrible. But we didn't know that yet, least of all poor Freddie who was still gazing up at her face, his own blankly glaikit.

'Freddie Goode, Miss,' he whispered, matching the teacher's tiny voice.

Then it all happened the way I said. I hung on to my bottom lip with my teeth and tried to switch off my ears, but they kept coming on.

How dare you, how dare you I scream . . . no one talks to me like that, no one talks . . . impertinent boy, oh boy what a voice . . . and what is more and more and more, ever more . . . straps for you, slaps too . . . and let this be a lesson, lessening now, humph, humph, sighing like a seal, poor Freddie's blubbing, we'll let him play tonight. Pig. Oh my head. The silence is tolling like Big Ben.

'Right then, now that I've made myself clear, I'll allocate you your seats. In the back seat, in the left hand corner, will sit . . . the Dux. (Trumpets sound.) Now, who's Mary Rose Lavery? Step out here.'

She looked at me sharply and didn't like what she saw.

'Take that look off your face, girl.' It was my normal look. Nobody had ever complained about it before. What kind of look did she want, for heaven's sake? I said:

'I'm not meaning to be rude, Miss Croal, but this is the look I have all the time. It's the way my face is.'

She stared at me for a minute without speaking. Then she snapped crossly:

'Go to your seat at once. And remember. There'll be a test every week, so you will have to fight to hold your place as the dux. Next, Flora McKechnie.'

A rather plump girl, wearing a greenish kilt and a white blouse, stepped forward very smartly.

'I am Flora McKechnie, Miss Croal.' She had a soft, pleasant voice, not Glasgow, and the way she said 'Miss Croal' it sounded like 'your honour'.

Miss Croal liked it. She beamed.

'That's the way. Right Flora, you take the place next to the girl Lavery, and remember. It's up to you to try and fill the dux position. You don't have to be content with second place.'

And that was it. Flora didn't often get the corner seat but in Miss Croal's heart, for people said she had one, Flora was the dux and I was the dunce, until we left primary school. The others were all arranged in their seats according to their marks from the previous year and there we sat, ready for judgement. Anybody coming into the class knew that Ronnie Gillis, sitting in the front seat on the extreme right, was the worst scholar in the room.

Lucky Jimmy Donleavy. He went into Miss Bright's class with all the boys and girls who wouldn't make the quali. This was the exam that decided the rest of your life: what kind of job you'd get, whom you'd marry, where you'd live and how many children you'd have. It was the exam that got you out of or barred your exit from the tenements. If you got an S1, S2 or S3 pass, you went to 'Bella', Bellahouston Academy. On the outside it was as bleak and depressing as the tenements, grimy stone walls topped with turrets. Stately and austere, they called it in the school song. It was the kind of prison, however, that people like me dreamed of breaking into, of wearing its black and gold uniform that would tell the tenements you had been sentenced to six years of glorious servitude. If my mother could get the uniform, that is. If I passed the exam, that was.

Those who didn't get an S pass went to Lambhill Street Junior where you studied sewing and cooking and office work, or woodwork if you were a boy. They were graded J1, J2, J3. Most people where I lived got M passes which promoted them to the advanced division of the primary school.

That's where Jimmy Donleavy would go. So they gave the kids like him Miss Bright for a teacher. She was the laughingest teacher in the school, everybody said, and she never used the strap. It was always summer in her class for she wore brightly flowered or striped smocks over her winter clothes. Not like Miss Croal who always dressed like a withered weed. The only season in her classroom was winter. Miss Bright was young and pretty with long thick brown hair like Debra Paget's in *Adventure in Paradise*. She kept it tied back with a ribbon, a different one for every day of each week, they said. I didn't see her much at school but once I got on the tram and there she was, wearing a tennis dress. It was short and showed her nice legs that were a bit tanned. She must have been away for a holiday somewhere. A chap was with her and she was laughing, as you might expect.

As the queue moved up the tram I arrived just in front of her and she saw me. She wasn't a bit embarrassed about being there with the man and holding his hand. She said:

'Hullo dear, you're a little girl from Lorne Street Primary, aren't you?'

Fancy that. She'd noticed me around. Miss Croal always treated you like the Invisible Man.

'Yes Miss.' Goodness, my face was heating up. I bet it was brick red. It was getting to be a terrible nuisance this business of blushing. I never used to do it.

'You're in the qualifying class, aren't you?'

Fancy that. She knew everything about you.

'Yes Miss. I'm in Miss Croal's class.' I tried to look mournful. In fact, I didn't have to try; just thinking about the old witch made me feel like dying.

'Well, keep up the good work,' Miss Bright went on, smiling right into my eyes, 'and you'll get into the top class at Bellahouston.'

Thank goodness it was my stop. Miss Bright was awfully nice but it was a strain talking to her like a human being. It made you right nervous.

Lucky Jimmy Donleavy. I never saw him again to ask him how lucky he was. Sometimes I searched for him in the lines when we were waiting to go in but if Miss Croal saw you with your eyes not straight in front, you copped it when you got inside.

Everybody said Miss Croal was the best teacher in the school. If you did what she told you, you always got a good pass, and she was one of the best teachers in Glasgow, at grammar. That's what the headmaster said, anyway. He used to come in and chat to Miss Croal. He was long and thin and flat as if he'd gone through a mangle. While he was talking, and his Adam's apple was blurting around, we waited nervously, because he had a trick, very funny he thought, of suddenly whirling round from Miss Croal and lunging with his pointer at someone—usually in the front seat:

'Thirteen at tuppence three farthings.' Or, 'Spell Uhlan. Too slow, too slow.'

Then shaking his head as if he didn't know what the world was coming to (he generally said it too) he'd give Miss Croal a short nod and float away like a giraffe. Miss Croal was always furious.

'For heaven's sake. You children have less life than the dummies at the waxworks. You're a disgrace. You make me ashamed. Ashamed.'

We were delighted.

On the following Friday we were to have Miss Croal's first test.

'Every Friday morning before recess, we will do thirty mental in thirty minutes, and forty sums in one hour.'

So on the first Friday morning, Flora McKechnie and I sat in silence waiting for the starting pistol. She was so calm and blandly indifferent, I was sure she already had the race in the bag. And what would I say to my father, then? He was never interested in marks. Ninety-eight or ninety-nine, it made no difference.

'Did ye come first?' If you didn't, a sigh of disappointment and vexation.

'Look, ah don't care aboot the marks. They mean nothing. What's important is to be the best there is. If ye're no' the best, the rest doesnae matter.'

'But ye cannae be the best a' the time, ye know. There's bound to be somebody, somewhere, who can beat ye.'

'Aye, well, ye can deal wi' that problem when ye come tae it.'

We were to do the mentals from a book Miss Croal passed around to us. At the end of thirty minutes, she said:

'Pens down. Put your name at the top of a new sheet and when I say "begin" you can start the arithmetic.'

She inverted the blackboard where she had laboriously written down the forty sums in her neat, curly writing, formed precisely, just like the curls on her head. Scribbling down the figures was time wasting, but we had to do it. I copied down the sums ten at a time, and then skimmed up and down the columns. Flora McKechnie was still writing when I finished, so I began checking my answers. I found one or two careless additions in the long multiplication sums. Flora was still writing. Her arm was spread over her page, hiding her work from view, obviously a deliberate action. I waited till she had to shift her arm to start a new page and sneaked a look at her answers to the more complicated divisions. Three of her answers were different. As many as that! I must have been very sloppy because she always went very carefully. Quickly I checked the divisions by multiplying

103

the answers by the divisor. The answer corresponded to the dividend. So she had three wrong it seemed. Later, I got another look at some of her additions. Different again. I checked and rechecked my answers. They were right. Well, little old Flora was in for a shock. Yet it seemed so strange. When we did our classwork, only an odd answer varied between us. Flora never bothered to look at mine. She had ample confidence in her own. Or maybe she was just honest.

The slower ones were starting to put their pens down now, so the hour must be nearly up. Sure enough, in a minute or so, Miss Croal yelped:

'Time. No more writing. Not a stroke.'

I waited, with the usual nervous rumblings in my stomach. Flora McKechnie sat with her plumpish, white hands folded together. Her nails were completely unbitten. Nicely rounded, too.

Finally, Miss Croal told us to change books and then she asked us to read out our answers. I had to read out some of Flora's answers to the mentals. Hers were all right. So were mine. Half-way through the correction of the sums, Miss Croal asked Flora to read out some of my answers. They were all wrong. I sat with my head hanging, nearly biting my tongue in two to stop the tears of shame and embarrassment. Some dux. The medal was starting to burn into my throat. It was hot with humiliation too. Any minute I expected it to throw itself round Flora's neck.

As other answers were read out, I watched Flora's hand. She was marking more crosses than ticks. God, what had happened to me? All of a sudden I must have become an imbecile. What would my father say? I would have to go into Miss Bright's class, and that prospect suddenly didn't seem so appealing. The colours in my tweed skirt were bobbing together in circular patches; I couldn't distinguish one from the other.

Miss Croal had her register open and was recording the marks as they were read out. I gave Flora her papers and took mine. She had got thirty for mental and thirty-eight for sums. Twenty-two was written at the top of my paper. I read it out in a whisper and the others turned round in surprise to look at me.

'Thirty-two or twenty-two?' Miss Croal asked with a frown in her voice.

When I repeated the mark she raised her eyebrows above her glasses and said:

'Bring your paper here.'

I took it out and handed it to her with my face averted from the class. Miss Croal looked at it, checking the sums with the tip of her pencil. When she'd finished, she started glancing over at the board, her eyes constantly shifting from it to the paper.

'Humph,' she kept grunting.

'Well, my girl,' she announced at the finish, 'you need glasses. You've got your figures copied down wrongly in so many sums it can't be coincidental. Go to the back wall and read out the first sum on the board.'

I did this and the class gasped and giggled. The teacher was right. I couldn't see properly. This was the first class where I had sat in the back seat so no one had noticed my shortsighted-ness before. It was a relief to know that I hadn't suddenly become an idiot, but after this sense of deliverance had passed I was afflicted by another nightmarish vision: me, with my short straight hair (cut, since I was separated from Jimmy Donleavy), cherry nose, as my family described it, and blubber lips (their image also of my overfull mouth), me with all these defects and nickel-framed glasses as well. What a sight! They would put me in the zoo or the circus. Glasses! You might as well be dead. Look at Freddie Goode. He was the only boy in the class, one of the few in the school, in fact, who wore glasses, and the names they called him! Specky, four eyes, owl face. That's why the girls didn't want to be caught by him. Glasses. They could say what they liked. I was never going to wear them. Never. Miss Croal would have to let me sit in the front seat.

'You can sit in the front for today,' she decided. 'I'll give you a note to go to the clinic. You can go this afternoon; the sooner the better. Tell your mother you may be a little late home.'

She glanced over the class, searching for someone. Her eye alighted on Freddie Goode who was self-consciously twiddling with his own glasses.

'Freddie Goode! You'll go to the clinic with Mary Rose,' she told him, 'as she'll need someone to bring her back to school. If they put drops in her eyes straight away she won't be able to see properly. Come to school first, after lunch, and I'll send you off with the card.'

I fetched my books from the back seat and was directed to one in the middle of the front row, only a few feet from the board. To my surprise Miss Croal, after recording the marks, announced that there would be no shifts in position that week. So my seat in the corner was left empty, but I felt guilty, keeping the medal.

'Could I put it in, please, for this week?' I asked the teacher.

'Yes, I think that might be the fairest thing,' she agreed. So for that week there was no dux.

After lunch, Freddie Goode and I marched off to the school clinic. My mother had been quite unperturbed by my funereal lament that I needed glasses, but Margaret exploded in mock horror.

'Wow, you'll be a right beauty then,' she cried. 'Fancy havin' tae get goggles. Everybody'll call you four eyes and all that the way they do tae ol' Freddie Goode. Boy, ah'm no' going tae be seen aroon wi' ye.'

I started to bawl. 'Ah'm never goin' tae wear the horrible things,' I vowed. 'Everybody'll laugh at me.'

My mother told Margaret to stop her nonsense and to stop exaggerating the situation.

'There's nothing wrong with glasses,' she assured me. 'Quite a lot o' people wear them. An' you're damn lucky to be getting them. It's better than no' bein' able to see at a'.'

'Och, Mammy,' Margaret interrupted, 'only old folk wear them. Ye hardly ever see kids oor age wearin' them. No wonder, they look like bloomin' gargoyles.'

This started me off again and I sat snivelling over my lunch till my mother warned me that if I didn't dry up she would give me something to cry for. She filled up the card requesting the eye test and I went back to school on one of the few specless days left on earth for me.

Freddie Goode wasn't much consolation.

'Aye, ah know, it's awful when ye wear specs. They make ye a proper laughin' stock. It's no' fair. If a' the world had to wear them, naebody would be able tae laugh then. An' you girls. Look at ye, the things ye say tae me, an' no' lettin' me catch ye or anything like that.'

'Well, ah've never called ye specky,' I rejoined with asperity. 'Ah always felt sorry for ye.'

'Aw well,' he said in an encouraging tone, 'ah'll still run after ye when we play C.C.K.'

The implications were obvious. No one else would. Tears of self pity began to pour down my face again.

'Shut up,' I said nastily. 'Ah'm never goin' tae play that game again anyway, an' ye'll no' need to chase me.'

When we arrived at the clinic which was in a terraced house in Rutland Crescent, I glared at the doctor as I handed him my card.

'Right you are my girl,' he said in a cheery voice that made me want to hit him. As if he were a real doctor and he was doing you a good turn. 'We'll have a look at those eyes straight away.'

He took us into a room where the blinds were drawn and left us by ourselves while he went out for a minute. The eye chart was right beside the door. I looked at the letters. They were all different sizes. Enormous at the top, like a baby's reading book, and tiny at the bottom. Minutes went by and the doctor hadn't returned. By this time without really knowing why I did it I had memorised all the letters on the chart.

'Right then,' the doctor said, hurrying into the room with a box of cards in his hand. 'Let's take a look, shall we?'

He put his hand over my right eye and told me to read the chart. I read everything. He said nothing. Then he covered my left eye and I read the chart again. Perfectly.

'Uh huh,' he said, stroking his chin and looking at me strangely. 'Uh huh.' He strode across the room and to my astonishment turned the chart around. In fact it was only one side of a lantern kind of thing which had charts on all four faces.

'Now,' the doctor said, covering my eye again. 'Read this chart.'

I could only see the very top letter. He turned the lantern round again. Still I could see only the top letter. Then he spun it round to the chart I had originally learnt by heart.

'I can't see that either,' I told him resignedly. 'I learned the letters off when you were outside.'

'Well now, did ye? That was a very silly thing to do,' he said gently. 'It's not the end of the world you know. You could have a wooden leg, or worse.'

I stared at him sullenly. He had a pleasant face, long and thin, with deep ruts and fair hair that fell in front of his eyes in a cow's lick. His own eyes, light blue with shiny whites, were quite naked.

'You don't wear them yourself, do you?' I said accusingly.

'If I had to, I would, you silly girl. You don't know how very lucky you are to get them. Your short sight could stop you from getting a good job later. You'd never be able to see well enough. But these glasses will let you see better than the best eyes.'

He turned to Freddie Goode.

'You're not sorry you've got them son, are you?' he asked.

'Aye, ah wish ah didnae have tae wear them,' Freddie muttered, pushing his specs high up on his nose.

'Och, ye pay too much attention to stupid people. They're ignorant, those folk that call you four eyes and such like. They belong in the Dark Ages. They're totally ignorant. You children are right up in the van of scientific development.'

He slipped a little white bullet into my eyes while he was talking. Then he made me sit down for a little while, explaining that I would see things blurrily for a bit.

'We've got to prepare your eyes for the glasses. Wait five minutes and then you can go back to school. We'll send your mother a card telling her when to come and get the glasses.'

'Can ye see the stairs all right?' Freddie asked me when we got outside.

'Och, of course ah can. Ah'm no' Blind Pew ye know.'

'Here, gie me yer hand,' he said, taking hold of my fingers and jumping onto the step below the one I was standing on. 'Come on noo, mind where ye put yer feet.'

Once we had put the steps behind us and we were walking down the Crescent, I stuck my hand into my pocket. But Freddie didn't seem to notice. He chatted on, in that airy, unseeing way he had.

'Will ye be goin' tae Bella in January?'

'Ah hope so, if ah pass all right. Will you?'

'No, no,' he said shaking his head positively from side to side.

'Why not? You're a good scholar. Ye'll be sure tae get an S pass.'

'Mah Da'll no' let me. He says Bella's only for rich folk. The ones that are goin' tae the University efter.'

'Och, but ye don't have tae be rich tae go tae the University. Mah Da says ye can get bursaries and exhibitions and things like that. That's what ah want tae get.'

'Aye, but mah Da says a trade's a good thing for a man. The universities arenae really supposed to be for people like us. Ah'm goin' tae Lambhill Street. Maybe ah'll go tae the Polytechnic after ah leave school and be a marine engineer.'

We went along in silence for a bit. What was he meaning by people like us, as if we had a disease or something?

'What dae ye mean by folks like us?' I asked him. 'We havenae got two heads, ye know. We're the same as other people. Mah Da says we're a' Jock Thamson's bairns on bath night.'

'Aye but we're poor,' Freddie said. 'That's the difference. Ye know the American ship we went on last month. At least you and some o' those kids from the other classes did. That's because you were poor.'

'What are ye talking aboot?' I demanded angrily. 'What's it got tae dae wi' the American ship? The navy invited us on for dinner and tae watch the pictures, that's a'.'

'Aye, but ah read aboot it in the paper,' Freddie said. 'Sixty poor and needy children from underprivileged areas of Glasgow were given a treat by the sailors of the U.S.S. what's its name. Ah've forgotten it. That was you and the others. The poor and needy.'

'Och, baloney,' I said rudely. 'We're no' a' that poor. We're no' starvin' are we? Anyway, mah Da says education is the great equaliser.'

Freddie scoffed. 'Aye, but mah Da says some folk try tae get above themselves an' ye know what happens then. Put the beggar on horseback and he rides tae hell.'

A sudden thought struck me.

'Is your Da no' a Communist then?'

Freddie's eyebrows rose so high, his specs all but slid right off his nose.

'Ye've got tae be joking,' he said in horror. 'Jings, they're terrible people. They're like the Russians. They turn everybody intae robots and send them tae Siberia. Mah Da hates them.'

'Och, that's a load of rubbish. Mah faither's a Communist an' he's no' a robot. He says a fair deal for everybody. If ye've got the brains tae go tae the Varsity they should let ye. Ah bet your faither's one o' these daft Tories like old Churchill. All warmongers.'

Freddie nodded his head vigorously. 'He's a Tory all right an' Churchill was a great man. He saved Britain from the Nazis.'

'That's havers,' I argued. 'Your Da's a traitor tae his class. The Tories are the ones that keep ye in the gutter. The poorer ye are the better they like ye. That's what mah Da says.'

Freddie looked embarrassed, but he was too kindly to continue the dispute with disparaging remarks about my father. Instead he said:

'If ye go tae Bella ye'll be at school for centuries. Till yer eighteen or something.'

I counted the years up on my fingers. 'Next year ah'll be twelve when ah'm at secondary school. Second year thirteen . . .' I went on counting. 'In sixth form ah'll only be seventeen, no' eighteen.'

'Are you only eleven?' Freddie asked in surprise. 'Ah'm just twelve. Ah'm older than you.'

We walked along in silence again. I was thinking about that American ship. I wouldn't have gone if I'd known why I was asked. As if ye needed their ice cream cake anyway. Freddie was pushing his glasses up his nose again, for the ten millionth time. Then he started dragging his ear lobe down.

'Can ah ask ye something?'

'Hm mm.'

'Dae you er, have you—um.' He stopped, and I looked at him curiously. What was the matter with him? 'Ah was wantin' tae ask ye,' he resumed, his cheeks slightly pink, 'ah was wantin' tae know . . . dae you wear a brassiere?'

My eyes widened to bursting point. Freddie was peering intently at me over his glasses which were down on the end of his nose again.

'Oh, why can't ye keep yer glasses still?' I demanded exasperatedly. 'An' ye shouldnae ask lassies that. It's no' nice.'

'Aye, ah know,' Freddie agreed candidly. 'But ah willnae tell anybody. Ah just thought it was interesting. Dae ye?' he pressed. There was no doubt about Freddie. He was shamelessly persistent, and he triumphed again as he did in the kissing game.

'Well, if ye really like tae know,' I said in my most sarcastic voice, 'ah don't. So there. Ye don't wear a brassiere till ye . . .' There I stopped with my hand over my mouth. I'd nearly said it.

'Aye, ah know that,' Freddie said confidently. 'The big lads told us. So—er, ye don't—um. Oh well. Thanks for tellin' me.'

He kicked at a stone in passing, then dropping his voice and looking at me from the side of his specs he said:

'I know a girl in our class who does.'

'Does what?' I queried, playing stupid.

'Wear a brassiere. That's what we were talking about, wasn't it?'

'You were, ye mean. I don't want tae talk aboot it.'

'Anyway,' he said, ignoring my reproof, 'it's Flora Mc-Kechnie.'

Well, that was interesting. So that's why she always sat with a secretive cat's look on her face. She made you think she knew something you didn't even though she got beaten in the tests. And she was such a lady, sitting all the time with her hands folded and her feet still. She never rattled her leg under the desk the way I did, so that the books kept stuttering away on it. Sometimes she would hold them down with her placid hand and I knew what she meant, so I tried to stop. But she never spoke to you about it. She was too good.

'And how dae you know all this, smart Alex?' I asked.

Freddie grinned. The dopey look had gone from his eyes and they were gleaming with little flecks of green and yellow light.

'Ah felt it,' he said. 'At the back, ye know, when we were dancing the St Bernard's waltz and the boy has tae put his hand on the girl's back? Ah felt it then.'

He was laughing with delight in his knowledge. Light was leaping and dancing off his eyes in brilliant slivers of golden green ice and his pale face was glowing redly in the flames of hair that licked around his head. I stared at him with wonder.

'Ye know, ol' Freddie, ah like you. Ah really do. You're a very funny boy, but ah like you.'

'Ah then,' he said, blazing away like a winter sun, 'ye'll let me chase ye when we play C.C.K.?'

'No no, ye silly fellow,' I cried, remembering the glasses with despair. 'Ah'm never goin' tae play that game again wi' anybody. When ah get mah specs.'

The letter came from the clinic one morning. I was at school and my mother went right then to get the glasses from the optician's that was mentioned in the letter. She didn't wait till I had sat down by the beans on bread we were having for lunch.

'Well ah've got them, hen.'

Margaret and I both looked at her questioningly.

'Got what?'

'Your glasses, for God's sake. What else? Here, take a look at them. They're in an awfy nice case.'

111

The case was dark brown and as hard and sharp as stone. It had a savage lid that slammed shut on your fingers if you left them there unawares and bit into them until you clawed it off with your uninjured hand. It was a horrible case. The glasses were lying across their folded legs whose feet hooked round like scythes. I picked them up by one leg and examined the lenses from the side. They were thick and the glass rippled.

'What are ye waitin' for?' my mother asked impatiently. 'Put them on and tell us what they're like.'

'Aye, hurry up,' Margaret urged me, 'ah'm bustin' tae see what ye look like. Boy, they're really freaky.'

But I wasn't going to let them have the first look at me with my glasses on. I wanted to see myself in the mirror, not in their faces. So I went to the foggy glass above the sink and put them on. The legs hooked right round my ears into the little depression under the bone. Then I looked at myself. The image was hazy, but ugly enough. Despite the cloudiness of the glass, the lines of my face had never been so sharply defined. Not a blurred edge to soften the ugliness. The kirby grip that pressed my hair down flat to the skull had always been a faint brown line before, but now it glittered, a hard and metallic clamp above the dark nickel of the wire that crawled round my ear like a spider's leg. I pulled my hair forward to hide them both. And what had happened to my eyes. They had shrunk to marbles. I lifted the spectacles up and pressed forward to see my eyes. They were definitely big. A rather mousy grey, but big. Now look at them. With the glasses on they halved and shrank into dark recesses in my head. Great. Just great. No wonder they called you owly with frames so perfectly round. They must have been drawn with a compass. They made you look as if you were frozen in astonishment, or just plain glaikit.

'Come on, come on,' Margaret demanded impatiently, 'gie's a look at ye.'

So I turned round. While they examined me, I in turn had a new look at them. They were shining and sparkling as if they had been newly washed and polished. Good heavens. Margaret had freckles across her nose and her hair was reddish. I'd always thought it was brown. And my mother. I had never noticed what a beautifully shaped mouth she had, long and clearly curved, perfectly balanced, the top and bottom lips. I glanced around the kitchen. Everything had been spring cleaned. The grain on the wood my mother had used to frame the fireplace. I had thought it was flat brown. Chips out of the hearth. A crack in a cup on the table and a line of dirt deeply packed into the join where the two halves of the table met. Now I could see the fantastic patterns of pink and green on the kitchen wall. My mother had dipped two cloths in dyes and rolled them over and over down the wall so that there was a whole forest of candied fronds waving madly round us. I was crowded in by objects that aggressively demanded my attention where before they had been content to remain mute in the shadow.

Margaret was laughing. 'Jings, ah don't know what tae say. Ah mean, we'll probably get used tae it.'

She cocked her head to one side and scratched behind her ear.

'What dae you think, Mammy?'

My mother was watching me carefully. 'Dae they make any difference tae the way ye see? Ah mean that's the important thing. That's the whole point o' it isn't it?'

My head was starting to feel giddy.

'Aye, Ma. They make a fantastic difference. It's like being in a new world, or switching on the light or something. It's terrible tae think ah havenae been seein' this before and everybody else has. Everything seems a wee bit smaller, mind you, but all scrubbed up. Margaret even looks clean, somehow, though ah know she's got a dirty face.'

I took the glasses off and returned them to their case, which snapped at my finger and got me unawares.

'But ah'm no' goin' tae wear them, just the same.'

My mother was indignant. 'Here, what kind o' stupid talk is this? Take them oot o' that case and put them on this instant.'

'No. Ah'm no' goin' tae,' I said, determinedly. 'They make me look like a freak. Ye'd need tae be Solomon tae see any beauty in them an' ah'm no' goin' tae suffer these kids callin' me specky an' four eyes an' all that.'

'Aye Ma, they will, ye know,' said Margaret. 'Here, can ah try them on?'

She tugged at the case to open it. 'Here, this bloomin' case is like that big clam we saw in *Wake o' the Red Witch*, ye know, the one that nearly broke that chap's leg in two and the black man had tae come and stab it open.'

'Oh my goodness,' she giggled, staggering around with her hands spread out in front of her, 'how can ye see wi' these? They nearly pull the eyes oot o' yer head like a poultice, and everything's all wriggling like worms. Wow!'

She pulled them off thankfully and put them back in the case, watching the lid carefully. 'No kiddin', ye'd think that lid was alive. Ah'm sure it tries tae get ye.'

'Look Mammy,' I said to my mother, placatingly, 'ah can see well enough ootside. It's just when ah'm readin' the board ah need specs. Ah'll wear them in the classroom.'

I put the case with the glasses into the pocket of my skirt. My mother gave me one of her suspicious looks.

'See that ye dae.'

At school I said nothing to anyone about the glasses. I was hoping Miss Croal would let me stay in the front seat and maybe not notice I was there. But not a chance. The test for dux would have to go on every week and if I sat in the front I would be spoiling the system. I thought of suggesting that maybe the dux could sit at the front and the other kids at the back, but the reasoning was that the ones who weren't good scholars talked more and fiddled around if they were sitting where they couldn't be seen. And even at the front, to tell the truth, I had to screw up my eyes a bit to be sure of getting the figures right. It was easier with words because you could nearly guess them from the words around.

Sure enough, on the Thursday, Miss Croal issued her weekly storm warning.

'Tomorrow, don't forget, is Friday. Make sure you have revised the score rule and the dozen rule, and the formula for simple interest.' An idea struck her suddenly. You could see it. She lifted her head sharply and pressed her forefinger against her bottom lip.

'It's over a week since you had the eye test, Mary Rose. Have you had no word from the clinic yet? They're usually very quick.'

The glasses were in my bag. I took a big breath inside myself and said so quietly, I had to repeat it:

'Ah've got them, Miss Croal.'

'Oh.'

The class sighed a long sigh and sat up with interest. I kept my eyes on my desk and waited. I hoped she wasn't going to speak in her tiny voice. Oddly enough, all she said, and quietly too, was:

114

'Then put them on at once, miss. Do you like going around like a blind man?'

'No Miss.'

'Then get them on.' As I didn't move straight away, she added: 'Hurry up. We haven't all day to wait for your glasses.'

I unbuckled my bag and felt along the bottom of it. The case was there, hard and cold and unfriendly, as if it didn't like being rejected. I hooked my fingers over the lid and stuck my nails in to prise it open. The lid was as cantankerous as ever and pulled with all its might to stay shut. Everybody was waiting. I kept tugging at the lid and suddenly it sprang open, taking me by surprise, muddling me. My fingers shook, and the case leapt from my grasp to the ground shaking up the glasses inside. But they remained firmly in their felted confines, absolutely secure in their property rights. I lifted them out, unfolded their legs and fitted them round my ears. The class was watching and waiting. Then I sat staring straight ahead at the board. It was empty at the moment. But the dark grey became black.

Miss Croal said nothing and went on talking about the test. Behind me, Jean Mackay prodded me on one of the little knobs of my spine with the sharp point of her ruler. I wriggled.

'Turn roon a minute, Mary Rose. Gie's a look.'

I sat with my face rigid.

Pst, pst. The whispers were everywhere and here and there, my ears carefully attuned to them, I heard an occasional snicker. When the bell sounded for lunch I grabbed the glasses off my face and thrust them into the case that I'd left open on my desk. Then I slapped the lid down defiantly and tipped the lot into my bag again. Freddie Goode was shuffling out alongside me. He gave me a disapproving look.

'Ye should be wearing them a' the time, ye know. Ah saw what ye couldnae see at the clinic. Your eyes are worse than mine.'

'Shut up. Ah don't care.' I retorted rudely. Then I pushed out ahead and ran down the stairs out of the school and along Craigiehall Street till I got home.

Of course, once I was back in the dux's position it was impossible to hide my face. Every boy and girl in the class had only to turn round when Miss Croal was writing on the board and they could see me, owlish and scowling for as long as they cared to stare. So far no one had called me any names because Miss Croal

115

always had her eye out, but I'd seen a few smirks and crossed glances. Flora McKechnie had said nothing except:

'Ye've got them now. Do they make you see better?'

When I nodded curtly, she just smiled and said pleasantly:
'That's good.'

7   The Message

It was clear that Miss Croal liked Flora more than anyone else in the class. I might get the highest marks in the test and sit with the medal but to Miss Croal the real dux was Flora. Whenever there was a message to do, Flora went. If another teacher asked to borrow someone sensible, capable, trustworthy and reliable, Flora was lent. She took round the notices, looked after the infant classes if the teacher had to leave them for a bit, and sometimes Miss Croal even sent her outside the school on messages. Never did she ask me, or anyone else for that matter. If I got a mistake in my sums, she frowned and admonished me:

'That's far too careless. Very careless. You'll have to do much better than that.'

If Flora made two mistakes she was patted on the head and praised for the ones she got right. Talk about one-eyed. Miss Croal wore an eye patch whenever I crossed her line of vision. What did Flora have that I hadn't? This preoccupied me for most of the year that we sat together. I didn't talk much. I'd given up playing under the desk. That would have called forth more than a tidal wave from Miss Croal. I was never rude. But Miss Croal detested me and thought I was an idiot.

So for a time I tried to be like Flora. I studied her face whenever I got a chance so that I could copy her expression. She had large pale blue eyes that were always tranquil in expression, mill-ponds, never stormy lakes. Her skin spread over her face like smooth milk, milk with that tinge of blue it gets from being watered down. Maybe it was just the colour of her eyes being reflected off her cheek bones. Her lips were never pressed tightly together, nor bitten, nor stuck out, nor chewed, the way mine were. No, they were contented lips, spread at their ease, touching, but lightly without the pressure of one on the other. And Flora's hairs. Happy hairs all of them. Not as blonde as mine and no more shiny, but content to lie where they fell, touching, never pushing, agreeably uniform in length, pleasant strands of a harmonious whole. When Flora sat listening to Miss Croal, her serenity flowed around me in waves like water warm as toast, smoothing out the tightness in my head and neck and stilling the tremor in my knees till I sprawled half floating along my chair and Miss Croal, her thick arms flapping and her stubby legs stiff with anger, hauled herself up the aisle screeching like an alarmed crow.

'Look alive there, in the back seat, sit up straight Miss Lavery, if you don't want to be standing up straight.'

Flora's look didn't wear so well on me, somehow. I hunched over the desk again. My neck knotted itself like before and my right leg took up its old rattle. Flora's hand poured over the desk and stilled the slithering books. And Miss Croal went on scowling and smiling at us both, first at me, then at Flora.

One fine day, Flora didn't come. She'd never been away before. She never got sick, it seemed. I was excited as if it had been my birthday. Before I had been the understudy for the messenger, now I should have a chance to be the star. Miss Croal must ask me. She must. But that day there were no messages. Maybe Miss Croal had decided she could wait. The next day Flora still didn't come, nor the next, nor the next, but Miss Croal had no errands to run. On the fifth day the seat beside me was still empty. Flora must really be sick. Maybe she was dying or something. I didn't know where she lived, nor did anyone else, or I might have gone to ask.

From time to time when I finished my sums or writing exercises, I would look up at Miss Croal. Usually I tried to avoid her eye because if she caught you doing nothing, she would make some humiliating, sarcastic remark. But I was determined, with Flora away, I should have my rights and I sat up as tall as I could, straight and rigid as cast iron and as bold as a magpie. Miss Croal, I'm looking at you and I'm not going to take my eyes off you till you send me on a message. I will have my due. I am not a fool. My mother sends me all her messages, even into the outer city to find her Woodbines. I never lose the change or forget the order though once I sat on a hot new loaf when I was tired and reshaped it into a horseshoe that my mother threw at me. But that was a long time ago when I was a little child and thoughtless. You must send me on a message. I insist on it. Otherwise I'll come and haunt you at night, you and your five little children. Oh yes, you didn't know I knew, did you, but I was listening with my elastic ears to Miss Bright and Mr Corbett talking about it.

'Isn't that marvellous of Miss Croal, taking over those chil-. dren? They belonged to her best friend, you know, and they were both killed in a car crash. The husband and the wife, I mean. So she's taken them in. The head says she means to adopt them.'

Poor kids. Fancy having crusty Croal for a mother. She's so ugly to start with. Always wearing that bottle green costume with the long jacket that buttons at the waist. And her legs. She'd never win a beauty contest for legs, like my mother. Straight as sticks they are, and dripping over the tops of those old-fashioned lace-ups she wears. My mother says, never marry an ugly man for if ye've nothing tae eat, ye've got something to look at. That goes the same for mothers and teachers. Ye like something to look at. Doesn't she realise we get sick of seeing the same clothes every day. I can count every little box on her jacket, and every fifth thread is yellow, but ye see it only when ye look close up. Look out, she's tapping her fingers on the desk the way she does before she calls Flora out. Me, me, Miss Croal. Ask me.

She did too. She hooked her finger towards her and jerked her head out the front. I jumped up though she hadn't said anything.

'Me, Miss. Do ye want me?'

'Oh hurry up girl and come out at once. Who else am I looking at?'

When I was standing beside her desk, she took a long yellow envelope from her bag and held it in one hand, thoughtfully, tapping it against the palm of her free hand.

'I hardly know if I'm doing the right thing, giving this to you,' she began in her grumbling manner, 'but it doesn't seem as if I have much choice.'

She was seeing things my way.

'Oh I won't lose it Miss Croal,' I cried. 'I'll hold it awfully tightly, I really will.'

'Och, it's not that I'm afraid of,' she said, waving her hand abstractedly, 'it's got to be registered. You take it to the post office and give it to the postmistress. The important thing is to remember not to put it in the box yourself. Now, do you understand that? Don't put it in the box yourself. Give it to the woman at the counter. She'll weigh it and tell you how much it'll cost and she'll keep it behind the counter. I want it registered, you're to tell her. Now do you understand clearly?'

'Oh yes, Miss Croal. Ah'm to give it to the woman at the counter and not to put it in the box myself.'

'That's right,' she said. 'It's to be registered.'

She gave me four shillings and the envelope and I dashed out of the classroom. I would be back from the post office far faster than Flora McKechnie ever would and show Miss Croal I could go messages too. I mustn't forget to give the letter to the woman and what was it she said? There was a word. Oh heavens I've forgotten it. Oh how could I be so stupid? Don't forget to . . . but what was it? Anyway, if I don't put it in the box myself, I'm doing the right thing.

At the post office I handed the letter to the woman and she weighed it.

'That'll be sixpence.'

I passed her two shillings and waited for the change. She gave me a stamp with the change and the letter.

'Oh no,' I said, dropping the letter on the counter and backing off. 'You're to keep the letter. You're definitely to keep it. I'm not to put it in the box.'

'Well, ah can tell ye, it'll be sittin' here at the millenium if ye wait till ah put it in the box,' the postmistress replied, leaning her fat elbows on the counter behind the grille. 'Ah only have tae weigh it. You post it. That's what the box is for ootside. Ye don't think for one minute ah'm supposed to be playing pop goes the weasel in and oot o' the shop dae ye, wi' letters the public are too lazy tae post themselves?'

'But you must,' I insisted desperately. 'My teacher told me fifty times you're to post it. I was to do something with it but ah've forgotten the word.'

'Your teacher told you, did she?' the postwoman exclaimed, her eyebrows and her voice rising in a duet. 'Well, you tell your teacher from me, kids go tae school tae learn things, no' tae be message boys for lazy teachers. And tell her also there's a perfectly good box here for the public tae post their own letters. Ah don't know,' she said disgustedly, turning to serve a customer who'd just come in with her family allowance book, 'teachers these days. They're no' what they were in mah time. They say more than their prayers, some o' them.'

The letter was still lying on the counter. If I just go away quickly, I thought, she'll have to post it, but the woman saw me turning to go and called after me.

'Here, take yer letter or somebody else'll snaffle it. Ah'm no' goin' tae lay a finger on it. Ye'd be better tae go back tae that teacher o' yours an' ask her tae write her message doon.'

Write it down! What a nerve she had, suggesting such a thing. Why Flora McKechnie had got all sorts of things at one time and had never written anything down. The woman thrust the letter at me.

'Put it in the box, hen,' she said in a more kindly tone. 'Yer teacher's probably made a mistake. Ah've weighed it.'

So I went outside and posted the letter.

I got into the class as Miss Croal was waving her pointer over a coloured map that was draped over the blackboard.

'This area here, in yellow,' she was saying, 'is the cotton belt of the USA.'

I stopped in front of her.

'Here's your change, Miss Croal.'

'Only cost sixpence, did it?' she asked, her eyebrows curving thickly. 'I thought it would have cost more. Good, thank you. Have you got the ticket?'

Now she asks me! What ticket? When did she ever mention a ticket? Whoever said anything about a ticket?

I was trembling like a ripple of water.

'What ticket, Miss Croal?'

Oh Flora, why were you away today? Miss Croal was leaning against the side of the board, her hand covering the long lapel of her jacket. She was breathing as if her jacket was too tight, like Doreen Smellie when she's having an asthma attack.

'You did register it, didn't you?' she asked me appealingly. 'You didn't forget—after all I told you?' Her voice was like a little girl's and for a minute I thought I was the teacher. That was the word, wasn't it? The one I had forgotten. Register. I knew now why Miss Croal had never asked me to go a message for her. She knew me better than I did. I was stupid and unreliable, only I had never known it.

'No, Miss Croal,' I said drearily. 'I couldn't remember the word you said, and the woman wouldn't tell me it. She weighed it and said I must put the letter in the box myself.'

Oh God, Miss Croal was using her tiny voice.

'Go girl,' she whispered so tinily, I had to lipread. 'Go and get that letter back and get it registered. Don't come back without the ticket.'

I thought she was going to add 'or I'll lay you in your own blood' but teachers don't speak like that. They can look it, though. Miss Croal's chest was starting to lift up rapidly so I grabbed the money that she'd put down on Ronnie Gillis's desk and fled from the room before the tidal wave came and swallowed me up. At the post office I remembered the word perfectly.

'The teacher had meant me to register the letter,' I told the woman behind the counter. 'That's why I wasn't to put it in the box. You could have thought of that, you know.'

She didn't like my accusing tone. 'Your teacher should send somebody who knows what's to do. Ah'm no' here to sort out jigsaws for dopey kids. Anyway,' she said, 'You've got no hope o' getting the letter back. Once it's in the box it's in the care of His Majesty and no one gets it except the addressee. It's a criminal offence to give it to anyone else.'

'You'll have to give it back to me,' I said slowly. 'Ah'm not going back to school, ever, without it.'

The woman just snorted and turned her back on me. I went outside and sat on the steps wondering what to do. There must be a way. But I didn't know how. I got up and crossed over to the pillar box and tried to shove my arm down its throat but the space was too narrow and I nearly couldn't get my arm out again. Dear God, omniscient God. Here we go again. Do something. You know what can be done. What could I bribe him with this time? Please God find a way of returning the letter and I promise I'll never want to go the messages again. I'll go to the Bethel on Thursday night instead of going to the Club and I'll try to say my prayers more often, not just when ah'm asking for something. Please God, send a miracle. If you don't I'll have to die. I can't go back to Miss Croal without the ticket.

Just then the red mail van turned the corner from Paisley Road into McLean Street and came up alongside the Post Office. The postie jumped out and raced over to the box, sorting out his keys on the run. He stuck one into the little keyhole on the door of the pillar box and wrenched it open. I could see all the letters lying behind a wire grid that was open at the bottom.

'Oh mister, mister,' I cried, looking over his shoulder. 'Please can you let me have my letter back that's in there.'

'Go and play trains, kid,' he said without turning round. He was scooping away at the letters, hurrying them into the mail bag though they were falling over each other to get there themselves. I stood chewing my bottom lip watching for the yellow envelope. If he didn't give it to me I would grab it and take off.

He was talking again.

'Dae ye no' realise it's a terrible crime for a postman to gie letters tae anybody other than the addressee. It would cost me mah job. They're awfy strict aboot interfering wi' His Majesty's mail.'

'It's no' His Majesty's at a',' I said, starting to bawl. 'It's mah teacher's and she wants it registered. Ah couldnae remember the word and the woman told me to put it in the box. How is it goin' tae hurt His Majesty if ah just get the letter and register it? You're just making things difficult.'

By this time I was sobbing hysterically and people were gathering to stare. The postman was embarrassed. He half turned to a small group of women who were watching me.

'She wants me tae gie her a letter from here, but for crikey's sake it's against the law.'

'Ah only want tae register it,' I said, crying more loudly. It occurred to me that I might be able to get some sympathy from the women.

'Ah mean he could come in wi' me an' see ah wouldnae steal it. It's mah teacher's an' she says ah've never tae come back withoot the ticket.'

'Aw gie the kid a go,' one woman, tall and hefty like my Granny Bygroves, said. 'Don't be such a damn fuddy duddy.'

Then I saw it. I stuck my hand into the bundle and pulled the yellow envelope out.

'That's it mister. Oh please let me take it. Ah'll run doon tae the Toll office then that woman in there won't know ye let me.' My nose was running and as usual I didn't have a hankie.

'Oh for God's sake.' The postman stopped scooping and turned to look at me. 'Take the bloody thing when mah heid's turned and get tae hell oot o' here.' He turned his head quickly to the side and I ran off with the envelope. It was a mile to the other Post Office but who cared? I was flying down the street reprieved from death. Registering the letter this time was no problem. I knew exactly what I was doing and the little slip the postwoman gave me I put in my pocket very carefully. Miss Croal would have nothing to worry about now. I sang to myself as I skipped over the cement dodging the cracks so as not to break my granny's back. I was so busy watching the ground that I nearly banged into Flora. She had just come out of Templeton's grocer's and was carrying a string bag with her rations in it.

'Goodness, it's you, Flora.' I was astonished.

'Yes,' she said, not surprised.

'Ye've been away a long time.'

'I know.'

I waited, but she wasn't going to say any more.

'Ye must have been awfy sick,' I said insincerely. She'd been well enough to go the messages, hadn't she?

Flora shook her head negatively. 'No, I haven't been sick at all.'

We both stood watching one another in silence, or at least Flora was looking in my direction, but she seemed to be staring through two glass eyes. There was something queer about her but at first I couldn't work out what it was. Then I realised her hairs were all askew, lying in disorder over her head and they were streaky with oil as if they hadn't been washed. The blue tinge that had whitened her milky skin was darkened to black streaks. Her eyes had lost their gleaming tranquillity. Their stillness was rigid and obscure as stone.

I tried again. A full frontal attack.

'Then why were ye off, Flora?'

At first I thought she wasn't going to answer me and I was getting ready to go on up the road, when she said suddenly:

'My father died.'

'Oh, he didn't!'

It's funny how when you say, 'he died', it sounds as if it were something a person actually did himself, an act of his own choice. Miss Croal had been teaching us active voice. If the subject of the verb performs the action then the verb is said to be in the active voice. You should use the active voice rather than the passive when it is important to be precise, because with the active voice there is no doubt whatever as to who has done the action. 'My father died.' Who or what died? My father. Did he do the dying?

124

Yes. Then died is in the active voice and the subject is clearly the father. My father. Our father. Who's going to give us our daily bread now? Did I tread on your toes? I'm very sorry. I'm sorry I'm late, Miss Croal, my sister ran off with my clean socks and left me with her dirty ones and I had to wash them. All right, I'll say I'm sorry if you do too; I'm sorry, we haven't any more Woodbines left. I'm sorry your father died. So I said nothing. We just stood. Then Flora sighed and began to walk off.

'I'll have to go now. My mother's waiting for the messages. She's not well at the moment.'

'I'll tell Miss Croal ye'll be coming back soon, shall I?' I asked.

'No don't do that. We'll write. We're going away. Up north. To my mother's relations.'

'Miss Croal will be sad,' I said. 'She likes you a lot.'

Flora smiled. It was the first time she'd ever really smiled at me.

'You'll be able to go the messages now, won't you?'

But a death to be a messenger. When I got back to school I was going to tell Miss Croal I didn't want to go the messages any more because it made me too nervous.

Flora didn't want me to tell the others, but I was shamelessly determined to walk among the desks and enact the news. I hung over Freddie Goode and stared straight ahead, ostentatiously vacant eyed, and in black-edged tones I murmured:

'Our father's dead.'

Of course, I said that Flora's father was dead but they all knew what I really meant. The scraping feet and crackling rulers stopped abruptly and everyone began to sweat fear. A father had died. Fathers could die. My father could die. They shrank away from each other into their centres but the whispers that followed, shuttling from one to another, up and down and across the aisles, bound them together again in clammy strands of shivering sound. Poor Flora. What will become of us? What will we do with a dead father? He will lie in his coffin on the kitchen dresser like a jewel in its box, padded at the sides. Old Pop did that. He was quiet and not listening any more. In the morning he wouldn't get up for work and there wouldn't be any need to pawn his suit any more. We could leave it with Archie. Maybe he would buy it. He bought things sometimes. Sally Lunney had no father. She got a free dinner ticket every single week whereas I had to pay one and ten on the Mondays that my mother had it. The Corporation gave her clothes which were quite posh. Heavy brogues,

125

good leather, my mother said, far superior to the ones she got from Bayne and Duckett's for five shillings, and a lovely dark green dress of soft wool, with long sleeves. But she had a way of holding her head to one side all the time that made her look like a bird with a broken wing. And there was a cast in her left eye.

They kept turning round to look at Flora's empty seat. It was almost as if she were dead herself. Well, the effect was the same, wasn't it? She wouldn't be around any more. We felt resentful of Flora for having a father who'd just died. You couldn't think of her father, only of your own.

8   The World's Afflicted

One Monday morning we were shuffling in from the playground and there was no sound:

'Lift your feet there, at the front.'

'Hold your head up, Ian McDonald.'

'March in time. In time, I said. Hup two, three four, hup two, three four.'

We were shuffling and listening in our morning dream when suddenly we noticed a man walking silently alongside us. He was shuffling too. He was very young. I had never seen such a young man teacher before. Even Mr Corbett who used to leave his room and his children and come into Miss Bright's class to laugh into her eyes, even he had only a triangle of hair and his chin and nose were growing towards one another. But this teacher had shaggy hair like a newly thatched roof and his chin slid backwards away from his nose, getting younger and younger every minute.

His voice was light and trembling.

'I'll write my name on the board, boys and girls,' he said, 'so that you can spell it properly.' He sounded slightly apologetic.

'Where's our teacher?' Ronnie Gillis asked cheekily. He would never have dared to use that voice with Miss Croal and he didn't say 'Sir'. But Mr Dalziel seemed to think he had a right to know.

'Miss Croal's gone into hospital for a little operation,' he answered. 'She'll be back in a few weeks.'

You could hear the words perfectly clearly, but your brain was beating out like a tom-tom: 'Be nice to me please, be nice be nice.'

For a second, the class reverberated with a silent roar.

'Make me!'

Some boys started to turn in their seats, grinning and winking behind them. The girls were already rummaging in their bags for their love comics or coloured pencils to make new dresses for their paper dolls. I was thinking of the book in my bag. Others were stretching happily, like cats awaking from a long sleep. They stuck their legs out under the chairs of those in front.

'Hey, Mr Dalziel, Donald Duck's kicking my heels under my chair.'

'Stop being silly,' the teacher said. 'There's no one in this class called Donald Duck.'

'Oh yes, sir,' Donald Devine called out. 'That's my baptismal name, sir.' And he started quacking. The whole class smiled and a thin sigh of ecstacy drifted lightly round the room.

Mr Dalziel's face went red. Fancy that, a grown man blushing. Like me. I never knew that teachers could blush.

'Come out at once,' he said without fire. The class laughed loudly this time, for Donald went out, waddling and quacking together and sticking his backside out like a duck's tail.

'If there's any more of this nonsense,' the teacher whimpered, redder than ever—it was going down his neck into his chest; I couldn't see his chest, but I knew the red was down there because that's how it was with me when I blushed—'If there's any more of this I'll take out the strap.'

The class went on smiling fondly. We heard the words starting off but they got twisted in the air and tumbled into our brains all upside down: 'Oh dear, this is a bit of a mess.'

After that, things were different at school. It was like being at home with your slippers on, you might say. When we got fed up sitting we went for a stroll down to the waste basket to sharpen our pencils or we squeezed between the desks to have a chat with someone at the other side of the room.

'Go back to your seat,' the teacher said.

'Oh sir, I can't do that. I've got to get some geography notes from Robert.'

In the back seats we played fortunes: 'Pick a colour. Blue. Pick a number. 94. Pick another. 21. When you grow up you will have ten children. You will be a beautiful film star when you grow up. You will die with a wooden leg.' Or we played hangman. With names of lakes, rivers, towns, countries. Lake Titicaca. What kind of lake's that? I never heard of that one. It's in

128

the Atlas, stupid. The Caspian. That's a sea. It's called the Caspian Sea and fine well you know it. Ah don't care. It's really a lake because it's drying up every year and seas don't dry up. Ah'm no' playin' wi' you any more, you're a cheat. Ah'm goin' doon the front tae have a chat wi' the teacher. Cathy Stuart's ay talkin' tae him. Ah think she has her eye on him. Och, he's showin' her how tae dae her problems. Let's play noughts and crosses.

Sometimes I sat in a front seat when Mr Dalziel was copying a poem on the board and I wrote with my eyes screwed up. Not too much, because his huge round letters lolled all over the board, slanting down and down and down until the day Ronnie Gillis dragged the giant blackboard ruler from the cupboard and staggered across the classroom floor pretending he was going to toss a caber.

'Quick, sir, quick, sir,' he panted, sagging at his knees, 'ah'm goin' tae drop it.' ·

The teacher took the straight edge (it was nearly as tall as him) and told Ronnie to stop acting the goat.

'Ah was only tryin' tae help ye, sir. Miss Croal always insists, insists,' he said, leaning heavily on the word, 'that those of us who can't write straight on blank paper have tae use a ruler. Ye see?'

'I see that you're going to get six of the best if you don't learn some manners,' the teacher said. 'I've just about had enough of this class.' But he took the ruler and drew lines across the board from then on.

Mr Dalziel never used the strap. He never gave tests either. When we told him it was Friday morning he shrugged and said:

'Oh, we'll just leave things as they are till Miss Croal comes back.'

It didn't seem to worry him at all if we were talking when he was. He just kept on alongside us and the two parallel lines of sound went round and round the classroom never meeting for a minute. They only time we shut up was when he told us a story. Miss Croal had never read to us but Mr Dalziel read us *Rob Roy*, acting out all the bits, and told us a few queer short stories: 'The Rocking Horse Winner' and 'Vendetta'. They made us scared. Not the way Frankenstein did when everybody screamed and threw their arms round each other half laughing. It was a different kind of fear that clung to you like wet fog on a dark day.

But after a few days of this I became restless. The quali was only two months away and I decided I'd better start working again, especially on my maths because the teacher said the exam was mainly maths and grammar. So when Mr Dalziel started to show us how to reduce fractions I went back to my own seat and concentrated with my glasses on.

'First you must find a factor common to both the numerator and the denominator,' the teacher was saying, and I leaned forward with chin in my hand, to understand better. But my concentration was sapped by the feeling someone was looking at me. I slewed my eyes to the side and saw Alec Thompson grinning at me like the advertisement for Gibbs Dentifrice.

'Got your specs on?' he said, holding his fingers to his eyes like binoculars. 'Toowit, toowoo,' he cooed loudly. The teacher went on cancelling out fractions on the board. I couldn't follow what he was doing. Others were turning round now, giggling and whispering.

'You look right funny wi' those specs.'

'Take a gander at four eyes.'

'Hey, goggles!'

They were nudging each other and pointing and my glasses began to steam over from the hot sweat on my cheeks. It was true, it was true, everything they were saying. That was the miserable part, but why did they have to put it into words? I wish I were dead, dead, dead. They say you get short sight from your parents. It's their fault. But my mother and father don't need glasses. It isn't fair. My cheeks were on fire and the water dammed up in my head was trying to burst its way through my lids. Some was seeping down my nose. I kept my lids shut by biting savagely into my tongue. Miss Croal, why did you go and get sick? They're at me because he doesn't care. I'll kill them all. I'll kill them. Oh I could smash these glasses into powder with a big hammer. Crunch them all up and cover them with a mountain. Why don't you tell them to shut up? Boring on with numerators and denominators and nobody listening to you.

I laid my head down on the desk and the waters broke through triumphantly, roaring in my ears and choking off my breath.

'Hey, sir. Mary Rose is greetin'.'

'Sir, sir, Mary Rose is greetin'.'

'Shut up you boys, it's your fault anyway, calling her names.'

'You're just as bad. You were laughin'.'

130

'Oh good gracious me, this is a to do. Dear me, dear me, what's all this tragedy? Sit up. What's her name?'

'Mary Rose.'

'Come on now, sit up, that's a good girl. Nothing's as bad as all that. You'll spoil your beauty crying like that.'

'It's already spoiled,' I said, snuffling into my arms. 'Everybody teases you with these horrible glasses.'

The teacher pushed a hankie under my cheek and patted me on the shoulder. His touch was light and without comfort.

'Here, wipe your face and blow your nose and I'll have something to say to these boys. Come on now, sit up and wipe your face.'

He went back down the aisle and I sat up, taking my glasses off first. I dried my face with my head turned to the wall. Then I sat with my eyes looking down at the desk.

'It's a very cruel and tactless thing to tease people for any handicap they might have,' the teacher began, 'whether it's glasses, or a limp or a withered arm. Is it not enough that these people are already suffering from their affliction? Nobody likes to wear glasses or have a wooden leg or a crooked back or suchlike. To make fun of them is to add to their unhappiness. Now I don't think you boys are so starved for fun that you really need to tease Mary Rose. There are hundreds of other ways you can enjoy yourselves. So don't let me catch you at it again.'

He went on talking but I wasn't listening any more. I was looking at myself in the great line-up of the world's afflicted: Johnny the lamplighter who had the crooked back, Freddie Freeling, the newsboy who'd lost his leg when the dock police chased him and he fell down onto spiked railings, Joe Barr, the dummy in Granny Lavery's street who made high grunting noises when the corner boys tried to cheat him at pontoon, that funny old woman who'd no nose, only a black hole. And me, with my glasses. It was funny how nobody teased Ann Bell and she had a glass eye. But it was a pretty good one and you could hardly notice the difference if you weren't looking closely and realised it never moved. Well, I had never in the world dreamed of teasing these people. Not even poor old Johnny who had an enormous keyhole in the door of his single end and dressed up in women's clothes in the afternoons before he came round to light the lamps. Sometimes he let us into his room if we called through the keyhole:

'It's me, Johnny, can ah listen tae your shell?'

And he would let us hold the huge shell that looked like rings stuck together, big rings that got smaller and smaller towards the centre and had the sounds of the sea encircled, high tides surging on to the rocks and the smell of seaweed. I smelt it once at Saltcoats. You felt pity for him and didn't look at the brassière hanging over his chair. But there were some people without pity, that's certain.

Never mind Mr Dalziel's talk. I didn't wear my glasses again while he was there. Ina Brogan who was sitting next to me, now that Flora was gone, let me copy figures from her book. She copied my answers sometimes in exchange. But I didn't care. You couldn't keep an answer to yourself. If it was right, everybody would get it.

Mr Dalziel was still with us when I saw the film *Robin Hood* with Richard Greene and Joan Collins. It was in technicolor. The green costumes and the pokey hats made the men look like fairies and the woods where they went riding with their arrows and quivers slung across their shoulders were fairy glens. So many things in the film were astonishing. It was another bad brother case. Prince John would have killed King Richard for his birthright. He was even worse than Jacob. And there was a fighting priest. Who ever heard of such a thing? A priest without manners who insisted on fighting Robin Hood with staves rather than give way to him on a narrow bridge. All the children were excited by this fighting with staves. It was much better than stones. For weeks after, the tenement mothers roared in their dens when they came upon broomheads without their bodies. Outside in the streets, narrow bridges were drawn with chalk while scores of Robin Hoods and Friar Tucks slammed each other with the decapitated brooms, the conflict ending when one side or another converted his stave to a battering ram and charged. There were those, too, who shot arrows from closes or upper windows, but they were shunned. Everyone remembered the last time bows had been in fashion and Ann Bell had stumbled out of a close, a red hand sticking to her left eye and her mouth wide open and staring.

More astonishing than anything else in the film, however, was the idea that the rich could be robbed to help the poor and the robbers might be considered goodies. The rich were bad. They got their money by cheating the poor. Maybe my father was right. Maybe the theft of scrap wasn't really theft at all.

The film so excited me that on Saturday night, while baby sitting for my Aunty Mary, I filled a small pad with the whole story, written in red biro, trying to remember every detail. This was a tremendous story. Everyone would want to read it. On the Monday morning I waited at Mr Dalziel's desk while he hung up his coat and scarf and then I handed the pad to him.

'I've written a story, sir,' I said. 'It's very exciting. I saw it at the pictures.'

The teacher turned over a few pages, reading them much more quickly than I had written them. He gave me a narrow sideways look and scratched his head.

'But this story is a famous one,' he told me. 'It's been written for a very long time: hundreds of years, in fact. That's why the picture was made. Lots of people like this story.'

I was completely flabbergasted.

'You mean, sir, they write the story first and then make the picture?'

'My word,' he said, smiling a little. 'Here you are,' giving me back my pad. 'You'll have to try again.'

I went back to my desk, flushed and confused. What an idiot I was. It was like Solomon's eye. Everybody knew about it except me, and there was I thinking I had discovered something. Why didn't people tell you these things? Wasting my time all the time. All that writing for nothing. And everybody knew except me. It was so exasperating. I gave a kick to the chair leg in front of me and the girl turned round indignantly:

'Hey, quit it.'

I just scowled at her and sulked over my sums till playtime. Then I threw the pad in the wastebasket on my way out.

A few days later we were chatting in the lines, standing, even when the order had been given to march. And we heard the grating voice again.

'Cease talking at once!' The last word was bellowed. Miss Croal had just come out of a side door and was stumping heavily towards us.

'How dare you stand there when the lines are moving in. Move immediately. Heads up, shoulders back, hup two three four, hup, hup.'

We marched off briskly, muttering, 'hup, hup, hup two three four, and as we turned into the hall out of sight, we did a little jig, threefour. Hup two three four, threefour. This was syncopated marching and generally brought the girl behind you into a sudden collision:

'Och look what you're doing, stupid appearance. Can ye no' march in time!'

Well, she was back. Old Crabbit Croal. In the classroom we raced to the desks we had been sitting at while Mr Dalziel was there and dragged our books out from under them, pushing each other out of the way to get back to our appointed places arranged in descending order of intellect.

Miss Croal stood, silently waiting till we were all still. Then she put her hands together and began the 'Our Father'. Goodness, I had hardly noticed we didn't say it with Mr Dalziel. I held my eyelids open a crack and squinted at her. She was definitely thinner. I could see that, even without my glasses. But her ankles were hanging over her shoes just the same as before.

The prayer was over, and business had begun.

'It's only two months now till the qualifying examination,' she was warning us. 'I understand Mr Dalziel has done some new work with you. I shall test that on Friday and then we'll find out how much you know—and how much you don't know,' she added darkly.

The wire was fully charged again. We filled exercise book after exercise book with problems and sums, and more exercise books with parsing and analysis. When Miss Croal wrote exercises on the board Ina Brogan held her arm down so that I could copy the figures. A few days after her return, Miss Croal noticed what I was doing and called me out.

'Where are your glasses, Miss?'

'I left them at home, Miss Croal.'

'You left them at home, or you leave them at home?'

I said nothing.

'Does your mother know you're not wearing your glasses at school?'

There was little point in lying. Knowing her, she'd be likely to go round and ask my mother. So I said no.

'And why, may I ask?'

What to say. If I said they made me ugly Miss Croal would think I was mad and start giving us one of her talks on vanity. But I couldn't think of a good story.

'I just don't like them. People call me names.'

She frowned. 'Bring your glasses to school from now on and don't let me catch you in class without them.'

As I turned to go back to my seat, she called after me:

'Stay behind at recess. I have something to say to you.'

'Boy, you're for it,' Ina Brogan whispered as I squeezed past her chair.

But I didn't really think so. After all, if she had been angry with me she would have punished me in front of the class. She liked making a spectacle of you. Maybe she was wanting me to go a message. Even after the registered letter business. I would tell her I couldn't go.

Recess came surprisingly quickly because we were analysing sentences half a page long and you really had to concentrate to pick out all the clauses. I waited beside Miss Croal's desk while the others were straggling out. She didn't make you march out. Probably because there was nobody to see us. She always wanted our class to put on the best show. I wished she would hurry up and talk to me. Five minutes had gone and she was still bending over the register, muttering as she rubbed out some of the figures Mr Dalziel had written in and substituting some of her own.

'Right then,' she said suddenly, abruptly slapping the register shut. 'What do they call you?'

I shrugged and said vaguely: 'Everything. The things you call people when they wear glasses.'

She ticked them off on her short fingers: 'Goggles, specky, glass eyes, owly, four eyes? That sort of thing?'

Fancy her knowing them.

'Yes, Miss.'

'You think your glasses make you look ugly?'

I raised my eyes to the ceiling. 'They make me look like a gargoyle. I hate them. I just hate them.'

Miss Croal tapped her fingers on the desk lid. 'All right then,' she said. 'Let's suppose they're not really cosmetic aids. How old are you?'

'Nearly twelve.'

'Now,' she said. 'You're not thinking of getting married right now, or engaged or anything like that?'

I giggled.

'Of course not,' she went on. 'At this stage of your life, you have only one problem. To get to Bellahouston and then to go

135

to the University. Now, I'm telling you, my girl, you won't do either without your glasses. With them you read faster and learn faster. You must wear them until at least you have completed your schooling. If you don't, you're going to stay in Plantation for the rest of your life.'

'We might be going to Australia,' I said.

'It makes no difference where you go. There are Plantations in every country in the world and the people who live in them are those that don't get to the academies. When you've got your education then you can turn your attention to other things and if you don't need your glasses to get those things, then you can put them away. But not now. Not now. Do you hear me?'

'Yes, Miss Croal. But I want to cry when they call me names.'

'Listen, you'll want to cry for much more serious things when you're grown up.'

What was she saying? It was grown-ups who used all the lip-stick and powder and curling tongs and went to the hairdresser for facials. My mother always laid two and six aside for a Friday facial, no matter what.

'If your mother and father were killed suddenly,' Miss Croal was saying, 'your glasses would be of secondary importance. You would be wondering how you ever came to think they were worth a thought.'

We were both thinking of the five children. Five go to Smuggler's Top, Five on a Hike, Five in a Caravan, Five on Their Own. But they had Miss Croal.

'People call me names too.'

Goodness, she knew about that.

'All sorts of names, different ones even from those you children use. Oh yes, I know them all,' she said firmly, holding up her hand like a policeman, to stop my lying denial. 'But there's an approach to these things. First you must make a distinction between the names that harm your reputation and endanger your livelihood—even your life, and those that are meant only to embarrass you. You can ignore the latter. They come from people who're either envious or miserable.'

She was silent then. A huge question mark, as sharp as a butcher's hook, hung dangerously above our heads. 'Specky' wouldn't damage your reputation or endanger your life.

'What about the others, Miss Croal? Like for instance, if you're a Catholic out on the streets during the Orange Walk and they start calling you "Fenian". You can get bashed up.'

Some people had had their heads smashed in with broken beer bottles. They died.

'Ah then,' she answered softly in a sigh that smoothed the sounds together, 'then you must fight, my dear, or if you can't —run.'

She began her heavy clump towards the door, pushing me a little in front of her and in her classroom voice said roughly:

'If the odds are fairly even, it's better to fight. You'll probably have to in the end, anyway. Well, I think you must agree that your real problem is to get through the qualifying exam. Right?'

She was very right. I hadn't been thinking about it enough lately. Fancy if I didn't get an 'S' pass and had to go to Lambhill Street. I would die with shame. My glasses I would wear in class all the time from now on.

'Off you go and play now,' Miss Croal said, turning down the corridor towards the teachers' common room. 'I'm not quite well yet and I need my cup of tea.'

Out in the playground I felt cold and afraid. Miss Croal hadn't said anything about if you weren't a good runner and they caught you. They'd caught Oliver Twist when he was running through the streets away from Nancy and Fagin's gang, and he was too little to fight. But in the end, the goodies won. That was the most important thing. So long as they won in the end you could live through the middle. And Miss Croal liked me now. Yes, she didn't think I was so glaikit, either, or she wouldn't have said that about going to Bella. Yes, everything comes out right in the end.

9 Up the Alley

Who's that bawling, there? Her again. I should have known. Bessie Bunter. Fat but not funny. No, she's too scary and Bessie Bunter was scared of everybody, but we're all paralysed by her. She turns us all to pillars of salt, pale but with no savour. Whose ball is that she's tossing up onto the roof? Ina Brogan's it must be. She's crying. Pig must have hit her, for Ina wouldn't cry for a lost ball. The Naughtiest Girl at School. We must be in the middle of the story for the baddies are doing awfully well right now. Who's going to make the end? That's what I would like to know. How shall it be made?

'Well, fight her then,' my father said later from behind his newspaper. 'It's no use complaining to me. If ye're all so gutless as to let her tramp over ye, ye must prefer lyin' doon tae standin' upright.'

'Och, but you don't know what a size she is. She's bigger than Mammy.'

'It's the iron in the blood that makes a fighter,' my father rejoined, 'no' his size. Ye wouldnae say Glaswegians were soft marks an' they're mainly wee nyaffs. Did ah tell ye that joke aboot the Germans and the Glesca razor boys that were in the H.L.I.?'

'Aye, fifty times. Look Da, could you no' go an' see her faither an' tell him ye'll bash him up if Sadie Bailey doesnae stop pestering us?'

My father laid the paper on his lap, something he rarely did before he'd finished reading it.

'Ye're no' really standin' there sayin' that tae me, are ye?' His face was all 'o's'. 'Ah would be ashamed. An' ah'd be damned

138

stupid tae pay attention tae ye. Gie' her a good kick in the shins. If one o' ye cannae manage it then gang together.'

He picked up the paper again and wrapped the sheets around his face like a mummy.

Miss Croal had said something the same. 'Fight if you can, and if you can't, run.' What if there was nowhere to run to? At every recess, morning and noontime, the words flickered on and off in my brain. I tried not to see them, but Sadie Bailey's heavy fist, spongy with jellied scunnersome warts, smashing our hands apart and pummelling pain in bright colours upon our upper arms, beat the words out in a blaze of white hot phosphorescence. You'll probably have to fight in the end, anyway.

Sadie Bailey. She was a giantess living with her old mother at the back of a fish and chip shop where they sold you pies and peas and wrung out the vinegar drop after drop and stop. You were never allowed to pick up the bottle yourself. Inside, the shop was all shadows like a dunney because sheets of grease-sogged cardboard were squeezed into the puttiless window frames. The glass had been gone before we came to Plantation. Mrs Bailey rose above the counter like a great, dark stone, her long, grey hair falling in greasy ropes around her shawl. The sounds of her speech, hissing and bubbling through the black spaces between her teeth, were absorbed into the hot furious sizzle of the dripping that boiled relentlessly above the gas jets arranged in rows of iridescent teeth. They were waiting, the dripping and the fire together, for the little white chips huddled inside the wire basket and for the pale, slack fillets lying in limp smears along the steel tray. Bailey's chips were roasted ferociously. They were cut-edge crisp and jumped about in your mouth like hot knives. Usually, however, we ate the flaccid greasy lumps from Joe's. The gas jets beneath his vats were worn down stumps and his dripping lay darkly and silently apathetic, barely sighing when the chips slunk beneath the surface.

'Ah don't care', my mother said adamantly, 'whether Bailey's chips are better or no'. Ah'm no wantin' the jaundice. Have ye seen those corners, and the window ledges! Scum as thick as your thumb and a' these deid flies stuck intae it like flypaper.'

'Well, if they're deid, they cannae dae ye any harm, can they?' Margaret demanded.

My mother was never impressed with that argument.

'The flies might be deid but the germs are alive an' kicking.
Don't gie me any o' your cheek an' if ye want chips get tae Joe's
or dae withoot.'

With our own money we bought chips from Bailey's shop.

Sadie Bailey came to our school. Why, nobody knew. We all
wished she would go away. Stride out of the playground and
over the river in her seven league black lace-ups and leave us in
peace to play our ring games and whirl our ropes. But every day
she prowled among us, like an angry Cyclops, snatching the
ropes and shaking them in the air above our heads while we
stood by helplessly, those who dared hissing vapid curses into
the absorbent flannel of their vests.

'Pig of a thing. Ah could kill that big pimply slob. Wi' mah
bare hands. Look at that. Mah new rope. Mah mother'll belt
me when ah get home.'

'She'd do better tae belt her. We should strangle her in her
bed wi' it.'

'We could gang together and kick her in the shins,' I said.
'My father said we should fight her.'

Dora's nose, long and thin like a dropper, sniffed upwards.
Her voice always seemed to come from the middle of her forehead
rather than her mouth and what with the sucking in and
squeezing out she was like a human bagpipe.

'Hmm—hmm. And did your father suggest what we could do
when we meet her on the streets by ourselves after we've been
busy kicking her in the shins?'

I shrugged.

'Okay, buy new ropes.'

It was Ellen Wallace's rope that had been taken that day, and
she spoke up now.

'Dae ye see what she's daein' wi' it? She doesnae really like to
play wi' it.'

We turned to where Ellen had jerked her head, and watched
fretfully. The new rope was fraying like spray as Sadie Bailey
slashed it savagely against the back wall of the playground,
drawing in the up thrusts, from the top of her head, the finest,
lightest hairs of a little girl who was playing marbles.

'Look at that. She nearly belted that wee lassie across the
heid. Bully.'

The little girl leapt suddenly into the air with a frightened squeak and her friends scuttled away on their hands and knees leaving their marbles behind them.

Ina Brogan sighed. 'It's no' fair that a great big gowk like her should be in our school anyway. She's nearly fifteen, somebody told me.'

Dora touched her bony forehead lightly with her pointed fingernail.

'She's an idiot, of course, that's why. They won't have her, even in the advanced division.'

'Well, if we cannae bash her all together, an' we cannae tell the teacher because she'll get us after school, what are we going to do?'

We were all silent, each with her extravagant fancies. Poison her playtime milk. Tip her into the chip vat, all covered in batter. Hex her with really sharp pins and tremendous concentration, but that really didn't work.

'There's one thing we've never thought of trying, you know,' Ina Brogan said suddenly, her long curling eyelashes that we all envied cast down thoughtfully. We waited, curious.

'We've never asked her to play with us. Maybe,' she said, glancing over at the shredded rope, now slung over the playground wall, 'maybe if we were nicer to her and asked her into the rings she would become friendly.'

'Hmm—hmm,' Dora sniffed. 'You mean like some wild dog? We should pat it on the head and offer it a biscuit? Well, you can. I'm not.' She stroked her long fingers tenderly, examining the pointed nails with affection. 'Get your own fingers bitten.'

'You could ask her, Mary Rose,' Ina said. 'You go into her chip shop sometimes, don't you? And she's never taken anything o' yours.'

'Well, it would be hard for her, wouldn't it?' I answered. 'It'd be like tryin' tae take the breeks off a hielanman. Ah mean ah've never got a rope or balls tae take, have ah, and she's given me a few punches tae.'

No other suggestions offered themselves though we stood for minutes silently reflecting and rejecting. Finally, Miss Croal's words being the only images my mind would release, I said:

'Okay. We'll try. Next time she comes up tae us ah'll ask her if she'd like tae play.'

The following day at playtime we decided we'd just stand

around and talk. Sadie Bailey was nowhere to be seen. At lunchtime, when we'd finished eating, Ina Brogan said:

'C'mon. We'll have tae play sometimes. Let's do "Old Roger".'

We joined our fingers together and began to shuffle round. Dora was on her knees in the centre. She was old Roger. The rhythm of the incantation hypnotised us and we swung our arms up and down, slowly together, rocking deeply, murmuring the words like old women keening by a graveside.

'Old Roger was dead and he lay in his grave,
Lay in his grave,
Lay in his grave,
Old Roger was dead and he lay in his grave,
Eeee-ali, lay in his grave.'

On the last tensed note our arms stretched up on fingertips into the centre, completely burying Dora's hunched up body and our heads bowed down towards the asphalt.

The moment of mourning, however, shattered in slivers of purple panic when someone gagged:

'Hey, she's coming.'

Dora sprang alive in a frenzy.

'Hey, I'm no' sitting here. She always goes for old Roger. She says since he does the kicking he should get a few kicks first.'

Ina Brogan grabbed her by the shoulders and pushed her down again.

'Stay there, ye great silly. We cannae stop playing and then ask her tae join us. It'll look funny. We have tae seem casual aboot it. Just keep goin' roon.'

So round we went, but at a pace that would never have arrived at a revolution, our necks and eyes brutally twisted to see across the playground. She was there all right, wedged in the doorway of the toilets. A dark stain of water had made a bib around the neck of her red jumper. She'd been using the bubbler and let the water dribble out of her mouth. Her head was lifted attentively, a little on one side, the two hot little eyes revolving like searchlights, crisscrossing the playground to seek out us, the ringplayers. To avoid her we turned our heads away, to the street, trying to fool her with facelessness. There were tremors, however, pulsing along our blood, pushing us together and making the air quiver with dis-ease. They told us we'd been caught in the light.

From somewhere in the centre a voice warned us.

'It's on its way.'

Tilting my head slightly to the left, I saw her in the peripheral vision. Like a giant doll with its works in bits and its legs and arms whirring, madly she came towards us, whooping the loop, banging into, bounding off, knocking over whatever failed to anticipate her erratic trajectory until she crashed into us, rocking wildly for a moment to regain her balance. Then:

'Break it up, break it up,' she yelled, breaking us up, slapping at our fingers, her face tremendous with destructive energy.

The others were gasping with fright. I could hardly breathe, myself. I felt as if a ball of fur was filling my throat.

'Quick, ask her, ask her,' Dora groaned.

So I called out, hardly thinking what I was doing.

'Hey, Sadie Bailey, come here a minute.'

She didn't hear me. The screaming and yelling in the playground absorbed identity from my voice. I shouted louder.

'Sadie, Sadie Bailey! I want to speak to you.'

That time, she heard me and swivelled round on one foot.

'All right. Speak, Ah'm here. What d' ye want?'

'Ah was wondering,' I said, wanting a cap to hold in my hand, 'we were wondering if ye would like tae play wi' us? The ring's really too small,' I added in a hurry as I saw the disbelief in her eyes.

'You were wondering,' she said, in a tone that soared with scorn, 'if ah would play wi' ye? Are ye stark ravin' mad!' She swung around and glared at the others. 'Who dae ye think I am tae play wi' a great lot o' ninnies? Bloody babies ye are, wi' yer silly kids' games. Ye make me sick.' She turned back to me and jabbed me with the wart on the end of her forefinger. It was full of little holes on the top, like a salt shaker, and was seething with germs, little warts really. When you touched somebody with a wart you made him get them. And she'd touched me with hers. I couldn't take my eyes off the horrible ugly thing, as big as sixpence it was and she saw me looking at it.

'What's wrong wi' your kipper?'

'You shouldn't have touched me with your wart,' I said, sick in my stomach. 'You could make me get one.'

She burst out laughing and held her finger up to the tip of her nose, crossing her eyes at it.

'So what. What's wrong wi' mah little wart? He an' me are

good buddies. We been together a long time. He's a nice wee wart. Look at him.' She stuck her finger right under my own nose, and then pushed my nose in with the big spongy excrudescence. She couldn't stop laughing, bending over and holding her stomach, her knees sagging so low that she nearly fell over and grabbed my waist to hold her up. 'Ye'll get,' she spluttered through her snickers, 'ye'll get a right wee bunch o' floo-ers on the end o' your snitch noo.'

I wanted to lie flat on the ground and groan and moan and beat her great fat head to pulp but the bells were ringing all round, the call to class. The others were already withdrawing, in nervous backward paces, watching Sadie Bailey with one eye and me with the other, warning me to get to lines. I was rubbing at my nose until it struck me that the warts might simply spread over a larger area and smit my hands too. So I stopped, holding my hand out and not knowing what to do.

Sadie Bailey was smiling at me. 'Here, here's another wee lot for ye', and she smeared both my cheeks with the wart. I slapped at her hand without thinking.

'Get off, you.'

'Hmm, hmm,' she said, her eyebrows going up. 'Little ol' cream puff's getting fashed.' Then she cuffed me over the ear, so hard I thought I was blinded for a minute.

'Watch it next time, or ah'll gie ye something ye'll no' forget in a hurry,' and she bounded off, shoving her way through the lines till she met up with her own class. There was nothing to do but sneak along the back lines, myself. I crouched down as I scurried from class to class, hoping no teacher would see me. Reaching my lines, I stood at the end, rubbing my face with the sleeve of my jumper. What if warts grew like grapes all over my cheeks and hung from my nose? I would kill myself. She was a pig, an animal, a wild beast. Rage and loathing filled out my head and I thought the blood was going to burst through my eyes. I looked across the lines and saw her class had just about reached the main door. Their teacher had gone inside. On the impulse, I broke away from my class and ran up to the beginning of the file, racing along the front of the lines. I just caught her in time.

'All right,' I said, clutching her arm and dragging her round. 'Ah'll do it.'

She looked at me hurriedly, impatiently, anxious to get to class in time.

'What are ye talking aboot, dopey? Ye'll do what?'

'Fight you.' I was afraid I would cry. 'Ah'll fight ye today, this afternoon, up the alley—after school. Okay?'

She grinned delightedly and snorted as she disappeared through the main door.

'Don't forget tae bring the troops, cream puff. Ye'll need them.'

Up the alley was a direction rather than a place. It was as short as an exclamation mark, the narrowest streak between the tenements whose skimpiest shadows were always expansive enough to secrete the alley in perpetual night. It was a thorough-fare for those who avoided going north or south on a long trek round the tenements to get to the bombed site where the fighting was done. This wasteland fronted the dry dock but was marked off from it by two metal lines drawn straight for half a mile. They were the tram tracks. When the trams rounded Paisley Road and turned into Govan Road they shrieked and rattled with screaming joy at the sight of the two straight lines and hurtled along them, buffeted furiously by their own gale, all their little wheels and springs and bolts jangling, their blue or yellow paint madly bright. One tram only reduced its speed on this stretch and slurred over the tracks with a quiet burble. This was the last tram of the night, on its way to Lorne Street Depot. Only then was the wasteland free of vibrations.

The fights, then, were conducted on this spare ground oppo-site the dry dock, irrespective of one's being challenged to go 'up the alley'. For me, this afternoon's spectacle would be the second. Part of the dread I felt in class derived more from memory of the last fight than anticipation of the one to come.

Jackie had caused it. He had let Joe Gibson take his jorries and then come in bawling so that my mother yelled at me:

'Here, Big Yin, go and get stuck intae him. Ye're the same age.'

I was horrified. 'You're crackers, Mammy. He's a boy. He could flatten me.'

But she wouldn't listen. If I didn't give it to him none of the younger ones could safely hold to their things again.

The only person I had ever punched before was Margaret and I had to shut my eyes to do it. When I found Joe Gibson and invited him up the alley, he burst out laughing. Friends of his were on the waste ground playing rounders and he called to them:

'Hey, fellas. Daddy longlegs wants a fight.'

'Well, give my brother back his jorries. You should be ashamed, pinching stuff from a wee laddie.'

'Ah havenae got them,' he said, grinning. And added softly, 'Ah hocked them wi' Archie.'

He started prancing around, punching the air and ducking, holding his stomach and gasping 'Oof. She got me.'

The other boys had already begun heading towards the alley to get good positions on top of the shelter. A few girls were there too, when I arrived, but all they could say was: oh jings, and wring their hands. Joe was still wearing his silly grin, standing with his hands in his pockets and bowing every time his friends clapped him. I shut my eyes and punched. Nothing happened. Joe just stuck out his arm as straight as a stick, and turned my fist away. Then he tapped me lightly on the face and everybody roared. In a rage, I dropped to my knees, ducking under his arms and before he realised what I was doing, I had grabbed his hair and was twisting it really savagely. He didn't like that one bit. His cheeks blew up and turned red. When he started digging his fingers into my throat I kicked him in the shin. The girls were cheering now: lay intae him! How do I stop, I thought in panic. It was like being stuck to the light switch. Pretty soon he would hit me hard and the thought made me weepy inside. Then all at once I felt a hot patch on my head and reached up to touch it.

At the same time my eye lit up a kind of madness, figures strangely inhuman, falling together like drunks and hanging upon one another. They were pointing at me and mouthing queerly.

Did ye see what he . . . did ye see her . . . ah never saw anything sae funny . . . ah cannae stop . . . haud me up.

They seemed to melt through my eyes like lumps of lard, sliding down each other on to the ground in gollops, their arms and legs aflutter before they dissolved in puddles of gurgles and rippling giggles. Oh, oh, oh, ah cannae stop. It's killing me. It's killing.

A boy on the shelter was peeing on me. It had burned the skin of my face and I put my fingers to it wonderingly. It was thick, and rank and sticky and was dribbling all down me. I was a toilet. I would have killed myself, but instead, shoved my fist into my mouth to stop shrieking and ran away down the alley that was pitch black. I would tell the polis. He would be hung, the foul fiend. They would hang him at Barlinnie.

Astonishingly, the police were unimpressed, even indifferent. They wanted murders, broken bottle fights, the theft of scrap.

'Well, my lass,' the sergeant at the bar said, buttoning on his jacket, for his relief was coming in behind me, 'if ye will fight wi' laddies that's what ye'll get. There's nae honour in war.' He wagged his finger at me over the counter. 'A wee kiss will take ye a lot further.'

I scowled at him. 'It's no' fair. One for one's the game. No two tae one. That's the coward's play.'

'True,' he agreed, with a nod of the head. 'But ye see what wins, don't ye?'

He came round the counter and patted me on the shoulder.

'Away hame tae your mammy, hen, an' get her tae gie your hair a guid wash. Ye're in a terrible mess.'

Now I should have to go up the alley again. All afternoon in the classroom I sent S.O.S. signals to God to get me off. Dear God, please visit me with pleurisy so that I can be taken to hospital and don't have to fight. Pleurisy is the ideal disease in situations like mine. It can leap on you from anywhere at any time, a sudden knifing in the back, shredding you into ribbons of pain until you jump up and down with your arms and legs flinging around like a maddened frog. Then I thought, slyly: there's a better idea. Dear God, send her the pleurisy. After all, I've had it. Oh, that's wicked. Only witches pray for pains to afflict their enemies. God won't listen. All the afternoon I waited. With ten minutes to bell time, not a twinge anywhere. I couldn't even bring on a vomit, though a big block of something was lying on my chest. Oh God, hurry and do something. I was so worried I didn't even offer a bribe. Finally, as the bell went and I left the classroom, strapping my bag to my shoulders on the way out, I changed my plea: dear God, don't let me be gutless.

Outside, I hurried away ahead of the others. I didn't want them crowding me, pushing me along like a gird the way they always did, keeping you pointed in the right direction, to make sure you didn't slink home after all and deprive them. Once they'd squeezed you through the alley they gave you a last shove and let you free on the spare ground. When I arrived, however, the entire waste was empty.

If they got there before you, they would take a pointed stick and score a ring in front of the air raid shelter, where they wanted you to stand. Then they'd stick their feet into someone else's cupped hand and spring up on the roof, squeezing together, legs hanging down the wall.

'Nae mair can fit in the front. Ye'll have tae staun at the back, you lot.'

So the dawdlers stood behind, leaning negligently on another's shoulder, the hard, wrinkled scale of bony elbows rasping an unprotected neck. They gnawed with slurps and splutters at apples and sleekit ones among them sometimes hurtled the cores at the fighter whom they opposed.

'Hey watch it up there, or ah'll take you on the morra.'

'Suits me,' spitting out a mouthful of pips. 'Keeps me in good nick.'

They weren't going to get me with apple cores as they did last time, or with anything else, for that matter. I measured the ground with my eye and drew my own ring, in a spot where no one could reach you with piddle or with pelted missiles. Then I stood inside the ring, listening to the alley's hum that sounded like a giant bee, coming aggressively nearer with its big sting ready if you didn't have something sweet for it. They all scrabbled out of the narrow opening, Sadie Bailey leading and being led, her arms pinned at her sides in friendly cameraderie, those behind nudging her along with remorselessly friendly little shoves in the back.

'Oh there you are,' they said. They were surprised to see me. 'We thought you'd buggered off.'

They ran over to the shelter and bounded up from the clasped hands. The ones who were too slow began to form a loose circle around me.

'Naebody at my back,' I said determinedly, 'or ah'm no' goin' tae be in it. Just stand where ye are. Ye can see fine well there.'

In a few minutes they were all ready, with their waiting, interested expressions. Justice was going to be done. Alley fights were always moral issues. To have beaten Sadie Bailey privately would have served no purpose. She could be felled only by public humiliation. Then even the smallest toddler in the street would be safe from her. Conversation was starting to pick up again as I made no move. Some had begun to blow huge bubbles with their gum, bursting them loudly, then clawing at the sticky grey mess that smeared their lips. Sadie Bailey was standing with her arms hanging by her side. I thought she would have been thumping her chest like King Kong.

'Well, come on,' an impatient voice shouted. 'We havenae a' day tae wait. Ah want mah tea the night no' the morra.'

'It's your go,' another said quietly.

So it was. I'd offered to fight and I was the one who had to lay my finger on Sadie Bailey. But I was too scared.

'Aw Jesus, this is like a bloody funeral. Gie her a shove, somebody.'

I glowered all round me. Nobody had better try. I would lay into him. In cold blood, however, it was too difficult.

'Do something, God,' I thought desperately, and on the instant someone hurtled me against Sadie Bailey and I had to throw my arms around her to keep my balance. She tore them off her and gave me a mighty swat across my face with her warty hand, so hard, bells started ringing in my right ear and I wanted to lie down and be done with it.

Then I heard my sister's voice yelling furiously:

'Ah'll paste you, you big pig.'

God, I couldn't have my little sister fighting for me. So I shut my eyes and swung out with my fist where for a brief second I had seen Sadie Bailey's face. It was still there. I felt it on my knuckles and her teeth met my bones like solid rock. Ouch. I wrapped my hand in my stomach to warm the pain away, not caring whether she hit me again or not. Nothing happened. Instead I heard someone whistle.

'Jesus, that's done it. Ye've knocked her teeth doon her throat.'

I hadn't. But I'd bled her lip and gums. We both ran home, terrified, she at losing her teeth, as she thought, and I from fear of being taken away by the police to the reformatory.

The police never came. Nor did Sadie Bailey's mother, though my mother was ready, waiting for her. I didn't see anything of Sadie Bailey at school again, but once when I was passing her chip shop she appeared suddenly on the pavement in front of me and thrust her hands right out under my nose so that I fell back, alarmed again.

'Look,' she said, proudly. 'No warts.'

They were all gone. Her mother had taken them off with black acid and now, she told me authoritatively, we could go together to the club on modern dancing night. Her mother wouldn't let her go by herself. I went once. After that she didn't need me. She found another girl her own size.

'How come, Da,' I asked my father, 'she asked me to go to the dance with her when I'd hit her in front of everybody? Ye'd think she would hate me.'

'They're a' the same, these bullies,' my father answered without hesitation. 'They go aroon looking for, hoping to find somebody that'll lick them. Then they can like ye withoot being ashamed.'

I will never forget that, or neglect to act on it.

10   Bellahouston Academy

There were no more fights up the alley for me, for not long after I began at the Academy. It was now called Bellahouston Senior Secondary but I resented the change. Why did they wait till I went to it, to stop calling it the Academy? In my area, however, it retained its old name. Most of the people in my class were posh sorts. They would have been flabbergasted to see a girl fighting up the alley. They went to dancing and elocution. So I said to Robert and Jackie:

'You'll have to fight your ain battles now.'

They were indignant. 'Just because ye're at Bella, ye think ye're something.'

In fact, at no other time in my life have I felt so concretely something. I was the luckiest person alive, the most privileged. I pitied the rest of the world. The only thing that modified my exultancy, though not much, was my not having the uniform. How could anybody in the streets around be expected to realise from my gaudy tartan coat, a gift from the Canadian Red Cross to Glasgow's poor and needy, or from the square-necked, short-sleeved blouse dyed gold, and the navy tunic, that I attended Bellahouston Academy. At least a badge, I protested to my mother, would be better than nothing, but even that outward sign to strangers of my extraordinary status was impossible.

In the school itself, however, standing at the back of the hall with two hundred other first year students, I felt like a Don Cossack, a Jesuit, a Janissary, a Mameluke, a crack servitor. Serving whom or what? The headmaster, our sultan, his white sausage curls carefully straddling his head like a barrister's wig? The teachers, long and black and serious in their gowns, their expressions neatly arranged for the solemnity of the weekly occasion? Or the elderly looking senior boys with their incredible moustaches and military bearing?

None of these. The headmaster was too remote. We rarely encountered him or the senior students. The teachers were too violent. Not only in words when they sneered at you or hissed severely, but physically as well.

Every morning a line of miscreants straggled across the front of the classroom, grinning embarrassedly, those nearest the desk crossing their hands in preparation for the strap. The teacher approached his task with disinterested briskness. Two each for all. These were yesterday's crimes. Today's would be dealt with tomorrow. That is, assuming the teacher could retain his brittle self-control. But the most violent one had a beautiful crippled daughter in the senior school, and he was obviously under strain, constantly nit picking, they whispered, watching him pluck his scalp, or tapping his straight nails on the lid of his desk. Nobody mutinied, therefore, the day he swung his fist down and knocked a girl unconscious to her desk.

'She wouldn't say it,' he cried to us, glancing round and round with his eyes popping and his skin taut to bursting point. 'I told her many times how to say it, but she just refused. There's nothing difficult about it, is there?' he begged us, while we stared at him with stricken faces. 'Acht tausend, acht hundert acht und achtig. Here, you say it,' he ordered, pointing threateningly at me. I mumbled it quickly, wanting to protect my chin. 'And you, and you.' The others gabbled it with downcast eyes. The girl decided to drop German after that and transferred to the Gaelic class. Between us and the German teacher there endured a fearful intimacy. We were accessories before and after the fact, conspirators, for having said nothing. When his nit picking became more agitated than usual we would warn him silently with our folded arms and he would excuse himself for fifteen minutes or so.

The women teachers found it too tiring to use the strap much, so a few of them devised other kinds of punishment. As soon as she learned that I might be going to Australia, the geography teacher slouched over her desk and announced spitefully:

'You'll end up marrying a black man. They're all black over there.'

'But I know some Scottish people who've gone there,' I protested not very confidently. 'There must be some white people too.'

The teacher shook her head. 'They're only white for a little while. They all turn black once they've been there a bit.'

'A lot of shit,' my mother assured me when I told her. 'She's having ye on. These bloody spinsters are a' the same. She's probably dreamin' o' some black man. They're supposed tae be gey sexy. Anyway I've seen pictures of the Prime Minister and he looked as white as we are. They're just a bit more sun tanned.'

At Bellahouston, therefore, it was knowledge we were eager to serve, and each other. For the first time I encountered in a limited geographical area a concentration of girls and boys who were as enthralled as I with books and discussion, who had ideas of their own that they were eager to defend and propagate with wit and conviction, forcing me to develop mine. If they noticed my irregular garb and Education Department shoes, they gave no indication. Nor did they blink at my glottal stops and street slang. Knowing and doing were their main preoccupations.

In Lorne Street I had amused the class by sewing sheets of exercise paper up the middle and filling them with silly space fantasies of which Mickey Mouse was the usual protagonist. At Bellahouston there were others interested in doing the same thing. We exchanged our works and strived to make some meaningful comment on them.

Within a few weeks we sorted ourselves into groups. I found myself friendly with Clarice Duncan, a short stocky girl with rather broad shoulders and a slightly jutting chin. Her manner of speaking was clipped and restrained, brusque almost, and the others considered her a bit intimidating. They consoled themselves for their timidity during the swimming period when, queuing up at the foot bath, they giggled and pointed out to everyone the hair that grew from Clarice's armpits and down the insides of her thighs. Clarice ignored them. But she always waited for an empty cubicle so that she could change in private.

One day she said: 'Why don't we start a class newspaper? Just one double sheet. You can do the writing and I'll do the illustrations. We can have a pets' column and a serial, and a short story and a leader, so's we can write about teachers punching girls on the chin and that kind of thing. And we'll get the others to write letters to us. Letters to the editor.'

'Well, yes,' I agreed, cautiously, however. 'But it'll take ages to write out even ten or twenty copies.'

Clarice had already considered that. 'Dad can get them printed.' The posh ones never called their fathers 'Da'. 'We write it on special paper, he's got lots, and he'll have copies made at work.'

Her father was a city journalist.

Obviously we would have to spend some time together to plan the layout of the paper. We couldn't do it at school.

'You can come out to my place,' she suggested, casually, 'if your mother will let you. On Saturday afternoon.'

She wrote down her address and told me what bus to catch. I was terrified. I never went on a bus except when I visited my Uncle Jim in Clarkston and that was only under duress, usually the threat of being laid in my own blood.

'Ah'm damned if ah know why ye squawk aboot goin' oot there,' my mother would complain. 'He's been gey good tae ye, and it gie's ye a chance tae see how the other half live. The trouble wi' you is ye've got a chip on yer shoulder, like a' they Laverys. They're aye resentful o' anybody who's made a few bob from his own efforts.'

My Uncle Jim was, as my mother argued, very good to me. Yet I distrusted him for no reason that was valid. His thick moustaches reminded me of music hall villains and the way he thumped his short leg on the floor seemed menacing. His constantly disdainful criticisms of my mother made me want to kick the gammy leg. On the rare occasions that he visited us, usually demanding contraceptives for which I shopped in Paisley Road where you asked for a packet of Durex, he would make some snide comment. Once, when my mother was pregnant with Anne, he drawled:

'God, another one below the belt. Some fools never learn.'

My mother was quite unperturbed.

'Tell me that when you're forty,' she said, scrubbing the potatoes, 'and ye've only got your money bags for company.'

Uncle Jim snorted: 'Listen, when poverty comes in, love flies out the window.'

'Well, there's more than one kind o' poverty,' my mother rejoined, 'if ye bothered tae read your bible.'

Uncle Jim didn't like me either. He much preferred to have Margaret or Susan visit him, but usually when he wanted us out at Clarkston it was to help clean the house, for the woman he lived with was sick and I could clean better than the other two. Not long after I had started at Bellahouston he borrowed me for a week to look after the lady. She was a very kind person. She cut up tiny little sandwiches that made me want to laugh and put eggs in egg cups and scattered bath salts in my bathwater. She used to sing, in a very refined voice, 'we are in love with you, my heart and I' and thought Ivor Novello divine.

I was glad to get home when the week was up, so that I could eat big slices of bread and lean my elbows on the table. About two weeks later, I was just leaving school and was crossing Paisley Road West with two friends, to get a penny bag of broken biscuits, when I saw my Uncle Jim's shooting brake parked by the kerb. It made me chilly all over. I drew away quickly from the others, saying: 'there's my Uncle, I'm off,' because I didn't want them to see him, he looked so fierce.

'Oh, hello, Uncle Jim,' I said, peeping in at the window.

He stared straight ahead and jerked his head like a gangster: 'Get in.'

We drove off in silence, me despairing at having to go back to Clarkston. But we went up the town, to Paisley's. Inside the shop, Uncle Jim stomped to a counter and pointed at me with his finger.

'A Bellahouston uniform for this girl, please. Everything.'

They piled all the clothes on the counter. I was ecstatic. Blouses: three, woollen socks: three pairs, navy knickers, tie, and blazer.

'Unfortunately, sir,' grieved the old man bending over us, 'we don't have a blazer with the ribbon. It will take a week or so to have the braid sewn to it.'

Uncle Jim was always impatient.

'Och, don't worry about it. Give me the ribbon and I'll sew it on myself.'

I was staggered. Who'd ever heard of a man sewing? Outside the shop, I trotted along beside my uncle, clutching the parcel and imagining myself decked out the next day.

'Gosh, thank you very much, Uncle Jim,' I murmured, feeling guilty for not liking him much.

Uncle Jim kept his eyes on the road ahead.

'That's for services rendered.'

He meant for cleaning the house for a week. I felt sick inside.

I thought of kicking the parcel under a double decker. What a horrible man. At his house that night, he dragged out an electric sewing machine and sewed the gold ribbon to the blazer, paying no attention to the corners of the lapels. He just lapped one piece over the other.

'It's no' a craftsman's job,' my mother commented, examining the work later, 'but he means well. It's better than nothing.'

Going out to Clarkston was like travelling to another country. You had to go up the town and catch a red S.M.T. bus. I was always afraid I would get off at the wrong stop. After a while, however, I noticed that the street lights changed when you entered Clarkston. They were the long orange kind instead of the round white bulbs. That meant you were in a new county. Then I selected landmarks that preceded Uncle Jim's stop. But I was never at ease out there.

Now I should have to go to Mosspark, to strangers. Mosspark was only a name to me, but it was a toffs' area and since you went to it by bus, it must be far away. My mother told me I was to be home by dark—or else, and gave me a list of instructions for my behaviour at the Duncans'.

'Say "how do you do" instead of "pleased to meet ye" That's the sort of thing your faither's side says. Don't look at anything, don't even keek. Somebody'll be watching you. Don't ask how much anything costs and don't pass remarks on anything. There's nothing more ignorant than somebody that's pass-remarkable. Get it? Don't eat too much, even if they offer ye more and don't eat with your mouth full or slurp when you're drinking tea, if they gie ye any. What else?' She tapped her teeth, false they were, since she was twenty-four.

'Christ, there couldnae be anything else, could there?' my father demanded. 'Ye'd think she was goin' tae a garden party at Buckingham Palace. You just be yourself, hen,' he said to me. 'They're only people, the same as us. Use your common sense. If ye listened tae everything yer mother told ye, ye'd be a heid case before ye got there.'

Just the same, it was my mother's words that impressed me, more than my father's, and my stomach was in a knot when I got off the bus. I was wearing my new salmon pink jumper and the grey skirt that my mother had got out of pawn, but I'd had to put on my school shoes. I hoped Clarice wouldn't notice.

Her house wasn't far from the main road. It was two-storeyed and semi-detached. Fancy that. Like the really rich folk at Clarkston. When Clarice opened the door, she seemed more aloof than ever, even hostile.

'Oh. You made it. Come down the back with me and I'll show you the paper and my tortoise.'

I followed her through a hall, carefully looking at nothing, and down a path to a hut at the bottom of the garden. I congratulated myself that I'd seen nothing by the time I got inside the hut. There was a table inside, piled high with blank newspaper, at which we sat all afternoon deciding how many columns and words could fit on each page and how big the pictures would be. Then Clarice got her tortoise from its box and placed it in my hand, pointing out the markings on its shell and the details of its tiny feet.

'I want to draw like Beatrix Potter,' she confided. 'Mummy and Daddy might send me to the Slade, when I finish school.'

The Slade must be some kind of an art school. I made a mental note to check that later. The little tortoise lay in my hand, barely moving, and Clarice sketched it painstakingly, including far more details than I could see, though I was examining the reptile closely.

When she'd finished I told her I would have to go. It was getting dark.

'All right. But come into the house for a minute and Mummy will give us something to eat. She's made some gingerbread, I think.'

Posh people always called their mothers 'Mummy' instead of 'Mammy'. I couldn't bring myself to do it. It sounded so English.

I stood in the middle of a very long room, with Clarice. It was carpeted in shades of dark brown, fairly recently, I thought, because the pile was so high, but I didn't dare to look around to see if the carpet was wall to wall.

Mrs Duncan came in with a tray. She'd made shortbread as well as gingerbread, and there were two mugs of cocoa. I nearly burnt myself trying not to slurp. Clarice introduced us and I said:

'How do you do, Mrs Duncan,' feeling like a poseur. I was sure she would guess that the words weren't natural to me. In fact I had never been introduced properly to anyone before.

'Oh hello, dear,' Mrs Duncan responded casually. She didn't

say 'how do you do' in return. 'You're Clarice's friend and rival, she tells me.'

Both labels were news to me.

'Am I?' I said, like a fool. After I'd taken two bites from the gingerbread and two drinks from the cocoa, I put the plate and cup back on the tray and excused myself. My mother would be anxious if I weren't home soon.

'Wait a few minutes, dear,' Mrs Duncan urged me, 'and my husband will be home soon. I'll get him to drive you. Where do you live? Is it far from here?'

'A million miles,' I wanted to say. What would Mr Duncan think if he saw our tenement! All the chalk on the walls, the smells, the kids all coming to climb on the car, for nobody at our place had a car. I edged my way out of the door, refusing Mrs Duncan's reiterated offers of transport. By the time I was seated on the bus, I was shaking all over, overwhelmingly relieved to have survived.

Our paper was a success. We sold about sixty copies a week for a few weeks, to pupils in other classes as well as our own. That meant half a crown for each of us. Clarice banked hers. I gave mine to my mother who was delighted with it.

'Good for you, hen,' she acclaimed me. 'We'll get some extra mince wi' that.'

I was obliged to visit Clarice's house four or five times. Little by little I came to feel more relaxed with her parents, especially with her father who gave us advice on laying out the paper and pointed out ways of compressing our language. In school, Clarice and I spent all our spare time together. We were working together on a story I had begun to write about a ship-wrecked brother and sister who discovered the lost city of Atlantis and became involved in a struggle for power between two rival groups who governed the people. The whole thing was derivative, pinched from accounts of the *Titanic*, the city of Atlantis and *The Prisoner of Zenda*. I'd begun the story for my own amusement, scribbling it in a pad that I carried around in my bag. One day, during an English lesson that was being spent on recitation, having gabbled off my own lines, I got the pad out and surreptitiously began writing in it. For about twenty minutes I wrote undisturbed. Then the pad was torn from my hand and the English teacher, usually a gentle woman, slapped me impatiently:

'How dare you, you naughty, naughty girl, rude girl, sly girl, how dare you.' Saliva dribbled from the corners of her mouth.

I slunk down into my chair and dropped my eyes.

'This will go straight into the bin.'

That was a pity. I had nearly finished. The next day, however, at the end of the lesson, the English teacher called me aside and handed me back the pad, together with a very thick note-book of unlined paper.

'You don't deserve this,' she told me. 'Copy your story into this book. Print it. Perhaps Clarice can be induced to illustrate it, and we'll see what we'll do later.'

So Clarice made a bright blue cover for the story and drew a marvellous picture of a city shimmering in water, all in black ink. I printed the words in violet. We borrowed copies of illuminated writings from the school library and every chapter was prefaced by a page with the heading surrounded by elaborate scrolls.

How could life be more enchanting! Any change could only be for the worse. And so it was. One day Clarice said:

'Why don't I come to your place for a change?'

'My place?' All my innards were tumbling. 'But I haven't got a hut where we can work.'

'We can work on a table. In your room, perhaps.'

In my room! My room. Well, actually, I considered saying, I haven't got a table in my room, and six other kids have equal rights to be there with me.

'Shall I come to your place next Saturday, then?'

'Why not?'

She'd never heard of Plantation, nor MacLean Street, but I told her how to find me. Her father was going to bring her. After that I made mental preparations for ending our collaboration. I didn't think of it as a friendship. Clarice wasn't very popular in class. Ann Bell, the girl with the glass eye, who had come to Bella-houston from a new housing estate to which her family had transferred soon after the accident, was constantly accusing Clarice of being a snob. Always looking down her nose at people, talking to them as if they were dirt. She never talked to me like that. I had to admit, however, that her manner was very reserved. Clarice rarely made small talk or indulged in frivolous activities. There were girls in the class who were richer than Clarice. A number of them were talking of going to Glasgow High, which was fee paying, or to Hutcheson Girls' Grammar, one of the élite schools. None of these, however, were felt to be snobs. None of them had hair under their armpits, either. Most of these others, too, thought Clarice strange.

I wasn't prepared to align myself wholly with either party, but Ann Bell kept urging me to dissociate myself from Clarice.

I became more and more gloomy before the Saturday. Will ye scrub the front doorstep last thing, Mammy? Shine the brasses. Wash the windows. Keep the bedroom door shut so that she can't see we all sleep in there together. We haven't got any trays, or a proper sugar bowl. Will ye buy a milk jug? Her mother doesn't pour it from the bottle. And Mammy, please, please don't say 'shit' or anything like that. Her mother doesn't swear. Oh, and don't call her 'hen'. Her mother says 'dear'. And can't Margaret take a' the kids to the park?

'You're kidding,' said Margaret. 'I want tae see this Queen o' the May.'

'Christ,' my mother protested, though she was cleaning vigorously, 'ye'd think it was the pope coming tae see us.'

By Saturday, I hated Clarice. I was barely civil to her in class and brooded over what Ann Bell said about her snobbishness.

'I'll wait till just before she comes,' my mother said, doing her best for me, 'before I light the fire in the living room.' It was also a bedroom, I reminded myself. 'Then it'll look just right.'

Her father dropped her outside the tenement. I went to the door as if to meet my executioner, feeling curiously abstracted, divorced from the situation. Whatever happened, it wouldn't be to me, but to this strange, mechanical creature who muttered stiffly:

'Oh, hello, Clarice. Come in.'

The living room was filled with black, smelly smoke. For the first time, the chimney refused to function. My mother had opened the windows. We could hear the noise of the children outside. But the smoke kept pouring down the lum instead of going up. We were all coughing and our eyes were stinging.

'We'll have tae sit in the kitchen, hen,' my mother told Clarice, 'until I get this a' cleared oot.'

In the kitchen I nearly swooned. My mother had hung up all the weekly wash on the pulley. The sheets, pillowcases, towels, trousers—every item of clothing in the house, apparently, was steaming above our heads. I got hold of my mother's arm and pinched it savagely.

'What did ye hang up the washing for?'

'Because it's been rainin' for the last three days. I need these things for the morra. I thought she would be staying in the living room all the time.'

Clarice was absolutely mute. I could have killed her. We sat down at the kitchen table—at least the sheets had stopped dripping, and pretended to plan the next issue of our paper, but I felt too miserable.

'I've got some nice apple dumplings in the oven, hen,' my mother announced, 'and I'll make a nice cup of tea.'

The apple dumplings hadn't cooked properly, though my mother was usually a wizard at making them. This time, however, the paste next to the apple was wet and sticky.

'Aw shit,' my mother exclaimed.

I was too frightened to look at Clarice to see how she was reacting. At last her father came to fetch her. We hadn't been able to do much work, for a gossipy neighbour had decided it was utterly imperative to inform my mother of some neighbour who had left his wife and was 'shacking up' with another dame. Merciful God. How much more?

Mr Duncan was his usual pleasant self at the door. No he wouldn't come in, he was due back at work. 'Thank you for having me,' Clarice murmured.

'Goodbye, Clarice.'

At school I avoided her. When some of the others made disparaging remarks about her, I joined them, disgusted with myself for doing it, just the same, for I thought their comments were unfounded. I was searching for a means of ending our relationship.

'She'll really look down on ye, now,' Ann Bell assured me.

So when Clarice offered a mild criticism of something I had written, with a suggestion for its improvement, advice that I had previously welcomed, I turned on her furiously.

'Who told you you're so smart! You think ye're cock o' the walk don't ye? Always putting on airs and graces. Everybody's right about you.'

'Right about what?' she prodded, her eyes narrowing slightly.

161

'Never you mind. Anyway, you're a snob. A snob o' the first water. Ye can find somebody else tae write the paper with.' I carried on, sickened by what I was saying, yet unable to stop myself. 'Your drawings aren't all that good anyway. Ye'll never be like Beatrix Potter in a million years.'

This made her face redden. 'You're no authority on drawing. How would you know?' She paused a minute, and then added, quietly, with a self-control that shamed me, 'You're the snob. Not I. You. And I despise snobs. I never mix with them.'

She turned her back on me and walked away.

'She's cracked, mad,' I babbled to Ann Bell who, surprisingly, made no response. 'How can poor people be snobs? That's ridiculous.'

'No it's not,' my mother said later. 'You were discriminating against her because of where she lived and who her parents are, in the same way that some of the rich won't associate with others because they live at the wrong address and have the wrong sort of job. You're what they call an inverted snob. So's your father, and all those Communists. They judge a man on his class, and no' by what he is as a person.'

My mother was right. Everything had been done by me. Clarice had never at any time remarked on anyone's style of living and both she and her parents had probably worked out my social standing by my accent. What a stupid fool I'd been. The next day I wouldn't go to school. Nor the day after. Then my mother pushed me out of the door.

'Do the right thing,' she ordered me.

But when I saw Clarice's face, I knew it would be useless. I was wiped from her existence. She had moved into a seat beside Ann Bell who also ignored me. Well, that's the biggest laugh of all, I thought. Yes, I deserve it. People like me should be sent to the galleys.

From then until I left Bellahouston, I functioned in a state of self-imposed isolation, in a prison cell to which I consigned myself for punishment. Consequently, my mother's increased agitation to get us to Australia was more welcome at the beginning than it would otherwise have been.

Every day she was writing letters, and every week reading them, throwing them away and cursing.

'Well, that's every bloody church I've tried noo,' she cried savagely, one night. 'Every church, the Red Cross, and even blasted radio stations. Do they want people oot there, or dae they no'? Ah'm damned if we're ever goin' tae get a sponsor.'

'What's a sponsor, Mammy?'

'Och, somebody who'll undertake tae let ye live at their place and find ye a job. The trouble is,' she added gloomily, 'naebody's got a place big enough for nine people plus their ain.'

My father was engrossed in a book. There were photographs in it. He'd brought it home wrapped in brown paper which meant it was a special book and I wouldn't be allowed to read it. I would have to keep my eye out to see where he put it, but say nothing, otherwise he would hide it where I couldn't find it.

'You want tae take a knife and fork tae that lot,' my mother nagged at him, irritably. 'Ye havenae lifted yer bloody heid since ye sat doon.'

'Aye, what's that ye were saying?' my father asked, turning the page back at its corner, to keep the place. He shut the book and I moved over to the fireplace pretending to be searching for something on the mantelpiece. I squinted downwards. *The Scourge of the Swastika* was the title.

'Ye cannae blame them, Rose,' he said, indicating he'd heard what she was saying. 'Ah mean, who can fit seven kids intae an ordinary hoose wi' another family as well?'

'Och, you gie me the shits,' my mother snapped, curling her lip, and starting to clear the table. She banged the cups and plates together in noisy discord, scraping the plates hard with a blunt knife and dropping them on the sink with an angry clunk. 'Ye're aye full o' excuses. Excuses, excuses, excuses. For you or for others. It's easier than trying tae change things. Wipe the table, you,' she snapped at me. 'They're wanting people tae go oot there, aren't they, and from what ah've heard they're no' too fussy aboot what they get so long as it's white. Well, here we are. Nine o' us. If they really need us they should get off their bums and find us a sponsor.'

'What do ye need tae go there for, anyway?' I asked, catching the crumbs from the edge of the table. 'Mah Da's getting good work noo, and ah like Bellahouston. The teacher wants me to finish my story.' Increasingly, every day, despite my attempts at self-flagellation, I was rediscovering my own worth, and I imagined that as time went by the breach between Clarice and myself might close.

Margaret had no desire whatever to leave. 'There's nothing

wrong wi' here. We'll soon get a house in a new estate, if we wait.'

My mother turned on us both. 'When ah want your five cents worth, ah'll send you a wire. Till then, shut up. Ye don't know the first thing ye're talking aboot. The Japanese shipyards'll soon empty the Clyde o' contracts, especially,' she added, looking darkly at my father who was staring into the flames, 'especially the way these Communists are rigging strikes. It's best tae get oot noo. In any case,' she continued, 'we need a bit o' sunlight. It's sunny a' the time in Australia.'

I had thought of something else. 'If we go ah won't be able to visit France or Germany on exchange. They pay for ye, if ye come top in languages. Ye go to a French school for six months the way they come to ours.'

But my mother wasn't listening. While her hand scoured the pots for every mote of food or grit, her mind was on the prowl, ranging over vast tracts of possibility, considering and rejecting, meditating, her lips tight with determination. It took her a few weeks more. Then one Saturday afternoon when my father was getting ready to go to the match, she spread the paper on top of the table and pointed to a paragraph she'd pencilled round.

'Here, Robert, hae a look at this. There's another ad. in the paper. You'll have tae go oot on your own.'

'Go where,' my father said, resting his foot on a chair to swish round it with a duster.

My mother scowled. 'Where dae ye think ah've been talking aboot a' this time. Australia, of course.'

And he went. First an interview up the town with officials from the steel company.

'Dae ye know,' my father remarked wonderingly, 'of all these blokes at the interview, ah was the only labourer?'

'Why, were the others Tories, Daddy?' Margaret said.

Then forms for my mother to sign for the protection of the British government. If my father died or ran away, she must promise not to be a burden on the state. Medical examination. Don't let on ye've got an epileptic in the family. For God's sake, he's aboot a fifth cousin. Aye, but it's in the genes. A' that insanity's catching, ye know.

Then he was ready to leave. Not much excited or greatly apprehensive, standing there quietly while they papered him over with money, staking their claim in the great adventure.

164

Uncle Jim tossed him a green flecked Harris Tweed sports coat with the price tag, fifteen pounds, hanging from a white string. Winter might be in the year, after all. Aunt Margaret strapped a big watch with a wide band round his wrist, to mark the time of his departure. January 1952. And the time of his homecoming again. Loaded with money and smooth with education. The others added their decorations and he went off like a Christmas tree, wearing all his presents next to his skin. Nobody could afford to go to Tilbury so my mother said to him at Central Station, comfortingly:

'Ye'll get yer hair back oot there. When the nerves go. That's a' it is, the doctor said. Nerves. The sun'll make it grow again, and if it doesnae, bald spots are better brown than white.'

My father grinned round the station at everybody, nodding all the time as if to say: 'Ah well, it's come tae this. Nothing tae be done. Cheer up. This too will pass.'

When he got to London he began the first of his many letters, writing in his perfect copperplate with the little pencil stub that he liked so much: dear wife!

It wasn't easy to get him off, you know. All the neighbours and friends and an odd relative came screaming into the house like spitfires, ready to bomb my mother's defences with deadly questions.

What will ye live on when he's on the ship? Who'll look after the kids if ye get a job? Who'll defend ye if men come around at night? And my Aunt Sally wheeled by, releasing bomb after bomb. He might no' come back, ye know, once he feels free again. They say it's a great country for deserting husbands. The police even help them out. Tell them tae get movin' when the wives are catching up. And who'll keep ye warm at night, Rose?

But my mother turned the heavy artillery of her will upon them and they went down in flames, screaming aaagh, she never would listen to reason.

My mother found a job in a bolt factory. She left before we got up in the morning. So I made the breakfast and while Margaret tidied up I took Jackie and Anne to the nursery about two miles away. After school I went to collect them and bring them home. My mother was tired, washing and working, cooking and cleaning. Little crises clotted time. Sadie drank a cup of bleach that was for my mother's false teeth. I broke the copper ball in the cistern pushing it up and down to see how the water rose and fell in the toilet bowl. All the water had to be turned off in the street to fix it.

Every week my father's blue aerogramme came. Dear wife: There are flying fish. Who would believe it? Your loving husband, Robert. Who would believe it? In Port Said they call the trading boats that rub the sides of the liner like ingratiating cats, bum boats. They're all smiles and wanting. An Englishman bought a watch and laughed as it was hauled up the side of the ship. He went away with it and didn't pay.

'That'd be their stretch,' my mother sniffed. 'They're a' the same, the English. Liars and thieves.'

'Even the King?' Robert asked.

'All o' them,' my mother repeated vehemently, 'and their kings are the worst o' the lot.'

Dear wife: in Perth when the buses are full the drivers call out. All children rise.

'And a good thing too.'

P.S. There are quiz kids here who are phenomenal. They know everything under the sun. At least in the southern hemisphere.

Dear wife: There are fifty-two radio stations on one network. A bit more than the B.B.C.'s got. I have found some cobbling work to do at night.

My mother began a new habit. Before she wrote her letter to my father, she put on all her makeup. When she'd finished writing she kissed the bottom of the page, on top of her signature. Two perfect lips. Gee Mammy, you could advertise lipsticks.

Dear wife: they all kidded me like hell. They saw the outline through the back.

Next week he sent her a pair of stockings.

Dear wife: I wish I were there to put them on. Your loving husband, Robert.

'Aaaahh,' my mother sighed.

'Dae ye think he's turning oot like Johnny the lamplighter?' I asked Margaret later, 'Wantin' tae put wimmen's stockings on?'

'Naw,' she said. 'Don't be daft. It's got tae dae wi' doin' dirty things.'

'I thought ye took stockings off for that,' I said wickedly, and we both fell on the bed laughing.

'Ah'm goin' oot the night,' my mother said, a few nights later.

'What for?'

'What dae ye mean what for? Ah'm goin' oot. Wi' Mary Perkin from upstairs. We're goin' tae the Plaza.'

'The pictures or the dance hall?'

She bent to fasten her black ankle-strap shoes before answering me.

'Tae the ballroom. Dae ye want tae make something of it?'

I just stared at her, and she went on, a bit fast, the way you do when you're embarrassed.

'Put the kids tae bed at eight. Nae fightin' and nae makin' tablet. There's no' enough sugar. An' don't answer the door tae any strange men.'

As she was going out, she put her head around the door and said:

'Ah might no' be home till late, so don't wait up for me.'

With the house quiet we sat in the kitchen reading until nine o'clock. But then Margaret, always impatient to be doing something, went off into the bedroom.

'Ah'm going tae see if there's anyone ootside in the street.'

A few minutes later she was back, tiptoeing in exaggerated fashion, her arms wobbling sideways for balance.

'Hey, Mary Rose. Somebody's kissing in the close. Ye can hear them. Ah think it's Catherine Turner and her boyfriend.'

Kissing. Goodness! I had never seen anyone doing it in real life. Every morning my father used to ask my mother for a 'peck', but that wasn't proper kissing, the kind that made you tremble and burn and say 'no, no' till you got a baby.

'We can put a chair in the lobby, under the letterbox, and keek through it.'

I was horrified. 'You're kidding. What if the lid slips from our fingers and bangs? She'd come and tell Mammy.'

The letterbox lid had a powerful spring. It was difficult to hold open and it always shut with a terrific snap. Margaret clicked her tongue with annoyance.

'Och, don't be such a feartie. It'll no' slip. We'll hang on tight. Come on. See if you can see what he looks like. I think he's black. He's got one of those furry voices that sound as if they're stroking you.'

There was no withstanding such an inducement. So I climbed up on the chair and prised the letterbox open with my nails, squeezing my face into the narrow aperture. It was Catherine all right. Standing in the corner opposite our door, under the gaslight. She was a pasty-faced looking girl, puffy round the eyes and white lipped when she had no makeup. Her hair was a dull yellow and crinkly. She never spoke to us if we met in the close but her mother sometimes said:

'Hullo, girls.'

I couldn't see anything of Catherine except her arms. They were round the man's back. He had his head bent and was certainly blackhaired, but it was difficult to see in the dim light if he was all black. Catherine's hands gave a little flutter from time to time, squeezing the air and then falling limp on the man's shoulder. They were making funny noises, the two of them.

Margaret stretched on tiptoe beside me.

'Can ye see them?' she whispered impatiently, 'What are they doin'? Here,' she tugged at my sleeve, 'come doon noo, ah want tae have a look,' but I shook her off because the couple were moving round a bit and now I could see Catherine side on. The man's face was darkish in the shadow.

'Shh, shh,' I hissed at Margaret, 'I can see them noo. They're really kissing.'

Margaret, however, could wait no longer. She climbed up on the chair beside me and I lost my balance. The inevitable happened. I let slip the letterbox lid and it slammed shut. Margaret and I froze with stupefaction, our eyes fixed on the door.

'God, what was that?' we heard Catherine's rather posh voice saying. She said all her 't's' at the end. There was silence then and they were obviously looking at our door since the bang had come from behind it and we were the only tenants in the close. Had they noticed the letterbox lid and worked out what we had been doing?

Margaret jumped down from the chair, indifferent to the noise she made. She raced into the bedroom and leapt under the clothes, pulling them over her head.

'Snib the door on the inside,' I heard her voice sounding from among the blankets, 'or they might turn the handle and come in.'

But even pushing the snib down made a loud noise. They would certainly know we were behind the door if they heard it. So I just stood waiting on the chair, staring at the letterbox and cursing Margaret for tempting me.

After a few minutes I heard footsteps going up the stairs.

What the couple thought, I couldn't tell, for they weren't speaking. That was even more ominous so far as I was concerned. I waited till I heard the footsteps walking along the first storey landing, then I got down and took the chair back into the kitchen.

Margaret hasn't come out of bed again, so she must be sleeping. What if Catherine Turner comes in the morning to tell Mammy? What will she say exactly, in her posh voice?

'Excuse me Mrs Lavery, las-te nigh-te I was with my boy-frien-de, my big black boyfriend with the dark, furry voice that licks your ear, I was with my boyfrien-de kissinggg in the corner opposi-te your door an-de your two daugh-t-ers were spyinggg on me from a narrow aperture through which pops your mail. The eevill dee-de was uncovere-de by acciden-te ...'

And Mammy will say:

'Did ye hear that, the way she speaks? Beautiful. Not like you. You'll have to stop gabbling all the time and concentrate on speaking clearly. Say all your tees and dees and en gees and that kind o' thing. Otherwise bein' a guid scholar will dae nothin' for ye. Dae ye hear me speakin' tae ye?'

I wonder what she was saying exactly when she was making sweet moan. Behold thou art fair my love (he might only be dark in the shadow) behold thou art fair. Thy legs are as marble set upon sockets of fine gold, thy mouth is most sweet. I'm never going to stand in a corner under the gas with anyone. Where men pee up against the walls like dogs. Mammy says drunk men have no control over their bladders. They come into our close and you never hear them The smell's there in the morning, however, and Mammy swears all the time she's scrubbing the steps with lysol. She listens at night for them:

Someone came leaking at my wee sma' door.
Someone came leaking, I'm sure, sure, sure.
I listened, I opened, I looked to left and right,
But nought there was a-stirring in the still, dark night.

She runs to the door every time, but she's never caught them yet. It's in the air. Makes the close like the world's toilet. You can't go scrubbing all the walls with lysol. Forty days and forty nights lysolling wouldn't drown the smell. It doesn't seem to bother them just the same, because they're always there, in the closes, the couples in the dark corners, kissing in the smell and saying no, no, no. When I get a boyfriend we'll kiss in the springtime up in the bluebell woods. Flowers up to Jackie's shoulder.

Walking on the sky blue in your moist, bare feet. Throwing up clouds of bluebells and frankincense, stretching out on bed-steads of cool petals, wearing mists of fine wet perfume. Never, never standing in the corner under the gas mantle. Mammy stood in the corner too, but she never said no. At the registry office in December she said yes again, and ten weeks later, in March, they all cooed:

'What a lovely baby!'

That was me.

Why had my mother said she would be late tonight? The dancing finished at eleven.

The next day, after Mammy'd come home from work, I asked her: 'Did ye enjoy yerself last night, Mammy?'

'Aye, no' bad,' she said.

'Did ye come straight home from the dancing?'

'Why wouldn't ah?'

'We heard Catherine Turner kissing in the close.'

My mother stared at me. 'You stick to your books.'

On the following Saturday afternoon, she called Margaret and me in from where we had been playing kick the can.

'Get washed,' she said. 'Ah want ye tae go up tae St Enoch's Station.'

A man was to be waiting there at the entrance. A tall man with fair hair and a light moustache.

'Tell him,' my mother said, 'that Rose changed her mind. That'll do. And hurry up,' she added before we could ask her what she was changing her mind about, 'he'll be there at half past seven.'

We waited impatiently, wondering. Margaret did handstands against the station wall.

'Quit that,' I told her. 'Ye're showin' everybody your drawers.'

Margaret was unabashed.

'Mah drawers are clean an' fit tae be seen. You're only jealous anyway, 'cause you cannae dae them.'

'C'mon,' I said, after a bit. 'It's just struck eight. Ah'm no' waitin' any longer.'

So we caught the subway back to Kinning Park and walked home.

'What will we tell her?' Margaret asked, flicking the corners of her eyes.

'He didnae turn up. What else?'

'She'll be offended, dae ye no' think?'

'Aye, she will. Serves her right.'

My mother was shutting the oven door when we got in. She turned round and without getting up asked quickly:

'Well, what did he say?'

Margaret leaned on me but I shook her off coldly.

'Naebody came.'

My mother stood up. Her forehead was sweating and she wiped it with the corner of her apron.

'Did they no'? Well fancy that. After a' the fuss. Are ye sure he didnae come? Maybe ye didnae recognise him?'

'Naebody was waiting for anybody. It could be', I said, staring at my mother, 'he's got a wife in Australia.'

Her eyes glittered at me and anger began to pull down the corners of her mouth. I prepared for battle. Then:

'Och,' she said, and the ugly expression vanished. She began to laugh and the good humour warmed all the room.

'Tae hell wi' it. Ye're probably right. Here, look hen,' swinging open the oven door, 'ah'm making apple dumplings for supper.'

She went to the dancing with Mary Perkin twice more, but after that the only visiting she did was to Granny Lavery, to help her clean the house. I was glad.

Men started coming. Sometimes late at night. Sitting in the kitchen we heard the quiet and steady knocks and watched my mother. Whatever she was doing she would stop and lift her head, listening like a cat. We waited, holding our breaths. The door was always snibbed. Then we heard the careful footsteps stepping quietly through the close and we rushed to the bedroom window to peep from behind the curtains. Mostly they walked away in the opposite direction and we couldn't see the visitor but once a shadow passed the window and my mother pulled the curtain back to look out.

'That's a mate o' your faither's.'

A knock muffled as if the fist were wrapped in a sock beat dully on the door one night when I was alone. My mother and Margaret had gone off to tap Granny Bygroves and they had stayed away. It wasn't a tentative, quizzical, I'm here on the chance you might be interested, kind of knock. Rather one that said, I'm here and I'm not going till you open the door. I might even stand all night. Afraid to breathe, I tiptoed into the lobby and waited. There was no sound of footsteps moving off. The knocking had stopped. I stood staring at the door with my mouth open. Then I crept back into the kitchen and got a stool that I laid carefully on the floor underneath the letterbox. Balanced on the stool, I hooked my fingernails behind the metal plate and drew it inwards. Two eyes, narrow and closely set, stared at me through the opening. My fingers stuck to the letterbox lid and my face sagged forward against the slot. The eyes remained fixed as if they had been nailed into the skull. Then, shockingly, without any warning, a voice shouted:

'Boo!'

And I fell off the stool, sobbing and only half conscious of the running feet.

'Bloody men,' my mother growled, shaking her head disgustedly, 'every wumman on her ain is a bitch in heat tae them.'

Little by little after that, the knocks grew fewer until we gave up listening for them. I was surprised, therefore, when one Saturday night, my mother stopped scrubbing and leaning on the sink, her hand still clasping the trousers she'd been squeezing, listened intently. I could hear nothing.

'Naebody knocked, Mammy.'

My mother paid no attention. Then suddenly, she threw the trousers into the water, splashing suds over the floor and rushed into the lobby.

'These dirty swine. They're oot there pissing up against the door again.'

She swung the outside door open, hard, so that it slammed against the wall.

'Get tae bloody hell oot o' . . .' and then her voice was cut off.

When I hurried into the lobby I saw a man standing over my mother, covering her mouth with his hand. My mother was pressed against the wall. I knew the man. He was a corner boy who often cheered us when we were playing 'doublers' against the grocer's wall with our worn out tennis balls. Now he glanced at me and said quickly:

'No' a sound, lassie.'

My mother was looking over his shoulder, so I looked there too. Gardiner's, the licensed grocer's, toilet was open and two men were crouched in it, on the floor. There was a hole in the wall and some bricks were scattered by the door. The man had taken his hand away from my mother's mouth and was fingering his shirt collar nervously.

'Ye know who I am, missus,' he said. 'No' a word, an' there'll be a hauf in it for yer Ne'e'rdy.'

'Jesus,' my mother sighed, 'ye scared a week's growth oot o' me. Ah thought ye were peein' on mah doorstep. The no-hopers aroon here think ah'm a public urinal.'

'Get inside, you,' she said, turning to me, 'an' don't go blabbin' tae the street aboot this.' She gave me a push and followed me into the lobby. As she was shutting the door, the man pressed his face into the opening.

'Noo mind. Nae tips. An' there'll be a bottle for ye.'

My mother nodded disbelievingly and shut the door.

The next day the police came round.

'The cobbler's was broken into last night, missus,' one said, holding a notebook in his hand. 'We thought you might have heard something.'

My mother shook her head.

'Like what?'

'Well they had to chip at cement tae get the bricks out. They must have made some noise.'

'Ah went tae bed early last night,' my mother lied. 'Ah wouldnae hae heard the last trumpet. Ah was dog tired.' Then cunningly she added: 'They must be desperate tae pinch auld shoes that need mending.'

'Ah well,' said the policeman. 'They had other things in mind ye know. But they took a wrong turning.'

After they'd gone, my mother sat by the kitchen table tapping her fingers on the oilcloth.

'Whit a bit o' bad luck. Nae bottle noo. Ah could've flogged it. These corner boys. They're good for nothing. They couldnae find an orange in the fruit market.'

I didn't play on that corner any more as I didn't want to look at that man. He might think I would tell the police one day, and be planning to murder me.

Later in the week Granny Bygroves came pounding on the door, bellowing like the coal man.

'It's me Rose,' she boomed through the letter box. 'Are ye up?'

'Well, what dae ye think o' that,' my mother asked her, telling her the story of the abortive break and entry.

Granny sniffed. She had Anne on her knee. Anne was awake because she had bronchitis. Now Granny was jigging her up and down and crooning that horrible little song that made my scalp prickle with embarrassment.

'Oh Mrs Goldielee,
Come tae bed an' lie wi' me
An' ah'll gie ye a cup o' tea
That'll make yer bel-ly warrum.'

'Och, that lot,' she snorted. 'They're a pack o' loafers an' thieves. They'd take the eyes oot o' yer heid and swear ye never had any. But ye were right', she went on, 'no' tae put them in. Be like the three wise monkeys an' ye'll no' go far wrong. Here, ah'm dyin' o' thirst, Rose. Are ye puttin' the kettle on?'

She'd brought some gammon with her, so Margaret and I went to the bakery for rolls. After she'd munched her way through four, the little hairs that sprouted from her chin bobbing up and down in time with her jaws, Granny sat back and loosened the belt of her gaberdine coat.

'That was stickin' oot, Rose,' she murmured, sighing gently with satisfaction. 'Ah havenae had a tightener a' day.' She burped loudly. 'Too busy at the hotel.' She burped again.

Margaret scowled.

'Why dae ye no' haud yer breath Granny? That sounds awful.' Granny folded her hands across her stomach and patted it gently.

'In the words o' that whoremaster poet: "wheree'er ye be, let yer wind gang free." Well then,' she said briskly, looking across at my mother, 'have ye got a sailin' date yet?'

My mother glowered down at the table.

'He hasnae drawn a hoose in the ballot. Six months since he left an' he hasnae drawn a hoose yet. There's nae luck attached tae anything that family does. They're a pack o' jonahs.'

'Well ye cannae blame him efter a',' Granny said, reasonably. 'A gamblin' government's no' an everyday occurrence. Ah mean, a Corporation that allocates hooses through a raffle instead o' a priority list . . .' she shrugged her heavy shoulders. 'Ye cannae see the reasoning in it. Does that no' mean, Rose, that a man can walk off a ship an' draw a hoose and another man can wait years an' years an' might never get his number up?'

'Well, no' exactly. There's what ye call a hard luck ballot. That's for people who've been waitin' more than a year. An' then, if ye're an ex-serviceman, your name gets put in two ballots each week. They have two ballots but normally yer name only goes in one.'

'Aye, ah see. They like tae make it dramatic, like. Ye get two thrills. One for getting a hoose an' the other for bein' in a raffle. Uh huh.' Granny nodded her head up and down. Then she peered into the teapot. 'Can ye fill this up again, Rose?'

My father usually sent twenty Australian pounds a fortnight. This was about seventeen pounds sterling. It was less than he'd been earning before he left but he had to pay for his board at a steelworks hostel and buy his cigarettes. As soon as his money began to arrive regularly, my mother stopped work. Then the money began to go up and down like a yo-yo.

'Another stoppage this week,' my father wrote. 'They had a pit top meeting and the management blew the stop-work whistle.'

'Bloody Communists, ah'll bet,' my mother snarled, glaring at the three five pound notes to be changed at the bank.

One week the letter was empty, except for writing.

'I'm trying to canvass shoes for mending,' my mother read to us, 'and I'll send you something as soon as I can. This is the third week we've been on strike.'

'Shit,' my mother said, and sat with her head in her hands.

It was nearly the end of May but the kitchen was freezing. Ne'er shed a clout, till May is oot. We sat silently in the room, not looking at the empty fireplace. It was very clean because it hadn't been used for three days. The coalman had been and gone but he wouldn't fill the bunker without cash in his hand. Granny Bygroves never seemed to be home. Nor was my Uncle Jim who sometimes helped us out.

'Food but no fags,' he told my mother sternly when she asked him for a 'loan'. 'Ye cannae expect the rest o' the world tae finance your indiscretions.'

Now he'd gone down to England on business for his firm and there was nothing in the cupboard but a packet of salt.

The rain started dripping outside. I got up and went to the kitchen window to look at the tenements in the next street. Grey, grey, grey. The ugliest colour in the whole world. When I grow up I will never wear grey or have anything grey about me. If I live in a grey stone house I'll paint the stones orange and if there are any grey cats howling on the midden I'll catch them and dye them bright yellow. I'll have curtains of ultramarine and cushions with splotches of green and red. To shake off the damp. The kitchen window was glazing over, and dark shadows were turning the room into a cave. We children sat motionless, like lumps of stone, waiting. Someone sniffed. Who could it be? Another sniff. My mother was crying behind her hands. Chaos. It was pouring inside and outside now. The walls were no longer a protection against the goblins and creepy things of the world. They were right among us.

The shopping bag was hanging on a nail behind the kitchen door. I took it down and went out and as I shut the door quietly I heard Margaret sobbing:

'Don't greet Mammy, don't greet, ye'll make us greet tae.'

In Rutland Lane, so I had heard, the briquette man had his store. I would go there and steal some briquettes. Fire was more important than food when it was raining and cold. But there were no briquettes in the yard. He must have taken them all away to sell.

Coal dust was piled high against a wall. That would do instead. We would make our own coal cakes. I gouged out the dust with my two hands and filled the bag quickly, patting it down tightly so that I could fit more in. When I was nearly finished I heard a horse and cart start to trundle down the lane. It might be someone just passing through, but it might also be the briquette man. I grabbed the bag and peeped out of the yard. It was him all right. Who cares? He won't catch me. Not when I'm in earnest and I was never so earnest in my life. Yell all you like.

'Hey you, come back here. Come back here!'

That big Clydesdale hasn't got a hope. Me, I'm a bird and I'm flying right out of this lane, skimming over the ground. The bag's full of feathers, no' flat irons. Jesus, ah nearly tripped. But in great long leaps I cleared the lane and soared over the dykes like a pole vaulter. Inside our close I sat on the bottom stair holding my chest with both hands. It was raw inside. I felt the dust anxiously to see if it had got wet. It was dry. The bag was a zip-up and the edges stuck together even if the zip wasn't working.

'Here, Mammy,' I said, opening the bag to show her. 'We can make briquettes.'

My mother wasn't as impressed as I had hoped for.

'Ye cannae make briquettes wi' that. Ye need cement tae bind it together.'

She stood looking down at the dust, thinking.

'Ah'll damp some newspapers and see if we can bind it tae them.'

So she did, drying off the round balls in the oven. Then we burnt them in the fireplace. At first there were little landslides and dust slid down into the tiny flames, trying to choke them. We hovered over them, hissing anxiously, cheering them on when they began to gobble up the dust and regurgitate it as hot coals. My mother made sticks of tightly wound newspaper and they bolstered the flames till they grew more aggressive and began to roar up the lum.

'Great,' we shouted. It had stopped raining inside.

Then the outside door opened and Robert came in. He laid four shillings on the table.

'Ah hope ye havenae been robbin' a bank,' my mother said anxiously.

'Naw, Ma. Mr Gardiner gie'd me the close money. In advance.'

My mother reeled backwards and slapped her forehead.

'Gie me strength. Ah've already got the close money from him —in advance.'

'Aye, but ah asked him would he like ye tae clean the close another time because it's been raining a lot and it's got mucky. People might think it hadnae been washed.'

Margaret reddened. 'Jings, ah'm no' goin' in there again tae buy anything. You've got a right cheek.'

Robert was completely unperturbed.

'We can get spuds and drippin' noo and hae chip sandwiches.'

He went off to get them and I said to my mother:

'Isn't that terrific, Mammy? We've got a fire and something tae eat.'

'Aye,' she said, mournful-looking just the same, 'but ah've nae tea an' mah tongue's hangin' oot for a smoke.'

Then I remembered something. I ran into the lounge-room and pulled myself up onto the shelf inside the big press. In the furthermost corner there were some little packages. I selected two and took them into the kitchen, dropping them triumphantly on the table.

'Look, Mammy. Tea and fags.'

My mother always used too much tea in the pot. People said she'd learned to make tea from the Arabs. So I had been sneaking some tea out of the new packets before I emptied them into the caddy and had hidden it in the press. When my mother got a twenty packet of Woodbines she didn't notice if you took one or two out, so I'd hidden them away too. They were emergency rations in case we got put in the concentration camps like the Jews I'd read about in *The Scourge of the Swastika*. And I'd read too that in these places people went around looking for douts.

They were always desperate for smokes as much as for food. If that happened to my mother she would be in a terrible state. But she was only going to get a few at a time. I would have to put the rest in a different place now, for she'd be scrounging around trying to find my plank.

Getting the cigarettes—there were five—was like winning the pools to my mother. She put the kettle on and the chip pan, and peeled the potatoes, singing that song of Harry Lauder's: 'Keep Right on to the End of the Road'.

When we'd finished eating and the younger ones were getting ready for bed, she murmured:

'Ah well, God looks after His own.'

I gazed into the flames that had turned the ribs of the grate into solid fire and tried to imagine God running down the lane with the briquette dust.

11 A Good Worker's Worth a Tomato

That June, when school holidays began, my mother agreed I could look for a job. I asked to speak to the manager of Country Dairies.

'Are you sure you're fifteen?'

Why does he doubt me? Everybody says I'm tall for my age. What's he looking at my chest for? Because I've no bust. That's why. When you're fifteen you've generally got big breasts.

'What school did you go to?'

Oh shame. If I say I went to Bella then he'll wonder why I want to work in a dairy. But if I say I attend Lambhill Street he'll think I'm a dope.

'I was in the top class at Lambhill Street.'

'Count up this list of figures.'

I was to report to Country Dairies at Govan Cross. Two spinster sisters ran the shop and one had broken her ankle. She would be away for another three weeks. I would work from half past six in the morning to six at night, Monday to Saturday, and from eight to twelve on Sundays. Wages. Thirty shillings a week.

Miss Mathieson looked at me very dubiously.

'You have to be quick here. Especially in the morning when the workmen come for their rolls.'

She wasn't looking at my chest but she said:

'Ye cannae have been fifteen very long.'

'Last week.'

'Aye?'

My mother bought me a dark green overall of polished cotton with brass buttons. It looked smashing. Really grown up. I was awake before the first tram left the depot. Trembling with excitement and dreaming of working the cash register. I would

179

be able to press the key down and the drawer would zip open and the figure appear in the glass at the top. Giving the change. All little compartments in the drawer. One for coppers, one for tanners, bobs and florins, two for the notes. Every time you pressed the key it went tinggg! Putting the rolls into the brown paper bags and twirling the bag by its two corners like a real shop assistant.

In the morning I climbed the brae with all the men going to the yards and sat on the tram with them, smelling their greasy coats and bunnets.

The shop was already packed when I got in. Miss Mathieson was ringing the cash register like a carillon and slamming the drawer so fast you would have thought that was all she was doing, but she was tearing the rolls off the huge sheets the baker delivered and cramming them in the bags.

'Here, dae ye know the prices o' rolls?' she asked me from the sides of her mouth, smiling at the wee man on the other side of the counter. 'Three for tuppence ha'penny, sir.'

I nodded, shivering inside.

'Well start serving; I'll show ye how tae work the cash register when ah get a minute.'

Until the rush finished at half past eight, I moved in an enchanted world. The arms that stretched backwards and forwards over the counter and the little drawer opening and shutting with its tinggg were part of a hectic dance. You twirled round on one foot from the bar to the drawer, dipping into the change, sliding the coins into the warm hands, bowing your head like a swan and smiling, smiling, a bland and creamy China doll.

When the shop was empty I woke up in a fright.

'No too bad, lassie.'

Miss Mathieson was watching me appraisingly.

'Ye can count.'

'Oh ah do like it,' I told her, watching the door impatiently. 'It's great fun. Exciting.'

At half past ten she forced me into one of the two chintz covered armchairs that brightened the dark back shop. There was a fire in the grate for the back part got no sun.

'Noo sit there,' she ordered, 'and hae this ham roll wi' a guid strong cup o' tea.'

I didn't want to sit for a minute.

'Och, but ah'm no' tired. I might miss a customer.'

Miss Mathieson put her neat little hand on my shoulder and held me down.

'A good worker knows when tae rest. Ye're nae use tae anybody burned oot.'

So the days lined up behind each other like dancers in a reel and I skipped by them, touching time lightly in the passing, welcoming each new partner with dizzy delight. I dusted the shelves in a frenzy and arranged the tins in new patterns so that their bright colours dazzled the sober walls. If a customer came in I scrabbled down the ladder and nearly fell into her lap.

'There's nae state o' emergency, ye know,' Miss Mathieson remarked drily. 'They don't mind waiting a whole second.'

'But ah cannae wait,' I said.

At night I couldn't sleep. When I sat by the table at lunchtime the others lamented that I rattled all the plates and slurped the gravy.

'She keeps shaking her legs, Mammy,' they complained.

'Oh it's great tae be young,' the customers said. 'Full of energy.'

I felt as if I were on an express rushing down the mountain at a terrific speed, hanging by my pinky from the footplate, going faster and faster for ever and ever. Hurry up, hurry up.

Then Mr Black came into the shop. He was like death dressed up. Wore a black suit with not a single coloured thread in it, a black hat, black shoes and black socks. His hands were furry with the black curls that sprouted from his knuckles even below the finger nails. His chin and cheeks under the hat were black too. Shaving shadow they called it. Only his eyes and teeth were coloured. Red in the whites and greenish yellow in the ball part. His teeth were yellow too. He had only three cutting teeth in the top so his eye teeth crouched closer together and stuck out over his bottom lip like a dog's. As soon as I saw him I shivered and the excitement hissed out of me like air from a balloon, leaving me flat and limp. He was something to do with the dairy and he came to see Miss Mathieson.

On the way into the back shop he saw me and paused beside me.

'So you're the new lassie I've been hearing about.'

I looked into his eye teeth.

'What's your name. Dear?'

'Baldy Bane. Stick your nose in an aeroplane.'

'Mary Rose? That's a pretty name.'

He paatted me on the arm. Like thaat. Then stroooke. I glanced down at the skin he'd touched. All the millions of pale hairs on my arms were standing straight up in furious protest.

The milk empties were piled up beside the counter. I grabbed the top one and held it between us.

'Excuse me, sir, I have to take the empties outside,' and I hurried out to the pavement. I'd swept it in the morning but it needed doing again. It was going to need doing until that man went away.

He came at least twice a week. On the way in or the way out he always caught you. Paaat. Stroooke. On the arm, on the neck, or somewhere.

One night at tea I told my mother about him.

'Ah hate that man who comes tae the shop. He gies me the creeps. Always touchin' ye wi' fingers like wet chamois.'

My mother ladled an extra doughball onto my plate.

'Has he ever tried tae put his hands up yer claes?'

'Mammy Lavery!' Margaret was scandalised. 'What a terrible thing tae say.'

'No half sae terrible as doin' it,' my mother retorted. 'Anyway,' she said, stabbing me with her finger to emphasise the point, 'you just tell him tae keep his hands on his ha'pennies.'

After a while I got smart at dodging Mr Black and my stomach gave up cramping when I saw his car stop outside. Miss Mathieson had told me I would shortly be transferred to another shop as her sister's leg was pretty well now. So I decided that before I left I would scrub out the back shop. Neither of the two old ladies had had the strength to do this and I knew Miss Mathieson would be pleased. It bothered her, wiping the stone floor over with a wet cloth instead of giving it a good scrub. One afternoon she went to the post office. It was pouring rain and there hadn't been a customer in all the afternoon. So I got a bucket of water and a scrubber and some newspapers to kneel on. Then I started doing the floor, beginning at the kitchen sink as I didn't want to walk over the wet parts if I had to serve someone. The warning bell must have rung but I didn't hear it, probably because I was thinking of staying with my granny that night. My mother had said I could spend the weekend with her. That meant bacon and egg in bed on Sunday morning and all the Sunday papers to read, including the *News of the World* that my father always hid away. All of a sudden when I was leaning over trying to reach into a corner with the scrubber, lying almost flat to the floor, I got this funny feeling up the back of my neck and in my shoulder blades. Like fingers walking up and down. It was him. That Mr Black. Standing right behind me. I heard his voice before I saw him.

'Ye're doing a great job there, lassie.'

I nearly jumped into the bucket with fright.

'Oh it's you, sir. You gave me a scare.'

I gave him a quick look upwards, still holding the scrubber in my hands. He was grinning with his horrible poky eye teeth hanging out and shaking his head from side to side.

'My word, ye're a touchy young thing. Nervous as a kitten. But there's nae need tae be feart o' me.' His voice was like snakes sliding over you. 'Ah like wee lassies.'

He glanced around the room and then out at the front shop.

'On your own today, I see. Is Miss Mathieson away the day, then?'

'Oh no,' I said quickly. I didn't want him thinking that for a minute. 'She's here, but she's just no' here at the moment, but she'll be right back. Any time.'

He wasn't listening. Looking down at my hand. The one with the scrubber in it.

'Ye know, ye oughtn't tae scrub floors like that. It isnae guid for your skin. Makes it rough—an' soft skin is a lassie's pride and joy.'

He leaned down and stroked my cheek, his fingers sliding round my neck.

'Ye've got lovely fine skin on your face.'

I dug the scrubber into the water and started to rub at the floor with it but the stone was nearly dry again and I couldn't scrub properly.

'Ah need more water,' I said, grabbing the cloth.

'Och, leave it alane.' He took hold of my hand in his dry fingers. 'Dae ye know there are places where the skin is softer than the one ye have on your face?'

I dropped my eyes to the middle button on his jacket.

'No, ah don't—and ah'm no' interested either.'

183

'Aye', he went on, ignoring my tart reply, 'inside your arm, for instance. There,' stroking inside my elbow. 'It's very soft in that part.'

I couldn't breathe. My tongue was choking the back of my throat. But I jumped up and wrenched my arm away from his furry fingers. Then I ran over to the sink and turned the tap on, not knowing what I was going to do with the water.

'Ah have tae wash my hands.' My voice was all dried out. 'The customers'll be comin' in a minute.' I held my hands under the tap, but the soap was in the bucket so I just rubbed them together.

He hadn't said another word and when I glanced across at him he was staring. And Breathing.

I thought, if he comes near me I'll put my thumb under the tap and squirt the water in his eye the way I do to Margaret.

Then the door bell went and Miss Mathieson came into the shop, her string bag full of potatoes and a cabbage. Mr Black was still standing there saying nothing. I couldn't stop myself taking a big breath. It sounded awfully loud in the shop. Miss Mathieson put down the bag on the floor. She didn't seem to have noticed anything.

'Ah hope ye havenae been waitin' long, Mr Black.' Then she turned to me. 'Just leave the rest o' the floor today, lassie. People'll be starting tae come in any minute.'

The next day she told me her sister was to start back at work on Monday. They were sending me to the Summerton Road shop.

'Mr Black doesnae visit that shop, lassie.'

I knew I wouldn't last at the Summerton Road Dairy as soon as I walked into it, and I didn't. By the end of the week I had sacked myself. It was a bigger shop than the one at Govan Cross. Two back rooms and back and front both mucky. Tins sticking together with dirt on the shelves. Gummed to each other and the wood. Scum filling the cracks in the flagstone floors. Shop-windows obscuring instead of displaying the goods. What a dump. And the two women working there. We disliked each other on sight. I mean they were pally but not with me. One was old, about my mother's age and the other was seventeen. She lived in Granny Lavery's street. Fat with lanky hair and a wet apron tied over her big belly.

'You're old McGiffin's grandkid, aren't ye?' she said for 'how do you do'. 'Ah've seen ye goin' up tae old Dorin's the money lender.'

'Ye'd see me goin' tae a lot o' places if ye watched long enough,' I answered, for 'pleased to meet you too'.

'Smartie!'

Funny, but the customers were the same. Bleak. Dirty. Sleekit looking with shabby scarves tied over their heads making their noses and mouths as sharp as bayonets, counting the change twice and glaring at you from their side of the counter as if it was visiting time at Barlinnie. So I decided to steal a tomato. I'd had my eye on it for a couple of days. It was home grown and very expensive. You might ask for a half pound of New Zealand or Danish fresh or Irish white salted if you were after butter, but if it was home-grown you hissed over it admiringly when you were buying tomatoes. This one I didn't touch to weigh it for I might have bruised its perfectly smooth skin. One of those with no seed or watery juice. Pale pink solid flesh as soft as butter in your mouth with the smell of fresh air and wet leaves coming from its middle.

'You should see it, Mammy,' I said. 'It's a smasher.'

I waited till Annie, the boss, and Lizzie Scullin had gone into the back shop. Then I slipped it inside my overall under my armpit and left for lunch, with my arm sticking out a bit, though not much. I didn't feel happy or guilty. Very strange in fact. Like punching Margaret or smashing the cups or throwing a brick through a window. I was halfway up Summerton Road going towards the tram stop when I heard Lizzie Scullin shout behind me.

'Hey Lavery, Annie wants ye!'

I didn't turn round. Just kept walking.

'What for?'

Her voice was as smooth as cream.

'She didnae say. But she wants ye tae come back straight away.'

She led the way like a warder and I dawdled behind, very little interested really. Maybe I should throw the tomato in a close. Now. But sleekit appearance was probably waiting for that and would catch me. In any case I didn't want to throw my tomato away. See it sputter all over the dirt. Nobody had seen me. I was sure of it.

In the shop Annie was standing in front of the counter with two customers. Two of her cronies. She smiled at me when I came in and I felt reassured.

'Oh there ye are, Mary Rose. Ah'm sorry tae drag ye a' the way back but it'll no' take a minute. Did ye take anything from the shop when ye went oot the day?'

Her tone was so casual I wondered if I had heard her properly and I didn't answer. Lizzie Scullin was lounging against the counter with a glaikit grin all over her mug and the two women were watching me as if they thought I was going out of fashion in a minute.

Annie waited. Then she said:

'Can ah see inside your overall please?'

I opened my overall and handed her the tomato without a word.

Oh, tisk tisk tisk. Their tongues rattled and clacked like rosary beads and their eyes, when I risked looking into them, gleamed like crosses of ice.

I wet my pants. Yes, it surprised me too. After all, I was two months past thirteen and had been toilet trained at an early age. But there it was.

'Can I go now please?' I asked.

I went round the back of the shop to the outside toilet. The wooden door was powdery with dry rot and slashed with cracks of light to look through when you were sitting on the bowl. I sat on the lid and stared at the rusty nail opposite. Small uneven squares of newspaper were spiked on it. My father said lascars are much cleaner than us. They have footprints on the sides of their toilets to crouch on and they wash themselves instead of using paper. But newspaper is more interesting. All the bits of news you miss are bundled together. I couldn't be bothered to read them. Just sat there. If only I could powder away with dry rot. And those wet pants. I couldn't go home without any. Someone might see me when I was getting on the tram.

My head was aching horribly and I had a pain low down in my back.

'My head's aching and I've got a pain low down in my back,' I said to myself.

There was something familiar about these words. Who had I heard saying them? My mother. My mother when she was explaining about growing up.

186

'I'll show ye how ye're built inside,' she'd said, smoothing out the paper from the tampon box. 'This is where the eggs are made and these two little roads are for the eggs to travel down . . .'

Margaret and I made faces at each other above my mother's head and wriggled our toes inside our shoes.

'Now here is where the man puts his . . .'

'Aw, dae ye mind!'

'Oh all right, all right. Ah'll tell ye that bit next time.'

Outside in the close Margaret stoated the balls against the walls as if she wanted to smash the tiles.

'Boy, she gives me the pip wi' all that creepy stuff.'

Just the same we looked and waited.

'Ye shouldnae hae told us so soon,' I grumbled after six months. 'Ah keep waitin' but nothing happens.'

My mother was surprised.

'Well, it doesnae come from mah family. We were a' early starters. Ye must be takin' after your father's side. They're retarded. Ah sometimes wonder if your father's started yet.'

My father, who was bent over the wireless, changing the accumulator, looked round incredulously:

'You're helluva smart. Where'll ye be next week?'

Sitting there in the toilet with my elbows on my knees and my chin wedged between my hands I suddenly became conscious of a radio blaring in my head. Three stations going at once. Zena, zena, zena, zena, can't you hear the music playing, in the city square. Put another nickel in, in the nickelodeon, here, here, the gang's all here, what the hell do we care, what the hell do we care. Music and fireworks were blowing my head off. Boy, wait till I tell my mother! I grabbed all the sheets of paper off the spike—that Lizzie Scullin would have to be a lascar next time she came here—and folded them into a thick, rectangular bundle. Then I hobbled out of the close away from that horrible shop, crackling like fire.

They were very forgiving at the head office when my mother turned up to collect my pay.

'Tell her,' they said, 'to come back.' And added, not unreasonably: 'a good worker is worth a tomato.'

'Ah can't,' I told my mother. 'Ah'm packed tight to the top o' mah head wi' shame.'

It's true. I wouldn't go out of the house for a few days,

thinking of those women shining with the purity of their scorn. They were very very good, and I was very bad. It was terrible to feel bad. No more thieving for me. No more briquette dust. We would freeze or starve honestly.

There wasn't much left of the holidays by now, but I played a bit. Once I met Freddie Goode down the street. He was thinner now and he had new glasses, the ones with the thick dark frames instead of the nickel. He was taller too, and shy and didn't play C.C.K. any more. None of us did.

'Hullo,' he said, with his hands in his pockets like a man. 'I thought you must have gone by now.'

'To Australia?'

'Aye.'

'We're waitin' for my father to tell us when to come. How dae ye like Lambhill Street?'

'No' bad. Dae ye think they've got a school like Bella, oot there?'

'If they havenae, ah'm comin' back. Ah'll ask mah faither tae find oot.'

But my father didn't want to wait any longer.

'Dear Wife,' he lamented, for what he thought was the last time. 'There's no future here for us. Too many strikes. This raffling of the houses could go on forever. I'm going to jump a ship and work my passage back.'

'Ho ho ho,' my mother said, laughing in a rage. 'We'll see aboot that.' She went to the post office and sent a cable:

'Stay put. We're coming.'

Then she bought a new nib for the pen and a new bottle of ink and sat over the table growling at us:

'Shut up, you lot, ah'm concentrating.'

When Granny came round later, Mammy was still black with indignation.

'What dae ye think o' that, Mother! He's had himself a good holiday while ah've been here knocking mah pork oot, an' noo he's fed up wi' the place he's coming back. Like bloody hell! Over mah dead body he is!' She pranced up and down the kitchen, whooping like a red Indian.

'Calm yerself, Rose. Calm yerself,' Granny admonished her. 'It's nae use gettin' yerself intae a state.'

'It'll be that Australia Hoose in London that'll be in a state when they get mah letter!'

We rushed at her.

'What did ye write, Mammy? Tell us what ye wrote.'

She put on her secret, cunning look.

'Never you mind.'

'Maybe she told them she'd gas us a',' Margaret said later when we were conjecturing. 'Dae ye mind that time she told the Corporation she was goin' straight oot tae throw herself over the Stockwell Bridge if we didnae get a hoose withoot rats? That man nearly wet himself, Mammy said.'

Out in the street the kids were playing, challenging the boy who stood in the middle of the road with his arms outstretched, barring the way.

'Charlie Chaplin, may I cross the wa-ter!'

'Not today, but maybe to-moooo-row.'

'When, exactly!' my mother nagged them in London. 'When? When?'

Only three weeks from today, the letter said, after being snatched from the box.

We somersaulted all over the beds and threw the pillows up in the air. We're off to see the beaches, the wonderful beaches of Aus. Then we ran out of the house half dressed and knocked on all the doors and windows like Wee Willie Winkie.

'September the sixteenth!' they cried. 'But that's awfy soon.'

'No' soon enough for me,' my mother muttered darkly. Then she cheered up. Four weeks holiday on a ship as big as a state. Relatives dived in among us, grabbing a leg here, an arm there and howked us off, holding tightly.

'It's nae use greetin',' they said firmly. 'Your mother has to sell the stuff now, and ye'll no' be split up for long.'

My Uncle Jim pointed proudly to his new television set. One of the first in Glasgow, you can be sure.

'Ye're lucky tae be staying with me, you know. Ye can watch the pictures every day.'

I sat with my back to the television set. Why couldn't the others have stayed with him? They liked him. At Uncle Jim's ye couldnae do anything except muck about on the piano. But he bought Sadie and me new clothes and the others got hand-me-downs. And he gave me an envelope at the station with twenty pounds in travellers cheques inside.

'Gie that tae your mother when ye're halfway to Australia,' he cautioned me.

12   September the Sixteenth

At the station my mother counted us carefully.

'Are they a' here noo?' she asked Aunty Margaret. 'What dae ye make o' that Carter woman, Margaret, wantin' tae keep oor Jackie? "Mah kid'll be that lonely when he goes," she said. "An' you've got seven, efter a'." The damned cheek. They think havin' a big family's the same as havin' a bag o' jorries. Ye can gie away a few an' no' miss them.'

The train was waiting there, at the station, patiently, like the milkman's horse, for everybody to say goodbye. The tenements in our street must have been empty because everybody was up at the station. A piper had come from somewhere and he began to play the Maoris' farewell. They all started singing and hanging on to us: nooooow is the hooour! People were holding your hand and talking at you all at once, voices at your knee and above your head. 'Ye'll send us a bottle o' sunshine, won't ye, hen?' 'Ye'll no' forget yer auld grannie, will ye lassie?' 'Can ye get me a pen friend? A good lookin' one. They say a' these Aussie laddies are terrifically handsome. Big and brown, ye know.'

Now the piper was playing 'Will ye no' come back again.' I pushed my way through to my mother. She had on a new suit, dark green and she'd got a perm. She looked great because she was so happy, laughing and shaking her head as if to say, 'Well, ah don't know.' Margaret Reid, from upstairs, was standing right beside her, looking into her face. She didn't play with me any more, her. She was going out with boys although she was only two years older than I.

'Hi, Margaret,' I said to her. 'Dae ye no' wish ye were comin' with us?'

She gave me a quick look and said brightly, but indifferently:
'Hullo there. Isn't this exciting?'

Then she put her hand on my mother's arm and patted it.
'Your husband'll fall in love wi' ye all over again, Rose.'

I nearly choked. 'Rose.' She'd called my mother 'Rose'. Since when? Since when did she stop saying 'Mrs Lavery'? My mother appeared not to have noticed it.

'Aye, dae ye like mah perm? It's no' too frizzy is it, Marg? Ah told her no' tae leave the neutraliser on too long.'

Talking to her as if she were a grown-up or something. It really made me mad. I could see our Margaret further up the platform. She was standing with her arm through Doreen Smellie's and they were whispering together.

'Hey, Margaret,' I hissed at her when I got through the crowd. 'Dae ye know what Margaret Reid called Mammy?'

'What?'

'Rose, she called her. Her first name.'

'Och!'

Margaret turned her back impatiently and started giggling again with Doreen Smellie.

I could have punched them. How come, it didn't bother Margaret. When I made my way back, Margaret Reid had disappeared and Granny Bygroves was talking to my mother.

'Ah'm tellin' ye, Rose,' she was saying earnestly, 'ye'll find it's the only true religion. Noo you take this rosary and . . .'

I grabbed my mother's arm.

'Mammy, did you hear Margaret Reid? She called you "Rose".'

My mother wasn't listening. I said more loudly, right into her ear: 'Mammy!'

She drew her head away, annoyed, and glared at me.

'Ah heard ye the first time. So what? What's the matter wi' ye? Go and say goodbye to yer Granny Lavery.'

'Och!'

I ground my teeth together and went up the train till I reached the platform outside our carriage. She had no right to call my mother 'Rose' as if she were a grown-up. She'd always said 'Mrs Lavery' before. Tears of anger and vexation began to dribble down my cheeks. Blow them all!

'Don't greet, hen,' my Aunty Mary murmured, giving me a hug. 'Ye can come back when ye're a big lassie.'

'Oh, ah'm no' crying for goin' away,' I wailed despairingly.

I wiped my eyes with my knuckles and stared down the platform into the darkness ahead of the engine, feeling absolutely desolate. If I'd been an Arctic wolf I would have howled and howled drearily and bleakly. For what, no one knew. I, least of all. But misery pressed crushingly on my chest.

The train was getting fed up waiting and everybody was pushing people on. Nobody was smiling much now. Some were having 'a good greet'. Ye felt so much better after, they always said. Then the piper suddenly changed his tune and the whole station roared so that you could hardly hear the engine as we started moving.

'For ah'm no' awa' tae bide awa',
Ah'm no' awa' tae leave ye.
Ah'm no' awa' tae bide awa',
Ah'll aye come back an' see ye.'

They were thumping the air with their fists and pounding out the words at the top of their voices. Defiant. Hopeful. Great stuff. Wha's like us. I huddled into a corner seat and listened to the pipes that played thinly in my head. They droned steadily, up and down, lamenting, and I tapped my foot in slow time, humming 'The Floo'ers o' the Forest are a' wede awa' '.

Part II   The Hostel

13 Dear Folks

I am waiting for Australia to enchant me. To distract me from the past. To become the hypnotic present.

Today I had my very first Australian cut. The first in the family. A sliver of raw steel was sticking out from the side supports of the gangway and it pricked me on the left calf as I put my right foot down on Terra Australis. Two gouts of blood blotched the concrete in tooth-edged circles before a path was found down my leg and into my sock. 'Take care,' my father warned, when I yelled 'Hey, look!' Cuts cannot be neglected here. The germs are ferocious in this water-sodden heat. I licked my finger and rubbed at the slit skin carelessly. What was the use of having a cut in Australia if it didn't develop its own unique characteristics? I would see how terrible the germs are.

Boys were punting a ball in a side street we passed on the way up from the ship. My father insisted they were ordinary kids like us, nothing special, and he wouldn't stop to stare. I wanted to see their faces close up and listen to their voices, but he loped away from us, bobbing up and down on what Mammy called his two left legs, opening and shutting them like scissors cutting up yard after yard of space. 'There's a train waiting,' he panted, when we grumbled in line behind him, straggling in and out like the tail of a kite.

He was wrong. The train had gone when we reached the station.

'Damnation. Two more hours.'

We consumed square pies with interest rather than hunger, prising open the lids and examining the gritty meat curiously.

'There's a lot o' empty space in here.'

'That's for people who're no' very hungry,' my father joked.

195

Bits of meat and gristle bloodied with red sauce began to dribble down best clothes.

'Christ, you eat like a pig. Here you, take him tae a bubbler and wipe that mess off his clothes.'

We couldn't find a bubbler in the Ladies' Waiting Room where eating food was strictly forbidden, but rows of wash basins with peeling taps and flaky porcelain were perched like cranes on single legs underneath dulled mirrors. Most extraordinary were the toilets with two bowls plonked side by side.

'This might be a toilet for twins,' Margaret suggested.

'Or best friends,' whispered hungry Susan who was always hiding at keyholes.

Margaret placed her two hands side by side between the bowls.

'Look at the wee space between them. Two fat women would be touching each other. Ugh.'

We looked at each other, horrified. Nae peace tae read a book, even.

Then, reluctantly, for we might need it again and would then have to pay another penny, we let the door slam and 'vacant' rushed round to shove 'engaged' into the lower half of the dial.

We wandered aimlessly over the station, stopping to read the headlines on the newspapers. The *Sydney Daily Telegraph*.

'Hey, look at that. You spell Sydney with a y not an i.'

Then we examined the yellow indicators above our heads, astonished at what we saw.

'They use other countries' names here: Newcastle, Hamilton, Toronto, Aberdeen, for goodness sake. Fancy using Scottish names.'

'Well, what about New South Wales?'

'Aye, and what if it had been called New West Scotland?'

Then we tried the Aboriginal names. 'What does "gatta" mean? This place is called Cool an gatta.'

'What's the opposite of Bulli?'

'Coweye, stupid.'

Robert, who was gazing around him, suddenly grabbed my father's arm.

'Hey, Da, there's an Aborigine!'

We all stared at the little dark man he was pointing to pushing an empty trolley. My father put down the paper he was reading (it was called the *Common Cause*) and glanced quickly at the little man.

'Don't go pointing at people like an ignoramus,' he snapped. 'And that man's no' an Aborigine. He's a Greek or an Italian. Jesus, did they no' teach ye anything at school, in geography?'

We played games in a frenzied squandering of time. Half an hour was spent, heedlessly running and taking wide stretched leaps over Susan's or Robert's bent back. But sometimes we ran, only to stop abruptly on the points of our shoes, pawing the air and holding in our stomachs to prevent a collision with a frozen-eyed man or woman whose sight was fixed on things inward.

My mother was fretful.

'Ye'll have tae stop playing leapfrog. Ye're getting in people's way and they're staring at us.'

And when we looked, so they were. Brown paper carrying bags lying on their ankles, or smallish suitcases with the corners pulled back and thick, ochre coloured cardboard exposed, clamped firmly between long, thin thighs and sharp chin. They were gaping at us. All along a red-brown seat. Sadie stuck her tongue out.

'Oh,' my mother said, affronted, and gave her a slap.

Waw—waw, and teeth grinding, ankles crossing and uncrossing, fingers beating restlessly and buttocks rotating on the hard wooden slats.

'Let's see who can spit the furthest.'

My mother jumped up from her seat and ran along the line, slap slapping, shake shaking.

'Ah've just about had you lot. Sit there and don't move a muscle or ah'll gie ye all a belting right here in front o' the world.'

Then only the eyes moved. Sliding sideways, crossing inwards, whirring round and round.

'Can you do it anti-clockwise?'

A sly look at my mother's tense face.

'Watch. Ah'm goin' tae pass mah hand over mah face and then ye'll see Dracula.'

'Och, that wasnae very scary. Ah can dae it better.'

My mother shut the *Readers' Digest* and glanced across at the waiting carrier bags and peeling suitcases.

'Christ, what are they doin' noo?' And she got up and hurried along to us.

'Dae ye have tae sit there making faces and makin' exhibitions o' yourselves? Look at these people watching ye.'

Susan sighed.

'Jings, ye cannae dae anything here except breathe.' Then she turned her head and looked across at the long seat opposite, carefully rolling her eyes and sticking her two eye teeth into her bottom lip.

My mother didn't see her. But the others did, and felt they had been avenged.

'Here, there's only twenty minutes left,' my father announced, standing up. 'The train'll be in. We can go and sit in it.'

It was leaving from platform 11. All stations to Gullawobblong.

'It's a slow train,' my father said.

And we all tried to push through the barrier at once.

'Christ, ah'm goin' tae kill that lot,' my mother swore.

In the train, however, she beamed happily when she came to inspect and found all the younger ones asleep, lying across each other like kittens.

'Thank God for that,' she said to Margaret and me. 'Ah can relax noo.'

And down the aisle she went to her own seat beside my father.

Though it was getting dark we could still see out of the window. Margaret had the window seat, so I watched from crab eyes the man sitting opposite us. He wore a cardigan and a hat. The skin on his face looked rough and tough and he had thin, drained lips. He sat with his knees spread open and his hands hanging between them, the fingers tapping each other restlessly. A few minutes after the train left the station he tapped his fingers together with a last flourish, one after the other as if he were running them down piano keys, and leaning forward, said:

'You kids mind if I smoke?'

Well, I nearly died. To ask us if we minded anything! The only time that was ever said to us was in the tone that meant quit it or I'll punch your nose. Do you *mind*, with a filthy look. Meaning, I blooming well mind what *you're* doing.

Margaret didn't hear him but I said:

'Good heavens, no.'

He dug around in the pocket of his cardigan and drew out a blue cellophane packet. I recognised it. It was a shag bag, and sure enough he opened it and took out a packet of cigarette papers. He tipped some shag along the fold of a smoothed-out paper, shaking it a bit to even it out, then he licked the edges of the paper and stuck them together. Some shag was hanging out both ends, so he nipped it off with his fingernails. They were black and long. Margaret had turned away from the window and was watching him the same as I was.

'Hey mister,' she said, embarrassing me and breaking the golden rule of silence with strangers, 'mah faither's got a wee machine for doin' that. It makes the cigarettes even all the way and they don't have wee bits hanging out the end.'

The man tugged at a few more threads of tobacco and lit the cigarette before he acknowledged the speech.

'Is that a fact?'

'My word.'

The man smiled with his eyes though the rest of his face was quite still.

'Well that sounds like a very fine machine. Very fine. But you see, I'm not all that keen on mass production. I like all my smokes to taste different, see. It's like having a cup of tea. Even with the same brand you can get a lot of different tastes. Depends on how you make it.'

We sat thinking. It made sense. Then the man spoke again. It was clear he felt comfortable with us now.

'Where are you kids going?'

'Gullawobblong.'

'Nice town. Lots of beaches. And steelworks for making money.' He flicked some ash on to the floor. Dirty thing. 'Poms, aren't you?'

What were Poms? Margaret never liked to show her ignorance.

'We're Protestants,' she said.

It was a useless attempt. I could see by the quick flicker of the man's lips that she'd said something stupid. He tried to cover it up.

'Then you're Protestant Poms.'

There was little point in going on with this game. It was like twenty questions. So I confessed that we weren't familiar with the word.

'Poms are short for Pommies. People from England.'

'From England or Britain?' I asked quickly.

He shrugged his shoulders and stared out of the window.

'What's it matter? They're all the same.'

Then he saw by my face I was annoyed and added:

'It's the English really. They're the Pommies.'

'Well,' I said, 'we're Scottish and there's a big difference, you know. But you haven't told us what Pommie means.'

He tapped his teeth with his long fingernail.

'I don't really know, kid. Something to do with their skins.'

'Is it good or bad?' I persisted.

He shook his head from left to right in a negative gesture.

'Bad. It means "I don't like you mate"!'

Then he changed the subject, wrenching it out of its ugly shape.

'What do you think of the bush?'

I felt anxious to please him somehow, so I looked along his wiggling fingers that pointed outside the window, and tried to single out particular leaves. It was impossible.

'Which one?'

'Which what?'

'Which bush?'

Oh dear. It was easier to talk broken English with Frank, the Italian fish shop owner. The man was exasperated. He made a queer sound in the back of his throat and withdrew into himself. His lids, drawing down over his eyes, said 'the end' and I folded my hands together on my lap, irritated because I didn't know what I'd done to be so annoying. From time to time I looked over at the man. A fine, dark glitter, sharp across his face, told me his eyes weren't perfectly shut. But he was sleeping, quietly soughing through his teeth. I nudged Margaret. She was dozing with her cheek on the hand that rested against the glass.

'That man,' I whispered, trying not to move my lips, 'that man is queer.'

She didn't answer.

We went into a tunnel that was longer than the others and fumes came rushing in through the open windows. I licked them off my mouth, trying not to breathe and then we were out again in the cold dusk, high above the sea, on the top of a scarp that was curving round like the bend in an elbow. Down below, tucked into the curve, was a tiny village. The sea was its boundary, like the stroke of the letter d. The few houses looked private and secure, propped up against the strong back wall. Quiet and cosy.

Then I felt fingers tapping on my knee. It was the man. He was leaning over to get my attention.

'It's the lot,' he said.

'The lot of what?'

'The lot—' he swung his arm widely this time. 'The grass, the trees, the ferns.' He swung again like a drunk man. 'Everything's the bush.'

'Och, is that what ye mean?'

He nodded deeply, pleased that I understood at last.

'Yeah, well what do you think?'

This time I did the shrugging. Grass and stuff. What could you say? We were going through a gorge now because the tops of the trees below the window looked like huge dark cauliflowers, and as I followed the growth up the slopes ahead the trees became a furry animal crawling on its belly.

'Everything seems to be coming or going,' I said, finally.

He sat up straight, his face watchful, and I sensed he was preparing to do battle for his bush. He was listening, not with interest but with ammunition.

'What do you mean?'

I swung my arm the way he had.

'The trees and the little bushes. They're all young, just growing, or they're all twisted, just dying. There don't seem to be any tall straight trees that are in the middle. Look at those,' I said, pointing. 'That tree's like an old hand springing out of the earth without a wrist, even. It hasn't got a proper trunk in the middle.'

'Maybe it's not a proper tree,' he argued craftily. 'It may be just scrub. But we've got mighty trees, you know. How do you think we get our telegraph poles?' he cried, delighted with his inspiration. There was nothing I could say to that. 'The bush', he went on like a salesman, as if he wanted me to buy it, 'goes on forever so that it never seems to move at all. All together, it is always there. Nobody saw its beginning, and it'll likely see our end. So you're wrong, you see. Got no understanding of it at all.'

And he sat back, satisfied. This time his lids dropped heavily, curtaining off his mind, There were to be no more encores. He was still sleeping when the train really stopped at Gullawob-blong. The other stops had only been pauses, but this was arrival.

Frowning, my mother swept the platform with her eyes. No one else had swept it, all day. Cold dry dust rushed up our noses making them twitch, jamming the narrow passages between our eyes. When you blew, nothing shifted and your head ached with the strain. Outside the station we huddled together eyeing the taxis, jealous of their warmth inside and hoping my father would see them. He wasn't looking at them.

'The Immigration Department said there'd be transport here,' he muttered, 'but it's probably gone, since we came on a later train.'

We were in a street shaped like a bottle opener, big and round at the station end with a narrow neck leading to another street which my father said was Gullawobblong. Some dark green buses were lined up behind a sign that said : Bus Stand Only. My father strode across to the front one, and called out to the driver who had a paper spread out across his steering wheel.

'Hey mac, do any of these buses go to Kershley Hostel?'

The bus driver just shook his head over the top of the paper.

'Shit,' said my mother. 'We'll have tae take a taxi. Here, Robert, go and ask how much it costs.'

The driver pushed his hat to the back of his head the way they do in F.B.I. pictures. The hat was an F.B.I. hat.

'Kershley Hostel, mate? That'll set you back about seventeen bob.'

My father scowled at him.

'That's a helluva lot, mate. It's in NSW, this hostel ah have in mind.'

The driver stared at my father without a word and then turned his head away.

'That's all ah've got,' my mother hissed under her breath. 'Have ye any money on ye?'

'A couple o' quid. The hostel'll feed ye till ah get paid next week.'

'Right, get in then,' my mother ordered us.

But the taxi driver had been watching us and he put his hand out arrestingly as I started to climb in, holding Anne.

'Sorry mate. You can't all fit in here.'

I ignored him and threw myself in, dropping Anne on the floor and falling on top of her.

'Aw come on Mister,' I said, trying to beg. 'They're mostly half sizes and we can sit them on our knees.'

We kept cramming in and cramming in. Sadie squeezed herself right under the driver's armpits and his arms were stretched up so that he had to rest them on the steering wheel. He was snorting and grumbling and then I heard the word the man had mentioned on the train.'

'Bloody Pommies.'

I was proud of my new knowledge and I rapped him on the neck.

'We're Scottish, mister,'

So he would know we knew. But he didn't like us just the same. You could tell. He drove angrily, pulling and hauling at the things in his car, bumping us up and down so we kept falling against each other and my father, after bouncing his head against the ceiling, cried:

'Take it easy, mac. Ye'd think ye were driving through paddocks.'

And up we went again. All in silence.

When we arrived at some lighted buildings miles and miles out in the country, the taxi stopped and we all clambered out. My mother counted the money and handed it to the driver.

'Thanks, laughing boy,' she said, 'ye'd be an ornament in any company.'

The driver grumbled something and slammed the door and my mother, in a rage, yelled at him:

'Aw, go and get stuffed!'

It's probably not a very nice thing to say, really, though the stuffed fox Archie had among his unredeemed pledges looked very lifelike, but my father gets boiling mad when my mother says it. Personally, I don't think it sounds nearly as bad as eff and see. Or even shit. It's not even a swear word. As soon as she said it my father dumped the bag he was carrying on the ground. It went squelch, and I realised that we were walking in some kind of a bog. Stuff was oozing into my socks.

'Look,' he bellowed, quietly, a lot of force but not much loudness. My father hates attracting attention. 'Look, is it necessary tae say that tae every stranger ye meet on the byways? Jesus, it sounds awful. Stick tae shit, will ye in future!'

'It's shit that sticks,' my mother said primly, but I could feel she was laughing. 'Och,' she spluttered, getting angry again, 'people like that gie me the jaundice. Goin' aroon as if they need a purge.'

We waited, at my father's admonition, while he squelched quickly towards the little building with the light. In a few minutes, the light came splashing the ground near our feet and we were beckoned over. He was with the manager of the hostel. Glad to meet you. Welcome to Australia. Hope you'll be happy here. You must be hungry. Fish and chips in the kitchen. Twice cooked, twice as tasty, eh? Stores first. Sheets, blankets, cutlery. Here, catch. Big family. Biggest we've had. We've allocated you a whole hut. Keys. I'll take you down and then you can eat. Sorry I've had to put you in with the Italians. British are at the other end. Just pile up the dishes in the sink. Breakfast starts at six. Goodnight. Goodnight. Goodnight.

14 Early Days

The sheets were freezing, but the camphor smell from the blankets loosened the tightness in my nose. It wasn't fair that I should have to be in here with my mother and the younger ones and Margaret in the other part with Susan and Robert and Sadie. They would have great fun. Their very own little house with its own keys. The sitting-room part was empty, that's true. They must have taken away the square table and the chairs my mother had in there, but just the same it was still their very own house. If they locked the door even my mother couldn't get in and if you could get your meals at the canteen then you hardly needed a mother. You could be completely independent. But:

'Aw no you don't,' she said when she saw me sneaking out. 'Ah want you in here tae help me keep an eye on these wee yins.'

And it would be worse when my father went back to his own hostel after tonight. I would have to sleep in the same room as her. You couldn't even turn round.

'Lie at peace,' she says.

You need to be in plaster of paris to please her.

Well, ah'm no' going tae sleep in the same room as her, ah don't care what. Anne can. My father's only going to come over at weekends. My mother's pretty mad about that but he says there isn't any bus from Kershley to the mine and he'd have to get up at four in the morning. I'm never going to heat up this bed. Every time I move, the sheet freezes me. It's so cold it feels wet and when I heat up a new bit, the old bit goes cold again. I'll have to lie like a dummy all night. There's a funny noise in here. I thought I heard it before but I wasn't sure.

I sat up in bed and concentrated on the noise. It was like a needle as fine as thread sewing loops and knots of high pitched screaming, drawing long strands away through the dark, then plunging down above my head, winding its shriek round and round in tightening circles. It was something alive. I climbed out of bed and patted the walls till I reached the light. The walls were cold and smooth like linoleum. When I put on the light, the sound switched off. Jackie and Robert were asleep with their arms thrown across each other. Even though I was cold, their faces were bubbled all over with sweat. I stood still, listening. Some tiny insects were flying about my face. Not vigorously the way flies or bluebottles do, but delicately, and out of them was spinning the faintest thread of sound. So they were it. Some alighted on the walls and as I pressed forward, stretching over the bed to have a closer look, I saw that the wall was in fact almost covered with them. On the other bed, Jackie snuffled and slapped his face and I saw an insect rise in the air above his head. Then I noticed one on his hand. I flicked it with my finger and when it danced away slapped it between my hands.

Then I went back to bed with the light on this time. The insects were pretty cunning because, except for the odd one, they didn't fly around much while the light was on. Then I had a thought and I sat up to have a look at the boys' bed. You wouldn't believe it but a few were hovering over their faces. So I jumped out of bed and tiptoed across and three were quietly feeding on Jackie's head. For some reason or other a line came into my head: sheep may safely graze. Well, these little black sheep would be grazing in an insect heaven in a minute. I flicked them lightly and caught them in my hand as they took off in fright, overloaded with cargo. After that I skulked around the room, getting the ones on the walls. The ones that hung around the light bulb were too inaccessible.

Once I had flattened all the ones I could see, I got into bed again and pulled the sheet over my head, tucking it in all round me.

My father's voice woke me in the morning. He sounded exasperated, which wasn't too common with him.

'What the hell's the matter wi' that yin?' he was grumbling. It was Margaret he was growling about. I could hear her shouting.

'Daaaaady! Daaaaady!'

She was shrieking like a scared rat. Ha! I was glad. Maybe

she'd do a swap with me. And I'd ask her while she was afraid.

My cardigan and skirt were lying across the bottom of the bed, so I grabbed them and hauled them on, buttoning up as I hurried through the little sitting-room that opened on to the path. Long, thick, spiky grass, two-edged, bushed out from under the hut like porcupine quills and overgrew half the path. Shorter, tougher stuff, fretted together, was elbowing the concrete slabs apart at their joins. I would have to watch out for the grass under the hut. Snakes could be hiding there. When I turned the corner, my legs streaked with wet, I nearly banged into my father who was up on his toes, trying to drag Margaret out of the window. She had pushed the small window up and out, but not far enough and was caught now between the frame and the sill, at her bottom. So more of her was out than in and she'd been hanging down, nearly bursting at the neck with the effort of holding her head up.

'What were you doing, you stupid?' I said into her upside down ear.

My father, grunting, had gripped her round the hips and was tugging. Finally her bottom came out with a rush and her legs, banging and clockering at the knees and the feet, tumbled after it. Standing on the ground, the right way up, she swayed a bit and shuddered.

'Ah couldnae come oot the door.'

She swiped her arm across her eyes and left two black smudges.

'The door was covered with mosquitoes and I was feart tae open it in case they attacked me. They can gie ye malaria and yellow fever.'

My father groaned. 'Christ, what a mentality!'

'Were there nane on your door?' Margaret asked me.

'Nope.'

Then I pointed to her arm. 'But I don't know why ye're making all that fuss. Ye're all bitten anyway. Look!'

Her arm was blotted with red bites, ugly like unripe boils. As soon as she saw them she started to scream and my father shook her hard.

'Don't be so damned stupid. There arenae any malarial mosquitoes here. Ye get them in the tropics. And no' even there very often since D.D.T. Ye can put some calamine lotion on them tae take away the itch and your mother'll buy citronella today at the wee shop.'

The others were all gathered round by now and Robert pushed forward, holding out his leg.

'Ah don't know what you're greeting for,' he said. 'Hae a look at mah ankle.'

There was an enormous lump just above his ankle bone. So much for my massacre.

'Aye well, c'mon then and we'll hae our breakfast,' my mother ordered us. 'Ah'll get some o' that stuff right after. And you,' she said to me, 'what's that on your leg?'

It was my cut. The slits had joined and there was now a dull red circle, yellowing in the middle.

'That's goin' tae fester, by the look o' it. Jesus, we're a' goin' tae be laid up wi' scabies if we're no' careful.'

Before long, hidden furnaces deep in our bodies began to throb and our skins made music that amazed us: zip-pop, zip-pop, before bursting open and throwing out blaringly red lumps of waste that burned slowly. The surrounding areas itched. In protest or sympathy? Who cared! We clawed at ourselves like madmen, with all the facility of rubber-limbed babies, but alone, in corners that we found away from our mother's irritated slaps and admonitions. Calamine lotion was cool. Also very costly to smear over seven blazing skins. Robert's lump and my festering cut raged in competition with each other and we both felt sick.

'What a mess ye are,' my mother sighed. 'If ye don't clear up soon ah'll have tae call a doctor. And nae National Health Service here, ah've been told.'

'It's no' clearing up, Mammy,' Robert announced one morning. 'Here's another lump noo.'

It was like an egg. In his groin.

'Ye'll have tae get the doctor straight away, Mammy,' I said. 'That's a bubo.'

'What the hell's that?'

'It's a lump ye get under your arms or in your groin when ye've got bubonic plague.'

My mother clapped her hands to her head and yanked at her hair.

'That's a' we need. Bubonic plague. Ye great blethering dolt, there hasnae been any bubonic plague for centuries!'

Actually, I couldn't remember if the plague lump was black or not, or if the bodies just turned black when they died.

'Oh well,' I said, reconsidering. 'Maybe it isnae that. We havenae seen any rats here, anyway, tae carry it.'

The doctor from Eugoberra, four miles away, was quite firm that Robert wasn't suffering from bubonic plague. He was suffering from blood poisoning, however, derived from a septic mosquito bite.

'And you've got a beaut ulcer there,' he told me, after examining my leg.

My mother leaned over him suspiciously. He was just out of medical school, she informed my father when he came at the weekend. But he had red hair and she favoured him for this. Injections for both of us, and Robert's lump would have to be removed.

'And what aboot a' the rest,' my mother asked, waving her arms over our scabby skins.

Boils, hives and prickly heat rash, probably aggravated by a change in diet. More injections, tablets and calamine lotion.

'It's a pity this stuff's pink,' said Margaret, shaking the bottle. 'If it were blue, we could pretend tae be Picts covered in woad.'

Robert's lump and my ulcer left scars. After that, all cuts were immediately doused with antiseptic. In Scotland, when my ankle had been gashed on an iron spike, soap and water was brought forth as treatment and the germs succumbed without a struggle. But truly, these Australian germs were a hardier breed.

Very smartly we noticed through open doors that a bright green cylinder with a black handle was a necessary ornament in the huts. This was the spray gun. It contained the D.D.T. to kill the mosquitoes. Push in the plunger, and pull it out and great clouds of choking drops stuck to the walls and light bulbs. Then you had the choice of sleeping with all the doors and windows shut, or of opening the windows and sleeping under the sheet with an air tube.

When we got a radio and heard the pest killer song I was really astonished to find that the mosquito was utterly ignored.

'How can you be sure there are no white ants in the door,
Borers in the floor,
Silver fish galore,
Get a Flick, man, that's your answer.
One Flick, and they're gone!'

'How come,' I asked my father, 'they don't mention the mosquito?'

'You're helluva soft,' he said, not answering the question.

'Well—why don't they?'

'First,' my father said, 'they cannae kill all the mosquitoes in a house for any length of time, and second, the mosquito doesnae really attack property. But anything that goes for property, you can bet your sweet life they'll have a cure for that. People don't matter.'

'Aw, here it comes, here it comes,' my mother cried. 'He's getting on his soap box again. My God, the ingenuity o' that man when it comes tae pluggin' Communism wouldnae be believed. If ye asked him the time o' day, he'd wangle it intae an attack on capitalism.'

My father raised his eyebrows to heaven and then gave my mother a grim look.

'You're the one that mentioned Communism. Ah havenae said a word aboot it.'

'Aw, don't think ah don't know the signs,' my mother jeered.

I got my towel and rushed out to have a shower. Fancy that, even talking about mosquitoes and it became a political brawl. As usual there was no one in the women's toilet block when I went in. We were in a section of the hostel that housed seventy Italians, all single men, and only my family seemed to use the women's part of the showers, though Margaret said she'd seen women coming out of it once or twice. The men's and women's facilities were back to back. I preferred to have my shower in the daytime because at night you couldn't dry yourself and fend off the mosquitoes as well. As I turned on the hot tap, I heard water running on the other side of the wall. Someone was having a shower there. Crikey, what if he could see me through the wall? What if I could see him? How embarrassing! Then the man started to sing. It was a foreign language, not French or German, so probably Italian. He had a deep voice and the song sounded very miserable. I wondered what the sadness was for. The end of love? Ae fond kiss, and then we sever. The doleful lament of the exile? And it's ooooh, but I'm longing for my aaain folk! Or was it that unspeakable, anonymous misery that slinks out of some monstrous subterranean receptacle of the world's griefs and folds itself about you, crushing your chest in panic and making madness in your mind? I wished he would shut up.

210

He was singing more quietly now, in a low, absent-minded monotone almost indistinguishable from the water gurgling down the drain. Then his shower went off. He started humming. It sounded angry, and shortly, out of the anger, words came forth again, pleading, indignant, pleading, declamatory, pleading, demanding and finally enraged, bursting out with a great roar of huge fists beating on the wall, or so it seemed. Good gracious! After the roar, a long, contorted cry, that went on and on getting more and more knotted before a final twist snapped it right off. Pow! The silence took my breath away. Hurrah. Hurrah! I stared in amazement at my hands that were clapping noisily and listened in disbelief to my voice shouting 'bravo', a word I had never pronounced aloud in my life.

Good heavens! What if he came rushing in to see who was being cheeky? I grabbed my clothes and leapt into a toilet where I hid for ages, holding the door shut, till I was sure the man must have gone. Afterwards, I peered round the corner of the main door but not a soul was on the path. So I raced back to our hut.

'Hey, there was a man singing in the shower today,' I told Margaret that night. 'He had a beautiful voice. He was singing something sad.'

'Aye, ah've heard somebody there, too,' Margaret said. She had taken her chair from the bedroom and was sitting astride it, staring out of the window. 'Ah wonder who it is? Do you know, more women go past this window than men. Ah've counted them. Ah was sorting them out. Five fat ones, two normal, only one pretty. Where do you think they go? This isnae the main path tae the village.'

'Probably to the laundry.'

'Well, they werenae carrying their washing.'

'No? Well . . . tomorrow, Mammy's going tae start us at school. You and Robert and Susan and Sadie will have to go to Eugoberra. Walking. Do ye know where it is? Over that great hill behind us. Mammy says it's about a four mile walk. There's nae bus to it because the bus that comes in the morning caters for shoppers and it's too late for primary kids. The factory people have tae walk as well. They leave early, too.'

'Och, ah don't care,' Margaret said, making a *moué* of indifference. 'There are cows and things and great big cactus. Daddy said ye can find huge lizards among these cactus. What makes me mad,' she growled, 'is having tae go back to primary again. Ah would've gone tae Bellahouston in September. It's no' fair.'

'It's because they have their summer holidays at Christmas; December's the end of the school year.'

Margaret brightened up at this.

'Och, well, it'll only be for a wee while then. And then we'll have another lot o' holidays.'

'They'll have tae be late the first day,' my mother said next morning, 'ah'm damned if ah'm walking over that hill in this heat. An' there are breaks in the fence along the road, Ah've seen cows wandering up an' doon.'

She looked them over quickly.

'Have ye a' got your cribs?'

They were all clutching the brown paper bags with their names and orders written on in indelible pencil: one peanut butter, one cheese, on Robert's. And everybody got a slice of cake and a piece of fruit.

'Ah wish we could have a crib for breakfast and tea as well,' Susan said, her eyes and lips narrow with annoyance. 'It's better than that other stuff they gie ye. Nae wonder we're a' scabby.'

My mother was checking her bag for her precious cigarettes. Thank goodness you could get any amount of Woodbines here.

'Listen, Lady Muck,' she said, 'if ye have nae worse tae eat before ye're dead ye can count yourself damn lucky. Noo get moving.'

'Aye,' I put in. 'Ye'd be glad o' it if ye'd been living in a concentration camp.'

My mother got annoyed at that.

'You've got concentration camps on the brain. Life's no' a preparation for living in one, ye know. But anyway, the food's no' much good because it has tae be made in bulk.'

She turned round again as she was moving out the door.

'How'd ye like tae earn a couple o' bob, hen? When your Da gets paid.'

I stared at her suspiciously.

'What for?'

'Daein' mah washin'. There's a good kid.'

My mother made me squirm when she was trying to be ingratiating. I would rather she had belted me. But I agreed, anyhow; the washing hadn't been touched at the weekend as my mother wanted to spend the time with my father. She gave me a long list of instructions: least dirty, first washed, no whites and coloureds together. Noo, mind the rinsing. That's more important than the washing. Ah don't want to be affronted wi' a grey wash hanging on the line. Aye Mammy. Aye. Aye, ah'll remember. What a relief when she'd gone.

She was home again when I finally left the laundry, too tired, she said, to go back into Gullawobblong on the afternoon bus, so we would go to the High School in the morning. After lunch I went for a walk around the hostel, just following the paths up and down. If there were any hut doors open and nobody to see me I looked inside. Some people had bright rugs on their walls instead of the floors and chintz curtains on the little high windows, the ones fixed into the curved sides of the hut. The big windows in the end walls usually had white curtains that you could see through. Net or nylon. Sometimes there were little plaster statues on top of the lockers. Catholics. If you drew your finger across the corrugated iron wall it made a noise like thunder. Once I did this and a man bounced out into his doorway and glared at me.

'Oh, I'm very sorry, mister, I wasn't thinking what I was doing.'

'Too noisee,' he said, wagging his finger at me.

I passed another doorway where a huge man was standing quietly, sniffing the air, almost. He was much taller than my father and heavier, with a massive head shaved like a brainy scientist's. I could feel him looking at me as I went past and I kept my eyes down, getting ready to turn right at the next space between the huts. Then a whistle blew, almost in my head. I leapt a foot into the air and turned round. It was him, the brainy scientist. He blew again, twice, on the whistle and waited, his lips pressed together impatiently. Feet were coming, from further up the hostel, near the swings, and two boys appeared, rushing along the path, one trying to get in front of the other. I jumped out of their way and watched.

'*Ja, Papa,*' the bigger one panted. '*Was ist?*'

Blooming Germans. The place was full of them. And blowing for their kids with a whistle! Like a dog.

Forward and to the right the British lived, so I wandered up that way and who should be coming out of her door but a Scotswoman whom I had met in the laundry.

'Oh, hullo,' she said, beaming at me in recognition. 'I thought

I might run into you again. Listen, you couldn't hold the baby a minute, could you, till I fix the pram?'

She had a little kid by the finger and this baby under her arm. I took the baby and had a squizz around her sitting-room while she was punching the mattress and the pillow.

'Is that Quo Vadis you've got there?' I asked, seeing the book among some others on top of a locker.

She lifted the baby out of my arms. It was a beautiful little girl with white blonde hair and brown eyes.

'Thank you. I'll put her in now. Yes, it is. Have you read it?'

'No.' I hesitated. Should I be pushy? 'But I would like to.'

'Take it then, if you like. Here, I'll get it.'

She crossed the tiny floor and drew the book out, pushing the piece of brick that acted as a book-end, to close the gap.

'There you are. Do you like reading?'

'Yes I do, a bit.'

'Well, I've only got a few books here, but you're welcome to any you'd like to borrow,' she said, generously. 'And there's a bookmobile comes to the hostel every week, from the town library. You can borrow from that.'

'That's great,' I said, 'but I'll be going to school soon, so I won't be here in the daytime.'

'Oh well, that's no problem. You can join the library in Gullawobblong. I suppose you're going to high school?'

'Yes, tomorrow I'm starting.'

She wanted to know how old I was, and where I came from.

'I'm from Airdrie. Have you been there?'

I hadn't, but I'd heard of it. Of Airdrie Academy, anyway.

'That's my old school,' she said.

It was time to go. She was going for a walk down the lake. Did I want to come? No, I would go back to my hut and read.

I went into Margaret's part of the hut so that my mother wouldn't know I was back.

By the time the others came back from school I'd had a good read. Margaret's face was nearly purple and her hair was drenched with sweat.

'Boy, what a walk.' She bounced onto the bed and threw herself across it like a sacrifice, staring up at the ceiling.

'Ah'm jiggered. These blooming flies. Dae ye know, they bite. They stick tae ye and bite ye. Ah didnae know flies had teeth. And they go intae the corners o' yer eyes and burrow into them. You have tae dig them oot, practically. And you should see the big lizards. Faither was right. They've got tongues that go inanoot like snakes. And guess what. We saw a snake. A real one, right across the road, puffing its head up like a cobra.'

'Och, stop havering,' I said, scornfully. 'Ye don't get cobras in Australia.'

'I know that, smarty. It was a copperhead, see. This taxi driver stopped and told us. He told us to get moving and quit looking at it. It's very poisonous.'

Thank God I wouldn't have to walk across that hill. I couldn't, with all these cows and snakes and flies with teeth.

'What was the school like?'

Margaret rolled herself over and sat up.

'Ah've got tae get these shoes and socks off. A lot o' kids wear bare feet. That's what ah'm goin' tae dae. It's a dump. One brick building and a few shacks wi' verandahs ootside. And the grass is that long stuff wi' the sticky bits that gie ye sores. Nae shade hardly. They havenae got a hall or anything, for P.T. or a swimming pool like Lorne Street. And we had tae queue up right in the sun for ages. And the milk was sour.'

'What did ye dae in class?'

'Nothing, hardly. They gie'd me some fractions and spelling. But ah'd done the fractions in Lorne Street and ah got the spelling right. So they told me to sit oot on the verandah and help some kids wi' their spelling. Aye, and they sent me messages. Across the street tae get the teacher's lunch.'

She eyed me suspiciously, suddenly.

'How come you're home. Did ye go tae school?'

When I'd explained what had happened and told her about the man who whistled up his kids, she picked up her towel from the back of a chair:

'Ah'm goin' tae have a shower and then some kids asked me tae go tae the lake wi' them. They say it's great for swimming in.'

'Don't tell Mammy I'm in here, will you?' I said. 'I want tae finish this book.'

She took it out of my hands and read the title.

'Where did ye get it?'

'From a Scotswoman I met in the laundry. Ah don't know her name.'

We opened the book at the first page and her name was written there. Isabelle Budinsky. A funny name for a Scot. Her husband must be a foreigner, we decided. I would ask her next time.

15   Getting to Know You

Next morning the others left early to walk over the hill and my mother and I caught the bus into Gullawobblong. The bus was a single-decker, bright red and blue like a toy out of a fairy story, and the bus driver, shining brightly with cleanliness and bonhomie, beamed upon each passenger who proffered a fare, uttering what was almost a benediction, his gleaming oiled hair and snow white side parting a manifestation of an uncluttered and readily coherent world. His wide open smile was an act of faith and assurance.

'G'day all you lovely lasses! Off to school again? Lucky teachers.'

He was nodding and kissing his hand to the girls who were climbing on ahead of us. There were about eight of them and a few boys, and they all rushed down to the back seats.

'Keep it clean down there,' he called to them over his shoulder. He recognised my mother.

'Another one for Eugoberra?'

'No, this one's going to the High School.'

He winked at me as I passed him.

'Do you belong to Glasgow?'

'I lived there,' I said.

We were last on and had to stand. The bus was full. When it had left the hostel and was raising soupy whirlpools of apricot dust on the Kershley Road, the bus driver glittered in his mirror and sang out:

'Right, you kids. Away we go. One two, three. Eins, zwei, drei.'

Giggles spurted and tickled in the back corner, and voices hissed and hushed. There was singing, a curious blend of light and dark, issuing from the giggles like carelessly thrown streamers of sound tossed into all the dusty corners of the bus and the bus driver, his teeth white with commendation, sat enchanted wearing a wreath of music, as gay as a crazy carillon. His bright red-blue bus lurched into the brittle pot holes, bouncing out of them again with a syncopated shrug so that we who were swinging from the silver pipe shook and shimmied in a fervour of rhythm, and rounding the corners the engine boomed like a tuba.

'Give it big licks!' the driver yelled, waving to someone gaping on the road.

If only I could sing too, I thought. But the songs were Dutch, my mother told me.

We passed through Eugoberra and my mother and I squeezed further up the aisle to make room for a fat woman with a basket that jabbed you with a broken cane.

'G'die, Ron.' She knew the bus driver very well.

'G'day, Goldilocks.'

Her hair was what my mother called 'brassy', the effect you got when you did it with a toothbrush dipped in peroxide. She curled her fingers around the steel and I stared right into her armpit. Oily bubbles of perspiration balanced on the ends of the bristles that sprang from her skin.

'Hot today, isn't it?' she remarked, trickling slowly.

My mother glanced at her, surprised. Was she speaking to us?

'Bit too hot for all that racket at the back, eh? Give you a headache. Always singing, these New Australian kids.'

The singing had toned down now. Two or three girls were kneeling on the back seat, waving at the driver of the bus behind. The buses were moving in convoy that grew bigger as we passed each new suburb where we picked up an additional driver and his load. All the drivers waved to each other and played some heavy game of touch, racing to be first at a stop so that they could pass it and leave the waiting queue for the bus behind. At the next stop, however, it was the laggard's turn to rush past hooting the klaxon, for the leader seemed to be morally obliged to pick up alternate loads. Or maybe the bus driver had to show a certain amount of money for the trip. And so they played this sliding and stopping to the cheers of the schoolkids who had gruesome faces saved up for jeering when their bus was taking the lead. I had never thought of bus drivers playing games.

'Hey, they're singing "The Happy Wanderer" now,' I whispered to my mother. Two girls were still active. Their sounds were unusual, strangely gritty and scraping, loosely filtered through husky voices that merged imperceptibly with each other in some kind of tonal rainbow.

'Think they were men, these girls, the way they sing.'

It was Goldilocks. She gave them cutting looks and shook impatiently the orange currants dangling from her ear. Orange grapes trailed around her neck. It was clear she intended no one to confuse her with a man.

When they began to sing 'valderee, valderaa', a new voice joined in, light and sweet.

'That should please her,' I said to my mother. 'Hasn't that girl got a lovely voice?'

'Aye. She's nice looking too, wi' that curly hair and fresh complexion.'

The bus went on for ages and ages. We rode up the middle of the remaining suburbs of Gullawobblong, for most of the houses and shops crouched along both edges of the highway, their tired gardens linked and roofs almost pressed together. In one garden, a woman, longboned and thin armed, held a drooping hose over dusty geraniums. Sloping banks from time to time obscured bushes tangled together like barbed wire and the camber dipped into high sharp tussocks, rank in patches where water was seeping up from broken pipes. Another suburb. I knew them now as we came to them, by the chemist shop, the milk bar and green-grocer and by the few streets that strayed timidly away from the highway into the unknown. Fields of cows. At last the hospital, that signalled the beginning of Gullawobblong proper and its main street, Bradman Avenue, whose eighth and last block was cut off from Chile by the Pacific Ocean, sprawled across the bus station.

We got off before the bus station, at the biggest intersection.

'They need lights here,' my mother grumbled, waiting for a break in the traffic. 'Fancy having nae traffic lights in a place wi' nearly a hundred thousand people.'

The school was at the top of Chifley Street, second in importance after Bradman Avenue. Two of its blocks, one on each side of the main street, had shops and it was the only secondary street with a big department store. It was also the site of two of Gullawobblong's three cinemas. Once you passed that first block, however, you were already among houses, mostly of dried weatherboard and all of them with front verandahs laid out over

218

little piles of bricks. Some of the verandahs were crumbling at the rims and choking tufts of grass clutched at the low foundations, boldly defying the blind thrusts of the lawn mower. We dawdled past an old lady sitting like stone in a cane chair, her knitting lying neglected in the sagging basin of her apron. Just beyond her house was the latticed wire fence that bounded the paddocks of the school. The gate whined as my mother pushed it, panting slightly, and we examined in silence the short scrubby grass on both sides of the path. Out of this rose long, tubular stems, bent down at the ends with the weight of sticky seeds.

'That's the grass that gie's ye the sores,' my mother said, frowning. 'What's its name, again?'

'Paspalum.'

'These wooden classrooms are the same as the ones at the primary school. They're very open-airish. Can ye see if they've got glass in the windows?'

'Aye, at the top, Mammy. The windows are pushed right up to let the air in.'

A boy, his face expressionless, glanced at us from his seat next to the window. Maybe he was trying to learn something and really didn't see us. There was a murmur of talk in the classroom and I saw two girls with their heads sloping into each other.

A two-storey building appeared just beyond the wooden structures.

'That must be the main building. The headmaster should be in there somewhere.'

He was sitting behind a big desk looking very old and empty. His eyes seemed drained of colour and glow. The tight raw red of his face spread beyond the roots of his woolly white hair. When he spoke we leaned forward and watched his lips, but we could still hardly hear him. His strange immobility made me feel as if I were petrifying little by crunch, and I sat rigidly with my hands motionless on my knees.

'Well, you're lucky today, because the counsellor just happens to be here. He generally has a few tests in his office, so if you take your daughter along to him it'll save you going down to the Education Department.'

He got up, stiffly, holding to his chair for a moment.

'I'll show you to his office.'

He took tiny, stilted steps as if his toes were nibbling at the

219

floor and we tottered behind him, in reluctant imitation. There were stairs to climb, drearily, holding your breath and your leg up over each step. I felt as old as my grandmother. At the top, the headmaster rested, leaning against the wall. The red of his face was purpling. We waited outside the counsellor's office while he was inside, explaining. It would be dark before he finished. But in a few minutes he was back in the doorway, propped against the jamb. Behind him a huge man with a yard of waist smiled and beckoned to us.

'G'day. Come in, will you please.'

Sitting opposite him, I noticed he too had the red in his face but it didn't reach his hairline yet.

'Well, we'll have to give Mary a test, Mrs Lavery [pronouncing it like slavery made me jump, slightly] to see if she'll be happy with us here. This is a highly selective school, you see, and it is possible that she might be better suited to the Home Science school in the next street.'

Home Science, for God's sake! I hated cooking and sewing.

'You've got her report there, from Glasgow,' my mother said, giving him the Gorgon stare.

'Ye-e-es.'

'And this test—when does she sit it?'

He waved his arms expansively. His shirt was tight around his neck.

'Now, if you like. Otherwise you'd have to bring her down to the Department's offices.'

It was one of those tests that we were always doing. Pig, cow, sheep, tiger. Who's the outsider? When I'd finished, he took the booklet into his office and we sat on chairs outside. It was like being at the doctor's. Cripes, if I had to do sewing and cooking I would plunk school every day.

'What if ah'm no' good enough, Mammy?' I whispered.

My mother snorted and scowled. 'Don't be bloody daft. Ye don't think they're a' Einsteins in a wee place like this. An' this school's no' Bellahouston. Jesus, it's like something oot o' the Wild West. Ye wouldnae piss on it if it were on fire.'

'But a school like Bella would look queer here, Mammy. Ah don't think those dark grey stony buildings would fit in wi' the sunlight.'

'Aye, well, maybe so. But a few more bricks wouldnae go

amiss. The buildings are too temporary looking. They don't gie ye confidence.'

Suddenly, the counsellor was there among us, looking down over his waist. He was smiling heartily, sort of, and spoke briskly, just the way doctors do when they're telling you the results of your X-ray.

'Well, no problems that I can see. We'll be delighted to have your daughter with us. The only thing is,' he added, as my mother got up to leave, 'Latin is studied here. We don't offer German, though it may come in one day. So Mary will have to take Business Principles and book-keeping. That'll be in one bee. She can go into first year again for the few weeks left. So you can come tomorrow, Mary,' he said to me. 'Fairfields' stock our uniform.'

When we were back in Chifley Street, I exhaled loudly, with relief.

'Thank goodness for that!'

My mother was angry, however.

'Did ye ever see such a condescending get! Thought he was doing us a favour. He read that report from Bellahouston, wi' your results in it, but he was trying to make oot that their Wild West school has got a higher standard. You make sure you get stuck intae the work here.'

I didn't listen to her mutterings all the way to Bradman Avenue. He could be as condescending as he liked so long as I didn't have to do cooking and sewing. No German. Well, that was a pity. You couldn't be a spy with only French. I would have to teach myself.

At Fairfields' my mother bought me the tunic and blouse. I would have to wait for shoes. Blast! That meant wearing my ghastly wedge-heeled sandals with the peep toe. They would look stupid with socks, and powder blue, of all colours! It would clash with the tunic. This was quite pretty, sleeveless with a round neck and a gored skirt. A belt fitted around the waist. It looked fresh and I felt excited to be wearing it. Pity about the shoes.

The next morning when I arrived at the bus stop, a long queue was already waiting. Everybody must be going to town to shop. The girls and boys who had been singing were grouped together, talking loudly and laughing. The one with the curly

221

hair who had the distinctive light voice noticed me suddenly and hurried across the grass.

'Hullo,' she said. 'You're Scottish. So am I.'

'Gosh, are ye!' I was delighted. 'How did ye know ah'm Scottish? Ah thought you were Dutch. Ye were singing on the bus wi' these Dutch kids.'

'Aye, ah ken,' she said, grinning. 'Ah don't know their songs but if they sing one we know in English, ah just join in the tune.' Then, in answer to my question:

'Ah heard ye last night in the canteen, talking tae another lassie. Was she your sister?'

'Did she have a blue checked dress on?'

'Aye, that's the one.'

'She's mah sister Margaret. She goes to Eugoberra over the hill.'

The girl glanced at my tunic.

'You're going tae the High School, aren't ye?'

She smoothed her jumper and kilt. I hadn't noticed it straight away.

'What clan are ye?'

'Buchanan tartan. Mah mother's family. But mah name's Harvey. Georgina Harvey. What's yours?'

I told her. She went to the High School too, but she was going to leave in a few months when she was fifteen.

'Are ye no' going tae stay on, then?' I was disappointed. 'Dae ye no' like school?'

She wrapped her arms round herself and swung back and forwards on her heels.

'Well ah did, in Edinburgh. Ah thought ah would like tae be a gym teacher. But—it's different here, ye ken. The folk are nice enough—naebody's nasty tae ye or anything like that. It's hard tae explain, but ye can feel something.' She took hold of my arm. 'Here, c'mon and ah'll introduce ye tae the gang afore the bus comes.'

The Dutch girls gathered round me and patted me on the shoulders.

'You very lucky girl.' The one who spoke had blonde crinkly hair and glasses thicker than mine. She peered into my face, smiling at me. 'You speak English. Oh, very difficult for us.' Then she grabbed my hand and squeezed it between hers. 'You teach us English tonight when we play ping-pong. Okay?'

They were crowding around me, the Dutch girls, like an embrace, touching me lightly with friendly and possessive fingers. Through the narrow gaps between their faces, I saw the frail contorted trees whose skinny wizened branches, starved for water, swayed like tentacles over the sharp yellow grasses, and for a dizzy moment I was a primeval ape, home with the tribe at last, though he hadn't known he'd been away. Strange, indistinct images jostled my senses, struggling to be loosed from oblivion and I held my breath to widen the crack in time, for something exciting and essential to my existence was demanding recognition.

'Okay?' she repeated.

There, it was gone from me, drawn away down into the darkness, driven off by the merciless all-prying light and the loud laughter, and the blustering ragings of the bus that was roaring, late and huffily defensive, along the road towards us. We got on the bus together, Georgina, the Dutch girls and I, rubbing skins and smiling, before settling on the back seat in a euphoria of affection. The bus driver today was different, grim like the taxi man. They sang just the same, and I sat, quietly happy, intent on recalling that pungent second of belonging.

We all got off at the stop nearest Chifley Street and split up. The Dutch girls, less brash now that they had alighted from the bus, and were being bunted around on the crowded pavement, shuffled off in a protective huddle, making for the Domestic Science School. All the foreign children went there, or to the Technical High, if they were boys.

'Ye'll have tae hurry,' Georgina urged me. 'That blooming bus gets you in so late, everybody's lined up when we come in. They a' stare at ye, and it's real embarrassing.'

The whole school was arranged in alternating files of boys and girls. They stood facing the main building and the old headmaster, who was supporting himself on the railing of the wooden platform from which he was addressing the school. Obviously he was saying something since it was inconceivable that he and the school should merely be staring at one another, but not a word of it reached my ears. Eventually he began to creep down the stairs leading from the platform and the lines moved off, to the right, to the left, up and down, radiating in all directions like the spokes of a wheel.

This dreary beginning at Gullawobblong High, and the

223

situations I encountered that day, the problems inherent in them, set me to the task of evolving a whole set of new responses in the search for which I was forced to ask myself, what will I be? whereas those around me kept quizzing, what will you do when you leave school?

First, there was the confrontation with a new kind of dialogue.

'Sorry about interrupting you, Mrs Mahon,' the Deputy said, drawing me behind him into the classroom. 'I've got a new wee girlie for you. A lass from Glasgow.' He turned to the faces above the desks. 'Good morning, one bee.'

His name, it seemed, was Mr Whittle, and the name must be used when saluting him. Miss and Sir were no longer acceptable titles. If you said: excuse me, Miss, you would hear giggles and if the lady were married she would react indignantly: MRS Brown, if you please.

'This is Mary Lavery. She's from Scotland.' Evidently he felt it necessary to locate Glasgow. 'She's probably feeling very strange.' This was an effort of imagination I wasn't often to encounter at school. The Deputy squeezed my arm. 'How long have you been out, lass?'

'A week, sir.'

'Uh huh. Well, you'll find this class a particularly nice lot of boys and girls who'll be only too pleased to help you settle in. You'll be an Aussie before you can say Robert Burns.' This statement contained a number of horrific assumptions that weren't immediately apparent to me, though it didn't take too long to work them out.

First, niceness is a virtue preceding all others. To be nice is better than being stimulating, or analytical, or witty. You must always say 'How are you', or 'how are you going,' nicely, but without expecting an answer. If some fool starts to tell you how he is, keep smiling but walk off and leave him with his jaw dropping, or keep smiling and stare at his right ear lobe. Then he will dry up and smile nicely, asking you how you are.

Second, people always want to settle, like old hulks settling into the mud. People don't crave drama or excitement or un-certainty. Make sure they set hard.

Third, people always want to be Australian.

If you aren't you can get by with a particular note of apology. 'I'm not yet, but I'm doing my best.'

The Deputy, his warm welcome at an end, spied me out a seat and directed me to it.

'There you are. There's a seat beside Wendy. She's a bit of a yakker, so don't let yourself be tempted.'

The girl he was portraying giggled and cooed:

'Oh, Mr Whittle, that's defamation of character. I'm as dumb as a mummy.'

All the class laughed at this, and the Deputy smiled benignly.

'Well, there's someone awfully like you, sitting in your seat, who never takes a breath.'

He looked across at the teacher, for support.

'Isn't that right, Mrs Mahon?'

It was, evidently. I sat down amid the confusion of laughter and noisy chat that erupted suddenly in the room, and the Deputy left. Another rule: seek out humour in the banal or you will be isolated from the fellowship of laughter.

'That will do, one bee.' The teacher was tightening her mouth. Little lines sprouted from her top lip. The Deputy had gone, leaving not one reverberation of his wit. 'We must get this prose finished or there will be no time for revision before the exams.'

During the lesson, Wendy began a non-stop monologue to which I responded with nods of the head. So you're Scottish. I'm English, from Kent. We came out in 1950. Have you done French? She's a real drip, Mrs Mahon. Always tired. All the teachers are, except Mr Whittle. He teaches maths. I'm going to a private school next year. Mum and Dad think this school's too rough. We have sport every Wednesday. That's today. It's compulsory. Do you like sport? You can choose between swimming, softball and tennis. I play tennis. Of course you wouldn't have your costume here. Swimmers, the Australians call them. So you'll probably have to play softball. How did you do at school in Scotland? Are you any good at French?

I was trying to remember the word for mourning. I'd seen it somewhere.

'Oh, all right,' I whispered. Was she never going to shut up? *Le deuil*, that was it. This passage was from *Jean Christophe*.

'Right, class, get on with it.' Mrs Mahon dropped her chalk into the groove under the board and moved sideways to her desk. 'If you don't get it finished before the bell goes, you can finish it for homework.'

'Aw geez, you're tough,' someone groaned.

Colloquial language and familiarity of tone are permissible when speaking to the teacher. A formal mode of approach will only make him ill at ease and he will avoid your eye. He might even think you are being insolent. You are not to exalt him. He doesn't think he is worth it. To obey him will be enough. It will establish the difference between you.

I couldn't remember the French for some words, so I left blanks and concentrated on the verb endings. When I lifted my head, I saw the teacher watching me. Blast. I've caught her eye. Now she's coming to examine my work. She's got a queer hair style. Flat to the head. I really hate that, especially when it's grey. Dreary. And those loose little curls all round the bottom. Pin curls, not very well formed, and straight bits poking out. Wonder why she wears such a low-necked dress when her skin's all shrivelled at the front?

The teacher wrote in the missing words for me and dangled her pen above each verb like a divining rod, seeking out the wrong inflections. Apparently satisfied there were none, she ticked the passage and initialled it. Then, in an embarrassingly loud voice that got the attention of the class, she said: 'Very good, girlie. I can see we won't have any problems with you.'

You don't see much then, do you?

Wendy stiffened beside me. Her whisper, despite its softness, was faintly disapproving.

'Are you a brain or something?'

It sounded like: Are you a Catholic?

Careful. 'Heavens, no. I've read some of the book that passage is from.'

'What! In French?'

Her whisper vanished in a squeak.

'Well, actually, our teacher read it to us.'

How is she taking it?

'Aw, you were lucky, then?'

Ah that was it. Luck, luck. I grinned with relief. 'Yes, I was, wasn't I?'

The bell drilled and Mrs Mahon wiped the chalk from her red and white striped dress with the square neck.

'Don't forget tomorrow's homework from Jones's *Grammar*,' she murmured, going out.

Nobody was listening. The hubbub was deafening, but there

were silent ones who stared at me curiously till they drew my own gaze, when their heads flicked down or round, guiltily. Watch those direct looks. They may be interpreted as acts of aggression.

I wanted a plain pin to fasten the top sheets of my writing pad together. They'd come loose.

'Excuse me.' I prodded Wendy in the back. She was leaning across the aisle giggling with a boy called Butch. 'Have you a spare pin, please?'

She twisted her neck around and spoke to me over her shoulder.

'Well, I've only got the one I use myself, but you can borrow it for a minute.' She reached over and picking her pen up from the groove on the desk, held it out to me.

I pushed her hand away, protesting: 'No, no, it's a pin I want, not a pen. A pin, the metal thing you use to hem dresses before you sew them. You know, plain pins and safety pins.'

'Aw, a pin! I thought you said a "pen". Hey kids, listen to the way she says "pin". Go on,' she pressed, giving me a dig of encouragement. 'Say "pin".'

The two girls in front of us had turned round and were waiting expectantly. Dutifully, I repeated 'pin' again and again until half the class was roaring and mimicking me. I sat, simpering bashfully, my cheeks and neck getting warmer and warmer. Really, it wasn't so very funny. I wished they would stop. But I didn't know how to make them. Not then, anyway. Not till three years later, when hunched in meditation upon the family chamber pot provided by the government and emptied by it once a week, I suddenly smote my knee and jumped up.

'A pox on being nice,' I cried, tearing off the toilet paper in exaggerated strips. 'I'll tell the truth and strike them dumb. The creeps.'

So that when the maths master roared at me:

'Why don't you learn to speak the King's English!'

I fixed him with a baleful eye and answered:

'From whom should I learn—here . . . sir?'

And, verily, he was struck dumb. But that was later. At the very beginning of the Age of Mirth.

On that first day I merely noted that differences are to be the subject of humour, not to merit serious consideration.

In the midst of all the laughter provoked by pin, the next

227

teacher came in. Another old one. Tall and thin, with a long, bald head. Purple spots were sprinkled over his head and hands. The girl, Wendy, hissed in my ear, wetting it:

'That's Mr Geraghty, the history teacher. Cranky, and boring as hell. What history did you do in Scotland?'

I dried my ear with my finger and eased my head forward, slightly.

'Scottish history, mainly.'

'Right, you, girlie.' It was me he was yelling at. Jesus. All those knobs bursting out between his eyebrows. 'Five pages, for the next lesson. Why I must not talk in class.'

Everybody wailed.

'Aw sir, that's not fair. She's new.'

Wendy spoke up prettily.

'It was my fault, sir. I asked her a question.'

The teacher shifted his scowl to her.

'Since when did you become your brother's keeper? She's responsible for her own actions and I don't give a damn whether she's new or not. In any case,' he continued, 'it's the best way to teach her the dangers of sitting next to you.'

The Wendy girl flushed. 'Beast.'

I put my hand up. The teacher glowered.

'Well, what's up with you?'

'Sir, am ah to write lines or a composition?'

'What? What! What the blazes are you gabbling about? Don't gabble.'

I repeated my question, terrified he might still not understand me.

'Composition, of course. And what's that appalling accent you've got.'

I shivered in my seat. I had been speaking my very best English, the one I kept for school, and here it wasn't acceptable.

'Ah'm Scottish, sir.'

He had lost interest in me and was grumbling at a boy in the front seat.

'Do you call that a margin, boy? Get it rubbed out and draw one with a ruler.'

Remember to honour the margin that thy peace may be long in the class the lord, thy Deputy, giveth thee. I was beginning to feel like a pencilled dot, almost invisible, at the centre of an infinity of lines of circumscription. Fortunately the bell went again.

Everybody stood up, slamming their cases onto the desks and hurtling their books inside with all the clatter possible. The teacher fled, mumbling to himself as he left. Wedged under his arm was a thick exercise book containing pages and pages of margins.

'C'mon.' Wendy was already pushing herself down the aisle. 'We've got pee ee now.'

In fact we had pee ee twice that week and every week thereafter. Plus sport, once a week, on Wednesdays. Every Wednesday a boy came to each class with a sheet of paper drawn up in columns. At the top of each column was the name of a sport: tennis, swimming, softball, in the summer. Every student signed his name in one column or another. There were about 750 students in the school and it took a minute for the sheet to go from one person to the next and a minute for him to write his name. So every Wednesday one thousand five hundred minutes passed like that. Plus fifteen minutes after recess when the pee ee master gave the latest bulletin on playing fields, team lists, the venue of matches, plus twenty minutes walking or bussing to the appointed spot, plus fifteen minutes ticking off the names at that spot to make sure everyone had arrived, plus fifteen minutes changing the tick to a cross, making sure everyone had stayed.

Some time was spent playing sport, but I've forgotten how much. Tennis, softball, basketball and swimming, all of this was compulsory. There were terrible penalties for evasion. I don't mean deportation or death or anything like that, but they had quite a subtle system of torture with which I became familiar during the Age of Mirth.

The lesson after pee ee (which is best forgotten) was English. Miss Ardlink, the teacher, was obviously very popular, since her entry was greeted with subdued wolf whistles. She was about thirty. Slim and straight with very neat ankles. Her rather faded blonde hair was curled a bit stiffly but tidily round her ears and she wore a simple beige suit. Her makeup was also creamy beige, that didn't completely mask her acne scars.

Her voice was low and pleasant, without any strain. She had an odd way of saying:

'Good morning, one buhee,' with no smile on her lips but one in her eyes. Then she stood calmly with her hands clasped lightly together in front of her, waiting for silence and willing it to be. Into the silence she said, casually:

229

'You haven't forgotten it's lecturettes today, one buhee?'

'Oh noooo, Miss Ardlink.'

They roared, too loudly.

'Easy, one buhee. Not too much noise, please. Well, whose turn today? Yours, Shirley?'

Shirley was the tall blonde girl I had noticed straight away in class. She wiggled her way down the aisle, one hand at a waist that was almost garotted by a savagely tight belt, and as she smoothed her tunic around her hips I noticed she was wearing pale pink nail polish. Her hair was hanging over one eye.

'Put your hair back from your face, please Shirley,' the teacher said.

She gave her head a toss that was somehow more significant than having an eye covered, and as the hair splayed out over her shoulders, its roots were displayed. Dark brown, like her eyes. She grinned widely at the class, fascinating me with the gold fillings that shone in her big front teeth. The only gold fillings I had ever seen before were in the mouths of Glasgow Filipinos. What on earth was a lecturette? It sounded foreboding.

It turned out to be a witty and confident peroration on the advantages of co-education, the main one, as Shirley worked it out, being that 'it makes it safe for women to walk the streets at night'. This conclusion was greeted with uproar. Miss Ardlink merely raised her eyebrows slightly and shook her head, as if to say: what shall I do with that girl? I smiled too, to join in, but I didn't know what I was laughing at.

Pretty smartly, however, I stopped smiling, after Miss Ardlink informed the class and me that I should have to give a lecturette the following week.

'A favourite poem will do,' she told me, patting me on the shoulder.

'Ah could never talk like that in a fit,' I moaned to Georgina at lunchtime. 'No kidding, that girl was like the Queen o' the May. She spoke like a blinking adult.'

Georgina's eyes widened sympathetically. 'Ah cannae blame ye for being feart. Ah would die tae get up in front of them a'. They laugh at ye as it is. These big laddies queue up ootside the verandah door and sort of blow through their noses as if they're playing the bagpipes. "What have ye on under your kilt," they say tae me. They're right ignorant. Ah'm even feart tae go tae the lavatory because they a' staun near the girls' toilets waitin' for ye and when ye come doon they whistle and shout: "Hoots mon, oot o' mah way, who dae ye think ye arrrr".'

'They're real comics,' I said drily, mentally noting never to go to the toilet while I was at school.

After lunch, at sport, I felt really lonely. Georgina had gone swimming and I was obliged to traipse along with four girls to whom she had introduced me. The footpaths were narrow and the numbers uneven so that I kept falling behind on my own. The girls tried to talk to me in those nice phrases that everyone kept for people like us, smiling at me as if I were feeble-minded. It was maddening. I wanted to punch their noses, and the most maddening thing of all was that I couldn't justify my anger, not until I imitated their smile in the mirror at home. Then I realised that the irritating agent was the eyes. They contradicted the smiles and bland tones, being narrowed with suspicion, defensiveness, a waiting for possible unpleasantness. When the Dutch girls smiled at you, their eyes lit fires inside you and made you glow with comfort.

Everyone disappeared when sport finished and I found my own way back to town, past trees like pineapples. The gravel kept getting in my wedgies and I had to stop every so often to shake it out of my toes. Eventually I saw a cross street about three blocks down. Cars and buses were scuttling along it, so I was back in town.

The buses weren't bright and shiny any more, or perhaps there was a mote in my eye now. I sat beside a window bleared with mud and gazed dolefully out at the tightly packed mass of school-kids squatting on their cases. They were strung across every doorway and recess like barricades. Angry shoppers tried to make a breach here and there but the barricades were three deep, so they withdrew again into the shops, muttering resentfully. Those who got out successfully were held immobile on the pavements, all movement proscribed by the powerful phalanx of determinedly indifferent bodies.

One fat woman battered a path for herself, using her massive shoulders like a club.

'Get out o' the bloody way,' she bellowed.

They leaned slightly to the side and she made it to the rail of the bus.

231

'There ought to be a law against these bloody kids,' she grumbled, rummaging in her purse for change. 'It's more than your life's worth to be in town this hour of the arvo.'

'It's not for lightweights, that's for sure.'

She glowered at the driver suspiciously. Was he slinging off at her? There was no time to debate the situation for they were climbing in right behind her, nudging her impatiently up the aisle and hurtling their cases ahead to book a seat, feeling in their blazer pockets for a cigarette before they sat down. Some blew smoke into the faces of those still pitched outside.

'Aaaah,' they sighed, sniffing it up with exaggerated longing, 'give us a puff, go on.'

My head ached with the noise and the smoke and the bodies that hung and swung all about me, clogging my pores with their greasy warmth and padding my mouth with the rough, fluffy serge of the blazers so that I gulped, panic stricken, for air. The fat woman collapsed heavily onto the seat in front of me, squeezing a little man right up against the metal side of the bus. I pressed my face against the muddy glass and kept it there even after we'd left Gullawobblong behind and the gutters were filling up with paspalum. The bus was almost empty when we got to Kershley but my head was screaming at the back, and my neck was rigid like steel.

In the hut my mother was sitting at the table writing a letter. She looked up as I came in.

'How did ye go, hen?'

'Oh, all right. I think I'll lie down for a bit.'

I kicked off my wedgies—one of the heels needed mending—and lay face down on the bed. Thank God for sleep.

Three weeks passed. People asked anxiously when they got to class:

'Did you do anything last night?'

'No, I didn't do a thing,' they said, lying blithely.

The teachers used the examinations to bring the recalcitrant ones to heel. Even Wendy was prevailed upon to be quiet at times, and in recognition of the new order, of the change in the power structure, the maths teacher faced the class. Previously she'd talked into the blackboard and pretended chaos was order. She bribed co-operation by hinting she might tell what was to be in the maths paper; she demanded it by threatening to fail the 'louts'. The examinations aroused little interest in me. I wasn't expected to do much because of the differences in subject matter. No one knew what the differences were exactly, but they were assumed.

'You can do it to fill in time,' the French teacher said, handing me a paper, 'or read a book if you like.'

When all the results were released, I topped the class on aggregate marks.

'So,' the girl Wendy said, accusingly, 'you *are* a brain!'

Shame.

'Well,' they all smiled, very nicely, 'you did do well, didn't you? Congratulations.'

The smiles made me feel uneasy. However, no one was nasty. They simply lost interest. If we passed, coming into or leaving class, they nodded and said: 'G'day, how are you.' Wendy shifted her seat without an explanation. After the exams Miss Ardlink remembered the lecturettes. 'Tam O'Shanter' was the only poem I knew well. I stared at the back of the class and read from my notes, boringly, monotonously, but they gave me all their attention. Their quietness clutched at my throat and stiffened my sounds and then suddenly, they were laughing. It was shocking. They laughed and laughed and threw themselves across their desks while I tore my notes to shreds in my hands. Even Miss Ardlink was smiling.

'It's all right,' she said, 'go on.'

'No, I shan't,' I told myself, and pretending I didn't hear her I went and sat down.

It was the devil, the teacher remarked, after the boy critic had chuckled through his report, it was the devil, sitting in the corner playing the bagpipes. Really, one never imagined the devil doing such a thing. It's an unusual image, though not, she added, in the context of the poem.

And I must give another one, Oh yes, I must. 'On a country road.' The boy critic stood up and said how interesting it had been, so pleasant to listen to, and he hadn't understood a single word of it. Ha ha ha. I gagged on their roars of derision and fell over the suitcases while I was rushing up the aisle. I'll kill them all, those 'nice' pigs, they'd better watch out!

Only with Georgina at playtime and lunchtime did I feel me. Once, when the bell went, I said: 'Let's go and hide in the toilet and we can chat a bit longer.'

She was aghast.

'Oh, ah couldnae dae that. What if they found out! Ye'd probably get hauled oot in front o' the whole school. Look,' she patted me on the arm, 'it's only a bit more than a week tae the holidays—nearly eight weeks. Don't let them get ye doon. Just ignore them.'

'That'll no' be hard,' I said, sighing. 'They ignore me anyway except when ah've got tae speak oot loud then they laugh themselves silly.'

'Aye, they're a great lot o' snobs. Aye blaahin' aboot how their faithers are managers o' this, that an' the other. Ye'd think that's the only thing ye're put on earth for, to be a blasted manager o' B.H.P. They make ye feel as if ye're a poor immigrant or something.'

This made me laugh: 'Well, they're right, Georgina. We *are* immigrants an' we're poor.'

Georgina's face grew redder than her jacket. It was curious how she was angry now.

'Well we're no' goin' roon wi' a beggin' bowl, are we? Naebody's giein' ye anything for nothing.' A sudden smile illuminated her prettiness. She was remembering something. 'Ye know how they keep askin' ye "where are *you* from", it gie's ye the pip, well, this morning I said tae one, "an' where are *you* from?". "Oh," says she, "ah'm a real Australian." "Are ye," says I, "well don't let it upset ye, ye'll probably survive it if ye eat yer porridge."'

I did a somersault over the grass, hugging myself with delight.

'Ye're no' sae timid as ye look, then, are ye, Georgina?' I cried, astonished at her boldness.

She grinned too. 'C'mon. They're startin' tae go tae lines. We'll just make it tae the lavatory if we hurry. These big lads'll be gone.'

16 Love-in-idleness

That afternoon I marched through the door of the hut and slung my books onto my bed, not noticing at first that my mother was sitting at the square table with a visitor. A man. He was sitting opposite my mother with a sheet of paper in front of him, and a pencil between his thick fingers. I stared at him curiously. Foreign, definitely. He was dressed in a brown suit, pinstripe, and he looked very heavy. The table protruded beyond his shoulders only a few inches on each side. His hair was black and grew down the sides of his cheeks and his eyes that flicked a shy look over at me were dark, too. Black hair, black eyes and dark skin. Everyman's Italian. What was my mother doing, sitting at the table with an Italian?

'This is Mr Gotardi,' she said, reading my thoughts, apparently. 'Ah'm teaching him English.'

I said nothing. So! That was the way of it. Teaching him English. My mother. And the band played. I stared at Mr Gotardi and glared at my mother. Then I just stood. They were embarrassed. Good. After a few minutes the man got up. He was shorter than I. He folded the paper carefully, there didn't seem to be much written on it, and slipped it into his pocket. Then he walked round the other side of the table, away from me and stuck out his hand to my mother:

'Thank you, Missus. You very good lady. I come again?'

'Yes, you can come tomorrow afternoon,' my mother said, shaking him by the hand. 'Tomorrow. Understand?'

You bet he understood. His lips stretched in a smile. A stainless steel tooth gleamed dully between his front molars. It would have a powerful bite, that one.

'Yes. Yes,' he said, nodding his head vigorously.

I had to stand aside to let him pass and I scowled at him, wanting to kick him in the bum. Creepy guy.

As soon as I'd slammed the door at his back my mother began her defence. Attack was her usual method.

'You were bloody rude tae that wee bloke, the way ye looked at him. If ye ever dae that tae an adult again ah'll gie ye a good cuff across the ear.'

It would depend on which one of us was most convincing to the other—and to ourself.

'Well, it's just as well there's somebody tae gie him the cold shoulder,' I retorted, carefully ignoring her threat. 'What are ye thinking of, bringing a strange man in here, and an Italian at that! Daddy wouldnae like it a bit.'

My mother humphed and tossed her head. That meant I was winning. She was going to change her tune in a minute.

'Look hen, he cannae speak English. He got talking tae me in the laundry an' ah said if ah had time ah'd help him a bit. He's harmless.'

'C'mon, c'mon Mammy. Who's always telling me there's nae such thing as a good man. Only men. He's just like those guys that were coming roon in Glasgow when Daddy was oot here. And what aboot that engineer on the ship. You were always ticking him off—so you said—and he was aye coming tae the door at two in the morning. He didnae stop till ah told him Daddy was getting on at Melbourne. Just as well he did. An' this wee guy's just the same. He can get English lessons anywhere. They have classes in the hostel at night.'

'Aye, but he works shift work,' my mother said. She was right on the defensive now.

'Well, ah don't care. He's nae right comin' after a wumman wi' seven kids.'

My mother raised her eyebrows in non-comprehension of my stupidity and denseness.

'Look, you don't understand what it's like in a situation like this. The man's lonely. He's naebody tae talk to.'

'What a lie!' I exclaimed indignantly. 'The hostel's full o' Italians.'

My mother spread her hands. Goodness. She was even picking up their mannerisms.

'But they need tae talk tae women noo an' again. Just for company.'

236

I glared at her with resentment.

'All right, Mammy Lavery.' I should have to threaten her. My eyes were beginning to prickle dangerously. 'If he comes in here again, ah'm goin' tae tell mah Da.'

My mother was beside me and over me in a second. She stood with her hand raised to smack my head.

'You open your mouth, my girl, and it'll be the last word ye'll ever utter. You're no mah keeper. Ah know what's right and wrong and ah don't need any snotty-nosed thirteen-year-old tae keep me on the straight and narrow.'

I tucked my head under my arm and grumbled into my armpit.

'Well, if ye know what's right and wrong why dae ye no' want me tae tell Daddy? He could probably teach him better English, anyway,' I added, keeping back a giggle. My mother really got mad if you implied my father was smarter than she.

She made a grimace of annoyance and snorted: 'The only English your faither could teach anybody is the end o' the Communist Manifesto. Noo go and get changed, and keep your trap shut if ye know what's good for ye.'

As I slunk off to the bedroom, I called over my shoulder: 'Hitler!'

For the next few days there was no sign of the man. Not that that meant anything significant. He was probably leaving before I got home from school. I tried to pump Jackie, asking him if a man came to do writing with Mammy. But he didn't know. He was always outside, wandering all over the hostel. I was too scared to mention it to my mother in case she swiped me. If she was in the hut when I got home, she would give me a smirking kind of look, as if to say: 'Hah, wouldn't you like to know?' but she was just as likely to do that even if the Italian weren't coming at all. To annoy me.

One Saturday afternoon, however, I encountered Mr Gotardi again, in very convenient circumstances for my purposes. I had gone to the laundry with Georgina to wash out my school tunic and socks. At first I thought the wash-house was empty. Then I saw a figure bent double, lighting the copper. It was him.

'Hey look,' I hissed to Georgina, pointing and making faces. 'That's that wee guy I was telling ye aboot, the one who's hanging aroon my mother.'

Georgina's eyebrows went up as she recognised him.

'Ah've seen him quite a bit. He's aye by himself. He's a bit queer because he wears a kind of bowler hat and carries a rolled umbrella, like an Englishman.'

'You wait here,' I told her, 'in the ironing room. Ah'm goin' tae talk to him.'

I walked down the wash-house, alongside the tubs, and he turned his head to see who was coming. Of course, when he saw me he got a wary look on his face and waited, without smiling. He must have sensed how I'd felt about him.

'Mr Gotardi,' I said.

'What you want?'

'I want...' I had a little think about what I wanted, 'I want you not to come near my mother again. Not to come to visit her.'

He didn't say a word. Maybe he didn't understand.

'You no come to my mother any more,' I said again.

He still made no response. It was my imagination, I think, that his eyes seemed to darken a shade. Then I thought of my father. I stretched my arms out sideways, first, and then held one arm above my head.

'My father very big man.' I did the pantomime again. 'Very big man. He very jealous. No like you to visit my mother. He go like this,' and I drew my hand across my throat, making a clicking sound.

The man moved quickly, like a watchful spider suddenly coming to life after you're convinced that you did kill it with the last swipe. He grabbed my wrist and held it tightly before throwing it down in disgust.

'Okay. I understand. Okay. You very bad girl. Go away.'

His eyes were raging and he was holding the edge of the tub as if he were going to wrench it from its base and throw it at me.

'Go!' he shouted. 'You bad girl. Go.'

Indignation made me blow out my cheeks.

'Go jump in the lake yourself. You've got a nerve.' My voice went up and up. 'You're the bad person, coming running after married women, and if I tell my father he'll come and knock your block off.'

I leapt backwards out of reach of his eyes. Something in them struck at me and made me suddenly unsure. Maybe my mother was right and he was just lonely. But that couldn't be so. Everything leads somewhere. My mother was a fool to forget it.

'Don't forget,' I reminded him. Then I turned and ran.

Georgina came rushing out after me.

'Jings,' she panted, when she'd caught up, 'ah thought he was going tae clobber ye for a minute. He looked sort of . . . desperate.'

We were moving up the path towards my place and I wondered if I should tell my mother.

'Ah wouldnae,' Georgina said fervently. 'Especially your mother. She might have wanted him to come, ye know.'

I glanced at her suspiciously. What was she getting at?

'Well, wi' your faither no' being here except at the weekends. She might be lonely, herself.' Then she added quickly: 'Mah faither would hae a fit if mah mother brought an Italian intae the hut, especially when he was oot.'

Yes. That was definitely the normal reaction. My mother was mad. I felt relieved now that I had done the right thing. The man's eyes I dismissed impatiently. His pride had been hurt.

We went up to the top laundry to look for the Dutch kids and try to talk them into playing a game of rounders. Karin, the one who was my age, was always reluctant to play at any game unless we had an audience of boys.

Today when we arrived there, she was swinging her bare legs on top of the ironing board, talking to Manfred, the German boy, whose father always whistled for him. What a serious fellow he was. Taller than I and very skinny. He was wearing those short leather trousers with the bib and his legs seemed to drop forever before disappearing into his big boots. Frontways he had a mass of yellow hair that hid his eyes. Tawny eyes like a lion's, but opaque, with no glitter in them. If you walked round the back of him he was as bald as a baby's bottom. His father shaved his head at the back.

He could speak very good English, slowly, a bit like a talking doll, with mechanical precision. People always shied away from him, however, because he kept analysing his grammar while he spoke, inviting their comments on his use of that particular tense or this particular preposition and sometimes even arguing that his choice was really more logical than the standard English usage. It didn't matter how the subject started off: it always ended as a discourse on language. Of course, he was most scholarly in analysing my accent, pointing out the similarity between certain German vowels and Scottish ones. We had a lot in common, he told me.

This made my blood run cold.

'Whatever similarities you see between Germans and Scots,' I told him once, very frigidly, 'are purely superficial. We've got nothing important in common at all,' and I gave him a meaningful look.

He gave me one back.

'That's history. It had nothing to do with me.'

'No, but . . .' I hesitated. Everybody said his father was an S.S. officer. 'Look at his height. Look at his build! And the way he trains those kids. Like Alsatians.' Some even whispered that his father had had plastic surgery to remove his S.S. number.

'Anyway,' I finished up, 'just don't keep saying we've got things in common. That's all.'

Manfred the Mad. King of Germany. And here he was, leaning his blue bony elbow on the ironing board, close to Karin's bare thighs. When she couldn't wear her navy swimming costume she wore red shorts. They were speaking in German. Most of the Dutch people in the hostel knew German though many refused to use it. Karin was laughing underground, because her teeth were shut, biting on her blonde hair which was nearly white, long and thick, and hung down over her brown back. She was always chewing it, pulling it across her cheek and stroking it with a finger like a blinking cat. When she'd sucked all the juice out of it then she'd start stroking herself, smoothing out imaginary wrinkles that always happened to be in embarrassing places. Personally, I could never see them. Her costume was always shrinking up her bum but she never bothered to pull it down though she was forever smoothing out the wrinkles there. She was the one that Goldilocks on the bus thought had a voice like a man. It was very deep and gravelly. When she laughed, it sounded like some subterranean spring boiling and slurruping deep down.

My mother didn't like Karin. For no reason at all, because she was always polite and very generous with paddle pops.

'Ah don't want ye hanging aroon that girl. The Dutch yin wi' the big mouth. She's away ahead o' her time. Her mother should be keeping her chained to the bed.'

'Whatever for? She never does anything.'

My mother looked down at me sideways, pressing her lips together and nodding her head up and down to signal: tell that to the Marines.

'Ah'm telling ye. She's going tae land herself a packet and ah don't want ye playing wi' her.'

To tell the truth, both Georgina and I preferred to chat with Karin's sister Irma who worked at the factory. Karin always seemed to be looking impatiently over your shoulder when you were talking to her, waiting for something secret. She was just tolerating you for the moment.

One hand was smoothing her shorts, absent-mindedly.

Manfred bowed: 'Good afternoon, ladies.'

I mean he was only fourteen. What did he think he was!

Karin leapt down from the board. Now she was glad to see us. She linked her arm in mine and bent over, beaming into my face. Her grey green eyes were images of magic.

'Come with me to the shop, please. My mother wants milk for Hannah.' Hannah was her baby sister. 'I don't like to go alone. You come too, mm?'

Why not? Time was elastic. She came into the middle between Georgina and me, her arms in ours, and we went back the way we came, briefly bidding Manfred farewell.

'Farewell, fair Manfred,' I called to him, dropping him a curtsy. 'We go to seek the precious milk that is found in yonder shop.'

As an additional touch, I clicked my wedgies together and scowled: '*Heil*—Manfred!'

He stood with his thin arms hanging, confused.

Georgina shook my arm reprovingly:

'Come on, Mary. Don't be cruel. You shouldn't tease him like that. He cannae see the funny side o' things.'

'Neither can I,' I answered sharply. 'Ah don't like Germans and ah'm no' goin' tae be nice tae them.'

Karin grabbed both our arms. 'My mother is waiting for the milk. She asked me one hour before.'

As we made our way back down the paths towards my own hut I said to her:

'Why do you speak German with him, Karin? I mean the Dutch didn't do very well with the Germans either. Your sister doesn't speak to them.'

Karin shrugged her shoulders in a gesture of annoyance.

'Oh her. She's too stupid. Too serious. Like my grandmother. I don't care if he is a German. To me he is—' she shrugged again and spread her hands, 'young. A young boy. I am a young girl.

That is enough.' She smiled slyly, glancing at us both. 'He was asking me to be his girlfriend.'

Georgina groaned. 'Ugh. Oh he's a nice enough boy, but he's too stodgy. Like potatoes,' she added, explaining to the Dutch girl. 'Too heavy.' She patted her stomach. 'In here.'

Karin grinned and shook her head in disagreement. 'You don't know these things?' She touched Georgina's stomach lightly. 'Not in there. Somewhere else.'

We all three burst out laughing.

'You're a very bad girl, Karin.' Georgina and I said this together, wagging our fingers at her.

'But what did you say to him?' I asked her.

She smoothed her hair back from her face, and shrugged theatrical fashion.

'I say. I don't want a boyfriend. I want many boyfriends. If I have one, I don't have the others.' She spread her arms wide. 'I like them all.'

She gave a little leap into the air and skipped ahead of us, down the path.

'C'mon. Hurry. Hannah needs the milk.'

We were past my place; I could hear my mother talking to my father through the open door, and we were just about to turn left from the ablutions block when I heard him singing again. Him. The one in the shower. I hadn't heard him since that other, first, time. Now he was having a shower again, probably getting ready to go out because it was Saturday. Or maybe he was going to church. He was singing Schubert's 'Ave Maria'. Georgina hummed along with him.

'Och, isn't that lovely. Ah wish ah knew the words.'

Karin had stopped and was looking back at us, curiously. I gave Georgina a little push.

'You go wi' her, Georgina, an' ah'll wait till he comes oot. Ah want tae see what he looks like an' ah might no' get another chance. Go on, Karin's coming back. Ah don't want her tae know.' Why shouldn't I want Karin to know? I was only going to listen to him. But she might like him for one of her boyfriends and although I hadn't even seen the melancholy singer I didn't want to share his existence with anyone. He belonged to my mind alone and I didn't want anyone else to have an image of him.

'Hurry up, Georgina. She's coming.'

'Oh all right then, if that's the way ye feel.' Georgina wanted to listen too and I would've let her if Karin had been elsewhere. She went, just the same, and I watched the two of them disappear down the road, one's arm carelessly slung across the other's shoulders.

Now I could listen in peace and wait to see him. Nobody else was around so I just lounged against the wall of the toilets. It was ages before the shower went off. If he didn't hurry they would be back from the shop. After another ten minutes I heard the slap slap of the thongs a lot of Italians wore. I ran on tiptoe to Margaret's window and then began to walk very slowly from there forward to the toilets, pretending that's where I was going.

The man who emerged from the entry, with a towel round his shoulders like a rainbow, was no one I had ever seen before. Thank goodness he wasn't Mr Gotardi. I didn't see him full face at all, only his profile for a minute, but he was beautiful, just like his voice. He was towelling his hair as he dawdled along the path and his uplifted arms drew the lightly tanned skin of his back over tight, neat muscles. He had a long torso, narrow at the waist, and strong, graceful legs. Not like that pee ee man's at school. His heavy, stolid legs made you think of raw beef. The singer was like a statue in the art books. Behold thou art fair, my love. Thy legs are like pillars of marble. His wet hair was hanging round his neck like black coins. What a pity his face was gone. I could only remember a high-bridged nose, a bit bent in the middle.

Well, so that was where he lived. In the hut, two down from us where all these men were, the ones who were always shouting and laughing and throwing each other out the door. I would be able to keep watch for him now. Karin and Georgina would be here any minute and I didn't want to talk to anyone. I hurried away to our part of the hut and lay down on my bed. My mother and father were still talking. Evidently my father had drawn a house in the ballot. That was very exciting. In two or three months we would be able to move into it.

'So what dae ye think o' that?'

'Great,' I answered mechanically, 'but ah like living here. There's plenty o' company. If we left I wouldn't be able to see the singer any more.'

'Aye,' said my father, 'it's good in that way, but it's nae

243

good for the family, me living in another hostel. It's too expensive anyway. Ye'll find plenty o' kids tae play wi' when we move intae a Commission hoose. They're usually people wi' young families.'

Lying down with my hands stretched behind my head I was reflecting that really I didn't want anyone to play with, exactly. Someone to look at, more likely. And touch. What a perfect figure he had, my singer-statue. I imagined him with a toga and leaves around his head. I wonder if that bent bit in his nose meant it was broken. I must try to get a look at his fingernails. If there's one thing I really can't stand about men it's dirty broken fingernails. Especially if they pick their noses, too. I thought of him sitting on a great rock out on the lake singing like the Emperor's nightingale. What would his name be? Not Tony, I hope. The man who came round with the ice cream cart in Plantation was called Tony and my mother used to make us laugh, singing about him while we licked our wafers:

'Roll-o, Anto-neeo
For he has gone away.
And left me on my owneeo
All upon my owneeo
Oh, I'd like to meet him
With his new—sweetheart!
Then up would go, Anto-neeo
And his ice-cream-cart?

No, he'd better not be called Tony. Nor Frank, neither. That was the fish and chip man. Some time or other I'd be bound to see him again.

17 Diversions

Christmas was coming. It made the adults very whingy. They complained about everything: the heat, the humidity and being cooped up like rabbits in Army Nissen huts covered with iron roofs that made ovens out of the rooms. 'If they'd shown us pictures of this place you can be sure I would never have left England (Holland, Poland, Scotland . . .). And the food. Gives you diarrhoea.'

One morning, in the canteen queuing up for breakfast, I saw Mrs Budinsky's husband ahead of us. She never seemed to come to breakfast. Her husband always took stuff back to the hut. He was an earthman, broad and heavy and careful moving. Very solid. Sometimes, when I heard his voice raised angrily and saw him swinging his right arm indignantly, he reminded me of Taras Bulba and I imagined him galloping through the canteen on a wild horse, brandishing a sabre and flashing fire, his bright purple and gold cloak wrapped around his arm and his horse nearly sagging at the knees from the great weight. When he spoke to his little girl, however, he was so quiet you couldn't hear him a yard away. Then he wasn't Taras Bulba any more, only Daddy Bear.

This morning he wasn't speaking to anyone. He was Mr Budinsky, quiet and absorbed in placing the bowls of sugared porridge on the tray. His head was bent down, examining carefully the cold, flat egg stuck to the plate. I must take that book back to Mrs Budinsky and get another one. Now he was moving along the line again, reaching out for the cups of milk allowed with each bowl of cereal. He glanced into one carelessly and threw a quick look at the Englishwoman behind the counter. Most of the canteen staff were tenants of the hostel. Then he lifted the cup and tossed the milk into the woman's face, roaring with rage at the top of his lungs. Taras Bulba rides again.

'You expect my baby to grow strong on this amount of milk! You thief! There's only half a cup. You want that my baby should have rickets! You insult me. Take this piss, yourself. I go to see the manager.'

He threw the tray of dishes on the benches and hurled himself, head down, along the wooden boards, Taras Bulba, the fierce protector of his line.

The silly woman, excessively shocked, reacted as if a huge funnel web spider had jumped on her and was biting into her neck. She screamed, high, hysterical shrieks from a rigid raw throat, slapping at her face and neck where the milk had wastefully been thrown and jerking her arms and legs in uncontrolled disintegration of her sanity. For God's sake. It put you right off your breakfast. There would be trouble about this. People don't have to put up with that kind of barbarism, you know. You're only doing your job after all. If the management decides to halve the milk allowance on economy grounds it's not my fault, is it? I've never been so insulted in all my life. I won't put up with it, I won't. I mean, it was for his country we came into the war, wasn't it? Gratitude, that's what!

That's how it was as Christmas approached; Christmas, the time of good cheer. And inside some of those huts, the shouting and bawling that went on! It was like the Muirs all over again. You could see them at the meal table, the ones who'd been rowing. The men, whitefaced and subdued, making dry balls out of the rubbery bread and flattening them into discs between their nervous fingers; the women, sulky and vengeful, little mouths drooping, discontented, tapping the table fretfully with their long, sharp fingernails, some red as blood.

My mother didn't quarrel much. After all, my father was only with us at weekends, but sometimes she managed to compress her irritations into a dense block of solid animosity and resentment with which she beat him around the head on Friday nights.

None of us kids paid any attention to the adults and their whingeing. We spent every spare minute down at the lake, Georgina, Karin and I, with the other Dutch kids and some English boys who'd just arrived. The lake was about ten minutes walk from the huts. Some yards ahead of the shop was a narrow jetty cutting into the water and on both sides of this Kershley fishermen ranged their boats along the sand. Low hills curved all round the lake's shores and the only part out of sight was its mouth, continually busy, swallowing great draughts of fresh seawater to replace that lost by evaporation. Alas, a fisherman told us, the lake was going to die one day, for a sandbank grew like a cancer across its mouth, steadily thickening and solidifying and insidiously repelling the eager tidal waters, condemning the lake to die of thirst and over-salting.

'It's going to cost more and more to root out the sandbank,' the fisherman said, 'and the council'll decide it's not worth the effort.'

He swung his arm widely, encompassing the range of hills behind us, the ones that cut off the hostel from the highway to Gullawobblong.

'The steelworks is only getting started. They'll cover these hills with Commission cottages for the ironworkers and when the lake starts to dry up, drain it for building on.'

'What'll happen to you then, mister? Where will you fish?'

'I fish mainly in the ocean, anyway, kid. Though it's good for prawning, this lake. But I've got land all round here. It's worth nothing right now. No people. Only you at the hostel and a couple of families here at the village. In a few years, but—maybe ten, maybe less,' scratching his neck, thoughtfully, 'my land'll be worth a fortune. And then I'll only fish for fun.'

Poor lake. You just couldn't imagine it dying. Such a lot of water drying up and disappearing. What would become of the islands?

'Will the islands sink down or something?' I asked. 'You know, after all the water's gone.'

The fisherman stopped rubbing at his boat with the sandpaper and looked at me curiously.

'Don't get you, kid.'

'The islands,' I said, amazed at his obtuseness. 'They'll be stranded like whales if the lake goes. What'll happen to them?'

'Bit of a comic, this mate of yours,' the fisherman commented, turning to Georgina. 'Do you think she's serious?'

What a great fool the man was! What was Georgina laughing at? She's an idiot as well.

'All right, what's so funny?' I demanded.

'Islands don't float, kid,' the fisherman said in an odd voice.

'They're mountains or hills lying on the ocean beds. You're seeing the top of them above the water. Have you', he asked curiously, 'ever seen an island floating?'

To tell the truth, I hadn't. But Sir Walter Scott describes islands in 'The Lady of the Lake'. I quoted the lines to them.

'And islands that empurpled bright,
Floated amidst the livelier light,
While mountains that like giants stand,
To sentinel enchanted land.'

'Very nice, too,' the fisherman said, nodding in affirmation. 'But I think that's just poetry. You know, they fiddle with things to make them pretty.'

So the two islands in the lake weren't lying at anchor. I could hardly imagine it. Oh well, if we ever got out to that big one I needn't be afraid it would move away with us like an ice floe. There was the floor of an old dance hall on that island, so we'd been told. People went out in motorboats and row boats to dance there. The women in their tulle with glittering sequins would lie back in the boats, trailing their hands in the warm water, and if they fell into the lake their white dresses would spread out about them. They would turn into water lilies, the pretty ones. The sour ones, pushing through the water with their rocky chins like the pee ee teacher, would stretch out their arms and legs behind them, roaming the dark lake forever and ever like marauding jellyfish. Then we would get them when they were slinking by the jetty. We would grasp their necks and smooth our hands over the marble heads. Then lay out their tentacles of tripe over the concrete slabs and dry them to death. It would be nice to turn all the pee ee teachers into jellyfish.

Someone was calling us. We clambered onto the jetty and stared back up the road, shading our eyes from the sun. Two women were outside the shop waving.

'Hi! Come on here a minute.'

Georgina bent down to tighten the strap of her sandal: 'Ah think it's Myra McFarlane and Lizzie Barker.'

'Lizzie must have the day off from the fruit shop,' I said. 'She usually works on a Saturday.'

Neither of us knew the two girls very well, really. They both worked. Myra was a checker at the woollen mills in Eugoberra and Lizzie worked for a Turkish shop in Gullawobblong.

'Oh, I couldn't stand that factory,' she'd told us. 'All that noise and forewomen breathing down your neck. And besides, the fruit shop pays thirty bob a week more. Three pounds ten's no good to me.'

'Hullo, you two.' They were waiting for us with their dimples showing. Myra's green eyes widened expertly, full of breathless astonishment. When she spoke, her lips traced out great areas of space for her vowels were broad and flat, much worse than mine, though she came from the country.

'Where have ye been a' this time?' she breathed. 'Lizzie an' me havenae seen ye for ages.'

She ought really to have smiled with her lips shut for her teeth were crooked, sagging together like a collapsing fence, but few people noticed this. It was her thick curly hair they commented on and her moist white skin. Even this they failed to observe once they saw her eyes. They were astonishing.

'Gosh, ah've never seen anybody wi' eyes like yours,' I exclaimed when I first met her. 'They're as green as lime drops.'

Myra giggled: 'Thanks a million.' She put her hand up to her face and made as if to pluck one out. 'Here, ye can a' have a suck.'

Everyone in the hostel praised her beauty to her mother and to Myra, herself. She was only amused by the compliments.

'But ah'm too fat. Look at mah ankles. Nae shape. And ah've hardly any bust.'

She was quick to draw attention to Lizzie's shape. 'Aw, hasn't she got a lovely bust-line? She looks great in a peasant blouse wi' that wee bit showin' at the top. Real seductive.'

Lizzie punched her friend affectionately and eased the pressure on her broad elastic belt with the gilt buckle. Today, in fact, she was wearing her peasant blouse and had the wee bit showing. Ah would never be able to do that at the rate I was going. My mother had bought me a brassière but I hadn't even taken it out of the paper yet.

'Gee, your skin looks a lot better, Lizzie,' I said to her. She had pink stuff on it and the crusts of acne were less noticeable. She was pleased, Lizzie, when I said that. So for good measure I added: 'And ah like your new hair style. It suits ye having all these wee curls across your forehead.'

'Ah think you're after one of my biscuits,' she said, laughing. Everybody liked to hear her laugh. It was a rare sound, full of well-being, warm and friendly. Not, mind you, that I would

249

trust any of the English. They're all very nice to your face. That's their profession my mother says, being charming so that they can diddle folk. But I liked Lizzie despite everything and she was from the north of England where the people were almost Scottish.

'We're going back to the hostel.' Myra was speaking now. 'We came tae get some odds and ends for Mrs Barker. Are ye going tae walk us back?'

'Aye, we will,' Georgina said. 'Ah couldnae stay at the lake much longer anyway, ah'm getting burned again an' ah've only just got rid o' the last lot o' blisters.' Her shoulders were flaming where they weren't darkly freckled.

'It's a blasted nuisance having this kind o' white skin. Ah'll never be able tae tan if ah stay here till ah'm a hundred.'

Myra nodded fervently, completely sympathetic.

'Ah ken, Georgie, it's the same wi' me. Us brunettes belong tae the olden days when they wore wet chiffon and bared their milky white shoulders. Naebody appreciates us here. Ye need a leathery look in this country.'

'Ye get it whether ye want it or no,' Lizzie put in, drily. 'Have ye noticed the skin o' these older women? They come in to my shop and some o' them wouldn't be more than thirty. But their skins are like worn-out pants elastic. Stretched to blazes and left quivering with those little brown knots on their necks.'

We had gone about twenty yards from the shop by this stage and Myra began to tell us about the film they'd seen on Wednesday night. She and Lizzie went to the pictures every Wednesday.

'And Mrs Bird came wi' us. She got her husband tae babysit for her. "Ah'm going mad here," she told us. "If ah don't get out for a bit ah'll blow mah stack".'

She was about to continue with her comments on the film when Lizzie caught her by the arm.

'God save us, Myra! Look who's coming. Quick, back to the shop. We'll ask them to hide us. C'mon,' she pressed urgently.

And there were the two of them going to run off, leaving Georgina and me open-mouthed.

'Where are ye going, Lizzie? There's nothing on the road except these Italians. They're from the hostel. Ah know them. Ah've seen them in the canteen.'

That's all there was. These men, bellowing at the top of their voices as usual, and punching each other on the shoulders.

Sometimes you couldn't sleep at night for the racket they kicked up playing cards, but it didn't bother us because they always sounded happy. I turned questioningly to Myra for some explanation and was shocked to see that she was stiff with apprehension. Her mouth had dropped open and her eyes seemed blind with fright.

'Oh, we cannae pass them,' she whimpered. 'Mah faither would kill me. He's warned me umpteen times.' She turned directly to Georgina and me and with unusual gravity said: 'Mah faither fought in Libya wi' them, ye see, during the war. A' they dae is go roon raping a' the wimmen. It doesnae matter the age. They're a' sex maniacs. That's why they lost the war, mah faither said. An' it's worse here because they havenae any wimmen o' their own. Mah faither reckons they ought tae take roon a petition tae get them oot o' the hostel. It's too dangerous, wi' a' the young lassies here.'

Georgina looked up the road at the approaching rapists and scratched the back of her neck. In her gentle voice she commented:

'Well, ah dinnae ken. They're been in the hostel a couple of months already and ah havenae heard o' anybody being raped yet. Have you, Mary? You live among them.'

I made a face: 'Look, they wouldnae let them intae the country if they were raping folk a' the time. Ye go tae gaol for that. The only time ah've ever heard o' them doin' it was in the rape o' the Sabine women. In any case, what about the Germans? They lost the war, too.' I nodded my head meaningfully. I was always meaningful when maligning the Germans. 'Everybody knows what they did. Much worse than raping. Ah would rather hide from them.'

The two girls were still poised to run away but doubt seemed to have unsettled them. Lizzie sucked at her finger.

'C'mon Lizzie,' Georgina said impulsively. 'We'll look after ye. Ye'll be safe wi' us Scots. At least some of us Scots,' she added, snapping her fingers at Myra. 'C'mon. Ye look as if ye've taken root.' She thrust her arm through Lizzie's and half dragged the English girl down the road, calling to Myra over her shoulder: 'Just look them in the eye.'

A gulp came from Myra but she started to follow us:

'Heavens, don't dae that, they'll think ye're gie'ing them an invitation.'

As we marched forward, at least Georgina and I marched, the

other two skulked and quaked, Georgina started humming under her breath:

'Rule Britannia, Britannia rules the waves,
Britons never never never, shall—be—slaves.'

'There,' I said, 'that should put iron in your soul. Ye should be ashamed, carrying on like that, big lassies like you.'

'Listen, Mary Lavery,' Myra retorted with asperity, tossing her dark head, 'if mah faither catches me breathing the same air as these Eyetalians, he'll flay me alive. Ah'm telling ye.'

These Eyetalians were now almost upon us—geographically speaking. There were six of them, strung out across the road.

'Like a net,' I murmured teasingly in Myra's ear.

They hadn't stopped shouting or slapping but I noticed we were under close scrutiny, just the same. A little pink with embarrassment we bundled each other onto the side of the road. Now the Italians had slowed to a stop beside us. They were staring quite openly and whispering through their grins.

'Keep moving,' Lizzie muttered, giving Georgina a push.

Then one of the group, the oldest in appearance and most confident in manner, stepped forward and made us a deep bow, like one of those rakes out of Georgette Heyer. He had an enormous barber's moustache that he tweaked a little before greeting us:

'Good day, young ladies!'

The formality of his address made me giggle and Georgina smile. The other two were in a stupor still. Encouraged by our response, the barber chap tried again:

'I say, what a lovely day it is today.'

His tone of voice was so like that of an elegant Englishman Georgina and I clung to each other and laughed till tears came in our eyes. The barber was looking confused and behind me Lizzie hissed: 'You shouldn't have laughed. You'll offend them!'

We didn't, though. They joined in after a moment and closed about us with their smiling white teeth and triumphantly shining eyes.

I murmured out of the side of my mouth:

'Here comes the rape of the Kershley women,' and Myra, trembling beside me, moaned:

'That's no' very funny.'

To tell the truth, it was difficult to see hideous passion and evil intent in the wide smiles and frank expressions of the two youngish men easing alongside Myra and Lizzie. But the closeness of the bodies around us was breathtaking: goose bumps popped out all over my arms and a strange shivery feeling made liquorice of my insides. We'd all stopped breathing. Not them, of course. The one standing right beside Lizzie now spoke carefully, almost into her ear. I saw her start.

'You . . . like . . . ice cream?'

Beware of Greeks bearing gifts, my father had said. And of Italians bringing ice cream?

'Answer him, Lizzie,' urged Georgina, 'it's you he's looking at?'

'No I don't, thank you very much,' she said loudly and over-grimly, I thought. 'And if you'll excuse me, I have to go.'

She was going to push through them, so I reached over and grasped her arm.

'Don't be so rude, silly,' I whispered quickly, and then aloud: 'Yes, we do like ice cream. You like ice cream, don't you Georgina?'

Georgina smiled, a bit nervously, and nodded.

'Aye, ah do, but it's nearly tea-time.'

Before any new complications could arise the barber dug into the back pocket of his blue shorts and tugged at his wallet.

'You wait. I go to buy ice cream.'

Lizzie and Myra were now standing like two great boobs, Myra twisting the front of her green skirt and Lizzie playing with the ribbon that drew shut her peasant blouse, a mistake, in my view, because that was the spot where the little bit showed, the snake's fangs, I mean, and the young chap who'd asked about the ice cream was hypnotised, it seemed, by the play of her fingers. She kept plucking at the blinking ribbon and letting it go with a ping, so that if your eyes didn't see, your ears would hear and another chap would start looking too. It's like my mother says. If you get raped you're usually asking for it. You shouldn't lead chaps on. Which reminds me, I wonder if that Mr Gotardi is still coming? Anyway, I gave her a nudge, a very obvious one, she complained later, and hissed:

'Quit playing with your ribbon, stupid, and say something. Friendly.'

She took a big breath. Another mistake, considering the size of her bust, and tucked her bottom lip under her top teeth.

'You Italian?' she said.

Did you ever hear of anything so stupid? Everybody knew they were Italians. But you would have thought from the way those chaps acted she'd said the wittiest thing under the sun. They beamed, they bowed. I thought they were going to turn cartwheels and at the end of it all, the one she'd spoken to—the blondish one, with blue eyes and wide cheekbones—said:

'Yes. I am Italian. You inglese?'

'English?' she repeated. 'Yes. Me English.'

By this time the barber had arrived back with the ice creams, a great load of doubles in a cardboard box. He handed them out all round, to us first naturally, and we began a slow shuffle back to the hostel, licking those big cones.

The blonde chap walked alongside Lizzie, and Myra fell behind with one who had enormous shoulders and great lumpy muscles in his back. She was looking up at him furtively, giving him quick peeps at her green eyes, I bet, but I could see she was talking a bit. The others stuck with Georgina and me, miming all the way. It didn't really encourage casual gossip. Georgina was laughing, spreading her fingers and shaking her curls as she and a small slim chap struggled to discuss the swimming pool at Steelhaven.

'Excuse me,' I said, an idea suddenly appearing, 'could you lend me your dictionary?' This was to the barber who had a small Collins Gem in his shirt pocket. I pointed as well, so he knew what I wanted. I turned over the corner of one page I'd found and flicked through the pages for the other word I wanted. Then I underlined both words with my fingernail. The barber said them aloud: *cantare, doccia*.

'Yes,' I said. 'Singing in the shower.' I held my hand up high, then pointed to my nose to indicate a bend.

There was a lot of discussion, but no result. So then I found 'who' and the barber slapped his head.

'*Capito*,' he cried. 'Emilio. *Si*, Emilio sings in the shower.'

So that was the name of the singer-statue. Emilio. Not bad. Not Tony or Frank. Very good.

Our ice creams finished, we reached the paddocks in front of the hostel. Lizzie and Myra were afraid someone they knew would see them talking to the Italians. They started backwards through the clammy paspalum, holding up their skirts. Both of them had thick knees.

'We have to go,' they said, united, looking directly at Georgina and me but speaking slowly enough to be understood by the two Italians from whom they were drawing away.

'Cheerio,' they finished and gave one or two frolicsome, backward leaps, a disastrous mistake for Lizzie, before turning and hopping away like little kangaroos, their giggles and shrill squeals a siren song for the two men left staring after them.

'We'll have to go too,' Georgina said to me, the apology in her tone meant for the ice cream donors. 'I want to have a shower before tea.' She uttered the last part much more quietly. It wouldn't do to talk in suggestive images.

'All right. But don't run backwards,' I warned her. 'Everything flops.'

We thanked the men for the ice creams and made off through the paddock at a quick trot. There was a hot spot between my shoulder blades where I could feel their eyes, boring like laser rays.

It was Thursday before we met Myra and Lizzie again, each picking at a lettuce leaf in the canteen. Hunched over the table, they murmured in our ears that Paolo and Sandro, the names of you know who, had risen up incredibly at the interval during the films with courteous offers of ice cream once more, supplemented, if they liked, by orange drinks. How the three of them found where we were sitting was a right mystery. Ah, your ears picked up the third man too! Who was he? They were very offhand about that. It was someone we both knew by sight, a man discussed and despised for his thick lips and the white horse he rode. But he had, I recalled later, a deep tan and perfect teeth in tactless contrast to his horse which was toothless. He would have been the odd man out, then? Well . . . no, not exactly. Don't forget Mrs Bird has been coming with us on Wednesday nights. Mrs Bird is the English lady whose nice husband is babysitting so that she won't blow her stack. (Mrs Bird, like the white horse, contrasts with the third man. He has thick lips and she has none: they were pressed into extinction, dissolved in a vinaigrette from a throat raucous with sour rage and vengeful lament. She is brittle and cracked at the tips of her blonde hair and her wonderful Saxon blue eyes if you touched them with your fingers would make you bleed. She cuts her husband with them every night at the tea table. A very proper person, nonetheless. She wears fifteen denier nylons even when she is washing and her seams are fearfully straight. She brings her Royal Doulton cup and saucer into the canteen and drinks from it, grinding her little teeth on the rim.)

It's less than nice, don't you think, for Mrs Bird to be one of you? She's old. She's married. She's a mother. But nothing happened, don't you see, and she's only twenty-six. We talked very little at the interval and we didn't see them after that. Nothing's happening. Then why all the excitement for nothing? I've read *Madame Bovary* and *The Red and the Black*, you know. The beginning is always recognisable by both of them, no matter what Stendhal says. She may pretend she is the victim of ineluctable forces, driven in innocence and ignorance into the demanding arms of her lover, waking up with a start and asking: how did I get here? Lies. She knows from the first glance and formal smile the significance of beginnings. That's why I had to save my mother from Mr Gotardi and watch her on the ship. Mrs Bird's daughter, however, can be of no assistance from her expensive Silver Cross pram with its swashbuckling mud-guards and noisy rattle dangling on a cord. Mr Bird would do better to find another babysitter.

Until the Christmas party all three relationships made progress on a horizontal rather than a vertical plane, that is, the meetings were repeated each Wednesday with hardly any variation. Sometimes they ate chocolate instead of ice cream.

Nonetheless, it was reported in the hostel that Mr Bird had waited by the men's toilet one night with a heavy piece of wood in his hand. He had risen up from his crouched position among the paspalum, seeds sticking to his brilliantine, when he heard Attilio come whistling towards the showers, and struck Attilio full force on the head, in silence. Attilio had staggered, dazed, into the light and Mr Bird, taken aback, apologised politely. Sorry, wrong man. It was that, rather than the blow, that made Attilio, weak at the knees, lurch back to his hut. They put wet cloths on the big lump and boiled him camomile on the little spirit stove that hid under the bed, laughing all the time as they dipped the cloths into the basin and wrung them out. They laughed for ages after, telling every new arrival of the English-man's apology. Sorry, wrong man. Without, mark you, inviting a blow in exchange.

Umberto, the real culprit, and his white horse, Garibaldi, ambled around the hostel, scar free. Garibaldi should have been dead. His teeth were gone, his muscles atrophied. His skin hung carelessly about his bones and his head lolled insensibly like that of Punch when the show is over. Sometimes it lay heavily on Umberto's shoulder, feebly snuffing up the carefully mashed apples and oats he was fed by hand. Yet Garibaldi's finest hour was still to come. That was after the party, when he participated in the elopement for which he was later sentenced to the knackery.

Some of them saw him that afternoon and wondered what he was doing, shambling down the forbidden paths between the rows of huts, till he stood before the Birds' place, waiting patiently for Umberto to stagger out with Mrs Bird's heavy black suitcase. She couldn't leave her wedding china behind, seeing as she was getting married again, so to speak. It took about twenty minutes to get the suitcase fastened to a secure spot on Garibaldi and another twenty to lead the horse out of the hostel, coaxing him forward with lumps of sugar. They were going to plod over the hill to Steelhaven where they could get a flat, but they were so slow Mr Bird finished his shift and was home in time to discover his loss and pursue the fugitives. He dragged the suitcase down from the horse, leaving Garibaldi panting on his knees, and swore at his wife, ordering her back to the hut before he bashed her bloody head in and blackened her Saxon eyes. But first he would deal with her fancy man, that wart-holed wog with the lascivious lips. He challenged Umberto to put his fists up and began dancing around, shadow boxing, so they said. Umberto was too busy trying to get Garibaldi up on his legs again. Finally he got the horse in a kind of fireman's lift and with a stupendous effort dragged it upright. He was out of breath himself now and leaned his head over Garibaldi's sagging spine, examining Mr Bird's exercises with wary interest. Mr Bird kept telling him to put them up and fight like a man but Umberto was fagged out. The expression in his thick brown eyes was quite benign.

Mr Bird had certainly won on a points basis. He gave up in disgust at Umberto's poor show. What could you expect from those cowards who'd lost the war? He left his sleeves rolled up in a devilish manner and strode off to the hut. His wife would certainly accept the challenge even if her lover refused it. But when he got there, he found only the baby, watching her fingers, cross-eyed. Mrs Bird had flown. She was hiding in another hut. The next day, determinedly, she wangled them a lift in the new utility of Mr Baldocci, and they were transported to Sydney.

Don't take on so, lad, they said, adding cautiously, she never were no good anyhow, goin' off and leaving her baby who aren't even past the cross-eyed stage. You're better rid o' her. But Mr Bird cried drily over his square table, ignoring the dadadas of his little girl who was, dammit, her mother's spit'n image. They went back to England, the two of them, to his ma.

18 Good Christian Men Rejoice

An invitation printed in gold lettering arrived in the mail for every family. In a spirit of peace and goodwill, the Italian members of the hostel would like to extend to every family a cordial invitation to the Christmas party, to be held in the canteen on December the twenty-third. Dancing till one a.m., it said in the fine print. Ah—hah! Dancing meant two people close together, touching. That in fact is the meaning of *tango*: I touch. The question is, who's going to be dancing with whom? *They* haven't any wives or daughters. It was only an excuse to get their olive oily paws on our women. If only it were possible, sighed Myra and Lizzie, trembling at the memories of brief pressures in the cinema crowd.

Nobody in my family was going. My mother and father were off to the pictures instead. What was the use, my mother complained; your father can't dance on account of his two left legs.

'You can come with us,' Georgina said, meaning her big brother and her parents, who loved to tango, 'and you can wear my pink dress if you haven't anything to wear. I'll wear my yellow one.'

It was a beautiful dress. Deep pink taffeta with a huge stand-up collar and a long row of tiny buttons at the front. It fitted perfectly at the waist and the colour, at least, matched my blushes. I was always blushing.

'It's no use,' I cried, tears making dark red stains on the collar. 'The top's too baggy.'

'Try putting socks in your bra.' I got the bra out of its cellophane and found a pair of clean socks. Even Georgina thought it looked funny. But people don't expect you to have a big bust when you're only thirteen.

She's so plausible, that Georgina. It's the only thing I don't like about her. She'll tell you anything to please you, like that time Karin dyed her hair and it came out all striped in black and white. It turned her into a zebra.

'Do you like it?' she asked us. Georgina looked at me first, then in that sort of smiling, anxious way she has at times, she said:

'Aye, it looks awfy nice. Different, ye ken, but ah think we'll probably get used tae it.'

I was disgusted with both of them.

'Och, you make me sick, Georgina Harvey. You're so plausible. It's blooming awful,' I said to Karin. 'Ye've gone and spoiled your lovely blonde hair and you look like a zebra crossing.'

That was the on'y time Georgina and I had a fight. She didn't like my calling her plausible. To her, it was almost the same as if I'd said prostitute. So now she gave me a wary kind of squint when I threw down my bra on the bed and shouted at her:

'Don't lie to me Georgina! You're lying. What were those two horrible German boys doing at the pictures the other night, feeling my blouse at the back? They wanted to see if I wore a bra. That's why the big fat one said: "No, she hasn't got one on." They didn't have to try with you, did they!' Then I felt ashamed. It wasn't Georgina's fault. She was trying to help.

'Look, it was good of ye tae lend me your dress,' I told her, changing my tone, 'but ah'm no' going. Ah'll stand on the boxes with the Dutch boys and watch through the windows. They've piled up fruit crates under the canteen windows so that ye can go from one spot to the other and get a different view. Like a moving camera, ye know?'

Georgina sighed and picked up her dress: 'Well, honest, ah think ye're daft. It's the dancing that counts and bein' wi' your friends no' how ye look. Ah'll away then, if ye've made up your mind. Ah'll gie ye a wave at the window.'

'Aye, do that. It'll be like spying, won't it, and that's what ah want tae dae when ah grow up. Ah can practise at the dance.'

Georgina went out then. The door shut behind her. A moment later, however, it was open again and her round cheek was pressed against the lintel.

'Ye'll no' change your mind, Mary? Wear your wine dress,' she urged coaxingly. 'It looks better than ye think.'

'If ah change mah mind, ah'll come,' I said, without lifting my head.

When she'd finally gone, emitting little spurts and puffs of secret vexation, I hauled the wine dress out of the closet and gave it a rough shake. They called it wine but it was more black, shot with purple. Some old woman had given it to us before we left. My mother kept telling me it had cost a fortune. She didn't bother to add 'a hundred years ago'. It was crepe and crepe was right out of fashion. So was the deep round collar, grown-up Peter Pan style, and the two belts at the side. Mind you, when you tied them at the back it made your waist look quite small and the bodice smoothed you over unobtrusively, modestly screening the changes your lazy body implemented only in fits and starts. Even Margaret was catching up on me. I fingered the inside of the collar. A line of grease gleamed silverly where the material had lain against my neck. I should have put the dress in the washing before. Still, nobody would see the grease and there was no smell under the arms. The trouble is, the whole hostel knew this dress. I wore it nearly every night. And then, blast it, there were those shoes, all marked at the sides and getting really baggy. I wasn't going to wear those wedgies to a dance. Oh well, that settled it. With the darkness came music, replacing the lights that usually assured you people were moving and breathing though their doors were shut tight. The lights were out tonight. Most of the Italians were at the canteen finishing off their decorations and squabbling over the cooking. A few had been working alongside the hostel cooks at tea-time but they all seemed to want the cooking done their way. My mother and father had gone off on the picture bus and the youngest kids were sleeping. Margaret was away somewhere. If I didn't go to watch the dance I would be annoyed tomorrow, I reflected, because Georgina left out too many things. When you asked her she'd say: 'Oh, it was real good.' Later, I would discover something very important had happened and she'd raise her eyebrows helplessly: 'Och, ah forgot about it. Ah didnae think ye'd be interested.' In any case, if I didn't go to watch, I should miss her in her new yellow dress. There was no point in changing now. Nobody would see me in the dark, anyhow. So I went up to the canteen in my uniform.

The Van der Kooi boys were standing in the doorway when I got there. They glanced at my school tunic and knew I hadn't come to dance.

'Nobody's here yet,' Jack said, over his shoulder. 'Haven't they made a beautiful sight!'

What strange things the Italians had done. The rafters of the canteen were looped about with fishing nets that hung down like enormous hammocks, all their little corks brightly painted, oranges, greens, reds and purples. Streamers were woven through the interstices, their variegated colours recklessly intertwined, harmony discarded for dazzling conflict. Bobbling below the nets, only a few feet above the tables that had been rendered stark white with butcher's paper, huge, grinning lanterns glowed and burned in blazing red crepe and balloons in constant movement twitched and touched each other, colliding on the ends of their coloured strings. The canteen had been a squat, ugly room before, inert and iron. Now it throbbed with tension and excitement, the hot, violent colours flailing the walls and roof while the air rushed mad with the music that relentlessly demanded whirling patterns of feet and hands.

The tables were a series of still lifes. No tomato sauce bottles tonight but strange lopsided bottles of heavy green glass leaning stiffly to one side, corseted in yellow straw. Between the bottles, spread flat on paper plates, were slices of dark red sausage, pale pink sausage, smooth light cheese and hard dry cheese (I tasted bits later), olives green and dark purple, raw ham, white and sweating cantaloupe, anchovies, bowls of bright green lettuce and oval platters of boiled lobster. Long black crusted loaves lay like clubs among the dishes. And things were cooking in the kitchen for I could see some of the Italians moving around with white paper hats on their heads.

'You like it?'

I jumped. It was Andrew the barber, the man with the moustache who had bought us the ice creams. (He was really a boilermaker but I liked him better as a barber. It suited his moustache.) He had been standing just inside the doorway beside a table almost covered with flat boxes containing rows of white camellias. I moved back into the shadows. It was terrible to stand in front of decorations in your school uniform.

'It's absolutely fantastic,' I said. 'I could eat it all up. Everybody will love it.'

Andrew shrugged and spread his hands, palms downwards.

'I hope *so*.'

They have a funny way of stressing things. I hope *so*. Behind me the gravel had begun to shift and crunch. People were coming. I slipped sideways right out of the light, and the Dutch boys came with me. A Scottish couple stepped into the doorway.

The man had on a dark blue lounge suit like my father's. His plumpish wife was in a tight fitting, sleeveless, white satin dress with slits at the side and a low, round neck. As soon as they got to the doorway Andrew bowed slightly, not in the exaggerated way he had done with us. He was a bit spivvy looking himself in his light grey suit and those pointed shoes that all the Italians wore.

'Good evening. You are very welcome.' He turned to the box beside him and took a camellia from it.

'For the lady,' he said, handing it to her.

'Och, isn't that nice o' the wee bloke, Alec,' the woman shrilled, looking up at her husband. 'Fancy goin' tae a' that trouble, giein' us floo'ers an' a'. Och, it's reely beautiful, but ah havenae got a pin, ye ken, tae fix it tae mah dress.'

Andrew had already handed a pin to the husband who was now rolling it between his fingers, a bit helplessly.

'Here, gie it tae me Alec, an' ah'll fix it mahsel',' the wife said, after waiting a minute impatiently. 'Oor men don't go in for this sort of thing, ye see,' she explained to Andrew. 'It's no' their style. There, that's it. The green leaves look nice against the white,' she went on, tucking her chin in so that she could look down on the flower. 'It's smashing. Thanks very much.'

The slit in her dress opened wide as she strode forward into the room where she began to go off like a whistling kettle.

'Och, isn't that a sight for sore eyes! Look what they've done tae it. Here,' she said to Andrew, 'they should have the canteen like this every day and it'd take your mind off the food.'

The husband rumbled in his throat and nodded to Andrew:

'Ye've got enough tae feed an army here, mac.'

We went round the side where Jack and his brother Frank had arranged the boxes, and climbing up on them, leaned on the narrow ledge that ran just beneath the window-pane. It wouldn't be comfortable for long, but it would do till we'd seen everybody come in. You should have seen the women when they got their camellias. A big fat one who'd been washing in the laundry beside me, screamed for joy and promptly stuck the flower between her breasts.

'Me no need pin,' she bellowed, so that everybody turned to look at her.

'Lucky it's not a rose,' Jack said to me. 'It would scratch her.'

Hah! There were Myra and Lizzie coming in with their

parents. I'm surprised Myra's father came at all, considering his fear of the Italians. Maybe Myra had insisted. She was sixteen, so she could probably insist a bit. She was in a bright red dress that went bang against her black hair and the black earrings that were dangling down. My mother says that's a prostitute's colour but I'm sure her mother wouldn't let her wear it if that were true. Her mother was in baby blue which suited her rosy cheeks. Lizzie was right behind her. It was a black do tonight. She was in black and white gingham, one of those folksy dresses with ribbons round the sleeves and lace all starched up about the neck which was pretty low. She had white flower earrings clipped on. She'd be sorry after. Her ears always swelled up and bled with those clip-ons, but as my mother says: vanity knows no pain. They both looked very pretty and they didn't shriek when they got their camellias, but smiled nicely at Andrew. Those loud-voiced women give me the pip.

The room was filling up now. There were those two chaps, no three, that went to the pictures on Wednesday night. I bet they'd be watching out for Myra and Lizzie. Georgina still hadn't arrived. That would be her mother's fault. Mrs Harvey always took hours to do herself up. One hour to put on all her creams and makeup, and another hour to smear most of it off with tissues and a spatula, so that in the end she didn't look much different. That was being 'subtle', she said. It rather surprised me that Georgina's mother was so fussy about her appearance. After all, she was white headed. But my mother said this was probably premature and she wouldn't be much more than forty.

A few Dutch girls had just arrived at the door, and two German sisters who lived near my hut were pinning camellias on their embroidered blouses, but Karin and Irma weren't there, and I knew Karin had a new dress. That meant her father had kept them both at home; she must have fought with him again. They were always fighting. I think he wanted her chained to the bed, too.

Everybody sat down to eat, some with wary expressions and tentative grumblings. The Italians took turns acting as waiters, popping the wine bottles and filling up the tumblers. I hoped they'd washed the tumblers themselves, for they were usually greasy.

'Chee, I would like a bit of that lobster,' Jack said. 'Or the rock melon. I'm going down to ask Andrew for something to eat.'

He jumped to the ground and disappeared into the dark. He was away a long time and when he came back the people inside were getting plates of little square things covered with red sauce. My stomach suddenly felt empty, though it was only a couple of hours since I'd eaten.

'Here,' Jack was whispering at my ankles, 'I got some things.'

Everything was mixed up on a big plate, lobster and sausage and cheese, but it tasted good. We now felt we weren't missing out on so many mysteries. My knees were sore from kneeling on the fruit crates and it was getting cool.

'Let's go to the tap and get some boiling water,' I suggested, 'and we can make some cocoa at my place and come back after. They haven't started dancing yet, anyway.'

Margaret was at home reading, when we arrived there with the bits and pieces. She spread some newspaper over the table and opened a tin of condensed milk for the cocoa.

'This is good fun,' young Frank spluttered, gulping over the hot drink. 'I don't like dancing, anyway.'

His brother was pulling the rind off a slice of baloney and said nothing. He was a bit too serious, really. Not crazy serious like Manfred, but he never liked you to know what he was thinking and he seemed to be thinking most of the time. He had a long thin face with a nose that was twisted off centre and he was always stroking it, maybe to straighten it. He chewed carefully at the sausage and when he'd finished remarked thoughtfully:

'Depends why you are dancing and on whom you are dancing.'

The Dutch were very good at speaking English but sometimes they said queer things like that. Neither Margaret nor I pointed out that you didn't dance *on* anybody. Instead, she said:

'I bet I know who you'd like to be dancing with, Jack.'

He took a swallow of cocoa.

'Who?'

'Karin.'

He was startled and discomfited. So Margaret was right! How did she know? Frank, too, was astonished. He said something in Dutch to his brother and the older boy glared at him.

'C'mon,' I said hurriedly, wrapping up the waste in the newspaper, 'we can take these mugs and wash them in the laundry and go back up. I want to see Georgina's new dress.'

There wasn't room for four of us on the boxes so Margaret stayed with Jack, and Frank and I went to another window near the top of the canteen.

'Does your brother really like Karin, do you think?' I asked him in a whisper, once we'd arranged ourselves.

'I think so.' Then he added, 'My mother doesn't.'

'Why not?'

'Because.'

His mother probably wouldn't. She was the one who went around looking queenly. Tall and straight and very aloof. His father was a bleached-out man with wispy hair. A big bible always sat on their table and sometimes I caught the father reading it if we passed their door.

It was coffee time now. The tables had been stripped and well, well, look who was sitting under this window! Myra, Lizzie and Mrs Bird. Mr Bird had his back to me, but I could see a bald spot shining like sixpence through his dark hair. Mr and Mrs MacFarlane were sitting beside him, still holding their tumblers of wine. I wondered why the girls weren't dancing. Lots of people were up on the floor dancing to La Cumparsita, a very slinky kind of tune. Goodness, there was Georgina in her new yellow dress. It was long, right down to her ankles, and she had golden sandals. She was dancing with Sandro, bending right back with her leg stretched forward. I didn't know she could tango. It tooked terribly difficult. My word, she was pretty. Look at Lizzie. She's staring down at the table, the way you do when you don't see anything, twiddling with her neckline as usual. She shouldn't have come if she didn't want to enjoy herself. Myra's got her chin hidden in her hand. I suppose her parents are there to make sure she doesn't get raped. Well they can see Georgina coming off the floor with her buttons still done up. Sandro's just glanced over at Lizzie but she hasn't seen him. I wonder why he doesn't ask her.

As soon as the music started again, two Italians rushed across the room to ask Georgina. One turned to Mrs Harvey and she pointed at her chest: 'Who me, the old duck?' But she got up and started doing a terrifically sizzly sort of samba. Fancy Scottish women dancing like that. And with white hair.

Mrs Bird was chatting to two friends of hers now. They were the same type: slim and hard with briskly curled blonde hair, grimly and determinedly pretty. She just ignored her husband. I wondered if she knew Umberto was at the table across the room from her. He'd taken off his jacket and his white shirt was open at the neck. It really did something for his tan. You wouldn't think white was a man's colour but if they've got very brown skin, it looks explosive. Next to Emilio—who hadn't come—Umberto is the handsomest man in the hostel, if you don't mind his thick lips. Emilio seems only to be in the hostel when he's in bed or having his shower. I wonder where he goes all the time.

There's Paolo, the one who likes Myra. He's sitting with his arm draped over the empty chair beside him, tapping its metal corner with his fingers. His eyes keep shifting around the room. They always seem angry, sharp and hard like black pebbles. Maybe that's because he's a boxer. He looks a real baby, sticking his bottom lip out like that. Somebody told me he's the youngest Italian in the hostel, only seventeen, and the others spoil him. I like Sandro better. He smiles more.

Now what? The two of them are discussing something. Sandro keeps looking across at Lizzie and Paolo just tosses his head. Oh, he's getting up and they're coming over here. Well, well, Mr MacFarlane. On guard! Here come the rapists.

What a pest that I can't see Mr MacFarlane's face, but I heard him sucking in his breath.

'May we dance?'

That was crafty of Paolo, looking at both father and daughter. He's gone red. So has Lizzie. He didn't say anything, probably because Mrs MacFarlane got in first:

'Get up and have a dance, hen,' she said. 'It's nae fun tae be sitting doon all the time, and Georgina's been having a great time,' she added, glaring at her husband.

I bet Mr MacFarlane wishes it were a reel. Then he could hold Myra's hand. Anyway, he can't complain. It's a waltz now and they're dancing very properly. Just as well it isn't a tango. And the two became one flesh. They should have it after weddings.

'What aboot you an' me havin' a fling at this?' says Mrs Mac-Farlane. So up they get and they're off, she in her baby blue. One two three, one two three. That leaves Mrs Bird. My word, isn't she a sour looking creature! Her husband hasn't taken his hands off that glass all night. He keeps staring down into it as if he's trying to read his misfortune. He's a bit wishy washy, mind you, pale and thin with a face like sand, shapeless and shifting. If I had a wife like that I'd give her a beating with a stick every morning when she woke up.

'Would you like to take a whirl, Minnie?' he says.

'Nope.'

Just like that. No please, or thank you not. Minnie Bird. The Italians would pronounce it Meanie Bird and they would be right.

Good Lord. Look who's coming over now. That Umberto. He's going to ask her to dance. Fool! He did too.

'Will you dance?' he asked, bowing slightly and cocking a bushy eye at Mr Bird.

Minnie Bird nearly knocked the chair over getting up, she was in such a hurry. I thought for a minute she was going to swing herself up onto Umberto.

'Ow yes, Umberto, ah'd be delaited.'

They always talk like that, those prissy ones. Just before she'd got off, however, digging into Umberto's elbows with her thin, dry fingers, Mr Bird emerged from the bottom of his glass and reached out for his wife.

'Oh no you don't. Come back here at once, Minnie,' he ordered her, rather loudly. 'If you're not dancing with your lawful wedded husband, then you're not going off with Romeo there.'

She stared at him, hating him steadily. Then she yanked her arm out of his grip, brushing away the traces of his fingers. Her voice came out like scalding steam:

'Don't go making a bludie fool of yourself in front of people. You know you can't dance anyway.'

The three of them were standing close together. Umberto kept glancing nervously from one to the other, running his tongue over his top lip. He moved slightly, about to break away, but Mrs Bird grabbed him.

'Don't mind him, Umberto. He's a bit tiddly.'

Her man got angry then. His pale cheeks flushed.

'Ah'm as sober as a judge, Minnie Bird. Ah've had one glass to drink all night. Now you come and sit down by me and tell that lad to go away.'

He took hold of the loose material of her white blouse and tugged at it, trying to drag her back to her seat. She kept her clutches on Umberto and stiffened her legs, having to bend over sideways where her husband was pulling her. Something ripped.

Her husband shifted his grip, but like a bulldog, to get a stronger one, and he tugged at her in increasing fury. People were watching the two of them with interest and apprehension. Next, she started shouting. Two red spots blazed on her cheeks and her mouth twisted in and out, sucking and spitting, projecting words sizzling in bile.

'You're not even half a man, you sod. You're a bludie old woman, you are. You never should have left your mam.'

She was writhing as if something had bitten her. Mr Bird was breathing loudly, I could hear him, and he was holding onto a chair with his free hand. Umberto eased himself away and disappeared. So he didn't see her false teeth fall out and her face cave in. Her jaw was convolving so violently it uprooted her teeth and they dropped onto the floor. That didn't stop her. She went on screeching while she was feeling around for them and stopped only for a second to put them back in.

'I haven't known a moment's happiness since I married you, you mealy mouthed bastard, and you only got me because o' me mam.'

Oops. They were out again. This time they had fallen under a table and a man sitting nearby darted beneath to get them. He tipped them quickly into his handkerchief and passed them over to her.

'Better put these in your bag, missus,' he said.

She dropped them into her handbag, snapping it shut with a vicious click.

'I'd like to put them right into his arse,' she gritted, 'and leave them there.'

Then she jammed her bag under her arm and marched out of the room. One of the men poured some wine into Mr Bird's glass.

'Here mate, get that into ye. She'll be all right in the morning.' He pushed the glass into Mr Bird's hand and gave him a little pat.

'Drink up man.'

Frank pressed my shoulder.

'Did you see her teeth fall out? Wasn't that funny!'

'Not very,' I said. 'I'm going home now.'

I jumped down from the boxes, shivering all over. Why did women have to be so horrible? My mother was the one who always started the fights. That Mrs Bird! If Umberto saw her so ugly, without her teeth, he would run away, and serve her right.

I couldn't sleep all night. For heaven's sake, why did people get married? Look at Lizzie and Sandro. You could see they were mad about each other. When they were dancing he was eating her up with his eyes. Would she marry him and then scream at him one day through her false teeth? You wouldn't catch me getting married when I grew up. I would have a baby and keep it myself and just visit the father sometimes, not too often.

19   The Boating Party

The morning after the party Georgina came to visit me. She shone and gleamed like polished crystal, her skin all soaped and towelled, her head alive with hundreds of tight wet curls and her teeth scoured white and phosphorescent. I used to wait outside the washroom for her while she cleaned her teeth. She would hang over the basin for ages with her eyes rolled up, spluttering chat through the foam of the toothpaste. Four times a day. You really ought to start cleaning yours, Mary. I will one day, when I'm not so busy. She bought a new toothbrush nearly every fortnight. Now here she was in her lime green shorts, ironed without a pucker, and her starched white blouse made lacelike by the hundreds of small holes pierced in the cotton. I felt grubby and tired.

'You're like Medusa with worms,' I said.

'Aye? We had a great time last night. You ought to have come. The Italians really did us proud, don't ye think? Everybody thought it was the best party they'd been to in a long time.'

'For some it was slightly less than marvellous,' I remarked, flapping my wings.

'Oh yes, the Birds.' Her voice slid away to an undertaker's whisper and we stood together, solemnly, for the fallen, our heads drooping. Poor Mr Bird. Naughty Missus. Silly Umberto.

Come down to the shop with me now, she commanded, and I'll buy you a paddle pop, one of the new banana ones, and tell you something. You know that wee chap, he's no' sae wee really, just very slim, the one I was discussing the pool with, when we got the ice creams from the Italians. Him wi' the cowboy boots? Well, he danced with me a terrific lot last night and he's asked us out today, in a rowboat. Out to the island that has the dance floor.

We'll hire a few boats, he said, and lots of us can go. Margaret too. Safety in numbers, she added shyly. True, I said. Yet crowds are not company and faces but a gallery of pictures, where, I elbowed her in her felt-covered ribs, there is no love. Bacon said that. Och, ye're aye teasing me. No kidding, though, he's a real nice bloke. Hey, don't ye think it's awfy hot? What if ah nick home for my costume and we'll go for a fling in the lake? Och, don't make faces like that. It's so drab. Ah mean, ye can dae dead man's float noo, and somersaults. If ye don't practise ye'll aye be standing in the shallow water looking at everybody. Go and get your costume and stop whingeing about it. It's nice and bright even if it's bubbly.

Thus spake Portobello's high diving champion, hockey captain, netball star, most popular girl in the tenements, her elbows eagerly coveted by school fans. It was all right for her to talk, tap dancing towards the shop in her rope-soled sneakers, sprung by her strong round calves into the air, effortlessly alighting accurately on the only patches of dirt that were free of cutting pebbles, making patterns with her feet to the dictates of her remarkable and remarked upon soprano.

'Oh hi, Georgina,' they yelled out to her from the jetty. She skipped along the concrete and cartwheeled to their feet.

Irma, Karin's sister, shook her head admiringly.

'My word, you're good at that.'

Her sister then pushed herself forward, rubbing arms with as many of the boys as she could reach without doing a detour. She tossed her hair back and stretched her arms above her head like a ballet dancer.

'I can do the splits,' she boasted, her legs sliding away from beneath her.

'Aye, so ye can,' Georgina responded, beaming at her in congratulation. 'Ah'm no' game tae try it though. Ah'm aye feart ah might hurt mahself. Inside, ye ken.'

Karin straightened herself up and started smoothing herself.

'Oh vy vorry about it? It vill go sooner or later.'

The elder Dickson boy, who had only been in the hostel about ten days, did a backward flip.

'With some people it'll be sooner rather than later,' he commented, back on his feet.

'Well,' Georgina said in her bright, let's change the subject voice, 'is naebody goin' in for a swim?'

272

'The water's full of jellyfish. Millions of them, babies, all over the place like a blinking pox.'

Will Dickson, the younger one, pointed straight down into the water. When Georgina and I pressed forward to the edge of the jetty we saw masses of tiny blue globules floating just below the surface.

'Jings, there's never been so many before. And the water's so lovely and warm,' Georgina lamented, trailing her finger in it. 'We'll have tae wait for the tide tae take them oot.'

Karin came up behind us and leaned on Georgina's shoulder. In her rasping voice she demanded:

'Why should we wait for the tide? We can take them out. Look, I show you.'

She lowered herself into the water which barely reached her hips, and stretched out her hand, covering one of the little blue jellies.

I shut my eyes:

'Don't, you'll get stung.'

'No I don't.'

When I opened my eyes an astonished jellyfish wobbled vulnerably beside my feet. Will picked up a discarded paddle pop stick and smeared the creature over the ground where it immediately began evaporating, roasted from beneath, for the white, hot jetty seared even through rubber shoes, and the sun's heat, diffused though it was, sought out the jellyfish to transform it.

Karin held out her narrow palm for everybody to see.

'Look, no sting. You put your fingers like this.' Her fingers drew together in a claw, exciting us with their boldly painted red nails. 'You touch the head. Only the legs sting.' She bent down and delved into the water again. 'Another one.'

It was slung beside the stain of the other.

'We all do it now and in half an hour they are gone.'

I thought this unlikely, considering the size of the lake, but everyone was now in the water, straddling the tall weeds and lunging after the baby jellyfish that continued to drift, placid and insensible, on the tide. Up into the air they went, uncomplaining, landing mute in rough piles on the jetty. Higher and harder they were thrown and we screamed with excitement watching them. The one that turned back we stared at blankly. How could that be? A boomerang jellyfish? It came like a fury.

Jesus Christ. Duck! And bored into Karin's eye that immediately poured tears of remorse, useless tears, down her burnt cheek where pain was ploughing furrows and throwing up tight white blisters right in front of your eyes.

'Lots of water, wash out your eye. Scrape off the tentacles. They must have broken off. We'll get a blue bag from the shop.'

We stepped over the little beasts, carefully, horrid clots of blue mucus shimmering repulsively as they oozed away defiantly into a new world.

'God, it makes ye ill tae think a' these hundreds o' wee things are going tae turn into those great big bags o' tripe. Ye'd never think the babies were so savage, would ye? How's your eye now, Karin? It doesnae look sae bloody.'

It was still watering though. The shop didn't have any blue bags. We hurried back to the hostel in silence. Arriving at the Italians' huts reminded Georgina.

'If ye feel better after lunch, Karin, would ye like tae come out with us in a boat? The Italians are going to hire a few and they'll take as many of us as want tae go.'

She turned to the Dickson brothers and to Jack and Frank.

'Dae you fellows want tae come?'

'Where are we going?'

'Out to the big island.'

They would all come. Karin too. Her eyes answered for her even before she spoke. The dark hub of her gory eye intensified in brilliance, while the red veins, fading slightly already, dilated momentarily, radiating like crimson spokes.

'I wouldn't miss it for anything,' she said huskily.

Frank spoke up, the mischief maker.

'If you can't see, Karin, Jack will take you by the hand.'

A dull red glowed for a moment through the yellow tints of Jack's long face. He clenched his fist and swung a punch at Frank, who danced backwards, laughing, teasing him in Dutch. Then the big brother strode off angrily, shouting threats over his shoulder.

'Ye shouldnae have said that, Frank,' Georgina reprimanded him. 'You've made him upset.'

Karin watched Jack disappear around a hut, then making up her mind suddenly, she yelled 'Oy', in her deep bay, and began to hurry after him, one hand covering her sore eye.

Ned Dickson started whistling 'When you are in love, it's the

274

loveliest night of the year'. He stopped in mid phrase, poised in surprise. 'Bit of all right, though, isn't she?' he said to the air. 'See you after lunch, then, down at the lake.'

My mother was very doubtful, at the table. What if the boat should capsise? People had drowned in that lake and I couldn't swim. Being able to do a dead man's float was quite the wrong sort of plea. Better to swim like a living man, she said. And I wouldn't be floating so calmly, Margaret put in, if one of those big jellyfish were to sit on my face and tickle my ear with its tentacles.

'Och, ah'm no' scared o' them any more. We pulled out hundreds this morning. Anyway, you keep your trap shut,' I warned Margaret 'or you'll no' be coming.'

There was a different lay to pipe then. She would save me. All the Italians could swim. Georgina was a champion. At least a hundred people would fight each other to rescue me if the boat should capsise, which of course was beyond imagination. Yes, it was true that southerly busters could blow in from nowhere and drive the lake crazy so that the waters ran this way and that, turning back on themselves and climbing upwards on the cool draughts, but the fishermen could tell you an hour beforehand. What about the Italians, cried my mother, shifting her line of attack. And what about them? Some were trusted inside the tight confines of a nissen hut, and nothing feared. Funny you should mention him. He's left the hostel, you know. He came to say goodbye to me. He was doing so well, too. Said he was taking a flat in town.

They all turned up at my door after lunch, since it was on the way to Alessio's hut. Irma came too, to look after Karin, whose eye was nearly normal. Irma was only seventeen, but she bore a resemblance to forty, in her hairstyle done up at the back, in the cheep cheeps of concern, in the awed anxiety that shadowed her short-sighted blue eyes or dragged her mouth open, in the protective squeeze of the arm that she was always throwing round someone or in the pressure of her fingers on yours. She was in a perpetual crouch of comfort to be offered, even squandered, from sources that seemed to be endlessly regenerating themselves. Good old Irma. In Dutch, English, German or Italian. The label appeared spontaneously. She was as pretty as Karin, though her teeth protruded slightly. Quite as slim and long in the leg. But she lacked the excitement and restless

275

vitality that made the town schoolboys call out when Karin swung past:

'Hey Daddy, buy me one of those!'

'What are you waiting for, Georgina?' That's Karin, impatient as usual. 'Knock on his door. He's *your* lover.'

'Och don't talk rot,' Georgina said peevishly. She hated cracks like that.

Well, we've made so much noise, his door's opened. No cowboy boots but he's wearing his Stetson. The Italian Tom Mix. Georgina's gone all pink. Her eyes are flitting away from each other, so I know she's embarrassed.

'We're all ready to go out in the boats, if it's still okay,' she says.

He's counting us with his eyes. 'Whew, too many.' That blasted Margaret's scowling at him. I hope he doesn't notice.

'What did ye tell us tae come for, Georgina Harvey? Ye should have made sure first.'

I could bash her for that. Such a quick temper. No wonder the doctor told Mammy to throw a bucket of water over her.

'Shut up, you. He means "many". They always say too many when they mean a lot. Not enough boats for everybody?'

'Oh yes,' he says, waving his arm over us. 'Too many boats.'

Now what's he crying 'oy, oy, oy' for? For his pals. They're all coming out of their doors like the children of Hamelin. Four and he makes five. Nine of us. Fourteen altogether. That's about three boat loads. Three dollars for the day, or what's left of it.

At the shop we waited for Alessio to hire the boats from the fisherman who also owned the shop. They came out together, and at their backs was Emilio, pushing a packet of cigarettes into his shirt pocket.

'Oy!' The Italians said together. They wanted him to come. When he shook his head, smiling to take the edge off his refusal, 'Oy', they said again, in a different tone, meaning, that's a feeble excuse.

I nudged Karin. 'Tell him to come, Karin. He's a great singer. He can sing while we're rowing out to the island. Go on. Ask him.'

She immediately glided forward and stroked Emilio's arm. 'Why you not come with us?' Her voice was smooth and vibrant like raw silk, cool but not too soothing. 'You don't like us, I think.' She tilted her face upwards, blinking at him from her fey green eyes. 'Please come. We like you to sing for us. After, we will sing for you.'

He drew a big breath. My goodness he was handsome. Let him come. *Let him*.

'When do you return?'

'About five,' I called out and slid behind Georgina.

'All right,' he said. 'I come too.' His friends slapped him on the back, joking with him in their deep, harsh voices.

The biggest boat was ours. Alessio and his friend Pino rowed. Emilio, Georgina, Irma and I sat at ease, at least on the outward journey. The bottom of the boat was crammed with our feet and legs, our toes lying close to each other within nudging distance. I kept mine to one side, for touching bothered me. Georgina never seemed to notice. When we played leapfrog or built pyramids at the direction of Ned Dickson, she hooked her arms through the boys', gripped their shoulders if we were playing at jousting, totally unaware of the contact, engrossed in the game whereas all I could think of was, I'm touching his flesh, and the thought burned me, made me tremble and want to run away. I never seemed to stop blushing. Karin didn't blush but she knew the significance of touching, investing it with something that at times, I noticed, made the boys redden too, though nothing was said.

I carefully located the positions of Emilio's feet and Pino's— Alessio was out of my way—and put a distance between us so that no thoughtless stretch could make their flesh burn mine. Emilio's toes were slim and straight, with neatly manicured nails. At Irma's instigation we began to exchange ages, for her role as comforter demanded she be busily curious.

'Oh,' she trilled at Pino with the Chinese eyes, 'you are very young. Only nineteen.' He said he was from Venice, and I wondered if his ancestors had come back from Cathay with Marco Polo and foreign wives. Alessio was the oldest at twenty-four; Emilio twenty-two. That was pretty old really, but he didn't look it.

He was facing Georgina and me. I pretended to look straight ahead, fascinated by the shoreline withdrawing from us. From the corners of my eyes, however, I examined Emilio's face. His nose was slightly hooked, dipping at the end. What a queer nose, so different from the spread-out ones of my father and uncle. His eyes were hazel and when he glanced down the lids were dark and heavy, deeply curved like those on the faces of corpses carved on tombs. I had seen pictures of them. How could anybody look like that and be alive today? The romance of his face made me almost breathless, so that when he leaned over and tapped me on the knee, I thought I'd snapped in two.

'Gosh, you're jumpy,' Georgina cried, tense herself now because of my nervy jerk.

'You are too serious.' Emilio nodded at me to underline his admonition. 'Thinking too much.'

I burst out laughing uncontrollably, till I hiccoughed and tears came into my eyes. If only he'd known what I was thinking.

Georgina gave me a curious glance and shrugged her shoulders.

'This is her mad half hour. Here, Emilio, now we've left the jetty and won't bother the village, are ye going to sing?'

'If you like.'

He sat with his head bent thoughtfully, listening to the beat of the oars. Alessio craned forward, his chin almost touching his knees. The oars swung out and hovered shakily over the water for a second before plunging backwards. On the downward thrust Emilio began his song. The long, opening phrase, dirge like, pointed up the strain in Alessio's face as his head rose, and he groaned, mockingly, shaking his head to denounce Emilio's choice. It was from Verdi's *Nabucco* though I didn't know it at the time. Pino and the Italians in the other two boats joined in. We others listened, transfixed, hypnotised by sight and sound. Our eyes, covert beneath the lids, flitted from man to man, intermittently blinking at the metallic sheen of the lake whose waters gleamed unevenly where restless fish squirmed just below the surface. The sombre voices wound our boats together in a dark chorus so exquisitely painful I could have cried, but didn't, for then I might have sobbed and thrown myself into a fit. I sat instead, holding my breath and when I glanced at Irma I saw the knuckles of her hands white where she was clasping her knees. Georgina's head was turned out towards the water.

When the singing ended, nobody said a word at first. The silence was like the brief pause at the end of a prayer. If it lasted too long, it would become embarrassing. So I was glad to hear Georgina's light, normal voice cry:

'That was a lovely song, Emilio. I would love to learn it.'

'Oh yes, but too sad.' Irma's face was all screwed up and her mouth turned down at the corners. 'It gives me a big pain here,' placing her hand on her chest.

On the island the scrub grew almost to the water's edge leaving only a scanty beach of burning rocks and sharp stones, but tall trees were visible further into the interior. We were to divide into two groups setting off in opposite directions. If we found a way into the centre we would look for the dance floor.

Irma was to accompany her sister and an Italian with sly eyes and an ingratiating smile. Margaret and Will Dickson came with us.

'Cheerio,' Georgina called to the others. 'Don't keep us waiting at the half-way mark.'

We were doing too much climbing for my liking. The sharp edges and points of rough boulders hurt even through the rubber of our thongs. Alessio had appointed himself Georgina's protector, clutching her elbow to push her up or leaping ahead to haul her over a ridge. He was constantly smiling encouragement or fond admiration for her nimbleness. She was constantly expressing her gratitude. Margaret was joking with Will Dickson and Pino of the Chinese eyes and happy grin. So I trailed behind Emilio. He was always stopping, poking among the ferns and nettles with a stick.

'What are you looking for?'

'Leaves. To make a salad. Sometimes there are very good wild leaves for eating, but I don't see any here.'

He had beautiful legs. My father had huge knees that hung over his shin bone and skinny ankles. They didn't look much of a support for his body though he could walk for miles and miles. Emilio's legs were like fine tree trunks, the colour of light bark.

'Do you like the hostel?'

He shook his head. 'Not too much.'

He was a Bolognese and they loved eating, but even to enter the canteen made him feel ill. The smell of the dripping and the sheep meat. No oil on the lettuce leaves which were bland and dull, anyway. No pasta. No olives. Cheese like soap. To build an empire on the terrible food they ate. He couldn't understand it.

'Maybe if you eat too well you don't feel like going out empire building,' I said, a bit annoyed by his criticism.

'And that's better too,' he answered.

279

I said nothing. He was jealous because he wasn't British. Even in Sydney, he went on, you could hardly get a decent meal. His mother wouldn't know him if she could see him. He was getting thinner and thinner. Well, I said, it was better than growing as stout as the fat Dutchwoman that everybody laughed at, and daringly I added that he looked like a statue. When I explained what I meant he threw his head back and laughed. His throat was hard and powerful, the skin taut. Some men had flabby throats with Adam's apples that floated soggily inside their loose skin. Emboldened, I got a penny from Margaret and told him I'd seen heads like his on pictures of medals and he laughed even more so that Alessio glanced back over his shoulder, curious.

'You are very diverting,' he said, patting me on the shoulder. His fingers were like his toes, long and brown and carefully manicured.

And what else did he do in Sydney when he wasn't hunting down food? Nothing much. He went out with friends. And when he left the hostel? Yes, that would be soon. You couldn't work in those steelworks too long. What filth. Hot and boring. Too little money. He would go north to the cane-fields and join a gang. There the money was tied to the labour. Or south to the fruit picking, not that he'd ever picked grapes. But for Australians, he shrugged, it was enough to be Italian. They thought you were born picking grapes, or digging ditches.

I would be very sorry if he went. He stared at me, his eyebrows arched in astonishment. Well, I bumbled on, there would be no one for me to listen to in the shower. Your voice enchants me, and you look so romantic.

He grabbed my ears and gave my head a little shake, laughing again. I was too diverting, he said. He caught hold of my arm and tugged me forward. 'Come on, *tesoro*. This island is too big and the sun is too hot.'

We persevered, however, until we found the path to the ruined dance floor. It was almost completely overgrown with dry foliage, tall grass, and the spindly branches of wiry trees. A long, thin, black spider with a crusty shell sat frozen faced in the middle of its great, sticky web, waiting. Not for us, I hoped, gulping. I watched it so fixedly all other forms of life escaped my notice till I blundered into something that ran red-hot up my leg and forearm. Oh God, what had touched me! Then Margaret screamed:

'Look at my arm!'

It was streaked with reddish purple lines. So were my leg and arm. Just beside us a nettle about three feet tall was vibrating gently where we had touched it, a delicate, unobtrusive creature covered not with spines but fine silky hairs that gave it a fluffy, feminine appearance. Margaret rubbed at her skin, furiously, her face red with the effort of holding back her tears.

'It was that bloomin' big nettle, there. Oh gee, it stings!'

Emilio patted my arm and clicked his tongue:

'Maybe wet sand will cool it.'

I nearly grinned, thinking that my arm would never cool while he was touching it. Finally, we persuaded the Italians to go on with their exploration of the island and Georgina came back to the beach with Margaret and me. Before long round dark clouds dragged themselves in from the sea, bloated and heavy with water, positioning themselves unhurriedly over our heads. The lake turned gunmetal grey and the water by our feet, previously quiet and still, began to slap against the rocks. The others were alarmed and came back to the boats quickly. First Karin, with her arm around the morose Van der Kooi boy who was making grim efforts to match her gaiety, like a butcher boy trying to dance a *pas de deux*. Behind them Irma tramped heavily, head thrust out and up, eyes peering earnestly into the face of the foxy-eyed Silvano whom she was counselling in the high pitched, clacking, sloshing syllables that made Dutch so unpleasant to listen to. Silvano kept nodding placatingly, his narrow eyes crinkling more tightly to mask his secret thoughts, but his lips betrayed him, flickering involuntarily at the corners. His left hand, thick and hairy to the fingernails, lay heavily on the Dutch girl's waist.

They started to push the boats into the water. What on earth was holding up Emilio and the others? I couldn't stop clenching and unclenching my hands and taking big breaths. Then Alessio appeared, scrabbling quickly over the rocks, and rushed to push the last boat into the lake.

'Hurry, Will! Help me.'

In two minutes we were all seated and Alessio grabbed one pair of oars.

'You take the others,' he directed Will.

'Hey, what about Emilio and Pino?' I demanded. 'We can't go without them.'

Alessio paid no attention and started rowing strongly.

Now I came to think of it, I didn't really like him, with that hairline moustache he wore as if he wanted to have a moustache but keep it secret. Georgina and I twisted round and yelled for the other two men. To our relief they responded with that 'oy' the Italians used to bellow through their cupped hands and a moment later they came running from the opposite direction to the one they had started from. So they had gone completely round the island.

'Alessio! Go back for Emilio and Pino.'

Will Dickson dumped his oars in the bottom of the boat and stood up angrily.

'Hey watch it,' I said. 'Ye'll capsise us.'

Pino was shouting behind us: 'Oy!' I squinted round and saw him with his hands on his hips. He shook his fist at Alessio and uttered a whole series of imprecations that made the horrid fellow go tut tut and grin.

'Look Georgina,' I said, shaking her arm, 'you'd better tell that peanut tae go back. By the time we fiddle around wi' his games the lake'll be goin' up like a water spout. Tell him ye'll no' be friendly wi' him if he doesnae quit being stupid.'

Georgina put on her gently reproving expression.

'Be fair, Alessio. This isn't the kind of weather to be fooling around. We might all get stranded if we waste too much time.'

The others by this time were half-way over the water.

Georgina put her hand on Alessio's wrist, a good move, I thought, and gazed at him like a golden spaniel.

'All right, all right.' He sighed and turned his eyes up as if to decry our poor sense of humour and then began turning the boat. Will picked up his oars again and we made for Pino and Emilio who were waiting, waist deep, at the water's edge. As we bumped up alongside them they both grabbed Alessio by the shoulders and yanked him out of the boat, into the water. Then they half dragged him, half carried him onto the rocks and dumped him, yelling and squirming, in a nettle patch.

'*Porca madonna,*' he kept bawling, clutching himself everywhere as he pulled himself up. '*Porca miseria.*' They were Italian swear words. Pino and Emilio bounded into the boat, nearly tipping us over, and Will, who was waiting with the oars ready, started pulling fast. Emilio picked up the other pair and we shot off again; no fooling this time.

'Ye're not going to leave him there, ye're not.' I was ashamed of my voice. It was a wail, a whine, and I couldn't stop tugging at my hair.

We would never get back to the hostel, having to turn again for Alessio. The clouds above us were intensifying in colour and substance. Their darkness was tinged with a dull green that made them seem like purulent sacs straining not to burst. Now and again, however, a solitary drop leaked onto your bare skin, shocking in its iciness. It was nerve racking not knowing where or when exactly the next drop would land. Much better to be poured on than dripped onto.

It was soon plain that nobody was going back for Alessio. He was leaping up and down like a dervish, flailing the air and cursing, but Pino just threw him a salute.

'He is always a silly fellow. Playing tricks too much. Next time he doesn't play any more with us.'

So Georgina's hero was a clown, though she hadn't said she'd liked him, only seemed grateful for his attentions. We were both uneasy. I glanced across at Emilio who was concentrating on his rowing. When I stared at him, biting my lips and frowning, he raised his head suddenly, aware of my perturbation.

'Don't worry, *tesoro*. He will be all right.'

I didn't smile back at him. Now I was having a good look at him in this greyish green light I saw his face cast in cruel shadows and the muscular lips that I had thought so perfect had a bleak droop to them. It was the old Jekyll and Hyde story again. How depressing.

By the time we tied up at the jetty, the others had gone. At the shop, Emilio and Pino halted. We heard them give the owner's wife a dollar so that her husband would row out and fetch Alessio about ten o'clock. The woman, astonishingly incurious, promised she would tell him when he came home.

Halfway along the road to the hostel the clouds finally unloaded themselves. The rain fell with the force of hail and in a few minutes we were saturated.

20   Falling Apart at the Centre

They were light-hearted times. Once we went to a famous beach lower down the coast in a bus ordered by the Italians. We dug for pippies and roasted them over fires of driftwood. A Neapolitan cooked a tomato sauce on one fire; spaghetti was boiled over another.

'Look,' he said, after watching our fumbling attempts to wind the pasta on a fork, and he seized in his fingers a few strands coated with the red fish sauce, held his head back, twirling the spaghetti just over his mouth, before dropping them straight down his gullet. None of us managed to be so accurate or so clean in our efforts, but the resulting comedy aided our digestions.

We played games all the time: horse racing and jousting. The men had wrestling matches and girls cheered. The Dickson boys put on a gym display, and the water was at our feet every minute, seductively cool and placid. On the way home we sang our national songs as boisterously offkey as drunks and, towards the end, as tricklingly sentimental.

But more and more, in the pauses, you became aware of tensions fine and grit-like, turning eyes to a wary red. Georgina and Alessio always sat beside each other or walked together. Sometimes Alessio laid his arms across Georgina's shoulder but almost inadvertently, not to be taken seriously, like his hairline moustache, so that you never knew if they were 'going together' or not. The same applied to Irma and Silvano. He pursued her with predatory grins and feinted caresses, always playing. She resolutely adhered to her role as big sister, slipping out from under his arm, scolding him, not too shrilly, when he tried to wrestle with her. Karin played a game of 'touch' with everyone,

284

inviting and rejecting in a way that set Jack Van der Kooi's teeth on edge and tinged greenish with bile the sallow juices of his skin. The tension was less apparent when everybody was active. It was in these breaks that occurred suddenly, spontaneously, when people flopped to the ground like rag dolls, it was in these lulls that a new kind of alertness, carefully unremarked upon, glowed in your brain and through your eyes though the rest of your face hung slack in an assumed manifestation of stupor. No one in the area missed being charged by the current. On the rare occasions that Emilio accompanied us I generated my own, completely obsessed, whatever activity was outwardly engaging my attention, with the romantic implications of his aloofness and his dark marbled face. He relaxed only when he joined in the singing. Then he was even more enchanting and I brooded over him surreptitiously, carefully guarding my rapture. Sometimes he called me *tesoro*, but absent-mindedly, even a bit patronisingly. This made me fume. Yet what were the desirable alternatives? I was dimly afraid of exploring the possibilities. So most of the time Emilio was part of the circle I sat far back on the fringes, safe out of his sight, vaguely annoyed with myself.

Uncertainty was the cause of all this tension. That became clear when I was confronted with the new boldness of Lizzie and Myra who promenaded around the hostel, their hands tucked out of sight inside the authoritative fingers of Paolo and Sandro who were newly christened Paul and Alec. Myra no longer giggled through her slipshod teeth:

'Och, mah faither would kill me if he knew!'

Now it was, 'But Paulie would kill me if he ever found oot.'

Myra's liaison with Paolo had in fact been made possible by Lizzie's struggle with her father, who often performed a caterwauling duet with Mr MacFarlane in expressing his loathing of Italians. Dagoes, he usually called them. By the time it occurred to him, however, to climb up the laundry wall and peer in the window, Lizzie and Sandro were well enough acquainted to kiss beside the gas copper, the flaming matches they had been rushing to the jet extinguished and wet, floating in the drain. Mr Barker slid down the curved iron wall on splayed fingers and ran the whole side of the hut, overshooting it in his hurry, Manfred told us. Then he rushed at the laundry door and slammed it open so hard, the handle clanged against the wall like a gong.

'Oh Dad,' said Lizzie, jerking straight up.

'Don't you Dad me, you slut,' her father returned. 'Ah'll bludie take me belt to ye when I get you inside.'

He thrust his finger tips into the flesh of her arm and dug deep so that Lizzie winced and began to cry hysterically.

'I weren't doin' nothin' wrong. Nothin' you and me mum h'aint done,' she added half defiantly.

This threw her father into a frenzy.

'You've got no call to talk about your mum like that. Your mum was pure when we got married—and I'm no Eyetalian. Git. Git home and I'll fix you when I'm finished with him.'

As soon as Lizzie vanished through the door, sobbing into the corner of her wet apron, Mr Barker clumped truculently across to Sandro who was waiting, his back to a tub and his thick arms folded across his chest.

'Right, man,' said the Englishman, snapping his teeth. 'What will it take for ye to go back to Italy? How much? I'll get you the fare and a hundred quid besides to go back to where you came from.'

Sandro rejected the offer with a raised palm.

'You go. You go to your country. I stay here.' He pounded on the copper lid with his fist and the lid bounced up and fell off, rolling along the floor like a hoop till it toppled over and hit the concrete with a grating clang. While the reverberations echoed and boomed inside the laundry, Sandro shouted at Mr Barker:

'Lizzie and I will marry. We will go away from here. Maybe to Darwin. Far away.' In a sudden change of tone and with a puzzled expression he asked, genuinely curious:

'Why you don't like me? I am a good boy.'

'Look, I don't even know you, fella. And I don't want to. People should stick to their own kind. That's what I say. You're Eyetalian. You've got different ways from us.'

'What you mean? Different? You English don't kiss?'

'Ah'm not talking about kissing. Other things.'

'What other things?'

Mr Barker made no reply. His face was red and sweating and he kept sucking his lips in and out. Finally he warned Sandro:

'Keep away from my lass. Right?'

'No.'

The refusal was unequivocal.

'Lizzie will be my wife.'

286

The Italian then turned his back on the gaping father-in-law to be and flip-flopped in his thongs out of the building.

Mr MacFarlane had nodded glumly on hearing the story, silently grieving. Horrid presentiments fluttered in his stomach and he waited in suspense. So there was little for Myra to do but announce casually that she was going to the pictures with Paolo and she liked him a lot. Her father shuddered behind his newspaper but made no comment. He tried not to see when Myra came home at night with her thick dark hair tangled, even at the roots, and her green eyes strangely luminous. Frank Van der Kooi invited Margaret to the pictures. They were free, he assured her, though you had to climb up on the laundry roof, the one in the block that was still empty. Such kissing, he murmured, wetting his lips. Better than the real pictures. You'd better remember Catherine Turner, I warned Margaret. So she didn't go.

By this time the holiday period was over and a certain fretfulness pervaded the hostel. The people in their huts seemed to be drawing closer and closer together though they longed to pull away. An obsessive inquisitiveness oozed from them like a spider's thread, and, glue like, drew them together, helplessly, forcing contacts that abraded their sensitivities, leaving them raw and vulnerable to infection.

Some women pressed the tips of their fingers together till they were quite white and paced round and round the square tables, throwing themselves down into a chair then leaping up again in seconds. Or they leaned tautly against the door jambs of their huts, doodling on the concrete step with a big toe.

'Nothing to do, nothing to do—if you're fed up with lakes.'

'I dreamed last night of mince and potatoes, made in mine own oven.'

'Ah've been up and down to that shop today at least fifteen times.'

Margaret had given up counting those who passed her window at night. We watched them in silence from behind the curtain. My mother told us to keep our traps shut, but people knew just the same. Sometimes a couple would leave the hostel suddenly, the husband abruptly having decided to rent a house even if it was more than he could afford. Sometimes a single man left hurriedly, having exhorted a promise from a friend to send on the luggage. In twos and threes, more and more often, the Italians were leaving, for Mildura, North Queensland, Sydney. Anything was better than the steelworks where they were confused with the dirt they were to sweep up. Their voices, raised at night, were not always bantering now, but more indignant, argumentative and blasphemous. Many came scowling to the canteen. One night they lit a fire in front of their section and beat morosely on empty garbage tins for hours and hours. I was shocked when I came on them tossing flying foxes carelessly into the burning logs. Poor harmless bats. The others, the 'Anglo-Saxons', cursed and ground their teeth and grumbled about 'consideration'.

Eventually, even those we liked best hired taxis to take their cases to Gullawobblong station.

'Are ye going tae come?' Georgina asked me. 'I'm starting work late. Alessio wants me to see him off.'

It would be embarrassing to get to school in the middle of a lesson. But the school had little to do with me. My world was breaking up. Everybody was going away and taking with him his peculiar warmth and colour, leaving me behind with spooks. Georgina had started at the factory with the Dutch girls. It's a wonder the school board didn't find out. They went off up the hill road laughing and singing, where a round-faced man with pale hair waited in his second-hand car to give Georgina a lift— and the others too if they wanted it.

At the station, Alessio gave Georgina a bracelet and promised to write when he learned English well enough. They were all excited at going away, you could tell. Their faces were dimpling again and their eyes crinkling in the semi-oriental way many of the Italians had. They were already looking to the future.

Oddly enough Emilio was still at the hostel, though he had been one of the first to mention leaving. Occasionally, when I walked past his window, I saw him sprawled across the bed, reading a magazine and smoking. Sometimes he came to chat if I called, but most of the time he was out of sight and I heard him singing in the shower less often. Just before we shifted to the Commission house I saw him for the last time. For a change, Georgina and I went to the swimming pool at Steelhaven one Saturday. We walked to it, up and down very steep hills, that seemed even more precipitous on the way back when we were tired out by the sun. There were dunes to be climbed before we reached the hills and we trudged up the first one none too happily, especially since Georgina's purse had been stolen from the change room.

On the top of the first dune we stopped, too puffed to speak, and looked across at the deep ripples of the second one. Then as we prepared to slide down the sand, Georgina suddenly pointed at two figures lying in the hollow of our dune, at the edge of it, almost on the beach.

'Isn't that Emilio doon there?' she said, squinting.

I squinted too.

'It's him, all right. I'd know his black and red striped trunks anywhere.'

Emilio was stretched out on the sand with his hands behind his head. A woman was kneeling beside him, her head bent over his. We could hear her laughing in the bass voice that commanded so much admiration in the hostel. Like Tallulah Bankhead, some said, or Marlene Dietrich. She was tickling his face with something long and slender, held in her hand, a straw perhaps, or blade of grass. While we watched, astonished, Emilio sat up with a sudden and quick movement and grabbed the woman, throwing her down on the sand. Her thick black hair, usually wound around her head like a turban, now spread out around her like a lacquered fan and we heard her murmuring some kind of mild reproof.

'Who would have thought it?' Georgina muttered. 'What would Jack say if he knew?'

'Aye, and her husband that studies his bible,' I said, wishing there was a huge boulder handy to hurl down on their heads. 'I hope he's been reading Hosea lately.'

We tramped along the crest of the dune, away from Emilio and Mrs Van der Kooi.

'And she was the one who disapproved of Karin,' I said, remembering suddenly. 'Talk aboot whited sepulchres. She makes me sick.'

I was sick from something else, actually, though Georgina wasn't going to know about it. The blood was rushing to my head and my eyes felt as if they were about to explode with the heat and pressure behind them. I covered my heart with my arms, that Georgina shouldn't hear its thudding.

'She'd get stoned to death in the olden times,' I said, relishing the thought. I would be in the front line.

'What gets me is that she's so old.' Georgina screwed up her face with distaste. 'She must be all of thirty-six.'

'She's a right old bag.'

'Och, ah wouldnae say that. She's got a neat figure in shorts and that white she's aye wearing shows up her tan. And there's a' that hair she's got.'

When we scrambled up from the hollow we had slithered into, Georgina said: 'Just the same, ah'm surprised at Emilio. Ah mean, he never flirted or acted the goat like the others. You would have thought he wasnae interested.'

Exactly what he was interested in, I preferred not to imagine and yet images sneaked through my mind, one by one, like a series of snapshots. You flicked through them hurriedly and then spread them out carefully for close examination, but each one enraged you so violently you slammed them all together and hurled them into the fire, dancing up and down like Rumpelstiltskin till your foot went right through the floor. Oh, to kill that woman. To strangle her with her thick, pitch black hair!

After that we smiled extra sweetly at the Van der Kooi boys, jumping to gratify their slightest whim, laughing at their heavy jokes at which hitherto I had rolled my eyes disdainfully, treating them like ignorant victims of some long fatal disease, till we drove the elder one to the edge of anger.

'What's the matter with you two girls?' he burst out impatiently. 'You make me feel as if you're praying over me.'

Our clubfooted pity! I was ashamed of my insensitivity and falteringly offered what I hoped was a plausible explanation.

'It's only because I'm leaving the hostel on Friday. I told Georgina I should make an effort to be nice to you. We're always arguing.'

Amazingly, he believed me, expanding slightly his lips in a short grin and shaking his head chidingly.

'Please. Be normal. I can understand that.'

The next Friday was the last time I ever slept in the hostel, and even on my visits, no mention was made of the Van der Koois' mother. Her relationship with Emilio must still be safe in the sand dunes. On school mornings I made sure I was late for the Eugoberra bus and waited for the hostel one. The Dutch girls sang no more. They chatted instead, in the subdued manner of the people at the front. One day, however, about a month after we'd moved, I noticed that Frank Van der Kooi's seat on the bus was empty. When it remained so for three more days, curiosity brought me to question Jack with whom I now exchanged only passing salutations.

'Is your brother sick?'

He didn't answer me straight away. Sulky fellow, I thought, he gets sourer by the day. Then he was mumbling through drooping lips.

'Frank has gone back to Holland with my father.'

And that's all I'm going to get, I decided. He jerked his head nervily back to the window, jumping his right shoulder up and forward, almost obscuring his face. Riding in the bus after that was like being in a hearse.

Part III   The Fibro Cottage

21 Oh, What a Lovely Garden

Our fibro cottage when we first saw it was stunning in its excellence. A complete house, *our* house, in its own garden, a garden resembling a miniature meadow, every grain of it sprouting tall paspalum that to us tenement dwellers could have passed for a field of unripe wheat. We walked all around the house, slowly, tentatively, disbelievingly, eyeing off the sharp corners with the pride of ownership. Not that we owned it, really, but we were its possessors, which was good enough.

'All ours,' we gloated.

I clambered up on the top rail of the back verandah from which I could look down upon a railway track gleaming like streaks of bright sun through the undergrowth. At the bottom of the garden an untidy looking shack lolled up against our back fence, its roof bitten away by rust. The top of one small window, a few inches of dirty glass framed in splintered wood, peered over our fence like a bleary eye. A missing brick in the chimney caused smoke to pour from two orifices, the nostrils of a misshapen nose. Down there, in the thick scrub, a neighbour was hiding and watching us.

'Oh what a lovely garden,' I cried, admiring everything. 'And it's ours, *ours*.'

My mother was turning on taps in the laundry which opened off the back verandah.

'Good pressure here. No' a bad copper. Nae coin in the slot gas meter. That's good.'

'Our very own laundry. No sharing. Our own, our own.'

Margaret had gone inside a funny little hut that stood like an upended coffin at the foot of the back path.

'Hey,' she yelled. 'Come here! Our very own potty.'

We all rushed down to look. She was holding the door back with one arm, pointing to a squat wooden box huddled almost out of sight in the shadows. 'Have a look inside.' She raised the lid.

'It's an iron pot, I think.'

We squeezed together, peering into the black depths of the tin and then let the lid drop.

Susan was biting her lips worriedly. 'I don't like that kind of toilet. No chain. Nothing goes away. It all stays inside. Even visitors'.'

'Getting higher and higher,' Margaret goaded, holding her nose expressively.

'What if. . .' We looked at each other. 'It wouldn't touch . . . would it?'

'That depends.'

Oh dear. Better not eat too many apples. Nor drink too much tea. And remember. Waste not, want not.

It was only then, gathered together outside the toilet, that we realised they had all come to watch us. The neighbours, I mean. They were fidgeting on their back verandahs, peeping at us from under their armpits or through the fingers that they used to push back their hair or scratch their head, if they were bald. We hurried away from their sight, jumping the back steps two at a time, rushing past the four bedrooms into the lounge. There they were again. Much younger ones, though, for they had taken up bold positions, hanging low on their shin-high fences, unabashedly observing us from across the narrow street. My mother, on seeing them, threw herself deep into the trunk in which we kept our bedding.

'Here, you two,' she cried, upside down. 'Take these sheets and tack them up on the front room window. A lot o' nosey parkers they are here. Jesus, they'll be able tae count the times ye go tae the lavatory. Nothing'll be sacred.'

Margaret and I, balanced on upturned suitcases, tacked a sheet up. When we had finished I felt it tauten and glanced over at Margaret to see what she was doing. She had thrust her head under the sheet and with her thumb touching her nose, was waggling her fingers through the glass. Before I could stop her she had stuck her tongue out and was crossing her eyes frantically.

'Quit it, you stupid,' I hissed at her. 'We've only just got here and there you are wanting to start a fight wi' people.' A quick flicker across the street told me her actions had not gone unobserved. The half dozen boys and girls who had previously been sitting quietly on the fence had now risen and were dithering around like discomfited cows.

We dropped the sheet immediately and set about covering up the remaining eight windows. Once we finished, we realised with a giggle that there were no sheets left to sleep in.

'Won't make any difference,' Susan muttered, pacing up and down, tight lipped. 'Got no beds—except that one in the middle room.'

'For God's sake, will ye stop that marching up and down,' my mother commanded her irritably. 'Ye'd think ye had St Vitus' dance. What the hell's the matter wi' ye?'

'Ah want tae go tae the toilet,' Susan said, crimsoning with annoyance.

'Well, away ye go then. Naebody's tying ye doon.'

'But ah'm scared it'll get filled up too quickly.'

'Let the government worry aboot that,' my mother retorted. 'They're the ones that have tae empty it.'

'Dae ye think the Prime Minister has a turn, Mammy?' I asked her slyly.

'Helluva funny, you are. The council does it. They pay people to empty the tins.'

So Susan went, reluctantly. We awaited her return with interest.

'What was it like.'

'Noisy. It booms inside the tin like a train goin' through a tunnel. Ah'm sure people can hear ye.'

'I hope ye didnae use up too much space,' I said to her teasing-ly. 'We'll a' have tae be economical.'

She still looked worried. 'Ah'm goin' tae use the school toilet as much as ah can.' Then another thought struck her. 'But they've got tins as well. And there are hundreds o' kids at school.'

When father returned from work that afternoon Susan immediately broached the subject to him. There were so many kids tae use the toilet tins. What if they filled up and spilled over?

My father regarded her gravely.

'Aye it's a helluva system. But did they no' gie ye your bottle at school?'

'What bottle?'

'Your toilet bottle. Everybody has tae carry a toilet bottle here.'

Susan started punching into my father's stomach.

'It's no' funny, Daddy Lavery.'

The initial distaste Susan felt for the waterless closet remained with her for years and the rest of us were not entirely unaffected by her anxieties. On Thursday mornings just before the sanitary carter came bounding down the path with an empty pan swung up on his shoulder, she would be ready with a warning if anyone made to head for the back verandah.

'Better be careful, if ye're going tae the lavatory. The man'll be here soon. He might catch ye on the pan.'

This was a possibility we all regarded with horror.

'If he comes when ah'm on it,' Margaret said, 'ah'm just goin' tae sit there for ever.'

'Ye should leap behind the door,' Robert suggested, 'and he wouldnae see ye.'

It was their sandshoes that worried me. They wore sandshoes with holes in the uppers, and socks with matching holes so that their toes protruded through both. Very often you didn't hear them at all. They should have been made to wear a bell round their necks.

'Ah'm aye terrified,' Margaret confided to us, 'that ah'll be sitting there in a daze, or reading a comic, and they'll just fling the door open. Ye know the way butlers do when they're announcing the next guest at a ball. Miss Margaret Lavery! And there'll be crowds of people tae see me.'

We all shivered, sympathetically.

At night we bargained heavily round the table to seduce a companion for evening evacuations. The verandah light did not extend as far as the hut which seemed even more coffin-like in the dark and all of us except Margaret were afraid to be alone on the iron pot. Or rather, we were afraid of not being alone. The corners of the hut were often battlefields for grim encounters between spiders and other beasts. Once I had watched a white spider plunge from a thread attached to a rusty nail and throw itself upon a frightened cockroach, turning it quickly on its back. The cockroach's legs flailed the air in panic, wildly at first, and then increasingly feebly as the spider bound it tightly with thread from its own mill, reels and reels of it, till the cockroach was cocooned, shimmering in fright, and the spider began to haul it, bumpity bump, up the rough lacerating door. Had the toilet man flung the door open then, he would have fled from my ghastly face.

In the night, in the toilet, the mind conceived its own terrors that turned the bowels costive. And so, Margaret was always in demand as an escort.

'Ah'll dry the dishes for ye, if ye'll come with me. Make the bed. Wash your socks. Press your tunic. Or take your turn at making supper.'

Sometimes she was fiendish, forfeiting payment and warranting a punch or a kick once she was dragged from her hiding place. That was when she waited outside until you were engaged and then ran away, shrieking: 'Ah'm going, ah'm going,' abandoning you to dark things, leaving you in a frenzy, rattling the toilet fixtures with fingers that kept tripping each other up until you snatched the door open and stumbled outside, praying for the moon. You were never confident when she accompanied you, though her slanted smile was meant to reassure you that this time would be different.

No wonder the radio was constantly exhorting people to take a Ford pill for instant relief. And lots of people did take them. Without paying.

'You know the item that's most often stolen from my shop,' the keeper told my mother. 'Those bloody Ford pills. Half the nation must be suffering from constipation. I lose more of these than chewing gum.'

After a time I discovered that there were some in Eugoberra who had a way, never mentioned aloud, of circumventing night-time trips to the iron pot. Most lawns in our suburb were yellowish, partly from inadequate rainfall at certain times of the year and partly because the tenants were constantly shaving the grass almost down to its roots. On some lawns, however, a bright swathe of grass, nearly a foot wide, never lost its greenness.

'How come the people across the street have that very green grass in the middle of the lawn?' I asked my mother.

'Peeing in the bath,' she answered briefly.

'You're not serious, Mammy?'

'Too right,' she said, speaking like an Australian. 'That strip's where the bath water runs. It's the ammonia in the urine that keeps the grass green. It's a kind of fertiliser.'

I was astonished. Thereafter, on my way to the station where

I caught a train to school, I examined carefully every lawn. Jesus. All those people peeing in their baths. Even the house at the bottom of the street that had venetian blinds and front steps solpahed red, where the little girl had her hair screwed into tight, lank ringlets and her mother weeded, wearing protective gloves and a turban over her coiffure, even that lawn was striped in green. In fact you couldn't miss it because the little plaster dwarfs were squatting on the bright part.

'Fancy that,' I said to the table one night.

'Aye, fancy,' they agreed, listening attentively.

Little by little, our front lawn also developed its distinctive band. My mother ranted, and scoured the bath with Ajax. Sometimes she lay in wait, her ear pressed beneath the door handle, but she caught no one, and no one would own up.

That first night, however, problems other than the absence of sewerage dominated our conversation. As Susan had pointed out, we had no beds, except for the big brass and iron frame left by the previous tenant. So, after tea, which was laid out on a wooden board meant to cover the laundry sinks, we piled all our coats and blankets together and slept on the floors, excited by the novelty of the situation. Where on earth were we to get beds and chairs? There weren't enough blankets to go round when we had to use some to lie on. We didn't even have the hire purchase deposit, for new beds would cost a fortune.

'Damned lucky it's summer,' I heard my mother growling at my father. He was wandering around in an aimless sort of way, at a loss to know what to do. About five o'clock, the second afternoon, there was a knock at our front door and we all rushed to open it. My mother squeezed to the front and we split up on both sides of her to examine the woman standing there. She was just finishing off a cigarette, drawing avidly at the last of the dout before flicking it onto the verandah and screwing her heel into it. We waited for about five minutes while she coughed, holding her head between her hands. Her hair was yellow and frizzy.

'Yes?' my mother asked, finally, when the coughing stopped.

The woman's voice was deep, and rusty, crackling like static.

'G'day. Doreen Glim's me name. Live across the street. Heard from your little fella you're a bit short of beds. Just remembered I've got one under the house. Used to be me and Fred's before we got our new suite. It's no good to us. Might do till you get something better.'

She waited expectantly, a faint smile fretting her reddish

pancake makeup with infinities of hairline cracks. Her eyes, half closed but missing nothing, looked behind us. Before my mother could answer, she went on:

'If your husband's home, maybe he and Fred can carry it over —after dark.'

Pride and necessity fought each other across my mother's face. She was furious and glad. After a minute's thought, she nodded her head and held the door open wide.

'Come in, Mrs Glim.'

'Doreen.'

'It's true we havenae any beds. We've only just moved across from the migrant hostel. Who was it told ye, did ye say?'

'Me. Ah did, Mammy,' Jackie spoke up proudly. 'Ah told all the kids we were sleeping on the floor. They said they were going tae ask their mothers if they could too.'

He was going to get a slap afterwards, blabbing our affairs outside. Susan pinched his arm as soon as the woman had gone.

'You're a right big mouth!'

His slap was postponed till later, however, for there was another knock at the door. Another neighbour. With another bed. And a table. And chairs. And a wardrobe. All evening long. And curtains. Some of the kids who had been watching us from the fence slunk in behind their parents and eyed us cagily before casting their beadies into the far-flung corners of our fibro realm. And not even hiding what they were doing. Talk about ignorant! We stared back at them, wooden faced, blocking off their vision where it was practicable.

When they had all gone, the house was full of dust and aglitter with alien cobwebs, the floorboards black from tramping feet. We were to sleep on the floor again that night, my mother decided, until she scrubbed the furniture down with lysol. She was terrified of bugs. Someone had given us a huge whitewood table. We covered it with newspaper and had our dinner from it, sitting on fruit boxes.

'Well, ye cannae say they've no' decent people.' That was my father. 'There's no' too many that'll come tae your door like that tae gie ye things. They've got big hearts, Australians.'

My mother agreed with him. 'Aye, they're good people.'

We sat round the table with our heads bowed, silently offering gratitude for our kind neighbours. They were hospitable too. The next night, Mrs Glim appeared again, devouring her cigarette, her eyes slitted against the smoke.

'C'mon over and have a drink with me and Fred. Go on,' she pressed, as she saw my mother getting ready to refuse. 'It'll do you good. And me and Fred are glad o' the company.'

So my mother and father went and returned about an hour later.

'What did ye do, Mammy?' I asked her. 'What did ye talk aboot?'

'Och, we had a couple o' glasses o' beer. Ah cannae mind what we talked aboot, tae tell ye the truth. They've got two girls aboot your ages and the man's a contract miner.'

That night, after setting the table for supper, I went outside onto the front path. It was nine o'clock. I looked up at the sky, speechless with admiration for its sumptuosity, a rich black fabric shot through with flashing ice. What I liked best about the stars was their distance. They were far out of touch. In Scotland, the sky pressed down upon you like a coolie hat, restricting your vision. I held my head up until I got a crick in my neck and then I glanced up and down the street. It was completely silent. Not a light was on in any house.

I went back inside, to Margaret, who was pouring tea in the kitchen.

'People go tae bed here, awfully early. There's nobody up in the street.'

'They cannae have much tae say to each other,' she said. And added, after a moment's reflection: 'Maybe their dreams are exciting and they rush tae them as soon as they can.'

People continued to be helpful and pleasant. They brought forks, spades, scissors and scythes so that we could cut down the paspalum and plant vegetables. We got blisters from wielding the scythes. My mother looked down on my father one afternoon, when he was bent over, his face purple with exertion. He needed a special scythe for he was left-handed.

'That's the right implement ye've got in your hand,' she called to him. 'A' ye need now is a hammer.'

My father just grinned.

'Never misses an opportunity, does she?'

The neighbours supervised our work with friendly approval, expressing appreciation as my father, in his stolid and unhurried way, turned over sod after sod, building the earth up in a series of burial plots, so it seemed. It's more than the abos ever did. Bunch o' no hopers they were. Drinking all the time. Never even mowed the lawn. Would you like a few tomato plants, morning glories, a bit of pig face? Here, have a few plums. Each morning for weeks and weeks, while conflict at the pit continually tapped my father's pay packet, a bucket of vegetables was deposited on our side of the fence by our pensioner neighbour. It wasn't always easy to thank him. He seemed to work in his garden when we were elsewhere. On the rare occasions that we managed to catch him, he listened sweetly to our professions of gratitude and smiled over our shoulders, nodding his head slightly.

'Uh huh.'

'They're such nice people,' my mother kept saying. You had to balk at that fact. There was no going past it or around it. Yet I didn't like them. I was ill at ease and resentful that I had to owe them gratitude. It was too much effort, the strain of smiling constantly, of agreeing all the time, anxiously agreeing, of saying: really? Is that so? Or, good gracious, imagine that, or I can hardly believe it. But they were so vulnerable nothing could induce you to tackle them. It would be offensive to question them, to imply you thought they were fools, or, at best, that their arguments were invalid. Some instinct warned us to pander to them and our jaws ached permanently from grinning. In the beginning, apart from the old pensioner, it was difficult to differentiate one from the other, for their speeches were all formulaic, and the set phrases were punctuated with niggling little irruptions of laughter that made you drop your eyes. It took time to work out that words should be discarded as identity markers.

To the left of us was a man with a very tidy garden. Most gardens in Eugoberra were tidy, but this was usually from emptiness: in the front, an oleander or two and shorn grass, a wild lemon or plum in the back. This was ambitious horticulture. Mr Billem's garden, however, was decidedly eccentric, sometimes provoking a wry face from the neighbours and, more rarely, mildly disparaging remarks.

'It's not what I would have in my own garden, mind you. All those wine bottles round the beds. Well, I suppose it's a bit artistic, maybe, but if you start asking where he gets the plonk bottles from, I mean there could be a couple of hundred there, people might get to thinking. Do I make my point? I'd rather keep me bottles under the house till the clean-up. What you drink's your own affair, don't you reckon? Don't get me wrong, mind. I'm not saying anything derogatory about Phil. He's a bonzer bloke. Terrific worker. Oh, my oath. Could set those young blokes half his age right back on their ears. Quiet fellow, but a bit o' the old pinko when he's had a few. Yeah. You wouldn't think it. Buys those coloured Chinese magazines with all the big tractors and red cheeked sheilahs. My oath. Oh, a terrific Federation man! But those shitty little beds he's got all over his lawn. That's his business I always say. Makes it difficult to mow, like. I like a straight go meself. Them beds and trees are more trouble than they're worth. Picking up leaves all the bloody time.'

In fact, Mr Billem had no trees at all in his garden. He had set out his lawn like the nine of diamonds with rigidly shaped flower beds arranged symmetrically throughout it, the soil bound tightly by inverted wine bottles that gleamed lushly after they had been hosed. The diamonds were set in a frame of low-growing annuals planted with precision: a dark blue margin of lobelia adjoining a line of red begonias that were in turn linked to white phlox, the square being completed by a border of multi-coloured portulaca. The eye scanned the pattern, missing the parts.

Mr Billem cursed and swore when he discovered the edges of his diamonds oftentimes ragged with holes where some mischief-maker had loosened a few bottles and thrown them all over the road. But he was never short of spare parts and the holes would be filled in immediately, the new bottles lovingly pressed down till they were level with the others. Admittedly, sometimes he would have to replace a green with a brown, but that little incongruity was usually attended to within days.

Mr Billem longed to protect his pretty pattern, but he didn't fancy lantana or blackberry as a hedge. Too difficult to control. So he planted a low hedge of elegant berry bush, not too thick, that bore delectable little balls of red and yellow. They glowed like suns in the sheen of your pupils, but once inside your mouth belched into flames that roared up your nose and in your ears in a second, turning your eyes into white hot cinders. And if you rubbed them with stained fingers, the pain bored into the back of your skull. Henceforth, for the little mischiefs, the gay berries assumed monstrous proportions of malevolence and the wine bottles remained inviolate in their protectorate, brittle guardians of order.

Mr Billem himself was very neat in his person, always clean-shaven to his bones which were very pointy. An F.B.I. hat shadowed his eyes and the pockets of his miner's cardigan sagged equally low on both sides. His speech was the most formulaic of all, and he tipped his hat when he spoke to you.

'Hot, coming up the hill,' in February.

'Windy, coming up the hill,' in August.

'Cold, coming up the hill,' in September.

To which I replied in despair: 'You can say that again.' If only I could see his eyes. But his head was usually tilted sideways when he spoke, or if he turned to look at you, he pulled his hat further down his forehead.

Then one night I came upon Mr Billem in chaos and I exulted. It was a Friday. I had finished washing the dishes and I went into the bedroom Margaret and I shared with Susan to make sure the window was shut, or the room would later be unbearable with mosquitoes. I stretched upwards to grasp the window frame and saw a light in the Billems' kitchen which was directly under our bedroom. Mr Billem was sitting in the middle of his kitchen floor singing angrily and thumping the linoleum with his sharp knuckles.

'Come and look at this, Margaret,' I hissed, tiptoeing to the door.

'He's drunk,' she said, reprovingly, pushing her head too far out of the window.

'The bitch!'

'Dae ye think that's his wife he's talking aboot?'

'She's a bloody fat bitch.' He had taken the saucepan that he was holding between his legs, and slammed it down with a thud. 'Bloody housie.' He was digging a big slotted spoon into the pot and gouging out some dark meat. 'Always burns me dinner. Never fails. And me working like a black in the pit. She doesn't give a—shit.' I giggled at the way he spat this out. He was chewing now, silent for the minute, staring straight at the cupboard doors, his hand absent-mindedly stroking the brown bottle beside the pot. Then he dropped the spoon on the floor and twisted the stopper from the bottle with greasy fingers. He lifted his head, stretching his scraggy throat upwards like a goose and the liquor poured straight down. We waited while he held his hand over his heart. And belched loudly. 'Three daughters, and a man comes home to burnt bloody tucker. Is it fair? I'm asking you.' I slapped my hand over Margaret's mouth to shut off her reply.

'That's a rhetorical question, you fool.'

'There's no justice. Three daughters... the bitch. I'll give her bloody housie when she gets back. And plenty bloody of it.' This sent him into a maniacal snickering on his back. Then he sat up abruptly, glaring all round him. 'Oh, fork 'em, fork 'em all,' and to our amazement he was weeping, banging the spoon on the floor again, an ineffectual beating that ended with the spoon falling from his fingers to the floor. His head was down, his eye fixed on the linoleum for a few minutes, before he too slid to the floor, forward on his face, and slightly twisted. In the russet browns of his pit cardigan, Mr Billem's arm curled round his head like an autumn leaf.

I couldn't stop thinking about it, coming up the hill on the following Monday. Things would be different now, now that we had seen him. He would have to say real things. Talk properly, because now I knew him. He was in the garden as you might expect, crouched on his hunkers, weeding in between the bottles.

'Hullo, Mr Billem.' I waited, breathlessly.

He turned his head towards me, not right round, and tipped his hat, nodding recognition.

'G'day. Bloody hot, coming up the hill today.'

Parlez moi d'amour. Speak to me Mr Billem. Not of love, but of feelings and thoughts. Tell me who you are. I'm your friend Mr Billem. I saw you when you were suffering and I love you for it. Oh Mr Billem, be mine this arvo! But he had turned his back and was patting the bottle, and I ran down our path, throwing my case ahead of me. How dare he insult me with his non-speak, his nothing today, thanks, no sale, nothing, nothing, nothing. I'll turn his heart out and have it beating in my hand.

Inside my room, I stretched out on the bed, drumming my heels on the top of the brass end, and mumbled to myself:

'I hate Australians, I hate 'em, I hate 'em.'

The others were substantially little different from Mr Billem. We were welcome any time at Mrs Glims, she told us.

'C'mon over and have a chinwag.'

So we did, one Saturday afternoon. In the living-room all the bits and pieces of furniture, the lean, bony lounge suite, the stools, even the pictures on the wall, were turned in obeisance towards a heavy, dark radiogram that straddled the middle of the floor, in front of the fireplace. It shone with a high french polish.

'Whaddya think o' my new radiogram,' Mrs Glim demanded, waving her arm towards it. A spot of liquor spilled from the glass in her hand and sank through the carpet.

The second daughter, Kathy, controlled a groan. 'Aw, Mum,' she muttered under her breath and in a flash was gone to the kitchen from where she reappeared carrying a wet cloth. She crouched down over the stain, rubbing at it with enormous vigour. A spot on the carpet meant a lot to her.

'What'll you have?' Mrs Glim asked, ignoring the carpet. 'Try some of this Williams Sweet Sherry, Rose. It really gives you a kick.'

My mother demurred: 'At this time of the day, Doreen? It's a bit early, isn't it?'

'Don't be bloody silly. There's Fred, gone off with his mates for a few beers and you can be sure they're not drinking in an empty hotel. If it isn't too early for them, it isn't too early for me. Us. Does that make sense, love?'

The question was directed at me and I blushed, not knowing what to say.

''Course it does,' she went on, answering herself. 'Dotty, get the girls a glass of orange each, and we'll play our new records.'

Whilst the youngest one was in the kitchen at her mother's behest, Kathy sprawled along the lounge, her face a crossover of disapproval and discontent. She stared at the ceiling, moon-faced, ignoring her mother's proud inventory of the living-room furniture. It was clear we were supposed to praise Mrs Glim's judgement, but after years of carefully ignoring articles in a house, it was difficult for me to reverse my attitudes so suddenly. I gave only quick, shifty glances at the carpet, genuine Axminster and only down six months, at the new curtains, made to measure, and with a prod from Dotty, who had shoved a glass of orange into my hand, I went over to examine the radiogram, a little emboldened by my mother's willingness to interest herself in it.

Half a dozen records could be played without having to touch the turntable, Dotty announced, starting off the first of the half dozen. So we sat, holding our orange drinks and listened to Bing Crosby in a duet with his son, followed by Vaughan Monroe singing 'The Night is Young and you're so Beautiful'. Mrs Glim swung her toe gently to the rhythm and tapped the arm of her chair with her glass. My mother, I could tell, was tense, impatient of sitting still and anxious to go home.

'Well, I'll be going then, Doreen,' she said abruptly, getting up. But Mrs Glim thrust her back into the chair. 'Just another drop, Rose,' filling my mother's glass and topping her own. 'No rush, is there? How ya goin' at school, love?' she called across to me.

'All right, thank you.'

'Geez, you're lucky to be going to the High. You've gotta be good to go there. Our Kathy goes. Doin' all right too, aren't ya, love? Why don't you and the kids get together more often? Go blackberrying up the bush. Geez, you get some lovely berries, this time o' the year. Take a billy, and your mum can make some tarts.'

We went up the bush a number of times with the Glim girls, carrying old kerosene tins that we filled with the berries, the bottom ones being pressed to juice by the top half before we got home. We could talk while there were objects to provoke questions. Have you ever seen a snake? No, but Des Rowles, two streets away, once came home with a dead diamond snake. Didn't he, Kathy? Have you always lived at Eugoberra? Yeah. We was born here, wasn't we, Kathy? Real good spot, I reckon. Got the beaches and the bush, both nearby. Ever gone swimming at the waterhole? Where? Up the mountain, near the road. Geez we've had some good times there, haven't we, Kath? Those fellas with Des Rowles always turn up when we're there. They duck you and everything. Don't they, Kathy? Hey, do you ever go to the flicks of a Satday? Come with us tonight, *Quo Vadis* it is. They have all these crucifixions and everything. Ask your mum. I know this fella who sells lollies at the interval. He'll give us some for nothing.

For Margaret, it was enough, on these outings, to be physically engaged. She gave all her time to the blackberries, rationing her rest periods, refusing to eat anything she had picked, thrusting her arms right into the centre of the bushes, indifferent to the thorns or the possibility of disturbing a snake.

'They run away if they hear ye coming,' she told me scornfully.

309

She barely listened to Dotty's prattle, answering briefly, but with a show of interest if she were addressed directly. When she was tired out and her tin full, she announced herself ready to go home. If no one else had finished, too bad. She went alone, carrying her burden effortlessly, striding easily through the paddocks, as much at home there as she had been in the streets around the docks.

I was tense all the time, up the bush, fearful of snakes, always picking the berries that grew on the outer surfaces of the bushes, careful never to wander too far from the others. Dotty Glim's unending prattle made my head ache. Once or twice I tried to interrupt it.

'Why do you like to see crucifixions?'

'Cause there's all that blood and stuff. It's exciting, see.'

'No I don't, exactly. Why is it exciting?'

She was annoyed at my persisting. 'Aw, you know why. Gawd, what d'ya think I am? Everybody likes that sort of stuff. Whaddya wanna harp about it for? You like it or you don't, doncha?'

It was absurd anyway, discussing a predilection for crucifixions among the blackberry bushes. Kathy Glim said very little. She seemed preoccupied with worrisome thoughts. She was fifteen, a year ahead of me at school.

'She's got a boyfriend,' her sister said, with awe. 'Have you met Russ?' Surely she would have known if I had met him. It could only have been at her place.

'Geez, he's a good lookin' fella. Isn't he, Kath? Works in a garage. He's got a car. Fixes Mum an' Dad's motor bike.'

Every afternoon, as soon as Mr Glim got home from the pit, Mrs Glim tied her headscarf under her chin and climbed on the pillion behind him. They went fishing at a creek about three miles away.

'Nothing like a bit o' fresh fish and a schooner o' beer,' she assured my mother. 'Why don't you and Bob take it up, Rose? Good sport, fishing.'

'What do you think about when you're fishing, Mrs Glim?' I asked her. 'It's a long time to be sitting doing nothing.'

'Aw, nothing much love. Nothing much to think about. Have a bit of a smoke and a snooze. The time soon passes.'

There wasn't a book in their house. Not even one borrowed

from Eugoberra library. The girls spent most of their spare time sewing their smart, new dresses, when they weren't out swimming. They were the only people our age in the street, if you didn't count Harold Brigon who lived next door to them.

We weren't allowed near him or his sisters and brothers. There were ten of them, eight still living at home, and the younger ones in Sadie's class had lice. My mother couldn't believe it when Sadie started scratching her head. We thought we'd left that all behind us. Every fibro cottage had a shower, after all. At the chemist's shop, two miles away, there was no D.D.T. emulsion to be had and the young chemist had never heard of a fine comb.

'It's short, with teeth on both sides, tightly packed together,' my mother explained. Adding in a lower voice: 'It's used for removing lice.'

'Oh,' the chemist said, drawing back a little. 'We don't use these things here.'

'That's obvious,' my mother rejoined curtly. Outside, she was white with humiliation and rage. 'Patronising get. Ignoramus. Who the hell does he think he's talking to!'

No green ladies came to the school to examine the heads. Finally my mother visited the headmaster and told him Sadie had to be shifted. It was his responsibility to ensure that the Brigon kids didn't infest other children. She had cleaned Sadie's head every night, and each day she had come home from the school with another lot. It was a problem he hadn't encountered before, the headmaster complained. In the end, he had to be threatened with the Public Health Department. What poor Mrs Brigon did, we never discovered—she had no fine combs, nor D.D.T. Someone mentioned kerosene. Though the infestations ceased, my mother forbade us to enter the Brigon house. We were very sorry, for Mrs Brigon was a homely little woman who spent most of her days cooking Anzac biscuits when she wasn't in bed with asthma. Her children, all of them born with turned-in feet and knock knees, shared her suffering anxiously, ever ready to dart to the cupboard for her tablets when her wheezing started and her lips turned blue. Mr Brigon was a truck driver whose vehicle was rarely parked in his own driveway. On those singular occasions his knees were seen to be knocking too, but the cause, one suspected, was a leakage of alcohol from the brain.

311

We had some contact with two or three other neighbours. The wife of our pensioner was a serene, gracious old woman who prided herself on her manners (which were, for that matter, unexceptionable), and was devoted to her grown-up children, especially to her daughter who was a music teacher. She was gentle voiced, unhurried in her movements, and took a quite kindly interest in our welfare. Dialogues between my mother and her took the form of a restrained exchange of their family's achievements: hers a reality, ours yet to come. It was a kind of duel, steely darts endorsed with a smile, each one indulging the other. It made me want to shout out:

'Stop it, stop it. why does there always have to be this desire to impress people?'

'She starts it,' my mother said, childishly.

Mrs Royale, our gracious neighbour, rarely entered our home. Unfortunately we could not say the same of Mrs Bockering from up the street, an enormous woman who carried around with her a separately enormous goitre that she uncoiled proudly to display before those who were lacking. The goitre pressed violently on her eyes and made them pop wildly. Her booming voice transformed our smallish rooms into echo chambers. She longed to take her husband and shake him till his teeth rattled. Every day, almost, she expressed this longing. Admittedly he's been through a lot, Rose. Changhi's no Sunday School picnic. But I have to do everything in the family. You see, and I wouldn't like this passed around, Rose, he's illiterate. Fair dinkum. Lived in the bush when he was a kid and his old man did his school lessons for him so the Correspondence School wouldn't catch on.

The dialogues never varied in substance, and very little in form. They talked unceasingly, demanding for their voices and their formulae time, attention and approval. Once I interrupted our neighbour with the goitre to ask her if she respected her husband when she married him first. She tossed her head indignantly.

'Love is blind. You'll know what I'm talking about when you're older. Won't she, Rose?'

They were always demanding support. Isn't that right? And if they didn't get it, they became peevish.

Sometimes when they'd gone, I crouched over our radio and

312

pressed my ear to the short wave broadcasts from China, the USA, France, Russia, anywhere outside. Thank God the world was still there. My father would complain: 'Turn that down, for God's sake. I'm trying tae read. What are ye listening tae China for when ye cannae understand it?'

'It makes me feel good, that's why.'

One morning we were sitting at our porridge when the back door was knocked and a woman walked in. We all looked at her, dumbfounded. She was a stranger who had only moved into her house a few weeks previously. We had never spoken to her but we had heard her talking to other neighbours, her chin resting on the back fence, her breasts enclosing the top of the front gate, her short heavy body barring the way, bailing up passers by on the footpath.

'Your money or your life.'

She was one of those acquisitive people who longed to know who your cousins were, your father's father, how much you lost on the strike last week, which neighbour had the most to give you when you moved in.

'The Eyes and Ears of the World,' my mother observed drily.

And now here she was incredibly, having reached the middle of our kitchen floor without a shot being fired. She was as reckless as a Turk, facing up to my mother with pale eyes, superficially bland, but finely honed steel in their depths, betraying their real awareness.

'Sick 'er, Mammy,' I urged silently.

'Yes?' my mother enquired. 'What do you want?'

The woman held out a rolled-up newspaper. Sound streamed through her nostrils. 'I was just going down the street and saw this in your front garden. Thought I would bring it in.'

My mother bit the air. 'Where we come from, a person waits till he's asked before he enters another's house. Couldn't you wait?'

'It was lying there,' the woman said. 'I thought a dog might chew it. There's been a lot of that recently.' After a pause, she bartered. 'Did you hear Mrs Billem got fifteen quid at the housie last night?'

'You've been up early this morning,' my mother answered, sneering a little, offering nothing.

The woman sighed and her gaze spread outwards like a fan,

tapping the stove, the sink, the table, flicking us all lightly.

'I have seven children,' my mother said, 'and there isn't one of them incapable of bringing in the paper.'

The fan closed. 'I'll be off, then. I was just going down the street and I saw it lying there. Thought I'd bring it in.'

She left the door open behind her.

My mother jumped up from her chair, twisting agilely to catch it before it fell over. She swept the kettle from the top of the stove and shoved it under the tap, filling it with a rush.

'Those bloody people. Ah cannae make them oot.'

'They are ubiquitous,' I said, transferring the meaning from the soya bean in Asia. 'Dostoevsky says they are a common class of people, ignorant and presumptuous, impervious to insult.'

It was comforting to me to think that Australia was visited by the same kind of romance as Russia, and that one could meet on a train, perhaps, the same clerk who accosted the Prince in *The Idiot*. But would one, I asked myself doubtfully, ever encounter a Rogojin? To cry fiercely:

'What an impertinent beast you are . . . I thought some creature like you would hang on to me.'

Among those pleasant people it didn't seem at all likely.

Then I will be like Rogojin, I vowed. But later. Not now, when I am so lonely.

23   School's Out

Loneliness made me hate school. Georgina was now a veteran checker at the woollen mills in the daylight hours, and at night, the evening star of a moon-faced little Australian who dragged her inexorably into his orbit with the powerful magnetism of a second-hand car. There was no one left for me to talk with easily; nothing to stop me from spending recesses in the school library, reading or doing my homework. But I shivered in my isolation, sick to belong to any group, no matter what, to be included in the laughter. Every time people laughed together in the classroom or out in the playground I felt deprived, like an orphaned waif numbed by social frostbite. Wherever I heard laughter I tracked it to its source, and went round and round the group of mirth-makers trying to find a way in. Only a joyless pride restrained me from wringing my hands and weeping. Yet every encounter was a disappointment. Within seconds of my arrival, the guffaws and grins that seemed so robust and cohesive a force at a distance rapidly dwindled and slipped away tangentially, totally unrelated, it seemed, to the words I managed to overhear for a minute. They couldn't have been laughing at what I heard! They'd hidden their wit away when they saw me coming. Each time I vowed I would be quicker and nail the mirth to its origins, but they were always quicker still and mocked me with banalities, till I wanted to brain myself on a paling, trying to find what I was missing.

I took to following two short girls in my class, maybe because I equated their lack of stature with diminished resilience. They were both dark. One with smooth black hair cut in a short heavy fringe across her face, to reduce its length, probably. Her cheeks were dry and rosy, her lips small. She was slim and flat all the way down. Her name was Ruby. The other had greyish brown hair that fluffed and curled down her back. Her skin was brown with overtones of yellow. A prominent nose, bumpy at the bridge, and thick black eyelashes cunningly underlined with pencil made her look very old and strangely foreign. She had a very sophisticated mouth, deeply curved, and her lips were always slightly open to show her tongue between her teeth. Looking at the two girls sitting together, you thought of squares and circles.

They shared the front seat near the door, most seriously, without ever trying to peer down the corridor outside the classroom, being most industrious with their rulers and red biros, talking only, and very quietly, at the change of lessons. Each recess, after removing small packets wrapped in tissue from their cases, they left the classroom silently and disappeared. I never saw them anywhere in the playground but when the bell went to return to class they were already at the front of the line, waiting.

So I said to myself: 'I'll follow them.' I found them at the front of the school hall, tucked into the corner of the bottom step, well repaired from the wind. They were eating steadily, in silence. I sat down behind them and they were surprised.

'G'day,' said the foreign-looking one. The other said nothing. They chatted together, serenely, and from time to time Anna turned round to see if I was still there. She smiled at me each time. The other kept her head bent over her sandwich, chewing deliberately, her jaw barely moving. The bell rang and we all got up together. I walked just behind the two girls for a yard or so and then, on an extra big breath, floated myself to Anna's side.

'Coming with us?'

'If you don't mind.'

'Do you know Ruby? This is Ruby.' The other girl responded with a blink. 'I'm Anna Laing.'

Each recess I followed them at a distance, not wanting to be too presumptuous. I sat on the steps behind them, at first. After a week I lowered myself down beside Anna, using her head as a partition between Ruby and me, for Ruby never spoke to me. Except when we discussed the White Australia policy after a class debate.

'I don't think it's white enough, meself. They should keep all the wogs and Balts out.'

I could only hear her voice, thin and peevish. So I said,

speaking to the tree across the steps, 'It would be even whiter if only blondes were allowed in. All the dark-haired people could be sent back to their origins.'

Anna's profile drooped slightly. Then the voice spoke up again, out of her other ear it seemed.

'I'm a bloody fifth generation Australian.'

Little Ruby got up and stalked across to the tree, flipping her scraps into the wire basket strung around the trunk.

'My mother's Scottish,' Anna whispered, giving me another quarter of her profile.

Your father is something markedly different, I thought, but I refrained from saying it.

By the end of a month, Anna and I exchanged words and, infrequently, simple sentences, falteringly, intimidated by the strength of Little Ruby's dark will which invoked silence where it could.

The westerlies blew up early that year. At least, so everybody said. Seasons were always out of sorts when they arrived, their confusion manifest in the broadcast of daily temperatures which were always one below or five above normal. It was astonishing that the quest for normality was so far-ranging and ambitious despite the non-co-operation of the elements, who, so far as I could tell from the weather reports, were almost frivolously eccentric.

That winter was cold all through, and the hairs on my arms were so erect for so long, I swore to myself I was developing a fur. There was no question of my getting a winter uniform. The most I could add to my summer tunic was a short-sleeved jacket almost the same colour that luckily, I had been given before we left. My mother offered me her heavy, powder blue coat. I hated this because of its conspicuousness and refused to wear it.

'Then freeze,' my mother commanded me.

There were times when, by intense concentration, I could banish my goose pimples. If a southerly from the alps, however, joined the westerly, it was time to retreat and attend to my teeth, forcing them to be still.

One lunch hour, Little Ruby, freshly black from head to foot in stockings, long-sleeved blouse, tunic, tie, jumper, blazer, gloves and fleecy-lined knickers, leaned forward and screwed her head round to examine my arms in their light blonde fur.

'I suppose you Scotch don't feel the cold.'

'Tape and whisky,' I said.

She darted back out of sight, momentarily flustered.

'Tape and whisky,' I repeated, leaning forward and twisting my head around Anna. 'They're the only things that are Scotch. The rest are Scottish or Scots.' Then I sat back.

'Oh, all right,' she said from Anna's far ear. 'Scots, if you're so fussy. You don't feel the cold?' and her black little head appeared by Anna's ankles.

'Well, it's like this,' I said, standing up and smiling at her. 'Scotland, as you probably know, is a land of perpetual sleet, ice and rain, battered by Arctic winds that know no rest. So, over thousands of years Scottish mummies have evolved a breast milk that's abnormally high in fat content, like the milk of the walrus or the seal. Without the fishy taste, of course. That makes us resistant to all sorts of cold.'

Shit to her, I thought, the next day, sitting at the beach. I had put on my mother's powder blue coat and continued in the bus right down to the terminus, where the tide was turning towards Chile. Inside the bus shelter, there was a wooden bench for you to stare right out at the horizon. After a few days I thought they might put the School Board onto me, so I left the blue coat at home, to my mother's disappointment, and returned to school, shifting to a seat at the back next to Shirley, the blonde girl. She was very friendly and told me what a wonderful game football was, especially the players. Shirley was always laughing with the boys behind her, mainly about dirty jokes that she traded with Butch, who had a crew cut, and George, who was still wearing short pants. Every chance she got, and there were many, she listened with a grin ready or related a story of her own, in her clear and melodious public speaking voice. Then, when she was joke teller, her big brown eyes glowed with excitement and the gold fillings in her teeth intensified their glitter. One day she dug me in the ribs with a slim elbow.

'Hear that one, kiddo?'

'What?'

'Butch's joke, you twit. Tell her it, Butchie.'

Butch was a bit wary, I could see.

He hung his head and shrugged, embarrassed.

'Aw quit it, Shirl. She doesn't want to hear it.'

What he meant was: keep out.

Shirley was more democratic. 'She does. She's been listening

318

before. Haven't you kid? I bet,' she went on, 'she even knows some, herself.'

Butch seized on this. 'All right, you tell us one and then I'll tell you one of ours.'

There it was. My membership card.

'All right,' I said. 'I do know one. Three men, a red Indian, a Negro and a Chinese, all loved the same girl. I'll marry, she told them, the one who can give me a white baby. She slept with the red Indian and had a red baby; she slept with the Negro and had a black baby; she slept with the Chinese and had a white baby. So she married him. How come, asked the first two of the Chinese, you gave her a white baby? The Chinese smirked before replying:

me no daft,
me no sill-ee
me whitewash
my till-ee will-ee.'

They smiled politely. 'Basically rib-tickling,' said Butch, 'but you don't tell it the right way. It sounds . . .'

'It doesn't sound lascivious enough,' Shirley broke in, flexing her vocabulary. 'Isn't that a beaut word! You can really lick it.' Her fleshy tongue came rolling out of her mouth, curling back on itself like a strawberry turnover, and her lips stretched in and out, in and out, squeezing it as she mouthed the word repeatedly: 'Lascivious, lascivious.'

From then on I was invited to listen to the dirty jokes. At the funny ones I laughed with the others, but I was instantly aware that the laughter meant nothing. There was no collusion between us.

However, I was invited to Shirley's place: 'C'mon over Satday. You can meet my boyfriend, John. He's a really great guy.'

'No thanks,' I said. 'I'm sure your boyfriend would find three a crowd.'

Shirley's gold fillings beamed out denials: 'You've got to be joking, kiddo. Three? There's me mum 'n' dad. Me big sister and her husband. John 'n' Dad usually talk footie, anyway.'

I liked her, so I went. Her parents were aged solid, ringed round with whorls of fat they'd accumulated like the annuli of trees. They were spread out over kitchen chairs, at opposite ends of a long, varnished table, their chairs turned sideways to face the radio which was one of those old-fashioned standard ones about three feet tall. The speaker was set behind a circular mesh as big as a dinner plate, and the people watching it so intently might have been mesmerised by a great mouth. Shirley and her boyfriend had their chairs drawn together, their knees scraping, directly in front of the radio looking deep down into the mesh. I placed myself at the side, facing all of them. There was nothing to see in the radio.

We were listening to football, which wasn't, after all, soccer.

'That's for women,' the boyfriend pshawed. 'Rugby's a man's game. You've got to be able to take it.'

'Take what?'

'Tackle. Throw a man down. Keep off the horde. Make away with the prize. John, John, the grey goose is gone and the fox is on the town-O. It's a man's game. Soccer's a dance.'

'You should see,' Shirley murmured, her eyes visionary, 'the damage when they come off the field. All the big bruises. And the smell,' she cried, after a pause, her nostrils steaming like a dragon's. She began to scrape at her boyfriend's knee and he rubbed back. They sat there, sanding their skins slowly in narrowing circles, burning each other with silent friction while her parents stretched their necks in towards the centre of the table, craning for a vista of radio between the heads.

Once the match was in play they all drew together, cheering and groaning as if to a metronome and I joined in when I could, usually on the off beat so that the dry, warped walls of the room shuddered and shook to syncopated mirth or protest.

It lasted for hours and hours. Then it was time to go. There was that kind of atmosphere. Leave taking was forcing itself on us. They were all expressing sorrow but I couldn't wait to break out of the place. Shirley got hold of my arm and gave it a squeeze:

'Geez, it was great having you over, wasn't it, John? Mum? Dad?'

We hadn't talked at all. The occasion had been too solemn for speech. The football and John's knee to rub. But it was great having me. There were the broad smiles and the invitations to come again as proof. They must be actors wanting an audience, I thought, and I hadn't even applauded. Only said: thank you for having me.

'Well,' my father explained, 'they enjoy themselves like that, and they assume you do too. They treat you like themselves.'

In practical terms, my relationship with Shirley hardly modified my condition at school. At recess she made straight for the prefects' room where, it was rumoured by the ugly girls in the class, she induced the boys to run their tongues along her teeth. It was some time before I realised that even the pretty girls regarded Shirley with some distaste though they called her Shirl as if they loved her and talked with her of common acquaintances. But they never sought her out or took her arm, or went home in the bus with her. She was never mentioned among the previous night's barbecue guests and I felt certain none of them had ever been to visit her. Their beams, when they encountered her, were only reflections of her own. From their lips that mimicked her huge grin, dry flakes of derision peeled away and they scratched at the corners of their mouths, glancing across at each other.

Every recess, when Shirley was in the prefects' room, I sat at a library table pondering how to make them like me. It couldn't be just my nationality that alienated them. That stupid Wendy girl was English and practically the leader of the biggest group. People didn't like you if you were nasty but Little Ruby was the only one I'd been sarcastic to. Admittedly I was useless at sport, but then, so were two others who were friendly with Wendy. No. It must be the studying. They didn't like you to say outright you enjoyed it. It was all right if you did it, for there were quite a few who were keen to do well, fighting the teachers for marks at the exams, but you had to pretend to hate it. So now, I promised myself, I too will play this game and shall scorn work. A man should lay down his mind for his adopted country.

For the next few weeks I deliberately sought the teacher's eye and responded consistently to every question in such a way as to bring a pained expression to his face.

'God, I'm an idiot,' I said aloud, many times.

Of course the biggest sacrifice would have to be made at exam time. My father would be horrified. It was really a question of swapping pains. But one thing was certain. I couldn't go on being by myself.

After giving my father the report card, I waited for him to swoon. He didn't, however. Merely checked it and handed it back to me.

'Eleventh? Gone off a bit, haven't ye?'

'Looks like it,' I said.

Later, I heard my mother discussing me with him.

'Dae ye think that primary teacher was right after a'?' she queried. 'According to her, Margaret was the one wi' the brains and the big yin was only a flash in the pan. Maybe she's burned oot or something. Had a brainstorm. I might take her tae a psychiatrist. See if she's having a nervous breakdown.'

At dinner she gave me an extra chop.

'Here, hen. You have that. Ah think ye're looking a bit run doon.'

Margaret howled indignantly: 'Baloney! She's as fit as I am. Ah'm the one that needs the extra chop. Ah have tae walk further than her from the station.'

Only Miss Ardlink among the teachers made any comment when she handed back the papers. She told me to come and see her at recess.

'Are you happy here?'

'Not much, Miss.'

'Why not?'

'Nobody likes me.'

'Do you like them?'

I thought a bit, and sighed with the truth: 'No, I don't like them at all.'

'Why not?'

'I want to punch them, Miss. They pretend all the time. They smile at me and that gets them off the hook. They've done their duty. But they don't want to be friends with me. If they'd say to me: I don't like you, you give me a pain in the bowels, buzz off, I'd think more of them. We could talk, then. But it's like being in a silent movie. Making faces all the time. I feel as if I could run amuck and bite them all. Then at least the sounds they'd utter would be natural.'

Miss Ardlink seemed not to be listening to me. She was staring over my shoulder down the corridor and I thought maybe she'd seen some kids. You're not allowed in the corridor at recess. I looked behind me but there was no one in sight. Then Miss Ardlink leaned forward and patted me on the shoulder.

'You know what I think?' she said, almost under her breath. 'Go ahead and bite. Hard.' And she gave me a little push down the corridor.

Some of the kids said she was a typical old maid. She was kind of tired and faded looking and her skin was pretty dry, what with the crusts of acne and that flaky makeup. But really she wasn't so old and someone had seen her on the beach one Sunday with the history teacher. He was crazy about her. He always carried a bottle of Listerine mouthwash with him. This was to keep the smell of plonk hidden. So they thought at first. Then we heard that the mouthwash bottle actually held brandy.

'Walter,' Miss Ardlink was reported to have told him, 'it's the drink or me.'

And the drink won every time, they chortled. For Miss Ardlink retired, defeated, to the country. Her mother was sick, she said. So I was really surprised that she could tell me to bite somebody.

After the exams I could hardly wait to get to class, now that I had shown them I was stupid. Every day I turned round in my seat, watching for something significant, a clue that things were changing. Pushing my way up and down the aisles I kept searching the faces for a real expression. I could hardly believe it, but not a single thing was different! The same old glaikit smiles and how are you going. What did they want from you, those people?

That same week, the business princip*les* teacher (there are no pals in business, tee hee) beckoned me to follow him out of the classroom. He was the next oldest to the headmaster and had the same shuffling walk. Some kids said he had been teaching for two hundred years but I can tell you, he was like most of those others at the High: he'd given in his notice on the second day. Spiritually, if you know what I mean. He didn't cry like some others, but trembled when the shadow of a cheeky girl splayed out in front of his heavy black shoes with the reinforced uppers. He fixed his eyes on the roof, determined not to see the froggy limbs jerking in time with his own. Where had his shadow gone? Blotted out by another.

'Geez, she's game, mimicking him like that,' they said, shaking their heads admiringly. 'Coming right up behind him and he can't even *feel* she's there.'

Oh, but he felt in intensely, like heartburn, make no mistake. There was sweat on his top lip. He would collapse into his canvas chair when he got home and mumble protests aloud, out there on his front verandah. That's where we saw him on our way to sport. We stopped beside his gate to contemplate the long, nut brown talking skull nibbling into the white singlet. Put a ring in his ear and he would be a Nubian slave.

323

The old bee pee teacher really looked crazy, crooking his finger at me like a witch. I noticed the others miming surprise as I got up and made ready to follow him. They were pushing their eyebrows up, forming ohs with their mouths, tapping their temples significantly.

'What's with the old guy?'

In the corridor he was edging his way backwards, drawing me along with him at the same pace.

'Yes, sir?' I said, curiously, when we came to a stop where the glass partition gave way to a plaster wall.

What was he staring round him for, spying out the land like that?

'Sir?' I said again. 'What did you want, sir?'

For answer he lunged forward and swiped me heavily across the face, hurting my nose and almost unhooking my glasses. One leg got pulled off my ear and ended halfway up a nostril.

'Hey, sir, you nearly broke my glasses,' I cried out involuntarily.

'That,' he retorted triumphantly, satisfaction turning his dark cheeks pink and bland like a baby's, 'is for cursing me.'

Jesus! It was useless trying to deny it, or to suggest that he might have misinterpreted my accent. We played, 'you did, I didn't' for a few minutes with him sort of lumbering over me, pointing his finger as if he were trying to cast out devils. Why, you silly old goat, I thought, if I'm going to start biting people then you may as well be first on the list. I'll get my mother to you. She'll knock your block off. I was glaring at him, preparatory to voicing all kinds of threats when all of a sudden, to my horror, a strange and rapid change came over him. His frame, a heavy and compact one, had begun to run at the edges and joints as if its insides were liquefying and draining away, leaving only an empty skin fastened to eyes that were milky with terror. He was dwindling so fast I was afraid to blink in case he might disappear altogether.

'Oh sir, sir', without thinking, I reached out and touched his sleeve. He stared right through me and I saw tears in his eyes. 'Sir', I gave his sleeve a little shake, curling my toes tightly in my shoes so that I shouldn't burst out crying. Oh God. Such misery. It was insupportable. If his heart didn't burst in a minute, mine would.

I shifted to the side of him and spoke directly into his ear, forming my sounds carefully.

324

'Really and truly, sir, I didn't swear at you. Nobody would want to curse you. It's just that I'm foreign, sir, and I speak strangely. That's why you thought I was swearing when I asked you the question.'

He seemed to be listening. At least his lids flickered and the tears slid out on to his cheeks, but he didn't move or say anything. I spoke up again, this time very loudly and abruptly, insolently, in fact.

'Sir, the bell will be going in a minute. Can I go back to class or am I to wait here all day?'

That was it. The change in tone brought a scowl to his face and a terse retort:

'No more of that cursing, girl, or I'll report you to the headmaster.'

'Yes, sir. I'm sorry, sir.'

He gave me a curt nod and set off back down the corridor grumbling to himself in his customary manner, with me walking slowly behind him, like a pall bearer, tired to death.

After that when we came across him, the bee pee teacher, nodding in his chair with his lower lip stuck out, I amused the others by crossing myself and murmuring: God rest his soul. Later, they said it too, crowding round his gate on the way to sport. But the seriousness of our invocation filled us with awe and eventually we left off snickering and giggling, and uttered it fearfully. Then he died and they took the chair away from the verandah.

You can probably imagine why I was terrified of becoming a teacher. Yet lots of kids in the class planned on aiming for teachers' scholarships when the time came. They thought the same as my parents. My mother drove me wild because she was always telling the neighbours that I was going to be a teacher when I finished school. Neither she nor my father could understand why this threw me into a rage.

'You could do a damn sight worse than be a teacher,' my father said once after I'd rushed up to the fence and shouted:

'Don't listen to her. I wouldn't be a teacher if I was dying of starvation. I'd rather be a prostitute.'

Of course this shocked Mrs Royale because she was a strict Catholic and also, her daughter was a music teacher.

'It's a good job for a woman,' my father said, 'short hours, long holidays, good wages. Security.'

'Look,' I said, gritting my teeth. 'Have you ever seen those

teachers in that school? They give me the shudders. They're all
sort of dead, they don't care. They sit with their feet out on the
desk and shout, 'Will you kids shaddup' and they've all got that
queer look in their eyes, like blind folk, scared folk, tired out
people. Is that to be for me? Never, I tell you. Maybe I'm scared
stiff out on that high tension wire, but at least my nerves are
twanging and I know I'm alive. I won't retreat from pain. How
else should I know pleasure?'

They said I was romancing again. What a load of codswobble
to say that a job makes you what you are. You don't have to
end up like the others. It's the height of folly, I argued, to reason
like that. Why should I be different from the others? Who's to
say that their weaknesses might not becoming mine a hundred-
fold, that I might not end up as a caricature of them, so that
people could pick me out in the street?

Forget about my teaching, I told them. Don't make false
prophecies to the neighbours.

Afterwards, they tried to talk to me reasonably.

'People in our situation can't afford to sneer at money and
security. You can see, can't you, that things are worse now than
they've ever been? It's true we've got more rooms and fresh air,
but the money's tighter. Because they're short of workers here,
the system of government and business is based on a man's
working full time all the time, but if you're having days off every
week, as I'm having at the pit, there's no relief.'

'And,' my mother put in, 'it's a vicious circle. Because there's
full employment the unions are tougher and there's more unrest.
People look at the theory of it—a chronic shortage of labour,
plenty of work and overtime. The reality is, never a week
without a day off. No bonus and a day's wages down the spout.
We've got no relatives to tap, no uncle, no granny, no money-
lender nearby, no corporation to help out with school clothes and
only one bloody pawnbroker who's too ashamed to hang his
balls ootside. Ah spent a whole morning goin' up and doon the
main street o' Gullawobblong, trying tae find a pawn, and ah
wouldnae hae discovered it if ah'd no' started tae look for
cubicles inside instead o' balls ootside.'

It was true. When you were broke here, you really were. In
Glasgow you knew that in a few hours you would be relieved,
but in Eugoberra, poverty laid siege to you, imprisoning you
within much narrower confines, battering at your defiance.

Relief was so far distant it could practically be discounted. When my school tunic washed first white, and then into holes, there was absolutely no way of getting another. The Gullawobblong store that gave lower income people carefully measured credit didn't stock the High uniform. Evidently there was little demand for it. It would have to be patched, my mother said, referring to my tunic, and she attached a huge, dazzlingly bright square of cloth to the seat of it. That was the only time my father took the belt to me, for I lay and screamed, refusing to quit the house wearing such a patch.

I wagged school again. Margaret came with me to the creek where the Glims went fishing and we stretched out on the coarse grass on the far bank, hidden from the highway. Margaret hated school too.

'They treat ye like dirt,' she grumbled moodily. 'They're a' snobs. Walking wi' their feet like Charlie Chaplin, just because the richest kid in the class is splayfooted. Ah wouldnae mind sae much if ah didnae have tae wear these shoes. The soles just embarrass me to death. Naebody here has crepe, two inches thick. And they're *never* going tae wear oot. Ah've already had them four years.'

I wasn't very sympathetic. 'Och, who goes aroon peering at the soles o' your shoes! How would ye like to carry a great patch on your seat like a blinking dartboard? It's a target for every-body's eyes. Not that they say anything, but ye should see the looks ye get.'

'It's your own fault for being sae fussy,' Margaret retorted. 'Ye're aye complaining ah'm dirty, but at least mah tunic isnae worn oot like yours. Ye shouldnae have washed it sae often.'

'Well, for somebody who's no' very fastidious,' I said, angrily, 'ye're aye pinching my clean socks and nicking off wi' them, so that ah have tae wash yours and wear them wet tae school. Why don't ye wear your own dirty, smelly things!'

Margaret just grinned. 'Why should I, when your clean ones are available? It's just a pity we don't wear the same coloured tunic and I'd leave ye mah dirty tunic too, in the mornings.'

This put me into a rage and I started pulling her hair. 'Ye're a dishonourable creature. Ye've got nae honesty in ye!'

We were punching into each other when Percy appeared, bearing offers of gifts. Sweets and ice cream. In the tone you use to suspicious dogs. Here, boy, good doggie.

'Oh, you two girls are larrikins, fighting like that. And wagging school too, I reckon.'

We sat up smartly and stared at him.

'What do you want?' Margaret asked, insolently.

'To find out what you want—and then, maybe, I'll show you what I want. There's a shop nearby, that sells ice cream and stuff. Come on, and I'll buy you something.'

'We don't want anything,' Margaret said, and added. 'So you don't get anything. Beat it. We know what you are. Blow.'

'What am I? he asked indignantly, reddening. He wasn't a working man, being dressed in a navy suit and wearing a collar and tie. He had a round moon face, like so many people here, and sparse hair. 'My name's Percy,' he announced in that ingratiating tone they use. We both grinned. 'It would be,' I said, cruelly. We backed off a bit for safety, and Margaret began to carol:

'Ah, Percy, dear Percy.
We'll show you no mercy,
Your face is like putty,
Your mind is all smutty,
Your hands are so oily and fat.

Your eyes are too shifty,
Your lips are too thrifty,
We'll have nothing to do with all that!'

Percy was flustered. 'Are you kids pommies?'

We burst out laughing. 'Never mind what we are,' I called to him. 'Think of what you are.'

'What am I, then?' he asked again.

Margaret cupped her hands around her mouth and shouted at the top of her voice: 'A dirty old man, a dirty old man.'

And I added, 'A seducer of little girls. A potential murderer. A menace. You're the fifth to date, Percy dear.'

'Go to your nearest doctor,' Margaret cried, tapping the side of her head. 'You're sick, Percy. My mother said.'

He started towards us, threateningly. 'If I get my hands on you...'

'Ah then, dear Percy,
You'd show us no mercy.'

We could hardly run for laughing. We felt mad. Wagging school, being at the creek, and that man. Fancy having a name like that. What a pity we couldn't tell my mother. At home we kept rolling around our bed thinking of it and the look on his face. Then we practised a few rhymes. 'Next time,' Margaret said, 'we'll ask them their names and have a rhyme ready. It nearly killed him.'

'He could've killed us,' I thought, 'if we were partial to ice creams.'

At Margaret's suggestion I bleached the patch on my tunic till it was less conspicuous, and I helped her slice through the crepe soles with a hacksaw blade. So we returned to school.

'But it makes no difference,' Margaret said, measuring the height of the crepe. 'I'm getting out as soon as I turn fifteen.'

24   Truth to Tell

All my world was a tunic, Margaret's a pair of shoes. The
limits of my mother's were more extensive.

'Look at that,' she cried, throwing the pay packet down on the
table. 'Nine quid for a fortnight and it's nearly eight for the
rent. Ah've got a light bill to pay and ah already owe the grocer
seven quid that ah couldnae pay last fortnight. How the bloody
hell dae ye expect me to manage on that?' she snarled, turning on
my father with hate on her face. 'It's a' you bloody Communists
that cause these strikes. Ah wouldnae be surprised if you were
putting them up to it. The woman across the street told me
they've never been so bad as they have, this last year. And that's
since you came.'

My father made no reply. His face was white with anxiety and
shame. There was no comfort or excuse he could offer to my
mother. In a voice that was almost a whisper, he murmured:

'You don't understand. Most of these stoppages are safety
issues. They're no' for money. A single pit doesnae strike for
higher wages. Ye cannae reduce pillars o' coal tae splinters that'll
no' haud the roof up. That's what causes fall-ins. It's dangerous.
B.H.P's too greedy. Anyway,' he said, letting out a sigh, 'Big
Brown's just got intae the Electricity Commission pit and as soon
as he's well in, he'll put mah name forward. They never have
days off there, and they get a good bonus.'

'Pigs might fly,' my mother retorted. She sat in silence, thinking and smoking. When that packet was finished there wouldn't
be any more, for the grocer had told her last time that in future
there would only be credit for necessities.

'Don't you smoke?' my mother had asked him bitterly.

'Never touch them,' he answered. He was a huge Dutchman who gave you a sermon with every order. 'Filthy things.'

My mother finished packing the tea and flour into her bag.

'There are filthier things in this world, Anton, believe you me.'

'Ye better go easy on your fags, Mammy,' I reminded her. 'Ye've only got two left.'

'Listen,' she said, not listening, herself. 'There's a meeting being held down on the oval tonight. It was in the paper. They've formed a progress association or something, and an M.L.A. is coming. They're going to discuss rental rebates for people who arenae working full time. Masses of people in Eugoberra are behind wi' their rents because o' these stoppages. So ah'm going doon to hear what they have to say. You can come wi' me, hen.'

The tone pointed to a favour being offered, but it was really a command. Nothing embarrassed me more than being in a public place with my mother. Shopping with her was an ordeal. She knew nearly every manager in town because she was always demanding access to him, wherever an assistant annoyed her or she couldn't get what she wanted. Once when a clerk in the Housing Commission tried to dismiss her in what she considered a patronising manner, she glared at him and said:

'Look, son, ah'm no' here tae talk business wi' the hoi-polloi. Get me the head bummer.'

When he blinked, uncomprehendingly, she spelled it out for him.

'The man at the top, son. Your boss, or preferably his boss, but best of all, his boss's boss.'

'Ye're wasting your time talking to these wee upstarts,' she explained to a tenant waiting at the counter.

The head bummer was ostentatiously polite but no more co-operative. They argued backwards and forwards and he kept saying: 'It's not our policy.'

'Listen, you,' my mother growled, stabbing her finger at him. Don't gie me that eyewash aboot policy. Ah'm going tae have questions asked in the House aboot you. Ye're a bloody little dictator. Power's gone tae your heid.'

She strode out of the office with me hurrying behind her, my chin tucked into my chest and my neck burning.

My mother had an almost mystic faith in the power of Parliament. I doubt if she had ever read Burke's pronouncements on the duties of an M.P. to his constituents, but she certainly had ideas of her own on the subject. 'Power is in Parliament,' she asserted regularly, 'and Parliament is a man in an office. And ye can do anything wi' a man if ye go the right way aboot it.'

Whether my mother's way was commendable is a bit dubious, but, in fact, the house we had in Craigiehall Street in Glasgow, with its own bathroom and hot water, resulted from her approach to our local member. Once she had decided that the house we formerly occupied, undesirable initially because of rats and continually bursting water pipes, and unbearable finally after two more births, once this house became unliveable to her, she decided to visit the chambers of the local member. These chambers were lodged in one of the corporate buildings up the town. Wide steps led to the entrance of this building and at the top of them stood a commissionaire, his gaze so alert in traversing the four double doors he might have passed for Cerberus.

'You should have seen him,' my mother reported, 'all done up in his brass braid and buttons like a tin soldier. "Have you an appointment, madam?" he called to me, nearly busting a gut to get to the door before me. Och, don't gie me your worries, I said to him. Away ye go and get yourself a decent job, instead of cavorting around like a clown. And ah was intae the building before he could draw breath. Well, ah marched down the corridor and opened the first door ah came to. Ah mean, ah didnae have any idea who might be there, but ah threw that door open, in any case. Here, there was this great round table wi' all these men sitting around. The meaty, respectable type. Councillors all. They stared at me as if ah were a spook. I want to speak to the member for Kinning Park, I told them. They were flabbergasted. Then this bloke got up, a bit slowly, and started moving round the table. "I am your member, Madam," he said, very nicely and politely. And I saw he had only one leg. Poor bloke. Still, we all have our problems and I told him mine. If you don't give me a promise of a decent house before I leave this room, I said, I'm going straight home tae gas us all. Ah mean it. We're better off dead than living like bugs in slime. Of course, ah was only being dramatic. He'd taken me into another wee office, and when I threatened to kill us all, he stared into my face. Ah looked half mad, ah suppose. Then he patted me on the shoulder. "Go home," he said, "and rest easy. Before the week is out, I'll have you in a decent house." He was dramatic too, ye see. So that was that. We got it. If ye want something, there's nae use whingeing or joining the Communist party. Just find the head bummer and get him on his own.'

The magnet drawing my mother to the oval, therefore, was the reported attendance of the M.L.A. About fifty people turned up to the meeting. The oval was just a big paddock with a brick toilet. The M.L.A. addressed us all from the top of a table which someone had provided. His voice was flat and monotonous as if he were reading out a shopping list. I found it difficult to concentrate so I had a look around to see if there were any kids I knew, but of course, there weren't. Mr Glim wasn't at the meeting, probably because he was a contract miner and made good money, but lots of men from my father's pit were standing around in their cardigans and open-necked shirts. 'Geez, it's bloody cold here, mate,' I heard one say. 'We'll need a warm-up after this lot.' I had the shivers, myself. I focused my eyes on a spot in front of my feet and began to imagine an enormous wood fire, with me stretched out at the edge of the flames, reading comics and eating chocolates, my favourite image of Paradise. In a few minutes I was off and the voices withdrew to the periphery of my consciousness. Dearly beloved, we are gathered here for the purpose of. Inside, I was glowing like a hot coal and comfort was wrapping me round in an eiderdown. My ears were muffed in warmth and melting images swirled smoothly through my mind.

'You're dozing off,' someone said, giving me a rough shake. 'You'll fall down.'

And at that moment I heard my mother's voice. Her out-loud public voice, strident with indignation, the clarion call to arms. Oh God, let me slip away.

'I would like to inform you,' she was proclaiming to the multitude, 'that if I had little to eat where I came from, then I've even less to subsist on here. In the six months I've been here, I've forgotten the taste of red meat. You've given me a big house but at a rent I can't afford to pay because of the industrial disturbances that plague this place. In Glasgow, I paid nine and fourpence a week for a flat with a hot water system, and if my husband was on short time my kids could get free meals at the school. Now they go to school without lunch. In Glasgow, my kids had all the exercise books they needed, provided by the school. Now my eldest daughter uses the old envelopes the bills

333

come in, to take notes. If we have to be poor, I'd rather be in a place where I'm no' swept under the carpet as if I didnae exist.'

Merciful God. How could she tell everybody this? No wonder faither stayed at home. Not that it would do him much good, anyway. A reporter was noting everything at my mother's elbow. When the meeting ended, the M.L.A. sought my mother out and promised her a rent rebate of a dollar a week till our income improved, whereupon the debt would have to be repaid. It was over fifty dollars that eventually we returned to the Housing Commission. Next day, in the local paper, 'No Meat for Six Months' blared hysterically from the headlines. I stayed home from school, it made me so taut.

'Why, why did you exaggerate like that, Mammy?' I kept moaning all day, restraining my tears in case she gave me a slap. 'Ye get a side o' lamb every fortnight. Telling people we havenae seen red meat. It's so humiliating. Ye never tell the truth. Even when it's necessary. Ye're not ashamed of lying.'

I got ready to duck in case my mother lunged at me, but she remained quite calm, wrapping up the potato peelings in thick layers of newspaper. 'Ye're another o' these Holy Wullies like your faither,' she said, sprinkling powder over the sink. 'Choked wi' false pride. Who the hell's interested in truth? So far as ah can tell, most people run a mile from it. It's a luxury. And the richer ye are, the less ye can afford it. It's excitement and drama people want. Something to make them say: "Fancy that, isn't that terrible?" 'That's why the *News o' the World* is the biggest selling newspaper in Britain. It gies the people what they want. And they're no' interested in the miserable poor, those white, peaky, stiff upper lip sorts who put a face on things. They want a spectacle. Calamity, preferably: that we should have a touch o' leprosy or only one leg between us. The poor, ye see, have tae learn tae be dramatic instead of snivelling. There's great possibilities in it. Look at us now. We've got a rent rebate. The Smith Family, whoever the hell they are, are going tae gie us some blankets. And that keeps us going another week or so. If you or your faither can do better, then do it. Till ye can, shut your trap and don't come whingeing tae me about truth and honour and that sort of shit.'

We were like a colony of winter sparrows: a little flutter here, an oblique hop there. And we had the same lack of perspicacity. As soon as something was scratched up we gobbled it down and cried: hurrah, winter's over! The famous, present-time orienta-tion of the poor. But the ground was pretty well bare by the time I came to prepare for the Intermediate exam. With six weeks to go, my mother decided I should leave school.

'When?' I asked, incredulously.

'Now. We're chasing our tails at the moment. There's no use waiting for those fools at the pit to come to their senses. I can't go tae work and let the house fall apart. We've got to make a break in the chain of our circumstances. If you go tae work, at least that's one mouth less to feed, and ye might be able to contri-bute something more if ye can get a good job. Ye know what the bible says: to them that hath shall be given, and from them that hath not shall be taken away even that which they hath. So if ye can add something, more will come.'

The bible adage infuriated me. It was so unjust. But, none-theless, it was true. I would have to find a job.

I could join the Public Service, my father suggested bleakly. That way I might be able to extend my education later. He was more disappointed than I at my leaving school and sat in the armchair, staring at the fireplace. It was a pity, I thought, having to go now, just when I'd arrived at a way of making school more entertaining. Now I should never be able to explore the possi-bilities of my discovery, or to determine its ultimate conse-quences.

This discovery was really quite simple. Once it was clear to me that no effort on my part would make me one with the others, there was no longer any need to pander to them. I need only please myself. The first encounter I had after drawing this conclusion was with a girl who constantly irritated me. One of those who asked you how you were going and was off at a gallop lest you tell her.

'Don't ask me,' I warned her, raising my hand as she made ready to fire her greeting. 'You couldn't give a damn how I'm going, even if I dropped at your feet, so don't waste your breath. You can tell me you see me, if you like, so's we don't collide, but keep your hypocritical claptrap for people with stronger stomachs.'

The girl was actually almost past me in her usual fashion, but hearing a suddenly non-formulaic response, she stopped abruptly, half-wheeling round. Her face was a picture of hurt disbelief.

'Hey, fair go,' she said, protestingly. 'What's all this about hypocrisy? What's wrong with asking anybody how he's going? It's just being friendly. Everybody knows that.'

'Bilge,' I answered rudely. 'It's nothing of the kind. It's making things pleasant for you, getting a cheap feeling of well-being for no effort. You're not interested in my welfare—so you're not greeting me for my sake, are you?'

She stood a minute, nonplussed, thinking.

'Oh well, then,' huffily now, 'if that's the way you feel about it, if you don't want to be friendly, you needn't,' and she hurried off, her face twitching resentfully.

I watched her, feeling elated, having begun to unburden myself of my own resentment.

We were to line up shortly after that. There was a very broad back in front of me. I stared at it curiously, not immediately recognising the body. Then the girl turned her head slightly and I remembered her. In spite of her great bulk she was a person easy to overlook in class, and most people, in fact, ignored her, not out of any hostility that I could detect, merely through lack of interest. A tall girl, even taller than I, she radiated an overall impression of whiteness. This stemmed from her very white, opaque skin, her pale wispy hair, her unusually white, thick eyelashes that brushed against the lenses of her round glasses in their white frames, and her white, pulpy lips. With her long sloping shoulders, fatly rounded, and her short neck tilting her head forward, she resembled nothing so much as a polar bear, a docile, bewildered creature.

On the left of us there was the usual commotion while the boys sorted themselves into some sort of line. Each 'possy' was territory to be contested. They pulled and hauled at each other, stretching jumpers like elastic, hooking their ankles round each other's legs and thudding one another in the ribs. Finally, the last whistle having blown and the prefects drawing ominously nearer, they stood quietly, slyly evaluating their surroundings.

Next to Jocelyn, that was her name, a good-looking Estonian boy found himself. He was rather shorter than the other boys, but very compact and hard, suntanned nearly black. His eyes, an incredible cornflour blue, were never still, reflecting, I thought, some inner edginess. In class, I'd noticed, his fingers were forever tapping the desk. The girls thought him attractive, I knew, and he joked with some of them in a heavy, clumsy manner, but I suspected he had little to do with anyone outside school. Now, he turned to inspect the surrounding company and his eyes immediately fell on Jocelyn.

'Oh my God,' he cried, slapping his hands over his eyes. 'Let me out of here.'

He started to wriggle his way down the line, repeating his cry 'Let me out of here' and had a scuffle with one or two boys before someone else agreed to take his place.

In front of me, the narrow white band that was Jocelyn's neck had turned bright red and when I leaned sideways for a better look I saw her ears and cheeks were scarlet too.

What a beast that fellow was! The girls ahead were beginning to shuffle off, with the boys marching more briskly alongside. As we started climbing the stairs the Estonian boy drew level with me. On impulse I touched the sleeve of his jumper and he turned to me with his eyebrows raised inquiringly:

'G'day.'

A note of surprise was in his voice.

'It's not a good day, one bit,' I said. 'You were absolutely disgusting to Jocelyn. How would you feel if someone did that to you, humiliated you in front of people. You're ignorant as dirt. If ye want to add inches to yourself, ye should try a pair of stilts or cowboy boots.'

'No talking up there,' a prefect called. 'Keep moving.' Others were listening curiously. I could feel their eyes on me. We all pushed into the classroom, with me still beside him.

'What are you getting on your high horse for?' he asked indignantly, stopping at the aisle leading to his seat. 'I wasn't doing anything to you.'

'And you wouldn't want to,' I answered frostily, 'for I'd spit in your eye.'

I'd never really done that to anyone, but I fancied I might like to one day. It sounded blood curdling, anyway.

He made a curious grunting sound of vexation and stomped up to his seat, throwing himself into it with a clatter.

Well, I thought, placing my hands over my stomach to soothe it, I'm on the roller coaster now. Things are going to be a lot less boring from now on.

I had one further confrontation that day, this time with a student teacher of mathematics, a former pupil of the High and reputedly one of Gullawobblong's wealthiest sons. He was twenty-two, handsome in a curly-headed, weak-chinned sort of way and reported to be secretly engaged to a fifth former. This teacher, on examining my exercise book, was appalled by the absence of margins which he considered the very essence of beauty. I pointed out to him that I used margins in those jotters that were corrected by teachers, to leave space for their comments, but since our maths books were never corrected, except by ourselves, a margin was a waste of space. The more space I had in a jotter, the less often I had to ask for a new one. For this reason too, I cultivated very tiny handwriting. I'd given up using exercise books for note taking at the library, using instead flattened out envelopes or blank pages that I regretfully tore from the backs and fronts of books I had brought with me from Scotland. So I had no intention of wasting precious space on margins.

The teacher insisted I draw wide margins in all the blank pages of my maths book. He flipped the pages over, thrust the ruler onto them and pointed to my pencil with a gracefully tapered finger.

'Now get on with it, while I'm here to watch you. Hurry up, draw the margins.'

Under the desk, I wriggled my fingers and toes to relax myself before making reply.

'No, sir. I won't.'

The class hissed, shocked altogether. They could laugh at the antics of a clown dancing behind a teacher's back, making faces, mimicking his gestures, or quite brazenly comment on another teacher's dress, his method of polishing his shoes, her newly laddered stocking, but a simple 'no' provoked apprehension and, one sensed, disapproval. This was the first time I had ever been bluntly defiant of authority and now that I had begun, I realised all at once that further confrontations would be inevitable. It was simply impossible to indulge so many people in their whims or obsessions or to continue allowing them to determine my good.

The teacher reacted immediately, without any thought. He yelled at me to get out of the class, gerrout, gerrout, gerrout, and swept past me in a rage after the bell went. But he didn't raise the matter again, nor come to inspect my exercise book.

So there, I thought. Three times now I've pleased myself, and three times met with resentment. If I am to play Rogojin, surely there will have to be Lebedeff, to reply when he is threatened with having his hide tanned: 'Aha! do—by all means! If you tan my hide you won't turn me away from your society. You'll bind me to you with your lash forever.'

Which one of all these pleasant people I've met here would ever dare assert such a connection between him and another, a stranger at that, met on the train? Why, I told myself, thinking of the Glims and the Billems, they wouldn't affirm it even of a blood relationship. They reject all bonds, all meaningful communication, muttering truculently: 'I take very grave offence.'

Well, I decided, you'll just have to. Take offence. No more smiles and empty salutations from me. Nor to me, either.

Having resigned myself to a single state within the class, I was taken aback one day when a pale, softly spoken girl, her teeth clamped into a metal bit, accosted me outside the classroom and invited me to join her and her friend at hand tennis. It seemed to me an absurdly infantile pastime for fifteen-year-olds, patting a ball backwards and forwards over a chalk line, mostly in silence, but sometimes with a slightly shocked pouf if one of them slid into the dust. However, I dutifully took my turn patting the ball, and was pleased to discover later that the action, mild and undemanding, was strangely soothing, a balm that produced a sensation of peaceful withdrawal.

Both girls were quite taciturn, giving most of their attention to this recess activity.

At the beginning of recess one would say, 'Your turn to start', including me and the other in her address, or 'our turn', if I were to wait. As we returned to lines they might exclaim in decorous tones, 'That was fun wasn't it?' and I would nod, a little bemused, but impressed with their seriousness.

The pattern was interrupted only by the absence of one or the other. Eunice, who wore the braces, was periodically confined to bed with sinus headaches, to ward off which her mother measured out three drops of Fisher's Phospherine every day. Her friend, Jane, would then talk to me in short, rather abrupt phrases punctuated with long dashes of silence when we just sat. She'd seen a perfectly round rainbow once, she informed me, on the way over here by flying boat. It was her own private miracle. It happened near the equator, ages ago, for she was five when they left Staffordshire. 'Of course, I'm quite happy here. People are all the same anyway.' This was added disconsolately

339

in the tone, not of one delighted by the unity of things, but of someone who'd given up hope of finding anything better. It was curious how such a sunny aspect could cast lengthening shadows of pessimism.

'You're an odd one,' I remarked once. 'All English tea rose on the outside, blonde and rosy cheeked like a kid on a calendar, and black inside.'

She resented such personal comments: 'I'm not a typical English rose. If you'll notice, I've got brown eyes. And in any case, people have worries they mightn't talk about.'

'Well, I won't ask you what yours are. You'd probably bite my nose off.'

'You're right.'

Eunice was equally defensive. Her voice was so soft and hesitant you often had difficulty making out what she said, a deliberate practice, I suspected, because it provided a ready retreat.

'Oh, I didn't say that at all. You're putting words into my mouth.'

She was going to be a teacher, like her elder sister who was aiming to reach Wagga Wagga Teachers' College.

'What's so attractive about teaching?'

'Oh, I don't know . . . I like little kids.'

'You don't know any.'

'How do you know who I know?'

'Well, do you?'

'Look, I don't have to be interrogated by you. I'm not going to discuss the matter any further.'

So then I said to the air: 'Frankly, it beats me why all you folk have such a vision splendid. Lord, make me like those. Like those deadbeats on a dung heap.'

'Really, I think you're cruel. In any case, none of my family would ever be deadbeats. We're from Prussian stock. With a von.'

'Ye Gods, junkers and scarred cheeks! They're a different sort of deadbeat.'

Then Eunice, who always presented her profile as part of her defence strategy, would jerk her head right round, and shake her pigtail.

Weeks passed like this, in a kind of sleep that belied the physical activity of our bodies, patting the little ball and running after it. I was alert only when reading, for then I could debate with characters whose vitality and passion far surpassed that of the people around me, people who by comparison were like the wooden creations of an inferior novelist, whose gestures and attitudes and characteristic dialogues were so mechanistic as to make them appear almost inanimate. Even my mother, with all her shrieks and shadow boxing, was nothing more than an outline of self, for when I attempted, on what might seem a specially propitious occasion, to draw from her more than the slogans that she offered to explain her stance in life, she would rage wildly and curse, so that you wondered, what goes on in there?

How then, I asked myself, becoming increasingly resentful, do these novelists get to know? Everything must be supposition. How bold they are to create so confidently from such scant material. What would Dostoevsky do with an Australian? Or maybe Russians are no different? Maybe they too say only, how are you going, hot today, except when they are alone on the kitchen floor, and Dostoevsky makes up the rest. There was no way of telling, since I knew no Russians.

Late in second term, however, a Latvian girl came to the school to throw the others into confusion, and me to enchant. She was new only to New South Wales, not to Australia, and striding in behind the Deputy, expressed neither wonder nor curiosity. While Mr Whittle formally introduced her to the class she stood with her arms folded across her chest and stared at each one of us in turn, saying very clearly: how loathesome you are! A vacant seat being indicated to her, she marched towards it with an 'out of the way, you turds' purposefulness, deliberately ignored by the boys who set to admiring her shining blonde pageboy and even tan. To me, her slanted grey eyes set in a head that sloped steeply outwards above the ears, had all the ferocity of a wolf. At change of lessons, her passage being obstructed by ditherers in the aisle, she called out, in precisely accented English:

'*Ex*—cuse me!'

and the way was cleared like magic.

'Bit of a nut, that one,' the girls said. 'The boys kept their counsel, but continued to gaze approvingly on the new girl's neat, spare figure and erect posture.

By coincidence I was late arriving at school the next day and

341

the playground, as I entered the gate, was almost deserted. The only other person in sight was the new girl, a few yards ahead of me on the path. I hurried to catch up with her, moving sideways onto the grass alongside her.

'Excuse me,' I said, 'you came into my class yesterday.'

She had a very vigorous, athletic walk, much more demanding than my own dawdle and I had to exert myself to keep up with her. Exasperated, I realised she was going to make no response.

A bit acidly, therefore, I said:

'Are you deaf, or something?'

She stopped so abruptly I nearly shot past her.

'Go away, will you. I don't like you.'

Now I was delighted. How brave of her, if a bit stupid.

'You don't even know me, so how can you not like me? If you dislike me without knowing me, then you must dislike everybody, in which case you should live in a cave, as a dirty old misanthrope.'

'I can like whom I choose and I loathe dirt.'

'You're not Russian by any chance?' I asked hopefully, ignoring the hostile set of her jaw.

'Good God, no. Don't even mention them to me. I hate them. They took my father away. I'm Latvian,' she added and I felt a lessening of her resistance.

'You came into class behind a bazooka,' I said. 'Why?'

'Because I know them already, my dear.' This tickled me, the assumption of an adult world weariness. 'They're all the same. Snobbish. Anti-Balt. In Victoria, Western Australia, New South Wales—the lot, their shoddy little minds are unvaried in their prejudices and pretensions.'

I was staggered by the girl's languid manner and her sophisticated style of expression.

'Goodness, you speak well,' I said, admiringly. 'Where did you learn English?'

'From my grandmother in Victoria. A highly educated woman. My bitch of a mother left me to her when I was three and dragged me from her when I had reached a useful age.'

Fancy anybody calling her mother a bitch!

'You know, I like you. I hope we can be friends.'

She turned her face towards me for the first time, and smiled, a little ironically.

'My dear young lady, how can you like me when you don't

342

know me? If you like me without knowing me then you must like everybody, in which case you should live in an asylum as a dirty old lunatic.'

This broke me up. I dropped my case and clapped my hands together with delight and gratitude, while Vera maintained her wintry little smile.

'You're terrific,' I cried. 'How marvellous you exist. I'm so glad you came here.'

'Hah,' she snorted. 'You might be sorry later.'

At recess, I rushed from the classroom to wait for Vera, already in my mind having discarded Eunice and Jane for ever. They'd picked me up as a lame dog to minister to, Eunice's mother being an ardent Presbyterian. But now I didn't need them any more, I was sure they would be glad to relinquish their burden. As Vera appeared in the corridor, I stepped towards her, astonished, however, to find a restraining hand on my arm. Irritated, I turned round, frowning. It was Jane.

'Coming?' she enquired, expectantly.

'Why, you must know I won't be coming any more,' I thought to say, but didn't. I should have to rid myself of this ridiculous notion that my mind was a moving neon, instantly read at a distance by any passer by. An explanation must be spelt out but it could be left for another time.

'All right, then,' I said. 'I'll come in a minute. I'd like to bring the new girl, too. Would you mind?'

Vera stood hesitatingly, a few yards away. If I didn't nab her quickly she would be off.

'Well, do you?'

She wasn't happy about it, Jane. You could see that. Who would imagine brown eyes could be so flat and opaque? In our monotonously blue and grey-eyed family brown eyes meant mystery, their centres suggesting whirling vortices that drew away secrets into some backless beyond, but Jane's eyes were curiously shallow, as if hard little discs had been slipped in just below the surface, blocking off your comprehension.

'I don't suppose I mind. It will be up to Eunice.'

Eunice, of course, was humanitarian and welcomed Vera.

Well, after all this, my mother's decision that I leave school was less welcome than it might have been a month or so earlier. It had taken so long for me to ally myself with someone in that place, the thought of starting all over again in another institution rather galled me. Still, there was no arguing against the fact of our financial inadequacy. So I applied to the Public Service for employment as a clerk and was asked to submit myself for an exam, three weeks hence. In the interim I made one visit to the school to tell the girls I was leaving. We talked through the railings, for once I had broken with the place I couldn't bring myself to enter the gates again.

Jane said nothing. Eunice was gently commiserating.

'An uncle of mine has made a great career in the Public Service. You can sit for exams there too like at Uni.'

'And who's going to sit beside me in French, now?' demanded Vera. 'I could kill you.'

I grinned, feeling better. That's what I liked about Vera. She gave the right value to every situation. She would survive quite well with the other two for she was, incredibly, an athlete who trained seriously, doing push-ups and running on the spot in a track suit. Despite her sophistication, she applied herself to the hand tennis with a ferocity that upgraded the game, unconsciously, thereby, defending the other two from my silent disbelief and earning their gratitude.

There was little to do while waiting for the exam but write letters to Sydney to discover the types of accommodation available, and help my mother about the house. My father all this time showed little interest in the new plans, refusing to echo my mother's enthusiasm for the revolutionary changes that were to be wrought by my joining the workforce. The night before the exam, however, he stirred himself suddenly, and announced:

'You're going back to school.'

'Wh-a-a-a-t!'

Yes indeed. And what's more, I was getting a new summer tunic. We could buy material from the credit store and have it made up. There were still three weeks to the Intermediate. I could catch up quickly and next year things would be easier, for I would undoubtedly win the bursary I had earlier applied to sit for, while my father had been assured he was next to be admitted to the State mine. It was self-defeating to throw away good prospects when we'd survived this far. My mother, astonishingly, offered no resistance.

'Aye, ye're right,' she agreed. 'Ah've felt sick aboot it, tae tell ye the truth.'

Hurrah! The teachers were ready to believe I had been sick.

Most of the others had barely noticed my absence. Everyone was preoccupied with the Intermediate, and some with the bursary.

Next year, I cheered myself, I shall have a proper uniform with a blazer as well.

25 Then There Were Five

Next year, however, was substantially little different.

'Don't get carried away wi' yourself. This bursary's only forty-eight pounds for the year, made in three payments.'

So my mother got the uniform from that credit store. A navy blue blazer instead of a black one, with no braid or anything. But at least I had two summer tunics now and a new pair of shoes. Margaret got a pair too and thankfully shoved her crepe soles to the bottom of the garbage bin, out of sight forever.

For the first time, returning to school in the new year, someone was waiting for me: Vera, Eunice and Jane, excited as I was to be in the senior school. Later, I discovered another in wait.

'G'day,' she said at my elbow, as we were changing lessons.

I looked down, surprised. It was Anna Laing. Strange, I hadn't noticed before, her own tunic was threadbare and the cuffs of her blazer split and frayed.

'Little Ruby's gone.'

'Uh-huh.'

'She's got a job in an office.'

I waited.

'I didn't think I would be coming back, myself. My sister wanted me to leave, but I told her I'd get a job in the shoe shop every holidays.'

'What's your sister got to do with it?'

'I live with her and her husband. My mother's dead.'

'Does your father live with her, too?'

Anna stared down at her shoes.

'I don't know where he lives.'

'Well,' I said, wondering what she wanted.

'I thought maybe we could go around together.'

346

Her eyes were proper brown ones, not like Jane's. The mysterious kind. There was something strangely old about her face, not wrinkles or sagging skin, but an inherited ancientness in the dark tones and high, bony nose.

'Your father's not Scottish, is he?'

'He's a Syrian. Well, what are you going to do?'

A Syrian. Coming down like a wolf on the fold.

'Well, I can't leave Eunice and Vera. But you can join us all. They won't mind. Okay?'

And so we were five. The rest of the time could be described under headings like those Enid Blyton used to woo dying generations. Five go for a paddle pop, together. Five plan a hitch hike together. Five peep at the new boy. Five strive for scholarships. My mother didn't like Anna. The only time she visited me my mother rushed her out of the house, flaying her with abuse, yelling at her not to have anything more to do with me, and Anna ran off, sobbing.

'She's evil, that girl,' my mother panted, after I had finished crying with humiliation and horror. 'She wants power over you, to destroy you. She's eaten up with jealousy.'

'You're out of your mind,' I moaned. 'How can you say such crazy things? You completely misinterpret her.'

Anna was concerned with saving my soul. A devout Presbyterian who never missed out on Sunday School teaching or evening service, a member of the Inter-School Christian Fellowship, she frowned upon what she considered my wilfulness and irresponsibility, for I had decided to do what I liked. Life's too short to let other people muck up my daily units, I used to announce and Vera, Jane and Anna would huddle together, protectively. Only Eunice gave me shy support.

'Look, you bitch, you're putting me in an embarrassing position.'

This was Vera, every Wednesday, complaining because I refused to put my name down on the sports list. 'I'll really have to report you.'

'Of course you must,' I answered sympathetically. 'You wouldn't be doing your job as sports captain, otherwise. I should have done it much sooner, in your position. But while you don't know where your responsibilities lie, I shall continue to study at the library.'

Anna fumed silently.

'You're not doing the right thing by Vera—or by anybody,' she muttered eventually, having intended to keep her mouth shut, but unable to contain her righteousness.

'You're wrong, Anna,' I said, 'I'm doing the right thing by me.'

Finally, Vera sorted out her loyalties and made her report. The sports mistress sent for me. She was a new one, an ex-captain of the school, less bulky than her predecessor, with stringier muscles and narrower ankles, but with a jaw, significantly pronounced and severe.

I stood in front of her desk.

'You've been absent from sport for six weeks, I understand. Have you a note to explain why you were away?'

What kind of game was this she was playing?

'I haven't any excuses, Miss. I avoided sport to study in town.' She didn't lift her head.

'You know the rules of the school. Sport is compulsory for all students unless there are certified medical grounds for non-participation. There are sound reasons for this rule.'

'I know that, Miss,' I said. 'Pardon me for interrupting, I knew I would get caught eventually and I'm quite prepared to be punished.'

This time she looked up. Her clear eyes were almost transparent with dislike.

'Are you, now? That's very magnanimous of you. Go to the headmaster at once, you impertinent girl, and tell him why I sent you.'

He was new, too, that year. The local press had praised his youth. He was only in his forties. Lean, trim, grey at the temples. Ambitious. It was whispered that he was a trouble shooter for the Education Department, sent by it to break up what was becoming a Catholic enclave.

'You're kidding!'

'My uncle's a Metho and he told me. Well, figure it out. A Catholic head, a Catholic Deputy, a Catholic French master. That's the ones we actually know of. Now we have a Pressie head, a deputy going—transferred, mind you, not promoted. French master going.'

'Who said? They haven't left yet.'

'My uncle. They'll be gone next year. You wait. And don't forget, we're having prayers and things like they have at the private schools.'

348

I explained to the headmaster the nature of my misdemeanour.

'What were you doing in the library?'

'Extra reading. Consulting past exam papers.'

'You'll have to be punished,' he said, not angrily. 'Go back and tell her she may dispose of you as she wishes.'

For the next six weeks I had to stand at attention, two inches from the wall on a field where first-year kids played netball.

'Don't move an inch,' she warned me coldly. 'Keep your hands pressed to your sides.'

The first week I fell down when it was time to go, but after that I used the time to recall my studies.

Anna felt that the punishment was too convenient for me, profitable in a way. A sinner should suffer.

Then I started missing lessons and hid in the toilets where you could read in peace. Eunice joined me without any fuss, and we sat in separate toilets, reading our novels.

'You're corrupting Eunice,' Anna complained, frowning.

'She's a free being.'

After a while, the English teacher noticed I was present at some lessons and not at others on the same day.

'You two are for it,' Jane told us, resentfully. 'He's looking for you.'

I sought him out at his staffroom.

'You've got to stop it,' he said. 'I know it's boring, having Shakespeare read around the class, but it's the only way to make sure the play's read by everyone.'

'But it isn't, Sir,' I protested. 'Everybody sleeps when it's not his turn. You can't get the meaning when people are reading aloud. It sounds like Chinese. They don't give it the right expression.'

'Promise me you won't skip lessons again.'

I promised only that I would sit in class to do my own work. In his classroom stroll, he came upon me making notes from a geography book and sighed. But said nothing.

Anna fumed some more. 'Why should rules be for some and not for others?'

'Some need to live by others' rules.'

'You have to live by rules or society can't function properly.'

'What makes you think I don't live by rules? Mine take more courage than yours. You're like a lot of people out here. You can hardly go to the toilet without wanting the approval of authority:

divine or temporal, it doesn't matter, so long as someone else can be responsible for your actions. It's your convict inheritance, this infantile dependence.'

This made Anna flush. 'You're so sure you know everything. Pride comes before a fall.'

I gazed at her for a minute, thinking. Then I said, slowly, 'How come you wear those funny little Miss Prim blouses and skirts that don't suit your personality a bit? But you exploded into that red dress you wore to the last school dance. That was really you. The low cut neckline and the hair hanging over your eyes. "Ah," everybody murmured, "look at Anna. She's blazing. She's burning up." And they left off what they were doing to come and warm themselves, so that there was a new intensity among them. They were more aware of each other. And you couldn't stop laughing. Neither could they. I bet you threw away that dress and wore a hair shirt afterwards.'

'A person's a better person for being disciplined and self-controlled.'

'A person's not a better person for falling unconscious on the classroom floor because of unresolved conflict.'

'The doctor said I've got low blood pressure.'

'Bull!'

At home, I complained to my mother. 'That Anna Laing. She's aye preaching to me.'

And my mother, who continually preached at me herself, was immediately resentful of someone's usurping her powers. So Anna didn't come to the party.

26 For Auld Lang Syne

The party was at my place, after the Leaving Certificate. At Hogmonay.

'We'll have a real humdinger,' my mother declared. 'We havenae had a decent Hogmonay since we've been here. Ah've asked Georgina Harvey's family, because her faither's got a good heid o' black hair to be oor first foot. And old Royale next door would like tae come. She's got a fiddle, she tells me, and can play all sorts of jigs. Her son's comin' doon at Christmas from the country. He's a jackeroo, and he's got a guitar.'

'What aboot the folk across the street? The Glims?'

'Och, ah invited them, but she says they'll probably go to bed. The Aussies don't pay much attention tae New Year. They're like the English.'

Before the festivities, the work.

'The whole place has tae be cleaned, remember. From top tae bottom. Thoroughly. In a' the corners. None o' this "face clean, arse not seen" business. You and Margaret get cracking on the walls. Get a' the maps and charts off your walls, and that picture o' Tito, burn it! Ah don't give a damn how handsome he is, ah'm no' having any Communists hanging up in my house. It's blasphemous. The exams are finished now, so no excuses. The other kids'll no' be interested in those quotations you've got stuck up all over the place. Get water and a paint scraper to remove them. Hang the mattresses out on the line. Wash down the springs. Share the windows between ye.'

'Jings, Mammy, we'll be going tae hospital after all this. Battle fatigue.'

'Don't gie me your worries. A day's work would kill ye. Ah've got tae get the food ready.'

Pork and veal and two ducks. Stuffing. Everything to be hot

351

at midnight. None o' this Australian cold meat and lettuce, thank you very much. Stones of potatoes for roasting. We might try pumpkin. It's quite tasty when you get used to it. Fruit cake. That's made. And dumpling. Lots of shortbread. Thank God butter's plentiful here. Apple pies. I'll make a big trifle. See if ye can buy some stale sponge at the cake shop. Jars of nuts and glacé fruit. Ah'll make a bowl of punch, but your faither'll look after the rest of the drinks.

On the afternoon of New Year's Eve, the house was in chaos and we were all snarling at each other.

'Get oot o' mah way, you fool. Can ye no' see ah'm in a hurry? Pick those marbles up off the floor before someone breaks his neck.'

'Mammy, that lazy Mary hasnae polished the lounge-room floor yet.'

Susan roamed the rooms trying to commit someone to the proposition that she should stay up all night.

'You're kidding,' I said. 'I didn't get staying up till I was thirteen.'

'But that was in the olden times.'

We skipped the evening meal, just grabbing a cup of tea and a sandwich.

At ten o'clock the table was stretched out in yards, almost reaching to the oven door.

'Push everything doon a bit,' my mother told us irritably. 'How the hell am ah tae baste the meat?'

Margaret and I danced around the kitchen touching everything excitedly, hugging each other.

'Wasnae that a good idea, Mammy, wrapping the milk bottles in coloured paper, tae hold the Christmas bush? It's so beautiful, like having flaming torches everywhere. Our Roman banquet!'

My mother straightened up and surveyed the kitchen with satisfaction.

'Aye, it looks very bright, right enough. Ye've done a good job, the two of ye.'

'Christ,' my father said, appearing at the back door with a box of beer. 'Ye need a pair o' sun glasses in here.'

Half an hour before midnight we were all dressed. At least Margaret and I, and my mother and father. The younger ones were to stay in their pyjamas for they would only be getting up to see the New Year in and have something to eat. My father went next door to fetch old Mr and Mrs Royale and I waited expectantly for my friends. They were to arrive about half past eleven.

Mrs Royale was wearing a dark blue dress with that low cut bodice a lot of old women favour. She had a string of beads round her neck. Maybe they were pearls. Her hair was newly washed and fitted in layers around her head like white down.

'You look really pretty, Mrs Royale,' Margaret said, leading her to the best arm chair.

'Oh, you are kind, my dear.'

Her son had gone out with some friends, but he would call in later. Then the girls arrived. Jane's father brought the three of them, for only he had a car. We put paper crowns on the heads of Mr and Mrs Royale who were to be the king and queen of the party, and then arranged ourselves round the kitchen. My father woke Susan and the others and they staggered in among us, blinking, visibly less pleased than they had thought to be at the great adventure. On the radio, they were playing Jimmy Shand. Even here, they regarded Hogmonay as a Scottish occasion.

'Oh,' my mother sighed, dramatically, 'we would hear the ships' sirens on the Clyde, if we were there now.'

'Not yet,' my father reminded her, 'it's still a minute or so tae midnight.'

He was hurrying round to see if everybody had his glass ready. We had been given punch. I was surprised to see him pouring whisky into Mrs Royale's glass.

'Oh dear, Mr Lavery. Only a little.'

'Och, this is medicine ye're getting, Mrs Royale. The water of life.'

Then the hooters went. Margaret and I started blowing the whistles we'd bought at Woolworth's and the kids threw streamers in the air. After 'Auld Lang Syne', it was kissing time. I didn't mind kissing the Royales but I felt idiotic exchanging cheeks with Margaret and the others. We shook hands with my father. And so to eat. But not for long. My mother had barely finished serving when Georgina's father burst in through the front door, yelling for us. We dashed up from the table and rushed into the lounge-room to greet him, and fell back amazed, at the long line of people uncoiling behind him.

'Happy New Year, Rose,' he cried, holding out a lump of coal. 'Ye'll no' mind if ah brought along Georgina's boyfriend and a few of his family.'

'Hell no,' shrieked my mother. 'Come on in everybody,' and in they came, hundreds of them, it seemed, the sisters with their husbands, the sisters with their boyfriends, the brothers with their fiancées, the brothers with their wives and the wives with their old mums.

'Ye Gods,' I whispered to Margaret, my eyes popping, 'when do they stop?'

'He comes from a farm, that friend of Georgina's, doesn't he?' she said meaningfully. 'They always have about twenty-two kids.'

The younger kids scuttled away to their beds like rabbits, overawed by the number of strangers and we reassembled at the table, almost two deep.

In a few minutes plates were whizzing through the air like spinning discs as they passed from hand to hand and from all parts of the table thick slices of pork and duck rose in flight like a flurry of startled birds. Roast potatoes bowled merrily along the tablecloth, oops, sorry, and out of season sprouts, faintly yellow, wriggled greasily off blunt knives. The sound of champing teeth and chewed-up speech nearly made me choke from laughing and tears came into my eyes.

'Hey, ye're already drunk,' my father whispered, passing by. 'Have ye been at my whisky?'

That was really very funny. I slid further down into my chair, laughing more than ever.

At the sink crouched my mother, cutting, cutting, cutting: 'Here, catch! More bread. Shit, I missed. More duck. Plenty of crackling here. Robert, that veal's still to be started.'

It was so gay and gaudy, but not really bawdy, and when another man appeared in the doorway our grins stretched out at both sides, like hammocks touching each other at the corners. All the room was crisscrossed with a lattice work of grins. Who's that guy?

'Oh Thomas,' peeped Mrs Royale, cheep cheeping feebly in the middle. 'Thomas, you've come.'

'Thomas has come, Thomas has come,' everyone chanted, taking his arm, and weaving in his grin.

'Have a bite to eat, man, and a drink.'

354

'Did ye bring your guitar, Thomas? Ah, we didn't doubt you Thomas, are you a rhymer, Thomas dear?'

By the time my mother was ready to bring the apple pies, the dumpling and the blood-curdling trifle spewing wine from every crumb, people were slipping just a little, their eyes a very little skewy.

'All right,' my mother said, briskly, 'we can eat the rest after. Let's go into the lounge and have a bit of a sing song.'

But dear Mrs Royale's white head was just crammed with jigs and we had to dance. The Gay Gordons, and the Dashing White Sergeant.

'C'mon Thomas,' I said, awash inside with trifle, 'I'll show you how to do it.'

'No, me, Thomas. Ah know it better than she does.'

'I'll teach you a Latvian folk dance, Thomas,' crooned Vera, peeking through her untidy pageboy.

Of course there were all those fiancées and boyfriends and wives Georgina had brought. We galloped up and down our little lounge-room which was all of a sudden as tiny as a telephone booth, banging into each other and jumping on toes, even our own.

'Oh, my arm,' wailed Mrs Royale, happily, laying down her fiddle and picking up her whisky glass.

So Thomas tucked his guitar under his blue-black chin and sang ballads of girls with blue velvet bands and of lovers who had met, kissed, wed and been buried, between two trees.

By this time my father was ready to sing 'Mother Machree' with his hand over his heart.

'Great stuff, Bob. Give us another one.'

Second on the list, 'Misty Islands', followed by weird street songs that made everyone giggle.

Mammy's turn now. 'Dark Lochnagar'.

'Your mother looks well, Mary,' Georgina whispered, coming up behind me.

'Aye, she suits that pink and white striped dress. Are you going to marry Johnny with the pale moon face?' I didn't say the last bit, of course.

'Och, ah dinna ken. Ah expect so. We seem to be going that way.'

'What happened to Alessio? Haven't you seen him since he left the hostel?'

355

'Well, he wrote me some terrific romantic letters. He learned English quite well, you know, but then,' she added, indignation raising her voice, 'I found out he'd written identical ones to all the Dutch girls at the factory.'

'Oh God,' I doubled up, holding my stomach. 'What a rascal. You're better off with Johnny.'

But you're not, you know, I tell myself. I've been watching him. You're marrying into soft affability, baby pink, another smiler with harried eyes, how are you going, already afflicted with creeping pomposity and raging self doubt that flares and singes him under his thin, transparent skin.

Then Georgina's turn to sing in her sweet, pure voice. Again and again. A duet with her sister-in-law to be. A duet with me. Then a big thud on the floor. What was that? A body has fallen. Good God, Johnny stretched out on the floor like a flaccid corpse. We all gather round him, bewildered. Oh dear, oh dear, what can the matter be? Johnny's so long on the floor.

'Somebody call an ambulance,' his sister said, with just a hint of sourness.

So all of their gang went out into the morning to look for a telephone and someone carried him on to the front verandah, Georgina anxiously wiping his brow and whimpering: 'Are you all right?'

We never did find out what was the matter with him, or at least what the doctor said, but they all surged away, thanks for a beaut night, and Thomas took up his guitar again, to sing of drovers and their dreams.

I wandered out into the kitchen where I found my mother bent over the sink, washing dishes. Millions of them.

'Here, gie me a hand, hen,' she beckoned me with a wave of her arm, 'ah want tae get these done, because ah'll have tae be starting the breakfast soon. Help me dry up, then you can take your pals up to the water-hole for a swim. It should be magic up the bush at this time of the morning.'

'How would you know, Mammy?' I asked her teasingly.

'Ah've read about it.'

'Well,' I said, collecting all the spoons together, 'it'll be bread and marge for the next three weeks, after this little lot. I suppose you've used up nearly all the holiday pay.'

My mother shrugged. 'Probably. So what! What will ye remember in twenty years' time—the party or the three weeks after? Didn't everybody have a good time? Ye cannae measure the cost of that. Look, when ye're poor, ye have tae live wi' a bit o' dash and bravado, if ye don't want, that is, tae end up wi' faces like those ye see aroon here. Nae fight left in them. Nae joy. Nae sense of adventure. That's a worse kind o' poverty than an empty tea caddy, believe me. Dae ye believe me?' she asked fiercely, in a swift change of tone.

'Well, I don't really know, Mammy. I'm too ignorant. Ask me in twenty years' time.'